William Henry Jones

Domesday for Wiltshire

SALZWASSER
VERLAG

William Henry Jones

Domesday for Wiltshire

Reprint of the original, first published in 1865.

1st Edition 2022 | ISBN: 978-3-75258-821-7

Verlag (Publisher): Salzwasser Verlag GmbH, Zeilweg 44, 60439 Frankfurt, Deutschland
Vertretungsberechtigt (Authorized to represent): E. Roepke, Zeilweg 44, 60439 Frankfurt, Deutschland
Druck (Print): Books on Demand GmbH, In de Tarpen 42, 22848 Norderstedt, Deutschland

DOMESDAY FOR WILTSHIRE

EXTRACTED FROM ACCURATE COPIES OF THE ORIGINAL RECORDS,
ACCOMPANIED WITH TRANSLATIONS, ILLUSTRATIVE NOTES,
ANALYSIS OF CONTENTS, AND GENERAL INTRODUCTION.

BY

WILLIAM HENRY JONES, M.A. F.S.A.

RURAL DEAN; VICAR OF BRADFORD-ON-AVON;
HON. CHAPLAIN TO THE LORD CHANCELLOR;
FORMERLY BODEN SANSCRIT SCHOLAR IN THE UNIVERSITY OF OXFORD.

BATH

MDCCCLXV.

SUMMARY OF CONTENTS.

INTRODUCTION

TO THE

DOMESDAY FOR WILTSHIRE.

INTRODUCTION.

CHAPTER I.

General plan of this work. Previous publication on the same subject. Difficulties in interpreting Domesday. Origin of Domesday Book. Powers of the Commissioners. Various accounts by Chroniclers. Proceedings of the Commissioners. Object of Domesday. Formal adoption of the Record at Sarum. Feudal tenures. Derivation of the name Domesday. Question as to the completeness of the Record. General plans and policy of the Conqueror.

General plan of this Work.

THE publication of the fac-simile of the Domesday Book for Wiltshire has suggested the desirableness of an accompanying volume, which shall interpret its contents, and make them accessible to the general reader. In this work, which, it is hoped, provides, as far as possible, a complete commentary on the Wiltshire portion of the Record, is given, first of all, an accurate copy of the Exchequer Domesday in extended Latin, with a close and literal translation, and to this are appended notes, illustrating peculiar words or phrases not otherwise explained, and, where they could be furnished, accounts of the principal or subordinate holders of the various Manors. Then follows (*p.* 153) a copy of the Exon Domesday for Wilts, with a list under each Hundred of such Manors as can be identified,—a necessary addition in consequence of the omission of the mention of the Hundreds in the Exchequer Domesday for this County. After this will be found (*p.* 193) a complete Analysis of the two preceding records, with an identification of the various manors, as far as such can be carried out, together with an indication of some sources whence further information may be obtained respecting them.

Previous publication on the same subject.

Nearly eighty years have now passed since Mr. Wyndham published his "Wiltshire extracted from the Domesday Book." In that volume he attempted little more than giving a copy of the text of the Exchequer Domesday with a translation, but, except in a very general way, did nothing towards identifying the manors referred to in the Record. Indeed, materials which have been largely used for the present work were not then accessible, and without the researches of Ellis, Kemble, Thorpe, Palgrave, and others, it was hardly possible to advance further in illustration of the general principles of Domesday than is done in the introduction to his volume. Neither had Sir Thomas Phillipps printed his most valuable work, "The Wilts Institutions," which has been found in many cases of great use in identifying some of the Domesday manors. Mr. Wyndham, however, may well claim the merit of having been the first to set on foot the important work of the compilation of a county history, and perhaps of having induced Sir R. C. Hoare to enter upon his great undertaking of the "History of Modern Wilts," to the contents of which the author has been indebted for many of the results which will be found in the succeeding pages. To Sir R. C. Hoare and his learned fellow-labourers, and to those who during the last quarter of a century have been following out similar investigations—to Mr. Poullet Scrope, who, in his history of Castle Combe, has given us so much that throws light on other Wiltshire manors;—to Canon Jackson, who, in his edition of Aubrey's Collections, has collected a mass of information valuable to every Wiltshire topographer;—to the various contributors to the Wiltshire Magazine,—the author would point as labourers who have preceded him in a similar field of enquiry, and without whose researches much in this volume must have been left untold. Nor must he forget to acknowledge the kindness with which in every part of the County access has been allowed to him to parish registers and other public documents. In short, it is in great part to the labours of others that he has been indebted for what success he may be judged to have attained in giving an accurate interpretation of much of the Domesday for Wiltshire.

Difficulties in interpreting Domesday.

Though some years have been spent in the preparation of this work, the author is only too well aware of its possible imperfections. Proverbially obscure in many parts, insomuch that even the Judges of the land, when appealed to in one instance, five centuries ago, to interpret some entries contained in it, openly set forth that they were "not able to explain them unless *just as the words sounded*,"[1]—something must be left to conjecture; and here others are as well qualified to form an opinion as himself. And then further, the identification of the manors has been a task of toilsome research, in which it is only too possible that, with every care, some erroneous conclusions may have been adopted. For the long period of a hundred years after the Conquest there is a blank in our national records; the link in the chain that connects the owners of estates at Domesday with those who possessed them in the time of King John is often hard to find. Moreover, as no archives but those of our ancient ecclesiastical establishments throw light to any extent on the Record, so it is only by a patient comparison of its entries with the chartularies of our earliest abbeys that we can reasonably hope to illustrate them; and when it is borne in mind that this is to be effected not merely by the examination of charters and partial surveys, but by the scattered details of an historical kind which are to be found in them, it will be acknowledged that as it is no light task which one who seeks to interpret the Domesday of any county imposes on himself, so it is one which should ensure for him the indulgent criticism of his readers. It is the testimony of Sir H. Ellis, to whose patient research we are indebted for the key that unlocks so many of the difficulties of Domesday, that "though he had passed years of labour on this Record he had only opened a way to a knowledge of its contents;" and further, that it was a "mine of information which had not yet been sufficiently wrought, containing illustrations of the most important and certain kind upon our ancient institutions, services, and tenures of lands, the metal of which could not be exhausted by the perseverance of any single labourer."[2] It will be a real satisfaction to the author to have been a pioneer in leading the way to a full interpretation of the Domesday for Wiltshire. He hopes to awaken the spirit of enquiry among his neighbours, so that local information may be brought to bear upon some points as yet undetermined, or left to conjecture, more or less probable. For it is only such investigations that can in many cases ascertain the sites of manors mentioned in Domesday, of which all memory seems to be lost, and the names of which, often in a corrupted form, are limited now to small and insignificant portions of land.

---

[1] The question submitted to the Treasurer and Barons of the Exchequer was, whether the lands of Roger de Huntingfield were held of the King *ut de Corona*, or *ut de Baronia vel Honore*. After calling to their help the Judges of the King's Council, they ended by giving a *verbatim* copy of what they found relating to the said lands in Domesday, adding—"Nescimus interpretationem facere nisi *quatenus verba inde sonant*."—Ellis I., 357.

[2] Preface to his Introduction to Domesday Book, *pp.* v. vi.

It is no part of the plan of this work to enter upon a full discussion of matters necessary to be understood in order to the accurate interpretation of the Domesday Book, regarded as a whole. Such as wish general information on the subject, will find it in the very valuable volumes by Sir H. Ellis, entitled "Introduction to Domesday." Our object is simply to consider those matters which, either directly or indirectly, are necessary to the elucidation of the Wiltshire portion of the Record, or which receive their illustration from entries contained in it. These will be found but a portion—though a considerable one—of questions necessary to be discussed by those who would fully understand Domesday. It is hoped, however, that by concentrating enquiry on one section of the Record, with the advantage of local information, we may be better able to evolve facts and principles applicable to the whole, than by an endeavour to grapple with the entire volume, which, on account of its vast extent and multifarious contents—each county having customs peculiar to itself—must be comparatively ineffectual.

Origin of Domesday Book.

It was in Midwinter, 1085, at the court of Gloucester, that Domesday, the 'grand Inquest' of all England, was projected and undertaken. In that year the king held a great council for the purpose of enquiring into the state of the nation, and adopting measures for putting it into a posture of defence against such invasions as they had recently been threatened with from Denmark. "The king," says the Saxon chronicler, "had a great consultation, and spoke very deeply with his 'witan' concerning the land, how it was held, and what were its tenantry. He then sent his men all over England, into every shire, and caused to be ascertained how many hundred hides of land it contained, and what lands the king possessed therein, what cattle there were in the several counties, and what revenue he ought to receive yearly from each. He also caused to be written down how much land belonged to his archbishops, to his bishops, his abbots, and his earls, and, that I may be brief, what property every inhabitant of England possessed in land or in cattle, and how much money this was worth. And so very narrowly did he cause the survey to be made, that there was not a single hide nor yard-land, nor—it is shameful to relate that which he thought no shame to do—was there an ox, or a cow, or a pig passed by, and that was not set down in the accounts, and then all these writings were brought to him." [1]

Limits of the powers of the Commissioners.

It must be borne in mind that this is the testimony of one of the Englishmen, who, at the time he wrote, in the position of the vanquished, was little disposed to do justice to the King's motives. There is certainly nothing in the Wiltshire portion of the Record to bear out this charge of inquisitorial minuteness laid at the door of the Conqueror. In the instructions given to the King's Commissioners there is also an absence of anything which can warrant the accusation of unnecessary harshness. Among the Cotton Manuscripts[2] there is preserved a copy of an Inquisition for Cambridgeshire, which shews clearly the limits of the powers of the Commissioners, and which is headed thus :—"Here followeth an Inquisition concerning the lands, &c.........on the oaths of the Sheriff of the county, and of the Barons, and their free-men (francigenarum), of the Hundred, of the Priest, of the Bailiff of the manor, and of six villans from each vill:—to wit,—what is the name of the estate (mansio), who held it in the time of King Edward, who holds it now, how many hides there are, how many

---

[1] Sax. Chron. A.D. 1085.

[2] MS. Cott. Tiber. A. VI. *fol.* 38. This manuscript, which is of the date of Henry II., relates to lands and demesnes of the Church of Ely in the counties of Cambridge, Huntingdon, Essex, Norfolk, and Suffolk. The first portion consists of the 'Inquisitio Eliensis' printed in a supplementary volume of Domesday, and then follows the "Inquisitio de terris," &c., to which allusion is made above.

carucates in demesne, how many vassals (homines), how many villans, how many cottars, how many serfs, what free-men, how many tenants in socage (sochomanni), what quantity of wood, how much meadow and pasture, what mills and fish-ponds, how much added or taken away, what was the gross value in King Edward's time, what is the present value, and how much each free-man or socheman had or has. The whole of this to be *triply* estimated;—namely, in the time of King Edward,—and when King William granted it,—and what it is now:—and further, if more could be fairly claimed from it than is now received."

Various accounts by Chroniclers.

A merely cursory glance at the entries in the Wiltshire Domesday will show that the King's Commissioners here carried out literally the royal precept. No doubt in numerous instances returns were framed of a more extensive nature than were absolutely required, and the opinion has been advanced that they were afterwards corrected and condensed by the clerks in the Exchequer, who omitted the tables of live stock, as not being of permanent importance. Hence we have those varying descriptions in different counties, which have led our old annalists to give what at first sight seem inconsistent accounts respecting the nature of the Domesday returns. Thus, whilst Ingulphus and Robert of Gloucester take no notice whatever of the return of live stock, Henry of Huntingdon and Knyghton state expressly that the number of animals (quot animalia) was to be recorded. Again, whilst Matthew Paris and Matthew of Westminster intimate that the enquiry under this head was limited to the number of animals that in each instance "would suffice for the cultivation of one hide of land," we have Hoveden, Florence of Worcester, and Simeon of Durham asserting that the Commissioners had to make an exact return of "every head of cattle in all the kingdom, from the greatest even to the least."[1] There are some, moreover, such as Bronton and Sprott, who state that a return had to be made respecting parish churches, and ecclesiastical dignities. There is nothing, it will be observed, in the terms of the royal precept, as implied in the heading of the inquisition above quoted, or in the contents of the Wiltshire portion of the Record, to warrant those statements. This varying testimony of historians is perhaps to be explained by the fact that they formed their opinions, not from any documentary evidence of what was the King's command respecting the survey, but from an inspection of partial extracts from different portions of it.

Proceedings of the Commissioners.

The King's Commissioners were Walter Giffard, Earl of Buckingham,—Henry de Ferieres,—Remigius, Bishop of Lincoln, the founder of the Cathedral in that city,—and Adam, brother of Eudo Dapifer (the Seneschal). The first two were land-owners in Wiltshire (*pp.* 98, 108). They made their several circuits, holding in every place of note or importance their council of enquiry. Summoning before them as a Jury those who were indicated as its component members by the King's writ, they received from them the information that was required. They appear to have accepted, without hesitation, as the materials of their survey, the sworn returns or presentments made by the Jurors. Though much discontent confessedly prevailed yet there certainly was no oppression in the way in which the enquiry was carried out. Indeed, regarded as a new basis for the assessment of the 'geld' due to the Crown, the last who had cause for complaint were those on whose information the materials for duly valuing the several estates were furnished. "Whilst Domesday secured the rights of the Crown, it also ensured a fair apportionment of the burden among those by whom it was to be contributed. The enquiry was made by the Royal Commissioners, but the repartition was made by the people:—the English taxed themselves."[2]

[1] Ellis, I., 28. [2] Palgrave's 'Normandy and England,' III. 576.

It would appear that the transcripts of the original depositions were afterwards methodised, and perhaps abbreviated, and then fairly transcribed in the Great Volume of Domesday. That volume " still exists, fresh and perfect as when the scribe put pen to parchment, the oldest cadastre, or survey of a kingdom, now existing in the world. The colophon—anno millesimo octogesimo sexto ab incarnatione Domini vigesimo vero Willelmi facta est ista descriptio—attests the date of this great record as well as the skill of those by whom it was completed. In the entries of the names of places, the inaccuracies and corruptions shew that the writers were not well acquainted with the Anglo-Saxon terminology, though in the more familiar designations of persons fewer errors are observed. The caligrapby betrays an Italian hand, and leads to the supposition that it was under the inspection and direction of the lettered Lanfranc that the work was compiled. Great force is given to this supposition from the circumstance that in Domesday we first find those abbreviations, afterwards so common in our legal documents, but which, in fact, are derived from the Tironian notes of the Romans, till then unknown in England."[1]

Object of Domesday.

The Conqueror had a two-fold object in view in causing the survey to be made. No doubt he wished, first of all, to obtain a complete census of his kingdom that he might be aware of its resources, and its means of defence against external enemies. And then, secondly, he desired to ascertain what really were the revenues to which in right of his crown he was entitled. Of course the estates and revenues belonging to the Confessor, as King of England, were now vested in him. Amongst the sources of the latter was the Dane-Geld,[2] a tax originally levied in the reign of Ethelred on each hide of ground iu the kingdom, for the purpose of raising the means of defending the country against the Daues, and afterwards continued as a regular impost, the proceeds being devoted to the requirements of the government, both military and civil. And no doubt it was the main intent of the survey to make a full and fair assessment of this charge. On every account such an investigation was necessary. The unsettled state of affairs during the latter years of the reign of Edward the Confessor,—the misfortunes necessarily attending the conquest,—the transfer of the land to new proprietors,—all were sufficient causes for the survey. Besides, the exemptions pleaded for non-payment of the tax, as is shown in a subsequent page (*p.* 154), were so numerous as seriously to interfere with its productiveness, and to place a heavy burden on those who were liable to it. Moreover, so long as the land remained untilled, no Dane-geld was payable, but when brought into cultivation, it became liable to the charge, and in many cases the assessment no doubt had been neglected or evaded. A mere glance at some of the entries in the Exon Domesday for Wiltshire (and the same may be observed in other counties) will show how partial was the incidence of the tax. Thus, out of *fifty-two hides* in STAPLE HUNDRED (*p.* 164) geld was paid only for *fourteen hides and half-a-virgate*. In BLACHEGRAVE HUNDRED (*p.* 166) out of a *hundred and sixty-five hides* it was assessed only for *ninety-one hides and three virgates and a half*. In SWANBOROUGH HUNDRED (*p.* 175) for more than half the land exemption was claimed; only *eighty-three*, out of a *hundred and eighty-three hides* paying the Dane-geld. It is impossible to deny the necessity of a revision, and certainly there is nothing in the way in which the enquiry was carried out to warrant the charge of the assertion of arbitrary right on the part of the Conqueror, of which the early annalists speak. It is true that he caused the Dane-geld, which, according to some, had been in abeyance during the latter

[1] Palgrave's 'Normandy and England,' III., 575.

[2] Information on the subject of this tax will be found in Webb's Short Account of Dane-Geld, 4to., 1756, reprinted from the Archæologia.

days of the Confessor, to be regularly levied, at the rate of *six shillings upon each hide* of land, but the necessities of his kingdom required it, and everything bears witness to his desire that the burden should be fairly proportioned among all who were liable to contribute to the tax. Indeed, in more instances than one, the enquiries of the Domesday Commissioners elicited from the 'men of the hundred' (homines de hundredo) as the local jurors are designated, information which led to the reparation of injustice or the correction of admitted errors.[1]

Formal adoption of Domesday at Sarum.

It is a matter of interest to us in Wiltshire, that it was at SARUM that the nation would seem to have formally adopted the Domesday Book, as a trustworthy account of the whole nation. The completion of the Record, and the great meeting at Sarum of all the landowners of the kingdom, so completely synchronize, and the two are so commonly joined together by almost all the historians of the times, that it is difficult not to believe them to have had an immediate relation to each other. "The King," says the Saxon Chronicle, under the year 1086, "came by Lammas to Salisbury, and there his 'witan' came to him, and all the landholders (landsittende men) that were of any account over all England, men (vassals) of whatever lord they might be, and they all submitted themselves to him and became his men (and wæron his menn), and swore to him oaths of fealty, that they would be faithful to him against all other men." Such was the multitude—they were no less than sixty thousand in number—that they could not have been assembled within the now silent ramparts of the ancient British city, but must have spread themselves over the surrounding plain. And then if our conjecture be feasible, they put their hand and seal, as it were, to the great volume, which was an 'extent' of the whole kingdom. That volume contained in some sort an abstract of the title-deeds to every estate throughout the realm, whether belonging to king or people. Each of the contracting parties here solemnly assented to a document by which henceforth all were to be bound, and the implied principles of which they pledged themselves to maintain. The King, on his part, covenanted to stand by the Record, and to deal justice fairly to all, whilst his subjects here accepted him as their lawful sovereign, and engaged to recognize him as such, and to render to him all the just rights implied in this relation. And this oath of fealty taken at Sarum was but the renovation of the bond of homage which became necessary as the recognition of the new lord and sovereign, when death had dissolved the previous engagements. Circumstances prevented such a public acknowledgment of William as King before this time. Down to our own day the repetition of the same ceremony by prelates and peers on the accession of a new sovereign attests that most ancient principle of our monarchy.

Question as to the introduction of feudal tenures

Much greater significance has been given indeed to this proceeding at Sarum. The English Chroniclers speak of it as the completion of their nation's disgrace, and an ignominious submission to the power of the Conqueror. And no less an authority than Sir W. Blackstone regards the completion of Domesday Book, and its adoption by the nation, as the era of formally introducing the *feudal tenures* by law. His words are—"This new polity seems not to have been *imposed* by the Conqueror, but nationally and freely *adopted* by the general assembly of the whole realm, in the same manner as others nations of Europe had before adopted it, upon the same principle of self-security. And, in particular, they had the recent example of the French nation before their eyes; which had gradually surrendered up all its allodial or free lands into the king's hands, who restored them to the owners as a *beneficium* or feud, to be held to them and such of their heirs as they previously nominated to the king; and thus by degrees all the allodial estates of France were converted into feuds, and the freeman became the

---

[1] One instance occurs under Warminster Hundred (*p.* 176) in which we are told, 'Here was found *one hide* which has paid no geld since King William had the kingdom.' See also under Heytesbury Hundred (*p.* 178).

vassals of the Crown. The only difference between this change of tenures in France and that in England was that the former was effected gradually, by the consent of private persons; the latter was done at once, all over England, by the common consent of the nation." [1]—But for neither of these opinions does there seem to be any real foundation. Most certainly William intended no dishonor to his subjects when he summoned them to Sarum, there to testify their allegiance to him. Doubtless he was anxious to consolidate his power, and to take all needful measures for the security of his person and his crown. The relation in which the greater nobles stood to the kings of the former dynasty was both uncertain and unsatisfactory. The Earls had independent powers, which were hardly consistent with the position in which they stood as subjects, and the King however much in theory, since the days of Egbert, he might be called monarch of England, was to a great extent after all but the head of a confederation. Naturally enough, therefore, William asked from those who through his bounty stood in the same position, a more defined allegiance to himself. He sought to draw closer the bonds which connected each one of his nobles with himself as their liege lord and king. And this is the simple meaning of the law made at the council of Sarum, which is couched in these remarkable words:—"Statuimus, ut omnes liberi homines fœdere et sacramento affirment, quod intra et extra universum regnum Angliæ Wilhelmo Regi domino suo fideles esse volunt; terras et honores illius omni fidelitate ubique servare cum eo, et contra inimicos et alienigenas defendere." [2]—And then, with regard to the opinion as to the completion of Domesday being the era for the introduction of feudal tenures, most certainly the Record itself testifies to no such change. The whole policy of the Conqueror was, as we shall have frequent occasion to shew, opposed to all needless alterations. As he found the land so he gave it,—the Norman was to hold it exactly as his Anglo-Saxon predecessor had done,—rendering the same services to the Sovereign, and, so far as William authorised or restrained him, entitled only to the same from the subordinate holders or the cultivators of the ground. Indeed, M. Guizot has given it as his deliberate opinion, that the feudal system of regular subordination never subsisted in the forms assigned to it by the jurists; and that feudal society, in its supposed entirety, is an imaginary structure raised only by the fancy of the learned, the materials of which, incoherent and broken, have been found lying in the soil. In this he is followed by Sir Francis Palgrave, who, after remarking that the feudal system never existed in its theoretical completeness, points out that the mistakes made by those who have advocated the opinion have arisen chiefly from confounding the *feudal tenure of land* with what is called *feudal government,* since, however paradoxical it may appear, there was no government in mediæval Europe founded on feudality. With reference to the point under discussion he says,—"Domesday, which was to fix all the territorial rights of the Crown, is wholly silent upon the subject of feudal tenures. The rendering military service for lands held of the Sovereign, a usage derived from the Romans, existed in Britain long before the conquest. That this was retained by William, when the same lands passed to his soldiery or followers, is in the nature of things. Whatever obligation the land was liable to in the days of King Edward, it was equally liable to in those of King William, and in this manner alone can we explain a fact which otherwise would be perplexing, viz., the total absence of any direct allusion to military tenure in the Record. In support of the rights of the Crown, resulting from the tenure of land, Domesday shews nothing. It only establishes a negative, and that in a very remarkable manner. Hugh Lupus, we are told, holds the Earldom of Chester by the sword, as freely as the King holds by his Crown. So also, no doubt, did other great lords. Matters altered entirely when we have over-leaped the reign of Henry

---

[1] Commentaries on the Laws of England, edit. 4to., Oxf. 1766, B. II. p. 49.

[2] Concil. Mag. Brit. cap. 52, Wilk. p. 228.

Plantagenet; but we are speaking of the rights, or rather no rights, of the respective parties before the generalization of the law. The hereditary descent of the "Laen Lands" continued as before the Conquest, a customary right of renewal to the son of the father's tenancy, which could not be enforced, but which, in the ordinary course of affairs, could not be denied.

"No doubt in the reign of Henry III. it was a received opinion and an axiom in the courts of Justice that 32,000 Knight's fees had been created by the Conqueror. But one Alexander de Swenford, Archdeacon of Sarum, who made due search on the subject, could find no account of them. Nigel, Bishop of Ely, treasurer to King Henry Beauclerc, knew nothing of them, neither had Richard, Bishop of London, stated anything about them, though he had fully expounded the business of the Exchequer. He therefore concludes that when Henry Fitz-Empress required acknowledgments from all the tenants *in capite* of what was due to him, he was ignorant of the rights of the crown. There is, in fact, no written document testifying to the creation of military tenures. When we find them afterwards they were a development of customary usages; some gradually reduced into regularity by the decisions of the courts of Justice, and others by compromises between the subject and the crown."[1]

Derivation of the name DOMESDAY.

There have been various opinions as to the derivation of the word DOMESDAY. Stow, in his Annals, tells us,—"The book of Bermondsey saith this Book was laid up in the King's Treasurie (which was in the church of Winchester, or Westminster,) in a place called *Domus Dei*, or God's House, and so the name of the booke, therefore called Domus Dei, and since, shortly, Domesday." Circumstances as accidental as this have at times given names to things, but against this theory as to the origin of the word in question is to be set the fact, that it is employed as a *generic term* to denote a number of other Records of similar character, to several of which, in its specific sense, as so interpreted, it would certainly not apply. Thus in the "Liber Evidentiarum Monast. S. Augustini Cantuarensis," a manuscript written by W. Biholt, a monk, about the year 1300, we have *four* distinct references to a DOMESDAY OF ST. EDWARD,[2] whatever that document may have been. In the Cathedral at York, too, there was a register called Domesday. A volume in the office of the Town-Clerk of Norwich, containing entries of sundry charters, customs, &c., is also called Domesday; and a similar volume at Ipswich bears a like appellation. The Domesday of Chester, a record more nearly approximating to the real Domesday, was preserved amongst the archives of the Earldom, and esteemed of high authority.[3] A manuscript note of Bishop Kennett in a copy of Cowel's Law Interpreter in the Bodleian Library, quotes the 'Domesday of the

---

[1] Palgrave's 'Normanday and England,' III. 610.

[2] This manuscript is in the Bibl. Arund. in the British Museum, No. 310. Thus at *fol.* 132, under the manor of 'Kenyntone,' after an account of the land, &c., it is added, 'sicut patet in *Domusdeio Sci Edwardi.*' So also at *fol.* 132 *b* under 'Sellinge.' In one case it is said to be 'in *Domusdeio Sci Edwardi Regis.*' See the extracts given in the Gentleman's Mag. for 1852, p. 369.

[3] In the Introduction to the Abbreviatio Placitorum, p. xii. the following account is given of the Domesday of Chester. "In the Archives of the Earl of Chester there formerly existed a Roll, denominated 'The Domesday of Chester;' the Entries in this Roll were esteemed of high Authority, and perhaps conclusive Evidence: For in an Assize of Darrein Presentment in the County of Chester, 38 Hen. 3, between Roger de Sandbach and the Abbot of Deulacrese, as to the Church of Sandbach, removed by Certiorari into the King's Bench, the Court, amongst other Grounds for pronouncing their Judgment, give the following Reason: 'Et quia convictum est per Domesday Cestr' quod perpetuam habet firmitatem & omnia quæ in eo continentur in perpetuum sunt stabilia in quo continentur quod, &c. confideratum est, &c.'"—Hill. 3 Hen. 3. Cestr' Rot. 10, p. 142.

Nuns of Haliwell,' which was simply a Leiger Book of the Monastery. And then we have a survey of the mauors belonging to St. Paul's in 1181, when Radulfus de Diceto was Dean, and which is called, "Domisday, Radulfi de Diceto." This last named document was published a few years ago by the Camden Society, under the able editorship of Archdeacon Hale, who, in his Introduction (p. x.), tells us,—"We know of the existence of *eight* books"—he might have said many more than that number—"subsequent to the Exchequer Domesday compiled at different intervals during two centuries, identical in character, and bearing the same denomination; those of them which have been brought to light being records of the inquisitions of the respective rights and duties of the lord of the soil, and of the tenants within the limits either of cities or manors."

Our English ancestors, however, invented another explanation of the origin of the name. For some centuries they would fain regard the Record as the evidence of their subjugation to a foreign power, and believe it to have been compiled with the sole object of extorting money from the people. Hence we have such statements as the following,—that the book was called Domys-day, *i.e.*, Judgment Day, 'because it spared no one, even as the great day of Doom.'[1] And the author of the 'Dialogus de Scaccario,' who lived in the time of King Stephen, and whose work will be found printed in Madox's 'History of the Exchequer,' enlarges on this supposed etymology of the word in the following manner:—"Hic liber, ab indigenis *Domesdei* nuncupatur, id est, *Dies Judicii*, per metaphoram: sicut enim districti et terribilis examinis illius novissimi sententia nulla tergiversationis arte valet eludi; sic, cum orta fuerit in regno contentio de his rebus quæ illic annotantur, cum ventum fuerit ad librum, sententia ejus infatuari non potest, vel impune declinari. Ob hoc nos eundem *Librum Judiciarium* nominavimus; non quod ab eo sicut a prædicto Judicio non licet ulla ratione discedere."

But here, again, the fact, which must be admitted, that the name is employed to denote Records which were anything but inquisitorial in their character, or of such a nature as to allow of no appeal from a decision based on entries contained in their rolls, is a sufficient reason for rejecting this explanation. In truth, the term DOMESDAY was used, in course of years, as *a denomination for any register of authority.* We must, therefore, seek another etymology which may better betoken the origin of the Book, and the special purposes for which it was compiled. And this, it is believed, is to be found in a consideration of the sources from which the materials in Domesday Book were obtained, and of the means by which they were collected together in one volume.

The entries in Domesday Book are clearly transcripts of the original depositions made in the Hundred and County Courts, or, at all events, abbreviations of them. When the clerks of the Exchequer, who condensed these returns, had occasion to quote them, they made use of expressions such as the following:—'Juratores dicunt,' or—'Dicunt homines de hundredo.' Now all who are familiar with ancient Court Rolls will at once perceive, that it must have been from documents of that kind that the 'men of the hundred' must have obtained a considerable portion of the information which they laid before the Domesday Commissioners. Indeed the Record itself might fitly be described as an abridgment of a series of manorial Court Rolls. To suppose that after a lapse of more than twenty years the jurors could describe minutely the value of the several estates, their owners and occupiers in the time of the Confessor, and the services due from them, is unreasonable. Many portions of the Wiltshire Domesday could not have been furnished without access to written records. Take, for

[1] "Vocatus Domysday .... quia nulli parcit sicut nec magnus dies Judicii."—Rudborne, in Anglia Sacra, I. 257.

example, the detailed statements that are given to us respecting the King's rights in the several Burghs (*pp.* 1, 6), and the recital of the various perquisites belonging to Edward of Salisbury (*p.* 65) as Sheriff of Wiltshire (evidently the same which his predecessor in office had enjoyed), and it will be clear that, without written documents, such returns could hardly have been made and certified to the Commissioners. Indeed it is distinctly implied in several entries of Domesday that charters were at times exhibited to them,[1] and it has been stated that a large portion of the forged Saxon charters which exist to this day are to be referred to the period of the Domesday Survey, the same having been fabricated by the monks, in their anxiety to make their title to their estates good, when the Norman commissioners came amongst them. Keeping these things in mind then, as far as they bear on the question of written records, and remembering also that the lordship of a manor or hundred in olden times commonly implied the holding of a Court Baron and Court Leet, and also certain days, called in later times Law-Days, at which all the tenants, free and customary, were bound, at the lord's summons, to attend,—and that at these courts not only pleas between man and man, within certain limitations, were heard and decided upon, but legal rights and duties appertaining to the various tenures ascertained, the whole being entered upon the Court Roll,—it is easy to see how such a record might well be termed the Law-day Book, or (which in olden times would be equivalent to it) the Domes-day Book. The step from the less to the greater is not difficult, and it was not unnatural that a volume, which contained a copy of the 'Court Rolls,' so to speak, of the whole kingdom, might also have a similar designation. As Archdeacon Hale has well expressed it:—"If, as is probable, the Exchequer Domesday, being the rental of all the manors of the kingdom in an abridged form, was compiled from inquisitions held on the *Domes-days* of the different manors, or on the *Law-days* of the hundreds, such a fact would illustrate the term DOMESDAY, when applied alike to the Liber Censualis of the Crown, and to the ancient Court Roll of Manors, as being records framed upon the oaths of Jurors in a Domes-day (or Law-day) inquisition."[2]

As corroborative of the probability of such an interpretation being correct, one fact may be mentioned, which is pointed out by Archdeacon Hale, in reference to the manor of Sandon, in Essex, which belonged to St. Paul's. In the inquisition of that manor we meet with three entries, from which it appears that the ancient form of the term, "by copy of court roll," was "per rotulationem," or "per rotulum Domesday." Thus, we have, "Willelmus Marescallus tenet xviii acras......per cartam Rotulacionem Domesday;"—again, "Galfridus Capellanus tenet v. acras......per Rotulum Domesday;" and "Dominus Vicarius de Sandone tenet i. acram per Domesday."[3] In all these cases the term 'Domesday' is evidently used simply for the 'Court Roll' of the manor.

Question as to the completeness of the Record.

It has been conjectured by some authorities, and amongst them by Camden and Kelham, that the Record is but an incomplete survey of the kingdom, and that many parts were left out because free from payments (quia pensitationibus liberæ). Whatever may be the case with regard to other counties, we can have but little hesitation in avowing our conviction, that, as regards Wiltshire, the survey is complete, and in the ensuing pages the evidence is set plainly before the reader. A few observations on this subject, with illustrations drawn from this portion of the Record, will perhaps remove some of the difficulties that students of Domesday

---

[1] Thus, under NIWETONE, in Devonshire, *fol* 101 *b.* it is said:—"De hoc manerio ostendit Osbernus episcopus *cartas suas* quæ testantur æcclesiam S. Petri inde fuisse saisitam antequam Rex Edwardus regnavit." Other instances are given by Ellis, I. 40, *note.*

[2] Introduction to Domesday of St. Paul's, p. xi.

[3] Ibid., p. cxxxvi.

have felt, who have been unable to trace in it estates which they knew to have existed as such before the eleventh century.

When estates were granted in olden times, they frequently consisted in part of lands lying some distance from the principal manor. Then out-lying lands were always considered integral portions of the one estate, and were included under its head in the Domesday Record. Hence, the *first* point to be remembered is, that among estates supposed to be omitted, are often *many that are not named separately because included in some larger manor.* Fortunately, we have in the Malmesbury Chartulary a deed which throws much light upon this very point.[1] At the request of Brihtric, Abbot of Malmesbury, a recital of the various lands and privileges belonging to his monastery was drawn up, in 1065, and received the approval and confirmation of Edward the Confessor. This, it will be observed, was in the last year of the Confessor's reign, and no long time before the decisive battle of Hastings. Such portions of the charter as illustrate the particular point which we wish to explain we will extract. Estates included in some larger manor.

After reciting the gift of NEWENTONE (Long Newnton) the deed goes on to describe, in these words, an estate at Kemble :—" Also KEMELE ; the land is *thirty hides*, of which *four* are in CHELLEWRDA (Chelworth); this land King Ceadwalla gave to the Abbot Aldhelm."—A reference to Domesday exactly corroborates this statement. The estate at CHEMELE (*p.* 36) is described as consisting of *thirty hides*, and CELEORDE (=Chelworth) is mentioned incidentally as containing *four of the said hides* which comprised the Manor.

Again, CRUDWELL is thus described: "Also, CREDDEWILLA, the land is *forty hides;* of this estate is EASTCOTUN,—HANEKYNTON,—MORCOTUN : this manor King Æthelwulf gave."—It will be seen, at *p.* 37, that CREDVELLE is reckoned at *forty hides*, and there is no specific mention in the Record of EASTCOT,—HANKYNTON, —or MORECOT.

The entry respecting BREMHILL is still more convincing :—" Also BREMELA, the land is *thirty-eight hides;* in this manor are included YWERIG,—SPEERFUL,—CHEDECOT,—FOXHAM,—and AVENE." The first of these is EWRIDGE, close by Colerne, and at some distance from Bremhill. Of the others, SPEERFUL (Spirit Hill), CHEDECOTE (Charlcott), and AVON are portions of the parish ;—FOXHAM, though in some respects an independent manor, is still attached, as it has been from time immemorial, to the living of Bremhill. Not one of these subordinate members of the Domesday manor of BREME (*p.* 38), is mentioned separately in the Record.

When reciting the gift of BROKENEBERGE, the charter is even still more explicit, as to the various manors comprised in that estate :—" Also the same church holds BROKENEBERGE (Brokenborough); the land is *fifty hides*, this was the gift of King Eadwy : of this land GRUTENHAM (Grittenham) counts for *one hide*, and SUTTUNA (Sutton Benger) for *ten hides*, RODBURNA for *ten hides*, CORSTUNA for *ten hides*, CUSFALDE for *three hides*, BREMELHAM for *two hides*."—Referring to *p.* 35, we have BROCHENEBERGE reckoned at *fifty hides*, and among the subordinate tenants is R. Flambard, who is said to hold six hides at CORSTONE, described as *a portion* of the same estate (de eadem terra). None of the other places are separately mentioned. With regard to one of them, Sutton Benger, it is an interesting fact, that though close to Chippenham, and at some little distance from

---

[1] Cod. Diplom. 817.

Brokenborough, it still preserves the tradition of its old connection with that manor by being reckoned in the same hundred; namely in that of Malmesbury.[1]

Another example may be taken from the chartulary of WILTON. In the year 955, King Eadwy granted to that monastery an estate of one hundred hides at CEOLCUM (Chalk).[2] This included several subordinate manors, such as ALVEDESTON,—TROW,—and SEMLEY—the last-named being at a considerable distance from the principal Manor, with several parishes intervening. In the charter, after the completion of the land limits of Ceolcum, there is added, "Đis synt ðа landgemæro on Semeleage" (these are the boundaries of Semley). Though locally situated in the hundred of Dunworth, SEMLEY, to this day, is reckoned as in that of Chalk. With regard to the other two subordinate holdings, a comparison of entries, at *pp.* 47 and 125, shews clearly that the one held by Richard Poingiant '*de eadem terra*' was at TROW,—whilst it is certainly a very probable conjecture that the two hides held by Aileva were at ALVEDES-TON.

A third instance is furnished by the WINTON chartulary. Among the earliest gifts to Winchester was one of *an hundred* hides at DOWNTON. In Domesday, DUNTONE is described as having paid geld for *ninety-seven* hides, because *three* were taken away in the time of Canute for the purpose of enlarging the royal forest. (See *pp.* 17 and 191.) There are several copies of the charter relating to this manor, given in the Codex Diplomaticus.[3] After completing the circuit of the present parish of DOWNTON (which includes CHARLTON,—NUNTON,—and REDLYNCH), it then goes on to give the land-limits of EBBESBOURN EPISCOPI, an estate some few miles distant. This last name is now superseded by that of BISHOPSTON. The parish still preserves the memorial of having originally formed part of the great manor of Downton by being still reckoned in the same hundred, though locally situated in that of Cawdon.

This principle observed of naming only the chief manor will account for the *apparent* absence of many names in Domesday. In the tabular analysis commencing at *p.* 195, will be found a number of similar instances, a few of which we will more particularly point out.

A reference to the Edingdon Chartulary compared with the entries in the Nomina Villarum, and other records, will show that in the manor of EDINGDON (the EDENDONE of Domesday, *p.* 52) were included BAYNTON,—WEST COULSTON,—and NORTH BRADLEY. In that of STEEPLE ASHTON—(AISTONE, *p.* 53)—were comprised SEMINGTON,—ROOD ASHTON,—WEST ASHTON,—and LITTLETON.

In like manner ALTON PRIORS would seem originally to have included PATNEY:—whilst NORTH NEWENTON included RAINSCOMB; indeed, the last-named estate, though some miles distant, is still connected with that parish. There can be little doubt moreover that in the large manor of SARISBERIE, which comprised no less than *fifty hides, p.* 23 (or possibly from eight to ten thousand acres), must have been reckoned several of the

---

[1] In the charter respecting BROKENEBERGE, this fact, of manors consisting of several subordinate members, comes out most clearly. Cod. Dipl. 460. Thus it is said,—"Et hii sunt termini 10 hidarum pertinentium ad manerium de Brokeneberge *quæ sunt de centum hidis nominatis; hoc est de Suttone*," &c. Then follow the land-limits of SUTTON BENGER.

[2] Cod. Dipl. 436.

[3] Cod. Dipl. 985, 1036, 1108.

neighbouring estates, such as STRATFORD, and WOODFORD. In the manor of BRADFORD were certainly comprised no less than *eight* subordinate estates,—LEIGH,—WOOLLEY,—(the ULF-LEGE of the Test. de Nev.),—TROWLE,—HOLT,—ATWORTH,—WRAXALL,—WINSLEY,—STOKE.

Meaning of the term 'Berwick.'

Whilst we are upon this point, it may be observed, that though we have in Wiltshire many places bearing the name of BERWICK, that name is not to be found in Domesday. The historian of the Hundred of Chalk, in Hoare's 'Modern Wilts,' notices the fact, and expresses his surprise, deducing from it the rather hasty inference that the Record was therefore incomplete. But the reason of the absence of such a word from Domesday is very evident, as soon as we arrive at its exact meaning. By BEREWICA (or BEREWITA) is meant a subordinate manor, or a remote hamlet, so far from the mother church as to need a chapel. In an ancient account of the lands of Peterborough, we read of Medehamstede and Oundle, "with their *berwicks*,"[1] Sometimes a '*berwick*' was a dislocated part of a manor, as Wyke in Surrey (the WUCHA of Domesday) is an insulated part of the parish of Worplesdon, wholly surrounded by the parish of Ash.[2] They are often alluded to in the Record as attached to manors: for example under STANES (Staines) in Middlesex (I., 128*b*) we have—'Ad hoc manerium pertinent 4 *berewicæ;*'—and under ADELMETONE (Edmonton) in the same county (I. 129*b*) we read—'Ad hoc manerium jacuit et jacet una *Berewica* quæ vocatur MIMES' (South Mimms). In like manner BROMESGRAVE in Worcestershire had eighteen Berewicks CHIDEMINSTRE sixteen, CEDESLAI eight;—RECORDINE in Shropshire had eight, MEMBREFELD eighteen;—SUDWELLE in Nottinghamshire had twelve Berewicks. In Yorkshire they occur in greater numbers, and more frequently than in most counties. In one or two places they are called *Members* of manors: thus, under RODOLIE in Leicestershire, we have, "Huic manerio pertinent subsequentia *membra*" to the amount of *twenty* (I. 230). So in Warwickshire, "Hæc duo *membra* jacent ad STANLEI manerium regis" (I. 238).

It will be easily understood, therefore, why we should not expect to find the name BERWICK in the Wiltshire Domesday. It implies, in fact, a subordinate manor, or member of a manor, which is *accounted for in the Record under the principal estate.* BERWICK ST. LEONARD, for example, is included in the entry relating to TISBURY (*p.* 42), of which parish it was without doubt originally a part. Thus in a recital of the various tithings of Tisbury in the Shaftesbury Chartulary (Harl. MS. 61, *fol.* 43), BERWICK is reckoned along with LINLEY,—HATCH,—and FERNHILL, which are still portions of the parish; and further it is added, "and from *all these places they bring bodies for burial to the church* at TISBURY," words which would seem to imply the common right belonging to every *parishioner*. Moreover, among the tenants at Tisseberie in the *Capellanus de Sancto Leonardo*, *i.e.*, the Chaplain of [Berwick] St. Leonard's.—Again, BERWICK ST. JOHN is accounted for under the large manor of CEOLCUM (Chalk), *p.* 47;—BERWICK BASSETT is included in CAUNA (Calne, *p.* 7), of which parish, like CHERHILL, it was, till quite recently, a chapelry;—BERWICK ST. JAMES was originally, it is conjectured, a portion of the large manor of WINTERBOURN STOKE.

---

[1] New Mon., I. 382.

[2] The following extracts will shew that such outlying portions as SEMLEY—EBBESBOURN EPISCOPI (= Bishopston), and SUTTON BENGER, to which allusion has been made, would be properly called '*Berwicks*' respectively to CHALK,—DOWNTON,—and BROKENBOROUGH. "Genouefæ Fornham (Fornham St. Genoveve) tempore Regis Edwardi tenuit Sanctus Edmundus *pro bereuita*......et aula cui pertinet est in alio hundredo..... Wlfpitam (Woolpit) tenuit Sanctus Edmundus tempore Regis Edwardi *pro bereuica* et aula cui pertinet est in alio hundredo."—See Domesd. II., 362.

Estates named under some generic appellation.

But a *second* point to be borne in mind, in judging of the completeness of the Domesday Record, is this: —that a number of places, too hastily concluded to have been omitted, are *included under some generic appellation*. Of these, the principal in Wilts are described under the term WINTREBURN, a name given to three different districts through which the *winter-bourns*, or streams, flow. By reference to the analytical table it will be seen that under this generic term are described the following manors:—WINTERBOURN BASSET,—WINTERBOURN MONKTON,—ROBSON, — WINTERBOURN STOKE, — ASSERTON, — ROLLESTON, — MADDINGTON, — SHREWTON, — GOMELDON, — WINTERBOURN EARLS,—WINTERBOURN GUNNER,—WINTERBOURN FORD, besides several others, some of which it is not easy to identify.

Again, under the generic term CLIVE, a name applied to the hilly country in the neighbourhood of Cliff Pipard and Helmarton, we have the following manors accounted for:—BUSHTON,—CLEVANCY,—FASTERN,—BROAD-TOWN,—besides several portions of CLIFF PIPARD, and HELMARTON.

A reference to the analysis, under DEVREL,—LANGEFORD,—and SUDTONE,—will exhibit other similar instances of manors being described under generic appellations.

Estates described without being specially named.

And then there is a *third* consideration to be taken into account before we too hastily conclude that the Record is incomplete. In a few cases a manor is not named, but *simply described as one which had been previously held by some Englishman in the time of the Confessor*. Thus, at *p.* 130, STEPHEN the carpenter is said to possess three hides held previously by Achil;—at *p.* 144, RAINBURGIS, as a King's Thane, is recorded as holding a manor which Godwin held in the time of King Edward;—at *p.* 142, SAIEVA is named as the owner of what had been the estate of Alwi;—and at *p.* 66, we have a manor of six hides, belonging in chief to Edward of Salisbury, described as 'in the *hundred* of WRDERUSTESELLE,' without any further clue to its exact locality.

Taking all these matters into account, added to the fact that we have been able to identify, with tolerable accuracy, all, save a very few, of the Domesday manors, we can have little hesitation in avowing our conviction, that, as far as Wiltshire is concerned, the Record is complete. We should expect as much from the systematic way in which the enquiry was conducted, and the care that the entries in the Exon Domesday evidently imply. Certainly the reason alleged in support of the presumed incompleteness of parts of the Record, namely that manors free from taxation were not named, does not hold here, since the estates, or the portions of them, which were free from geld, are especially mentioned. As regards nearly every existing parish or tithing in Wilts, it is hoped that some reference will be found in the General Index which will point out the entry in Domesday under which it is accounted for. The exceptions are so very few, as to lead to the fair presumption that the deficiency is not in Domesday, but in our own inability to trace out the precise form in which any manor, as yet undiscovered, may have been entered in the Record.

General policy of the Conqueror.

A few observations may here be added on the Conqueror's policy, as attested by entries in this, as well as in other portions of Domesday Book. There is no doubt that the great principle for which William contended, and on which he acted throughout, was that of his undoubted right to the Crown of England. He did not claim the throne by virtue of the conquest, but as the lawful heir of the Confessor. As Edward's adopted son, and inheritor of his throne in right of the bequest made by his cousin, he sought and obtained the blessing of the Holy See upon his enterprise. The consecrated banner,—the gonfalon,—sent to him by the Pope, seemed to admit by implication the justice of his claim. Indeed, as far as any claim could be alleged, William's was at least as good as his rival's, for certainly the realm was not Harold's by any legal title. If one was a usurper, so was the other. Edgar Atheling, if kindred had weight, the son of Edward the Outlaw, was the real heir; for he, as the lineal descendant of Edmund Ironside, was the only male left of the house of Cerdic.

We can easily understand, therefore, much of the phraseology of Domesday. Claiming the throne by lawful inheritance, William directed that all respect should be paid to rights acknowledged in the days of the Confessor. Hence, throughout the Record, the memory of King Edward is treated with the greatest respect. In more than one passage he is termed 'gloriosus Rex Edwardus.'[1] In like manner his Queen Editha was treated with all honor,—she was allowed to retain the possessions which she enjoyed as Queen till the day of her death, in 1075, after which time they reverted to the Crown. On the other hand, there is not the slightest recognition in Domesday of Harold as King; he is simply designated as the Earl Harold (Comes Heraldus), and his efforts to maintain his short-lived dominion are spoken of as an '*invasion*' ("quando regnum *invasit*"). Of William it is as constantly said "Postquam *venit* in Angliam,"[2]—*came*, that is, as a matter of course, to assume the sovereignty that of right belonged to him. In truth, as Sir F. Palgrave has well, and, it is believed, correctly expressed it:—"As William the Conqueror assumed the royal power as the lawful successor of Edward the Confessor, it followed, as a natural consequence, that he would support his own authority by respecting Edward the Confessor's law. This constituted what we may term the technical principle of his government. Every prescriptive right was to be held as it had been in the days of the Confessor: the laws of Edward the Confessor were to be observed in all respects, except so far as he had caused them to be amended for the benefit of the English people; and at first sight there was no intentional innovation, or change. . . . . Whatever aspects William's policy assumed, he never departed from the principle that he had placed himself in the position of a legitimate sovereign asserting legitimate rights. William did not present himself as a barbarian stranger, a Sweyne or a Canute, wielding his battle-axe, slaying old and young, thirsting for blood, greedy of gold, seeking rapine, pursuing revenge; but as a lawful claimant, contesting the inheritance withheld by an unjust adversary; and it is hardly possible to deny but that, on constitutional grounds, he had a better title than he who was vanquished by the battle-trial at Hastings. When, therefore, William, as such lawful claimant, obtained the dominion, the reign of the usurper was blotted out from the legal and constitutional annals of England. In the same manner as the ordinances of the Commonwealth have no place in our statute-books, and the patents of the Protector are expunged from our records, so was the reign of Harold passed over, and never recognized by the law. Even as King *de facto*, he was not acknowledged. Domesday, which was to establish the territorial rights of the Conqueror, the record by which he was willing to be concluded, that great memorial, not of an arbitrary power, but of the principle of establishing the rights of the crown, so far as property was concerned, by an immutable law, always dates them "*tempore Regis Edwardi.*" William wanted nothing more than what King Edward had; he would take nothing as from Harold; he ascended the throne not as the victor of the son of Godwin, but as succeeding the Confessor. Therefore, he was to be bound to the responsibility of the monarch of whom he claimed to be the adopted son, the constituted heir."[3]

A similar principle may be observed in the distribution of the lands amongst his Norman followers. Much indeed of the property in Wiltshire was left undisturbed. There would seem to have been no interference, or at all events to a very trifling extent, with the estates belonging to the Church, which in themselves comprised a large portion of territory. The Crown lands, comprehended under the term 'Terræ Regis,' as a matter of course, became vested in the King. Among the holders of land in Wiltshire were not a few who had possessed the same,

---

[1] Domesd. II. 416 *b*, 425 *b*. [2] See below, pp. 102, 176. [3] Normandy and England, III, 620, 630.

as King's Thanes, under the Confessor. In some cases, as in the instance of Alured of Marlborough, considerable estates were bestowed on Englishmen, though in this particular instance the gifts may have been an acknowledgment of his services as an active opponent of Godwin's family. But even the forfeited lands were not assigned to the Normans indiscriminately. An English lordship was generally handed over in its entirety to the new proprietor. Thus William de Ow succeeds to the various estates that had been previously held by Alestan de Boscumb (*p.* 101);—Alured of Marlborough obtains a number of manors which Carlo had possessed in the time of the Confessor (*p.* 83);—sundry estates held before by Spirtes, a priest, are bestowed by the Conqueror on Nigel his physician (*p.* 123);—five manors belonging to Ednod, the steward, are granted to the Earl Hugo (*p.* 61);—the lands of Harding and Azor become the possession of the Earl Aubrey (*pp.* 62, 63). And just as William claimed to reign as the lawful heir of King Edward, so the Norman baron affected to be the representative of the English Thane whom he succeeded, and whom he designated his 'antecessor.' Thus, in the Domesday for Hampshire, we have a portion of land claimed as belonging to the manor of CERDEFORD (Chardford), as part of the fee of Hugo de Port, 'per hæreditatem *sui antecessoris.*" In some cases, the Norman's connection with his 'antecessor' is much less like usurpation. Thus, we have Milo Crispin, the son-in-law of Robert de Oily, possessed of REDBORNE (*p.* 92), and of MANETUNE (*p.* 93), the same having originally been given to Robert de Oily himself, as the son-in-law of Wigod de Wallingford, the possessor of them in the days of King Edward. (See note, *p.* 91.) Moreover, as we shall have occasion to shew in subsequent pages, all these estates were given to their new proprietors, subject to the same customs as regarded the subordinate tenants, or the cultivators of the soil, as heretofore,—no more power was given to the one, no less privileges reserved to the other. The probability would seem to be, that the villans and other subordinate occupiers of the lands, except in parts of the country which had been desolated by war or afforested, remained for the most part undisturbed. They had changed masters, but still held and cultivated their lands, on similar conditions, and with like services, as in the days of the Confessor.

Indeed, there is but small necessity for ascribing the changes effected by the Conquest to national subjugation and hostile influence. The whole stream of events for some years before William set foot on the shores of England had been naturally drifting into a ready acceptance of the rule of the Norman, whose language and customs had for some years been in fame in high places. The long residence of the Confessor in Normandy had created a partiality for the customs of the country, and many such usages had been adopted by him. He surrounded himself with men of that nation, and of the few castles that were built in his time the most important were garrisoned by French and Norman soldiers. Hence everything was prepared for the success of the Norman, and the conquest, when calmly considered, is rather to be regarded as an event to be expected, than as an overwhelming catastrophe involving the destruction of independence and nationality. As Palgrave has said,—"William never strove to Normanize the English people. He was cruel, though perhaps not unnecessarily so, yet never interfered except when he needed to interfere. He never attempted to introduce a new religion, new language, new laws. Let us but refer to the Laws of the Conqueror, and to the 'custumal' ascribed to Henry Beauclerc, and we have therein an assured testimony, that, as far as direct and positive legislation is concerned, William effected the smallest possible alteration. In regard to the assertion that in the very frame of his laws he made a distinction between Norman and English, we may appeal to the fact that they were received by the nation not only without reluctance but with zealous joy. Thus the very means by which William was able to accomplish the conquest prevented him from ruling otherwise than as an English king."[1]

---

[1] Normandy and England, III., 595.

CHAPTER II.

Meaning of the word Manor. Two-fold character of ancient manors. Inalienable manors. Domesday manors not always co-extensive with the present parishes. Their correspondence in many cases with tithe-districts. Land-limits in ancient charters still applicable. Hundreds and Tithings,—opinions as to the origin of them, how far to be ascribed to Alfred the Great. Evidence as to the antiquity of the Wiltshire Hundreds. Ragged Hundreds. The Hide and Virgate,—their probable average extent. The Hide as an assessment. The Carucate, and Bovate,—their extent. Measure of the Leuca and Quarentena. The Wood-land and Forests. The Mills. The Vineyards.

Meaning of the word 'Manor' Two-fold character of the ancient manors.

IN order to understand the entries in Domesday, it is necessary to bear in mind the precise character of a MANOR in olden time. By this term, which, it is contended by some authorities, is of Norman origin and derived from the French *manoir*,[1] though certainly the thing signified was not unknown to the Saxon constitution, is denoted not only a landed estate, but also a seignory or lordship, extending in some cases over several subordinate manors. Archdeacon Hale, in his introduction to the Domesday of St. Paul's, has well explained this *two-fold* character of the ancient manors. "Manorial property," he says, "was a possession differing in many respects from what is now called landed estate. It was not a breadth of land, which the lord might cultivate or not, as he pleased, suffer it to be inhabited, or reduce it to solitude and waste, but it was a dominion or empire, within which the lord was the superior over subjects of different ranks, his power over them not being absolute, but limited by law and custom. The lord of a manor who had received, by grant from the Crown, saca and soca, tol and team, &c., was not merely a proprietor but a prince; and his courts were not only courts of law, but frequently of criminal justice. The demesne, the assised, and the waste lands were his; but the usufruct of the assised lands belonged, on conditions, to the tenants, and the waste lands were not so entirely his, that he could exclude the tenants from the use of them. The lord stood to his tenants in a double capacity as the arbiter of their rights, as well as the owner of the land, and a Manor was both a Seignory and also a Farm; a Seignory as respected the occupiers of the lands held by the payment of services, rents, and heriots; and a Farm as respected the demesne lands; the Seneschallus, or Steward, being the representative of the lord, and the judge of the manorial courts; and the Ballivus being the officer who exacted the services due from the tenants for the cultivation of the demesne."[2]

---

[1] See Ellis, I. 224. The primary idea conveyed by the word 'MANOR' is, that it was the usual *residence* of the owner on his land. Ordericus Vitalis (Book iv.) when speaking of the possessions bestowed by the Conqueror on the Bishop of Coutance, describes them as "ducentas et octoginta *villas*, quas *a manendo* vulgo vocamus." So in the Domesday for Chester (I. *fol.* 268) we read, "Homo *manens* in isto hundredo;" and in that for Surrey (I., *fol.* 30) we have the expression, "abstulit rusticum qui ibi *manebat*."

[2] Introduction to the Domesday of St. Paul's, pp. xxxiii., xxxvii.

Principal and subordinate manors

In the ensuing pages it will be observed that in the case of the greater land-owners a certain number of estates are entered in the Record as *possessed by themselves*, others as simply *held under them* as chief lords by some subordinate tenant. Thus, to take one instance out of a large number that might be adduced, of LACOCH (*p.* 71) it is said, "Edward [of Salisbury] *himself* holds Lacock,"—whilst of LANGEFEL (*p.* 71) it is said, "Borel holds Langley [Burrell] of Edward of Salisbury." This distinction must be borne in mind, especially in seeking to trace out the descent of the various estates. The latter class of manors is not alluded to in the Exon Domesday, except incidentally, inasmuch as only the demesne lands of the great lords and barons,[1] and not those held by subordinate tenants under them, were exempt from payment of the Dane-geld. Of course, in cases where the seignory alone appertained to the chief lord, all the benefits accruing to him, though sometimes they were substantial, were the profits derived from heriots, or fines, or the dues payable on Law-days, when the tenants were bound to give their attendance at his court. The spirit of the feudal system, which was based on the mutual dependence of class on class, required that every possessor of a manor should render service to some superior lord. This explains entries we find frequently in the Wiltshire Domesday (as, for example, at *p.* 72, under DEPEFORD), in which it is said that a tenant *could go whither he wished* (potuit ire quo volebat),—that is, he could transfer his feudal allegiance to any chief lord he chose. One instance, recorded at *p.* 77, is singular; a Thane holding a small estate at CHEIESLAVE (Chedglow), who had the power of thus transferring his allegiance, and, as seems to be implied, had exercised it, again, "of his own accord returned to Ernulf de Hesding" (sponte se vertit ad Ernulfum). In other instances the smaller manors were *inalienable* from some particular chief lord. Hence, we meet with the phrase, 'non potuit recedere a domino suo,' that is, he "could not depart from his lord," or separate himself from the principal manor. In the case of lands belonging to the Church this condition seems always as a rule to have attached to them. Examples such as we have at *p.* 17, respecting some of the under-tenants at DUNTONE,—"Qui has terras tenebant T. R. E. non se poterant ab ecclesia separare,"—are frequent throughout the Record. A remarkable entry, however, at *p.* 110, under HIWI seems to imply that, during a lease on lives of church property, the lessee might at times claim the liberty of doing suit and service at what lord's court he pleased. "Toti," it is said, "purchased Hiwi, in the time of King Edward, of the Church of Malmesbury, for the *lives of three men*, and *within that term he could go with the land to what lord he pleased.*"

Inalienable manors.

Domesday manors not always co-extensive with the present parishes.

Another thing to be remembered in considering the entries in Domesday is this,—that the manors mentioned there are by no means necessarily co-extensive with the present parishes. The manor is at times more extensive than the parish, or the parish comprises more than one manor. Examples of the former are given in the preceding chapter (*p.* xix); we there see how an entry in Domesday corresponds often with *several* manors, some of which even as early as 1290 (the date of the taxation of Pope Nicholas), had become independent parishes, or at least free-chapelries dependent upon the mother church. On the other hand, one of our present parishes is sometimes accounted for in the Record under several entries. Thus, in GREAT BEDWIN are included not only Bedvinde (*p.* 7),—but also Haredone (*p.* 145)—Ulfela (*p.* 146)—*two* entries under Mertone (*pp.* 145, 146)—and no less than *four* entries under the head of Graftone or Grastone (*pp.* 100, 145). In HELMARTON are comprised the Domesday manors of Adhelmertone (*p.* 100)—Helmertune (*p.* 134)—Helmerintone (*p.* 96)—Clive (*p.* 83)—and Gategram (*p.* 142). CLIFF PIPARD, in like manner, comprises several entries under the generic term Clive, references to which may be seen in the Analysis at *p.* 207. And

[1] See below, p. 154.

then the larger part of the present parish of AVEBURY is accounted for, not under the entry Avreberic (*p.* 16) but under those of Bachentune (*p.* 95), and Chenete (*p.* 84). It is of course most important, that, before we draw any deductions from the entries in Domesday, we should be quite clear that we are dealing with *the precise area of the manorial district* which King William's commissioners undertook to survey. A neglect of this precaution has led Kemble into error (at least as far as his Wiltshire examples are concerned), in his remarks on the extent of the 'hide.' Thus, whilst under BROKENBOROUGH he gives the bidage as it is in Domesday, he makes the estate consist only of 2950 acres (about the extent of what is *now* included in that parish)—whereas in the *fifty hides* at which it was assessed, as has been already shewn (*p.* xix), lands at Rodburne,—Grittenham,—and Sutton [Beuger] were included, the actual extent of the Domesday manor amounting to at least 6000, or perhaps 7000 acres.[1] Without doubt, many of the smaller holdings have, in the course of centuries, been absorbed into the larger estates, and it is now impossible accurately to mark out their original boundaries. Still, a considerable number remain, as they were at the time of Domesday, in the various *tithe-districts* which are kept as distinct portions of the several parishes of which now they are considered part. Fortunately we have preserved to us a large collection of Anglo-Saxon charters relating to Wiltshire, and to this day many a manor may be traced out by means of the land-limits given in a grant of Alfred or Edgar.[2] In several instances has the author gone over the boundaries of such manors with an ancient charter, and the Ordnance Map divided into parishes, or rather tithe-districts, as his guides, and most striking has been the way in which boundaries described, now some thousand years ago, may still be accurately traced. To this day the names originally given to hills and brooks survive, though those names may be unknown even to the proprietors of the estates themselves, and are treasured up only in the memory of the shepherd that tends his flocks on the Wiltshire downs, or the labourer that tills the soil. And in cases where we have no ancient charters as our guides, there can be little doubt but that the Ordnance Map, divided, as we have intimated, into Tithe Districts, and supplemented where it is deficient from the parish maps and terriers, is the safest guide in forming a judgment as to the actual extent of land included in many of the manors mentioned in the Domesday Survey.

Ancient manors often correspond with tithe districts.

In the returns for many of the counties, the King's Commissioners placed the several estates under the respective HUNDREDS, within the limits of which they were situated. In the Exchequer Domesday for Wiltshire

---

[1] Kemble's "Saxons in England," I., 107. The other Wiltshire examples given in the same passage are also incorrect. NEWNTON is said to be assessed at *ten hides* and to consist of 810 *acres*. There are two places of this name in Wilts, Newnton next Tetbury, and North Newnton near Pewsey; the former is the NEWENTONE (p. 36) which contains 1570 acres, and is reckoned at *thirty hides*,—the latter the NEWETONE (p. 45) which is assessed at *thirteen hides and a half*, and contains some 1080 acres. Again, Kemble gives two entries under KINGTON, each assessed at the large amount of *forty hides*, and containing respectively 2320 and 3950 acres. Certainly this description cannot apply either to Kington St. Michael, or to West Kington, as the reader may soon convince himself by turning to those names in the general index to this Volume, and examining the references there given to various entries in the Exchequer Domesday.

[2] One instance I cannot help mentioning. No long time ago, I was perambulating, together with a friend, who was well acquainted with the locality, the parish of ALTON PRIORS, a charter relating to which is contained in the Codex Winton. At starting, we learnt that the largest of the several streams which are to be seen there, and from which the parish, originally called *Æwel-tún*, that is, "the village by the springs," derives its name, was called (spelling it as it was pronounced to us) *Brad-ells*. Our charter soon interpreted this, for the starting point in its description was—First, from the western-most spring (or stream) that is called *Bradewyll*, *i.e.*, simply the "broad spring." At another point we came upon what tradition marks out as an old British road; on enquiring from a shepherd the names of places in that immediate locality, we found that a hill just above the ancient track-way was (as he pronounced it) called *Walo-way* hill. Our charter here described a *weala-wege*, that is a *Welsh-way*, the ordinary name for the old British roads. In the ordnance map the name has been tortured into *Walker's Hill*.—I may add that we were able to identify with accuracy nearly every boundary-point indicated in the Anglo-Saxon charter.

the Hundreds are omitted, and this circumstance makes our portion of the Record more difficult of accurate interpretation. Fortunately a list of them, and of the principal holders of manors in them, is supplied to us in the Exon Domesday; and hence we have been able, though the task of tracing them out has been long and wearisome, to identify with tolerable certainty by far the greater number of the estates. On the Wiltshire Hundreds, in particular, information will be found at *p.* 155, in the introduction to the Exon Domesday. Some remarks, however, may be here introduced on Hundreds and Tithings in general, and on a few matters incidentally arising out of the consideration of those for Wiltshire.

Hundreds and Tithings; opinions as to their origin.

Much has been written on the subject of the first institution of HUNDREDS and TITHINGS in England. At what time they were originally established here, and for what object, as well as the way in which they were formed,—these questions have been discussed by scholars of learning and weight. Lambard and Spelman, no mean authorities, have contended that the Hundred is to be understood of a Hundred heads of families. Bromton, Abbot of Jervaux, considered that it comprised a Hundred villages.[1] The author of the "Dialogus de Scaccario,"[2] on the other hand, was of opinion that it consisted of a number of Hides, sometimes more and sometimes less, but of no certain quantity. His words are,—"Hundredus vero ex Hydarum aliquot centenariis sed non determinatis; quidam enim ex pluribus, quidam ex paucioribus Hidis constat."—Ellis, however, brings forward extracts from a very ancient Leiger Book of Peterborough Abbey, "containing an enumeration of the Hundreds of Northamptonshire and their contents, referring to the time of the Confessor, in which *every Hundred is made to consist of one hundred hides:* the hides paying geld being particularly distinguished from those in the royal occupation, and the waste uncultivated land."[3] This opinion thus sustained, is corroborated, he contends by a passage in Domesday itself, in its account of the lands belonging to Evesham Abbey and which is as follows:— "In Fissesberge Hund. habet ecclesia de Evesham lxv. hid. Ex his xii. hidæ sunt liberæ. In illo Hund. jacent xx. hidæ de Dodentreu, et *xv. hidæ de Wirecestre perficiunt hundret.*"[4] The last few words in which the fifteen hides are spoken of as *making up the hundred,* coupled with his extract from the Leiger Book of Peterborough, he considers as conclusive evidence as to the real origin of the Hundred. But after all, as Hallam truly remarks, and the varying size of the Wiltshire Hundreds gives much weight to his words:—"there is one circumstance observable which seems to indicate that the division of the country into Hundreds could not have taken place at one time or on one system, namely, the extreme inequality of Hundreds in various parts of England. Whether the name be considered to denote the number of free families, or of land-holders, or of petty vills forming so many associations of mutual assurance of frank-pledge, we can hardly doubt that when the term was first applied, a

---

[1] See Ellis, I. 188.

[2] The document is printed in Madox's History of the Exchequer, 4th edition; vol. i., 399.

[3] The document is in the library of the Society of Antiquaries. Ellis (I. 184) prints it entire in a note. He is, however, mistaken in saying that '*every Hundred is made to consist of one hundred hides.*' In many instances it is so, and there are several cases in which the division is called *a hundred and a half,* and made to consist of 150 hides. Still, SPELHOH Hundred had but 90 hides, POCABROC 62 hides, STOCK 40 hides. See Morgan's 'England under the Normans,' p. 181.

[4] Domesday, i., 184. See Ellis, I. xix.

hundred of one or other of these were comprised, at an average reckoning, within the district. But it is impossible to reconcile the varying size of hundreds to any single hypothesis."[1]

The most careful examination of the subject is perhaps to be found in Kemble's valuable work, "The Saxons in England." His views may be expressed in brief as follows. From the first, we find the inhabitants of the Mark classed in *tens* and *hundreds*, each probably comprising respectively a corresponding number of members, together with the necessary officers, viz., a Tithing-man for each tithing, and a Hundred-man for each hundred.[2] The Frankish law names the officers thus alluded to; in it the tithing-men are DECANI (which appear to be the same as the DECIMALES HOMINES[3] alluded to in the Laws of Æthelred) and the Hundred-men CENTENARII. Now though the Anglo-Saxon laws do not mention these divisions by these names till a comparatively late period, when this signification had become altered, they do seem to imply them under the term GEGYLDAN, that is, brothers, or fellows of the *gyld*. Thus it is provided in the laws of Alfred, that, in the case of aggravated crime, the offender's relations should pay one third of the fine, his *gegyldan* one third, the remaining third being paid by himself, and in the event of his not being able to pay his proportion he is to forfeit his land, and flee from the country.[4] This law of course implies that *gegylda* was a general name borne by every individual in respect of some *gyld*, or association of which he was a member. The most probable meaning of the world *gegylda* is *one who shares with others in paying;* and, adopting this interpretation, we may suppose that certain contributions were made by a number of persons to a common purse, as a mutual guarantee fund, for the expenses of reciprocal aid and defence, or for general charitable purposes, or, as is possible, for the outfit of armed men who attend in the *fyrd*, or military expedition,[5] on behalf of them all.

In later times the Tithing and Hundred appear as local and territorial, not as numerical divisions. We hear of tithings where there are more, and tithings where there are fewer people. But this does not necessarily invalidate the doctrine, that originally the numbers were calculated according to the heads of families, or that the extent of territory formed at first the varying quantity. In truth the difference in size and number of hundreds in different counties is only intelligible if we assume population, and not space, to have been the basis of the original calculation. Moreover, to a late period, in one part of England the abstract word Teoðung (Tithing) was replaced by the word Tyn-manna-tæl (Ten-man-tale), to which it is impossible to give

---

[1] Europe in the Middle Ages. Chap. viii., part 1.

[2] Hundreds are first *mentioned* in the laws of Edgar, and Tithings in those of Canute. In both passages, however, they seem to be alluded to as institutions already recognized, and so no light is thrown by such mention on their first establishment. Thorpe's Ancient Laws &c., I. 258, 269, 387.

[3] Laws of Æthelred, ch. viii., § 2. [Thorpe, I. 338.]

[4] Laws of Alfred, § 27. [Thorpe, I. 79.]

[5] The opinion held by some that the hundred was at the first a military organization, seems to derive support from the term used in some of the northern counties, as equivalent to it, viz., *Wapentake*. The meaning and derivation of this word are thus explained in one of the Laws of Edward the Confessor:—"Cum aliquis accipiebat prefecturam Wapentagii die statuto in loco ubi consueverant congregari, omnes majores natu contra eum conveniebant, et descendente eo de equo suo, omnes assurgebant ei. Ipse vero erecta lancea sua, ab omnibus, secundum morem, fœdus accipiebat: omnes enim quotquot venissent cum lanceis suis ipsius hastam tangebant, et ita se confirmabant per contactum armorum, pace palam concessa. Anglice vero arma vocantur *wæpen* (= weapon) et *taccare* confirmare, quasi armorum confirmacio, vel ut magis expresse, secundum linguam Anglicam, dicamus Wapentac, *i.e.*, armorum tactus; *wæpen* enim arma sonat; *tac* tactus est. Quamobrem potest cognosci quod hac de causa totus ille conventus dicitur WAPENTAC, eo *quod per tactum armorum suorum ad invicem confœderati sunt*."—Thorpe, I. 455. See also, Ellis, I. 161.

any meaning but the simple one the words express, *viz.*, the 'tale or count of ten *men.*'—And so too, in the city of London, where men, and not acres, became necessarily the subjects of calculation, we find the citizens distributing themselves into Friðgylds, or associations for the maintenance of the peace, each consisting of *ten men;* while ten such gylds formed the HUNDRED.

After giving other illustrations of his views, Kemble adds,—" It is true that no division founded upon numbers can long continue to coincide with the first corresponding territorial allocation, however closely they may have been at first adjusted. In spite of every attempt to regulate it, population varies incessantly; but the tendency of land-divisions is to remain stationary for ages; a holy horror prevents the alteration of that which has been sanctified in men's minds by long continuance, and was perhaps more deeply sanctified at the first by religious ceremonies. The rights of property universally demand the jealous guardianship of boundaries. Moreover the first Tithings, or at all events the first Hundreds, must have had elbow-room enough within the Mark to allow for a considerable elasticity of population without the necessity of disturbing the ancient boundary; and thus we can readily understand two very distinct things to have grown up together out of one origin, namely, a constantly increasing number of gylds, yet a nearly, or entirely, stationary tale of territorial tithings and hundreds." [1]

How far the origin of Tithings and Hundreds can be attributed to King Alfred.

It is often said that we owe the institution of Shires, Tithings, and Hundreds to Alfred the Great. As to the divisions of the counties, and their government by aldermen and sheriffs, these certainly existed long before his time, for they are alluded to in the laws of King Ina, *c.* A.D. 700. And with regard to tithings and hundreds, the first writer who attributes their institution to Alfred is Ingulphus, who lived at the time of the Conquest. It is true that in a manuscript, entitled 'Cronicon Wintonense,' we have, under the date 882, the following entry, 'Aluredus Rex instituit hundredos et tethingas ad latrones investigandos,' [2] but literally true the statement cannot be, for as Alfred was never master of more than half the kingdom, the complete distribution of England into these districts cannot upon any supposition be referred to him. Moreover, the silence of cotemporary writers on the subject, and the absence of all allusion to these institutions in the laws of Alfred, are the strongest argument against the opinion that he was the first to establish them. The ready willingness to believe him to have been their author is an instance of the strength of national feeling, which, in reverence for the memory of that great man, makes him the representative of every thing that is good, and connects every institution of worth with his name. Possibly, as Kemble suggests, the tradition may be *in part* true, for he may have found it necessary, after the devastation of the Danish wars, to make a new muster or regulation of the tithings, nay, even to cause, in some districts of his kingdom, a new territorial division to be established on the old principle. It may be, that the words of the old Winchester Chronicle are susceptible of the interpretation, that as Tithings and Hundreds were first established for mutual protection, so Alfred utilized them for the purpose of ensuring the internal security of his kingdom. We know at least, that on these was based the institution called Frank-pledge, [3] which is also attributed to Alfred, though the principle of it was as old as the

---

[1] 'Saxons in England, I.' pp. 237—241, 245.

[2] MS. Cott. Domit. A. 13, *fol.* 10. See New Mon. I. 205.

[3] See 'Saxons in England,' I. 249.

Anglo-Saxon monarchy itself. But still he carried out that principle into active exercise, and this circumstance may have given rise to the tradition that Hundreds and Tithings were first of all instituted by him.

Evidence as to the antiquity of the Wiltshire Hundreds.

There are one or two points connected with the Hundreds for Wiltshire, which seem to throw light incidentally on the antiquity of this institution, on which we must in passing offer a few remarks. By referring to the list of them given at *p.* 155, it will be observed, that, out of 40 which are enumerated, there are but 12 which are called from the chief town contained within their limits. These are—Ambresbury, Bradford, Cricklade, Chippenham, Calne, Downton, Heytesbury, Melksham, Mere, Ramsbury, Warminster. The comparatively small places, Alderbury, Cannings, Damerham, and Worth (Highworth), give names to Hundreds; but neither Bedwin, Wilton, or Malmesbury are found assigning their names to such divisions of territory; and of the rest, the meaning of some of the words is so obscure as to be beyond our power to explain, whilst of others the interpretation seems to point to a remote time when the county was but thinly peopled, and there were but few towns or villages of any note in it. Thus BLACHE-GRAVE means the dark grove or wood; THORN-GRAVE and THORN-HILL, the wood and hill respectively covered with thorns or brambles; STAN-FORD, the *stone* (paved) ford over a stream, the old name for the present hundred of Chalk; STOD-FALD, the fold, or place, for horses (Anglo-Saxon *stód-fald*); EL-STUB, in Anglo-Saxon *ellen-stub*, the stump or stowl of the elder, of very common occurrence in the recital of ancient boundaries; STAPLE (A. S. *stapol*), literally an upright post or pillar, designating, at the first perhaps, the place where the Hundred Court was held, when, meeting in open-air, they transacted the business of which that ancient court took cognisance; RUGEBERG, *i.e.*, the *rough*, or hoar barrow; WHER-WELS-DON, (originally perhaps *hár-welles-dún,) i.e.*, the hill by the hoar, or ancient well. And it is hard to explain, except by the merest conjecture, such names as FERSTESFIELD (Frustfield),—STERKLEY,—BRENCHESBERG (Branch),—DOLESFELT (Dole),—and SELKLEY,—all traces having for the most part long since perished of the sources from which they were originally derived. Most certainly such names tell of great antiquity, and point to a time when Wiltshire had but few places of note which might give names to the Hundreds in which they were situated. And a very early and primitive state of things must be indicated, when the ancient barrow or tumulus, the elder-stowl, the hoar or ancient well, the staple or stone pillar, give names to Hundreds.

Add to this the following facts, and they are not without weight in giving colour for the belief, that the institution of Hundreds in Wilts was perhaps some 200 years before Alfred's time. Up to the close of the 11th century, the date of the Exon Domesday, there is no such hundred as that of Malmesbury. In the year 1340 as we learn from the Inquisitiones Nonarum, what is now the town of Malmesbury was situated in *two hundreds*, the dividing line running through it. The Church of St. Mary, together with Brokenborough and Charlton, was in the hundred of CHEGGELEWE; the Church of St. Paul, together with Rodbourn and Corston, was in the hundred of STERCHELEE. If the town of Malmesbury existed at the time when the hundreds were formed, is it likely that it would have been parted between *two* hundreds, especially when we bear in mind that the lordship of both, as well as all the neighbouring estates, belonged from an early period to the Abbot of Malmesbury? In fact, is it not almost certain that had it so existed it would have given its name (as it did in after times) to the hundred, like Bradford, Westbury, Calne, Warminster, &c.? Now, Malmesbury is mentioned as a town by Bede, who calls it "Maildulfi urbs," under the date of A.D. 705. If therefore there be any force in the facts on which we have been dwelling, they would furnish, to say the least, a strong probability that the Wiltshire Hundreds were formed before the town of Malmesbury was built, and, consequently some 200 years before Alfred the Great was born. As far as they go they would give some confirmation to the opinion advanced by Hutchins and others.

that their first institution is, with far more likelihood, to be attributed to Ina, the friend and kinsman of Aldhelm, who was king of Wessex, A.D. 688–725.[1]

Ragged Hundreds.

A few words must be added upon the subject of what are called RAGGED HUNDREDS, a name employed to denote Hundreds composed of a number of estates lying in different parts of the county, and yet reckoned as portions of one and the same Hundred. In a preceding page (*p.* xix), mention has been made of the custom of including in the same estate outlying portions granted with it, and, so to speak, appurtenant to the principal manor. These outlying portions came afterwards to be regarded as in the same Hundred with the chief manor. Hence SEMLEY is in the hundred of Chalk,—and BISHOPSTON (in South Wilts) in that of Downton,—and SUTTON BENGER in that of Malmesbury,—though all these places are locally situated in other Hundreds. In some instances we are quite unable to explain, especially at this distance of time, why these eccentric arrangements should have prevailed. No doubt, even as early as the time of Domesday, lands were taken from one manor, or hundred, and attached to another, many of the Thanes, as we have already remarked,[2] having power to remove their lands and change their lords, and many of these changes may have been the result of simple caprice. A close connection between BRITFORD and BRAMSHAW may account for the latter place, like the former, being in the Hundred of Cadworth.[3] But why COMPTON CHAMBERLAIN should be in the hundred of Damerham, or FISHERTON DELAMERE and DINTON in that of Warminster, it is not easy to say. It was, however, in the course of the 13th century that these anomalous arrangements increased. The Hundred Rolls are full of complaints respecting some of the greater land-owners,—and in almost every instance they were ecclesiastical persons,—who withdrew their estates from the hundred to which they properly belonged, and attached them to some distant hundred in which was situated their principal manor, or, as it was technically termed, '*caput baroniæ*,' the head of their barony. Thus the Bishop of Winchester, *c.* 1330, removed EAST KNOYLE and FONTHILL, both of which belonged to his see, the one from Mere, and the other from Dunworth, and attached them to the hundred of Downton, the lordship of which was vested in him. In like manner a previous Bishop of Winchester had attached all the estates which belonged to the Priory of St. Swithin, of which he was, so to speak, a trustee, such as ALTON (Priors),—HAM,—WESTWOOD,—STOCKTON, and some few others, to the hundred of Elstub, in which was situated ENFORD, one of the largest of them. In one case we have a deed preserved to us, showing that sometimes the transfer was made in a business-like way, and with no attempt to defraud the lord of the hundred, in which they were properly situated, of his rights. The document in question relates to certain estates belonging to the Abbot of Glastonbury, which at the time (A.D., 1319) were in the hundred of Chippenham. It is as follows;—"To all &c. Edmund Gascelyn, Lord of the Hundred of Chippenham, greeting. Know &c., that I have quite claimed for myself and my heirs for ever to Godfrey by the Grace of GOD, Lord Abbot of Glastonbury and to the Convent there, all summonses, attachments, distraints, and execution of all briefs, precepts and mandates of our Lord the King, his Justices, Sheriffs, and all other his officers, in Kingston St. Michael,—Christtemalforde,—Gritelington,—and Netelington, and all lands and fees thereto belonging in Wiltshire. Witnessed &c.—Dated at Glastonbury, Monday after Feast of Purification, 13 Edward II."[4] The Abbot at once formed

---

[1] History of Dorset. Vol. iv. Dissertation on Domesday. [2] See above, p. xxvi.

[3] See Sir R. C. Hoare's 'Frustfield Hundred,' p. 93, on outlying portions of the hundred of Alderbury.

[4] See Jackson's Aubrey, p. 124.

a new hundred called that of NORTH DAMERHAM (after the name of his principal estate in South Wilts,) in which he placed the *four* manors so ceded to him.

These irregularities, of which we have been speaking, exist even to the present day. It says much for the dislike to change and innovation which is the characteristic of our countrymen, to observe how for centuries they have patiently acquiesced in such anomalous arrangements, too often at first the result of the exercise of arbitrary power. It needed but the memory of one generation to make them accomplished facts, and the next reverences them as memorials of the past, which no rude hand is hastily to obliterate.

The HIDE and VIRGATE.

Many and conflicting are the accounts given to us respecting the HIDE and VIRGATE. The former was a very ancient denomination of land among the Anglo-Saxons. It is mentioned repeatedly in the laws of King Ina, which were promulgated at the commencement of the eighth century. Kemble's account of the derivation of the word appears to be the true one. He says, "The ordinary Anglo-Saxon words are *Higid*—(in its contracted and almost universal form *Híd*)—and *Hiwisc*. The Latin equivalents, which we find in the chronicles and charters, are *familia, cassatus, mansus, mansio, manens,* and *terra tributarii.* The words Híd and Hiwisc are similar, if not identical, in meaning; they stand in close etymological relation to Higan, Hiwan, the family, the man and wife, and thus perfectly to justify the Latin terms *familia* and *cassatus* by which they are translated. The Híd then, or Hide of land, is the estate of one household, the amount of land sufficient for the support of one family. It is clear, however, that this could not be an invariable quantity, if the households were to subsist on an equal scale: it must depend on the original quality and condition of the soil, as well as upon manifold contingencies of situation—climate, aspect, accessibility of water and roads, abundance of natural manures, proximity of marshes and forests, in short an endless catalogue of varying details."[1]

Varying statements as to the extent of the Hide.

It is owing to this circumstance that the accounts given to us concerning the *extent* of the Hide are so various. Selden no doubt was quite right in saying that 'the just value of a Hide that might fit the whole kingdom never appears from Domesday, and was ever of uncertain quantity.'[2] The author of the Dialogus de Scaccacio makes it *one hundred acres*:—"Ruricolæ melius hoc norunt; verum, sicut ab ipsis accepimus, Hida a primitiva institutione ex *centum acris* constat." Spelman, citing a Malmesbury manuscript, computes it at *ninety-six* acres. Agard again quotes several ancient documents which seem to prove that *one hundred and twenty* acres, both before and after the conquest, went to the Hide.[3] Such varying statements, for each of which no doubt there are good grounds, are only to be explained on the supposition that *at first* the Hide was of *uncertain quantity.* In fact, as Sir Francis Palgrave has well explained it, "Land was measured by a compromise between superficial extent and productive value. Instead of trundling the theodolite, they yoked the oxen and sped the plough. The carucate consisted of so much land as the ploughshare could furrow in the course of the season; the half-drowned plashes which sunk beneath the tread, or the soil studded with jutting rocks, where the husbandman could not turn up the glebe, were no portion of the plough-land. The bents and sedges where the ox could not feed were excluded from the ox-gang. The ridges and balks over which the scythe could not

---

[1] 'Saxons in England,' I. 91. See also Cod. Dipl., vol. iii., in the glossary at the commencement of the volume, *sub voce* Híd.

[2] Selden. Tit. Hon. p. 622. See also Kelham, p. 231.

[3] See all the authorities given in Ellis I. 145—148.

mow the grass, were not reckoned in the 'day-math,' and, generally speaking, no land uncultivated at the time of the Domesday survey was included in the calculation of the Hides. Hence the very unequal admeasurement of the plough-land, carucate, or hide, in subsequent times, when by usage it became a regular sum total of acreage; the same denomination of measure, a 'hide-land,' or its synonyms, being applied to 60, 80, 100, 112, 120, or 150 acres."[1]

Within a very few years of the completion of Domesday, William Rufus, urged on by his minister Flambard, ignored this *equitable* mode of reckoning the extent of the Hide, and caused the land to be remeasured by *the rope or line*,[2] thus rendering superficial extent alone the basis of calculation. The crown officers formed a new cadastre according to the new principle, which took no account whatever of the *quality* of the soil. The land was meted out according to an invariable geometrical standard without any reference to its productive worth. The result of course exhibited a much larger Hidage than the Domesday Survey, and the tax increased accordingly, to the great injury, in many cases, of the land holders.[3]

Admitting the fact, that the Hide was at the first a *conventional* rather than any *fixed* amount of land, and that it so continued to the time of Domesday, we nevertheless meet with statements that seem to imply that some rule was adopted in settling the number of Hides in each estate. Bede speaks in several places of manors consisting of so many hides '*juxta mensuram Anglorum.*' And such entries as we have under Adelingtone (*p.* 79), which consisted of eleven hides and a half, *and five acres*,—and Dobreham (*p.* 29), where one of the subordinate tenants is said to possess one hide, *and eight acres*;—and Devrel (*p.* 56), in which three hides and a half, *all but three acres*, are said to be in demesne, seem to imply some attempt at accurate valuation or measurement. However much the Hide may differ in average extent in various counties, there is of course a strong antecedent probability that in one and the same county it would approximate, more or less, to some fixed amount of land. The question we have to try to solve is,—"What was the average extent of the Hide in Wiltshire?"

---

[1] History of Normandy and England, iv., 60.

[2] Flambard was not without a precedent for this step, for the territorial divisions in Sussex, which are still called *Rapes*, are so designated from the fact that the Conqueror from the first divided that county by '*the rope*' as it was termed, that is, by actual measurement. As Palgrave says: "He divided that county into six districts, extending right down from the northern border, each possessing a frontage towards the sea, each effecting a ready communication with Normandy, and constituting, as it were, six military high roads to his paternal duchy. But few Norwegian or Teutonic terms can comparatively be found preserved among the Normans, but the '*hreppar*' seems to have been retained almost unaltered among them. Hence these demarcations were, and still are called, '*rapes.*' Each possessed within its bounds some one castle or other important station for defence or protection, and each appears to have been placed under some military commander. Sussex alone, of all the counties in England, sustained this great territorial alteration, being dealt with from the first moment entirely as a conquered territory."—Hist. of Normandy and England, II., 394.

[3] Ordericus Vitalis, who was living at the time, gives us an exact account of this transaction, and of the hardships that it inflicted. "Hic [Flambard] juvenem fraudulentis stimulationibus inquietavit Regem, incitans ut totius Angliæ reviseret descriptionem, Anglicæque telluris comprobans iteraret partitionem, subditisque recideret, tam advenis quam indigenis, quicquid inveniretur ultra certam dimensionem. Annuente Rege, omnes *carucatas*, quas Angli *hidas* vocant, funiculo mensus est et descripsit; postpositisque mensuris, quas liberales Angli jussu Edwardi Regis largiter distribuerant, imminuit, et regales fiscos accumulans colonis arva retruncavit. Ruris itaque olim diutius nacti diminutione, et insoliti vectigalis gravi exaggeratione, supplices Regiæ fidelitati plebes indecenter oppressit, ablatis rebus attenuavit, et in nimiam egestatem de ingenti copia redegit."—Order. Vital. Lib. viii. cap. 8. (A°. 1089).

Probable average extent of the Hide in Wiltshire.

The Exon Domesday gives us material help in this enquiry. We gather from it, in the first place, that each HIDE consisted of *four* VIRGATES :—in every instance the 'geld,' which was *six shillings* on the Hide, is calculated at a proportionate sum on the Virgates. Thus, at *p.* 181, we have this entry,—"Saulf retained the tax of *one hide* and *one virgate*, to wit, *seven shillings and sixpence.*" Again, at *p.* 159, we are told,—"Of the land of Ernulf de Hesding, for *half-a-hide* and *half-a-virgate*, there have been retained *three shillings and ninepence.*" And, at *p.* 161, it is said,—"Turstin retained the geld of *three virgates*, to wit, *four shillings and sixpence.*"—And then, from an entry under CALNE (*p.* 172), we are able to infer what number of acres there were in each Virgate; for in *two* out of the three manuscripts of the Exon Domesday, *two parts of a virgate* are interpreted as *seven acres*, and the *third part of a virgate* as *three acres;* and that these were intended to be equivalents is clear from the fact of the geld payable being in either case the same sum. We arrive, therefore, at this result, that the HIDE, in Wiltshire, consisting of four Virgates, each of some ten acres, contained in round numbers *forty acres*. Assuming, as Kemble has endeavoured to show,[1] that an acre implied ordinarily a quantity of land not very different in extent from our own statute acre, we have at all events a starting point.

But on applying these calculations as tests to the correctness of the Domesday entries, we see at once that such a measurement cannot apply to the *whole* of each parish or manor. Thus, to take a few of the present parishes of which we can have little doubt as to their corresponding in extent with the Domesday manors,—WOCHESIE (*p.* 131), is said to have paid geld for ten hides, and as it contains 1490 acres, the average extent of each hide on this reckoning would be 149 acres ;—STERTE (*p.* 83), which contains 615 acres, is assessed at 5 hides, thus giving 123 acres for each ;—BISCOPESTREU (*p.* 76), with 1029 acres, is reckoned at 7 hides, each on this calculation with 147 acres ;—CRISTEMELEFORD (*p.* 30), with 2750 acres, is assessed at 20 hides, thus shewing an average 137 acres to each.

These apparent discrepancies are at once explained by reference to the customs of our Saxon forefathers as to the distribution of land when they first settled in England. "The district," says Kemble, "occupied by a body of new settlers was divided by lot in various proportions. Yet it is certain that *not all the land* was so distributed; a quantity sufficient to supply a block of arable to each settler was set apart for division ; while the surplus fitted for cultivation, the marshes and forests less suited to the operations of the plough, and a great amount of fine grass or meadow-land, destined for the maintenance of cattle, remained in undivided possession as commons. At first, too, considerable tracts were left purposely out of cultivation to form the marches or defences of the several communities."[2]

It is easy to understand how, in the course of centuries, from various causes, these lands thus *common*, in the first instance, to all who lived in a certain district, became apportioned amongst those who held the *arable*

---

[1] Kemble argues thus much from a passage in the dialogue attributed to Ælfric, where the ploughman is made to say, "Having yoked my oxen, and fastened my share and coulter, I am bound to plough *every day a full acre or more.*" He adds, that experience proves that a plough drawn by oxen will scarcely exceed this measure on average land at the present day; an acre and a quarter being a very hard day's work for any ploughman under such circumstances. (Saxons in England, I. 96.) In early times, however, the 'acre' was of uncertain quantity. It depended on the length of its perch, which varied by custom. In Cooke's 'Description of the County of Wilts,' (p. 46) he speaks of the perch in this county being of *three* lengths,—15, 18, and 16½ feet; the *first*, now nearly out of use, but commonly employed throughout England in the twelfth and thirteenth centuries; the *second*, the ancient forest measure, an acre derived from it consisting of no less than 5760 square yards; the *third*, the present standard measure. See, on this subject, Ellis' Introduction to Domesday, I., 157; and Morgan's England under the Normans, pp. 18—26.

[2] Saxons in England, I. 90.

land. They became, in fact, partible and appurtenant to private estates in a certain proportion to the arable. Thus Kemble quotes an Anglo-Saxon charter, bearing date 982, in which he finds the following grant;—" the millstead, and the mill, and so much of the mark-land *as belongs to three hides*."[1] A glance at a map of Wiltshire divided into tithe-districts, which, as we have intimated, so often correspond with the ancient manors, will at once show how much care was taken to assign to each a due quantity of arable land, and also of pasture and meadow. In several instances they run down in thin strips to the river from the hills, for the purpose of securing this necessary apportionment of lands.

The inference that we should draw would be this,—that the *forty acres* of which the Hide consisted (as we have gathered from the Exon Domesday) comprised simply the *arable land* contained in it, but that every HIDE *implied* a certain amount of pasture, meadow, and, it might be, of wood, as *necessarily appurtenant* to it. And this inference is confirmed by an entry in the Wiltshire Domesday. Thus, under EDENDONE (*p.* 144), Hervey is said to hold *one hide;* the land is described as being *one carucate,* and there is said to be as much meadow and pasture *as is sufficient for one hide* (tantum prati et pasturæ *quantum convenit uni hidæ*). In some instances it would appear that, in estimating the assessment of an estate in Hides, the smaller extent of the arable land was compensated for by a larger quantity of meadow and pasture. A comparison of two entries under CLIVE (*p.* 58) shews this clearly; each estate contained *a carucate and a half* of arable land; but, in the one case, geld was paid for *three hides,* in the other, for *three hides and three virgates;* and the explanation would appear to consist in the fact, that, in the former instance, there were but *ten acres of meadow,* in the latter, *sixteen acres of meadow,* and *fourteen acres of pasture.*

If we could trust the account given in the Exon Domesday as an accurate estimate of the number of hides in Wilts, it would not be difficult soon to arrive at a fair conclusion as to average number of acres included, or implied, in each. It is a question, however, how far the Exon Domesday takes notice of several large estates belonging to the Crown, such as Calne, Bedwin, Ambresbury, Warminster, and Chippenham, of which we are told in the Exchequer Domesday that they '*never paid geld, neither were assessed in hides.*' In some instances, we have the number of carucates that paid no geld, but not under any of the hundreds in which the manors just named were situated.[2] In one case, too, in which we have the means of comparing the entries in the two Records, there is a discrepancy which we cannot account for, since whilst under Wherwelsdown Hundred the Exon Domesday gives a total of *seventy-eight* hides, the Exchequer Domesday, as will be seen in the note below,[3] where the hidage of the several estates is given, makes it more than *ninety.* Taking it however for what it is worth, the estimate given in the Exon Domesday of the number of hides in Wiltshire, including in them

[1] 'Saxons in England,' I. 50. Cod. Dipl. 633.

[2] See above pp. 7—9, and compare the entries in the Exon Domesday under the Hundreds of CALNE (p. 171), KINWARDSTONE (p. 180), AMBRESBURY (p. 185), WARMINSTER (p. 176), and CHIPPENHAM (p. 161).

[3] Compare the entries at p. 172 with the following:—

EDENDONE	(p. 52)	reckoned at	30	hides.
EDENDONE	(p. 144)	,,	1	,,
COVELESTONE	(p. 131)	,,	5	,,
CHIVELE	(p. 74)	,,	16	,,
AISTONE	(p. 53)	,,	30	,,
		Total	92	hides

the 'carucates paying no geld,' that are reckoned under several of the Hundreds, amounts to 3996. The number of acres in our County is about 866,000, and, dividing these by the number of hides registered in the Exon Domesday, we get as a result an *average* amount of some 216 acres to each hide. This can hardly be accepted as a trustworthy result, even though we admit that a very large part of Wiltshire at the time of Domesday was forest or waste land. We must rather look for an explanation to the probable incompleteness of the Exon Domesday, and to another reason (on which we shall presently have more to say),—the fact that many of the estates were assessed at a less number of hides than they actually contained.

Fortunately we have a document preserved to us, of the date of Henry III., which may be deemed of better authority as to the actual number of hides in Wilts, inasmuch as though Flambard's re-measurement of them in the time of William Rufus, to which we have alluded, may in some cases have been atteuded with harshness, it at all events gives us the means of forming a more accurate judgment as to their average extent. In this document we have the following entry:—"In Wiltescyre continentur 4800 Hidæ."[1] Taking this as the actual number, the average extent of each hide, with its appurtenances of pasture and meadow (and including also in the calculation the forests and waste land), amounts to 180 acres. There can be no doubt but that the wood and waste land amounted to little less than *one-fifth* of the county, and, if allowance be made for this, and we reckon only the land which could more or less be profitably occupied, we arrive at a result which we believe to be near the truth, namely, that the Hide in Wiltshire implied an amount of arable land with meadow and pasture, varying, according to the quality of the soil, from 120 to 160 acres.

One interesting fact we may at all events deduce from the eutries in the Exon Domesday, compared with the statement of the ancient manuscript to which reference has been made. Reckoning each hide as containing *forty* acres of arable land, and the number of hides at 4800, this would give a total of 192,000 acres, or rather more than *one-fifth* of the whole land in Wiltshire, under the plough at the time of the Domesday survey.

The extent of the Hide according to ancient terriers and customs of parishes in Wiltshire.

These general conclusions respecting the extent of the Hide in our county are fairly borne out by reference to ancient terriers, and, where such can be ascertained, the custom of parishes. In the course of centuries, extensive clearing of wood-land has taken place, and much that was formerly waste or down land brought into tillage, and the proportion consequently borne by the arable to the rest of the land increased. As regards, however, the *total* number of acres included in the Yard-land (= Virgate), or the Hide, there is a remarkable agreement, whether our data are drawn from ancient or modern records.

The two following examples, taken from a Survey of the Manor of Bradford-on-Avon [*c.* 1629], will illustrate the point we are discussing:—

> "Henry Babshen holdeth by copy dated 16° May A° 39° Elizabethæ Reginæ one messuage and one *halfe yard-lande* containing in Arrable vii acres I yarde, mead half an acre, and pasture xii acres and halfe," &c.
>
> "Margaret Mathews widdowe holdeth by copy dated primo April, A° 4° Elizab. one messuage and 1 *yard-lande* in Lighe containing in Arrable xvi acres [and a half], mead half an acre, pasture xii acres xvii perches and wood 1 acre," &c.

[1] Cott. MSS. Claud. B. vii. *fol.* 204 *b.*

Taking these figures as trustworthy, the extent of the Hide, consisting of four yard-lands, in the *former* case would consist of some 160,—in the *latter* of about 124 acres.

Again, we find that in the reign of George III., according to Report to the Board of Agriculture (*p.* 17), there were at that period many instances in Wiltshire where "a yard-land contained about 2 acres of meadow land, 18 acres of arable, and a right of pasture,"—perhaps equivalent to from 30 to 35 acres altogether, and thus representing a Hide as comprising from 120 to 140 acres.

It is no long time ago, since the tenants at Stockton, in South Wilts, were assessed to the parochial rates according to the number of *livings* or *yard-lands* which they held. These yard-lands consisted, I found on enquiry, of some 25 acres of arable land, more or less according to its productive value, together with a certain amount of meadow, and pasture. The extent of the Hide, according to this reckoning, would be from 130 to 150 acres.[1]

The CARUCATE, its identity with the Hide as a measure of land.

Much that has been said respecting the Hide is applicable also to the CARUCATE. The latter word is of Norman origin and is derived, as Bishop Kennet suggests, from the old French word *carrue*, a plough. Like the former it is, as Sir Edward Coke observes, a 'word compound,' and denotes as much arable land as could be managed with one plough and the beasts belonging thereto in a year and containing also, as *appurtenant to it*, meadow and pasture necessary for such tillage. There can be little doubt that regarded as actual *measures* of the extent of land, the Hide and Carucate were identical. Thus, Ordericus Vitalis, who was living at the time of Domesday, speaks of the two terms as synonymous,—"*carucatas* quas Angli *hidas* vocant."[2] Agard, moreover, as Ellis tells us,[3] quotes Walter Wyttlesey, a monk of Peterborough, who, as far as one county is concerned, writes, "In provincia Lincolniæ non sunt Hidæ sicut in aliis provinciis, sed pro Hidis sunt *Carucatæ terrarum*, et *non minus valent quam Hidæ.*" He also cites a passage from Knyghton, "de qualibet *Hida*, id est *Carucata* terræ."

---

[1] The following examples taken from different parts of the county will suffice to show the general correctness of the conclusions arrived at respecting the extent of the Hide in Wilts. The instances selected, as well as others given at *p.* xxxv., are those in which we may be tolerably sure that the Domesday manor is co-extensive with the modern parish, and in which the *assessment* in Hides fairly corresponds with its actual *extent* in acres. It must, however, be borne in mind that in the *total acreage* given is included, as indeed the Record itself shows, much that was wood or waste land at the time of Domesday, and allowance in each case must be made for this, in attempting to arrive at anything like accurate conclusions.

			Hides	Acres.	Acres in each Hide.				Hides.	Acres.	Acres in each Hide.
BROMHAM	*p.* 13	*Bromham*	20	3522	176	JERCHESFONTE	*p.* 51	*Erchfont*	30	6102	203
CANINGE	*p.* 52	*All-Cannings*	18½	3234	178	LIDIARDE	*p.* 15	*Lydiard Millicent*	10	1850	185
CHENVEL	*p.* 47	*West Knoyle*	10	1913	191	LITELTONE	*p.* 27	*Littleton Drew*	5	904	180
CHILMERC	*p.* 46	*Chilmark*	20	3137	156	MERESDENE	*p.* 10	*Marden*	10	1257	125
COLEBURNE	*p.* 40	*Collingbourn Kingston*	50	7142	142	NEWENTONE	*p.* 80	*Newton Tony*	11	2336	212
COLINGEBURNE	*p.* 14	*Collingbourn Ducis*	20⅓	3188	155	RODE	*p.* 80	*Rowde*	20	2555	127
COVELESTONE	*p.* 131	*East Coulston*	5	868	173	SOPWORDE	*p* 101	*Sopworth*	5	790	158
DEVREL	*p.* 34	*Monkton Deverel*	10	1735	173	STANTONE	*p.* 137	*Stanton Fitz-Waryn*	10	1420	142
EBLESBORNE	*p.* 113	*Ebbesbourn Wake*	14	2700	190	STAPLEFORD	*p.* 143	*Stapleford*	10⅓	1990	189
EDINTONE	*p.* 65	*Heddington*	10	1550	155	STOTTUNE	*p.* 21	*Stockton*	10	2085	208
ESSITONE	*p.* 20	*Ashton Keynes*	20	3820	191	SUMREFORD	*p.* 28	*Somerford Keynes*	10	1640	164
FEBEFONT	*p.* 50	*Fovant*	10	1990	199	UPTONE	*p.* 55	*Upton Lovell*	10	1384	138
FONTEL	*p.* 1 7	*Fonthill Episcopi*	10	1733	173	WADONE	*p.* 138	*Whaddon*	3	580	193

[2] See the whole passage in the note to p. xxxiv.

[3] Introduction to Domesday, I. 150.

One distinction however may be drawn between them,—the HIDE would seem to take into account *all* the land comprised within a manor, the CARUCATE, strictly speaking, was that which might be ploughed "terra arabilis,"—it comprehended fallows, and pastures, but not woods.[1]

As confirmatory of the opinion that as *measures* of land the Hide and Carucate were identical, we may refer to a manuscript preserved in the British Museum containing an 'extent' of the Wiltshire manors belonging to Malmesbury Abbey in the year 1396.[2] Thus under CRUDEWELLE, we have registered *four carucates* containing 200 acres of arable, together with 20 acres of meadow, and the right of pasture for 200 sheep and 38 oxen, &c. Under KEMELE (Kemble) there are said to be *two carucates* containing 110 acres of arable, 12 acres of meadow, and the right of pasture for 260 sheep and 20 oxen, &c. Under CHERLTON (Charlton) we have *two carucates* containing 90 acres of arable, together with 12 acres of meadow, and the right of pasture for 140 sheep and 22 oxen, &c. Under BROKENBERGH there are *three carucates* containing 180 acres of pasture, together with 15 acres of meadow, and pasture for 200 sheep 30 oxen. Under BREMELE (Bremhill), within which manor are included the hamlets of FOXHAM and AVON,—we have *three carucates* containing 145 acres of arable, together with 16 acres of meadow, and the right of pasture for 61 oxen, &c.—Taking these five examples as a basis for calculation, we find that a Carucate in Wiltshire towards the end of the fourteenth century, comprised on an average some 50 *acres of arable land.* There is in this result no great discrepancy from the conclusions to which we came as to the extent of arable land comprised in the Hide, especially if we have in mind the fact already mentioned, namely, the greater proportion that, as centuries passed on, through the process of clearing woods and reducing what at the time of Domesday was waste or unprofitable lands into tillage, the arable came to bear to the other descriptions of land.[3]

Several interpreters of Domesday have been sorely perplexed at observing the varying numbers of the Hides and Carucates that are registered under the several manors. There appears to them to be a great discrepancy, which at first sight it is hard to explain. Hence they have contended that the well known abbreviation *Car'*. does not usually represent 'carucata' (a *plough-land*), but 'caruca' (a *plough-team*), and denotes not the quantity of land occupied, but the number of plough-teams employed.[4] Thus they would render 'Terra est 6 car'. not as we have uniformly done, 'Terra est 6 *carucatæ*,' but 'Terra est 6 *carucis*,' that is, as they would interpret the words, 'the arable is sufficient for 6 *plough-teams*.' This view has been adopted by Thorold in his General meaning of the abbreviation CAR'

---

[1] The usual formula "*Terra* est [totidem] carucatæ" would seem to imply thus much; since "*Terra*," when put singly, uniformly implies *arable* land. A Wiltshire peasant would speak of crossing a ploughed field, in contradistinction to walking along the road, as going over the *ground.*

[2] Add. MS. 6165, *fol.* 109.

[3] It would appear that the word 'carucate' was used at times to denote much larger quantities of land. "We meet," says Mr. Morgan, "with *compound* plough-lands, double or threefold. Fleta, temp. Edw. I., says, 'if land lay in three common fields, then nine score acres to a carucate, *sixty* for winter tillage, *sixty* for spring tillage, and *sixty* for fallows. But if land lay in two fields, then eight score acres to a carucate, *one half* for tillage, and the *other* fallow. In modern times, Trinity fields, as they were called, have been more frequent than the two-fold arrangement."—England under the Normans, *p.* 34. More information is given on this subject in Mr. Morgan's work, which is full of useful matter, and well deserving of an attentive perusal.

[4] Of course such a phrase as we meet with under Newentone, p. 45,—"Totum manerium possunt arare 10 *car'*.—can only admit of one rendering, namely that 10 plough teams (*carucæ*) can till the whole manor." A reference, however, to the earlier part of the same entry will show that under the general formula in which the extent of the manor is given there are but 7 *car'*. accounted for, and in this case it is contended the word must be an abbreviation for *carucatæ*, i.e., *carucates*, or *plough-lands.*

History of Northamptonshire, by Brady in the general preface to his History of England, and by Nichols in his History of Leicestershire.[1] The translator of the short extracts, prefixed to the copies in fac-simile issued of the Domesday record of the various counties, appears to have adopted the same opinion.

Now against this interpretation may be urged the simple fact that a return of *plough-teams* employed on each manor does not seem to be required by the terms of the King's precept. The enquiry would appear to have been 'Quot carucatæ' and 'Quot carucatæ in dominio.'[2] It is not denied that in some cases full particulars were taken, no doubt with the view of accurately testing the productive value of the land, and so of making a fair calculation as to its proper assessment. But all that they needed in a Record such as Domesday was a brief chronicle of the *result*, as regarded the number of plough-lands in each manor respectively. And then further, there is no little awkwardness in explaining, on such an interpretation, entries which frequently occur, in which *half*, or *three quarters*, or some other proportion of a *car'*. or *caruc'*., is registered as held. Thus, under DRAICOTE (*p.* 26), sundry subordinate tenants (they are no less than *eleven* in number) are described as having *dimidium car'*. In such cases possibly the advocates of the opinion we are combating would interpret the phrase as *half a plough-land*, but surely where the expressions are precisely identical there should be a uniformity in their rendering, and it should not be left to the judgment, we had almost said caprice, of a translator, to decide for what the abbreviation in question stands.

Apart, however, from these general considerations, there are, in the Domesday for Wilts, a number of entries which seem to be conclusive against such a rendering of the ordinary formula which is so familiar to all students of the Record. We will name a few, and venture to think that they quite warrant us in adhering in this work to that interpretation which certainly has on its side, as far as authorities are concerned, the greater weight. Under CHINTONE (*p.* 110) we have,—"Terra est 1 car'. *quæ est ibi in dominio*;"—under WIFLESFORD (*p.* 60), "Terra est 1 car'. et *ipsa est in dominio.*" Under HESTREBE (*p.* 16), we have "Terra est 2 car'., *ipsæ sunt ibi* cum 6 villanis et 6 cotariis et 6 *acris prati.*"[3] Under CADEHAM (*p.* 61) "Terra est 4 caruc'.; *de his* sunt in dominio 3 *hidæ.*" Under CHELSTANESTONE (*p.* 54) "Terra est 1 car'. et dimid., et *tantum* est ibi;" and an entry of the same character occurs under CELDRINTONE (*p.* 77). One more example shall be given, which would certainly seem tolerably conclusive on the matter. Under ULFELA (*p.* 146), we have, "Terra est 3 car'., *et nil pecuniæ*," that is, 'and there are *no cattle*.' It will be observed that every one of the examples we have quoted, and others of like character might be produced, commences with the usual formula, "Terra est...car'."[4]

The Hide as the measure of the assessment of manors.

But after all, the needless difficulty which, as we venture to think, such interpreters of Domesday have created for themselves arises from their forgetfulness of this important fact, that though the HIDE was in the first instance more or less a measure of the *extent* of the various manors, it had at the time of Domesday become practically the measure of their *assessment*, which by no means in many cases corresponded with their real acreage,

[1] Introduction, p. xlvii. [2] See above, p. xii

[3] This entry relates to the land belonging to the *Church* at Heytesbury. In the Inq. Non., 155, we have this entry, which at all events interprets this example in the way for which we are contending:—"Rector habet *duas carucatas terræ*."

[4] The whole question is well discussed in Manning and Bray's 'History of Surrey,' I. 113. The conclusion to which they come is in favor of the interpretation adopted in this volume.

the fair presumable value of the estate. Many entries in the Wiltshire Domesday imply clearly that the Hide is to be regarded in this light of an assessment. Hence, under OPETONE (*p.* 78) we have a small holding described as 'tantum *quod valet* 1 hidam.' Indeed, strictly speaking, the Record gives us in most cases only the number of hides for which each estate *paid geld* (geldabat), which might, or might not be, a fair criterion of its extent or value. Under COSSEHAM (*p.* 11), we have an entry in which the actual number of Hides which it contained is contrasted with those for which it paid geld,—"there are *thirty-four* hides, but it pays geld for *eighteen* hides."—Under CHEPEHAM (*p.* 9) and THEODULVESIDE (*p.* 10) we have in either case the entry "it paid no geld, neither was it assessed in hides." Under CAUNA (*p.* 7), we have the still more decisive entry, "it never paid geld, *therefore it is not known how many hides are there*" (nunquam geldavit, *ideo nescitur quot hidæ sint ibi.*) Then, again, under SOMREFORDE (*p.* 68) and HERTHAM (*p.* 72) we have entries in which it is intimated that in those cases the *assessment* was equal to the actual *measurement;* for, after naming the number of Hides, it is added in each instance, "*et pro tanto geldabat,*" words which imply that this agreement might be exceptional. Moreover we have such statements as STANDENE (*p.* 108) containing *five carucates* and paying geld only for *one hide;*—and COLECOTE (*p.* 130), which contained *five* hides, assessed at *half-a-hide.* On the other hand, examples may be brought forward in which the assessment in hides seems excessive. Thus HIWEI (*p.* 34), paid geld for *eleven* hides, though there were but *five* carucates contained in it, which gives only some sixty-seven acres for each hide;—AWLTONE (*p.* 18) paid geld for *twenty* hides, with only *fourteen* carucates, giving seventy-five acres to each hide;—GRETELINTONE (*p.* 32) had only *twenty* carucates, and yet was assessed at *thirty* hides, giving only sixty-five acres to the hide.[1]

Taking these circumstances into consideration, even though all difficulties connected with the subject may not be removed, we at all events get rid of some of them. We at least can understand the apparent discrepancy in many instances between the number of hides and carucates, and can comprehend why it was necessary, in compiling a national Record, which was afterwards to be a standard of appeal, to take account alike of the former, which marked the assessment of the whole estate, as well as of the latter, which indicated the quantity of land contained in it that was under the plough.[2]

The BOVATE or OX-GANG.

Mention has already been made (*p.* 81, note) of the BOVATE or OX-GANG. We recur to it simply for the purpose of giving a short extract from the Malmesbury Manuscript, to which reference has been already made (*p.* xxxix), which shews its extent in Wiltshire in the time of Richard II. Under the manor of SUTTON (Sutton Benger) we have registered, "*four* bovates of land, containing in them *thirty acres* of arable," and appurtenant to them four acres of meadow, and the right of pasture for five oxen, &c. This gives for each Bovate some

---

[1] Instances of disproportionate assessment are frequent. Thus the estate of CHILCOMBE belonging to Winchester is reckoned at *one hundred* hides, but the monks succeeded in getting it rated to the public burdens at *one hide* only.—Cod. Dipl., 642.

[2] The fact of the Hide being an assessment dependent on the *quality* rather than the *quantity* of the land is made very evident by taking an instance or two of parishes which coincide with the original manors, and where we can ascertain correctly the acreage and the *present assessment.* Thus, ALLINGTON near Ambresbury (which consists of the two Domesday manors entered at pp. 54, 62, under ALENTONE) is now assessed as £1032, and contains 928 acres, thus giving an average rateable value of rather more than 22 shillings per acre; in Domesday this was assessed at eight hides, giving some 116 acres to each hide. On the other hand PERTWOOD, which contains 450 acres, is now assessed at £315, or some 14 shillings per acre; in Domesday (p. 27) this was reckoned at two hides, thus giving some 225 acres to each hide.

seven acres and a half of arable land. Two passages in the Wiltshire Domesday would seem to imply that there were *six* bovates in each carucate, or plough-land. Thus, under DARNEFORD (*p.* 46) we have an entry, 'ibi sunt 6 *bovatæ* in carucata dominica,' and under HERTHAM (*p.* 72), where there is said to be one carucate, it is added, 'terra est 6 *bobus*.' On this reckoning we arrive at a result singularly like that which has been shewn in the preceding pages,—namely, that the plough-land in the fifteenth century consisted of from 45 to 50 acres of arable land.

The LEUCA and QUARENTENA.

The LEUCA and QUARENTENA which we have translated *mile* and *furlong*, are most commonly applied as measures to wood-land. In the Register of Battle Abbey, there is a passage from which we learn that the Leuga, or ancient English 'league' consisted of *twelve* 'quarentenes,' and that a quarentene (or furlong) comprised *forty* perches, each *sixteen* feet in length. This will bring the Domesday mile to 2560 yards, whereas there are but 1760 yards in an English mile of the present day. In making an estimate of manors it is necessary to bear in mind that the mile represented by the term 'leuca' was as nearly as possible *a mile and a half* of the present standard.

The WOOD-LAND always registered in Domesday.

The portion of each manor occupied by WOOD-LAND (Silva or Nemus) is always carefully entered. It is generally described as so many '*quarentenæ*' or '*leucæ*' in length and breadth. When we have the simple expression a 'quarentene of wood' it means usually a square furlong, or some ten normal acres; in like manner a 'mile (leuca) of wood' implies a mile in length and breadth, according to the reckoning already intimated some 1440 acres.[1]—It was not that the timber was of any great value that this care was taken in giving the extent of the woods, but because they supplied the swine of the villagers with food. For this privilege the swine-herds had to pay either in money, or kind, to the lord of the manor, and this charge was called *pannage* (pannagium).[2] In the manor of Bradford-on-Avon this same payment was called *larder-money*, (lardarium).[3] Our ancestors even estimated the value of a tree by the number of hogs that could stand under it. In the laws of Ina a man who cut down a tree under which thirty hogs could stand, was condemned to pay a fine of sixty shillings.[4] Other instances might be adduced from the same ancient code of laws showing the importance attached to this right of the lord of a manor, by the very heavy fines and penalties exacted from trespassers.

In two instances in Wiltshire, LITTLECOTE (*p.* 92) and BREME (*p.* 38), we have allusions to a few acres of what the Record designates 'spinetum,' that is 'bramble wood;" in the latter case it is accidentally interesting as giving us a clue to the etymology of the name of Bremhill.[5] We have mention also of the right which

---

[1] See Morgan's 'England under the Normans,' p 29.

[2] At Leominster in Herefordshire the *pannage* was every *tenth* pig "Quisque villanus habens x. porcos dat unum porcum de pasnagio." Domesd. I. 180. At Ringwood in Hampshire the payment was made in money. "Silva de cxlix porcis de pasnagio; hoc quod Rex habet valet vii. libr. et x. solid. numero." Ibid. I. 39. See other instances in Ellis I. 99, and 'England under the Normans' p. 56. The importance of pannage or masting was such as to cause the introduction of a clause in the Charta de Foresta; see § 9.—Fleta (Lib. II. p. 80), thinks it necessary to devote a chapter to the subject. 'Saxons in England,' II. 84.

[3] See Wilts. Mag. v. 69. [4] Laws of Ina, p. 44. [Thorpe I. 131.]

[5] See the note at p. 38. In the manuscript concerning the estates of Malmesbury Abbey (2 Rich. II.) already cited, we have the following entry under BREMELE:—"pastura bosci et gravæ nihil valet per annum *propter multitudinem spinarum* et umbram ramorum arborum."—Add. MSS. 6165, *fol.* 110.

appertained to some manors of cutting as much wood as was necessary for the repairs of buildings or fences, and also for fuel.[1] Thus under NEWENTONE, *p.* 48, we have the entry,—"To this manor belongs by custom the right to 80 cart-loads of wood, and the feed of 80 hogs in Milchet Wood, and what may be necessary for the repairs of the houses and fences." Precisely similar rights are recorded as belonging to the manor of WAISEL (*p.* 50).

The FORESTS in Wiltshire.

We have few allusions in Domesday to the FORESTS in Wilts. A forest was a district 'foras,' out of ordinary jurisdiction, and the foresters were free from many burdens borne by others, and exempt from 'hundred law.'[2] Among the rights of royalty enumerated in the laws of Henry I. are 'forestæ,' and hence, as they were no objects of assessment, but were subject to special jurisdiction, they are omitted from the Record.[3] A few are incidentally mentioned,—that of GRAVELINGES (Groveley) *p.* 144,—CETUM (Chute) *p.* 15,—what was afterwards called the NEW FOREST under Duntone, *p.* 17,—and that of CLARENDON under the entries of Lavrecestohes, *p.* 50, and Meleford, *p.* 90.

Much reproach, as we know, has been heaped on the memory of the Conqueror for the destruction of many villages and churches for the purpose of increasing the New Forest. The fact of his having done so is too clearly admitted to be denied. His own chaplain, William of Jumieges, speaks of the deaths of his two sons, Richard and William Rufus, as having been regarded by the people in general as a judgment of God on him for this act.[4] The passion for the chase led the Norman kings into many an act of cruelty, and the seizing a compass of territory not less than 50 miles in extent is a lasting monument of the Conqueror's tyranny.[5] At the same time it must be remembered that he was not the first to commence this wanton mode of proceeding. Thus by comparing the entry in the Exon Domesday, *p.* 191, with that concerning Duntone at *p.* 17, it is evident that some *five* hides in all were taken away in the time of King Canute from the Bishop of Winchester, on account of the King's forest (propter forestam Regis). William adopted the severe code promulgated in Canute's "Constitutiones de Foresta," and followed the example first set to him by his predecessor. This fact does not of course justify the Conqueror's act, but it at least exonerates him from the guilt of having first commenced this course of cruelty and injustice.

The MILLS, a source of profit to the Lord of the manor.

In Domesday we have a careful account of the MILLS belonging to each manor. These were a source of profit to the land-holder, inasmuch as tenants were permitted to grind their corn only at the lord's mill. In the larger estates some mills seem to have been used exclusively for the corn grown on the demesne lands; in other cases they were let out at a rent which was returned in money or kind. Of course the mills were of very

---

[1] See the note at p. 48.

[2] Thus in the document entitled 'Constitutiones de Foresta,' § ix., of the date of Canute, we have the following description of immunities enjoyed by those who had the guardianship of the forests entrusted to them: 'Sint omnes liberi et quieti ab omnibus provincialibus summonitionibus et popularibus placitis, quæ 'hundred laghe' Angli dicunt, et ab omnibus armorum oneribus, quod 'warscot' Angli dicunt, et forinsecis querelis."—Thorpe's Ancient Laws, I. 427.

[3] "Forestas communi consensu baronum meorum in manu mea sic retinui sicut pater meus eas habuit."—Laws of Henry I., printed in Thorpe's Ancient Laws, I. 501; see also I. 509.

[4] Histor. Norm. Script. Duchesne, (*fol.* 1619), p. 296. See also Ellis I. 107.

[5] See on this point the notes to the 'Red King' by W. Stewart Rose, pp. 204–208.

unequal value. In some of the larger manors, especially when they were situated on one or other of the various streams in Wilts and water-power was abundant, they were valuable; in the case of the smaller manors, or when they were on the down-land, the rent paid to the lord was proportionately less. A mill at RUSTESELLE (Lushill, near Swindon) (*p.* 86), returned only *one shilling* yearly, and the six mills at CAININGHAM (Bishop's Cannings,) (*p.* 22), paid only *fifteen pence* each. Those also at WERTUNE (*p.* 85),—WILDEHILLE (*p.* 81),—LIDIARDE (*p.* 15), LEDENTONE (*p.* 44),—BLONTESDONE (*p.* 69),—were of small value, paying on the average only some *ten shillings and six-pence* yearly. On the other hand, the two mills at BOLTINTONE (Bullford) (*p.* 53), yielded *thirty-two shillings and six-pence* each yearly; and those at BRADEFORD (*p.* 43), OCHEBURNE (*p.* 93), MILDENHALE (*p.* 31), and CROSTONE (*p.* 80), were each worth *thirty shillings* annually. The common range of mills in Wiltshire, appears to be from *five* to *fifteen* shillings; in Somersetshire, however, we have several returning but *six-pence* a year to their lord; a few only *four-pence*; and one no more than *three-pence*.[1]

Mills frequently hadmore than one owner. Thus, under LANGEFORD (*p.* 58),—TEDRINTONE (*p.* 62),—CHEVREL (*p.* 74),—and CALDEFELLE (*p.* 75), we have entries in each case of *half a mill* (dimidium molini). Two lords of adjoining manors, that is, had equal shares in the mill. So sometimes we have a mill divided into several shares. Thus, to the manor of SUMREFORD (*p.* 87), belonged *one third* of a mill,—to that of TEDELINTONE (*p.* 84), *two parts* of a mill,—whilst under the two entries of CONTONE (*pp.* 85, 97), we have recorded, as belonging to either of the manors, *one third part of two mills*, worth in each case *ten shillings*. Perhaps the most valuable of these shares in mills was the *half mill* registered as belonging to Bishop Osmund at SARISBERIE (*p.* 23), which yielded the large annual rent of *thirty shillings*.

In most cases, no doubt, the mills were water-mills. In the Agricultural Report for Wilts (*p.* 259) a Mill-ham, the equivalent to the Domesday phrase 'sedes molini,' by which is designated the miller's home-stead and portion of meadow attached to the mill, is defined to be 'a narrow strip of ground by the side of a river.' In some cases, however, as in that of THEODULVESIDE (Tilshead,) *p.* 10, where there were no less than *nine* mills, they must have been worked by some other motive power. A natural suggestion would be that they were wind-mills, were it not the fact that there is no genuine evidence that they were used in the eleventh century. In the Boldon Book, printed in the supplementary volume of Domesday, under the date 1183, we have notice at Oxenhall, near Darlington, in Durham, of a mill worked by horses.[2]

A mill might belong to a manor, though not situated within its proper bounds. Thus to this day there is a mill belonging to CHILMARK, which is locally situated in the parish of Tisbury,—the mill and its appurtenances are nevertheless deemed as an outlying portion of the former parish.

The VINEYARDS. We have several notices of the VINEYARDS in Wiltshire. Thus, at TOLLARD (*p.* 123) there were "*two arpens* of vineyard,—at LACOCH (*p.* 71) there was *half an acre*. Some years ago a doubt was expressed by some authorities whether by Vineæ, in Domesday, we were to understand orchards. The idea first started by Agard was taken up by Atkins in his history of Gloucestershire, and by Daines Barrington in the Archæologia.[3] Dr.

---

[1] Domesd. for Somerset. I. 93, *b*.

[2] Boldon Book, p. 583. [3] Archæol. III. 67.

Pegge, however, replied to their arguments and proved undeniably that they were mistaken, and that the entries in Domesday could only apply to true and proper vineyards.[1]

There can be no doubt that Vineyards existed long before the Norman conquest. They were most probably introduced by the Romans during the later period of their stay in this country. According to Vopiscus[2] the Emperor Probus, about the year A.D. 280, restored the privilege of the Vineyard. They are mentioned moreover, in the laws of Alfred the Great,[3] and as Ellis shows in the context to the passages referred to in the foot-notes are repeatedly alluded to in ancient deeds and charters, and often as distinct from orchards. It is more difficult to prove the neglect of the culture of the vine as to the period and the cause. But even admitting that we had recourse to foreigners for the main portion of our consumption, it may be proved that to a certain extent, even in the reign of Edward I., we were not without a home supply. The various places at which ecclesiastics in particular cultivated the grape often occur in records, and the vineyards at Hereford, Ledbury, Gloucester, Tewkesbury, and Worcester testify to the fact, in that sunny and well-cultivated part of England. Bishop Cantilupe, in a letter of instructions to his steward, expressly mentions that of Ledbury at the time that it was formed, or re-planted, and we have it bearing fruit in the vintage of 1289. That which was cultivated seems to have been the green grape, and some of it was converted into verjuice, for which it was probably better suited than for wine, though the proportion of the latter to the former was considerable.

Sir H. Ellis quotes a passage from the life of Bulleyn, in the Biographia Britannica, in which it is stated, "It is affirmed we have still upon record some treaty of peace between France and England, in which it is stipulated that we should root up our vineyards, and be their customers for all our wine. If such extirpation of the English vineyards was not owing to this, it might be the falling of Gascony into the hands of the English, whence wine was imported better and cheaper than we could make it." On this passage it is then remarked :— "The quantity of wine produced in England never could have been sufficient for the consumption of the inhabitants; and its inferiority is probably a better reason for it having been supplanted by foreign produce than any stipulated destruction of the vines by treaty."[4]

When Aubrey visited Bradford-on-Avon some two hundred years ago, he was struck at the fitness of the sloping hill on the western side of the town as a site for a vineyard. In his Natural History (ch. ix.) he says, "At Bradford all the side of the high hill above Mr. Paul Methwin's house is covered with elders. I fancy that that part might be turned to better profit, for it is situated as well for a vineyard as any place can be, and is on a rocky, gravelly ground." And in his Wiltshire Collections, he says, "This high hill [above Mr. Methwyn's] is rock and gravel, faces the south and south-west, therefore is the best site for a vineyard of any place I know: better in England cannot be." It is not impossible that when gossiping with some of the inhabitants whom he

---

[1] See Ellis, I. 116.

[2] Ibid. p. 119. "Gallis omnibus, ac Hispanis, ac *Britannis* hinc permisit *ut vites haberent* vinumque conficerent."

[3] "Gif hwa gewerde oðres monnes win-geard oþþe his æcras, oþþe his landes awiht, gebete swa hit mon geeahtige." [If any one injure another man's vineyard, or his fields, or aught of his lands, let him make recompence as it may be valued.] Laws of Alfred, § 26. (Thorpe I. 50).

[4] Ellis I. 121.

chanced to meet, they told him that once, as people said, the vine flourished on that hill ; and so that there was the 'arpen of vineyard' recorded in Domesday as belonging to the manor of BRADEFORD (*p.* 48). Certain it is, that the older inhabitants of Wilcote, or the shepherds that tend their flocks on the neighbouring downs, will tell you to this day, that the peculiar indentations you may observe in some of the sloping ground are marks of ancient vineyards that in olden times were planted there. One can hardly be incredulous when he finds the tradition thus handed down by these sons of the soil confirmed by the entry in Domesday, which records as belonging to WILCOTE, (*p.* 65,)—'a new church, and excellent house, and a *good vineyard.*'

CHAPTER III.

Manors commonly divided into two parts; the lord's part or demesne, and the tenantry part or villans' land. The lands belonging to the Crown, or Terræ Regis; some belonging to the King as his private property, others belonging to the nation and held by him for the public. The King's Barons,—distribution of lands among them. The Sheriff,—duties and perquisites of his office. The Thanes,—various classes of them. The King's Officers. The King's Servants. The Huntsmen or Foresters. Thanes of the Shire. Cultivators of the demesne,—the Serfs and Coliberts. The Villans,—Cotsetlers,—Cottars,—Bordars. The Bee-keepers or Honey-men. The Swine-herds. General Condition of the English Tenantry in the olden time.

Manors divided into two parts, the demesne and the tenantry part.

MANORS in olden times were commonly divided into two portions, the one held by the lord *(dominus)* for his own use, and hence called the demesne *(dominium)*, the other let out to various tenants who paid rent in money or kind, and were bound to render certain customary services for the enjoyment of the same.[1] Spelman, after remarking that the word '*dominium*' is sometimes used in a larger sense as signifying generally the lord's property in the whole estate *(patrimonium domini)*, thus defines the more limited usage to which we now refer. He states that it is employed,—"ad significandum manerii partem, hoc est terras et prædia quæ dominus hæreditarie non tradit suis tenentibus, sed aut sui ipsius manibus retinuit aut ad annos aliquot sive voluntatem elocavit, vulgo terræ Dominicales"—lands or estates, that is, which the lord did not grant to tenants in fee, but which he either kept in his own hands or let out for a term of years or at will, what in fact are commonly called 'Demesne Lands.'[2]

The portion of a Manor held by the lord for his own especial benefit seems to have been cultivated partly by his serfs, and partly also by the tenants of the *out-lands*, who had to render certain prædial services to the lord. In a few entries the coliberts are joined with the serfs, as employed on the demesne lands. The rest of the manor, the *out-land* in fact, was apportioned among the Villans, the Bordars, the Cottars, and other classes of which we shall presently make more particular mention. From some entries indeed it would almost

---

[1] This arrangement is well described in the Agricultural Report of Wiltshire (p. 17),—"In general there was in each manor one great farm called the lord's farm, which usually had its land in severalty and distinct from the tenants. The rest of the manor, called the tenantry part, was divided into small copyhold tenements or farms, called yard-lands, each of which was originally of nearly equal value, and enjoyed equal rights of commonage."

[2] The *demesne* corresponded with the *in-land* of olden times; the other part of the manor was originally called *út-land* (i.e., *out-land*), and sometimes *geneat-land*, for the two terms seem to be synonymous. Thus, in the laws of Edgar, tithe is directed to be paid, "ægðer ge of þegnes in-land ge of geneat-land," *i.e.*, both from a Thane's *in-land* and from *geneat-land*.—Thorpe's Ancient Laws, I. 263. It would seem, however that all demesne land was not necessarily *in-land*, and that the latter was sometimes restricted to the several and enclosed part of the demesne which the tenants were obliged to 'ware,' that is, to guard or fence.—'England under the Normans,' p. 73.

appear that the Villan was a sort of middle man between the other tenants and the chief owner of the estate, and that some services due ultimately to the lord were, in the first instance, paid mediately to him.

Terræ Regis, or Crown Lands.

The King himself was the greatest land-owner in Wiltshire. Under the head of Terræ Regis, or Crown Lands, is registered *one-fifth* of all the land in the county. The large estates of Calne, Bedwin, Ambresbury, Warminster, Melksham, and many others, belonged to the king either as his private property, or were vested in him as the representative of the state and so the holder of the *folc-land*, under which term were comprised those estates which belonged to the nation at large. Like other freemen the King depended for much of his subsistence on the cultivation of those estates which he held in absolute possession. These were furnished with dwellings and storehouses in which the produce of his farms might be laid up, and from one to another he proceeded as political exigencies, or the need of supplies, or in some cases perhaps simple caprice, rendered expedient. Sometimes, as at Warminster, he could by custom demand a night's entertainment for himself and his suite, when he conferred on his faithful subjects residing there the honor of a royal visit. In each *villa* or *wic* was placed a Bailiff (*prepositus* or *villicus*), the old *wic-gerefa*, whose duty it was to watch over the King's interests, to superintend the processes of industry, and look after the labourers employed in production; above all, to represent the King as regarded the freemen and the officers of the county court.[1]

It will be observed that the King's Lands are almost uniformly those which the old royal family had previously held. They had belonged to King Edward, Harold, Earl Godwin, Ghida, the mother of Harold, Tostig his brother, or Editha the Confessor's queen. No doubt much that is entered as having belonged to King Edward, and which afterwards became vested in the Conqueror, was the *folc-land*, or public property of the state, to which we have just alluded, of which, though the nominal proprietor, he was the usufructuary possessor, and, with the license and consent of his Witan, the distributor on the part of the public. Hence the land which in the Exchequer Domesday is called Terra Regis, is in the Exon Domesday termed, 'Dominicatus Regis *ad regnum pertinens*.'[2] A similar form of expression indeed is found in the Exchequer Domesday, for a manor granted by the King to Earl Ralph is described as having previously *belonged to the kingdom*."[3]

On this point the following pertinent remarks are found in Allen's valuable work on the Royal Prerogative (*p.* 150). "When the King became the representative of the state, the *folc-land* came to be considered his property. It was his land in the same sense that the servants of the public were his servants, the laws his laws, the army his army. In his politic or ideal capacity he was the state, and whatever belonged to the state belonged to him. If *folc-land* was assigned to any one for life, or for a shorter term, it was given by his authority, and apparently for his service. Where it was converted into *boc-land*, or land of inheritance, the deed was executed in his name, and though the grant was of no validity without the concurrence of his Witan, the donation seemed in form the spontaneous act of his munificence. Whilst it continued *folc-land* it was subject to payments and other burdens which were due to him, or to other persons who by law were termed his servants. When bestowed on military men employed in the national defence it was called *Thane-land* (or *Tain-land*), and said to be held by his Thanes. When applied to the services of the person entrusted with the civil administration

---

[1] See Kemble's 'Saxons in England' I. 155. In the laws of Canute, § lxx., is an enactment, "De victu ex Regis prædiis."—Thorpe's Anct. Laws. I. 412.

[2] Exon Domesday (Devonshire) p. 75.

[3] Domesday II. 119*b*.

of the shires it was called *Reve-land*, and said to be possessed by his *ealdormen* and *gerefan*. When appropriated to his own subsistence, and the maintenance of his household, it was said to be held in demesne, or let out to farm. The same lands, it is probable, were constantly or usually destined to the same use and occupied by persons of the same degree."

The principal holders of lands are spoken of in the Exon Domesday for Wilts as the KING'S BARONS, (Barones Regis). We meet with a similar title in other parts of Domesday, but by it we generally understand the King's Justiciaries, before whom claims respecting property were litigated.[1] The title seems to have been of Norman introduction, and to have included, as a generic term, various degrees of nobility and gentry. These were Barones Majores, and Barones Minores. Amongst the laws of Henry I., is one 'De privilegiis *procerum* Angliæ,[2] and in the body of the law we have as an equivalent expression, 'Barones habentes socnam,' *i.e.*, Barons having the right of holding courts: in both cases the words denoting simply lords of manor, who might of course be of many different degrees of rank. Then again, the citizens of London, as also those of York, Norwich, Chester and some other places, were dignified with the title of Baron. In the charter of Henry III., concerning the liberties of the citizens of London, we have the following:—"BARONES civitatis London elegant sibi singulis annis de seipsis Majorem."—The citizens bore the same title also on their common seal.[3]

The BARONS, various classes of them.

Of the Norman nobles, the Earls and others, among whom the lands of the vanquished English were distributed, some account is given in foot-notes to the various sections in which we have a list of the manors bestowed on them. Those estates seem to have been distributed by the Conqueror among the officers of his army, either in proportion to their rank in Normandy, or to the supplies they furnished in the expedition. A liberal share fell to those who were more or less connected with his family, such as the Earl Morton, the Earl Roger, Walter Giffard, Richard Fitz-Gilbert, Radulf de Mortemer, and others. The chief promoters of William's plans were not forgotten, and hence the names of Milo Crispin, Gilbert de Breteville, William de Ow, and William de Moiun are found amongst the proprietors of Wiltshire manors. Including under this head, all the King's Thanes, Officers, and Servants, who are recorded as holding lands directly from the King, there were in Wilts *one hundred and fifty-six* principal land-owners, or Tenants in Capite.

Of these, the owner of the most extensive estates was EDWARD OF SALISBURY, or, as he is also termed, EDWARD THE SHERIFF (Vice-Comes). Some account of himself, as well as of the profits belonging to his office, will be found at *p.* 64. The office itself is no doubt of the highest antiquity. The SCIR-GEREFA, as his name denotes, was the person who stood at the head of the shire or county; hence he is often called Scírman or Scírigman.[4] He was probably the holder of the county court, the *scír-gemōt*, or *folc-mōt*, which was assembled twice in the year, and before which was brought all the important cases, and such as exceeded the competence of the Hundred. He had also to see to the execution of the law, and to exercise a supreme police in his county. Moreover he was the principal fiscal officer in the county; the mints and coinage were under his superintendence;

The SHERIFF, duties and perquisites of his office

---

[1] See Ellis, I. 44. [2] Thorpe, I. 530.

[3] Stowe's Survey, edit. 1603. p. 307. [Ellis, I. 50.]

[4] Kemble ('Saxons in England,' II., 158) gives several quotations from the laws of Ina and Athelstan, as well as from charters in the Cod. Dipl., in which this office is thus designated. In the same chapter much interesting information is contained regarding the office itself.

he had to levy all fines that accrued to the King from offenders, and to collect such taxes as the land paid for public purposes. He was no doubt charged with certain disbursements, required by the public service, and, we may fairly presume, had to render a periodical account of receipts and expenditure, to the officers who then represented the royal exchequer.[1]

Among the perquisites of this office were the receipts from what is called, at *p.* 64, *Reve-land,* to which allusion has been already made. We meet occasionally in Anglo-Saxon charters with such words as *geréf-land* and *geréf-mæd,* where, as Kemble observes, 'the form of the composition denotes, not the land or meadow of some particular sheriff, but of the sheriff generally;'[2] in fact, land which he enjoyed in virtue of his office. The mention of Reve-land is not frequent in Domesday; it occurs but in five or six entries, one of which is found in the Wiltshire portion of the Record. Complaints are made in one passage of *Thane-land* having been fraudulently converted into *Reve-land,* subtracted, that is, from the military service of the state and appropriated by its civil servants, the 'gerefan,' to the increase of their own emoluments.[3]

It would appear that the Sheriff occasionally took charge or possession of the estates of private persons, sometimes holding them in farm, sometimes in mortgage (*in vadimonio*) as in the case of WIVELESFORD (*p.* 133), either on account of misdemeanours, or because the owners neglected the land, or because the dues were in arrear.[4]

The THANES, various classes of them.

The Anglo-Saxon title of nobility was Đegn (Thane), a term which, like the Norman name of Baron that in time supplanted it, included various ranks. Originally, no doubt, it was a title, not so much of dignity as of service, for this seems to be implied in the word 'þegnian,' the primary meaning of which is, to *serve.* At first a military follower of the King, and so attached to his person and acquiring rank, the Thane became the possessor of land, the natural reward of his services to the Crown. Hence, in course of time, the possession of territory became itself the title to rank, and any one who held lands of a certain value could claim a corresponding social position with its accompanying privileges.

There would seem to have been two great divisions of Thanes. First of all there were the KING'S THANES (Taini Regis, or Taini Majores) who served the King in places of eminency either in court or commonwealth, or ranked with such; and then there were the LESSER THANES (Taini Minores) who filled subordinate offices either under the king or some of the nobles of the kingdom, or who were judged worthy of such a position. The distinction between these classes is clearly shewn in one of the provisions of Canute's 'Constitutiones de Foresta.' In every county there were to be chosen as Head Foresters *(primarii forestæ)* four persons "ex *liberalioribus hominibus* qui habent salvas suas debitas consuetudines quos Angli 'þegenes' *(Thanes)* appellant;" under each of these chief foresters were to be chosen four "ex *mediocribus hominibus* quos Angli

---

[1] 'Saxons in England,' II. 164. [2] Ibid. II. 166.

[3] Thus, in the Domesday for Hereford (I. 181), 'Hæc terra fuit Tainland T. R. E. sed postea conversa est in Reveland et ideo dicunt legati Regis quod ipsa terra et census qui inde exit furtim aufertur Rege.' Other passages in Domesday in which Reveland is named will be found in Vol. I. *fol.* 57*b* (Berks),—*fol.* 69 (Wilts),—*fol.* 179*b* (Hereford),—*fol.* 208 (Hants),—and Vol. II *fol.* 29 (Dorset) in the account of land belonging to Aiulf, Sheriff of that County.—See Morgan's 'England under the Normans,' pp. 196—204.

[4] Thus, in the Domesday for Bedfordshire, I., *fol.* 216*b*, Ralph Tallebosc, Sheriff of that county, is said to have seized land for dues not paid,—"ille gablum de hac terra dare noluit, et Radulfus Taillgebosc gablum dedit et *pro forisfacto* ipsam terram sumpsit."

'les-þegenes' (*Lesser Thanes*) nuncupant, Dani vero 'yoongmen' vocat," whose duty it was to look after the vert and venison.[1]

It would appear that success in one of the inferior classes might entitle a person to claim the privileges of a Thane, or even of an Earl. Thus in an old Anglo-Saxon document entitled 'Of People's Ranks and Law,' we have the following entries:—§ 2, "If a 'ceorl' thrived so that he had fully five hides of his own land, church and kitchen, bell-house and burh-gate seat,[2] and special duty in the king's hall, then he was henceforth of *thane-right* worthy." § 5, "If a Thane so thrived that he became an 'eorl,' then was he henceforth of *eorl-right* worthy." § 6, "If a merchant so thrived that he fared thrice over the wide sea in his own vessel, then he was thenceforth of *thane-right* worthy."[3]

A comparison of the entries in the Laws of Canute (§ lxxii. De Hereotis), of William the Conqueror (§ xx. De Releviis), and of Henry I. (§ xiv. De Relevacionibus)[4] will show very accurately the rank held by the two classes of Thanes. The *heriot*[5] payable on the death of a King's Thane is the same as the *relief* due on the death of a Baron; and in like manner, the Lesser Thane and the Vavassour are chargeable with precisely the same *heriot* or *relief*. The law of Canute, which is the earliest enactment now existing by which the amount of such heriot was determined, was probably only a confirmation of older customs, and promulgated for the purpose of putting an end to disputes on the subject. As regards Thanes it declares as follows:—"Let the heriots be as fits the degree. From a King's Thane, of those who are nearest to him, four horses, two saddled, two unsaddled, two swords, four spears, four shields, a helmet, a coat of mail, and fifty mancuses of gold. From a medial Thane (medemra þegna) a horse equipped and his arms, or his heals fang[6] in Wessex, and in Mercia and East Anglia two pounds. Among the Danes, the heriot of a King's Thane who has his socn (= baronial court) four pounds; if he stand in near relation to the King, two horses, one equipped, a sword, two spears, two shields, and fifty mancuses of gold. And from a Thane of the lower order, two pounds."

---

[1] Thorpe, I. 426.

[2] Thorpe, in his glossary at the end of his second volume, explains 'Bel-hús,' which we have translated *bell-house*, as equivalent to the Latin *tympanarium* and the French *tinel*, and as meaning a common hall in which the servants of the household took their meals. He interprets the word 'Burh-geat-sete' as literally a seat at a town gate, but used as a court for trying causes of family and tenants.

[3] Thorpe, I. 191.

[4] Thorpe, I. 415, 475, 525.

[5] Kemble thus clearly explains the difference between the '*heriot*' and the '*relief*,' though as far as their practical effect they were identical. "The horse and arms which in theory had been the loan of the chief were to be returned at the death of the vassal, in order that, according to the same theory, they might furnish some other adventurer with the instruments of service. These technically called *here-geatwu*, i.e., literally *military equipments* have continued to our own day under the name of *Heriot*, and strictly speaking consist of horses and weapons. In later imitation of this, those who were not called on to perform military service were bound on demise to pay the best chattel *(melius catallum)*, probably on the theoretical hypothesis that the lord, at the commencement of the tenancy, had supplied the necessary implements of agriculture. And this differs from a Relief, because Heriot is the *act of the leaving*, Relief the *act of the incoming* tenant or heir. Relief *(relevium)* is from *relevare*, to lift or take up again. It is a sum paid by the heir to the lord, on *taking*, or *lifting up again* the inheritance of an estate which has, as it were, fallen to the ground by the death of the ancestor." 'Saxons in England,' I. 178.'

[6] Heals-fang is explained by Thorpe (in his Glossary to Ancient Laws, &c.) to mean literally a 'pillory.' It does not occur, however, in this sense in any of the Anglo-Saxon laws, but is used to denote a certain fine, graduated according to the degree of the offender, and a commutation for a degrading punishment. 'Heals-fang' he conceives may therefore be defined:—'The sum a man sentenced to the pillory would have to pay to save him from that punishment, had it been in use.'

Manors held by King's Thanes.

A large number of Manors in Wiltshire, though many of them were but of small extent, were held by various persons as King's Thanes. In many instances the same manors had been held, either by themselves or by members of their families, in the days of the Confessor. Some difference, however, would seem from sundry entries to have existed by custom with regard to the tenure of lands thus held in their own hands by King's Thanes. Probably many of such holdings were allodial lands, (though this expression is not met with in the Wiltshire Domesday), free lands, that is, of ancient inheritance, for which could be claimed an immunity from 'geld.' This, however, was not the case with all, for in the Record, over several of the entries, is written the word 'geld.' (= *geldantem* or *geldabilem*), as though this liability were an exception to what was a general rule with regard to the lands held by King's Thanes. Examples may be seen under TOCHEHAM (*p.* 135),—MERE (*p.* 137),—BRAMESSAGE (*p.* 141),—and GATEGRAM (*p.* 142).

MINISTRI REGIS, or the King's officers.

Amongst those who held rank as King's Thanes must be reckoned the MINISTRI REGIS, or KING'S OFFICERS. These were the principal officers of the Court, or members of the Royal Household, or held lands originally attached to such offices. Several of such persons had filled the high and honorable post of Camerarius (or Chamberlain of the household); amongst them were ODIN (*p.* 148),—TURSTIN (*p.* 148),—and ALBERIC (*p.* 149). Another, by name WARIN, was the King's bow-man (*p.* 149); GUNDVIN was the keeper of the royal granaries (*p.* 149); a third is described (*p.* 147) as JOHANNES HOSTIARIUS (= Ostiarius), *i.e.*, the usher, or door-keeper. A comparison of an entry at *p.* 146, with the Exon Domesday, *p.* 163, shews that TEDBALD, who is reckoned among the king's officers, was one of the royal physicians. GEOFFREY, the holder of Draicote (*p.* 147), as we learn from a passage in the Exon Domesday (*p.* 160), was possessed of the high dignity of Marescallus (or Marshal), an office corresponding with that of the 'Steallere' and 'Horsþegn' among the Anglo-Saxons, the duties of which consisted in taking charge of everything connected with the royal equipments, and so led naturally enough to its holders becoming the head of the active and disposable military force of the palace.

VENATORES, or the Huntsmen.

Under this head, also, of Taini Majores are certainly to be reckoned the VENATORES, or HUNTSMEN, mention of whom is so frequent throughout the Survey. As guardians of the Royal Forests, many of them were not only of good rank,[1] but were well endowed with lands. WALERAN, the Huntsman, from whom descended several well-known families in Wilts, was possessed of considerable estates (*pp.* 104–107). Many of the manors granted to this class of persons were in the vicinity of one or other of the forests. Thus CROC held a manor at Todeworde (*p.* 146), close by the forest of CHUTE,—ULURIC at Scaldeburne (*p.* 140), near that of Savernake,—GODRIC at Mera (*p.* 137), in the neighbourhood of that of SELWOOD. A reference to the lands belonging to WALERAN will shew that many of them were also in the vicinity of forest-land. Under Chepeham (*p.* 9), we have notice of a manor which the Confessor had granted to ULVIET his huntsman: another of the royal huntsmen in the days of King Edward held a small estate under the Abbess of Wilton at Newetone (*p.* 45). In one entry we have a manor belonging to the KING'S FORESTERS in the forest of GRAVELINGES (*p.* 144).

---

[1] The position held by the VENATORES is well defined in Canute's 'Constitutiones de Foresta.' All those engaged in 'warding' the forests were out of 'Hundred-Law,' that is, quit and free of all summonses, county courts, and military dues. Thus, among the 'Constitutiones de Foresta" § 9 [Thorpe, I. 427], we have the following:—"Sint omnes......liberi et quieti ab omnibus provincialibus summonitionibus et popularibus placitis quæ 'Hundred-laghe' Angli dicunt, et ab omnibus armorum oneribus quod 'Warscot' Angli dicunt, et forinsecis querelis." The persons of the Head-Foresters were guarded by severe penalties. The Court of the Forest was to be held four times a year, and exercised a jurisdiction such as belonged only to the higher and royal courts. See 'Saxons in England,' II. 81.

It may be observed, in passing, that occasionally we find the same persons holding lands in different capacities. Thus William Corniole held Helprintone (*p.* 129), as one of the King's servants, and Wicheford (*p.* 149), as one of the King's officers. Humfrey de L'Isle is, as we learn by a comparison of the entries in the Exchequer and Exon Domesday (see *pp.* 121, 163), recorded separately as holding Schernecote (*p.* 121), under the title of Humfrey the Chamberlain. So too, whilst most of the Huntsmen are entered as holding lands as King's Thanes, Croc held Stoche (*p.* 149), as one of the King's Officers.

It is possible that though the Servientes Regis, or King's Servants, comprised a class of officers of the court of an inferior relative position to those just described, they may have been included, as far as rank was concerned, among the Taini Majores, or Higher Thanes. Amongst them was Ansger, the King's cook, the holder of Helprintone (*p.* 129);—and Stephen, his carpenter, the possessor of a small estate at Ardescote (*p.* 130);—and Osmund, his interpreter [1] (if indeed we may draw such a conclusion from the entry in the Exon Domesday) the holder of Ponberie (*p.* 130). In one case we have Tedbald, the physician, and Humfrey, the cook, numbered among the Ministri Regis as joint-owners of Widehille. [See *p.* 146 compared with *p.* 163.] In this last instance, possibly by *cook* may be intended the office of Disc-þegn or Thane of the table, which corresponded with that of Steward or Dapifer, such as was held by Ednod in the days of the Confessor (*p.* 61). All the officers of the King had much deference paid to them, and even the lower situations about the court entitled the holders to much social rank. Thus, when Hardicanute sent certain persons to dig up the body of Harold, he is said to have appointed 'Ælfric, Archbishop of York, Earl Godwin, Styr master of the household, Edric the steward, Troudh his *cook*, and *others of high dignity*." [2]

Servientes Regis, or the King's Servants.

We have spoken of the Lesser Thanes as corresponding with what in some portions of the Record are called Vavassours. This last title does not occur in the Wiltshire Domesday, though no doubt in this class were included very many who are named as principal under-tenants. Thus the subordinate holders of Boltintone (*p.* 53), are described as Thanes; the demesne of the Abbess of Ambresbury as chief owner is said to be worth £13; and then "quod *Taini* tenent" is valued at 15 shillings. Selden conjectures that they held their lands either of a mesne lord, or not immediately of the King, or at least of the King as of an honour or manor and not in chief. And Sir H. Spelman gives us much the same account when he says,—"The grantees who received their estates from the Barons or Tenants in chief and not from the King were called Valvasours, and were with their lords as they, the Tenants in chief, were to the King." They corresponded with what were called Frankleins at a later period, for Chaucer calls his Franklein a Vavassour. The position held by them is explained in an early account of the services of the tenants of Ramsey Monastery, in which they are thus distinguished from the 'milites;'—"Præter hos milites sunt *Franklani*, quorum quidam tenent dimidiam hidam, quidam plus, quidam minus, et solent adjuvare milites ad servicium faciendum." [3] According to Morgan they

The Lesser Thanes, who corresponded with the Vavassours.

---

1 The Exon Domesday (p. 170) gives the name as Osmund *Latimar.* Ellis (I. 91) quotes from a register of Abingdon (MS. Cott. Claud. C. ix. *fol.* 139*b*) the following explanation of the term, "Gilbertus *Latemer*, id est *interpres.*" Latin-arius (= Latin-er) would seem to be the origin of the word; one, that is, whose skill in Latin was presumed to enable him to understand other languages. Hugo Latinarius occurs among the tenants in Hants (Domes. I. 50*b*). Blount says, "Beneath Whittington in Shropshire one Wrenoc, son of Meuric, held lands by the service of being *latimer* (i.e., interpreter) between the English and the Welshmen."—See Kennett's Paroch. Antiq. (Glossary); also, 'England under the Normans,' p. 207.

2 Quoted from Simeon of Durham, by Ellis, I. 92.

3 New Monast. II. 579.

were "not very unlike the sochemen of a previous period, and seem to resemble the class of yeomen freeholders, called statesmen, now becoming extinct, whose name perhaps indicates that they form a middle class, or estate."[1]

Confirmation of the accuracy of these opinions seems to be derived from several of the entries in the Wiltshire Domesday. Thus all the subordinate holdings under the Abbot of Glastonbury in DOBREHAM (*p.* 28), are called 'Terra Tainorum.' Under BREME (*p.* 38), we have land granted 'cuidam Taino.' Siward, a Thane, is registered as holding land at CHEGESLAUE (*p.* 93), under Milo Crispin. So in the Exon Domesday, at *p.* 174, we have among the land holders, the 'Thanes of Edward the Sheriff,' and at *p.* 185, the 'Thanes of Ernulf de Hesding.'

THANES OF THE SHIRE.

Of this class were no doubt the TAINI SCIRÆ (Thanes of the Shire), by whose evidence the Commissioners seem to have been commonly guided in making their returns. They are very frequently alluded to in the Wiltshire portion of the Record. See under WINTREBURNE (*p.* 33),—ALENTONE (*p.* 63),—LANGEFORDE (*p.* 73). In one case, under CAUNA (*p.* 7), we have the expression 'testimonio Sciræ.'

We have already stated that the demesne land was cultivated by the lord himself for his own especial use. In each estate he seems to have placed a Prefectus or Prepositus, that is a Bailiff or Steward, answering to the Anglo-Saxon 'Wicnere,' whose position varied with the rank of his employer and the extent of his jurisdiction, for he represented the lord in his manorial court and had to see that the various services due to him were properly rendered.

Gathering our conclusions from the entries themselves, the demesne lands in Wiltshire would seem to have been chiefly cultivated by the SERVI or SERFS. With them are sometimes associated the 'COLIBERTI,' which we have translated COLIBERTS.

The SERFS, their condition in olden time.

The Anglo-Saxon word for a serf was Ðeów or Esne, for, though there seems to have been some difference between the two, they are used as identical in meaning in the laws ascribed to Ina.[2] The name by which they are designated in the laws of William the Conqueror,—namely Naifs or Neifs,—the latin word for which is *Nativi*,—[3] seems to justify the inference, that they were originally the lowest class of the natives engaged in the cultivation of the soil, when the country was subdued by the Saxons, who were retained by the conquerors in a state of bondage. From this circumstance, no doubt, it was that the terms *Wealh* and *Wyln* were also used for this class. Certainly nothing is more unlikely, or opposed to facts, than the notion once commonly entertained of the total expulsion or extermination of the British by the Anglo-Saxon invaders. No doubt, as regards the irresponsibility of the master in the eye of the law, as to all dealings between himself and his þeów, the lot of the serf was a hard one. As far as legal position was concerned, he was in fact "the absolute property of the lord, a chattel to be disposed of at the lord's pleasure, and having a value only for the benefit of the lord, or of some public authority

---

[1] 'England under the Normans,' 224.

[2] The one is used in the rubric and the other as its equivalent in the text of the law alluded to. See Thorpe, I. 121. The Esne seems to have belonged to the class of poor mercenaries who served for their hire on their land, and not to have been reduced so low in the social scale as the Ðeow, or, as he was also sometimes called, the Wealh. 'Saxons in England,' I. 215.

[3] Thorpe, I. 480.

in his place. The serf could not represent himself or others; his interests had to be guarded by others, for he himself had no standing in any public courts."[1] Even as late as in the time of Ethelred and Canute the law ventured no further in favour of the serf than to prohibit his being sold into heathendom, or without some fault on his part.[2] At the same time the mere material condition of the serf was not necessarily one of great hardship.[3] Many alleviations of his condition had in course of centuries been obtained through the kind offices of the clergy. They procured for him respite from labour at certain times, from sun-set on Sunday-eve till sun-set on Monday-eve, on certain high festivals and on the days which preceded or followed them, and by the laws of Ina it is expressly enacted that if the lord compelled his 'þeów-man,' or serf, to work on the Sunday, the serf was to be declared free, and the lord to pay a fine of 30 shillings.[4] No doubt to the same influence it must be ascribed that in the wills of the Anglo-Saxon proprietors, we so often find directions for the manumission of a certain number of serfs, for the 'soul's heal' of the testator. The privilege given by the laws of Alfred[5] to the serf to bequeath to whomsoever they wished whatever any one might give them in God's name, or what they might earn in their own permitted times of work, implies also a protection from the exercise of arbitrary power on the part of the lord, in removing a labourer from a plot of ground well cultivated by his own industry, or in depriving him of all interest in his own efforts. Hence the conclusion to which Kemble comes seems a just one; "it seems doubtful whether the labour of the serf was practically more severe, or the remuneration much less than that of an agricultural labourer in this country at this day. His lord was bound to feed him for his own sake, and if, when old and worn out, he wished to rid himself of a useless burden, he could by an act of emancipation, hand over his broken-down labourer to the care of a Church, which, with all its faults, never totally lost sight of the divine precepts of charity. We are not altogether without the means of judging as to the condition of the serf and the provision made for him. In the prose version of Salomon and Saturn it is said that every serf ought to receive yearly seven hundred and thirty loaves, that is, two loaves a day, besides morning meals and noon meals; this cannot be said to be a very niggardly portion. Again, the valuable document entitled, "Rectitudines singularum personarum," gives details respecting the allowance made to the serfs in various prædial or domestic capacities, which would induce a belief not only that they were tolerably provided for, but even enabled by the exertion of skill and industry to lay up funds of their own towards the purchase of their freedom, the redemption of their children, or the alleviation of their own poverty."[6]

The number of Serfs registered in the Wiltshire Domesday, as attached to the various manors, is about *sixteen hundred.*

In the laws of William the Conqueror is a form for the emancipation of a serf. It runs thus:—"We forbid any one selling a man out of his own county. If any one wishes to give freedom to his serf, let him deliver him to the Sheriff by the right hand, in full county (in pleno comitatu), and proclaim him free from all

---

[1] 'Saxons in England,' I. 209. [2] Thorpe, I, 305, 317, 379.

[3] Care must be taken in drawing conclusions respecting serfs not to form them exclusively from statements which have reference to the condition of the wite-þeow, or penal slave,—a convict, that is, reduced to slavery for crime, and expiating his offences by his sufferings. Kemble (I. 210—213) gives a long and careful description of the various classes of the *unfree* population.

[4] Thorpe's Ancient Laws, I. 39, 105, 173, 388. [5] Ibid. I. 93.

[6] 'Saxons in England,' I. 214.

yoke of servitude by manumission, and show him open roads and doors, and give him the arms of a free man, (namely a lance and a sword. Thenceforth he shall be free."[1] One instance occurs in the Domesday for Gloucester I. 167*b*) of this manumission of serfs. Under the land of William Leuric at Heile, it is said, "Ibi erant 12 servi *quos Willelmus liberos fecit.*"

The COLIBERTS, their semi-servile condition.

It is not easy to give an exact account of the COLIBERTI.—According to Ducange "they were called Coliberts in the civil law who had been presented with their freedom by the lord whose serfs they had been." He explains the word as though it were *con-libertus*, and describes their condition as being reckoned neither amongst the altogether free, nor amongst those who are wholly serfs.[2] They corresponded with the *coloni* of a former age. Having been serfs admitted to freedom, though not fully and completely, they were called *conditionales*. And Cowell, in his Law Interpreter, also explains the word as denoting 'a middle class of tenants, between servile and free, or such as held their freedom of tenure under condition of such works and services." They were in fact a semi-servile class, occupying a position between the *servi* and the *liberi*, doing many of the works of the former but holding by the tenure of the latter. Such persons, as Heywood remarks, "who had been slaves, are found after their manumission uniformly on the demesnes, probably those which they had worked on before, and therefore the bare act of manumission did not discharge them from all connexion with the lord's demesnes, or entitle them to be placed among the villans and bordars. They seem to have been compulsorily attached to the same spot, and, as far as can now be traced, to have been obliged to associate with the same persons, and perform the same labours as in their originally servile state."[3]

In Domesday Book there are several entries from which it would appear that the COLIBERTS held much the same position as the BURI or BURES. Thus in an entry relating to the manor of DENE, in Hants (I *fol.* 38*b*), *Bures* is an interlineation in a coeval hand above the word *Coliberti*. Again, in the Domesday for Worcestershire (I. 174*b*), under POIWIC, we have the word *Coliberti* in like manner written above *Buri*. The Anglo-Saxon word *ge-búr* whence comes our modern *boor*, is, as we shall have occasion presently to show, used generically for all free labourers or occupiers below a certain grade. It is equivalent to *colonus* (whence comes the modern word *clown*), which is used in the laws of William the Conqueror[4] to denote the lower class of free agricultural labourers.

This semi-servile character of the Coliberts is borne out by the entries in the Wiltshire Domesday. Very frequently they are associated with the Serfs in the cultivation of the lord's demesne. Examples may be seen under AMBLESBERIE (*p.* 8),—ALDBORNE (*p.* 11),—MELCHESAM (*p.* 12),—WESTBERIE (*p.* 13),—POTERNE (*p.* 22),—DOBREHAM (*p.* 28),—CHETRE (*p.* 69),—and elsewhere. On the other hand there are instances, though they are by no means so numerous, in which they are named together with the tenants who occupied and cultivated the 'out-lands,' or those portions of the manor not included in the lord's demesne. Thus, under CAUNA (*p.* 7), and EDENDONE (*p.* 52), we have the Coliberts classed with the Villans and Bordars, in contradistinction to the Serfs.

---

[1] Thorpe, I. 493.

[2] "Coliberti nec inter omnino liberos nec inter omnino servos accensebantur, nec liberis nec servis annumerarentur, licet ad servorum statum proprius accederent, cum eorum instar essent in commercio, dominos haberent, quibus censum de more exsolvebant, et ab iis in libertatem non secus ac servi affererentur. Patet non multum aberrare qui colibertos ejusdem fuisse conditionis dicunt, quos ætas anterior *colonos* appellavit. Erant servi in libertatem, non quidem plenariam sed conditionalem asserti: unde etiam *conditionales* dicuntur ejusmodi homines alicui vel servituti obnoxii, a qua rursum afferebantur interdum in potiorem libertatem." Ducange *sub voce* COLIBERTUS.

[3] Heywood on the Ranks of the People under the Anglo-Saxons, p. 314.

[4] Thorpe, I. 481.

There are some 263 Coliberts registered as connected with the various manors in Wiltshire. They seldom occur on any but crown or church lands, and are confined to the western counties. No doubt there were different grades in this class, some of the coliberts being evidently possessed of more land than others. Thus, in the Hants Domesday (I. 38), under COSEHAM (as part of the larger manor of WIMERINGES), we meet with eight Bures, or Coliberts, possessed of four carucates of land, and paying as rent nearly fifty shillings yearly; whilst at POIWIC (Powick, in Worcestershire) three Coliberts paid only forty-five pence and three sextaries of honey. (Domesd. I. 174*b*).

We come now to a consideration of those classes who occupied and cultivated that part of the estate which the lord did not keep in his own hands, which was called the *ût-land* (out-land).

The VILLANS, the position held by them as a class.

The chief of these were the VILLANI, which we have uniformly translated VILLANS. These occur in nearly every entry, and are the most numerous of all the classes, about 3500 being registered under the various manors. When they are not expressly named, it may in some cases be almost inferred that the principal under-tenant, especially if the holding be a small one, was himself the VILLAN.

Much has been written on the subject of the position held by the Villans. Blackstone, in a long passage cited by Ellis,[1] regards them as bondsmen just raised above absolute servitude. "On the arrival," he says, "of the Normans here, it seems not improbable that they, who were strangers to any other than a feudal state, might give some sparks of enfranchisement to such wretched persons as fell to their share, by admitting them, as well as others, to the oath of fealty; which conferred a right of protection, and raised the tenant to a kind of estate superior to downright slavery, but inferior to every other condition. This they called *Villenage* and the tenants *Villeins*, either from the word *vilis*, or else, as Sir E. Coke tells us, *a villa*, because they lived chiefly in villages, and were employed in rustic works of the most sordid kind."

A merely cursory glance at the entries in the Wiltshire Domesday will show that in this county the Villans were certainly no bondsmen.[2] In some instances they must have had a considerable quantity of land for cultivation. The fact, moreover, that *six villans* from each manor formed part of the jury or inquest, on whose information, given upon oath, the Domesday returns were framed, is also conclusive on this point. And then further, among the Conqueror's laws, there is one concerning the 'Relief' due from the Villan, which is altogether irreconcilable with the idea of his being a bondsman. It runs as follows:—"The relief of a Villan:—the best animal that he has, whether it be an ox, or a horse, shall come to the lord: and all the Villans shall be in frank-pledge."[3]

---

[1] Introduction to Domesday, I. 75.

[2] In one of the laws of William the Conqueror the word *villanus* is given as the equivalent to '*li socheman*.' Thorpe, I. 475. The 'Sochemanni,' as Ellis tells us, were those inferior land-owners who had lands in the *Soc* or franchise of a great baron; who though their tenures were really copyhold, yet had an interest equal to a freehold. Their services were fixed and determinate. They could not be compelled to relinquish their tenements at the lord's will, nor against their own; 'et ideo,' says Bracton, 'denominantur liberi.' A certain number of such men were necessary in every manor to hold the pleas of the Manor Court. Soc-men were consequently those who owed suit and service to the lord's court, and it is from the word *Soc*, which gives them their name, that we derive our tenures in free and common *socage*. Ellis, I. 69. A full and interesting account of Sochemen will be found in 'England under the Normans,' pp. 128—138. This class of persons is not expressly named in the Wiltshire Domesday; in truth such an appellation seems to be confined to the midland and eastern counties.

[3] Thorpe, I. 476.

Fortunately we have, in a very valuable document entituled 'Rectitudines singularum personarum,'[1] the position of the Villan defined with tolerable accuracy. Both the Anglo-Saxon version of that document and its Latin translation are of ancient date, and when we find therefore the one giving *villanus* as equivalent to *ge-neát,* we can have little doubt as to his true character and position. "The geneát-right (*villani* rectum) is various according to the custom of the land. In some places he must pay land-gafol (= rent), and a grass-swine yearly; ride and carry and lead load;[2] he must work and feed[3] his lord; he must reap and mow; he must hew the deer-hedge and hold *sæte*;[4] he must build and enclose the burh [or mansion]; he must make new roads to the farm; he must pay church-shot and alms-fee;[5] he must hold head-ward and horse-ward;[6] he must go on errand far and near, whithersoever he is directed."

Such services as these could only be rendered by a free-man, and one also who was in a substantial position. It is not implied that all these services were to be performed in each instance, as it is expressly said that these depended on the custom of the particular land which was held. In any case, however, the villan must have had many dependents under him, in order to enable him to pay the services due to the lord. We are not informed of the amount of such services that might be demanded for a given quantity of land. Possibly we might obtain a tolerably accurate idea on this subject by an examination of ancient Court Rolls, or Custumals of Manors.

There can be no doubt that in Wiltshire the villan represented the principal of the subordinate tenants or cultivators of the land. The name *Villanus* was assigned to him no doubt because he held his land according to the *custom of the Vill*, or Manor, and hence its synonym *Custumarius*,[7] that is, 'customary tenant.' And in time these customary tenants became what we know by the more familiar name of *copy-holders*. The process is thus described by Blackstone:—"Villans in process of time gained considerable ground on their lords, and in

---

[1] This document is printed in Thorpe's Ancient Laws, I. 432. A later edition was published by Dr. H. Leo, of Halle.

[2] The Anglo-Saxon reads 'and lade lædan,' which the Latin translates 'et summagium ducere.' By *summagium* is denoted a service which consisted in supplying the lord with beasts of burden, or, as Roquefort explains it, 'Service qu'un vassal devoit a son seigneur, et qui consistoit a faire quelques voyages par ses betes de *somme*. See Thorpe's Glossary, *sub voce* Lád.

[3] And hlaford *feormian* [et dominum suum *firmare*];—that is, the villan was bound to give a certain portion of the '*feorm*,' or produce of the land, to the lord.

[4] And sæte haldan [et stabilitatem observare]. Kemble (I. 322) interprets this service as consisting in helping to make park-paling, and perhaps keeping watch for game. Ellis (I. iii.) says that *stabilitio* meant stalling the deer. To drive the deer and other game from all quarters to the centre of a gradually contracted circle, where they were compelled to stand, was *stabilitio*.

[5] And cyric-sceat syllan and ælmes-feoh [et ciricsceatum dare et almesfeoh, id est, pecuniam elemosinæ]. Cyric-sceat or Church-shot was, according to Bishop Kennett, a quantity of corn paid to the priest on St. Martin's day as the first-fruits of harvest, and hence called '*Primitiæ seminum*.' The payment was enjoined in the laws of King Ina and also in those of King Canute. Thorpe, I. 105, 367. See also Ellis, I. 300. Some further remarks on this payment will be found in the next chapter.

[6] The Latin equivalent for the service called *heafod-ward* is *custodia capitis*. Ducange defines *custodia* as 'obligatio qua tenentur vassalli *excubias facere* in castris dominorum, quas vulgo *gardes* vocant.' Hence this expression may signify holding watch at the tent of the lord.—*Hors-weard* would seem to have been a service which consisted in watching the *horses* of the lord.

[7] See Hund. R. II. 512, where, as elsewhere, *villani* and *custumarii* are used as synonymous.

particular strengthened the tenure of their estates to that degree that they came to have in them in many places an interest full as good, in others better than their lords. For the good nature and benevolence of many lords of manors having, time out of mind, permitted their villans aud their children to enjoy their possessions without interruption, in a regular course of descent, the common law, of which custom is the life, now gave them title to prescribe against their lords, and, on performance of the same services, to hold their lands, in spite of any determination of the lord's will. For though in general they are still said to hold their estates at the will of the lord, yet it is such a will as is agreeable to the custom of the manor; which customs are preserved and evidenced by the rolls of the several courts baron in which they are entered, or kept on foot by the constant immemorial usage of the several manors in which the lands lie. And as such tenants had nothing to show for their estates but their customs, and admissions, in pursuance of them, entered on those rolls, or the copies of such entries witnessed by the steward, they now began to be called *tenants by copy of court roll*, and their tenure itself a copyhold."[1]

The Cotsetler or Coscet.

Next in social position to the Villan, according to the document already quoted, was the Cotsetler, or as he is commonly termed in the Wiltshire Domesday, the Coscet. We meet with this class of tenants only in Devonshire, Dorset, Shropshire, Somerset, and Wilts. There are in the whole of Domesday but about 1750 registered, and of these more than 1400 are found in the Wiltshire portion of the Record. They were no doubt cottagers who held small portions of land, generally about five acres, as attached to their tenement, for which they were to render certain services to the lord. It will be observed that in the following extract, which describes his rights and duties, it is expressly implied that the Coscet was a freeman:—"The Cotsetler's right is according to the custom of the land. In some places he must work for the lord every Monday throughout the year; or three days each week in harvest. He need pay no land-gafol [i.e., *rent*]. He ought to have five acres; more if it be the custom of the place. If it be less it is too little, because his service is often called upon. He must pay his hearth-penny[2] on Holy Thursday, as is the duty of *every freeman*. He must acquit his lord's inland,[3] when summoned to do so, at sea-ward and at the King's deer-hedge, and at such things as are in his competence. He must pay his church-shot at Martinmas."

Such services as these were by no means of a servile character, especially those which required the Coscet in his own person to supply the liabilities of the lord in hewiug the king's deer-hedge, or performing the duty of coast-guard.

It is commonly said that the Cottar is much the same as the Coscet, or, at all events, that the difference between them was so trifling that it cannot now be discovered.[4] But against this theory is to be set the fact that the Coscet aud the Cottar are repeatedly mentioned in the same entries. Examples may be seen under

---

[1] Blackstone's Comment. 4to. Oxf. 1766, vol. ii. 95. See Ellis, I. 78.

[2] According to the glossaries, Heorð-penig was the same as what was also called Rom-feoh, Rom-sceat, and in Latin 'denarius Sancti Petri' (or Peter's-pence), a due payable to the see of Rome, and consisting of one penny from every hearth. See Thorpe, I. 170.

[3] The Anglo-Saxon has 'werige his hláfordes inland,' which the old Latin version translates '*adquietet* inland domini sui.' The meaning is that he shall *acquit* the lord of the duty (in other words perform it for his lord) of *sea-ward* (i.e., of coast-guard) and at *the King's deer hedge* (i.e., of attending the King's hunt, or perhaps in repairing the park-paling). See Kemble, I. 323.

[4] Ellis, I. 84.

COSEHAM (*p.* 11),—DANTESIE (*p.* 34),—BRECHEORDE (*p.* 35),—NEWETONE (*p.* 36),—CERLETONE (*p.* 37),—BOLTINTONE (*p.* 53),—BOSCUMBE (*p.* 54),—ALLENTONE (*p.* 54),—EDINTONE (*p.* 65),—LANGEFEL (*p.* 71),—LACOCK (*p.* 71),—HASEBERIE (*p.* 94). Moreover, in each of the counties in which the Coscets are mentioned, the Cottars occur as a distinct class. We must therefore assume that there was a difference between them, and in what that consisted we must seek now to ascertain.[1]

The GE-BUR, the class of labourers indicated by this term.

In the 'Rectitudines singularum personarum' there is no distinct mention made of the Cottar or Bordar. But we have a long description of the *Ge-búr* (= Boor), of which class, as such, there is no mention in the Wilts Domesday, which is so comprehensive in its character as to appear rather to include several classes of much the same grade, than to be limited to any one in particular. And some expressions in it seem to throw light on the relative position of the classes which we are now considering. The entry is as follows :—" The customs of the Ge-búr are very various. In some places they are heavy, in others moderate. In some places it is usual that he shall do two days' week-work, whatever work may be commanded him, every week throughout the year; and three days' week-work in harvest, and three from Candlemas to Easter. If he does haulage, he need not work himself while his horse is out. He must pay at Michaelmas 10 gafol-pence, and at Martinmas 23, and a sester of barley,[2] and 2 hens; at Easter one young sheep or two pence; and he shall lie out at the lord's fold[3] from Martinmas till Easter, as often as it comes to his turn. And from the time when they first begin to plough till Martinmas he shall plough one acre every week, and himself prepare the seed in the lord's barn; in addition to this he must plough three acres *on request*, and two of grass-ploughing.[4] If he requires more grass, let him earn it on such conditions as he may. For his rent-ploughing [gafol-yrðe], he shall plough three acres, and sow them from his own barn. He shall pay his hearth-penny; and two and two shall feed one stag-hound. And every Ge-búr shall give six loaves to the In-swán[5] when he drives his herd to masting. In the same land, where this custom prevails, the Ge-búr has a right, towards first stocking his land, to two oxen, one cow, and six sheep, and seven acres in his yard of land ready sown. After the first year, he must do all the customs that belong to him; and he is to be supplied with *tools for his work* and *furniture for his house*. When he dies, let his lord again have all that is left behind.

---

[1] In the Shaftesbury Chartulary (Harl. MS. 61) under Heutoun, in Dorset, we have a clear distinction drawn between the Cotsetli and the Cotarii, different lists being given of those who held on the respective tenures. See *fol.* 65*b*. The former seem there to have commonly had *four acres* of land, paying at the same time certain rent, and performing certain services.

[2] The Anglo-Saxon reads 'on Martinus mæsse-dæg xxiii systra beres,' i.e., "at Martinmas 23 *sesters of barley*." This seems so immense an amount that we have preferred to follow the old Latin version, which gives the version in the text.

[3] The fold being often at a great distance from the homestead required careful watching, especially during the winter-months. See Kemble, I. 324.

[4] The Anglo-Saxon reads 'þreo æceras to béne and twá to gærsyrðe,' which the Latin translates 'tres acras *precum* et duas de herbagio,' the general meaning of which is, that if he has to work on old arable ground he is to plough *three*, if on meadow land (which would be harder to work, as it would have to be broken up) *two* acres. These works, thus given *on request* were what were called *precations*. At first, 'according to the oldest custom, such work was freely offered, then *precariously* requested, lastly despotically demanded.' Thorpe's Glossary, *sub voce* Feorm. In the north of England, the days on which the tenants gave such labour to their lords were called *boon* days, evidently from the Anglo-Saxon *bén*, which primarily means simply a *request*. There were precations of ploughing, or as they were termed bén-yrð (precariæ carucarum) in winter or spring, and precations in autumn for gathering in the crops called bén-rip. See Introduction to Domesday of St. Paul's, p. lxvii.

[5] The In-swán was the *swain*, or swine-herd, of the in-land or demesne.

"This land-law prevails in some lands, but, as I have before said, in some places it is heavier, in some lighter, because the customs of all lands are not alike. In some places the Ge-bûr has to pay *honey-gafol*, in some *meat-gafol*, in some *ale-gafol*. Let him that holds the shire take heed to know always what is *the old arrangement about the land*, and what is *the custom of his country*."[1]

It cannot be supposed for an instant that any *one* Ge-bûr could be called upon to render all these services. The concluding words, which qualify the whole passage, plainly intimate that the above extract is to be regarded as the description of a *class* of cultivators of the soil, and of the *kind* of services that could be required by the lord, the special ones demanded, both as to number and extent, being settled by the custom of each particular manor. A notice of the words italicised will shew how the peculiar tenure of the classes included in it is described.

The Cottars. First among these, it is believed, was the COTTAR. The *cottage* given to him by the lord, and also furnished by him, may well account for his name. A comparison of the services due from the Coscet and the Cottar will shew that those rendered by the former were of a much higher character than those demanded from the latter. Moreover, the Coscet, though his portion of land was small in extent, might at all events call the stock, and produce of the same, bis own, provided he performed his customary services. The Cottar, as a Ge-bûr, received what land he held only as a loan from the lord, who, as he had stocked the land, and furnished the cottage, and even supplied tools for his poor dependent, took possession again of all on the tenant's decease.

The Bordars. To this same class, also, it is conjectured, belonged the BORDARIUS or BORDAR. That the Cottar and Bordar were of the same social grade appears tolerably clear from the fact that in the Ely MS. we find the term *bordarii* where the breviate of the same entry in the Exchequer Domesday reads *cotarii*.[2] They derived their name from the fact of their paying their *gafol* (or rent) in kind,—in provisions, that is, to supply the lord's table. In letting out land to under-tenants, care was always taken to reserve a sufficient quantity to supply the lord's table with provisions. Lands so appropriated "were styled *bord-lands*, the occupiers *bordarii*, and the rents bord-land rents, and sometimes *table-rents*—for whether we construe the Anglo-Saxon *bord* by *domus* with some, or by *mensa* with others, it is not material, since to supply the house or table with provisious conveys precisely the same idea."[3]

According to Mr. Morgan, a bordar's usual tenement was five acres in Norfolk, Cambridgeshire, Middlesex, and Somerset. "In a few cases," he says, "tenants of three acres, and of seven acres and a half are called bordars. They assisted the villans in husbandry, but were not always themselves owners of ploughs and oxen. It is possible that their yards, or gardens, may have been, not shares in the common fields, but small parcels severed from the true villenage, and surrounded by the lord's free-hold land. Out of Domesday, bordars are not

---

[1] Thorpe, I. 435.

[2] Ellis, I. 83.

[3] Gentleman's Mag. (1792) p. 1188. Bracton's explanation is much of the same character, when he says:—"Est autem dominicum, quod quis habet *ad mensam*, et proprie sicut sunt *Boordlands* Anglice." Fleta also speaks of the same as 'terra *ad mensam* assignata.' In similar manner we have John Daincourt, in the year 1169, saying of a plough-land at Branston, 'una de carucatis fuit de dominio meo, *mensæ meæ*.' New Mon., iv. 421. The same writer adds, "It is common in *our days* (i.e., at the close of the last century) for tenants to supply their landlords with so many hundreds of cheese annually, and so many pounds of butter weekly."

often mentioned in English records; their name had been brought into England by the Normans, and it disappears at the end of the twelfth century. In Normandy they were principally employed in domestic labours, while the services of the other peasants were directed to the cultivation of the land. This is quite consistent with some entries in Domesday; we read of bordars being servants at the court at Evesham (I. 175*b*), and of bordars who abided about the hall at Tewkesbury (I. 163)."[1]

The same author tells us, that very frequently, when the value of a mill was not large, its keeper was a bordar. "We frequently find a single bordar in lands which have a small mill: this is most remarkable in particular counties, such as Oxford, Gloucester, Northampton, Warwick, and Leicestershire, and several lands with two mills have likewise two bordars."[2]

There are two other classes of peasantry named in the Wiltshire Domesday of which we must make mention, the MELLITARII, or Bee-keepers, and the PORCARII, or Swine-herds.

The MELLITARII, or BEE-KEEPERS.

The Anglo-Saxon name of the MELLITARIUS was *Beo-Ceorl* (=Bee-Churl). His duties and privileges are thus defined in the document already so frequently quoted,—"The Bee-keeper, if he have a gafol-herd (that is, hold them at an annual *gafol* or rent), shall pay all the customary dues of the place. In some places it is usual for him to give five sesters of honey as gafol, in others, he has commonly to pay more. He must also often be prepared to do many works at the will of his lord, and must render service of ben-yrðe[3] and ben ripe,[3] and help in mowing the meadow. And if he have good land he shall have a horse with which he may do haulage for his lord, or lead himself whithersoever it may be told him. And there are many things of like character that must be done by the Bee-keeper which cannot now be narrated. When he dies, the lord shall have what is left behind, with the exception of any part of it which is free."[4]

The Mellitarii are named but once in the Wiltshire Domesday, under WESTBERIE (*p.* 13). Among the perquisites of Edward of Salisbury, as Sheriff of Wilts, were 'sixteen sextaries of honey, or instead of honey, sixteen shillings' (*p.* 64). It must be borne in mind that there were, among the servile class, some who were Bee-keepers, or Honey-men as they have been called. The Saxon name for such a person was Ðeów-beoceorl, or as the Latin gives it, 'Servus custos apum.' These in the various entries in Domesday, are, no doubt, accounted for under the Serfs.

The PORCARII, or SWINEHERDS.

The PORCARII were the Swine-herds. As in the previous case, there was the Ðeów-swán, or as he is also called, Æhte-swán, the 'Servus porcarius qui dominicam gregem curiæ custodit;' and also the Gafol-swán, who was a freeman, and who paid a certain *gafol*, or rent in kind, to the lord for the privilege of masting his swine in the common fields, or the woods belonging to the manor. Of the former, we have no doubt very many included among the Serfs. Of the latter, there are but 87 named in the Wilts Domesday, and these were attached to the

---

[1] 'England under the Normans,' p. 64.

[2] Ibid. p. 100, where a number of references to various passages in Domesday are given in corroboration of the truth of the above statement.

[3] On the meaning of these terms, see note on p. lx.

[4] Thorpe, I. 436.

large manors of Bradford, Westbury, Chippenham, and Warminster. The Gafol-swán had not only to give to the lord a certain number of porkers yearly,—in many places, according to the 'Rectitudines singularum personarum,' fifteen—ten old and five young,—but was liable to be called upon to perform similar services with the Beo-ceorl. Amongst other things he had to provide a horse for the lord's work when required to do so, at certain times.

General condition of the tenantry in olden time.

This review of the various classes mentioned in the Wilts Domesday will probably lead many persons to the conclusion that the lot of the dependent freeman was no enviable one in olden time. Still it must be borne in mind, that, however subject he might be in some instances to the tyranny or caprice of the lord under whom he held his land, the law protected him fully in the enjoyment of all the privileges which custom had assigned to his particular tenure or condition. The duties of lord and vassal, even to the lowest class, his very serfs, were within certain limits well defined, and the law provided that ample justice should be meted out to all. In strict truth, the lord of a manor in the eleventh century was but the head of a confederacy, the subordinate members of which held their lands by a tenure not less certain than his own. It was assumed as a fact, that, on the estate which they helped to cultivate, the husbandman and the labourer should have both house and provisions, and no lord could either neglect the proper cultivation of his estate, or eject without due cause those by whose labour it was tilled. For thus ran the law of the Conqueror,[1]—"Coloni et terrarum exercitores non vexentur ultra debitum et statutum; nec licet dominis removere colonos a terris, dummodo debita servicia persolvant." . . . . "Si domini terrarum non procurent idoneos cultores ad terras suas colendas, justiciarii hoc faciant."

[1] "Cil qui custiuent la terre ne deit lum trauailer se de lour droite cense; noun le leist a seignurage de partir les cultiuurs de lur terre; pur tant cum il pussent le dreit servise faire"......"Si les seignurages ne facent altri gainurs uenir a lour terre, la justice le facet." Laws of William the Conqueror, I. §§ 29, 31. [Thorpe, I. 480].

CHAPTER IV.

Estates belonging to the Church at the time of Domesday. Confiscation of Church property, how far to be attributed to the Conqueror. The tenure in frankalmoigne. Gifts to the Church recorded. Estates held by foreign monasteries. The Churches in Wiltshire, —very many not named because no land belonging to them chargeable with geld. Churches held in moieties and other shares. Titles of ministers,—presbyter,—clericolus. Vicars of parishes, their position and income. Revenues of the Church. Alienation of Tithes. Leases of lands granted on lives. Cyric-sceat. State of the clergy in the tenth century.

Estates belonging to the Church. A VERY large portion of the land in Wiltshire was, at the time of Domesday, in the hands of the Church. Manors assessed at no less than 1750[1] hides, representing probably some 260,000 acres, or more than *two-fifths* of the whole county, belonged to one or other of the great religious houses, or to persons holding high office in the church. In the north was Malmesbury Abbey with its 13 manors, some of them of large extent, embracing several subordinate ones, assessed at well-nigh 300 hides, and so implying the possession of some 50,000 acres. In the south were the two abbeys of Ambresbury and Wilton, each with a number of estates; those held by the latter monastery being nearly as extensive as those possessed by Malmesbury. The abbey of St. Edward at Shaftesbury moreover had considerable estates in Wilts, situated principally in the western portion of the county. The famous abbey at Glastonbury, and the three religious houses at Winchester, had goodly endowments here, whilst a few manors belonged to the abbeys of Romsey in Hants, and Cranbourne in Dorset.

Of high ecclesiastics the Bishop of Sarum was the greatest proprietor, holding as he did the estates belonging to the old Bishopric of Ramsbury, which but a few years before the Conquest had been united with that of Sherborne, and, with it, transferred to Sarum. Next came the Bishop of Winchester, who, either in right of his see, or as trustee for the monks of St. Swithin, held manors assessed at no less than 249 hides. Some foreign ecclesiastics, the Bishops of Baieux, Coutance, and Lisieux possessed a few manors, though none of any extent, amounting in all to hardly more than fifty hides, and the first two owed them, no doubt, as much to the services they rendered to William in his invasion of England, as to the sacred office which they held.

---

[1] It has been sometimes supposed that the estates belonging to the Church were assessed considerably below their real value, and examples may no doubt be brought forward which seem to favor such a view. See above, p. xli. Ingulphus distinctly states that the possessions of Croyland Abbey were under-rated. Ellis, I. 30. As regards Wiltshire, as far as I have been able to carry out the enquiry, the valuation of Church estates seems on the whole a fair one. Compared with those belonging to laymen, they often seem over-rated; though no doubt they were in a better state of cultivation, and therefore more valuable. Thus GRETELINTONE (p. 32) (Grittleton,) which belonged to Glastonbury, and CHIVELE (p. 74) (Keevil), which belonged to Ernulf de Hesding, contain respectively 1973 and 2049 acres, and yet the former paid geld for *thirty*, and the latter for *sixteen* hides.

Confiscation of Church lands not frequent in Wiltshire.

This recital will shew that up to the date of Domesday, as far as Wiltshire was concerned, there was no violent interference with the property belonging to the Church. Indeed, with regard to Malmesbury, we have a deed bearing date 1065, to which reference has been made in a previous page (*p.* xix), which enables us to institute a comparison between its estates before and after the conquest. The variation between the statements of that charter and the record in Domesday is so trifling, that the difference may fairly be accounted for without the supposition of royal confiscations. We know, for instance, that sometimes the Abbots themselves, for various purposes, would alienate some of the estates of their monasteries. Thus, under NEWENTONE (*p.* 36), we are told expressly that an Abbot of Malmesbury gave one hide to one of his own retainers. Under BREME, too, it seems implied that in the time of King Edward certain portions were alienated. [Compare *pp.* 38, 101.] Such proceedings were not always unwarranted: for Bishop Walchelin raised funds for the rebuilding of his cathedral at Winchester by disposing of several estates belonging to the monks of St. Swithin. (See *p.* 17, *note.*)

Instances of confiscations.

Some confiscations undoubtedly there were, but they seem, for the most part, to have been the acts of others rather than of the Conqueror. Thus the *five hides* taken away from the estate of the Bishop of Winchester at DUNTONE to increase the royal forests were appropriated to that purpose by King Canute. [Compare *pp.* 17, 191.] Under ALENTONE (*p.* 63) it is stated that there were four hides which *Harold had unjustly taken away* from the Church of Ambresbury. Under LANGEFORD (*pp.* 73, 33) we have an instance of invasion—such is the usual term—on the part of Edward of Salisbury, one hide held by him being distinctly stated to belong of right to the Abbey of Glastonbury.[1] Under OGEFORD (*p.* 118) we are told that Earl Godwin took that estate from the Church of Wilton, and that it was afterwards recovered by Ednod; at the time of Domesday it was held by Gunduin under Osbern Gifard.

Other examples may be seen under TOCHEHAM (*p.* 96), held in the time of the Confessor of the Church of Malmesbury, but afterwards possessed by Durand of Gloucester as chief lord;—TROI, which once belonged to Wilton, but was held at Domesday by Richard Puingiant (*pp.* 47, 125);—POTERNE, where Ernulf de Hesding held lands which were claimed by the Bishop of Sarum (*pp.* 22, 74, 132);—CHINTONE (*p.* 110), said to have been held, in the time of King Edward, of Glastonbury, and afterwards of Radulf de Mortemer;—WINTRESLEU, where the Earl Morton *unjustly* held two hides belonging to Ambresbury (*pp.* 54, 58);—LITELTONE (*p.* 99), which was once *tain-land* appertaining to the church at Sarum, and afterwards held by William de Aldrie, under William de Ow as chief lord.

It may therefore fairly be allowed, as far as Wiltshire is concerned, that King William respected the rights of the Church. The entries of lands belonging to various religious bodies or persons seem almost universally to imply that they were so held in the time of the Confessor. In the case of ESSITONE (*p.* 41) it is expressly stated that the Abbey of Cranbourn held it also in the days of King Edward.[2]

---

[1] The Bishop of Coutance held in like manner the manor of LITELTONE, *p.* 27, which had been held in the time of King Edward by Alward, of the church of Glastonbury. See also *p.* 32, where the Bishop of Coutance is registered as an under-tenant of GRETELINTONE. In Somerset, several manors which had belonged to Glastonbury are registered as belonging to the Bishop of Coutance. Domesd. I. *fol.* 88. 88*b*. Ellis, I. 400.

[2] In some instances William the Conqueror ordered the restitution of lands taken away from the Church. Thus in the Domesday for Dorset, I. *fol.* 78*b*, under Cesehurna, it is said, "Istum manerium et Sture abstulerat Heraldus comes tempore Regis Edwardi sed Willelmus Rex eam fecit resaisari, quia in ipsa ecclesia inventus brevis cum sigillo Regis Edwardi precipiens ut ecclesiæ restituerentur." So too in the Hants Domesday I. *fol.* 48, of the manor of Icene, which had been alienated from the Abbey of St. Mary Winchester, we read, "Rex Willelmus reddidit eidem ecclesiæ."

The tenure of Frankalmoigne.

All the estates belonging to the Church were held in Frankalmoigne, or 'free alms,' as it was termed. The Latin phrase is 'in elemosina,' or 'in libera et pura elemosina.' Some difference seems to have existed between these two tenures just named, but only in degree, not in kind, those who held lands 'in elemosina,' in charity, or by divine service, being bound to offer certain prayers on certain days, whilst those who held land in frankalmoigne,' in libera elemosina,' were bound to pray only at their discretion. Such prayers for the soul of the donor of their lands and his heirs were supposed to be a sufficient return, and so exempted the monastic bodies from all secular burdens but that of the 'trinoda necessitas,' or the three imposts of *bryge-bôt* (the repairing of bridges), *burg-bôt* (the repairing of castles or fortresses), and *fyrd* (helping to maintain the military force of the kingdom).

This tenure would seem, from one entry, to have been continued as to manors belonging to the Church, even though they were afterwards alienated. Thus Girald of Wilton is said to hold UPTONE of the King 'in elemosina' (*p.* 55). The estate alluded to is Upton Lovel, which at one time belonged to the Abbey at Wilton.

Gifts to the Church recorded.

A few gifts to the Church are noticed in the Wiltshire Domesday. Thus, at *p.* 50, we have an account of a small estate at DECHEMENTONE, which had been given to the Abbey at Wilton by a Thane named Toret, but which at the time of Domesday was unjustly held by the Bishop of Baieux. Again, under JERCHESFONTE (*p.* 51) we have an instance of the surrender of what was by no means necessarily an unjust possession, a certain Bailiff of the Abbess of St. Mary, Winton, to whom the principal estate belonged, restoring two hides of the same which he had held, together with all his stock of cattle, to the Church. In like manner, under BICHENESTOCH (*p.* 42), we are told that Harding, who had a life-interest in the estate, willingly surrendered the same to the Abbey at Shaftesbury.

Possessions of foreign monasteries.

The possessions held by foreign monasteries were but few. The Abbey of St. Michael de Monte in Normandy held the two churches of OTONE (*p.* 13); the Abbey of St. Wandragisil the Church of RUSTESELLE (*p.* 11); and that of Fontenay possessed a small estate at MIDELTONE (*p.* 117). The Abbey of St. Mary de Monteburg is registered as holding under Nigel 'the physician' (who seems to be the same as Nigel 'the priest' referred to at *pp.* 7, 172) some land at SUDTONE (*p.* 124). One donation only is recorded, and that has some interest attaching to it: a manor at DEVREL (*p.* 55) which had once belonged to Brictric, is spoken of as belonging to the Abbey of Bec, by the gift of Matilda, the Conqueror's Queen. The Exon Domesday (*p.* 177) speaks of it as having been given 'for the soul of the Queen.'

Churches named only incidentally in Domesday.

The precept which directed the formation of the Survey required no return to be made of Churches. To refer to Domesday therefore, as in any way giving us correct information as to the number of Churches, is useless. A few cases are named, but they are invariably those in which some land belonged to them as an endowment, which lands were subject to geld. Where such glebe lands did not exist, the mention of churches in Domesday is to be regarded only as incidental.

Proofs might easily be multiplied to shew that many churches did undoubtedly exist, of which no mention is made in the Record. Thus, in the churches of Bremhill and Burcombe there are, as all authorities are agreed, undoubted remains of Saxon work, and yet no notice of them occurs in Domesday. Again in the Church of East Knoyle, there are in the external wall of the south side of the chancel evident traces of a very early arcade, and there was also a church at Bradford of a date anterior to the conquest, and yet we have no account of either. Again, in the Anglo-Saxon charter of King Edgar, A.D. 972,[1] respecting West Overton,

[1] Cod. Diplom. 571.

where again Domesday is silent as to the existence of a church (*p.* 47), we have distinct mention of the *cyric-stede*, i.e., the *church-stead;* and we are quite sure that at Sarum there was one, if not several, churches, and yet even under SARISBERIE (*p.* 13) we have no notice whatever taken of them.

There can be no doubt that a large number of churches, or chapels, though many it is admitted were but of small extent, did exist at the time of Domesday. The four-fold distinction of churches specified in the laws of Canute[1] implies a considerable number of such sacred edifices in his reign, and there is a statement in one of the laws of Edward the Confessor which shows that there had been a large increase within a few years, there being in many places *three* or *four* where there had been but *one* previously.[2] Kemble's opinion, that the number of churches in Anglo-Saxon times was very great, is no doubt correct.[3] Some of them were built of wood; and were what our ancestors called *Stocken* Churches. One example only of such a Church occurs in Domesday, and that was at Begeland in Yorkshire, where we have recorded,—"Ibi presbyter et *ecclesia lignea.*"[4] They are often alluded to in early charters. Thus, in the grant from King Edgar to the Abbey of St. Peter, Westminster, we have notice of the 'old wooden church of St. Andrew, above London fen, or the valley of the Fleet.'[5] In the the History of Crowland, moreover, we have the following entry,—"De dono Algari comitis *ligneam capellam* Sanctæ Mariæ per Spaldelyng quæ Anglice *Stokkym* appellatur."

Number of Churches named in the Wiltshire Domesday.

There are only some *thirty* churches distinctly mentioned in the Wilts Domesday. Nearly all of them are registered under the 'King's Land' and will be principally found at *p.* 16.—A few others, such as that at ALWARBERIE (*p.* 56),—DUNTONE (*p.* 17),—DEVREL (*p.* 55),—and WILCOTE (*p.* 65) (in which last place it is stated that there was a *new church*) are mentioned incidentally. In a few passages we have *presbyteri* mentioned, where there is no church named, but we may fairly consider the entry of the one as implying the existence of the other. Examples may be seen under RAMESBERIE (*p.* 23),—ENEDFORDE (*p.* 20),—RODE (*p.* 80),—and BROMHAM (*p.* 13). The presbyter, or parish priest, of the last-named place is said to hold land, '*de terra villanorum.*' From other parts of Domesday it would appear that some *presbyteri* were holders of stock, and farmers of portions of the out-lands, like the villans. Mr. Morgan reminds us that Chaucer's "Good Parson" was the ploughman's brother, and certainly there are many entries in Domesday in which the parish priest is numbered with the villans and bordars. The tenement of a parish priest was, it is conjectured, about equal to the tenement of a villan, not usually more than half a plough-land, and sometimes as little as twelve or fifteen acres.[6]

In one entry we have *half a church* recorded as held by Bishop Osmund, *p.* 16. This is the only instance in Wiltshire, but in other portions of Domesday we are told of churches divided into moieties, and other fractions. The following examples are taken from Mr. Morgan's book:—"At Sibson, in Huntingdonshire, the church and mill were equally divided between the Abbot of Thorney and Earl Eustace (I. 205). Several

---

[1] There was the "Heafod mynster," that is, the chief or *head minster*;—the "medemra mynster," translated *mediocris ecclesia*;—then one described as somewhat less in extent, translated *minor ecclesia*, 'where there was a little service and a burial place;'—and then there was the Feld-cirice, literally *field church* (ecclesia campestris)—where there was no burial place. Thorpe, I. 361. The last two correspond, respectively, it is believed, with the *capellæ* and the *ecclesiolæ* of the survey.

[2] The statement occurs at the end of the enactment respecting the due payment of tithes,—'in multis locis sunt modo iv. vel iii. ecclesiæ, ubi tunc temporis non erat nisi *una*. Thorpe, I. 445.

[3] 'Saxons in England,' I. 425.

[4] Domesday, I. *fol.* 320*b*.

[5] New Mon. I. 291.

[6] 'England under the Normans,' p. 110.

churches in Nottinghamshire were divided into halves; and two, Bole (I. 286*b*), and Clistone (I. 284*b*), were quartered. Edward Cilt had a third part of the Archbishop of York's church at Wime in Lincolnshire (I. 340). At Londonthorpe there was half a church with *half a priest* (I. 357); and at Boxford, in Suffolk, we meet with a fraction as small as the twelfth part of a church (II. 291). At the present day there are several advowsons held in shares, and some of the examples above given may amount to nothing more."[1]

Titles given to ministers of the Church.

The usual title given to ministers in the Wilts Domesday is *presbyter*. In other parts of the Record we meet also with *capellanus* and *diaconus*. The *clericolus* who held the church at Westbury was, perhaps, a sub-deacon. Churches were too often entrusted, for some succeeding centuries, to persons who held but some one or other of the minor orders.[2] Indeed, many contentions arose between bishops and patrons, especially when the patronage was vested in a Religious House, on the score that parishes were neglected by being left to the occasional services of curates or chaplains entirely dependent upon the patrons themselves. In the annals of Tewksbury will be found an account of a memorable attempt made by Bishop Cantelupe, in 1242, to found a permanent vicarage in that church, which was for a time strenuously, and successfully, resisted by the Abbot.[3] It was not until the commencement of the fifteenth century that impropriators of tithe were compelled by Act of Parliament to maintain a perpetual vicar in each church. It was not wonderful, as it has been well remarked, that the parochial clergy, thus placed at last in their true position, should become opponents of the monastic system, and heralds of the Reformation.

The Revenues of the Church.

A little information is given to us incidentally respecting the revenues of the church. A small portion only was allotted to the Vicar. In some cases a third of the tithe was given to him, in others his portion was fixed by a special episcopal ordinance. Very often the tithes were alienated from the church, and held by some ecclesiastic, or layman, at a distance. Thus Girald, a priest of Wilton, held the tithes of Colingeburne (*p.* 15), and Nigel, the physician, those of the church of Nigravre (*pp.* 14, 124), to which the goodly manors of Stratone and Chesigeberie were appurtenant. It is instructive to note the remarks in Domesday on the state of the fabrics of the churches in those parishes where the tithes had been thus alienated; that of Colingburne is described as *ruinous and decayed* (vasta est et dissipata);—that of Nigravre was *so ruinous, and the roof so out of repair as to be almost tumbling down* (vasta est et ita discooperta ut pene corruat). Much as we may lament this evil of alienating tithes from the purposes to which they were originally given, we must at least acknowledge

---

[1] England under the Normans, 102. Mr. Morgan adds another example which is the more interesting as the arrangement was continued to our own times;—"At Lymm, in Cheshire, the benefice was in medieties at the time of the Norman Survey; in that portion of the township which belonged to Gilbert de Venables was half-a-church, with half-a-yardland (I. 267); in the other portion belonging to Osbern, the son of Tezzo, was half-a-church, with a priest, and half-a-yardland, quit of geld (I. 267*b*). The sections of this church had not been united in 1810; the duty was performed on alternate Sundays by the Incumbents of the two medieties."

[2] There were *seven* ecclesiastical degrees. They are thus enumerated in the Canons of Ælfric,—(1) Ostiarius, or door-keeper;—(2) Lector, or reader;—(3) Exorcista, or adjurer [se halsigend], 'who reads over men diseased and the infirm;'—(4) Acolitus, 'who bears the candle or taper in God's ministries;'—(5) Sub-diaconus, or sub-deacon;—(6) Diaconus, or deacon;—(7) Presbyter, or priest. Thorp, II. 379, see also *p.* 346. No attempt to enforce the rule of celibacy seems to have been made except in the case of the Priests and Deacons. Hence possibly some of the Sub-deacons or Acolites did not advance to a higher order. It is but too probable that many of the Incumbents of parishes, described in the Institutions under the generic term of "Clerici," belonged to one of the minor orders.

[3] See 'Annales de Theokesberia,' in one of the volumes published under the direction of the Master of the Rolls, edited by the Rev. H. R. Luard.

that it is not one of modern date. The vicious custom ante-dates the Conquest; many laymen and churchmen enriched with such spoils existed in the days of the Confessor. Such was Reinbald (*p.* 56), who had been King Edward's chancellor. Such were Spirtes and Alsi, both described as 'presbyteri,' who owned the lands and churches which were afterwards bestowed on Nigel the physician. Many enactments had been promulgated for the purpose of putting an end to the system. As early as A.D. 994, we find, among ecclesiastical institutes[1] then put forth, one thus headed;—'Ut sacerdotes aliorum parochianos ad se non alliciant ob contrahendas decimas.' Still the practice was common, for, as Selden tells us, tithes were frequently, even up till the end of the twelfth century, consecrated to any church or monastery at the owner's choice. Persons would often assign tithes, or a portion of them, to the place at which they desired to be buried, and out of this custom the moieties or other portions of tithe belonging to the various churches had their beginning. In the year 1199, Pope Innocent put a stop to this arbitrary consecration of tithe by a decretal epistle, in which he directed,—'ut ecclesiis parochialibus justæ decimæ persolvantur.'

Leases granted for lives.

We have also, in the Wilts Domesday, several illustrations of the custom of leasing out lands, especially those belonging to the Church, for one life, or for three lives. Thus one hide at NEWETONE (*p.* 46) was held by Aluric the huntsman, for his life, of the Abbess of Wilton. HIWI (*p.* 110) was held for three lives by Toti, under the Abbot of Malmesbury, in the days of the Confessor. Three hides at HANINDONE (*p.* 29) were held in like manner at the same period by a Thane, under the Abbot of Glastonbury. Kemble shews that this custom of granting out lands for lives is a very ancient one, and quotes many examples from ancient charters of the ninth century and downwards.[2] Thus, in 902, Bishop Denewulf leased fifteen hides of church land at Eblesburn (now Bishopston) to his relative Beornwulf, for forty-five shillings yearly, with liberty to Beornwulf's children to continue the lease.[3]

Cyric-sceat not distinctly named, but implied.

There is no distinct mention of Cyric sceat, or, as it was afterwards called, Cherchesed (or Church-sed), and Church-shot, in our portion of the Record, but the payment of this due is *implied*, as has been shewn in a previous page,[4] in the tenure of every villan. It is named in connection with several estates in a neighbouring county. Thus under ESSEBORNE, in Hampshire (I. *fol.* 39), we have,—"Circesset quod appreciatur xiii. solid.;" and under WALLOPE (I. *fol.* 38*b*) we are told,—"Ibi ecclesia cui pertinent una hida et medietas decimæ manerii et totum *Curset*," &c. Kemble considers that this payment was 'at first a recognitory rent paid to the particular churches from estates leased under them, not so much in the nature of a fair equivalent, but as a token of beneficiary tenure.' He quotes a passage from the Worcester Domesday, in corroboration of his views, in which, under LAPPEWRTE (I. *fol.* 174), it is said,—'De hac terra per singulos annos redduntur viii. denarii ad ecclesiam de Wirecestre pro *Cirsette* et *recognitione terræ*.' In process of time, according to his views, a new character was assumed for it, and it was claimed, of all men alike, as a due to the clergy. Then it was ordered, by several enactments of Edmund, to be paid on pain of excommunication. In the time of Edgar it was directed to be paid from the hearth of every freeman to the old minster, and so became a fixed charge on the land. In very many cases it

---

[1] Thorpe, II. 411. See also directions to the same effect, in other ancient documents, at pp. 64, 100, 237.

[2] Saxons in England, I. 316.

[3] Cod. Dipl. 1079.

[4] See above p. lviii. and the accompanying note.

had passed into the hands of secular lords with lands that had once belonged to the church.[1] Archdeacon Hale, on the other hand, argues thatthe payment was in the nature of an offering of first fruits to the church at Martinmas, that is at the beginning of July, the origin of which dates back even to British times. He brings forward several passages from the Hundred Rolls, which he considers as conclusive on the point, not only that Cyric-sceat was a tax borne by all, even the lower order of tenants, but also that, at the close of the thirteenth century, the lords of manors had converted to their own use the payments *anciently due to the church*."[2] Certainly the words of Fleta, even though we reject his etymology of the word itself as untenable, seem to confirm the last opinion :—"Churchsed certam mensuram bladi tritici signat, quam quilibet olim sanctæ Ecclesiæ die sancti Martini tempore tam Britonum quam Anglorum, contribuerunt. Plures tamen magnates, post Normannorum adventum in Angliam, illam contributionem secundum veterem legem Moysi, nomine *primitiarum*, dabant, prout in brevi regis Knuti ad summum pontificem transmisso continetur, in quibus illam contributionem appellant *Churchsed*, quasi *semen ecclesiæ*."[3]

General state of the Church at the time of Domesday.

Though little can be gleaned from Domesday respecting the state of the Church in the eleventh century, yet there is enough to corroborate the accounts that are given us of the sad contrast which it presented to its condition some centuries previously. The 'clerklet' (*clericolus*) at Westbury (*p.* 14), and the ruinous churches at Nigravre and Colingeburne, and the alienation of tithes from the parishes to which they were properly payable, are all symptoms of that neglect of the best interests of the people that is too justly charged against the clergy of that period. As Palgrave has forcibly said, "The tenth century may be emphatically denoted the 'sæculum obscurum.' The attempts of Alfred had failed, and the priesthood had settled on their lees. It is with communities as with individuals; those who do not advance in goodness decline, and we seek in vain for any token of redeeming vitality. Learning altogether decayed, and he who could read Latin was accounted a prodigy. Morals declined fearfully.......The English clergy were viciously corrupted. The reforms so zealously and honestly attempted by Popes and Councils in other portions of the Catholic Church in the west had not reached them. Very many of the Bishops and Abbots had obtained their dignities by simony. The open and shameless barter and sale of ecclesiastical dignities throughout this period is scarcely conceivable to us, amongst whom this abuse at least has ceased. The Bishop was a judge, bound to attend to the reformation of manners, but he had *bought* his office, and so would *sell* impunity to the opulent transgressor. Hence the universal relaxation of all discipline, and the prevalence throughout England of the lowest immorality. In all these transactions the clergy were assuredly the most guilty. Every simoniacal promotion they obtained was accompanied with perjury; the higher the standard of morality which the priesthood were bound to affect, the greater was their guilt, and the more deleterious their example on the rest of the community. There were some holy men among them, but they were not sufficient to avert the destiny of the people, and all were involved in one common ruin. The empire seemed to exist under Edward the Confessor, but it was really on the verge of dissolution."[4]

---

[1] 'Saxons in England,' II. 492, 559.

[2] Introduction to Domesday of St. Paul's, p. cxxiv.

[3] Fleta, l. *c.* xlv, § 28. He is hardly right in his etymology. The second portion of the word is clearly the Anglo-Saxon *sceat*, which means *payment*. In like manner *sawl-sceat*, i.e., *soul-shot*, was a *payment* made at the open grave for the repose of the soul of the deceased.

[4] 'History of Normandy and England,' III. 334, 637.

CHAPTER V.

The Cities and Boroughs in Wiltshire—reason why so little information is given respecting them. Payments from towns in lieu of the King's geld. The privilege of a Mint. Various Classes of Burgesses. Prædial services due from them. Burgesses often attached to particular manors. Domesday Book an imperfect guide as to population. The value of the several estates, the mode of estimating them, and how far such values can be compared with their value at the present time. The value of estates increased in Wiltshire between the days of the Confessor and of William the Conqueror. Descent of various manors through successive centuries,—how far traceable. Names of ancient owners or occupiers still preserved. Concluding observations.

The Cities and Boroughs in Wiltshire.

VERY little information is given to us in Domesday respecting the cities and boroughs in Wiltshire. In other portions of the Record we have a notice of the services and customs appertaining to several of the more important towns, and these form a valuable illustration of the Anglo-Saxon laws. The Conqueror appears to have made little, if any, alteration, in the ancient institutions of the people, and in this, as in other respects, to have followed out the policy of keeping as closely as possible to the customs that prevailed in the days of the Confessor.[1]

The term *burgus* is expressly given only to two towns in Wiltshire, namely Wilton and Malmesbury. No doubt under the term, which we translate 'Burgh' or 'Borough,' must be included many others, such as Sarum, Marlborough, Cricklade, and a place called Bade,[2] in each of which 'the third penny,' or third part of the taxation, belonged to the King. To these must be added Calne, Ambresbury, Warminster, Chippenham, and perhaps Tilshead, from each of which the King could demand one night's entertainment (firma unius noctis) for himself and his suite. Others might be named, such as Bradford, Westbury, Melksham, Mere, Ramsbury, and Aldbourn, which would also come under such a designation. In general, all large towns seem to have been called *burh*, or *byrig*, though the strict meaning of either word appears to be a fortified place or stronghold, and the former is certainly applied to a single house or castle as well as to a town.

1 This fact is sometimes expressly stated. Thus, in the account of Dover (I. *fol.* i.) we are told,—"Omnes hæ consuetudines erant ibi quando Willelmus Rex in Angliam venit." So, under Wallingford (I. *fol.* 56) we have the entry,—"Modo sunt in ipso burgo consuetudines omnes ut ante fuerunt."

2 A suggestion has been made, at p. 16, that *Bed*-win was the place intended. Morgan ('England under the Normans,' p. 191) considers it to have been Bath, which was thus placed in the 'farm' or collectorship of Wiltshire. He refers to the Somerset Domesday (I. *fol.* 87) where, under BADE, Edward is said to pay £11 to the King from 'the third penny,' the precise sum which was payable from BADE entered in the Wilts Domesday. It is not, however, distinctly stated that this Edward was Edward of Salisbury. He nevertheless had possessions in Bath. See Domesd. I. *fol.* 98.

It must be borne in mind that the entry of burgesses (burgeuses) under a manor in Domesday by no means necessarily implies that the place was a borough. Thus Domnitone (Dinton), Draicote, Gardone, Smitecote, and Sudtone (Sutton Mandeville), at each of which places there were burgesses, could never have been more than small market towns at the most; and these, in early days, were little more than villages, in which a number of handicraftsmen dwelt side by side with the agricultural population.

Reasons why so little information is given respecting towns in Wilts.

In some portions of Domesday we have minute and detailed accounts of the principal towns in the county. Thus in the Domesday for Dorset, we have a particular description of Bridport, Wareham, and especially of Shaftesbury. In the Cheshire portion of the Record, we have a long and interesting statement of the customs of Chester as they existed in the days of the Confessor. This is by no means the case in the Wiltshire Domesday; the only attempt here at a detailed account is in the case of the borough of Malmesbury, and that after all is but a meagre statement. That town, like Wallingford in Berkshire, furnished soldiers for the army; the 'third penny' arising from it belonged to the King; from two divisions of it Walter Hosed paid £8 to the King, the same sum which had been paid in the time of the Confessor. We have an enumeration of the number of 'masures,' or tenements with a plot of ground annexed to them, contained in the borough, with the names of their respective owners. The military service of the town consisted in either paying twenty shillings to the King for the support of his sailors (ad pascendos suos buzecarlos), or in furnishing him with one man for each honor of five hides, a statement which seems to shew that twenty shillings was the commutation for the service of one man.[1]

The omission of many of the principal towns from some portions of Domesday is accounted for partly from the charters of immunity granted to them. Others, no doubt, compounded for all dues and customary payments, and hence concerning them all that we need expect to find in the Record is a statement of the sum so paid. Thus, Westbury paid annually the large sum of £100,—Aldbourn paid £60,—Wilton £50,—towards the King's geld.

The privilege of a Mint appurtenant to Burghs.

Amongst the privileges of a Burgh was the right of having a mint. By a law of Æthelstan, at the commencement of the tenth century, large cities and towns were permitted to have a certain number of mints, according to their size and importance, and then it is added that all other burghs should have one [elles to þam oðrum burgum, I.][2] The only notice in Domesday of a mint in Wilts is under Malmesberio (*p.* 6). We meet however with coins of Edward the Confessor, bearing the mint-mark of Bedwin, and coins of William the Conqueror with the mint-mark of Marlborough, Wilton, and Salisbury. Ellis (I. 177) accounts for the omission of such and other places of mintage from the Record, by supposing the places named on the different coins to be those of the moneyer's residence, and that the name of a town on a Saxon or Norman penny does not necessarily imply that a mint was established there. But this is by no means a satisfactory solution of the difficulty, inasmuch as in the same code of laws, by which the number of mints is fixed, it is expressly enacted, under severe penalties, that no man may mint money excepting within port (butan on porte),[3] that is, within the town to which the privilege was so conceded. It is far more likely that the mints are omitted because in the total amount

[1] See below, pp. 3, 6.

[2] Laws of Æthelstan, I. § 14. [Thorpe, I. 207.]

[3] *Port* means strictly an enclosed place, for sale and purchase, a market; for "Portus est conclusus locus, quo importantur merces et inde exportantur. Est et statio conclusa et munita." Thorpe, I. 158. Kemble, II. 550. *Port-wall* is often used as synonymous with *Borough-wall*.

whether in money or kind, said to be payable to the King from the various Burghs is included the sum due for the privilege of the mint. The 'firma unius noctis' at Bedwin, and the £50 due annually from Wilton, may fairly be taken to include such payments, and in such a case there was no need of specific mention of the mints in those places.

Various classes of Burgesses.

By a Burgess (burgensis) would seem to be meant one who, by residence or settlement in a borough, acquired certain rights and privileges. The burgesses of Domesday were, however, not tradesmen in all cases, but often husbandmen, or at all events men liable to render prædial services. Thus at Battle, in the time of Henry II., a number of burgage tenements were occupied by men of various crafts, each of whom, besides paying a small annual rent, had to find a man to do certain work in repairing the lord's mill, making malt for the court, and mowing the lord's meadow, and the men of the said town, on account of *the superior dignity of the place*, were called *burgesses*.[1]

There were great inequalities of condition among the burgesses entered in Domesday. In some places we find a distinction made between burgesses within the walls, and out-burgesses or suburbans. At Malmesbury there were a number of coscets without the borough (foris burgum) who paid geld with the burgesses. At Derby there were 140 burgesses, of whom 40 were called 'burgenses *minores*.' At Norwich such persons seem to have been called *mein-burgenses*; and at Tatteshale, in Yorkshire, *burgenses minuti*. At Ipswich there were 100 poor burgesses who could return nothing towards the King's geld except a poll-tax of one penny.

To many of the more important towns there were fields attached. At Totness, for example, there were ninety-five burgesses within the borough, and fifteen without, cultivating the land.[2] The burgesses of Exeter had twelve plough-lands without the city, which rendered no custom except to the city.[3] Morgan suggests that such tracts of land were in all likelihood occupied as common fields or pastures. "Malmesbury common," he adds, "may still be shared in this manner: not many years ago each landowner in the borough had an acre of the common; a member of the common council about two or three acres; a capital burgess about fifteen or sixteen acres."[4]

Prædial services rendered by Burgesses.

The condition annexed to burgage tenements of rendering prædial services is well illustrated by the customs of Hereford, which are very fully enumerated in Domesday (I. 179). If any one wished to depart from the city, he might, with leave of the Bailiff, sell his 'masure' to any one who engaged to perform the proper services. If any one from poverty could not perform such services, he relinquished his 'masure' to the Bailiff without reward, and that officer took care that it should be occupied by another tenant, and that the King did not lose his geld. Every entire 'masure' paid seven pence halfpenny, and four pence toward hiring horses, and the tenants did the personal service of reaping three days in August, and of gathering hay one day wherever the Sheriff directed.

It is ingeniously argued by Turner, that the manumission of serfs increased the numbers of the independent part of the lower orders. Whilst some of the emancipated became agricultural labourers, and took

---

1 'England under the Normans,' 152. 2 Domesd. I. *fol.* 108*b*. 3 Domesd. I. *fol.* 100.

4 'England under the Normans,' 156.

land of the clergy and the great, many went to the towns, and, as the King was the lord of the free, resided in these under his protection, and became free burghers or burgesses.[1] It is certain that, by a law of the Conqueror, serfs might acquire their freedom by residing for a year and a day, 'sine calumpnia,' in a city or borough.[2] This may possibly give us the solution of a difficulty we can hardly help feeling when we find burgesses described as belonging to certain manors. Thus at CRICHELADE, in addition to many burgesses (plures burgenses) in the borough itself that belonged to the Abbey of St. Peter, Westminster, there were no less than thirty-three burgesses who were attached to the manors of Aldeborne (*p.* 11), Badeberie (*p.* 31), Chiseldene (*p.* 41), Clive (*p.* 87), Colecote (*p.* 130), Ledentone (*p.* 44), Lediar (*p.* 81), Piritone (*p.* 37), and Ramesberie (*p.* 22). So at WILTUNE there were burgesses who belonged to Come (*p.* 89), Fifhide (*p.* 82), Nigravre (*p.* 14), Odestoche (*p.* 132), Sarisberie (*p.* 22), Scarentone (*p.* 118), and Stradford (*p.* 63). At CAUNA there were burgesses that belonged to the neighbouring manors of Calestone (*pp.* 75, 125),—and at MALMESBERIE, some that were attached to Sumreford (*pp.* 34, 87), Sorestone (*p.* 90), Come (*p.* 89), and Werocheshalle (*p.* 72). Such burgesses may have acquired their social position, if so we may term it, by residence in a borough, but may still have been liable to render prædial services to the lords of the manors with which they had been previously connected; or, which is more likely, such services in some of the neighbouring estates may have been annexed to a tenement in a borough by the owner of the same. It would appear probable also, that burgesses entered under some of the smaller manors, such as Draicote (*p.* 147), Smitecote (*p.* 87), and Gardone (*p.* 37), were really residents in a neighbouring town. In the case of the three just named, the town may have been Malmesbury, for certainly among the owners of 'masures' in that borough (see *p.* 3) were Geoffrey Mariscal, Humfrey de L'Isle, and the Abbot of Malmesbury, to whom as chief lords those manors respectively belonged. There is certainly no difficulty in such a supposition, because it does not appear that the ordinary prædial services due from certain classes were invariably required to be performed in person. In many cases, indeed, they were commuted for a money payment. At Bury St. Edmunds, for example, there were, according to Domesday (II. 372), some seventy-five persons of various trades,—bakers, brewers, shoe-makers, skinners, tailors, &c.,—who were accustomed to cut corn like servants. In course of time this service was commuted for what was called *reap-silver*, which consisted of the payment of one penny from each household.[3]

Burgesses attached to particular manors.

There are but 271 burgesses enumerated in the Domesday for Wiltshire. We cannot for a moment suppose that this was anything like an approximation to their real number, since amongst the matters on which Domesday is comparatively silent must certainly be reckoned the population of the cities and towns. The object of the Record was simply to ascertain the amount due, whether in money or services, from a borough to the King; and where this was commuted for a given payment, as in the case of Wilton, (see *p.* 6), there was no need to register the number of burgesses and other inhabitants. Hence every burgess entered as resident in Wilton

---

[1] See Ellis, I. 156.

[2] "Si servi permanserint sine calumpnia per annum et diem in civitatibus nostris, vel in burgis muro vallatis, vel in castris nostris, a die illa liberi efficiantur, et liberi a jugo servitutis suæ sint in perpetuum."—Laws of William the Conqueror, III. § 16. [Thorpe, I. 494.]

[3] See 'England under the Normans,' 152. The gradual way in which the various prædial services due to the lords of manors were commuted into money payments, and the ultimate effects of the change, are well described by Archdeacon Hale in the Introduction to the Domesday of St. Paul's, pp. lvi.—lix.

was attached to some one or other manor in the neighbourhood. This is the reason why in Domesday we have many boroughs or towns paying geld, in which no residents are mentioned at all. At SARISBERIE (*p.* 22), for example, there are no burgesses registered, the seven recorded as belonging to that manor being inhabitants, as it would appear, of Wilton.

Domesday an imperfect guide as to population.

Indeed we may say generally that it is but a very imperfect view of the population of Wiltshire which we obtain from Domesday. For the owners and occupiers of land, and for the agricultural population, it may possibly be considered a fair record, but in other respects it gives us but an unsatisfactory account. Not only are the inhabitants of towns unaccounted for, but there are a number of other omissions. We have no notice whatever of the tenants and inmates of monasteries; and the number of priests and other parochial clergy omitted must very much exceed those enumerated. In the case too of very many of these smaller holdings, as may be seen by a reference to the lands of the King's Thanes (*pp.* 132–144), no subordinate occupiers or labourers are entered at all. Taking the statement for what it is worth, we may mention that the number of persons actually registered in the Wilts Domesday is about 10,500; if each of those be regarded as heads of families, it would represent a a total population accounted for, of about 40,000,—but this must be very short of the real number of inhabitants of Wiltshire in the eleventh century.

Mode of estimating the value of manors.

In estimating the value of the estates, the Domesday Commissioners usually employ the terms 'valet' and 'valuit.' Nash, in his observations on the Domesday for Worcestershire, and some other writers, have interpreted these phrases as indicating the whole value of the manor, or, as we might say, the value of the fee simple of the estate. It would, however, seem far more probable that these terms denoted only the annual profits of the estate. In several passages the terms 'reddit' and 'redditus' supply the place of 'valet.' Thus, in the two consecutive entries of FOSTESBERGE and BEDESDENE (*p.* 112), we have the two used clearly as convertible terms. Moreover, under the 'Terræ Regis' (*pp.* 7–11), we have several distinguished from the rest as ancient Royal manors which had never paid 'geld,' but which "*reddiderunt* firmam unius noctis cum omnibus consuetudinibus," the value of this *redditus* being at Chepeham £110, and at Theodulveside £100. The value of sundry other manors, some of which had belonged to Harold, is estimated in most of them as 'redditus,' but in others by the term 'valet.' Many other examples might be adduced to shew that by 'valet' the commissioners meant to denote the annual value, or the sum the estate was worth when let to farm.

How far a comparison can be made between the value of estates now, and at the time of Domesday.

An attempt is made by Wyndham, in the Introduction to his Domesday for Wiltshire, to institute a comparison between the nominal value of estates in the eleventh century and their value some eighty years ago, when he published his work. He proposed to multiply the sums given in Domesday by 67½. The way in which he arrived at this multiple is as follows: he first multiplied the Domesday shillings and pounds by 3—(the ancient shilling being three times the weight of the present one),—and this sum he then proposed to multiply by 7½ to make it accord with the modern value of gold and silver. As he considers the real and intrinsic value of the lands themselves to have increased three-fold, he then adds a further multiplication by 3,—thus $3 \times 7\frac{1}{2} \times 3 = 67\frac{1}{2}$. He gives, as an illustration of the correctness of his proposed method, the manor of ODESTOCHE (Odstock, near Salisbury), which at the time of Domesday was worth £10. This sum multiplied by 67½ would give £675, which he supposed would be a fair annual return of the manor in 1788. There can be no doubt that some portions of this theory are reasonable, but, as it has been remarked, it fails to take any account of the value of the prædial services of the tenantry.[1]

---

[1] 'England under the Normans,' p. 44.

The rental of the kingdom, as a whole, reduced at the time of the conquest.

In some counties the Domesday commissioners reported a considerable decrease in the value of very many of the estates as compared with their value in the time of the Confessor. Ellis tells us, as the result of his researches into Domesday as a whole, that in general, at the survey, the King's lands were more highly valued than before the Conquest, and his rent from the cities and boroughs was increased, and that a few of the larger Tenants in capite had improved their estates,—but that, on the whole, the rental of the kingdom was reduced, the estates, twenty years after the Conquest, being, on medium, valued at little more than *three-fourths* of the former estimate. It was not so, however, in Wiltshire. There are, of course, some few instances in which estates had decreased in value; but in by far the majority of cases, the value, if not the same as in the days of King Edward, is reported as greater. This is made very evident by the following examples taken from different portions of the Record, in which we have the estimated value of a large number of manors, held by various persons, at either period:—

The value of Wiltshire estates much increased at the same period

	Number of Hides.	Annual Value. T. R. E.	Annual Value. T. R. W.
Bishop of Winchester ...	260	£196 0 0	£268 10 0
Bishop of Sarum ...	267	231 10 0	233 10 0
Abbot of Glastonbury ...	258	167 10 0	223 0 0
Abbot of Malmesbury ...	194	154 19 0	170 19 0
Edward of Salisbury ...	157	158 7 0	220 17 0
Humfrey de L'Isle ...	157	108 9 3	115 19 0
Waleran, the Huntsman ...	43	42 6 0	45 16 0
Osbern Gifard ...	69	43 10 0	52 0 0
	1405	1102 11 3	1330 11 0

This statement, which refers to estates comprising nearly *one-third* of the land in Wiltshire, shews that there had been an increase to the amount of some *twenty per cent.* in the annual value of land in the time of the Conqueror as compared with the days of the Confessor; and further, that at Domesday the annual value in our county of a hide of land at farm averaged about *nineteen shillings.* We may also gather, as a probable inference, from the fact of such an increase in the value of land, that Wiltshire enjoyed an immunity from some of those evils which necessarily attended the Conquest, and which caused much depreciation of property in other parts of England.

Descent of various manors through successive centuries.

An attempt has been made in the latter portion of this volume to show the descent of many of the manors mentioned in the Wiltshire Domesday. As the examples are all given in the Analysis (*pp.* 195–244) we need not lengthen these introductory remarks by more specific mention of them. It is most interesting, however, to observe with what accuracy many of the estates may be traced through successive centuries. Often, indeed, through forfeitures to the crown, during some of the turbulent and eventful reigns, the connecting link is broken, but it is surprising how frequently a manor, after the lapse of many years, is found in the possession of owners descended from the Domesday proprietor, or deriving their title from some connection with his family. And even when a manor may not be possessed by any of his actual descendants, it is very frequently held as 'of the honor' of which he or some of his immediate successors were chief lords.

Names of ancient owners or occupiers still preserved.

Another matter, on which an endeavour has been made to throw a little light in this volume, and which deserves a passing notice here, is the way in which, in the names of several of the parishes or tithings, we have still preserved the memory of their owners or occupiers in the eleventh century. Aileva, who in the days of the

Confessor held a small estate at Chelche (Chalk), and Girard, who possessed property at the same place in the days of the Conqueror, have left traces of themselves in *Alvedes*-ton, and Guston (originally *Girardes*-ton). Brictric has stamped his name on *Brixton* Deverel, spelt in old records *Brictrices*-ton. From Vitel, its owner in the time of King Edward, would seem to come the name of *Vitele*-ton, now Fittleton. Littleton *Drew* is a memorial of *Drogo* Fitz-Ponz, or of some of his family, who, under the name of *Dru*, were lords of the manor in the thirteenth century;—Langley Fitz-*Urse* reminds us of Urso, one of its subordinate occupiers in the time of Domesday. Fonthill *Giffard*, and Cowlesfield *Esturmy*, still tell of Berenger Gifard, and Richard Sturmid, their owners at the same period. Langley *Burrel* preserves the memory of *Borel*, whose family, or at least whose namesakes, continued to hold the manor till the commencement of the fourteenth century. Other examples of a similar character will be found in several of the notes scattered throughout this work, and in various pages of the analysis at the end of the volume.

Concluding observations.

In bringing these observations to a close, and sending forth his work to the public, the author must once more bespeak the indulgent criticism of his readers. Only able to devote to its preparation such intervals as could be spared from the more important duties of his sacred calling, it has been to him, for some years past, a source of no little toil and anxiety. Future research, or information obtained from those who from local knowledge may be able more accurately to illustrate particular portions of the Record, may modify some of the conclusions at which he has arrived. During the progress of the work through the press, a few typographical and other errors have been noticed, a list of which is given on a page preceding the general index. It is hoped, however, that due care has been taken to avoid careless and hasty conclusions, and to give, wherever it was possible, the grounds on which opinions in all doubtful cases were formed. The author has often been like one travelling, with but an imperfect chart, over a country to a considerable extent unexplored, and therefore it will be hardly surprising if some steps have to be re-traced. But it will be a real satisfaction to him, if, in the judgment of those competent to form an opinion, he has succeeded in throwing some little additional light on the past history of a portion of England so full of interest to the archæological student, in which a kind and guiding Providence, now some fourteen years ago, cast his lot, and which his children are privileged to call their native county.

The Vicarage, Bradford-on-Avon;
May, 1865.

THE

EXCHEQUER DOMESDAY

FOR

WILTSHIRE.

[The Marginal Notes at the head of each page refer respectively to the pages in the fac-simile issued by the Ordnance Office, and to the corresponding folio in the original Record.]

DOMESDAY BOOK.

WILTESCIRE.

I a 64 c In Burgo *MALMESBERIE* habet Rex 26 masuras[1] hospitatas,[2] et 25 masuras in quibus sunt domus quæ non reddunt geldum plusquam vasta[3] terra. Unaquæque harum masurarum reddit 10 denarios de gablo; hoc est simul 43 solidi et 6 denarii.[4]

De feudo Episcopi Baiocensis est ibi dimidia masura vasta quæ nullum servitium reddit.

Abbas Malmesberie habet 4 masuras et dimidium, et foris burgum 9 coscez qui geldant cum burgensibus.

Abbas Glastingberiensis habet 2 masuras; Edwardus Vicecomes 3 masuras; Radulfus de Mortemer, 1 et dimidium; Durandus de Glowecestre, 1 et dimidium; Willelmus de Ow, 1; Hunfridus de Insula, 1; Osbernus Gifard, 1; Aluredus de Merleberge, dimidiam masuram vastam; Goisfridus Mariscal, similiter; Tovi, 1 et quartam partem unius masuræ; Drogo filius Ponz, dimidium; Uxor

In the Borough of *MALMESBERIE* the King has 26 masures, which pay a rent, and 25 masures in which are dwellings which do not pay geld, any more than as waste land. Each one of these masures pays 10 pence for rent; this is altogether 43 shillings and 6 pence.

There is half a decayed masure, part of the fee of the Bishop of Baieux, which renders no service.

The Abbot of Malmesbury has 4 masures and a half, and outside the borough are 9 coscets, who pay geld with the burgesses.

The Abbot of Glastonbury has 2 masures; Edward, the sheriff, 3 masures; Ralph de Mortemer, 1 and a half; Durand of Gloucester, 1 and a half; William de Ow, 1; Humfrey de L'Isle, 1; Osbern Giffard, 1; Alured of Marlborough, half a decayed masure; Geoffrey Mariscal, the like; Tovi, 1, and the fourth part of 1 masure; Drogo Fitz-Ponz, half a masure; the wife of Edric, 1; Roger de

[1] Kelham defines "Masura" to be "a house belonging to, or which goes together with, some land in a borough."—*Domesday Illustrated, p.* 268. The Anglicised form of the word in the translation, is adopted, for the sake of convenience, by Kelham and Ellis.

[2] Ducange, in his Glossary, under "Hospitatus," says,—"De fundo vel domo dici videtur quæ *hospiti* sub certis conditionibus conceditur." Kelham explains the term as denoting "messuages, or tenements, let to a tenant at an annual rent, and in which the tenant (*hospes*) was bound to reside."—*Domesday Illustrated, p.* 236.

[3] By "vasta terra," is usually meant waste or uncultivated ground. Sometimes, however, according to Ducange, it implies a common pasture,—"terra pascendis animalibus destinata."

[4] It is so entered in the original, but the proper amount would seem to be 42 *shillings and sixpence.*

Fol. { 1 a / 64 c } Edrici, 1; Roger de Berchelai, 1 masuram de firma Regis; et Ernulfus Hesding, 1 similiter, de firma Regis, quam incaute accepit. Hæ duæ nullum servitium reddunt.

Rex habet unam vastam masuram de terra quam Azor tenuit.

HIC ANNOTANTUR TENENTES TERRAS IN WILTESCIRE.

I. Rex Willelmus.
II. Episcopus Wintoniensis.
III. Episcopus Sarisberiensis.
IV. Episcopus Baiocensis.
V. Episcopus Constantiensis.
VI. Episcopus Lisiacensis.
VII. Abbatia Glastingberiensis.
VIII. Abbatia Malmesberiensis.
IX. Abbatia Westmonasteriensis.
X. Abbatia Wintoniensis.
XI. Abbatia Creneburnensis.
XII. Abbatissa Shaftesberiensis.
XIII. Abbatissa Wiltuniensis.
XIV. Abbatissa Wintoniensis.
XV. Abbatissa Romesiensis..
XVI. Abbatissa Ambresberiensis.
XVII. Ecclesia Beccensis.
XVIII. Giraldus, presbyter de Wiltune.
XIX. Canonici Lisiacenses.
XX. Comes Moritoniensis.
XXI. Comes Rogerius.
XXII. Comes Hugo.
XXIII. Comes Albericus.
XXIV. Edwardus de Sarisberie.
XXV. Ernulfus de Hesding.
XXVI. Aluredus de Merlebergh.
XXVII. Hunfridus de Insula.
XXVIII. Milo Crispin.
XXIX. Gislebertus de Bretevile.
XXX. Durandus de Glowcestre.
XXXI. Walterius Gifard.
XXXII. Willelmus de Ow.
XXXIII. Willelmus de Braiose.
XXXIV. Willelmus de Moiun.
XXXV. Willelmus de Faleise.

Berchelai, 1 masure of the King's manor; a Ernulf de Hesding, in like manner, 1 masure the King's manor, which he incautiously accept These two render no service.

The King has one waste masure which belon to the land which Azor held.

HERE ARE NOTED THE LAND-HOLDERS IN WILTSHIR

King William.
The Bishop of Winchester.
The Bishop of Salisbury.
The Bishop of Baieux.
The Bishop of Coutances.
The Bishop of Lisieux.
Abbey of Glastonbury.
Abbey of Malmesbury.
Abbey of Westminster.
Abbey of Winchester.
Abbey of Cranbourne.
Abbess of Shaftesbury.
Abbess of Wilton.
Abbess of Winchester.
Abbess of Romsey.
Abbess of Ambresbury.
The Church of Bec.
Girald, Priest of Wilton.
The Canons of Lisieux.
The Earl Morton.
The Earl Roger.
The Earl Hugo.
The Earl Albericus. (Aubrey)
Edward of Salisbury.
Ernulf de Hesding.
Alured of Marlborough.
Humfrey de L'Isle.
Milo Crispin.
Gilbert de Bretevile.
Durand of Gloucester.
Walter Giffard.
William de Ow.
William de Braiose.
William de Moiun (Mohun).
William de Faleise.

{I a 64c} XXXVI.	Walscinus de Dowai.	Walscin de Dowai (Douay).
XXXVII.	Waleran, venator.	Waleran, the Huntsman.
XXXVIII.	Willelmus, filius Widonis.	William, son of Widon (Fitz-Widon).
XXXIX.	Henricus de Fericres.	Henry de Fericres.
XL.	Ricardus filius Gisleberti Comitis.	Richard, son of Earl Gilbert.
XLI.	Radulfus de Mortemer.	Ralph de Mortemer.
XLII.	Robertus filius Girold.	Robert son of Girold (Fitz-Girold).
XLIII.	Robertus filius Rolf.	Robert, son of Rolf (Fitz-Rolf).
XLIV.	Rogerius de Curcelle.	Roger de Curcelle (Churchhill).
XLV.	Rogerius de Berchelai.	Roger de Berchelai (Berkeley).
XLVI.	Bernard Pancevolt.	Bernard Pancevolt.
XLVII.	Berenger Gifard.	Berenger Giffard.
XLVIII.	Osbernus Gifard.	Osbern Giffard.
XLIX.	Drogo filius Ponz.	Drogo, son of Ponz (Fitz-Ponz).
L.	Hugo Lasne.	Hugo Lasne.
LI.	Hugo filius Baldrici.	Hugo, son of Baldric (Fitz-Baldric).
LII.	Humfridus, camerarius.	Humfrey, the Chamberlain.
LIII.	Gunfridus Malduith.	Gunfrid Malduith.
LIV.	Aluredus de Ispania.	Alured of Spain.
LV.	Aiulfus, Vicecomes.	Aiulf, the Sheriff.
LVI.	Nigellus, medicus.	Nigel, the Physician.
LVII.	Osbernus, presbyter.	Osbern, the Priest.
LVIII.	Ricardus Puingiant.	Richard Puingiant.
LIX.	Robertus Marescal.	Robert Marescal.
LX.	Robertus Flavus.	Robert Flavus (the Fair).
LXI.	Ricardus Sturmid.	Richard Sturmid.
LXII.	Rainaldus Canud.	Rainald Canud.
LXIII.	Maci de Moretania.	Maci of Moretania.
LXIV.	Gozelinus Riveire.	Gozelin Riveire.
LXV.	Godescal.	Godescal.
LXVI.	Herman et alii servientes Regis.	Herman, and other of the King's Servants.
LXVII.	Odo et alii Taini Regis.	Odo, and other of the King's Thanes.
LXVIII.	Herveus et alii ministri Regis.	Hervey, and other of the King's Officers.

Fol. { I a 64 c } Rex habet de Burgo *WILTUNIE*, 50 libras. Quando Herveus recepit ad custodiendum reddebat 22 libras.

De *WILTESCIRE* habet Rex 10 libras pro accipitre, et 20 solidos pro summario, et pro feno 100 solidos et 5 oras.[1]

De dimidio molino apud *SARISBERIE* habet Rex 20 solidos ad pensum. De tercio denario *SARISBERIE* habet Rex 6 libras. De tercio denario *MERLEBERGE*, 4 libras. De tercio denario *CRICHELADE*, 5 libras. De tercio denario *BADE*,[2] 11 libras. De tercio denario *MALMESBERIE*, 6 libras. De cremento 60 libras ad pondus; hoc reddit EDWARDUS Vicecomes.

WALTERIUS HOSED de 2 partibus burgi *MALMESBERIE*, reddit 8 libras Regi; tantundem reddebat ipsum burgum tempore Regis Edwardi, et in hac firma erant placita Hundretorum de Cicemertone[3] et Sutelesberg, quæ Regi pertinebant. De moneta reddit ipsum burgum 100 solidos. In eodem burgo habuit Heraldus Comes 1 agrum terræ, in quo sunt 4 masuræ et 6 aliæ vastæ, et 1 molinum reddentem 10 solidos. Hoc totum reddebat 100 solidos tempore Regis EDWARDI. Quando Rex ibat in expeditionem, vel terra vel mari, habebat de hoc burgo, aut 20 solidos ad pascendos suos[4] buzecarlos, aut unum hominem ducebat secum pro honore 5 hidarum.

The King has, from the Borough of *WILTO*[...] £50. When Hervey undertook the custody of t[...] town, it paid £22.

From *WILTESCIRE* the King has £10 inste[...] of a falcon, and 20 shillings for a sumpter-hors[...] and 100 shillings and 5 ores for fodder.

From half a mill at *SARISBERIE*, the Ki[...] has 20 shillings by weight. From the third penny [...] *SARISBERIE* the King has £6. From the thi[...] penny of *MERLEBERGE*, £4. From the thi[...] penny of *CRICHELADE*, £5. From the thi[...] penny of *BADE*, £11. From the third penny [...] *MALMESBERIE*, £6. From improved rents 6[...] pounds by weight; this, Edward the sheriff pays.

WALTER HOSED, from two parts of the boroug[...] of *MALMESBERIE*, pays £8 to the King; th[...] borough itself paid a like sum in the time of Kin[...] Edward, and in this holding were included the ple[...] of the Hundreds of Cicemertone, and Sutelesber[...] which belonged to the King. From its mint th[...] Borough pays 100 shillings. In the same Boroug[...] the Earl Harold had one field of land, in which ar[...] 4 masures, and 6 other waste masures, and one mil[...] paying 10 shillings. The whole used to pay 10[...] shillings in the time of King Edward. When th[...] King was going on an expedition, whether by lan[...] or sea, he was either wont to have from this Boroug[...] 20 shillings for the support of his sailors, or too[...] with him one man for each honor of 5 hides.

---

[1] The "Ora" seems originally to have represented 16 pence; therefore 16 oræ = 1 pound. In the Domesday Survey, however, it is used for the ounce, or twelfth part of the nummulary pound, and hence was worth 20 pence. Thus in the Domesday for Kent we find, as indeed in many other parts of the record, "125 libr. et 10 solid. *de* 20 *in Ora*," *i.e.*, "125 pounds and 10 shillings, every ore calculated at the value of 20 pence." It was simply money of account; in fact the penny was the *only coin* known in England till long after the date of the Domesday Book.—*See Ellis's Introduction to Domesday Book*, I., 165.

[2] This is most probably intended for *Bed*-vinde (Bedwin), which is often spoken of in early writings as a '*regia villa.*'—See below, p. 7.

[3] The Hundred of "Cicemertone," afterwards called, as it would seem, "Cheggelewe," comprised a number of places in the neighbourhood of Malmesbury. There was no name like "Sutelesberg" given to a hundred. The one alluded to wa[...] probably that of "Sterchelee," in which were included Brinkwort[...] Hullavington, and several other places in the same locality. [...] is, however, difficult to regard the one word as a corruption [...] the other. See below, in the accounts given in the Exon Domes[...] day, of the two Hundreds of "Cicemethorn," and "Sterchelec[...]

[4] This word is from the Anglo-Saxon "Bútsé-carl," a sailo[...] Bosworth interprets the word as "*bát-sæ-carl*," *i.e.*, literally, "*boat-sea-churl.*" When Earl Tosti was driven from the Hum[...]ber, where he had arrived with sixty ships, by Earl Edwin, it [...] said in the Saxon Chronicle, Anno 1066, "þa butsecarlas hi[...] forsocan,"—then the *sailors* forsook him. Thorpe, in a note [...] a passage in which the word occurs in the Saxon Chronicl[...] under A.D., 1052, says, "The first component of this word i[...] no doubt, our '*bus*,' as in '*herring-buss*;' old Norman '*bússa*[...] a large boat; old high German, '*buso*.'"

I b
64 d

TERRA REGIS.

Rex tenet *CAUNA*. Rex Edwardus tenuit, et nunquam geldavit; ideo nescitur quot hidæ sint ibi. Terra est 29 carucatæ. In dominio sunt 8 carucatæ et 8 servi. Ibi 37 villani, et 78 bordarii, et 10 coliberti habentes 21 carucatas. Ibi 45 burgenses, et 7 molini reddentes 4 libras et 12 solidos et 6 denarios, et 50 acræ prati, et pastura 2 leucis longa et 1 leuca lata. Hæc villa reddit firmam[1] unius noctis cum omnibus consuetudinibus.

Hujus Manerii ecclesiam tenet Nigellus de Rege cum 6 hidis terræ. Terra est 5 carucatæ. In dominio sunt 2, et 6 servi. Ibi 7 villani, et 2 bordarii, et 11 cozets cum 3 carucatis. Ibi 2 molini de 20 solidis, et 25 burgenses reddentes 20 solidos. Silva 2 quarentenis longa et 1 quarentena et 24 acris lata. Pastura 4 quarentenis longa et 2 quarentenis lata. Totum valet 8 libras.

Aluredus de Hispania tenet 5 hidas terræ quas Nigellus calumniatur. Hæc terra, testimonio Sciræ, pertinuit ad ecclesiam tempore Regis Edwardi.

Rex tenet *BEDVINDE*. Rex Edwardus tenuit. Nunquam geldavit, nec hidata fuit. Terra est 80 carucatæ, una minus. In dominio sunt 12 carucatæ, et 18 servi. Ibi 80 villani et 60 cozets, et 14 coliberti, cum 67 carucatis. Ibi 8 molini reddentes 100 solidos. Duæ silvæ habentes 2 leucas longitudine et 1 leucam latitudine. Ibi 200 acræ prati, et 12 quarentenæ pasturæ longitudine, et 6 quarentenæ latitudine. Huic manerio pertinent 25 burgenses. Hæc villa reddit firmam unius noctis cum omnibus consuetudinibus. In hoc manerio fuit tempore Regis Edwardi lucus habens dimidium leucæ longitudine, et 3 quarentenas latitudine, et erat in dominio Regis. Modo tenet eum Henricus de Ferreres.

THE KING'S LAND.

The King holds *CAUNA*. King Edward held it, and it never paid geld; hence it is unknown how many hides are there. The land is 29 carucates. In demesne are 8 carucates and 8 serfs. There are 37 villans, and 78 bordars, and 10 coliberts having 21 carucates. There are 45 burgesses and 7 mills, paying £4 12*s.* 6*d.*, and 50 acres of meadow, and pasture 2 miles long and 1 mile broad. This vill provides one night's entertainment with all its customs.

Nigel, holds the Church of this Manor of the King, with 6 hides of land. The land is 5 carucates. In demesne are 2, and 6 serfs. There are 7 villans and 2 bordars and 11 coscets with 3 carucates. There are two mills worth 20 shillings, and 25 burgesses paying 20 shillings. The wood is 2 furlongs long, and one furlong and 24 acres broad. The pasture 4 furlongs long and 2 furlongs broad. The whole is worth £8.

Alured of Spain holds 5 hides of land which Nigel claims. This land, according to the testimony of the Shire, belonged to the Church in the time of King Edward.

The King holds *BEDVINDE*. King Edward held it. It never paid geld, nor was it assessed in hides. The land is 80 carucates, wanting one. In demesne there are 12 carucates and 18 serfs. There are 80 villans, and 60 coscets, and 14 coliberts, with 67 carucates. There are 8 mills paying 100 shillings. Two woods, having 2 miles in length, and one in breadth. There are 200 acres of meadow, and of pasture 12 furlongs in length, and 6 furlongs in breadth. To this manor belong 25 burgesses. This vill provides one night's entertainment with all customs. In this manor there was in the time of King Edward, a grove, having half a mile in length, and 3 furlongs in breadth, and it was in the demesne of the King. Now, Henry de Ferreres holds it.

---

[1] Kennet derives this word "*firma*," which usually means a "*farm*," or land and tenements hired at a certain rent, from the Anglo-Saxon "*feorm*," meal or entertainment; "Whence," he says, "the Latin *firma*, for the reception and entertainment of the King, or any other lord and his retinue; as frequently in the Domesday Book a condition of tenure was *pro firma unius noctis*," &c.—*Parochial Antiquities* (*Glossary*).

Fol. { I b / 64 d }

REX tenet *AMBLESBERIE.* Rex Edwardus tenuit. Nunquam geldavit, nec hidata fuit. Terra est 40 carucatæ. In dominio sunt 16 carucatæ, et 55 servi, et 2 coliberti. Ibi 85 villani et 56 bordarii habentes 23 carucatas. Ibi 8 molini reddentes 4 libras et 10 solidos, et 70 acræ prati. Pastura 4 leucis longa et 3 leucis lata. Silva[1] 6 leucis longa et 4 leucis lata.

THE KING holds *AMBLESBERIE.* King Edward held it. It never paid geld, nor was it assessed in hides. The land is 40 carucates. In demesne are 16 carucates, and 55 serfs, and 2 coliberts. There are 85 villans, and 56 bordars, having 23 carucates. There are 8 mills paying £4 10*s.*, and 70 acres of meadow. The pasture is 4 miles long, and 3 miles broad. The wood is 6 miles long, and 4 miles broad.

Hoc manerium, cum appendicibus suis, reddit firmam unius noctis cum omnibus consuetudinibus. In hoc manerio numerantur terræ trium Tainorum quas ipsi tenebant tempore Regis Edwardi. Has dedit Willelmus[2] Comes, in Amblesberie, pro mutuatione BOVECOME.[3] ☞

This Manor, with its appendages, provides one night's entertainment with all customs. In this manor are included the lands of three Thanes, which they held in the time of King Edward. These lands in Amblesberie, Earl William gave in exchange for Bovecome. ☞

De hujus manerii terra, 2 hidas dedit Rex Edwardus, in sua infirmitate, Abbatissæ Wiltuniensi, quas nunquam antea habuerat; postea vero eas tenuit.

Of the land of this manor, King Edward, in his sickness, gave two hides to the Abbess of Wilton, which she never had previously; afterwards, however, she held them.

☞ [Willelmus Comes dedit *QUINTONE* et *SUINDONE* et *CHEVREL*, quæ erant Tainlandæ, pro terra de Insula de With, quæ pertinebat ad firmam[4] de Amblesberie.]

☞ [Earl William gave *QUINTONE* and *SUINDONE*, and *CHEVREL*, which were Thanelands, for land in the Isle of Wight, which belonged to the estate of Amblesberie.]

REX tenet *GUERMINSTRE.* Rex Edwardus tenuit. Non geldavit, nec hidata fuit. Terra est 40 carucatæ. In dominio sunt 6 carucatæ, et 24 servi, et 13 porcarii. Ibi 15 villani, et 8 cozets, et 14 coliberti, cum 36 carucatis. Ibi 7 molini de 4 libris, et 80 acræ prati. Pastura 1 leuca longa, et dimidio leucæ lata. Silva 2 leucis longa, et 2 lata. Ibi 30 burgenses.

THE KING holds *GUERMINSTRE.* King Edward held it. It paid no geld, nor was it assessed in hides. The land is 40 carucates. In demesne are 6 carucates, and 24 serfs, and 13 swine-herds. There are 15 villans, and 8 coscets, and 14 coliberts, with 36 carucates. There are 7 mills of the value of £4, and 80 acres of meadow. The pasture is one mile long, and half a mile broad. The wood 2 miles long, and 2 broad. There are 30 burgesses.

---

[1] WYNDHAM suggests that this large wood was probably Bentley Wood, near Winterslow. That wood certainly belonged to Amesbury, and it was by no means unusual for manors to have woods allotted to them which were not included within their proper boundaries. See Sir R. C. Hoare's "Modern Wilts"—*Hundred of Heytesbury*, p. 168.

[2] This Earl William, who is frequently named in Domesday, was William Fitz-Osbern, a kinsman of William the Conqueror. He was one of the chief advisers of his attempting the conquest of England, and had a principal command at the battle of Hastings. He was created Earl of Hereford, and appointed Justiciar for the North of England. He was slain in battle against the Earl of Flanders, in the year 1070, together with Arnulf, Earl of Hainault, whose cause he was sent to support.

[3] This is no doubt BOWCOMB, in the Isle of Wight. See *Domesday for Hampshire*, p. 30 *b*.

[4] This paragraph seems introduced as a supplementary note to the statement just made with regard to Bovecome. It is given above as it stands in the original text, though its more correct place would perhaps be in a foot-note.

{I b 64 d} Hoc Manerium reddit firmam[1] unius noctis cum omnibus consuetudinibus suis.

This manor provides one night's entertainment with all its customs.

Rex tenet *CHEPEHAM.* Rex Edwardus tenuit. Non geldavit, nec hidata fuit. Terra est 100 carucatæ. In dominio sunt 16 carucatæ, et 28 servi. Ibi 48 villani, et 45 bordarii, et 20 cotarii, et 23 porcarii: inter omnes habent 66 carucatas. Ibi 12 molini de 6 libris, et 100 acræ prati. Silva 4 leucis in longitudine et latitudine. Pastura 2 leucis longa et una leuca lata.

The King holds *CHEPEHAM.* King Edward held it. It paid no geld, neither was it assessed in hides. The land is 100 carucates. In demesne are 16 carucates, and 28 serfs. There are 48 villans, and 45 bordars, and 20 cottars, and 23 swine-herds. Between them all they have 66 carucates. There are 12 mills of the value of £6, and 100 acres of meadow. The wood is 4 miles in length and breadth. The pasture is 2 miles long, and one mile broad.

Hoc manerium, cum appendicibus suis, reddit firmam unius noctis cum omnibus consuetudinibus, et valet 110 libras ad numerum.

This manor, with its appendages, provides one night's entertainment with all its customs, and is worth £110, by tale.

Hujus manerii ecclesiam, cum 2 hidis, tenet Osbernus[2] episcopus ex tempore Regis Edwardi. Una ex his hidis est Tainlande,—altera pertinet ecclesiæ. Totum valet 55 solidos. Huic manerio pertinet una terra quam Rex Edwardus dederat Ulviet venatori suo, et erat de dominio suo. Hæc in firma Regis est modo, et pro una hida habetur. Terra est 2 carucatæ, et ipsæ ibi sunt, et 3 servi; et 4 villani, et 4 cozets, cum 1 carucata. Pastura 4 quarentenis longa et 1 quarentena lata. Valet 3 libras. In firma hujus manerii est dimidia virgata terræ quæ fuit Tainlande. Edricus tenuit tempore Regis Edwardi.

Bishop Osbern holds the church of this manor, with 2 hides, from the time of King Edward. One of these hides is Thane-land,—the other belongs to the church. The whole is worth 55 shillings. To this manor belongs a certain land which King Edward had given to Ulviet, his huntsman, and which was part of his demesne. This is now in the estate of the King, and it is reckoned for one hide. The land is 2 carucates, and they are there, and 3 serfs; and 4 villans, and 4 coscets, with one carucate. The pasture is 4 furlongs long, and one furlong broad. It is worth £3. In the estate of this manor is half a virgate of land, which was Thane-land. Edric held it in the time of King Edward.

{II a 65 a} Rex tenet *BRETFORD.* Rex Edwardus tenuit et pro una hida geldavit. Terra est 20 carucatæ. In dominio sunt 2 carucatæ, et 6 servi, et 10 coliberti. Ibi 12 villani, et 6 bordarii, et 14 cozets, cum 17 carucatis. Ibi 2 molini, de 20 solidis, et 100 acræ prati. Pastura 1 leuca longa et dimidio leucæ lata.

The King holds *BRETFORD.* King Edward held it, and it paid geld for one hide. The land is 20 carucates. In demesne are 2 carucates, and 6 serfs, and 10 coliberts. There are 12 villans, and 6 bordars, and 14 coscets, with 17 carucates. There are 2 mills worth 20 shillings, and 100 acres of meadow. The pasture is one mile long, and half a mile broad.

---

[1] This obligation to find the king a lodging, with his suite, for one night was demanded, and paid by the Lord of the Manor and Baron of Warminster to King George the Third, on Monday, the 13th September, 1786, the King, Queen, and Princesses, being entertained at Longleat by the Lord Viscount Weymouth.

Charles the Second was likewise entertained in the same way, in 1663, when Sir James Thynne possessed the manor. See Sir R. C. Hoare's "Modern Wilts," *(Hundred of Warminster)* p. 1.

[2] Unless, as Wyndham seems to take for granted, this be a mistake for Osbernus *presbyter*, (as in the next entry,) the bishop alluded to can be no other than Osbern, who was consecrated Bishop of Exeter in 1074, and died in 1103. He is said to have been a kinsman of Edward the Confessor, and allied to William the Conqueror. He was brother to William Fitz-Osbern, Earl of Hereford.

Fol. { II a / 65 a } Hoc manerium reddit 30 libras ad pensum. Silva est in manu Regis, et inde habet 40 solidos in firma sua.

Hujus manerii ecclesiam tenet Osbernus presbyter, cum una hida terræ pertinente ecclesiæ. Valet 40 solidos.

Rex tenet *THEODULVESIDE.* Rex Edwardus tenuit. Non geldavit, nec hidata fuit. Terra est 40 carucatæ. In dominio sunt 9 carucatæ, et 22 servi, et 10 coliberti. Ibi 34 villani, et 32 cozets, cum 18 carucatis. Ibi 9 molini, de 100 solidis et 30 denariis, et 66 burgenses reddentes 50 solidos. Ibi una leuca prati in longitudine et dimidium latitudine. Pastura una leuca et dimidio longa et una leuca lata. Silva 2 leucis longa et una leuca lata.

Hoc manerium reddit firmam unius noctis cum consuetudinibus suis. Valet 100 libras ad numerum.

Rex tenet *CONTONE.* Heraldus Comes tenuit, et pro 10 hidis geldavit. Terra est 10 carucatæ. In dominio sunt 2 carucatæ, et 2 servi; et 28 villani, et 2 bordarii, cum 8 carucatis. Ibi molinus de 12 solidis et 6 denariis, et 20 acræ prati, et 8 acræ pasturæ, et 15 acræ silvæ. Hoc manerium reddit 12 libras ad pensum.

Rex tenet *RUSTESELVE.* Ghida[1] tenuit tempore Regis Edwardi, et geldabat pro 37 hidis cum appendicibus suis. Terra est 27 carucatæ et dimidium. In dominio sunt 19 hidæ, et ibi 12 carucatæ, et 37 servi. Ibi 28 villani, et 40 bordarii, cum 14 carucatis. Ibi 5 molini, de 72 solidis, et 112 acræ prati. Pastura 3 leucis et dimidio in longitudine, et 1 leuca et dimidio in latitudine. Silva 1 leuca longa et dimidio leucæ lata. Valuit et valet 32 libras et 10 solidos.

This manor pays £30 by weight. The wood is in the hands of the King, and thence he has 40 shillings in his own estate.

Osbern, a priest, holds the church of this manor, with one hide belonging to the church. It is worth 40 shillings.

The King holds *THEODULVESIDE.* King Edward held it. It paid no geld, neither was it assessed in hides. The land is 40 carucates. In demesne are 9 carucates, and 22 serfs, and 10 coliberts. There are 34 villans, and 32 coscets, with 18 carucates. There are 9 mills worth 100 shillings, and 30 pence, and 66 burgesses paying 50 shillings. There is one mile of meadow in length, and half a mile in breadth. The pasture is one mile and a half long, and one mile broad. The wood is 2 miles long, and one mile broad.

This manor provides one night's entertainment with its customs. It is worth £100 by tale.

The King holds *CONTONE.* The Earl Harold held it, and it paid geld for 10 hides. The land is 10 carucates. In demesne are 2 carucates, and 2 serfs; and there are 28 villans, and 2 bordars, with 8 carucates. There is a mill worth 12 shillings and 6 pence, and 20 acres of meadow, and 8 acres of pasture, and 15 acres of wood. This manor pays 12 pounds by weight.

The King holds *RUSTESELVE.* Ghida held it in the time of King Edward, and it paid geld with its appendages for 37 hides. The land is 27 carucates and a half. In demesne are 19 hides, and there are 12 carucates, and 37 serfs. There are 28 villans, and 40 bordars, with 14 carucates. There are 5 mills worth 72 shillings, and 112 acres of meadow. The pasture is 3 miles and a half in length, and 1 mile and a half in breadth. The wood is one mile long, and half a mile broad. It was worth, and is still worth, £32 10s.

---

[1] Ghida was the wife of Earl Godwin, and the mother of Harold. She was sister to Sweyn, King of Denmark. In the annals of the Church of Winchester, under the year 1052, she is spoken of as a generous benefactor. She was in Exeter, in 1068, when William the Conqueror laid siege to that city, but succeeded in effecting her escape to Flanders. She held in different counties of England, in the time of Edward the Confessor, more than 330 hides;—possibly as much as from 40,000 to 50,000 acres of land.

II a 65 a Hujus manerii ecclesiam habet Sanctus Wandregisilus[1] cum 2 hidis terræ, et ibi est 1 carucata et dimidium. Valet 40 solidos.

The Abbey of St. Wandregisil holds the church of this manor, with 2 hides of land, and there is there one carucate and a half. It is worth 40 shillings.

Rex tenet *ALDEBORNE*. Ghida tenuit tempore Regis Edwardi et geldabat pro 40 hidis. Terra est 45 carucatæ. In dominio sunt 18 hidæ, et ibi 10 carucatæ, et 25 servi, et 14 coliberti. Ibi 73 villani, et 38 cozets, cum 26 carucatis. Ibi 4 molini, de 16 solidis et 8 denariis. Pratum 1 leuca longa et 5 quarentenis lata. Pastura 1 leuca longa et dimidio leucæ lata. Silva 2 leucis longa et dimidio leucæ lata. Huic manerio pertinent 6 burgenses in Crichelade reddentes 64 denarios.

The King holds *ALDEBORNE*. Ghida held it in the time of King Edward, and it paid geld for 40 hides. The land is 45 carucates. In demesne are 18 hides, and there are 10 carucates, and 25 serfs, and 14 coliberts. There are 73 villans, and 38 coscets, with 26 carucates. There are 4 mills, worth 16 shillings and 8 pence. The meadow is one mile long, and 5 furlongs broad. The pasture is one mile long, and half a mile broad. The wood is 2 miles long, and half a mile broad. To this manor belong 6 burgesses in Crichelade, paying 64 pence.

Hoc manerium reddit 70 libras[2] ad pensum, sed ab Anglis non appreciatur nisi 60 libris ad numerum. Ad ecclesiam hujus manerii pertinent 2 hidæ. Terra 2 carucatæ. Has habet presbyter ejusdem ecclesiæ, et valent 40 solidos.

This manor pays 70 pounds by weight, but by the English it is not valued at more than 60 pounds, by tale. To the church of this manor belong 2 hides. The land is 2 carucates. These the priest of the same church holds, and they are worth 40 shillings.

Rex tenet *COSSEHAM*. Tosti Comes tenuit tempore Regis Edwardi. Ibi sunt 34 hidæ, sed pro 18 hidis reddit geldum. Terra est 50 carucatæ. In dominio sunt 11 hidæ, et ibi 7 carucatæ, et 10 servi. Ibi 65 villani, et 48 cozets, et 9 cotarii, cum 38 carucatis. Ibi 2 molini de 8 solidis et 6 denariis, et 32 acræ prati, et 1 hida pasturæ, et 2 leucæ silvæ in longitudine et latitudine.

The King holds *COSSEHAM*. Earl Tosti held it in the time of King Edward. There are 34 hides, but it renders geld for 18 hides. The land is 50 carucates. In demesne are 11 hides, and there are 7 carucates and 10 serfs. There are there 65 villans and 48 coscets and 9 cottars with 38 carucates. There are 2 mills, worth 8 shillings and 6 pence, and 32 acres of meadow, and one hide of pasture, and 2 miles of wood in length and breadth.

Hoc manerium cum appendicibus reddit 30 libras ad pensum. Angli vero appreciant ad 31 libras ad numerum.

This manor with its appendages pays 30 pounds by weight. The English, however, value it at 31 pounds by tale.

---

[1] "The Abbey of Vandrille, anciently called Fontenelle, in the diocese of Rouen, situated about six or seven leagues from that city. It was founded, by St. Wandregisillus, A.D. 654. The Dukes of Normandy were considerable benefactors to it, particularly Duke Richard II. William the Conqueror's benefactions to it, in Normandy, are recited in Neustria Pia, p. 167."—*Ellis' Introduction to Domesday* I., 507.

[2] The *Libræ*, or Pounds, were of three kinds. There were, first of all, the *Libræ ad pensum*, which were by weight;—then the *Libræ ad numerum*, or pounds of ready money, made up not of shillings but of oræ (see above, p. 6 *note*), and, as we ascertain by various entries, valued at the rate of twenty pence to the ora;—and lastly, the *Libræ ad ignem et ad pensum*, which formed the payment when, in consequence of the coins offered at the Exchequer being deficient in fineness as well as in weight, the Receivers either melted a sample of the money paid, or received sixpence or a shilling over every twenty in lieu of actual combustion. When Domesday was compiled there was always, it is said, a fire ready in the Exchequer, in which, if the alloy of the money was not approved, they burnt it, and then weighed it.—*Ellis' Introd. to Domesday*, I. 163. *Kelham's Domesday illustrated*, *p*. 157.

Fol. { II a / 65 a } Hujus manerii ecclesiam habet S. Stefanus[1] Cadomi, cum 2 hidis terræ. Terra est 5 carucatæ. Has habent ibi 3 villani, cum 6 cozets. Valet 7 libras. Ecclesiam de Paveshou,[2] quæ adjacet huic manerio tenet Edgar, et pater ejus tenuit. Valet 5 solidos.

The Abbey of S. Stephen of Caen, holds the church of this manor with 2 hides of land. The land is 5 carucates. These 3 villans, with 6 coscets, hold. It is worth £7. Edgar holds the church of Paveshou which adjoins this manor; his father held it. It is worth 5 shillings.

Rex tenet *MELCHESHAM.* Heraldus Comes tenuit et pro 84 hidis geldavit cum appendicibus suis. Terra est 60 carucatæ. In dominio sunt 34 hidæ, et ibi 19 carucatæ, et 35 servi, et 31 coliberti. Ibi 100 villani, 8 minus, et 66 bordarii habentes 39 carucatas. Ibi 8 molini, reddentes 7 libras et 6 solidos, et 130 acræ prati, et 8 leucæ pasturæ in longitudine et latitudine. Silva 4 leucæ inter longitudinem et latitudinem.

The King holds *MELCHESHAM.* The Earl Harold held it, and, with its appendages, it paid geld for 84 hides. The land is 60 carucates. In demesne there are 34 hides, and there are 19 carucates and 35 serfs and 31 coliberts. There are 100 villans save 8, and 66 bordars having 39 carucates. There are 8 mills paying 7 pounds and 6 shillings, and 130 acres of meadow, and 8 miles of pasture in length and breadth. The wood is 4 miles between length and breadth.

Hoc manerium reddit 111 libras et 11 solidos ad pensum. Angli vero appreciant ad totidem libras ad numerum. Hujus manerii ecclesiam cum 1 hida terræ habet Rumoldus presbyter et valet 40 solidos.

This Manor pays £111 11*s.* by weight. The English, however, reckon it at the same number of pounds by tale. Rumold, the priest, holds the church of this manor with 1 hide of land, and it is worth 40 shillings.

Fol. { II b / 65 b } Rex tenet *CUMBE.* Ghida tenuit tempore Regis Edwardi, et geldabat pro 23 hidis et dimidio. Terra est 20 carucatæ. In dominio sunt 11 hidæ, et ibi 3 carucatæ, et 7 servi. Ibi 28 villani et 7 bordarii, et 43 cozets, habentes 17 carucatas. Ibi 2 molini reddentes 25 solidos, et 60 acræ prati, et pastura una leuca longa et alia lata, et 10 acræ parvæ silvæ.

The King holds *CUMBE.* Ghida held it in the time of King Edward, and it paid geld for 23 hides and a half. The land is 20 carucates. In demesne are 11 hides, and there are 3 carucates, and 7 serfs. There are 28 villans and 7 bordars and 43 coscets, having 17 carucates. There are 2 mills paying 25 shillings, and 60 acres of meadow, and pasture 1 mile long and another wide, and 10 acres of small wood (coppice).

Hoc manerium reddit 24 libras ad pensum. Tempore Regis Edwardi tantundem ad numerum. Ecclesiam hujus manerii cum dimidia hida terræ tenet Leuricus presbyter, et valet 20 solidos.

This Manor pays 24 pounds by weight. In the time of King Edward it paid a like sum by tale. Leuric, the priest, holds the church of this manor with half a hide of land, and it is worth 20 shillings.

[1] The Abbey of St. Stephen, at Caen, was founded by William the Conqueror, about the year 1064, though not dedicated till after 1066, as in the foundation charter William takes the title of King, and among his donations are enumerated properties and privileges in various parts of England, which shew that he was at the time in possession of the island. William of Jumieges, who was living at the time, states that this monastery, as well as the Convent of the Holy Trinity, at Caen, were both founded as an act of penance enjoined on him by the Pope, as the condition of his granting him absolution for having contracted a marriage with Matilda, daughter of Baldwin, Earl of Flanders, the son of his father's sister, which was within the prohibited degrees of affinity. Lanfranc, afterwards Archbishop of Canterbury, was the first abbot of St. Stephen, Caen. *Ellis' Introduction to Domesday*, I., 391. See the Charters relating to these monasteries in the New Monasticon, VI. pp. 1070, 1072.

[2] This is clearly *Pewsham*, which is close by Corsham. It takes its name from the *Pewe*, a little stream rising at Lockswell, and flowing into the Avon, near Lackham.

b
5 b
REX tenet *BROMHAM.* Heraldus Comes tenuit et pro 20 hidis geldavit. Terra est 10 carucatæ. In dominio sunt 10 hidæ, et ibi 2 carucatæ, et 4 servi. Ibi 14 villani, et 6 bordarii, et 30 cozets, cum 8 carucatis. Ibi 2 molini de 5 solidis, et 40 acræ prati, et 12 acræ pasturæ. Silva 5 quarentenis longa et 3 quarentenis lata. Valuit 20 libras, modo 24 libras. De terra villanorum tenet presbyter unam hidam, et unam virgatam terræ de Rege. Valet 15 solidos.

The KING holds *BROMHAM.* The Earl Harold held it, and it paid geld for 20 hides. The land is 10 carucates. In demesne are 10 hides, and there are 2 carucates and 4 serfs. There are 14 villans and 6 borders and 30 coscets with 8 carucates. There are 2 mills worth 5 shillings, and 40 acres of meadow and 12 acres of pasture. The wood is 5 furlongs long and 3 furlongs broad. It was worth £20; now £24. Of the land of the villans a priest holds 1 hide and 1 virgate of land under the King. It is worth 15 shillings.

REX tenet *OTONE.* Eddid Regina[1] tenuit et geldabat pro 30 hidis una virgata minus. Terra est 30 carucatæ. In dominio sunt 13 hidæ et una virgata terræ, et ibi 2 carucatæ et 12 servi. Ibi 40 villani, et 17 coscez, cum 14 carucatis. Ibi 6 acræ prati, et pastura 6 quarentenis longa et 3 quarentenis lata. Silva 6 quarentenis longa et tantundem lata. Valuit 26 libras, modo 30 libras.

The KING holds *OTONE.* Queen Editha held it and it paid geld for 30 hides, less one virgate. The land is 30 carucates. In demesne are 13 hides and 1 virgate of land, and therein are 2 carucates and 12 serfs. There are 40 villans and 17 coscets with 14 carucates. There are 6 acres of meadow, and the pasture is 6 furlongs long and 3 furlongs broad. The wood is 6 furlongs long and as much broad. It was worth £26, now £30.

Hujus manerii ecclesias duas, cum 1 hida terræ tenet[2] S. Michael de Monte.

The Abbey of S. Michael de Monte holds the two churches of this manor with one hide of land.

REX tenet *WESTBERIE.* Eddid Regina tenuit et geldavit pro 40 hidis. Terra est 47 carucatæ. In dominio sunt 17 hidæ, et ibi 7 carucatæ, et 28 servi, et 16 coliberti. Ibi 38 villani, et 23 bordarii, et 9 mellitarii. Inter omnes habent 40 carucatas. Ibi potarii reddunt 20 solidos per annum, et 6 molini reddunt 70 solidos, et 6 denarios; et 80 acræ prati. Pastura 3 leucis longa et 3 leucis lata. Silva 3 leucis longa et dimidio leucæ lata. Ibi 29 porcarii et ibi habent 7 carucatas. Hoc manerium reddit 100 libras ad numerum.

The KING holds *WESTBERIE.* Queen Editha held it, and it paid geld for 40 hides. The land is 47 carucates. In demesne are 17 hides, and there are 7 carucates and 28 serfs and 16 coliberts. There are 38 villans, 23 bordars, and 9 bee-keepers. Among all of them they have 40 carucates. The potters pay 20 shillings by the year, and 6 mills pay 70 shillings and 6 pence; and there are 80 acres of meadow. The pasture is 3 miles long and 3 miles broad. The wood is 3 miles long and half a mile broad. There are 29 swine-herds and they have there 7 carucates. This manor pays 100 pounds by tale.

---

[1] This was EDITHA, the Queen of Edward the Confessor. She seems to have been permitted to hold the whole of the possessions which belonged to her as Queen, till the time of her death in 1075, when they reverted to the crown. In the different surveys, she is spoken of as Edid, Eddid, Eddida, or Eddied Regina.

[2] The Abbey of St. Michael in Periculo Maris, in Normandy, was founded, according to tradition, about the year 708. Rollo, the first Duke of Normandy, dispersed the secular canons of the first foundation, A.D. 966, and put Benedictine monks in their room. Richard II. Duke of Normandy, rebuilt the church in 1024. The Priory of St. Michael's Mount, in Cornwall, which was founded by Edward the Confessor, was subsequently annexed to the Abbey of St. Michael, in Normandy. *Ellis' Introduction to Domesday*, I., 453.

Fol. { 11 b / 65 b } De eadem terra hujus manerii, habet ecclesia hidam et dimidium; Willelmus Scudet 4 hidas et dimidium. Ecclesia valet 50 solidos: [quidam clericolus[1] tenet.]

Rex tenet *WINTREBURNE*. Eddid Regina tenuit, et geldabat pro 2 -hidis et 1 virgata terræ. Terra est 12 carucatæ. In dominio est dimidium virgatæ terræ, et ibi 3 carucatæ, et 11 servi, et 5 coliberti. Ibi 15 villani, et 15 bordarii, cum 8 carucatis. Ibi molinus de 10 solidis, et 8 acræ prati. Pastura 2 leucis longa, et tantundem lata. Valuit et valet 33 libras. Ecclesia ejusdem manerii habet 1 hidam de ipsa terra. Abbatia Gemmeticensis[2] tenet hanc ecclesiam cum terra, et valet 60 solidos.

Rex tenet *NIGRAVRE*. Heraldus Comes tenuit, et geldabat pro 20 hidis. Terra est 22 carucatæ. In dominio sunt 2 hidæ, et ibi 6 carucatæ, et 46 servi, et 8 coliberti. Ibi 30 villani, et 40 bordarii, cum 16 carucatis. Ad hoc manerium pertinent 5 burgenses in Wiltune reddentes 6 solidos. Ibi 3 molini reddentes 30 solidos, et 70 acræ prati. Pastura 3 leucis longa et dimidio leucæ lata. Valuit 40 libras, modo 57 libras. De hac terra hujus manerii tenet Herveus hidam et dimidium, et ibi habet 1 carucatam. Unus Tainus habet 2 hidas et dimidium, et ibi habet 1 carucatam.

Ecclesiam hujus manerii cum una hida tenet Nigellus medicus. Hæc cum omnibus appendicibus suis valet 32 libras. Ipsa vero vasta est, et ita discooperta, ut pene corruat.

Rex tenet *COLINGEBURNE*. Heraldus Comes tenuit et geldabat pro 20 hidis. Terra est 45 carucatæ. In dominio sunt 5 hidæ, et ibi 5 carucatæ et 12 servi. Ibi 49 carucatæ,[3] et 26 bordarii,

Of the same land of this manor the church has one hide and a half. William Scudet four hides and a half. The Church is worth 50 shillings, [a certain chaplain holds it.]

The King holds *WINTREBURNE*. Queen Editha held it, and it paid geld for 2 hides and 1 virgate of land. The land is 12 carucates. In demesne is half a virgate of land, and there are 3 carucates, and 11 serfs, and 5 coliberts. There are 15 villans, and 15 bordars, with 8 carucates. There is a mill worth 10 shillings, and 8 acres of meadow. The pasture is 2 miles long, and as much broad. It was, and still is worth £33. The church of the same Manor has one hide of the same land. The Abbey of Jumieges holds this church with the land, and it is worth 60 shillings.

The King holds *NIGRAVRE*. The Earl Harold held it, and it paid geld for 20 hides. The land is 22 carucates. In demesne are 2 hides, and there are 6 carucates and 46 serfs and 8 coliberts. There are 30 villans and 40 bordars with 16 carucates. To this Manor belong 5 burgesses, in Wilton, who pay 6 shillings. There are 3 mills paying 30 shillings, and 70 acres of meadow. The pasture is 3 miles long and half a mile broad. It was worth £40; it is now worth £57. Of the land of this manor Hervey holds a hide and a half, and there he has one carucate. A Thane has 2 hides and a half, and he has there one carucate.

Nigel, the physician, holds the church of this manor with one hide. This with all its appendages is worth £32. The Church itself, however, is ruinous, and the roof so out of repair, that it is almost tumbling down.

The King holds *COLINGEBURNE*. The Earl Harold held it, and it paid geld for 20 hides. The land is 45 carucates. In demesne are 5 hides, and there are 5 carucates and 12 serfs. There are 49

[1] *Clericolus*, or, as he writes it, *Clericulus*, is interpreted by Ducange, as "junior clericus" or "puer choralis." It is not easy to say what is its exact meaning in this passage.

[2] This was the Abbey of St. Peter, at Jumieges, a town situated on the river Seine, in the diocese of Rouen. It was founded, A.D. 664, by St. Philibert and Clovis II. It was burnt by the Normans, in the middle of the ninth century, and the church rebuilt in 1400, by Abbot Robert II., afterwards Archbishop of Canterbury. See the New Monastic. VI. p. 1086. The estate of Helingay (*Hayling*), in Hants, belonged to this monastery. See *Domesday for Hants*, p. 43.

[3] It is so written in the original, but it seems clearly to be a mistake for "*villani*," and is so rendered in the translation.

II b 65 b cum 15 carucatis, et 20 acræ prati. Pastura 2 leucis longa, et una leuca lata. Silva 1 leuca longa et tantundem lata, et tercia pars silvæ quæ vocatur *CETUM.*[1] Valuit 40 libras, modo 60 libras.

Ad ecclesiam pertinet dimidia hida. Hujus ecclesiæ decimam tenet Giraldus, presbyter de Wiltone, et valet 10 solidos. Ecclesia vasta est et dissipata.

Rex tenet *CHENVEL.* Eileva tenuit tempore Regis Edwardi, et geldavit pro 30 hidis. Terra 15 carucatæ. In dominio sunt 17 hidæ et dimidium, et ibi 5 carucatæ et 10 servi. Ibi 16 villani, et 10 bordarii, et 18 coscez, cum 10 carucatis. Ibi 15 acræ prati, et pastura 1 leuca longa et dimidio leucæ lata. Silva dimidio leucæ longa et tantundem lata. Valuit 28 libras, modo 30 libras. De hac terra habet Gislebertus 1 hidam. Ibi sunt 3 bordarii. Valet 7 solidos et 6 denarios.

Rex tenet *LIDIARDE.* Godricus tenuit tempore Regis Edwardi, et geldabat pro 10 hidis. Terra est 8 carucatæ. In dominio 6 hidæ, una virgata minus, et ibi 4 carucatæ et 9 servi. Ibi 10 villani, et 6 bordarii, habentes 6 carucatas. Ibi molinus de 32 denariis, et 20 acræ prati. Silva 1 leuca longa et dimidio leucæ lata. Valuit 10 libras; modo 12 libras.

Hæ duæ villæ fuerunt Willelmi Comitis.

III a 65 c Rex tenet *OCHEBORNE.* Tempore Regis Edwardi geldabat pro 30 hidis. Terra est 25 carucatæ. In dominio sunt 18 hidæ, et ibi sunt 4 carucatæ, et 6 servi. Ibi 24 villani, et 14 bordarii, habentes 10 carucatas. Ibi 6 acræ prati, et pastura dimidio leucæ longa et 4 quarentenis lata, et tantundem silvæ. Valet 25 libras.

Radulfus, presbyter, tenet ecclesiam de *WRDE*, et ad eam pertinent 3 hidæ quæ non geldabant

villans, and 26 bordars, with 15 carucates, and 20 acres of meadow. The pasture is 2 miles long and one mile broad. The wood one mile long, and as much broad, and there is a third part of the wood which is called *CETUM.* It was worth £40; it is now worth £60.

To the church belongs half a hide. Girald, priest of Wilton, holds the tithe of this church, and it is worth 10 shillings. The church itself is ruinous and decayed.

The King holds *CHENVEL.* Eileva held it in the time of King Edward, and it paid geld for 30 hides. The land is 15 carucates. In demesne are 17 hides and a half, and there are 5 carucates and 10 serfs. There are 16 villans, and 10 bordars, and 18 coscets, with 10 carucates. There are 15 acres of meadow, and the pasture is 1 mile long and half a mile wide. The wood is half a mile long and as much wide. It was worth £28; it is now worth £30. Of this land Gilbert has one hide. There are 3 bordars. It is worth 7 shillings and 6 pence.

The King holds *LIDIARDE.* Godric held it in the time of King Edward, and it paid geld for 10 hides. The land is 8 carucates. In demesne are 6 hides less one virgate, and there are 4 carucates and 9 serfs. There are 10 villans and 6 bordars having 6 carucates. There is a mill worth 32 pence, and 20 acres of meadow. The wood is 1 mile long and half a mile broad. It was worth £10; it is now worth £12.

These two vills belonged to the Earl William.

The King holds *OCHEBORNE.* In the time of King Edward it paid geld for 30 hides. The land is 25 carucates. In demesne are 18 hides, and there are 4 carucates and 6 serfs. There are 24 villans, and 14 bordars, having 10 carucates. There are 6 acres of meadow, and the pasture is half a mile long and 4 furlongs broad, and there is the same quantity of wood. It is worth £25.

Ralph, the priest, holds the church of *WRDE*, and to it belong 3 hides, which did not pay geld in

[1] The wood alluded to is "Chute."

Fol. { III a, 65 c } tempore Regis Edwardi. Terra est 2 carucatæ. Has habet ibi presbyter cum 6 bordariis, et 10 acris prati. Valet 100 solidos.

the time of King Edward. The land is 2 carucates. These the priest has, with 6 bordars, and 10 acres of meadow. It is worth 100 shillings.

VITALIS, presbyter, tenet ecclesiam de *BURBETCE* cum una virgata terræ. Valet 20 solidos.

VITALIS, the priest, holds the church of *BURBETCE*, with one virgate of land. It is worth 20 shillings.

RAINBOLDUS, presbyter, tenet ecclesiam de *PEVESIE* cum una carucata terræ. Valet 20 solidos.

RAINBOLD, the priest, holds the church of *PEVESIE*, with one carucate of land. It is worth 20 shillings.

RAINBOLDUS, presbyter, tenet ecclesiam de *AVREBERIE*, ad quam pertinent 2 hidæ. Valet 40 solidos.

RAINBOLD, the priest, holds the church of *AVREBERIE*, to which belong 2 hides. It is worth 40 shillings.

ALWARDUS, presbyter, tenet ecclesiam de *HESTREBE*, ad quam pertinent 3 hidæ. Terra est 2 carucatæ. Ipsæ sunt ibi cum 2 villanis, et 6 cotariis, et 6 acris prati. Valet 60 solidos.

ALWARD, the priest, holds the church of *HESTREBE*, to which belong 3 hides. The land is 2 carucates. They are there with 2 villans, and 6 cottars, and 6 acres of meadow. It is worth 60 shillings.

OSBERNUS Episcopus habet ecclesiam de *HASEBERIE*, cum dimidia virgata terræ. Valet 10 solidos.

Bishop OSBERN has the church of *HASEBERIE*, with half a virgate of land. It is worth 10 shillings.

SANCTUS WANDREGISILUS tenet ecclesiam de *SORSTAIN*, ad quam pertinent 3 virgatæ terræ. Valet 28 solidos. Similiter tenet ecclesiam de *OPPAVRENE*, ad quam pertinent 2 hidæ et dimidium. Terra est 2 carucatæ. Valet 10 libras et 15 solidos.

The Abbey of ST. WANDREGISIL holds the church of *SORSTAIN*, to which belong 3 virgates of land. It is worth 28 shillings. In like manner it holds the church of *OPPAVRENE*, to which belong 2 hides and a half. The land is 2 carucates. It is worth £10 15s.

OSMUNDUS Episcopus tenet de Rege dimidiam ecclesiam in elemosina ad quam pertinet dimidia hida. Ibi est 1 carucata cum 5 bordariis, et molinus de 6 solidis. Valet 25 solidos.

Bishop OSMUND holds of the King half a church in frank-almoigne to which belongs half a hide. There is 1 carucate with 5 bordars, and a mill worth 6 shillings. It is worth 25 shillings.

WILLELMUS DE BELFOU habet 1 hidam cum una ecclesia in *MERLEBERGE*. Valet 30 solidos.

WILLIAM DE BELFOU has 1 hide, with a church in *MERLEBERGE*. It is worth 30 shillings.

BRISTOARDUS, presbyter, tenet ecclesiam de *BEDVINDE*. Pater ejus tenuit tempore Regis Edwardi. Ibi pertinet una hida et dimidium. Terra est 1 carucata quæ ibi est. Valuit et valet 60 solidos.

BRISTOARD, the priest, holds the church of *BEDVINDE*. His father held it in the time of King Edward. To it belongs one hide and a half. The land which is there is 1 carucate. It was, and still is worth, 60 shillings.

III a 65 c

II. TERRA EPISCOPI WINTONIENSIS.

EPISCOPUS WINTONIENSIS tenet *DUNTONE.* Tempore Regis Edwardi geldavit pro 100 hidis tribus minus. Duæ ex his non sunt Episcopi, quia ablatæ fuerunt, cum aliis tribus, de ecclesia, et de manu Episcopi, tempore Cnut Regis. Terra est 46 carucatæ et dimidium. De hæc terra sunt in dominio 30 hidæ, et ibi 13 carucatæ et 40 servi. Ibi 64 villani, et 27 bordarii, habentes 17 carucatas. Ibi 7 molini reddentes 60 solidos; et 60 acræ prati. Pastura 2 leucis longa, et 1 leuca lata. Silva una leuca et dimidio longa, et dimidia leuca lata.

De eadem terra hujus manerii tenet Willelmus de Braiose 14 hidas; Walerannus 5 hidas; Radulfus 5 hidas; Ansgotus 3 hidas et dimidium; et Rex habet, in sua foresta, 4 hidas; Ecclesia ejusdem manerii habet 4 hidas; et omnes hi de Episcopo tenent. Qui has terras tenebant tempore Regis Edwardi non se poterant ab ecclesia separare.

Quando Walchelinus[1] Episcopus hoc manerium recepit, valebat 60 libras. Modo quod habet in dominio valet 80 libras; quod milites, 23 libras; quod Ecclesia, 3 libras.

Idem Episcopus tenet *FONTEL.* Tempore Regis Edwardi geldabat pro 10 hidis. Terra est 7 carucatæ. In dominio de hac terra sunt 5 hidæ, et ibi 2 carucatæ et 5 servi. Ibi 8 villani, et 5 bordarii, cum 3 carucatis. Ibi molinus de 5 solidis, et 8 acræ prati. Pastura dimidio leucæ longa, et 3 quarentenis lata, et tantundem silvæ. Valuit 10 libras, modo 14 libras.

II. LAND OF THE BISHOP OF WINCHESTER.

The BISHOP OF WINCHESTER holds *DUNTONE.* In the time of King Edward it paid geld for 100 hides, less three. Two of these hides are not the Bishop's, because they were taken away, with other three, from the church, and out of the hand of the Bishop, in the time of King Canute. The land is 46 carucates and a half. Of this land 30 hides are in demesne, wherein are 13 carucates and 40 serfs. There are 64 villans, and 27 bordars, having 17 carucates. There are 7 mills paying 60 shillings, and 60 acres of meadow. The pasture is 2 miles long, and 1 mile broad. The wood is one mile and a half long, and half a mile broad.

Of the same land of this manor William de Braiose holds 14 hides; Waleran 5 hides; Ralph 5 hides; Ansgot 3 hides and a half; and the King has, in his forest, 4 hides; the Church of the same manor has 4 hides; and all these hold under the Bishop. Those who held these lands in the time of King Edward could not separate themselves from the Church.

When Bishop Walchelin received this manor, it was worth £60. What he has now in demesne is worth £80; what is held by military tenure is worth £23; what the Church holds is worth £3.

The same Bishop holds *FONTEL.* In the time of King Edward it paid geld for 10 hides. The land is 7 carucates. In demesne are 5 hides of this land, and therein are 2 carucates and 5 serfs. There are 8 villans, and 5 bordars, with 3 carucates. There is a mill worth 5 shillings, and 8 acres of meadow. The pasture is half a mile long, and three furlongs broad, and there is the same quantity of wood. It was worth £10; now £14.

---

[1] Walchelin was related to William the Conqueror, and was chaplain to the royal household. On the deprivation of Stigand in 1070 he was promoted to the Bishopric of Winchester. He undertook the re-building of his cathedral, with the adjoining monastery, 1079. He completed the latter in 1094. According to extracts given by LELAND (*Collect.* i. 430) he obtained funds by disposing of sundry estates belonging to the monks. It is said,—"multa maneria a monachis Walkelinus abstulit usque ad valorem trecentarum librarum terræ."

Fol. { 111 b / 65 d } Idem Episcopus tenet *FIFHIDE*, et Edwardus de eo, et geldabat pro 5 hidis tempore Regis Edwardi. Hæc terra fuit Capicerii ecclesiæ. Alsi, monachus, tenuit de Episcopo. Terra est 3 carucatæ. De hac terra 3 hidæ sunt in dominio, et ibi 2 carucatæ cum 1 servo. Ibi 3 villani, et 9 bordarii, cum 2 carucatis. Ibi 3 acræ prati, et 30 acræ pasturæ. Silva 3 quarentenis longa, et 1 quarentena lata. Valuit, et valet, 100 solidos.

The same Bishop holds *FIFHIDE*, and Edward holds of him, and it used to pay geld for 5 hides in the time of King Edward. This land belonged to the Sacrist of the church: Alsi, a monk, held it of the Bishop. The land is 3 carucates. Of this land 3 hides are in demesne, and therein are 2 carucates with 1 serf. There are 3 villans, and 9 bordars, with 2 carucates. There are 3 acres of meadow, and 30 acres of pasture. The wood is 3 furlongs long, and one furlong broad. It was, and still is worth 100 shillings.

HÆ [TERRÆ] SUNT DE VICTU MONACHORUM.[1]

THESE [LANDS] ARE FOR THE SUPPORT OF THE MONKS.

Idem Episcopus tenet *AWLTONE*, et geldabat pro 20 hidis tempore Regis Edwardi. Terra est 14 carucatæ. De hac terra sunt 6 hidæ et una virgata terræ in dominio, et ibi 4 carucatæ, et 8 servi. Ibi 27 villani, et 15 coscez, cum 8 carucatis. Ibi 2 molini de 12 solidis et dimidio, et 100 acræ prati. Pastura 6 quarentenis longa, et 4 quarentenis lata. Silva 7 quarentenis longa, et 2 quarentenis lata. De eadem terra tenet Willelmus Scudet 3 hidas de Episcopo, et ibi habet 2 carucatas. Quod monachi habent, valet 24 libras; quod Willelmus, 100 solidos.

The same Bishop holds *AWLTONE*, and it paid geld for 20 hides in the time of King Edward. The land is 14 carucates. Of this land there are 6 hides and one virgate of land in demesne, and therein are 4 carucates and 8 serfs. There are 27 villans, and 15 coscets, with 8 carucates. There are 2 mills worth twelve shillings and sixpence, and 100 acres of meadow. The pasture is 6 furlongs long, and 4 furlongs broad. The wood is 7 furlongs long, and 2 furlongs broad. Of the same land William Scudet holds 3 hides under the Bishop, and he has there 2 carucates. What the monks have, is worth £24; what William has is worth 100 shillings.

Idem Episcopus tenet *HAME*. Tempore Regis Edwardi geldabat pro 10 hidis et dimidio, et dimidia virgata terræ. Terra est 7 carucatæ. De hac terra 5 hidæ et dimidium sunt in dominio, et ibi 3 carucatæ, cum 1 servo. Ibi 9 villani, et 10 coscez, cum 3 carucatis. Ibi 8 acræ prati. Pastura 3 quarentenis longa, et 1 quarentena lata. Silva 6 quarentenis longa, et 3 quarentenis lata. De eadem terra tenet

The same Bishop holds *HAME*. In the time of King Edward it paid geld for 10 hides and a half, and half a virgate of land. The land is seven carucates. Of this land 5 hides and a half are in demesne, and therein are 3 carucates, with 1 serf. There are 9 villans, and 10 coscets, with 3 carucates. There are 8 acres of meadow. The pasture is 3 furlongs long, and one furlong broad. The wood is 6 furlongs long

---

[1] These were the monks of the Benedictine Monastery, which was connected with the Cathedral at Winchester. They are usually spoken of as the monks of St. Swithin, though the Cathedral was dedicated, at different times, to St. Amphibalus, St. Peter, St. Swithin, and to the Holy Trinity. New Monast. i. 190. The estates enumerated, of which the Bishop of Winchester was, so to speak, a Trustee, were let to farm to various tenants, who were bound to furnish food of a certain amount for the supply of the inmates of the monastery.

III b
65 d
Willelmus 2 hidas de Episcopo. Qui ante eum tenuit non poterat ab ecclesia recedere.

and three furlongs broad. Of the same land William holds 2 hides under the Bishop. He who held them before him could not recede from the Church (as his feudal lord).

Valuit hoc manerium 6 libras, quando Episcopus recepit; modo dominium valet 9 libras; quod Willelmus tenet, 3 libras.

This manor was worth £6 when the Bishop received it; the demesne is now worth £9; what William holds is worth £3.

Idem Episcopus tenet *WESTWODE*. Tempore Regis Edwardi geldabat pro 3 hidis. Terra 5 carucatæ. De hac terra 2 hidæ in dominio, et ibi 3 carucatæ et 3 servi. Ibi 6 villani, et 4 bordarii, cum 1 carucata. Ibi molinus, reddens 10 solidos, et 6 acræ prati. Silva 2 quarentenis longa, et 1 quarentena lata. Quando recepit Episcopus valebat 6 libras; modo 4 libras.

The same Bishop holds *WESTWOODE*. In the time of King Edward it paid geld for 3 hides. The land is 5 carucates. Of this land 2 hides are in demesne, and therein are 3 carucates, and 3 serfs. There are 6 villans, and 4 bordars, with 1 carucate. There is a mill paying 10 shillings, and 6 acres of meadow. The wood is 2 furlongs long, and 1 furlong broad. When the Bishop received it, it was worth £6; now £4.

Idem Episcopus tenet *ELENDUNE*. Tempore Regis Edwardi geldabat pro 30 hidis. Terra est 12 carucatæ. De hac terra sunt in dominio 15 hidæ, et ibi 4 carucatæ, et 3 servi. Ibi 25 villani, et 14 bordarii, habentes 7 carucatas. Ibi 6 molini, reddentes 42 solidos et 6 denarios, et 60 acræ prati. Pastura dimidio leucæ longa, et 3 quarentenis lata, et 20 acræ silvæ.

The same Bishop holds *ELENDUNE*. In the time of King Edward it paid geld for 30 hides. The land is 12 carucates. Of this land there are, in demesne, 15 hides, wherein are 4 carucates, and 3 serfs. There are 25 villans, and 14 bordars, who have 7 carucates. There are 6 mills, paying 42 shillings and 6 pence, and 60 acres of meadow. The pasture is half a mile long and 3 furlongs broad, and there are 20 acres of wood.

De hac terra habet unus miles 1 hidam et dimidium, et habet ibi 1 carucatam. Godricus, qui tenuit tempore Regis Edwardi, non potuit ab ecclesia separari. Quando Episcopus recepit valebat 14 libras; valet modo 18 libras.

Of this land, a tenant, holding by military tenure, has 1 hide and a half, and has therein 1 carucate. Godric, who held it in the time of King Edward, could not be separated from the church. When the Bishop received it, it was worth £14; it is now worth £18.

Ipse Episcopus tenet *CLIVE*. Tempore Regis Edwardi geldabat pro 10 hidis. Terra est 5 carucatæ. De eadem terra sunt in dominio 6 hidæ et dimidium, et ibi 2 carucatæ et 3 servi. Ibi 7 villani, et 3 coscez, cum 2 carucatis. Ibi 30 acræ prati. Silva 2 quarentenis longa, et una quarentena lata. Quando Episcopus recepit, valebat 3 libras; modo 6 libras.

The Bishop himself holds *CLIVE*. In the time of King Edward it paid geld for 10 hides. The land is 5 carucates. Of the same land there are in demesne 6 hides and a half, and therein are 2 carucates and 3 serfs. There are 7 villans, and 3 coscets, with 2 carucates. There are 30 acres of meadow. The wood is 2 furlongs long, and one furlong broad. When the Bishop received it, it was worth £3; it is now worth £6.

Fol. { III b 65 d } Idem Episcopus tenet *WEMBERGE.* Tempore Regis Edwardi geldabat pro 19 hidis. Terra est 10 carucatæ. De eadem terra 9 hidæ sunt in dominio, et ibi 3 carucatæ et 6 servi. Ibi 19 villani, et 13 bordarii, cum 5 carucatis. Ibi molinus, reddens 5 solidos, et 40 acræ prati. Pastura dimidio leucæ longa, et 15 quarentenis lata. De hac terra tenet Richerus 1 hidam. Quando recepit Episcopus valebat 15 libras; modo 18 libras.

The same Bishop holds *WEMBERGE.* In the time of King Edward it paid geld for 19 hides. The land is 10 carucates. Of this same land 9 hides are in demesne, and therein are 3 carucates, and 6 serfs. There are 19 villans, and 13 bordars with 5 carucates. There is a mill, paying 5 shillings, and 40 acres of meadow. The pasture is half a mile long, and 15 furlongs broad. Of this land Richer holds 1 hide. When the Bishop received (this land) it was worth £15; it is now worth £18.

Idem Episcopus tenet *ENEDFORDE.* Tempore Regis Edwardi geldabat pro 30 hidis. Terra est 24 carucatæ. De eadem terra 10 hidæ sunt in dominio, et ibi 3 carucatæ et 6 servi. Ibi 12 villani, et 15 bordarii, cum 10 carucatis. Ibi 2 molini, reddentes 25 solidos, et 17 acræ prati. Pastura 2 leucis et dimidio longa, et una leuca et dimidio lata. De eadem terra tenet Willelmus 5 hidas, et Heraldus 2 hidas. Unus Anglicus 3 hidas. Ibi habent 10 carucatas. Presbyter habet 1 hidam. Qui tenuerunt tempore Regis Edwardi non poterant ab ecclesia separari. Quando Episcopus recepit valebat 34 libras. Modo dominium valet 20 libras. Quod presbyter et milites tenent 19 libras.

The same Bishop holds *ENEDFORDE.* In the time of King Edward it paid geld for 30 hides. The land is 24 carucates. Of this same land, 10 hides are in demesne, and therein are 3 carucates and 6 serfs. There are 12 villans, and 15 bordars, with 10 carucates. There are 2 mills, paying 25 shillings, and 17 acres of meadow. The pasture is 2 miles and a half long, and one mile and a half broad. Of this same land William holds 5 hides, and Harold 2 hides. An Englishman has 3 hides. They have there 10 carucates. The priest has one hide. They who held these lands in the time of King Edward could not be separated from the church. When the Bishop received this estate it was worth £34. The demesne is now worth £20. What the priest and those who hold by military tenure have, is worth £19.

Idem Episcopus tenet *OVRETONE.* Tempore Regis Edwardi geldabat pro 15 hidis. Terra est 7 carucatæ. De ipsa terra sunt in dominio 8 hidæ et dimidium, et ibi 2 carucatæ. Ibi villani habentes 5 carucatas. Ibi 15 acræ prati. Pastura 8 quarentenis longa, et 4 quarentenis lata. Silva 5 quarentenis longa, et 2 quarentenis lata.

The same Bishop holds *OVRETONE.* In the time of King Edward it paid geld for 15 hides. The land is 7 carucates. Of this land there are in demesne 8 hides and a half, and therein are 2 carucates. There are villans having 5 carucates. There are 15 acres of meadow. The pasture is 8 furlongs long, and 4 furlongs broad. The wood 5 furlongs long, and 2 furlongs broad.

De eadem terra tenet Durandus 2 hidas, dimidia virgata minus. Qui tenuit tempore Regis Edwardi non poterat ab ecclesia separari. Valuit et valet 20 solidos. Dominium valet 8 libras. Quando Episcopus recepit valebat 6 libras.

Of the same land Durand holds 2 hides, all but half a virgate. He who held them in the time of King Edward could not be separated from the church. It was, and is, worth 20 shillings. The demesne is worth £8. When the Bishop received it, it was worth £6.

III b 65 d Idem Episcopus tenet *STOTTUNE*. Tempore Regis Edwardi geldabat pro 10 hidis. Terra est 6 carucatæ. De ipsa terra sunt in dominio 3 hidæ et dimidium, et ibi 2 carucatæ et 3 servi. Ibi 4 villani et 6 bordarii, cum 2 carucatis. Ibi molinus de 10 solidis, et 10 acræ prati. Pastura 5 quarentenis longa, et 2 quarentenis lata, et 40 acræ silvæ.

The same Bishop holds *STOTTUNE*. In the time of King Edward it paid geld for 10 hides. The land is 6 carucates. Of this land there are in demesne 3 hides and a half, therein are 2 carucates and 3 serfs. There are 4 villans and 6 bordars, with 2 carucates. There is a mill worth 10 shillings and 10 acres of meadow. The pasture is 5 furlongs long, 2 furlongs broad, and there are 40 acres of wood.

De eadem terra tenet Richerus 2 hidas, et Anschitil 2 hidas et dimidium. Ibi habent 2 carucatas.

Of the same land Richer holds 5 hides, and Anschitil 2 hides and a half. They have there 2 carucates.

Hoc manerium quando Episcopus recepit valebat 8 libras. Modo dominium valet 100 solidos et 10 solidos.[1] Quod homines tenent valet 4 libras. Terra, quam tenent, non poterat ab ecclesia, tempore Regis Edwardi, separari.

The manor when the Bishop received it was worth £8. The demesne is now worth 100 shillings and 10 pence. What the vassals hold is worth £4. The land which they hold could not be separated from the church in the time of King Edward.

IV a 66 a

III. TERRA EPISCOPI SARISBERIENSIS.

Episcopus Sarisberiensis[2] tenet *POTERNE*. Tempore Regis Edwardi geldabat pro 52 hidis. Terra est 40 carucatæ. De hac terra 10 hidæ sunt in dominio, et ibi 6 carucatæ, et 4 servi, et 5 coliberti. Ibi 29 villani, et 40 bordarii, cum 30 carucatis. Ibi 6 molini, reddentes 43 solidos et 4 denarios, et 40 acræ prati. Pastura 2 leucis et dimidio longa, et una leuca et 3 quarentenis lata. Silva 1 leuca longa, et 10 quarentenis lata. Dominium Episcopi valet et valuit 60 libras.

III. LAND OF THE BISHOP OF SALISBURY.

The Bishop of Salisbury holds *POTERNE*. In the time of King Edward it paid geld for 52 hides. The land is 40 carucates. Of this land 10 hides are in demesne, and there are 6 carucates, and 4 serfs, and 5 coliberts. There are 29 villans, 40 bordars, with 30 carucates. There are 6 mills paying 43 shillings and 4 pence, and 40 acres of meadow. The pasture is 2 miles and a half long, and 1 mile and 3 furlongs broad. The wood is 1 mile long, and 10 furlongs broad. The demesne of the Bishop is, and was, worth £60.

---

[1] It is so written in the original, but it is no doubt a mistake for "*denarios*," i.e., "*pence*," and it is so rendered in the translation.

[2] This Bishop, at old Sarum, at the time of Domesday, was the celebrated St. Osmund, the father and founder of the first cathedral church. He not only built and endowed his church, but also framed the well known "Use of Sarum," according to which the worship of God was for some centuries offered up in the Church of England, from which circumstance, it is said, the Bishops of Sarum enjoy the office of Precentor of the Province of Canterbury. He died in 1099. In the year 1457 he was canonized, when his remains were disinterred with great respect, and the 5th of December assigned to his memory.

Fol. {IV a / 66 a} De eadem terra hujus manerii tenent 2 Angli 6 hidas et unam virgatam terræ. Unus ex eis est miles[1] jussu Regis, et nepos fuit Hermanni Episcopi.[2] Et Alwardus tenet 3 hidas quas Wlwardus,[3] tempore Regis Edwardi, ab Episcopo Hermanno emit in vita sua tantum ut postea redirent ad firmam Episcopi, quia de dominio Episcopi erant. Hi Taini habent 4 carucatas ibi cum 2 servis et 9 bordariis. Valent 7 libras.

Of the same land of this manor 2 Englishmen hold 6 hides and one virgate of land. One of them is a 'Miles' by the command of the King, and was nephew of Bishop Herman. And Alward holds 3 hides which Ulward, in the time of King Edward, bought of Bishop Herman, but only for his own life, so that they should afterwards revert to the Bishop's manor, because they were part of the demesne of the Bishop. These Thanes have there 4 carucates, with 2 serfs and 9 bordars. They are worth £7.

Quod presbyter hujus manerii tenet valet 40 solidos.

What the priest of this manor holds is worth 20 shillings.

De terra ejusdem Manerii tenet Arnulfus de Hesding 3 hidas et unam virgatam de Regc. Episcopus vero calumniatur eas, quum qui tenuit tempore Regis Edwardi non poterat ab Episcopo separari.

Of the land of this same manor Ernulf de Hesding holds 3 hides and one virgate of land of the King. The Bishop however claims them, because he who held them in the time of King Edward could not be separated from the Bishop.

Idem Episcopus tenet *CAININGHAM.* Tempore Regis Edwardi geldabat pro 70 hidis. Terra est 45 carucatæ. De hac, 10 hidæ sunt in dominio, et ibi 5 carucatæ et 6 servi. Ibi 48 villani, et 40 bordarii, cum 28 carucatis. Ibi 6 molini, reddentes 7 solidos et 6 denarios, et 30 acræ prati. Pastura 1 leuca

The same Bishop holds *CAININGHAM.* In the time of King Edward it paid geld for 70 hides. The land is 45 carucates. Of this, 10 hides are in demesne, and there are 5 carucates and 6 serfs. There are 48 villans, and 40 bordars, with 28 carucates. There are 6 mills, paying 7 shillings and

---

[1] The term "Miles" does not appear to have had a precise meaning in the eleventh century, and is therefore left untranslated. It sometimes denotes persons of distinction, such as knights or thanes,—those, in fact, who had to render knight-service; at other times it implies soldiers generally, and some who are called "milites," are, in the survey, classed with the inferior orders of tenantry. In all cases it seems to imply obligation to render services to a feudal lord, and, through him, to the king, and so to confer rank in proportion to the services required. Perhaps in this passage, "Esquire," as understood in olden time, would be the best translation of the word.—See *Ellis, I.* 58.

[2] HERMAN is generally called the last Bishop of Wilton, though his see was fixed at Ramsbury, and that town would more fitly give a title to the bishopric. He was a native of Flanders, and was advanced by Edward the Confessor, whose chaplain he was, to the episcopal dignity. He made great efforts to remove his see to Malmesbury, but was opposed by the abbot of that monastery, aided by the powerful Earl Godwin. He retired, it is said, for a time from his bishopric to the celebrated monastery of St. Bertin, in France. On his return a few years afterwards, he had influence enough, in 1058, to procure the union of the bishopric of Sherborne with his own; and, in 1076, immediately after the decree of a synod held in London under Archbishop Lanfranc, to the effect that the episcopal sees which were established in obscure villages should be removed to considerable towns, he changed his residence to Old Sarum, and so became the first bishop of Salisbury. In the Anglo-Saxon Chronicle (A.D. 1078) he is called "Hereman, bishop of Berkshire, and of Wiltshire, and of Dorsetshire." The title "Bishop of Sunning" is sometimes given, in old records, to the occupants of the see of Salisbury, from their episcopal residence at Sunning, in Berks.

[3] In the original, over "Wlwardus" is written, in very small characters, the word "*albus*" i.e., "*white.*" This would seem to be a translation of the Anglo-Saxon holder's name, which was, in fact, "Ulward *White.*" In the Exon Domesday we frequently meet with surnames, but seldom in the Exchequer Domesday, and what there are will be found generally in a translated form. See below, in § lx., under the holding of "Robertus Flavus."

IV a 66 a longa, et 8 quarentenis lata. Silva 1 leuca longa, et 10 quarentenis lata. In burgo *CAUNE*, una domus pertinet huic manerio reddens 20 denarios per annum.

De eadem terra hujus manerii tenet presbyter 2 hidas; Ebrardus 10 hidas; Hermannus 4 hidas; Quintinus 3 hidas; Walterus 2 hidas; Brictwardus 5 hidas; Alwardus 1 hidam; uxor præpositi 1 hidam. Hi habent 8 carucatas, cum 3 villanis et 30 bordariis habentibus 4 carucatas. Dominium Episcopi valet 60 libras. Quod alii tenent valet 35 libras.

Idem Episcopus tenet *RAMESBERIE.* Tempore Regis Edwardi geldabat pro quatuor viginti et 10 hidis. Terra est 54 carucatæ. De hac terra 30 hidæ sunt in dominio, et ibi 8 carucatæ, et 9 servi. Ibi 68 villani, et 43 bordarii, habentes 29 carucatas. Ibi 80 acræ prati, et 10 molini reddentes 6 libras et 30 denarios. Pastura 14 quarentenis longa, et 5 quarentenis lata. Silva 16 quarentenis longa et 4 quarentenis lata.

De eadem terra hujus manerii tenent presbyteri 4 hidas: Otboldus 12 hidas; Herbertus 5 hidas; Quintinus 5 hidas; uxor præpositi 1 hidam. Hi habent in dominio 11 carucatas; et 31 bordarii cum 6 carucatis.

In Crichelade 5 burgenses pertinent huic manerio reddentes 5 solidos.

Dominium Episcopi valet 52 libras et 15 solidos. Quod alii tenent, 17 libras et 5 solidos.

Idem Episcopus tenet *SARISBERIE.* Tempore Regis Edwardi geldabat pro 50 hidis. Terra est 32 carucatæ. De hac terra 10 hidæ sunt in dominio, et ibi 8 carucatæ. Ibi 25 villani, et 50 bordarii, cum 17 carucatis.

In Wiltune 7 burgenses pertinent huic manerio reddentes 65 denarios.

In manerio 4 molini de 47 solidis et 7 denariis, et dimidium molinum de 30 solidis, et 142 acræ

6 pence, and 30 acres of meadow. The pasture is 1 mile long and 8 furlongs broad. The wood is 1 mile long and 10 furlongs broad. In the borough of *CAUNE*, a house belongs to this manor which pays 20 pence per annum.

Of the same land of this manor the priest holds 2 hides; Ebrard 10 hides; Herman 4 hides; Quintin 3 hides; Walter 2 hides; Brictward 5 hides; Alward 1 hide; the wife of the bailiff 1 hide. These have 8 carucates, with 3 villans and 30 bordars having 4 carucates. The demesne of the Bishop is worth £60. What the others hold is worth £35.

The same Bishop holds *RAMESBERIE.* In the time of King Edward it paid geld for 90 hides. The land is 54 carucates. Of this land 30 hides are in demesne, and there are 8 carucates and 9 serfs. There are 68 villans, and 43 bordars, having 29 carucates. There are 80 acres of meadow, and 10 mills paying 6 pounds and 30 pence. The pasture is 14 furlongs long and 5 furlongs broad. The wood is 16 furlongs long and 4 furlongs broad.

Of the same land of this manor the priests hold 4 hides; Otbold 12 hides; Herbert 5 hides; Quintin 5 hides; the wife of the bailiff 1 hide. These have in demesne 11 carucates; and there are 31 bordars with 6 carucates.

In Crichelade five burgesses paying 5 shillings belong to this manor.

The demesne of the Bishop is worth £52 15*s.* What the others hold is worth £17 5*s.*

The same Bishop holds *SARISBERIE.* In the the time of King Edward it paid geld for 50 hides. The land is 32 carucates. Of this land 10 hides are in demesne, and there are 8 carucates. There are 25 villans, and 50 bordars, with 17 carucates.

Seven burgesses in Wiltune belong to this manor paying 65 pence.

In the manor are 4 mills worth 47 shillings and 7 pence, and half a mill worth 30 shillings, and 142

Fol. { IV a 66 a prati. Pastura 20 quarentenis longa, et 10 quarentenis lata, et alibi 5 quarentenæ pasturæ longitudine, et una quarentena latitudine. Silva 4 quarentenis longa, et 2 quarentenis lata.

De eadem terra hujus manerii tenet Edwardus 5 hidas; Odo 5 hidas; Hugo 3 hidas una virgata minus. Qui has tenuerunt tempore Regis Edwardi non poterant ab Episcopo separari. Ibi sunt in dominio 5 carucatæ; et 6 villani, et 17 bordarii, cum 2 carucatis.

Dominium Episcopi valet 47 libras. Quod homines tenent valet 17 libras et 10 solidos.

Idem Episcopus tenet *CHEDELWICH.* Algar tenuit tempore Regis Edwardi, et geldabat pro 5 hidis. Terra est 3 carucatæ. De hac terra 4 hidæ sunt in dominio, et ibi 2 carucatæ; et 3 villani, et 6 bordarii, et 2 coscez, cum 1 carucata et dimidio. Ibi 10 acræ prati et dimidium. Pastura 3 quarentenis longa, et 2 quarentenis lata. Silva 2 quarentenis longa, et una quarentena lata. Valuit 40 solidos; modo 4 libras.

Hoc est de excambio *SCEPELEIA.* Hugo tenet de Episcopo.

acres of meadow. The pasture is twenty furlongs long and 10 furlongs broad, and elsewhere there are 5 furlongs of pasture in length and 1 furlong in breadth. The wood is 4 furlongs long and 2 furlongs broad.

Of the same land of this manor Edward holds 5 hides: Odo 5 hides: Hugo 3 hides all but one virgate. Those who held them in the time of King Edward could not be separated from the Bishop. There are in demesne 5 carucates; and there are 6 villans, and 17 bordars, with 2 carucates.

The demesne of the Bishop is worth £47. What the vassals hold is worth £17 10*s.*

The same Bishop holds *CHEDELWICH.* Algar held it in the time of King Edward, and it paid geld for 5 hides. The land is 3 carucates. Of this land 4 hides are in demesne, and there are 2 carucates; and 3 villans, and 6 bordars, and 2 coscets, with 1 carucate and a half. There are 10½ acres of meadow. The pasture is 3 furlongs long and 2 furlongs broad. The wood is 2 furlongs long, and 1 furlong broad. It was worth 40 shillings; it is now worth £4.

This is in exchange for *SCEPELEIA.* Hugo holds it of the Bishop.

Fol. { IV b 66 b

IV. TERRA EPISCOPI BAIOCENSIS.

EPISCOPUS BAIOCENSIS[1] tenet *TODEWORDE,* et Odo de eo. Eddulfus tenuit tempore Regis Edwardi, et geldabat pro 5 hidis. Terra est 3

IV. LAND OF THE BISHOP OF BAIEUX.

The BISHOP OF BAIEUX holds *TODEWORDE,* and Odo of him. Eddulf held it in the time of King Edward, and it paid geld for 5 hides. The

[1] ODO, BISHOP OF BAIEUX, was half brother to the Conqueror, being the son of Herluin de Contaville and Harleta, the mother of William, by Robert Duke of Normandy. He took an active part in the invasion of England, celebrating mass and giving a blessing to the soldiers on the morning of the battle of Hastings. His fidelity and zeal were rewarded with no less than 439 manors, in various parts of England, and the title of Earl of Kent. He also held several high and lucrative offices. For some ambitious designs he seems, at length, to have fallen into disgrace, and to have been sent, in 1084, to Normandy, as to an honorable exile. He died at Palermo, in 1097, on his way to the Holy Land. An engraving of his seal, appendant to a deed, is given in the Archæologia I. 337. On one side he is represented as an Earl mounted on his war horse, clad in armour, and holding a sword in his right hand; and on the reverse, as a bishop, dressed in his pontifical robes, pronouncing a blessing.

V b carucatæ. De hac terra sunt in dominio 4 hidæ una
6 b virgata minus, et ibi 2 carucatæ et 2 servi. Ibi unus villanus, et 6 bordarii, cum 1 carucata. Ibi pastura 3 quarentenis longa, et 2 quarentenis lata. Valet 4 libras et 10 solidos.

land is 3 carucates. Of this land there are in demesne 4 hides all but one virgate, and there are 2 carucates and 2 serfs. There is one villan and 6 bordars, with 1 carucate. The pasture there is three furlongs long, and 2 furlongs broad. It is worth £4 10*s*.

Idem Episcopus tenet *WADHULLE*, et Odo de eo. Eddulfus tenuit tempore Regis Edwardi, et geldabat pro 6 hidis. Terra est 3 carucatæ. De hac terra sunt in dominio 5 hidæ, et ibi 2 carucatæ, et 6 servi. Ibi unus villanus et 4 bordarii cum 1 carucata. Ibi 12 acræ prati, et pastura 1 quarentena longa et tantundem lata. Silva una quarentena longa, et 3 acris lata. Valet 4 libras.

The same Bishop holds *WADHULLE*, and Odo of him. Eddulf held it in the time of King Edward, and it paid geld for 6 hides. The land is 3 carucates. Of this land there are in demesne 5 hides, and there are 2 carucates, and 6 serfs. There is one villan, and 4 bordars, with 1 carucate. There are 12 acres of meadow, and the pasture is one furlong long, and as much broad. The wood is 1 furlong long, and 3 acres broad. It is worth £4.

Idem Episcopus tenet *SVINDUNE*, et Wadardus de eo. Leuiet tenuit tempore Regis Edwardi, et geldabat pro 5 hidis. Ex his una est in dominio, et ibi 1 carucata, et 4 servi. Ibi 5 villani et 2 bordarii cum 2 carucatis. Ibi molinus de 4 solidis, et 30 acræ prati, et tantundem pasturæ. Valuit 40 solidos; modo 4 libras.

The same Bishop holds *SVINDUNE*, and Wadard of him. Leuiet held in the time of King Edward, and it paid geld for 5 hides. Of these one is in demesne, and there is 1 carucate, and 4 serfs. There are 5 villans and 2 bordars, with 2 carucates. There is a mill worth 4 shillings, and 30 acres of meadow, and as much pasture. It was worth 40 shillings; it is now worth £4.

Idem Episcopus tenet *DECHEMENTONE*, et Robertus de eo. Azor tenuit tempore Regis Edwardi, et geldabat pro 2 hidis. Terra est 2 carucatæ. Has habent ibi 18 cotarii; et 4 molini sunt ibi, reddentes 27 solidos, et 4 acræ prati, et 10 acræ pasturæ. Valuit 100 solidos; modo 8 libras.

The same Bishop holds *DECHEMENTONE*, and Robert of him. Azor held it in the time of King Edward, and it paid geld for 2 hides. The land is 2 carucates. These 18 cottars have there; and there are 4 mills, paying 27 shillings, and 4 acres of meadow, and 10 acres of pasture. It was worth 100 shillings; it is now worth £8.

Fol. { IV b
66 b

V. TERRA EPISCOPI CONSTANTIENSIS.

Episcopus Constantiensis[1] tenet *DRAICOTE*, et Rogerius de eo. Alwardus et Elnod tenuerunt pro 2 maneriis tempore Regis Edwardi, et geldabant pro 5 hidis. Terra est 2 carucatæ et dimidium. De hac terra sunt in dominio 4 hidæ una virgata minus, et ibi 2 carucatæ, et 3 servi. Ibi 4 bordarii, et 7 coscez, habentes dimidiam carucatam. Ibi 60 acræ pasturæ. Valuit 30 solidos; modo 60 solidos.

Idem Episcopus tenet *WITHENHAM*, et Rogerius de eo. Aluet tenuit tempore Regis Edwardi, et geldabat pro 5 hidis. Terra est 5 carucatæ. De hoc terra 3 hidæ sunt in dominio, et ibi 1 carucata, et 3 servi. Ibi 5 villani, et 5 bordarii, cum 4 carucatis. Ibi molinus, reddens 12 solidos et 6 denarios, et 10 acræ prati, et 16 acræ silvæ. Pastura 2 quarentenis longa, et una quarentena lata. Valuit, et valet, 4 libras et 10 solidos.

Idem Episcopus tenet *WINEFEL*, et Rogerius de eo. Azor tenuit tempore Regis Edwardi, et geldabat pro 3 hidis et dimidio. Terra est 3 carucatæ. De hac terra 2 hidæ sunt in dominio, et ibi 1 carucata. Ibi 3 villani, et 9 bordarii, cum 2 carucatis. Ibi molinus, reddens 20 solidos, et 7 acræ prati, et 20 acræ silvæ. Pastura 3 quarentenis longa, et 2 quarentenis lata. Valuit, et valet, 70 solidos.

Idem Episcopus tenet *MAMESBERIE*. Gislebertus tenuit tempore Regis Edwardi, et geldabat

V. LAND OF THE BISHOP OF COUTANCE.

The Bishop of Coutance holds *DRAICOTE*, and Roger of him. Alward and Elnod held it for 2 manors in the time of King Edward, and paid geld for 4 hides. The land is 2 carucates and a half. Of this land there are in demesne 4 hides all but 1 virgate, and there are 2 carucates and 3 serfs. There are 4 bordars and 7 cosccts, having half a carucate. There are 60 acres of pasture. It was worth 30 shillings; it is now worth 60 shillings.

The same Bishop holds *WITHENHAM*, and Roger of him. Alvet held it in the time of King Edward, and it paid geld for 5 hides. The land is 5 carucates. Of this land 3 hides are in demesne, and there is one carucate, and 3 serfs. There are 5 villans, and 5 bordars, with 4 carucates. There is a mill, paying 12 shillings and six pence, and 10 acres of meadow, and 16 acres of wood. The pasture is 2 furlongs long and 1 furlong broad. It was, and is, worth, £4 10*s*.

The same Bishop holds *WINEFEL*, and Roger of him. Azor held it in the time of King Edward, and it paid geld for 3 hides and a half. The land is 3 carucates. Of this land 2 hides are in demesne, and there is one carucate. There are 3 villans, and 9 bordars, with 2 carucates. There is a mill, paying 20 shillings, and 7 acres of meadow, and 20 acres of wood. The pasture is 3 furlongs long and 2 furlongs broad. It was, and is, worth 70 shillings.

The same Bishop holds *MAMESBERIE*. Gilbert held it in the time of King Edward, and it

---

[1] This was Geoffrey de Montbray, who became Bishop of Coutance, in Normandy, in the year 1048. He was appointed subsequently to the high office of Chief Justiciary of England, and presided at the great trial in the County Court, held at Pinendene, in Kent, between Lanfranc, Archbishop of Canterbury, and Odo, Bishop of Baieux. He had also acted, Kelham tells us, (*p.* 46) as William the Conqueror's Lieutenant-General after the battle of Hastings. He was possessed of no less than 280 manors. He was one of the party who joined in Duke Robert's favor, in 1088, against William Rufus. He died in 1093. In the Gloucestershire Domesday (*fol.* 165) he is designated, "Episcopus de Sancto Laudo," which Kelham (*p.* 85) explains,—"St. Lo, a vill in Lower Normandy, in the diocese of Coutance." In the New Monastic: (I. 144), among the witnesses to King William's charter to the monastery of St. Augustine, at Canterbury, we have, "Episcopo Golfrydo de Seynt Loth" (Geoffrey de Montbray).—Ellis' Introduction to Domesday, i. 400.

V b 66 b pro una hida. Terra est dimidium carucatæ. De hac terra sunt 3 virgatæ terræ in dominio, et ibi dimidium carucatæ cum 3 bordariis. Ibi 4 acræ prati, et pastura 2 quarentenis longa, et una quarentena lata. Valet 13 solidos.

paid geld for 1 hide. The land is half a carucate. Of this land there are 3 virgates of land in demesne, and there is half a carucate with 3 bordars. There are 4 acres of meadow, and the pasture is 2 furlongs long and 1 furlong broad. It is worth 13 shillings.

Idem Episcopus tenet *PERTEWORDE*, et Osbertus de eo. Wlwardus tenuit tempore Regis Edwardi, et geldabat pro 2 hidis. Terra est 2 carucatæ. De hac terra in dominio est hida et dimidium, et ibi 1 carucata. Ibi 2 villani, et 3 bordarii, cum 1 carucata. Ibi 20 acræ pasturæ, et 4 acræ silvæ. Valuit, et valet, 40 solidos.

The same Bishop holds *PERTEWORDE*, and Osbert of him. Ulward held it in the time of King Edward, and it paid geld for 2 hides. The land is 2 carucates. Of this land there is in demesne 1 hide and a half, and there is 1 carucate. There are 2 villans, and 3 bordars, with 1 carucate. There are 20 acres of pasture, and 4 acres of wood. It was, and is, worth 40 shillings.

Idem Episcopus tenet *LITELTONE*, et Robertus de eo. Alwardus tenuit tempore Regis Edwardi de abbate Glastingberiensi,[1] et non poterat ab ipsa ecclesia separari, et geldabat pro 5 hidis. Terra est 8 carucatæ. De hac terra in dominio sunt 2 hidæ, et ibi 2 carucatæ, et 4 servi. Ibi 6 villani, et 6 bordarii, cum 5 carucatis. Ibi molinus, reddens 7 solidos et 6 denarios, et 15 acræ prati. Valuit, et valet, 7 libras.

The same Bishop holds *LITELTONE*, and Robert of him. Alward held it in the time of King Edward of the abbot of Glastonbury, and he could not be separated from the church, and it paid geld for 5 hides. The land is 8 carucates. Of this land there are in demesne 2 hides, and there are 2 carucates, and 4 serfs. There are 6 villans, and 6 bordars, with 5 carucates. There is a mill, paying 7 shillings and 6 pence, and 15 acres of meadow. It was, and is, worth £7.

Idem Episcopus tenet *WINTREBURNE*. Lessida tenuit tempore Regis Edwardi, et geldabat pro 2 hidis et dimidio. Terra est 2 carucatæ. De hac terra in dominio est hida et dimidium, et ibi 1 carucata, et 2 servi. Ibi 5 villani, et unus cotarius, et 4 bordarii, cum 1 carucata. Ibi molinus, reddens 12 solidos et 6 denarios, et 20 acræ pasturæ. Valuit 30 solidos quando recepit Episcopus ; modo 4 libras.

The same Bishop holds *WINTREBURNE*. Lessid held it in the time of King Edward, and it paid geld for 2 hides and a half. The land is 2 carucates. Of this land there is in demesne 1 hide and a half, and there is one carucate, and 2 serfs. There are 5 villans, and 1 cottar, and 4 bordars, with 1 carucate. There is a mill, paying 12 shillings and sixpence, and 20 acres of pasture. It was worth 30 shillings when the Bishop received it; it is now worth £4.

---

[1] The Bishop of Coutance seems to have possessed several manors which previously belonged to the Abbey of Glastonbury. Thus in the Somersetshire Domesday *(Fol. 88)*, after an account of HOTUNE, LILEBERE, and WINTRETH, it is added :—"Hæc 3 Maneria erant de Ecclesia Glastingberie, tempore Regis Edwardi." The manors also of STRATONE, and MILLESCOTE *(Fol. 88b)*, in the same county, which are amongst those belonging to the Bishop of Coutance, appear also originally to have been the property of Glastonbury.—*See below, p.* 30, *note* 2.

Fol. {IV b 66 b

VI. TERRA EPISCOPI LISIACENSIS.

Episcopus Lisiacensis[1] tenet *ETONE.* Levenot tenuit tempore Regis Edwardi, et geldabat pro 2 hidis et 3 virgatis. Terra est 3 carucatæ. De ea, sunt in dominio 2 hidæ, et ibi 1 carucata; et 2 bordarii, et 6 coscez, cum 1 carucata. Ibi molinus, reddens 10 solidos, et 3 acræ prati. Silva 2 quarentenis longa, et tantundem lata. Valuit, et valet, 40 solidos. Turstinus tenet de Episcopo.

Idem Episcopus tenet *SUMREFORD.* Alwardus tenuit tempore Regis Edwardi, et geldabat pro 10 hidis. Terra est 7 carucatæ. De ea, sunt in dominio 5 hidæ, et ibi 3 carucatæ, et 5 servi; et 14 villani, et 8 bordarii, cum 4 carucatis. Ibi molinus, reddens 10 solidos, et 100 acræ prati. Silva 3 quarentenis longa, et 2 quarentenis lata. Valet 7 libras.

VI. LAND OF THE BISHOP OF LISIEUX.

The Bishop of Lisieux holds *ETONE.* Levenot held it the time of King Edward, and it paid geld for 2 hides and 3 virgates. The land is 3 carucates. Of this there are in demesne 2 hides, and there is 1 carucate; and there are 2 bordars, and 6 coscets, with 1 carucate. There is a mill, paying 10 shillings, and 3 acres of meadow. The wood is 2 furlongs long, and as much broad. It was, and is, worth 40 shillings. Turstin holds it of the Bishop.

The same Bishop holds *SUMREFORD.* Alward held it in the time of King Edward, and it paid geld for 10 hides. The land is 7 carucates. Of this, 5 hides are in demesne, and there are 3 carucates, and 5 serfs; and 14 villans, and 8 bordars, with 4 carucates. There is a mill, paying 10 shillings, and 100 acres of meadow. The wood is 3 furlongs long, and 2 furlongs broad. It is worth £7.

Fol. {V a 66 c

VII. TERRA ECCLESIÆ GLASTINGEBERIENSIS.

Ecclesia S. Mariæ Glastingeberiensis[2] tenet *DOBREHAM,* et geldavit, tempore Regis Edwardi, pro 52 hidis. Terra est 30 carucatæ. De hac terra 16 hidæ sunt in dominio, et ibi 4 carucatæ, et 6 servi,

VII. LAND OF THE CHURCH OF GLASTONBURY.

The Church of St. Mary at Glastonbury holds *DOBREHAM,* and, in the time of King Edward, it paid geld for 52 hides. The land is 30 carucates. Of this land 16 hides are in demesne, and there are

---

[1] In the Gloucestershire Domesday *(Fol. 166b.)* under "Redmartone" this same Bishop is called "Gislebertus Episcopus Lisiacensis. In the Exon Domesday he is repeatedly referred to as "Gislebertus de Maminot." He was chaplain, and one of the physicians, to the Conqueror. On the decease of Hugh de Eu, son of the Earl of Auge, who died whilst engaged in a visitation of his diocese in 1077, Gilbert de Maminot succeeded to the Bishopric of Lisieux. He assisted at the Council of Rouen in 1096, and died in 1101. *Ellis* i. 424.

[2] This was the Benedictine Abbey at Glastonbury, in Somerset. One of the most ancient churches in Britain is said to have been erected here. As early as A.D. 435, there was a religious house in this place. At the close of the seventh century it was liberally endowed by Ina, King of Wessex, and its revenues were afterwards increased by Edmund the Elder, and other Saxon kings and nobles. In the year 954, the celebrated Dunstan, afterwards Archbishop of Canterbury, was its abbot, and by him Benedictine monks were introduced, and the rules of their order adopted in the monastery. The principal estate in South Wilts belonging to Glastonbury was at Damerham, where the Lordship of the Hundred was vested in the abbot. In the course of years their estates in North Wilts, which, at the time of Domesday, were in the old hundreds of Thorngrave and Sterkeley, (those in Thorngrave hundred, being subsequently included in that of Chippenham,) were formed into a separate hundred, which was called North Damerham.—*See Jackson's Aubrey,* 124.

V a 66 c et 38 coliberti. Ibi 14 villani, et 17 bordarii, cum 19 carucatis. Ibi 4 molini, reddentes 20 solidos, et 26 acræ prati. Pastura 3 leucis longa, et una leuca lata. Silva 5 quarentenis longa, et 4 quarentenis lata.

De eadem terra tenet Serlo 5 hidas; uxor Hugonis 3 hidas; Rogerius unam hidam, et 8 acras. Qui tenuerunt, tempore Regis Edwardi, non poterant ab ecclesia separari. Ibi sunt 3 carucatæ et dimidium.

Totum manerium, tempore Regis Edwardi, valebat 36 libras. Modo reddit 61 libras; sed ab hominibus[1] non appreciantur plus quam 45 libris propter confusionem terræ, et propter firmam, quæ nimis est alta. Terra Tainorum valet 7 libras et 15 solidos.

Eadem ecclesia tenet *HANINDONE*, et Robertus de Abbate. Ibi sunt 15 hidæ. Terra est 10 carucatæ. In dominio sunt 3 carucatæ, et 7 servi; et 18 villani, et 10 coscez, cum 6 carucatis. Ibi 2 molini, reddentes 8 solidos, et una domus reddens 5 denarios. Pratum 3 quarentenis longum, et 3 quarentenis latum. Pastura 4 quarentenis longa, et 3 quarentenis lata. In omni valentia valet 15 libras.

De hac eadem terra 3 hidas vendiderat Abbas cuidem Taino, tempore Regis Edwardi, ad ætatem trium hominum, et ipse Abbas habebat inde servitium, et postea debebat redire ad dominium. Ita modo cum aliis 12 hidis sunt.

4 carucates, and 6 serfs, and 38 coliberts. There are 14 villans, and 17 bordars, with 19 carucates. There are 4 mills, paying 20 shillings, and 26 acres of meadow. The pasture is 3 miles long, and one mile broad. The wood is 5 furlongs long, and 4 furlongs broad.

Of the same land Serlo holds 5 hides; the wife of Hugo 3 hides; Roger one hide, and 8 acres. Those who held these lands, in the time of King Edward, could not be separated from the church. There are there 3 carucates and a half.

The whole manor, in the time of King Edward, was worth £36. It now pays £61, but by the assessors the lands are not valued at more than £45, on account of the confusion of the land, and on account of the farm-rent, which is too high. The land of the Thanes is worth £7 15*s.*

The same church holds *HANINDONE*, and Robert holds it of the Abbot. There are 15 hides. The land is 10 carucates. In demesne are 3 carucates, and 7 serfs; and there are 18 villans, and 10 coscets, with 6 carucates. There are 2 mills paying 8 shillings, and one house paying 5 pence. The meadow is 3 furlongs long, and 3 furlongs broad. The pasture is 4 furlongs long, and 3 furlongs broad. Its whole value amounts to £15.

Of this same land the Abbot had sold 3 hides to a certain Thane, in the time of King Edward, for the lives of three men, and the Abbot was to have meanwhile the service due to him [as the chief lord of the fee], and the land was afterwards to return to the demesne. So these three are now [reckoned] with the other 12 hides.

---

[1] By the "Homines" are most probably to be understood the Jurors that were called together in each hundred to give information to the Domesday Commissioners as to the extent and value of the several estates, and on the other points into which it was their duty to enquire. In the introduction to this volume will be found an account of their mode of procedure in compiling materials for this record. By the term "confusionem terræ" is probably meant the inter-mixing of the lands of the various tenants above enumerated, with the land appertaining to the principal manor, which would of course lessen its value to the occupants of the latter.

Fol. { V a / 66 c }

Eadem Ecclesia tenet *DEVREL*. Tempore Regis Edwardi geldavit pro 10 hidis. Terra est 8 carucatæ. De hac terra sunt in dominio 5 hidæ, et ibi 2 carucatæ, et 2 servi. Ibi 10 villani, et 8 coscez, cum 5 carucatis. Ibi molinus, reddens 5 solidos, et una acra prati. Pastura dimidio leucæ longa, et tantundem lata.

De eadem terra tenet unus Tainus hidam et dimidium; nec potuit, neque potest, ab ecclesia hæc terra separari. Valuit mancrium quando Turstinus[1] Abbas recepit, 8 libras; modo 10 libras.

Eadem Ecclesia tenet *CRISTEMELEFORDE*. Tempore Regis Edwardi geldabat pro 20 hidis. Terra est 10 carucatæ. De hac terra 14 hidæ sunt in dominio, et ibi 3 carucatæ, et 2 servi. Ibi 11 villani, et 12 bordarii, et 12 coscez, cum 6 carucatis. Ibi 2 molini, reddentes 40 solidos, et 36 acræ prati. Silva 1 leuca longa, et dimidio leucæ lata. De eadem terra tenet Robertus dimidiam hidam, et Edwardus unam virgatam. Hæc terra Teinlande non poterat ab ecclesia separari, tempore Regis Edwardi.

Totum Manerium valet 10 libras et 10 solidos.

Abbas Glastingeberiensis præstitit 6 acras prati Brictric, tempore Regis Edwardi, in *STANTONE*. Osbernus Gifart tenet modo. Similiter præstitit 4 acras prati, in *LITELTONE*, Alwardo. Goisfridus Episcopus tenet modo. Hæc 10 acræ prati debent jacere in *CRISTEMELEFORDE*.[2]

The same Church holds *DEVREL*. In the time of King Edward it paid geld for 10 hides. The land is 8 carucates. Of this land, 5 hides are in demesne, and there are 2 carucates, and 2 serfs. There are 10 villans, 8 coscets, with 5 carucates. There is a mill, paying 5 shillings, and one acre of meadow. The pasture is half a mile long, and as much broad.

Of this same land a Thane holds one hide and a half; and this land neither could, nor can it now, be separated from the church. The manor, when Abbot Turstin received it, was worth £8; it is now worth £10.

The same church holds *CRISTEMELEFORDE*. In the time of King Edward it paid geld for 20 hides. The land is 10 carucates. Of this land 14 hides are in demesne, and there are 3 carucates, and 2 serfs. There are 11 villans, and 12 bordars, and 12 coscets, with 6 carucates. There are 2 mills, paying 40 shillings, and 36 acres of meadow. The wood is 1 mile long, and half a mile broad. Of this same land Robert holds half a hide, and Edward one virgate. This land being Tain-land could not be separated from the church, in the time of King Edward.

The whole manor is worth £10 10*s*.

The Abbot of Glastonbury granted 6 acres of meadow to Brictric, in the time of King Edward, in *STANTONE*. Osbern Giffard holds them now. In like manner he granted 4 acres of meadow in *LITELTONE* to Alward. Bishop Geoffrey holds them now. These 10 acres ought to be considered as lying in *CRISTEMELEFORDE*.

---

[1] TURSTIN (or THURSTAN), was a Cluniac monk of Caen, in Normandy, who, on the deprivation of Egelnoth, by the Conqueror, was appointed Abbot of Glastonbury in his room. He was a weak, but withal a busy and prodigal man, wasting the revenues of the convent, and perverting its statutes. He so tyrannized over the monks that they refused to obey him. On one occasion he introduced a party of soldiers, for the purpose of compelling their submission, when an unseemly contest took place in the Church, which ended in the death of three of the monks, and the wounding of eighteen others. [*Chron. Sax.* A.D. 1083.] An enquiry taking place as to the cause of the dispute, and the Conqueror finding that the Abbot was alone to blame, Thurstan was removed, and sent back to Caen in banishment. After the Conqueror's death, he again obtained his abbey from William Rufus by the payment of £500 in silver. Many of the monks however left the monastery and did not return till the death of Thurstan, in 1101.—*New Mon.*, i. 3.

[2] According to this passage, the Abbot of Glastonbury, lord of the manor of CHRISTIAN MALFORD, had some small portion of land in the two neighbouring parishes of STANTON [ST. QUINTIN] and LITTLETON [DREW]; which outlying pieces, the Record adds, ought to be reckoned as in Christian Malford. It is probably to this ancient state of things that Aubrey is really

V a 66 c Ipsa Ecclesia tenet *BADEBERIE.* Tempore Regis Edwardi geldabat pro 20 hidis. Terra est 10 carucatæ. De hac terra 13 hidæ et dimidium sunt in dominio, et ibi 3 carucatæ, et 4 servi. Ibi 11 villani, et 10 bordarii, cum 3 carucatis. Ibi molinus, reddens 40 denarios, et 100 acræ prati. Pastura 1 leuca longa, et 3 quarentenis lata. In Crichelade 1 burgensis reddit 5 denarios. Valuit 8 libras; modo 10 libras.

The Church itself holds *BADEBERIE.* In the time of King Edward it paid geld for 20 hides. The land is 10 carucates. Of this land 13 hides and a half are in demesne, and there are 3 carucates, and 4 serfs. There are 11 villans, and 10 bordars, with 3 carucates. There is a mill, paying 40 pence, and 100 acres of meadow. The pasture is 1 mile long, and 3 furlongs broad. In Crichelade one burgess pays 5 pence. It was worth £8; now £10.

Ipsa Ecclesia tenet *MILDENHALLE*, et Edwardus de ea. Hugolinus ante tenuerat. In manu Abbatis erat, tempore Regis Edwardi, et geldabat pro 10 hidis. Terra est 10 carucatæ. De hac terra sunt in dominio 4 hidæ, et ibi 2 carucatæ. Ibi 15 villani, et 5 bordarii, cum 4 carucatis. Ibi molinus, reddens 30 solidos, et 10 acræ prati. Pastura dimidio leucæ longa, et 3 quarentenis lata, et tantundem silvæ.

The Church itself holds *MILDENHALLE*, and Edward holds of it. Hugolin had held it previously. It was in the hand of the Abbot, in the time of King Edward, and paid geld for 10 hides. The land is 10 carucates. Of this land there are in demesne 4 hides, and there are 2 carucates. There are 15 villans, and 5 bordars, with 4 carucates. There is a mill, paying 30 shillings, and 10 acres of meadow. The pasture is half a mile long, and 3 furlongs broad, and there is as much wood.

Valuit 12 libras; modo 18 libras.

It was worth £12; now £18.

Ipsa Ecclesia tenet *WINTREBORNE.* Tempore Regis Edwardi geldabat pro 25 hidis. Terra est 15 carucatæ. De hac terra sunt in dominio 10 hidæ, et ibi 4 carucatæ, et 7 servi. Ibi 17 villani, et 8 bordarii, cum 7 carucatis. Ibi 6 acræ prati, et 100 acræ pasturæ.

The Church itself holds *WINTREBORNE.* In the time of King Edward it paid geld for 25 hides. The land is 15 carucates. Of this land there are in demesne 10 hides, and there are 4 carucates, and 7 serfs. There are 17 villans, and 8 bordars, with 7 carucates. There are 6 acres of meadow, and 100 acres of pasture.

De eadem terra tenet Gislebertus 3 hidas et dimidium. Orgar tenuit, tempore Regis Edwardi, nec potuit ab ecclesia separari.

Of the same land Gilbert holds 3½ hides. Orgar held them in the time of King Edward, and he could not be separated from the church.

Totum manerium valuit 12 libras; modo 20 libras.

The whole manor was worth £12; it is now worth £20.

Ipsa Ecclesia tenet *NITELETONE.* Tempore Regis Edwardi geldabat pro 20 hidis. Terra est 12

The Church itself holds *NITELETONE.* In the time of King Edward it paid geld for 20 hides.

---

alluding when he mentions [*See* "*Jackson's Aubrey*," *p.* 286] that Stanton St. Quintin had some few acres in Christian Malford, belonging formerly to an abbot. Of the two conflicting authorities, Domesday Book is the more likely to be correct, especially as Aubrey has still further confused his story by making the Abbot of *Cirencester* owner of the manor of Stanton, which is not known to have been the case. There is at present no outlying piece of land within the boundaries, either of Christian Malford or Stanton, that belongs to the other parish, nor any land at Littleton Drew that belongs to Christian Malford. See above, p. 27, under the estates of Bishop Geoffrey, [of Coutance]; and in § xlviii, under the lands of Osbern Giffard.

Fol. { V a 66 c } carucatæ. De hac terra sunt in dominio 10 hidæ, et ibi 4 carucatæ, et 2 servi. Ibi 10 villani, et 12 bordarii, cum 6 carucatis. Ibi 3 molini, reddentes 22 solidos et 6 denarios, et 4 acræ prati. Silva dimidio leucæ longa, et 2 quarentenis lata. Valuit 8 libras; modo 13 libras.

The land is 12 carucates, of this land there are in demesne 10 hides, and there are 4 carucates, and 2 serfs. There are 10 villans, and 12 bordars, with 6 carucates. There are 3 mills, paying 22 shillings and sixpence, and 4 acres of meadow. The wood is half a mile long, and 2 furlongs broad. It was worth £8; it is now worth £13.

Fol. { V b 66 d } Ipsa ecclesia tenet *GRETELINTONE.* Tempore Regis Edwardi geldabat pro 30 hidis. Terra est 20 carucatæ. De hac terra sunt in dominio 10 hidæ, et ibi 13 carucatæ, et 2 servi. Ibi 10 villani, et 11 bordarii, cum 7 carucatis. Ibi 10 acræ prati, et 8 acræ pasturæ.

The church itself holds *GRETELINTONE.* In the time of King Edward it paid geld for 30 hides. The land is 20 carucates. Of this land there are in demesne 10 hides, and there are 13 carucates, and 2 serfs. There are 10 villans, and 11 bordars, with 7 carucates. There are 10 acres of meadow, and 8 acres of pasture.

De eadem terra tenet Episcopus Constantiensis 5 hidis, et Urso 4 hidas et dimidium. Qui tenebant, tempore Regis Edwardi, non poterant ab ecclesia separari. Ibi sunt 10 carucatæ.

Of this same land the Bishop of Coutance holds 5 hides, and Urso 4 hides and a half. Those who held them, in the time of King Edward, could not be separated from the church. There are 10 carucates.

Dominium Abbatis valet 12 libras; Episcopi, 7 libras; Ursonis, 40 solidos.

The demesne of the Abbot is worth £12; that of the Bishop, £7; that of Urso, 40 shillings.

Ipsa Ecclesia tenet *LANGHELEI.* Tempore Regis Edwardi geldabat pro 29 hidis. Terra est 16 carucatæ. De hac terra sunt in dominio 11 hidæ, et ibi 4 carucatæ, et 4 servi. Ibi 15 villani, et 5 bordarii, cum 8 carucatis. Ibi 15 acræ prati, et 10 acræ pasturæ. Silva 1 leuca et dimidio longa, et dimidio leucæ lata. In Malmesberie, unus burgensis, reddens 15 denarios, pertinet huic manerio.

The Church itself holds *LANGHELEI.* In the time of King Edward it paid geld for 29 hides. The land is 16 carucates. Of this land there are in demesne 11 hides, and there are 4 carucates, and 4 serfs. There are 15 villans, and 5 bordars, with 8 carucates. There are 15 acres of meadow, and 10 acres of pasture. The wood is one mile and a half long, and half a mile broad. In Malmesbury, one burgess, paying 15 pence, belongs to this manor.

De eadem terra tenet Urso 2 hidas et dimidium; Rogerus 2 hidas una virgata minus; Radulfus hidam et dimidium. Ibi habent 3 carucatas. Qui has terras tenebant, tempore Regis Edwardi, non poterant ab ecclesia separari.

Of the same land Urso holds 2½ hides; Roger, 2 hides all but one virgate; Ralph, a hide and a half. They have there 3 carucates. They who held these lands, in the time of King Edward, could not be separated from the church.

Dominium Abbatis valet 14 libras et 10 solidos; hominum vero 100 solidos. Quando recepit Abbas, valebat 8 libras.

The demesne of the Abbot is worth £14 10*s.*; that of the tenants 100 shillings. When the Abbot received it, it was worth £8.

b 6 d In *LANGEFORD* tenet Abbas ejusdem Ecclesiæ 2 hidas, et Edwardus de eo. Duo Taini tenuerunt de Abbate, tempore Regis Edwardi, et geldabant pro 2 hidis. Terra est 1 carucata et dimidium. In dominio est hida una et 3 virgatæ de hac terra, et ibi 1 carucata, et 2 servi, et 7 bordarii; et 17 acræ prati, et 20 acræ pasturæ. Valuit, et valet, 60 solidos.

In *LANGEFORD* the Abbot of the same Church holds 2 hides, and Edward holds them of him. Two Thanes held them of the Abbot, in the time of King Edward, and paid geld for 2 hides. The land is 1 carucate and a half. Of this land 1 hide and 3 virgates are in demesne, and there is 1 carucate, and 2 serfs, and 7 bordars; and there are 17 acres of meadow, and 20 acres of pasture. It was, and is, worth 60 shillings.

In eadem villa tenet Edwardus de Rege 1 hidam quæ jure pertinet Abbatiæ ad Tainlande.

In the same vill Edward holds 1 hide of the King, which by right belongs to the Tain-land of the Abbey.

Ipsa Ecclesia tenet *EUNESTETONE*. Tempore Regis Edwardi geldabat pro 10 hidis. Una ex his jacet in Hantescire. Terra est 7 carucatæ. De hac terra sunt in dominio 3 hidæ, et ibi 1 carucata, et 2 servi. Ibi 8 villani, et 5 bordarii, cum 2 carucatis. Ibi 6 acræ prati, et 10 acræ silvæ. Pastura 1 leuca longa, et 3 quarentenis lata.

The Church itself holds *EUNESTETONE*. In the time of King Edward it paid geld for 10 hides. One of these lies in Hampshire. The land is 7 carucates. Of this land there are in demesne 3 hides, and there is 1 carucate, and 2 serfs. There are 8 villans, and 5 bordars, with 2 carucates. There are 6 acres of meadow, and 10 acres of wood. The pasture is 1 mile long, and 3 furlongs broad.

De eadem terra tenet Hunfridus 2 hidas et dimidium, et ibi habet 1 carucatam, et 4 acras prati, et 20 acras pasturæ. Qui tenebat, tempore Regis Edwardi, non poterat ab ecclesia diverti. Valet 40 solidos.

Of the same land Humphrey holds 2½ hides, and has there 1 carucate, and 4 acres of meadow, and 20 acres of pasture. He who held them, in the time of King Edward, could not be separated from the church. It is worth 40 shillings.

Dominium Abbatis valet 6 libras. Quando recepit, valebat 100 solidos.

The demesne of the Abbot is worth £6. When he received it, it was worth 100 shillings.

Ipsa Ecclesia tenet *WINTREBURNE*. Tempore Regis Edwardi geldabat pro 5 hidis. Terra est 3 carucatæ. De hac terra sunt in dominio 2 hidæ et dimidium, et ibi 1 carucata, et 2 servi. Ibi 6 villani, et 3 bordarii, cum 1 carucata et dimidio. Ibi molinus, reddens 15 solidos; et 6 acræ prati, et 60 acræ pastura. Valuit, et valet, 4 libras.

The Church itself holds *WINTREBURNE*. In the time of King Edward it paid geld for 5 hides. The land is 3 carucates. Of this land there are in demesne 2½ hides, and there is 1 carucate, and 2 serfs. There are 6 villans, and 3 bordars, with 1 carucate and a half. There is a mill, paying 15 shillings; and 6 acres of meadow, and 60 acres of pasture. It was, and is, worth £4.

De his 5 hidis tenet Waleranus unam virgatam terræ, quam testificantur Taini ad ecclesiam debere pertinere, et Abbas calumniatur eam.

Out of these 5 hides Waleran holds 1 virgate of land, which the Thanes allege should belong to the church, and the Abbot claims it.

Fol. { V b / 66 d }

Ipsa Ecclesia tenet *DEVREL*. Tempore Regis Edwardi geldabat pro 10 hidis. Terra est 9 carucatæ. De hac terra sunt in dominio 5 hidæ, et ibi 3 carucatæ, et 2 servi. Ibi 14 villani, et 24 bordarii, et 12 cotarii, cum 6 carucatis. Ibi 3 molini, reddentes 14 solidos et 10 denarios, et 6 acræ prati. Pastura dimidio leucæ longa, et 2 quarentenis lata. Silva 2 leucis longa, et dimidio leucæ lata. De eadem terra tenet unus miles unam hidam et unam virgatam terræ de Abbate. Eisi qui tenuit, tempore Regis Edwardi, non poterat ab ecclesia separari. Totum manerium valet 12 libras.

The Church itself holds *DEVREL*. In the time of King Edward it paid geld for 10 hides. The land is 9 carucates. Of this land there are in demesne 5 hides, and there are 3 carucates, and 2 serfs. There are 14 villans, and 24 bordars, and 12 cottars, with 6 carucates. There are 3 mills, paying 14 shillings and 10 pence, and 6 acres of meadow. The pasture is half a mile long, and 2 furlongs broad. The wood is 2 miles long, and a half a mile broad. Of this same land a "miles" holds 1 hide, and 1 virgate of land of the Abbot. Eisi who held this land, in the time of King Edward, could not be separated from the church. The whole manor is worth £12.

VIII. TERRA ECCLESIÆ MALMESBERIENSIS.

ECCLESIA S. MARIÆ MALMESBERIENSIS[1] tenet *HIWEI*. Tempore Regis Edwardi geldabat pro 11 hidis. Terra est 6 carucatæ. In dominio sunt 3 carucatæ. Ibi 3 villani, et 6 bordarii, et 4 cotarii, cum 1 servo, habentes 3 carucatas. Ibi 15 acræ prati, et totidem acræ pasturæ. Valuit 100 solidos; modo, 8 libras.

Ipsa Ecclesia tenet *DANTESIE*. Tempore Regis Edwardi geldabat pro 10 hidis. Terra est 6 carucatæ. Robertus tenet de Abbate. Alwardus qui tenuit de Abbate, tempore Regis Edwardi, non poterat ab ecclesia separari. In dominio sunt 2 carucatæ, et 2 servi; et 10 villani, et 11 coscez, et 3 cotarii, cum 4 carucatis. Ibi molinus, reddens 20 solidos, et 12 acræ prati. Silva dimidio leucæ longa, et tantundem lata. Valuit, et valet, 6 libras.

VIII. LAND OF THE CHURCH OF MALMESBURY.

THE CHURCH OF ST. MARY AT MALMESBURY holds *HIWEI*. In the time of King Edward it paid geld for 11 hides. The land is 6 carucates. In demesne are 3 carucates. There are 3 villans, and 6 bordars, and 4 cottars, with 1 serf, having 3 carucates. There are 15 acres of meadow, and as many acres of pasture. It was worth 100 shillings; it is now worth £8.

The Church itself holds *DANTESIE*. In the time of King Edward it paid geld for 10 hides. The land is 6 carucates. Robert holds it of the Abbot. Alward, who held it of the Abbot in the time of King Edward, could not be separated from the church. In demesne are 2 carucates, and 2 serfs; and 10 villans, and 11 coscets, and 3 cottars, with 4 carucates. There is a mill, paying 20 shillings, and 12 acres of meadow. The wood is half a mile long, and as much broad. It was, and is, worth £6.

[1] The Monastery at MALMESBURY is said to have been founded by Maildulf, about the middle of the seventh century. It owed its permanent establishment however to Aldhelm, the successor to Maildulf, and afterwards first Bishop of Sherborne. A series of papers on Malmesbury will be found in Vol. viii. of the Wilts Archæol. Mag. Some few years ago, a valuable essay by J. Y. Akerman, Esq., on the "Possessions of Malmesbury Abbey" was published in Vol. xxxvii of the "Archæologia."

VI a 67 a Ipsa Ecclesia tenet *SUMREFORD*, et Gunfridus de Abbate. Tempore Regis Edwardi geldabat pro 5 hidis. Alwardus qui tenuit tempore Regis Edwardi non poterat ab ecclesia separari. Terra est 6 carucatæ. De hac terra sunt 2 hidæ in dominio, et ibi 3 carucatæ. Ibi 7 villani, et 5 bordarii, et 12 coscez, et 3 servi, habentes 4 carucatas. Ibi molinus, reddens 20 solidos, et 40 acræ prati, et 8 acræ silvæ. Ad Malmesberie unus burgensis reddit 12 denarios. Valuit 60 solidos; modo 100 solidos.

The Church itself holds *SUMREFORD*, and Gunfrid holds it of the Abbot. In the time of King Edward it paid geld for 5 hides. Alward who held it in the time of King Edward could not be separated from the church. The land is 6 carucates. Of this land there are 2 hides in demesne, and there are 3 carucates. There are 7 villans, and 5 bordars, and 12 coscets, and 3 serfs, having 4 carucates. There is a mill, paying 20 shillings, and 40 acres of meadow, and 8 acres of wood. At Malmesbury a burgess pays 12 pence. It was worth 60 shillings; it is now worth 100 shillings.

Ipsa Ecclesia tenet *BRECHEORDE*. Tempore Regis Edwardi geldabat pro 5 hidis. Terra est 8 carucatæ. De hac terra in dominio est una hida, et ibi 2 carucatæ, et 3 servi. Ibi 9 villani, et 13 coscez, et 18 cotarii, cum 6 carucatis. Ibi 12 acræ prati. Silva 2 quarentenis longa, et una quarentena lata. De eadem terra tenet unus miles 1 hidam. Valuit, et valet, 4 libras. Terra militis 15 solidos.

The Church itself holds *BRECHEORDE*. In the time of King Edward it paid geld for 5 hides. The land is 8 carucates. Of this land there is one hide in demesne, and therein are 2 carucates, and 3 serfs. There are 9 villans, and 13 coscets, and 18 cottars, with 6 carucates. There are 12 acres of meadow. The wood is 2 furlongs long, and one furlong broad. Of the same land a "miles"[1] holds 1 hide. The principal estate was, and is, worth £4. The land of the "miles"[1] is worth 15 shillings.

Ipsa Ecclesia tenet *NORTONE*. Tempore Regis Edwardi geldabat pro 5 hidis. Terra est 8 carucatæ. De hac terra sunt in dominio 2 hidæ et dimidium, et ibi 2 carucatæ, et 5 servi. Ibi 7 villani, et 3 coscez, cum 3 carucatis. Ibi molinus, reddens 15 solidos, et 6 acræ prati. Pastura 2 quarentenis longa, et una quarentena lata. Valuit 6 libras; modo 4 libras.

The Church itself holds *NORTONE*. In the time of King Edward it paid geld for 5 hides. The land is 8 carucates. Of this land there are in demesne 2½ hides, and there are 2 carucates, and 5 serfs. There are 7 villans, and 3 coscets, with 3 carucates. There is a mill, paying 15 shillings, and 6 acres of meadow. The pasture is 2 furlongs long, and 1 furlong broad. It was worth £6; it is now worth £4.

Ipsa Ecclesia tenet *BROCHENEBERGE*. Tempore Regis Edwardi geldavit pro 50 hidis. Terra est 60 carucatæ. De hac terra sunt in dominio 8 hidæ, et ibi 5 carucatæ, et 16 servi. Ibi 64 villani, et 7 cotarii, et 15 coscez, habentes 59 carucatas. Ibi 8 molini, reddentes 6 libras et 12 solidos et 6 denarios, et 50 acræ prati, et 30 acræ pasturæ. Silva 3 leucis longa, et 2 leucis lata.

The Church itself holds *BROCHENEBERGE*. In the time of King Edward it paid geld for 50 hides. The land is 60 carucates. Of this land there are in demesne 8 hides, and there are 5 carucates, and 16 serfs. There are 64 villans, and 7 cottars, and 16 coscets, having 59 carucates. There are 8 mills, paying £6 12*s.* 6*d.*, and 50 acres of meadow, and 30 acres pasture. The wood is 3 miles long, and 2 miles broad.

De eadem terra tenet Ranulfus Flambard in *CORSTONE* 6 hidas. Terra 5 carucatæ. Ibi habet 2 carucatas, et 2 villanos, et 2 coscez, et 2

Of the same land Ranulf Flambard holds in *CORSTONE* 6 hides. The land is 5 carucates. He has there 2 carucates and 2 villans, and 2 coscets,

[1] On the meaning of the word "Miles" see a note on *p.* 22.

Fol. { VI a / 67 a } servos cum 1 carucata; et molinum de 12 solidis et 6 denariis, et 10 acras prati, et 15 acras pasturæ, et silvam 3 quarentenis longam, et una quarentena latam.

De eadem etiam terra tenet Robertus 3 hidas et dimidium; Willelmus 2 hidas; una Anglica mulier 1 hidam. Qui has terras tenuerunt, tempore Regis Edwardi, non poterant ab ecclesia separari.

De dominio monachorum, et terra villanorum, tenent 2 milites 3 hidas et dimidium.

Dominium Abbatis, quando recepit, valebat 26 libras; modo 30 libras. Quod Ranulfus et alii tenent, valet 11 libras et 4 solidos.

Ipsa Ecclesia tenet *CHEMELE.* Tempore Regis Edwardi geldabat pro 30 hidis. Terra est 30 carucatæ. De hac terra sunt in dominio 12 hidæ, et ibi 2 carucatæ, et 6 servi. Ibi 30 villani, et 15 coscez, cum 18 carucatis. Ibi 2 molini, reddentes 15 solidos, et 40 acræ prati. Silva una leuca longa, et 3 quarentenis lata.

De eadem terra tenet Tovi 2 hidas et unam virgatam terræ, et Willelmus 4 hidas, in *CELEORDE.* Qui tenebant, tempore Regis Edwardi, non poterant ab ecclesia separari. Ibi sunt 2 carucatæ, et 6 servi, et 6 bordarii, et molinus de 10 solidis, et 8 acræ prati.

De terra villanorum tenet Anschitil 1 hidam.

Dominium Abbatis valet 13 libras. Quando recepit valebat 10 libras. Quod homines tenent valet 8 libras.

Ipsa Ecclesia tenet *NEWENTONE.* Tempore Regis Edwardi geldabat pro 30 hidis. Terra est 23 carucatæ. De hac terra sunt in dominio 15 hidæ, et ibi 4 carucatæ, et 4 servi. Ibi 19 villani, et 5 cotarii, et 2 coscez, cum 9 carucatis. Ibi 2 molini, reddentes 30 solidos, et 18 acræ prati, et 80 acræ pasturæ.

and 2 serfs, with 1 carucate; and a mill of the value of 12 shillings and 6 pence, and 10 acres of meadow, and 15 acres of pasture, and a wood 3 furlongs long, and 1 furlong broad.

Of this same land also Robert holds 3½ hides; William has 2 hides; an Englishwoman 1 hide. They who held these lands, in the time of King Edward, could not be separated from the church.

Of the demesne of the monks, and of the land of the villans, two "milites" hold 3½ hides.

The demesne of the Abbot, when he received it, was worth £26; it is now worth £30. What Ranulf and the others hold, is worth £11 4*s*.

The Church itself holds *CHEMELE.* In the time of King Edward it paid geld for 30 hides. The land is 30 carucates. Of this land there are in demesne 12 hides, and there are 2 carucates, and 6 serfs. There are 30 villans, and 15 coscets, with 18 carucates. There are 2 mills, paying 15 shillings, and 40 acres of meadow. The wood is 1 mile long, and 3 furlongs broad.

Of the same land Tovi holds 2 hides and one virgate of land, and William 4 hides, in *CELEORDE.* They who held them, in the time of King Edward, could not be separated from the church. There are 2 carucates, and 6 serfs, and 6 bordars, and a mill paying 10 shillings, and 8 acres of meadow.

Of the land of the villans Anschitil holds 1 hide.

The demesne of the Abbot is worth £13. When he received it, it was worth £10. What the vassals hold is worth £8.

The Church itself holds *NEWENTONE.* In the time of King Edward it paid geld for 30 hides. The land is 23 carucates. Of this land there are in demesne 15 hides, and there are 4 carucates, and 4 serfs. There are 19 villans, and 5 cottars, and 2 coscets, with 9 carucates. There are 2 mills, paying 30 shillings, and 18 acres of meadow, and 80 acres of pasture.

VI a 67 a De eadem terra tenet Osbernus 3 hidas, et Willelmus 2 hidas. Ibi habent 6 carucatas. De terra villanorum dedit Abbas cuidam militi suo 1 hidam. Quando Abbas recepit valebat 10 libras; dominium ejus modo valet 12 libras. Quod homines tenent valet 6 libras.

Of the same land Osbern holds 3 hides, and William 2 hides. They have there 6 carucates. Of the land of the villans the Abbot gave 1 hide to one of his own retainers. When the Abbot received the estate it was worth £10; his demesne is now worth £12. What the vassals hold is worth £6.

Ipsa Ecclesia tenet *CERLETONE*. Tempore Regis Edwardi geldabat pro 20 hidis. Terra est 13 carucatæ. De hac terra, 12 hidæ sunt in dominio, et ibi 2 carucatæ, et 7 servi. Ibi 23 villani, et 13 cotarii, et 2 coscez, cum 5 carucatis. Ibi molinus, reddens 15 solidos, et 12 acræ prati, et 15 acræ pasturæ. Silva 2 quarentenis longa, et una quarentena lata.

The Church itself holds *CERLETONE*. In the time of King Edward it paid geld for 20 hides. The land is 13 carucates. Of this land, 12 hides are in demesne, and there are 2 carucates and 7 serfs. There are 23 villans, and 13 cottars, and 2 coscets, with 5 carucates. There is a mill paying 15 shillings, and 12 acres of meadow, and 15 acres of pasture. The wood is 2 furlongs long, and 1 furlong broad.

De eadem terra tenet R. Flambard unam hidam
VI b 67 b et dimidium, et ibi habet 1 carucatam et dimidium. De terra villanorum tenet Radulfus hidam et dimidium, et ibi habet 1 carucatam. Quando Abbas manerium recepit valebat 8 libras; modo dominium ejus tantundem valet. Quod homines tenent valet 40 solidos.

Of the same land R. Flambard holds one hide and a half, and has there one carucate and a half. Of the land of the villans Radulf has one hide and a half, and has there 1 carucate. When the Abbot received the manor, it was worth £8; his demesne is worth as much now. What the vassals hold is worth 40 shillings.

Ipsa Ecclesia tenet *GARDONE*. Ulveva tenuit tempore Regis Edwardi, et geldabat pro 3 hidis. Terra est 6 carucatæ. De hac terra in dominio est una hida et dimidium, et ibi 2 carucatæ, et 6 servi. Ibi 5 villani, et 5 coscez, cum 3 carucatis. Ibi 2 molini, reddentes 25 solidos, et 10 acræ prati, et 10 acræ pasturæ. Silva dimidio leucæ longa, et 2 quarentenis lata; et unus burgensis reddit 3 solidos. Valuit 60 solidos; modo 100 solidos.

The Church itself holds *GARDONE*. Ulveva held it in the time of King Edward, and it paid geld for 3 hides. The land is 6 carucates. Of this land there is in demesne one hide and a half, and there are 2 carucates, and 6 serfs. There are 5 villans and 5 coscets, with 3 carucates. There are 2 mills, paying 25 shillings, and 10 acres of meadow, and 10 acres of pasture. The wood is half a mile long, and 2 furlongs broad; and one burgess pays 3 shillings. It was worth 60 shillings, it is now worth 100 shillings.

Ipsa Ecclesia tenet *CREDVELLE*. Tempore Regis Edwardi geldabat pro 40 hidis. Terra est 25 carucatæ. De hac terra sunt in dominio 18 hidæ, et ibi 4 carucatæ, et 5 servi. Ibi 48 villani, et 24 bordarii, et 10 cotarii, et 7 coliberti, cum 18 carucatis. Ibi 24 acræ prati. Silva 2 leucis longa, et tantundem lata. Valuit, et valet, 16 libras.

The Church itself holds *CREDVELLE*. In the time of King Edward it paid geld for 40 hides. The land is 25 carucates. Of this land there are in demesne 18 hides, and there are 4 carucates, and 5 serfs. There are 48 villans, and 24 bordars, and 10 cottars, and 7 coliberts, with 18 carucates. There are 24 acres of meadow. The wood is 2 miles long, and as much broad. It was, and is, worth £16.

De eadem terra tenet Ebrardus 3 hidas, et ibi habet 3 carucatas, et 7 villanos, cum 1 bordario, et 5

Of the same land Ebrard has 3 hides, and he has there 3 carucates, and 7 villans, with 1 bordar, and

Fol. { VI b / 67 b } servis, et 1 carucata. Guerlinus qui tenuit tempore Regis Edwardi ab ecclesia non poterat separari. Valet 4 libras. Ibi 9 acræ prati.

5 serfs, and one carucate. Guerlin who held this land in the time of King Edward could not be separated from the church. It is worth £4. There are 9 acres of meadow.

Ipsa Ecclesia tenet *BREME.* Tempore Regis Edwardi geldabat pro 38 hidis. Terra est 30 carucatæ. De hac terra sunt in dominio 17 hidæ, et ibi 7 carucatæ, et 12 servi. Ibi 32 villani, et 13 bordarii, cum 20 carucatis. Ibi 2 molini, reddentes 30 solidos, et 12 acræ prati. Silva 2 leucis longa, et 2 quarentenis lata. Valuit 14 libras quando Abbas recepit; modo 16 libras.

The Church itself holds *BREME.* In the time of King Edward it paid geld for 38 hides. The land is 30 carucates. Of this land there are in demesne 17 hides, and there are 7 carucates, and 12 serfs. There are 32 villans, and 13 bordars, with 20 carucates. There are 2 mills, paying 30 shillings, and 12 acres of meadow. The wood is 2 miles long, and 2 furlongs broad. It was worth £14 when the Abbot received it; it is now worth £16.

De eadem terra tenet Edwardus 4 hidas, et Teodricus 4 hidas. Terra est 7 carucatæ; et totidem carucatæ ibi sunt, et 2 villani, et 9 bordarii, et 7 cotarii, et 4 servi. Ibi molinus inter eos de 16 solidis, et 10 acræ prati, et 4 acræ spineti,[1] et silvæ una quarentena longitudine, et tantundem latitudine. Valet 100 solidos utrumque. Qui tenebant has 8 hidas, tempore Regis Edwardi, ab ecclesia non poterant separari.

Of the same land Edward holds 4 hides, and Teodric 4 hides. The land is 7 carucates, and there are as many carucates there, and 2 villans, and 9 bordars, and 7 cottars, and 4 serfs. There is a mill between them worth 16 shillings, and 10 acres of meadow, and 4 acres of bramble-wood, and of wood one furlong in length and as much in breadth. Either of these holdings is worth 100 shillings. They who held these 8 hides, in the time of King Edward, could not be separated from the church.

De terra villanorum tenet idem Teodricus 1 hidam quam dedit ei Abbas. De eadem etiam tenet Edwardus 2 hidas de Rege, et Gislebertus de eo. Has abstulit de dominio ecclesiæ quidam Abbas Anglicus, et dedit cuidam proposito, et postea uni Taino, qui nullo modo separari poterat ab ecclesia. Valet 40 solidos per annum.

Of the land of the villans the same Teodric holds 1 hide, which the Abbot gave him. Of the same land also Edward holds 2 hides of the King, and Gilbert holds them of him. These a certain English Abbot took away from the demesne of the Church and gave to a certain bailiff, and afterwards to a Thane, who could by no means be separated from the church. It is worth 40 shillings by the year.

Willelmus quoque de Ow tenet de eadem terra unam hidam quam præstitit Abbas Alestano tempore Regis Edwardi. Valet 6 solidos.

William de Ow also holds 1 hide of the same land which the Abbot granted to Alestan in the time of King Edward. It is worth 6 shillings.

---

[1] This description would seem to give us the key to the etymology of the word which is now commonly spelt BREMHILL. This is however a comparatively modern corruption, an older form being BREMELE or BREMEL, and in more recent times BREMBLE, which is clearly derived from the Anglo-Saxon word "*bremel*," or "*brembel*," a brier, or *bramble*. In like manner BREMILHAM was originally BREMEL-HAM; and BRAM-SHAW is the contracted form of *Bremel-sceaga*, i.e., literally, "*thorn-wood*" or "*bramble-wood*." It may be added that there is "*Brimble* Farm" not far from Maiden Bradley, and that two of the neighbouring hundreds to that in which Bremhill is situated, were, in olden times, called "THORN-HILL," and "THORN-GRAVE" respectively.

VI b
67 b
Ipsa Ecclesia tenet *PIRITONE.* Tempore Regis Edwardi geldabat pro 35 hidis. Terra est 24 carucatæ. De hac terra sunt in dominio 21 hidæ et dimidium, et ibi 2 carucatæ, et 5 servi. Ibi 20 villani, et 12 bordarii, et 13 cotarii, cum 19 carucatis. Ibi molinus, de 5 solidis, et 60 acræ prati. Silva 2 leucis longa, et tantundem lata.

In Crichelade unus burgensis, reddens 6 denarios, pertinet huic manerio. Valuit, et valet, 16 libras.

The Church itself holds *PIRITONE.* In the time of King Edward it paid geld for 35 hides. The land is 24 carucates. Of this land 21½ hides are in demesne, and there are 2 carucates, and 5 serfs. There are 20 villans, and 12 bordars, and 13 cottars, with 19 carucates. There is a mill worth 5 shillings, and 60 acres of meadow. The wood is 2 miles long, and as much broad.

In Cricklade a burgess, paying 6 pence, belongs to this manor. The whole estate was, and is, worth £16.

IX. QUOD HABET SANCTUS PETRUS WESTMONASTERIENSIS.

Ecclesia S. Petri Westmonasteriensis[1] tenet ecclesiam de *CRICHELADE,* et habet ibi plures burgenses, et tertium denarium ejusdem villæ. Totum simul reddit 9 libras.

IX. WHAT THE CHURCH OF ST. PETER AT WESTMINSTER HOLDS.

The Church of St. Peter at Westminster holds the church of *CRICHELADE,* and has there many burgesses, and the third penny of the same vill. The whole together pays £9.

X. TERRA ABBATIÆ SANCTI PETRI WINTONIENSIS.

Ecclesia S. Petri Wintoniensis[2] tenet *MANEFORDE.* Tempore Regis Edwardi geldavit pro 10 hidis. Terra est 10 carucatæ. De hac terra sunt in

X. LAND OF THE ABBEY OF ST. PETER AT WINCHESTER.

The Church of St. Peter at Winchester holds *MANEFORDE.* In the time of King Edward it paid geld for 10 hides. The land is 10 carucates.

[1] A church, dedicated to St. Peter, was built at Westminster, on the ruins of an older church, by Sebert, king of the East Saxons, about the year A.D. 610, at the instigation of Mellitus, Bishop of London, and the encouragement of Ethelbert, king of Kent. This church having been destroyed in the Danish wars, a new one was erected on the same site by King Edgar, and Dunstan, then Bishop of London, in the year A.D. 958. In connection with this church, or minster, a foundation for twelve monks was formed, though the provision for them was but slender. See Leland's Collect. ii. 250. About a hundred years afterwards, Edward the Confessor began to re-build the church, which he completed and endowed before the year A.D. 1066. Monks of the Benedictine order were then established here. *Leland's Collect.* iii., 72.

[2] This was the Benedictine Monastery called Hyde Abbey or, as in ancient times, New Minster. It was originally situated within the precincts of the cemetery on the north side of the Cathedral, at Winchester. After having stood there for two hundred years it was removed to a spot called Hyde without the city walls.

This monastery seems to have been projected by King Alfred.

Fol. { VI b / 67 b } dominio 5 hidæ et dimidium virgatæ terræ, et ibi 2 carucatæ, et 5 servi. Ibi 8 villani, et 7 coscez, cum 2 carucatis et dimidio. Ibi molinus, de 12 solidis et 6 denariis, et 10 acræ prati. Pastura 4 quarentenis longa, et una quarentena lata. Valuit 6 libras; modo 8 libras.

Of this land there are in demesne 5 hides, and half a virgate of land, and there are 2 carucates, and 5 serfs. There are 8 villans, and 7 coscets, with 2½ carucates. There is a mill, worth 12 shillings and 6 pence, and 10 acres of meadow. The pasture is 4 furlongs long, and 1 furlong broad. It was worth £6; it is now worth £8.

Ipsa Ecclesia tenet *COLEBURNE.* Tempore Regis Edwardi geldabat pro 50 hidis. Terra est 32 carucatæ. De hac terra sunt in dominio 10 hidæ, et ibi 4 carucatæ, et 13 servi. Ibi 40 villani, et 13 coscez, cum 15 carucatis. Ibi 2 acræ prati. Silva una leuca longa, et dimidio leucæ lata, et tantundem pasturæ.

The Church itself holds *COLEBURNE.* In the time of King Edward it paid geld for 50 hides. The land is 32 carucates. Of this land there are in demesne 10 hides, and there are 4 carucates, and 13 serfs. There are 40 villans, and 13 coscets, with 15 carucates. There are 2 acres of meadow. The wood is 1 mile long, and half a mile broad, and there is as much pasture.

De eadem terra tenet Croc de Abbate 10 hidas et dimidium virgatæ terræ; et Fulcredus 2 hidas. Qui tenebant, tempore Regis Edwardi, ab ecclesia non poterant separari. Ibi sunt 8 carucatæ. De Tainlande habet Abbas in suo dominio 1 hidam.

Of the same land Croc holds under the Abbot 10 hides and half a virgate of land; and Fulcred, 2 hides. Those who held these lands, in the time of King Edward, could not be separated from the church. There are 8 carucates. Of Thane-land the Abbot has, in his demesne, 1 hide.

Dominium Abbatis totum valet modo 28 libras. Quod homines tenent valet 12 libras. Quando recepit minus valebat 100 solidos.

The whole demesne of the Abbot is now worth £28. What the vassals hold is worth £12. When the Abbot received this estate it was worth less by 100 shillings.

Fol. { VII a / 67 c } Ipsa Ecclesia tenet *PEVESIE.* Tempore Regis Edwardi geldabat pro 30 hidis. Terra est 24 carucatæ. De hac terra sunt in dominio 6 hidæ et una virgata terræ, et ibi 3 carucatæ, et 6 servi. Ibi 46 villani, et 24 coscez, et unus bordarius, cum 18 carucatis. Ibi 7 molini, reddentes 4 libras et 5 solidos, et 15 acræ prati. Pastura una leuca longa, et tantundem lata. Silva 3 quarentenis longa, et dimidio quarentenæ lata.

The Church itself holds *PEVESIE.* In the time of King Edward it paid geld for 30 hides. The land is 24 carucates. Of this land there are in demesne 6 hides and 1 virgate of land, and there are 3 carucates, and 6 serfs. There are 46 villans, and 24 coscets, and 1 bordar, with 18 carucates. There are 7 mills, paying £4 5s., and 15 acres of meadow. The pasture is 1 mile long, and as much broad. The wood is 3 furlongs long, and half a furlong broad.

It was finished by Edward the Elder (the son of Alfred) in 903, that King placing therein secular canons, and the church being consecrated by Archbishop Plegmund. In the year 959 a number of Benedictine monks, from Abingdon in Berkshire, were placed in the stead of the secular canons, and the monastery was freshly endowed by King Edgar, who also furnished it with the new code of statutes.

At the time of the Norman invasion, Alwy, brother to Earl Godwin, was abbot of this monastery. He accompanied his nephew Harold to the field of Hastings, and was there slain with twelve monks and twenty soldiers. Hence William the Conqueror, it is said, felt especial anger against the inmates of Hyde Abbey, and confiscated many of their estates. *New Monast.* ii., 428–434.

VII a
67 c De eadem terra tenet unus Tainus 2 hidas una virgata minus, et non poterat ab ecclesia separari; et Ernulfus de Hesding 2 hidas tenet de Rege, quas Abbas dedit uni Taino tempore Regis Edwardi, qui tamen non poterat ab ecclesia separari. Valet 30 solidos.

Dominium Abbatis valuit 26 libras. Modo valet 28 libras.

Ipsa Ecclesia tenet in *WINTREBURNE* 2 hidas. Terra est 2 carucatæ. De hac terra in dominio est una hida; et 1 carucata, et 3 servi. Ibi unus villanus, et 4 bordarii, cum 1 carucata; et 4 acræ prati, et 60 acræ pasturæ. Valuit 10 solidos; modo 40 solidos.

Ipsa Ecclesia tenet *CHISELDENE*. Tempore Regis Edwardi geldabat pro 40 hidis. Terra est 22 carucatæ. De hac terra sunt in dominio 17 hidæ, et 5 carucatæ, et 6 servi. Ibi 45 villani, et 13 bordarii, cum 10 carucatis. Ibi molinus, reddens 40 denarios, et 40 acræ prati. Pastura dimidio leucæ longa, et 4 quarentenis lata. Silva 3 quarentenis longa, et 2 quarentenis lata. Valuit 18 libras; modo 24 libras.

Huic Manerio pertinent 6 burgenses in Crichelade reddentes 4 solidos et unum denarium.

Of the same land a Thane holds 2 hides all but 1 virgate, and he could not be separated from the church; and Ernulf de Hesding holds 2 hides of the King, which the Abbot gave to a Thane in the time of King Edward, who however could not be separated from the church. It is worth 30 shillings.

The demesne of the Abbot was worth £26. It is now worth £28.

The Church itself holds 2 hides in *WINTREBURNE*. The land is 2 carucates. Of this land there is in demesne 1 hide; and there is 1 carucate, and 3 serfs. There is 1 villan, and 4 bordars, with 1 carucate; and there are 4 acres of meadow, and 60 acres of pasture. It was worth 10 shillings; it is now worth 40 shillings.

The Church itself holds *CHISELDENE*. In the time of King Edward it paid geld for 40 hides. The land is 22 carucates. Of this land there are in demesne 17 hides, and 5 carucates and 6 serfs. There are 45 villans, and 13 bordars, with 10 carucates. There is a mill, paying 40 pence, and 40 acres of meadow. The pasture is half a mile long, and 4 furlongs broad. The wood is 3 furlongs long, and 2 furlongs broad. It was worth £18; it is now worth £24.

To this manor belong 6 burgesses in Cricklade paying 4 shillings and one penny.

XI. TERRA ECCLESIA CRENEBURNENSIS.

Ecclesia S. Mariæ Creneburnensis[1] tenet *ESSITONE*, et tenuit tempore Regis Edwardi, et pro

XI. LAND OF THE CHURCH OF CRANBOURN.

The Church of S. Mary at Cranbourn holds *ESSITONE*, and held it in the time of King Edward,

[1] The Monastery at Cranbourne in Dorsetshire, was founded by one Aylward Mere, or Meaw,—in some accounts it is written Snew. About A.D. 980, Algar, the son of the founder, completed the foundation, and Brictric, his grandson, is also recorded as a benefactor. To his new monastery Aylward annexed the lands and endowments of the ruined priory of Tewkesbury in Gloucestershire, which for more than 100 years was a cell to Cranbourne. Early in the reign of Henry I., Robert Fitz-Haymon, Earl of Gloucester, patron of both monasteries, preferring the situation of Tewkesbury, enlarged its buildings and increased its possessions, and finally, in 1102, removed thither the great body of the monks of Cranbourne, leaving at the latter place a Prior and two monks only as residents. *New Monast.* iv., 466.

Fol. { VII a 67 c } 20 hidis geldavit. Terra est 16 carucatæ. De hac terra sunt in dominio 10 hidæ, et ibi 2 carucatæ, et 5 servi. Ibi 20 villani, et 12 bordarii, et 4 coscez, cum 13 carucatis. Ibi molinus, reddens 5 solidos, et 200 acræ prati. Pastura una leuca longa, et dimidio leucæ lata. Silva habet tantundem. Valuit, et valet, 15 libras.

and it paid geld for 20 hides. The land is 16 carucates. Of this land there are 10 hides in demesne, and there are 2 carucates, and 5 serfs. There are 20 villans, and 12 bordars, and 4 coscets, with 13 carucates. There is a mill, paying 5 shillings, and 200 acres of meadow. The pasture is 1 mile long, and half a mile broad. The wood is of like extent. It was, and is, worth £15.

Ipsa Ecclesia tenet in *DOBREHAM* unam hidam. Terra est 1 carucata et dimidium. Ibi habet Abbas 1 carucatam; et 5 bordarii cum dimidia carucata. Valet 20 solidos.

The Church itself holds 1 hide in *DOBREHAM*. The land is 1 carucate and a half. The Abbot has there 1 carucate; and there are 5 bordars with half a carucate. It is worth 20 shillings.

XII. TERRA ECCLESIÆ SCEPTESBERIENSIS.

XII. LAND OF THE CHURCH OF SHAFTESBURY.

Ecclesia S. Mariæ Sceptesberiensis[1] tenet *BICHENESTOCH*. Turstinus tenet de Abbatissa. Harding tenuit de ecclesia, tempore Regis Edwardi, et geldabat pro 5 hidis. Terra est 5 carucatæ. De hac terra sunt in dominio 3 hidæ, et ibi 2 carucatæ, et 2 servi. Ibi 6 villani, et 6 coscez, cum 3 carucatis. Ibi molinus, reddens 12 solidos, et 28 acræ prati, et 40 acræ pasturæ. Valuit 60 solidos; modo, 100 solidos.

The Church of S. Mary at Shaftesbury holds *BICHENESTOCH*. Turstin holds it of the Abbess. Harding held it of the church, in the time of King Edward, and it paid geld for 5 hides. The land is 5 carucates. Of this land there are 3 hides in demesne, and there are 2 carucates, and 2 serfs. There are 6 villans, and 6 coscets, with 3 carucates. There is a mill, paying 12 shillings, and 28 acres of meadow, and 40 acres of pasture. It was worth 60 shillings. It is now worth 100 shillings.

Hanc terram reddidit sponte sua ecclesiæ Hardingus, qui in vita sua per conventum debebat tenere.

Harding, who by agreement was entitled to hold this land in his own life-time, of his own accord restored it to the church.

Ipsa Ecclesia tenet *TISSEBERIE*. Tempore Regis Edwardi geldabat pro 20 hidis. Terra est 40 carucatæ. De hac terra sunt in dominio 5 hidæ, et

The Church itself holds *TISSEBERIE*. In the time of King Edward it paid geld for 20 hides. The land is 40 carucates. Of this land there are in

[1] The Abbey at Shaftesbury, which eventually became one of the richest and most distinguished in the kingdom, was founded by Alfred the Great, about A.D. 880. Its first Abbess was Ælgiva, the daughter of Alfred. In the seventh volume of the Wiltshire Archæol. Mag., pp. 250–301, are several papers relating to the ancient history of Shaftesbury, and the Wiltshire possessions of the Abbess.

II a ibi 3 carucatæ. Ibi 40 villani, et 50 bordarii, cum
7 c 25 carucatis. Ibi 4 molini, reddentes 35 solidos, et 40 acræ prati. Pastura 1 leuca longa, et dimidio leucæ lata. Silva una leuca longa, et tantundem lata.

De eadem terra tenet de Abbatissa Turstinus 3 hidas; Gunfridus 3 hidas; Albericus 2 hidas. Ibi habent 9 carucatas. Edwardus, vice-comes, habet 3 carucatas in terra villanorum. Dominium Abbatissæ valet 30 libras; militum vero 13 libras.

Ipsa Ecclesia tenet *DUNEHEVE.* Tempore Regis Edwardi geldabat pro 40 hidis. Terra est 32 carucatæ. De hac terra sunt in dominio 12 hidæ, et ibi 2 carucatæ. Ibi 35 villani, et 25 bordarii, cum 25 carucatis. Ibi 8 molini, reddentes 66 solidos et 8 denarios, et 15 acræ prati. Pastura 1 leuca longa, et tantundem lata. Silva 6 quarentenis longa, et 2 quarentenis lata.

De eadem terra tenet Turstinus 6 hidas, et quidam Tainus 1 hidam, et ibi sunt 6 carucatæ. Qui tenebant tempore Regis Edwardi non poterant ab ecclesia separari.

Dominium Abbatissæ valet 22 libras; hominum vero 10 libras; et prius tantundem valuit.

Ipsa Ecclesia tenet *BRADEFORD.* Tempore Regis Edwardi geldabat pro 42 hidis. Terra est 40 carucatæ. De hac terra sunt in dominio 13 hidæ, et ibi 8 carucatæ, et 9 servi, et 18 coliberti. Ibi 36 villani, et 40 bordarii, cum 32 carucatis. Et ibi 22 porcarii, et 33 burgenses, reddentes 35 solidos et 9 denarios, et unus serviens reddens 7 sextaria[1] mellis.

demesne 5 hides, and there are 3 carucates. There are 40 villans, and 50 borders, with 25 carucates. There are 4 mills, paying 35 shillings, and 40 acres of meadow. The pasture is 1 mile long, and half a mile broad. The wood is 1 mile long and as much broad.

Of the same land Turstin holds 3 hides of the Abbess; Gunfrid, 3 hides; Alberic, 2 hides. They have there 9 carucates. Edward, the sheriff, has 3 carucates in the land of the villans. The demesne of the Abbess is worth £30; that which is held by military tenure is worth £13.

The Church itself holds *DUNEHEVE.* In the time of King Edward it paid geld for 40 hides. The land is 32 carucates. Of this land there are 12 hides in demesne, and there are 2 carucates. There are 35 villans, and 25 bordars, with 25 carucates. There are 8 mills, paying 66 shillings and 8 pence, and 15 acres of meadow. The pasture is 1 mile long, and as much broad. The wood is 6 furlongs long, and 2 furlongs broad.

Of the same land Turstin holds 6 hides, and a certain Thane has 1 hide, and there are 6 carucates. Those who held them in the time of King Edward could not be separated from the church.

The demesne of the Abbess is worth £22; that of the vassals is worth £10; and it was of the same value previously.

The Church itself holds *BRADEFORD.* In the time of King Edward it paid geld for 42 hides. The land is 40 carucates. Of this land there are in demesne 13 hides, and there are 8 carucates, and 9 serfs, and 18 coliberts. There are 36 villans, and 40 bordars, with 32 carucates. And there are 22 hog-keepers, and 33 burgesses, paying 35 shillings and

[1] The "Sextary" was a measure of uncertain quantity. In most of the entries in the Survey in which it occurs it is mentioned as a measure of honey, though it was used also for corn or flour. See § xxiv. under the "Rents of Edward of Salisbury." The Gloucester Sextary for honey, in the Conqueror's time, was peculiar to the place; thus at Domesd. I., *fol.* 162, we meet with the expression," "12 sextaria mellis ad mensuram ejusdem burgi." At 'Chenemartune' (Kemerton), in the same county, we have "8 sextaria mellis ad mensuram Regis." Ibid, *fol.* 166. And at Warwick we have, "24 sextaria mellis cum *majori mensura*, . . . sextarium scilicet pro 15 denariis." Ibid. *fol.* 238. Ellis. I., 134.

Fol. { VII a 67 c Ibi 2 molini, reddentes 3 libras. Mercatum reddit 45 solidos. Ibi una arpenna[1] vineæ, et 50 acræ prati. Pastura 11 quarentenis longa, et 3 quarentenis lata. Silva dimidio leucæ longa, et 2 quarentenis lata.

9 pence, and 1 customary tenant paying 7 sextaries of honey. There are 2 mills, paying £3. The market pays 45 shillings. There is an arpen of vineyard, and 50 acres of meadow. The pasture is 11 furlongs long, and 3 furlongs broad. The wood is half a mile long, and 2 furlongs broad.

Fol. { VII b 67 d Ad eundem[2] manerium Bradeford pertinet *ALVESTONE.* Tempore Regis Edwardi geldabat pro 7 hidis, exceptis 42 superioribus hidis. Terra est 6 carucatæ. De hac terra sunt in dominio 4 hidæ, et ibi 3 carucatæ.

To the same manor of Bradeford belongs *ALVESTONE.* In the time of King Edward it paid geld for 7 hides, besides the 42 hides above mentioned. The land is 6 carucates. Of this land there are in demesne 4 hides, and there are 3 carucates.

Totum Bradeford, cum appendicibus, valuit, et valet, 60 libras.

The whole of Bradeford, with its appendages, was and is valued at £60.

Ipsa Ecclesia tenet *LEDENTONE.* Tempore Regis Edwardi geldabat pro 38 hidis. Terra est 16 carucatæ. De hac terra sunt in dominio 24 hidæ, et ibi 4 carucatæ, et 6 servi. Ibi 23 villani, et 17 bordarii, cum 7 carucatis. Ibi 2 molini, reddentes 5 solidos. Pratum 4 quarentenis longum, et 3 quarentenis latum. Pastura dimidio leucæ longa, et 3 quarentenis lata. In Crichelade unus burgensis reddit 6 denarios. Valuit 18 libras; modo 22 libras.

The Church itself holds *LEDENTONE.* In the time of King Edward it paid geld for 38 hides. The land is 16 carucates. Of this land there are in demesne 24 hides, and there are 4 carucates, and 6 serfs. There are 23 villans, and 17 bordars, with 7 carucates. There are 2 mills, paying 5 shillings. The meadow is 4 furlongs long, and 3 furlongs broad. The pasture is half a mile long, and 3 furlongs broad. In Cricklade 1 burgess pays 6 pence. The manor was worth £18; it is now worth £22.

Ipsa Ecclesia tenet *DOMNITONE.* Tempore Regis Edwardi geldabat pro 20 hidis. Terra est 15 carucatæ. De hac terra sunt 7 hidæ et 3 virgatæ terræ in dominio, et ibi 2 carucatæ, et 4 servi. Ibi 21 villani, et 10 bordarii, cum 11 carucatis. Ibi 2 molini, reddentes 12 solidos et 6 denarios, et 20 acræ prati, et totidem acræ silvæ. Pastura 1 leuca longa, et dimidio leucæ lata. Duo burgenses reddunt 10 denarios.

The Church itself holds *DOMNITONE.* In the time of King Edward it paid geld for 20 hides. The land is 15 carucates. Of this land there are 7 hides and 3 virgates of land in demesne, and there are 2 carucates, and 4 serfs. There are 21 villans, and 10 bordars, with 11 carucates. There are 2 mills, paying 12 shillings and 6 pence, and 20 acres of meadow, and as many acres of wood. The pasture is 1 mile long, and half a mile broad. Two burgesses pay 10 pence.

---

[1] The "Arpenna," or "Arpent," is the usual measurement of vineyards in Domesday. It is met with in several entries in Wiltshire, as applied also to measures of wood, and meadow land. See below in § lxviii., under 'Grastone,' and 'Buberge,' and in § l. under 'Scaldeburne, and 'Mertone.' The "arpen" properly signified an acre or furlong of ground. Cowel, however, quotes the Register of Wormsley Priory, in a passage where it seems to be a quantity something less than an acre. No doubt, both in England, as well as in France, the measure of the arpen was various. Sir H. Ellis gives as a quotation from Ducange (voce *Acra*) who derived it from an official and trustworthy source,—"xl. perticæ terræ faciunt virgatam; duæ virgatæ faciunt *Arpentum.*" *Ellis*, I. 117.

[2] *Sic*, in the original.

VIIb 67 d De eadem terra tenet Gunfridus 2 hidas, et ibi habet 2 carucatas. Qui tenuit, tempore Regis Edwardi, non poterat ab ecclesia separari.

Dominium Abbatissæ valuit, et valet 18 libras; Gunfridi, 40 solidos.

Of the same land Gunfrid holds 2 hides, and has there 2 carucates. He who held them in the time of King Edward could not be separated from the church.

The demesne of the Abbess was, and is, worth £18;—that of Gunfrid, 40 shillings.

XIII. TERRA ECCLESIÆ WILTUNIENSIS.

Ecclesia S. Mariæ Wiltuniensis[1] tenet *STANTONE.* Tempore Regis Edwardi geldabat pro 20 hidis. Terra est 12 carucatæ. De hac terra sunt in dominio 10 hidæ, et ibi 4 carucatæ, et ibi 8 servi. Ibi 16 villani, et unus bordarius, et 21 coscez, cum 8 carucatis. Ibi 2 molini, reddentes 12 solidos et 6 denarios, et 60 acræ prati, et 3 acræ alneti. Pastura 1 leuca longa, et dimidio leucæ lata. Valuit 16 libras; modo 24 libras.

Ipsa Ecclesia tenet *NEWETONE.* Tempore Regis Edwardi geldabat pro 13 hidis et dimidio, et dimidio virgatæ terræ. De hac terra sunt in dominio 3 hidæ, et ibi 2 carucatæ, et 4 servi. Ibi 13 villani, et 16 coscez, cum 5 carucatis. Totum manerium possunt arare 10 carucæ. Ibi molinus, reddens 12 solidos et 6 denarios, et 30 acræ prati. Pastura 4 quarentenis longa, et 2 quarentenis lata. Silva 1 leuca longa, et tantundem lata.

XIII. LAND OF THE CHURCH OF WILTON.

The Church of S. Mary at Wilton holds *STANTONE.* In the time of King Edward it paid geld for 20 hides. The land is 12 carucates. Of this land there are 10 hides in demesne, and there are 4 carucates and 8 serfs. There are 16 villans, and 1 bordar, and 21 coscets, with 8 carucates. There are 2 mills paying 12 shillings and 6 pence, and 60 acres of meadow, and 3 acres of alder-wood. The pasture is 1 mile long, and half a mile broad. It was worth £16; it is now worth £24.

The Church itself holds *NEWETONE.* In the time of King Edward it paid geld for 13½ hides and half a virgate of land. Of this land there are in demesne 3 hides, and there are 2 carucates, and 4 serfs. There are 13 villans, and 16 coscets, with 5 carucates. Ten plough-teams could plough the whole manor. There is a mill, paying 12 shillings and 6 pence, and 30 acres of meadow. The pasture is 4 furlongs long, and 2 furlongs broad. The wood is 1 mile long, and as much broad.

---

[1] The first founder of a religious house at Wilton seems to have been Wulstan, who, about the middle of the eighth century, repaired an ancient church of this place dedicated to St. Mary, and having built a chantry in it, placed therein a college of priests. The said Wulstan was married to Elburga, the sister of Egbert, king of Wessex, and by her influence, after her husband's death, that king was persuaded to change it into an abbey, she herself becoming the superior, with twelve nuns under her. It was, however, Alfred the Great that appears to have been the principal founder. At the instigation of his queen, he built a new monastery on the site of his own palace at Wilton, and transferred thither the religious of the old nunnery, adding some twelve or thirteen more to the foundation. Successive kings became benefactors to the abbey, and largely increased its revenues. A metrical chronicle, detailing the life and virtues of St. Editha, a daughter of king Edgar, who was its Abbess towards the close of the tenth century, was printed from the Cotton MS., under the title of "Chronicon Vilodunense," by Sir R. C. Hoare, in 1830. A short time previously he had printed the "Registrum Wiltunense," from the Harl. MS. 436. See '*New Monast.*' ii. 315.

Fol. { VII b / 67 d } De terra villanorum dedit Abbatissa uni militi 3 hidas et dimidium virgatæ terræ. Ibi habet 2 carucatas, et villani ejus 1 carucatam.

Of the land of the villans the Abbess gave to a 'miles' 3 hides and half a virgate of land. He has there 2 carucates, and his villans have 1 carucate.

De eadem terra tenuit Aluric venator de Abbatissa unam hidam et unam virgatam terræ et dimidium, ea conditione, ut post mortem ejus rediret ad ecclesiam, quia de dominica firma erat. Modo tenet Ricardus Sturmid. Totum manerium valuit 14 libras quando recepit; modo 18 libras.

Of the same land, Aluric, the huntsman, held of the Abbess, 1 hide and 1 virgate and a half of land, on the condition, that after his death it should return to the church, because it was part of the demesne farm. Richard Sturmid holds it now. The whole manor was worth £14 when he received it; it is now worth £18.

Ipsa Ecclesia tenet *DARNEFORD.* Tempore Regis Edwardi geldabat pro 4 hidis. Terra est 3 carucatæ. Edwardus tenet de Abbatissa. Tres Angli tenuerunt tempore Regis Edwardi, et non poterant ab ecclesia separari. Duo ex eis reddebant 5 solidos, et tertius serviebat sicut Tainus. Ibi sunt 6 bovatæ in carucata dominica, cum 4 bordariis. Ibi 2 Angli habent 2 carucatas. Ibi molinus, reddens 7 solidos et dimidium, et 12 acræ ibi prati. Pastura 4 quarentenis longa, et una quarentena lata. Valuit 100 solidos; modo 9 libras.

The Church itself holds *DARNEFORD.* In the time of King Edward it paid geld for 4 hides. The land is 3 carucates. Edward holds it of the Abbess. Three Englishmen held it in the time of King Edward, and they could not be separated from the church. Two of them paid 5 shillings, and the third rendered such services as are due from a Thane. There are 6 bovates in the carucate belonging to the demesne, with 4 bordars. Two Englishmen there have 2 carucates. There is a mill, paying 7 shillings and sixpence, and 12 acres of meadow. The pasture is 4 furlongs long, and 1 furlong broad. It was worth 100 shillings; it is now worth £9.

Ipsa Ecclesia tenet *SVALOCLIVE.* Tempore Regis Edwardi geldabat pro 4 hidis, et una virgata. Terra est 2 carucatæ. Ibi est unus villanus, et 2 bordarii, et 2 acræ prati. Valuit, et valet, 40 solidos.

The church itself holds *SVALOCLIVE.* In the time of King Edward it paid geld for 4 hides and 1 virgate. The land is 2 carucates. There is 1 villan, and 2 bordars, and 2 acres of meadow. It was, and is worth, 40 shillings.

Ipsa Ecclesia tenet *CHILMERC.* Tempore Regis Edwardi geldabat pro 20 hidis. Terra est 14 carucatæ. De hac terra sunt in dominio 8 hidæ, et ibi 2 carucatæ. Ibi 15 villani, et 12 bordarii, et 12 coliberti, cum 12 carucatis. Ibi molinus, reddens 10 solidos, et 5 acræ prati, et 10 acræ runceti. Pastura una leuca longa, et dimidio leucæ lata. Valuit 14 libras; modo 15 libras.

The Church itself holds *CHILMERC.* In the time of King Edward it paid geld for 20 hides. The land is 14 carucates. Of this land there are in demesne 8 hides, and there are 2 carucates. There are 15 villans, and 12 bordars, and 12 coliberts, with 12 carucates. There is a mill, paying 10 shillings, and 5 acres of meadow, and 10 acres of thorns. The pasture is 1 mile long, and half a mile broad. It was worth £14; it is now worth £15.

Ipsa Ecclesia tenet unam hidam terra in *WERDORE,* et Britmarus de Abbatissa tenet. Terra est 1 carucata. Ipsa est ibi, cum 4 bordariis,

The Church itself holds 1 hide of land in *WERDORE,* and Britmar holds it of the Abbess. The land is 1 carucate. It is there, with 4 bordars,

VIII a 68 a et 3 acris prati. Pastura 1 leuca longa, et dimidio leucæ lata. Silva 2 quarentenis longa, et una quarentena lata. Valet 20 solidos.

Ipsa Ecclesia tenet *CHENVEL*. Tempore Regis Edwardi, [geldabat] pro 10 hidis. Terra est 7 carucatæ. De hac terra sunt in dominio 4 hidæ et dimidium, et 3 servi. Ibi 11 villani, et 9 coscez, cum 5 carucatis. Ibi 5 acræ prati, et pastura dimidio leucæ longa, et 3 quarentenis lata. Silva dimidio leucæ longa, et tantundem lata. Valuit 6 libras; modo 8 libras.

Ipsa Ecclesia tenet *OVRETONE*. Tempore Regis Edwardi geldabat pro 10 hidis. Terra est 4 carucatæ. De hac terra sunt in dominio 7 hidæ et dimidium virgatæ terræ, et ibi 2 carucatæ, et 2 servi. Ibi 3 villani, et 8 bordarii, cum 2 carucatis. Ibi molinus, reddens 10 solidos, et 5 acræ prati, et 20 acræ pasturæ, et 20 acræ silvæ. Valet 100 solidos.

Ipsa Ecclesia tenet *CHELCHE*. Tempore Regis Edwardi geldabat pro 77 hidis. Terra est 66 carucatæ. De hac terra sunt in dominio 10 hidæ, et ibi 10 carucatæ, et 20 servi. Ibi 86 villani, et 50 bordarii, et 10 coliberti, habentes 50 carucatas. Ibi 5 molini, reddentes 65 solidos, et 12 acræ prati. Pastura 3 leucis longa, et una leuca lata, et tantundem silvæ.

De eadem terra tenet Girardus 3 hidas. Qui tenebat, tempore Regis Edwardi, non poterat ab ecclesia separari. Ibi sunt 2 carucatæ. Valent 3 libras.

Dominium Abbatissæ valet 67 libras.

De eadem terra tenet Ricardus Poingiant 7 hidas et dimidium de rege. Ex his, 2 hidas tenebat Aileva, tempore Regis Edwardi, et alias tenebant homines ecclesiæ servientes sicut villani. Abbatissa calum-

and 3 acres of meadow. The pasture is 1 mile long, and half a mile broad. The wood is 2 furlongs long, and 1 furlong broad. It is worth 20 shillings.

The Church itself holds *CHENVEL*. In the time of King Edward [it paid geld] for 10 hides. The land is 7 carucates. Of this land there are in demesne 4½ hides, and 3 serfs. There are 11 villans, and 9 coscets, with 5 carucates. There are 5 acres of meadow, and the pasture is half a mile long, and 3 furlongs broad. The wood is half a mile long, and as much broad. It was worth £6; it is now worth £8.

The Church itself holds *OVRETONE*. In the time of King Edward it paid geld for 10 hides. The land is 4 carucates. Of this land there are in demesne 7 hides and half a virgate of land, and therein are 2 carucates, and 2 serfs. There are 3 villans, and 8 bordars, with 2 carucates. There is a mill, paying 10 shillings, and 5 acres of meadow, and 20 acres of pasture, and 20 acres of wood. It is worth 100 shillings.

The Church itself holds *CHELCHE*. In the time of King Edward it paid geld for 77 hides. The land is 66 carucates. Of this land there are in demesne 10 hides, and therein are 10 carucates, and 20 serfs. There are 86 villans, and 50 bordars, and 10 coliberts, having 50 carucates. There are 5 mills, paying 65 shillings, and 12 acres of meadow. The pasture is 3 miles long, and 1 mile broad, and there is as much wood.

Of the same land Girard holds 3 hides. He who held them, in the time of King Edward, could not be separated from the church. There are 2 carucates. They are worth £3.

The demesne of the Abbess is worth £67.

Of the same land Richard Poingiant holds 7 hides and a half of the king. Of these, Aileva held 2 hides, in the time of King Edward, and the vassals of the church held the others, rendering

Fol. { VIII a / 68 a } niatur. Ibi habet Ricardus 5 carucatas, et valent 7 libras.

Ipsa Ecclesia tenet *NEWENTONE.* Tempore Regis Edwardi geldabat pro 19 hidis et 3 virgatis terræ. Terra est 14 carucatæ. De hac terra sunt in dominio 2 hidæ, et ibi 2 carucatæ, et 6 coliberti. Ibi 20 villani, et 16 bordarii, cum 12 carucatis. Ibi 2 molini, reddentes 40 solidos, et 20 acræ prati, et 150 acræ pasturæ, et 200 acræ silvæ. Ad istum manerium pertinet habere per consuetudinem in silva Milcheti 80 caretedes lignorum, et paissonem 80 porcorum, et ad domos et sepes reemendandas[1] quod opus fuerit. *NEWENTON* valet 16 libras.

Ipsa Ecclesia tenet *WILGI.* Tempore Regis Edwardi geldabat pro 10 hidis. Terra cst 5 carucatæ. De hac terra sunt in dominio 5 hidæ, et ibi 2 carucatæ, et 2 servi. Ibi 9 villani, et 10 bordarii, cum 3 carucatis. Ibi molinus, reddens 10 solidos, et 12 acræ prati, et 100 acræ pasturæ, et 10 acræ silvæ parvæ. Valuit 6 libras : modo 8 libras.

Ipsa Ecclesia tenet *WICHEFORD.* Temporc Regis Edwardi geldabat pro 4 hidis. Terra est 3 carucatæ. De hac terra sunt in dominio 2 hidæ, ct ibi 2 carucatæ. Ibi 1 villanus, et 16 bordarii, cum 1 carucata. Ibi 2 molini, reddentes 24 solidos, et 8 acræ prati, et 9 acræ pasturæ. Valuit 3 libras ; modo 4 libras.

services such as are due from villans. The Abbess claims them. Richard has there 5 carucates, and they are worth £7.

The Church itself holds *NEWENTONE.* In the time of King Edward it paid geld for 19 hides and 3 virgates of land. The land is 14 carucates. Of this land there are in demesne 2 hides, and there are 2 carucates, and 6 coliberts. There are 20 villans, and 16 bordars, with 12 carucates. There are 2 mills, paying 40 shillings, and 20 acres of meadow, and 150 acres of pasture, and 200 acres of wood. To this manor belongs by custom the right to 80 cart-loads of wood, and the feed of 80 hogs, in Milchet Wood, and what may be necessary for the repair of the houses and fences. *NEWENTON* is worth £16.

The Church itself holds *WILGI.* In the time of King Edward it paid geld for 10 hides. The land is 5 carucates. Of this land there are in demesne 5 hides, and there are 2 carucates, and 2 serfs. There are 9 villans, and 10 bordars, with 3 carucates. There is a mill paying 10 shillings, and 12 acres of meadow, and 100 acres of pasture, and 10 acres of coppice-wood. It was worth £6 ; it is now worth £8.

The Church itself holds *WICHEFORD.* In the time of King Edward it paid geld for 4 hides. The land is 3 carucates. Of this land there are in demesne 2 hides, and there are 2 carucates. There is 1 villan, and 16 bordars, with 1 carucate. There arc 2 mills, paying 24 shillings, and 8 acres of meadow, and 9 acres of pasture. It was worth £3 ; it is now worth £4.

---

[1] These privileges of cutting as much wood as was needed for the repair of the dwelling-house, and for maintaining the fences and hedges, were what are now commonly called, (and indeed to this day they are still in some leases of farms so termed) HEYBOTE, and HOUSEBOTE. The latter portion of each word is the Anglo Saxon '*bót*' or '*bôte*' which signifies 'repair,' or 'compensation.' The word '*Haye*,' a 'hedge' or 'enclosure,' is the origin of the former part of the term '*Hey-bote*.' The officer whose duty it was to preserve the *fences* and grass of enclosed grounds from injury, was hence called the *Hay-ward*;— a name, and office which still exist in many manors.

VIII a 68 a Ipsa Ecclesia tenet *LANGEFORD.* Tempore Regis Edwardi geldabat pro 3 hidis. Terra est 2 carucatæ. Has habent ibi 2 Angli, cum 2 bordariis, et 2 servis. Ibi molinus, reddens 5 solidos, et 25 acræ prati, et 20 acræ pasturæ. Valuit 40 solidos; modo 50 solidos.

The Church itself holds *LANGEFORD.* In the time of King Edward it paid geld for 3 hides. The land is 2 carucates. These, 2 Englishmen have there, with 2 bordars, and 2 serfs. There is a mill, paying 5 shillings, and 25 acres of meadow, and 20 acres of pasture. It was worth 40 shillings; it is now worth 50 shillings.

Pater eorum qui nunc tenent, tenuit tempore Regis Edwardi, nec potuit ab ecclesia separari.

The father of those who now hold it, held it in the time of King Edward, and could not be separated from the church.

Ipsa Ecclesia tenet *OCHEFORDE.* Tempore Regis Edwardi geldabat pro 4 hidis. Terra est 3 carucatæ. De hac terra sunt in dominio 3 hidæ, et ibi 1 carucata. Ibi 2 villani, et 4 bordarii, cum 1 carucata. Ibi molinus, reddens 5 solidos, et 6 acræ prati. Valuit 40 solidos; modo 60 solidos.

The Church itself holds *OCHEFORDE.* In the time of King Edward it paid geld for 4 hides. The land is 3 carucates. Of this land there are in demesne 3 hides, and there is 1 carucate. There are 2 villans, and 4 bordars, with 1 carucate. There is a mill, paying 5 shillings, and 6 acres of meadow. It was worth 40 shillings; it is now worth 60 shillings.

Ipsa Ecclesia habet dimidiam hidam terræ in *DICEHANTONE.* Valet 30 denarios.

The Church itself has half a hide of land in *DICEHANTONE.* It is worth 30 pence.

Ipsa Ecclesia tenet *BREDECUMBE.* Tempore Regis Edwardi geldabat pro 6 hidis. Terra est 4 carucatæ. De hac terra sunt in dominio 2 hidæ, et ibi 2 carucatæ. Ibi 13 bordarii, et molinus, reddens 15 solidos, et 18 acræ prati. Pastura 8 quarentenis longa, et una quarentena lata. Valet 100 solidos.

The Church itself holds *BREDECUMBE.* In the time of King Edward it paid geld for 6 hides. The land is 4 carucates. Of this land there are in demesne 2 hides and there are 2 carucates. There are 13 bordars, and a mill, paying 15 shillings, and 18 acres of meadow. The pasture is 8 furlongs long, and 1 furlong broad. It is worth 100 shillings.

De eadem terra tenet Edwardus 1 hidam quæ non potest ab ecclesia tolli. Valet 15 solidos.

Of the same land Edward holds 1 hide which cannot be alienated from the church. It is worth 15 shillings.

Vol. VIII b 68 b Ipsa Ecclesia tenet *BABESTOCHE.* Tempore Regis Edwardi pro 3 hidis geldabat. Terra est 3 carucatæ. De his sunt in dominio 2 hidæ, et ibi 1 carucata cum 1 servo; et 4 bordarii cum 2 carucatis; et 6 acræ prati, et 4 acræ pasturæ. Valet 60 solidos.

The Church itself holds *BABESTOCHE.* In the time of King Edward it paid geld for 3 hides. The land is 3 carucates. Of these there are in demesne 2 hides, and there is 1 carucate, with 1 serf; and there are 4 bordars with 2 carucates; and 6 acres of meadow, and 4 acres of pasture. It is worth 60 shillings.

Ipsa Ecclesia tenet *WAISEL.* Tempore Regis Edwardi geldabat pro 8 hidis et dimidio. Terra est 7 carucatæ. De hac terra sunt in dominio 2 hidæ,

The Church itself holds *WAISEL.* In the time of King Edward it paid geld for 8 hides and a half. The land is 7 carucates. Of this land there are in

Fol. { VIII b, 68 b } et ibi 1 carucata. Ibi 9 villani, et 10 coliberti, cum 6 carucatis. Ibi 12 acræ prati. Pastura 8 quarentenis longa, et 6 quarentenis lata. In silva Milchete pastura 80 porcis, et 80 caretedes lignorum, et ad domos et ad sepes quod opus est. Valet 7 libras et 10 solidos.

demesne 2 hides, and there is 1 carucate. There are 9 villans, and 10 coliberts, with 6 carucates. There are 12 acres of meadow. The pasture is 8 furlongs long, and 6 furlongs broad. In Milchet Wood there is pasture for 80 hogs, and they are entitled to 80 cart-loads of wood, and to what is necessary for repairing the dwellings and fences. It is worth £7 10s.

Ipsa Ecclesia tenet *FEBEFONTE.* Tempore Regis Edwardi geldabat pro 10 hidis. Terra est 7 carucatæ. De hac terra sunt in dominio 5 hidæ, et ibi 2 carucatæ, et 7 coliberti. Ibi 8 villani, et 7 bordarii, cum 5 carucatis. Ibi 2 molini, reddentes 17 solidos et 6 denarios, et 8 acræ prati. Pastura 4 quarentenis longa, et una quarentena lata. Silva 2 quarentenis longa, et una quarentena lata. Valet 7 libras et 10 solidos.

The Church itself holds *FEBEFONTE.* In the time of King Edward it paid geld for 10 hides. The land is 7 carucates. Of this land there are in demesne 5 hides, and there are 2 carucates, and 7 coliberts. There are 8 villans, and 7 bordars, with 5 carucates. There are 2 mills, paying 17 shillings and sixpence, and 8 acres of meadow. The pasture is 4 furlongs long, and 1 furlong broad. The wood is 2 furlongs long, and 1 furlong broad. It is worth £7 10s.

Ipsa Ecclesia tenet *LAVVRECESTOHES.* Tempore Regis Edwardi geldabat pro 2 hidis. Terra est 3 carucatæ. De hac terra est in dominio 1 hida, et ibi 1 carucata. Ibi 6 villani, et 8 bordarii, cum 2 carucatis. Ibi molinus, reddens 7 solidos et 6 denarios, et 18 acræ pasturæ. Valuit 100 solidos; modo 6 libras.

The Church itself holds *LAVVRECESTOHES.* In the time of King Edward it paid geld for 2 hides. The land is 3 carucates. Of this land there is in demesne 1 hide, and there is 1 carucate. There are 6 villans, and 8 bordars, with 2 carucates. There is a mill, paying 7 shillings and 6 pence, and 18 acres of pasture. It was worth 100 shillings; it is now worth £6.

Hujus terræ quarta pars in foresta Regis est posita.

Of this land a fourth part is situated in the King's forest.

Ipsa Ecclesia tenebat 2 hidas,[1] tempore Regis Edwardi, quas Toret dederat ibi cum duabus filiabus[2]

The Church used to hold 2 hides, in the time of King Edward, which Toret had given them with his

[1] These *two hides* are clearly those entered under the head of 'DECHEMENTONE' at p. 25, as belonging to the Bishop of Baieux. Together with the *half hide* at DICEHANTONE, recorded at p. 49, as still belonging to the Abbess of Wilton, they make up the *two hides and a half*, which, according to the Wilton Chartulary, were granted by King Edward the Confessor, in the year 1045, to his Thane by name Ðorð—evidently the same as is intended by 'Toret' in this entry—and which seem afterwards to have become part of the possessions of the Abbey. The charter concerning 'Dichæmatune' is printed in *Hoare's Regist. Wiltun.*, p. 29, and in the *Cod. Dipl.*, *No.* 778.

[2] It was usual, when any person of substance devoted a daughter or kinswoman to the office of a Nun, that she should bring a "portion" with her, the proceeds of which afterwards formed part of the general revenues of the Abbey. On this custom see *Wilts Archæol. Mag.*, vii. 278.

VIII b 68 b suis, et ex eis semper fuerunt vestitæ, donec Episcopus Baiocensis injuste abstulit Ecclesiæ.

Omnes redditus, quos habet Ecclesia de ipso burgo Wiltunensi, appreciantur 10 libris, et 17 solidis, et 6 denariis.

two daughters, and from them the nuns were always clothed, until the Bishop of Baieux unjustly took them away from the Church.

All the rents which the Church has from the borough of Wilton, are valued at £10 17s. 6d.

XIV. TERRA ECCLESIÆ SANCTÆ MARIÆ WINTONIENSIS.

Ecclesia S. Mariæ Wintoniensis[1] tenet *JERCHESFONTE.* Tempore Regis Edwardi geldabat pro 30 hidis. Terra est 20 carucatæ. De hac terra sunt in dominio 6 hidæ, et ibi 7 carucatæ, et 17 servi. Ibi 33 villani, et 26 bordarii, et 6 cotarii, cum 9 carucatis. Ibi 3 molini, reddentes 21 solidos et 3 denarios, et 64 acræ prati. Pastura 1 leuca longa, et dimidio leucæ lata, et tantundem silvæ.

De eadem terra tenet Edwardus hidam et dimidium, et tertiam partem dimidiæ hidæ; Walterus 1 hidam; Angli tenent 2 hidas, et duas partes dimidiæ hidæ.

De 6 hidis quæ sunt in dominio, tenuit prepositus Abbatissæ 2 hidas tempore Regis Edwardi; postea vero reddidit eas ecclesiæ cum omni pecunia[2] sua, et nunc usque sunt in dominio.

XIV. LAND OF THE CHURCH OF SAINT MARY AT WINCHESTER.

The Church of S. Mary at Winchester, holds *JERCHESFONTE.* In the time of King Edward it paid geld for 30 hides. The land is 20 carucates. Of this land there are in demesne 6 hides, and there are 7 carucates, and 17 serfs. There are 33 villans, and 26 bordars, and 6 cottars, with 9 carucates. There are 3 mills, paying 21 shillings and 3 pence, and 64 acres of meadow. The pasture is 1 mile long, and half a mile broad, and there is the same quantity of wood.

Of the same land Edward holds a hide and a half, and the third part of half a hide; Walter, 1 hide; some Englishmen hold 2 hides, and 2 parts of half a hide.

Of the 6 hides which are in demesne, the bailiff of the Abbess held 2 hides in the time of King Edward; afterwards, however, he restored them to the church with all his cattle, and at this time they are in demesne.

---

[1] The Abbey of St. Mary at Winchester, which is also called Nunna-Minster, was founded by Alfred the Great, and his Queen Ethelswitha. It was completed by their son, Edward the Elder. It was subsequently re-founded, and restored, by Bishop Ethelwold, in 932. It was destroyed, in 1141, in the war between King Stephen and the Empress Maud. In 1536 it was once again established, just four years before it was dissolved. A list of the Abbesses is given in the *New Monast.* ii. 452.

[2] The word *Pecunia* (which is derived from *Pecus* cattle, the principal source of wealth in olden times,) seldom occurs in Domesday Book as denoting *money*. Ellis (I. 171) mentions three instances in which it seems to imply *money*, but adds, that in all the rest it evidently denotes *cattle*. "Pastura ad *pecuniam* villæ," *i.e.* "pasture for the *cattle* of the village," is a common entry in the accounts of Middlesex, Hertfordshire, Herefordshire, Cambridgeshire, Huntingdonshire, and Bedfordshire. Ellis notices one instance in the Exon Domesday, (*p.* 19, *l.* 34,) in which *Pecunia* is used for money, with a specification of pounds, shillings, and pence, but this meaning of the word is very unusual.

Fol. { VIII b / 68 b } Quando Abbatissa recepit manerium, valebat 15 libras; modo, 27 libras, quod habet in dominio; quod milites, 3 libras.

Ipsa Ecclesia tenet *CANINGE.* Tempore Regis Edwardi geldabat pro 18 hidis et una virgata terræ et dimidio. Terra est 15 carucatæ. De hac terra sunt in dominio 4 hidæ, et ibi 5 carucatæ, et 8 servi. Ibi 27 villani, et 17 bordarii, et 6 cotarii, cum 10 carucatis. Ibi molinus, reddens 13 solidos, et 108 acræ prati. Pastura una leuca longa, et 3 quarentenis lata. Silva 4 quarentenis longa, et 2 quarentenis lata. Valuit 20 libras; modo 30 libras.

When the Abbess received this manor, it was worth £15; what she has now in demesne is worth £27; what the 'milites' hold is worth £3.

The Church itself holds *CANINGE.* In the time of King Edward it paid geld for 18 hides and 1 virgate and a half. The land is 15 carucates. Of this land there are in demesne 4 hides, and there are 5 carucates, and 8 serfs. There are 27 villans, and 17 bordars, and 6 cottars, with 10 carucates. There is a mill, paying 13 shillings, and 108 acres of meadow. The pasture is 1 mile long, and 3 furlongs broad. The wood is 4 furlongs long, and 2 furlongs broad. It was worth £20; it is now worth £30.

XV. TERRA ECCLESIÆ ROMESIENSIS.

Ecclesia S. Mariæ Romesiensis[1] tenet *EDENDONE.* Tempore Regis Edwardi geldabat pro 30 hidis. Terra est 35 carucatæ et dimidium. De hac terra sunt in dominio 2 hidæ et dimidium, et ibi 7 carucatæ, et 10 servi. Ibi 21 villani, et 23 bordarii, et 10 coliberti, cum 15 carucatis. Ibi 2 molini, reddentes 19 solidos, et 100 acræ prati. Pastura una leuca longa, et dimidio leucæ lata. Silva 10 quarentenis longa, et 5 lata.

De eadem terra tenet Willelmus 4 hidas et dimidium; Osmundus 4 hidas; Herveus 2 hidas; Angli 5 hidas et unam virgatam terræ. Qui tenebant, tempore Regis Edwardi, has 15 hidas et 3 virgatas, non poterant separari ab ecclesia. Ibi sunt 12 carucatæ et dimidium.

Dominium ecclesiæ valet 30 libras; quod homines tenent, 18 libras.

XV. LAND OF THE CHURCH OF ROMSEY.

The Church of S. Mary at Romsey holds *EDENDONE.* In the time of King Edward it paid geld for 30 hides. The land is 35½ carucates. Of this land there are 2½ hides in demesne, and there are 7 carucates, and 10 serfs. There are 21 villans, and 23 bordars, and 10 coliberts, with 15 carucates. There are 2 mills paying 19 shillings, and 100 acres of meadow. The pasture is 1 mile long, and half a mile broad. The wood is 10 furlongs long, and 5 broad.

Of the same land William holds 4½ hides; Osmund 4 hides; Hervey 2 hides; some Englishmen 5 hides and 1 virgate of land. They who held these 15 hides and 3 virgates, in the time of King Edward, could not be separated from the church. There are there 12½ carucates.

The demesne of the church is worth £30; what the various vassals hold, is worth £18.

[1] Edward the Elder, or Ethelwold, a Saxon nobleman, built a monastery at Romsey, in which King Edgar, about the year 967, placed Benedictine Nuns, under the government of the Abbess Merwenna. It was dedicated to the Blessed Virgin, and St. Elfleda, daughter of the said Ethelwold, who had been a nun and Abbess here. There is no chartulary of Romsey known. *New Monast.*, ii. 506.

{VIII b 68 b} Ipsa Ecclesia tenet *AISTONE.* Tempore Regis Edwardi geldabat pro 40 hidis. Terra est 37 carucatæ. De hac terra sunt in dominio 10 hidæ, et ibi 9 carucatæ, et 8 servi. Ibi 40 villani, et 30 bordarii, cum 20 carucatis. Ibi 3 molini, reddentes 32 solidos et 6 denarios, et 100 acræ prati. Pastura 19 quarentenis longa, et una quarentena lata. Silva 2 leucis longa, et dimidio leucæ lata.

De eadem terra tenet Edwardus 3 hidas; Willelmus 1 hidam; Angli 4 hidas. Qui tenebant, tempore Regis Edwardi, non poterant ab ecclesia separari. Dominium ecclesiæ valet 30 libras; hominum vero, 6 libras et 13 solidos.

The Church itself holds *AISTONE.* In the time of King Edward it paid geld for 40 hides. The land is 37 carucates. Of this land there are in demesne 10 hides, and there are 9 carucates, and 8 serfs. There are 40 villans, and 30 bordars, with 20 carucates. There are 3 mills, paying 32 shillings and sixpence, and 100 acres of meadow. The pasture is 19 furlongs long, and 1 furlong broad. The wood is 2 miles long, and half a mile broad.

Of the same land Edward holds 3 hides; William 1 hide; some Englishmen 4 hides. They who held them, in the time of King Edward, could not be separated from the church. The demesne of the church is worth £30; the holdings of the vassals are worth £6 13s.

XVI. TERRA ECCLESIÆ AMBRESBERIENSIS.

{IX a 68 c} Ecclesia Ambresberiensis[1] tenet *BOLTINTONE.* Tempore Regis Edwardi geldabat pro 12 hidis. Terra est 9 carucatæ. De hac terra sunt in dominio 6 hidæ, et ibi 3 carucatæ, et 13 servi. Ibi 3 villani, et 20 coscez, et 3 cotarii, cum 5 carucatis. Ibi 2 molini, reddentes 65 solidos, et 35 acræ prati. Pastura 1 leuca longa, et dimidio leucæ lata.

De eadem terra tenet Alwardus 3 hidas. Qui tenebat tempore Regis Edwardi non poterat ab ecclesia separari.

Dominium Abbatissæ valet 13 libras; quod Taini tenent valet 15 solidos.

XVI. LAND OF THE CHURCH OF AMBRESBURY.

The Church of Ambresbury holds *BOLTINTONE.* In the time of King Edward it paid geld for 12 hides. The land is 9 carucates. Of this land there are in demesne 6 hides, and there are 3 carucates, and 13 serfs. There are 3 villans, and 20 coscets, and 3 cottars, with 5 carucates. There are 2 mills paying 65 shillings, and 35 acres of meadow. The pasture is 1 mile long, and half a mile broad.

Of the same land Alward holds 3 hides. He who held them in the time of King Edward could not be separated from the church.

The demesne of the Abbess is worth £13; what the Thanes hold is worth 15 shillings.

---

[1] There would seem to have been a very ancient monastery at Ambresbury, which was in existence as early as the fifth century. The reasons for this belief are given by Dr. Guest, in the Salisbury volume of the Archæol. Inst., p. 58. The monastery alluded to above was a later foundation, ascribed to Elfrida, who, repenting of the murder of her son Edward the Martyr, founded two monasteries, the one at Ambresbury, and the other at Wherwell, in Hants. In the year 1177, King Henry I. is said to have expelled the nuns from Ambresbury in consequence of their misconduct, and to have bestowed the monastery on the Abbey of Fontevrault, in Normandy. See Sir R. C. Hoare's 'Ambresbury Hundr.' 58—72. *New Monast.*, ii. 333.

Fol. { IX a / 68 c

Ipsa Ecclesia tenet *BOSCUMBE*. Tempore Regis Edwardi geldabat pro 4 hidis. Terra est 2 carucatæ. De hac terra sunt in dominio 2 hidæ et dimidium, et ibi 1 carucata, cum 1 servo. Ibi 2 villani, et 5 coscez, et 2 cotarii, cum 1 carucata. Ibi 4 acræ prati. Pastura una quarentena longa, et dimidio quarentenæ lata. Valuit, et valet, 3 libras.

Ipsa Ecclesia tenet *ALLENTONE*. Tempore Regis Edwardi geldabat pro 4 hidis. Terra est 2 carucatæ. De hac terra sunt in dominio 3 hidæ una virgata minus, et ibi 1 carucata, et 3 servi. Ibi 3 villani, et 5 coscez, et unus cotarius, cum 1 carucata. Ibi 8 acræ prati. Pastura 1 leuca longa, et una quarentena lata. Valuit 3 libras; modo 4 libras.

Ipsa Ecclesia tenet *CHELESTANESTONE*, et Alwardus tenet de Abbatissa. Tempore Regis Edwardi geldabat pro 2 hidis et dimidio. Terra est 1 carucata et dimidium, et tantum est ibi, cum 2 servis, et 3 coscez. Ibi 8 acræ prati. Pastura 5 quarentenis longa, et una quarentena lata. Valuit 30 solidos: modo 40 solidos.

Ipsa Ecclesia tenebat 2 hidas tempore Regis Edwardi, et post tenuit tempore Regis Willelmi, et sunt de victu monialium. Has tenet Comes Moritoniensis[1] injuste.

Ipsa Ecclesia tenet in *WINTREBURNE* 6 hidas. Terra est 4 carucatæ. De hac terra sunt in dominio 3 hidæ, et ibi 3 carucatæ, et 2 servi. Ibi 5 villani, et 10 bordarii, cum 1 carucata. Ibi 3 acræ prati. Pastura dimidio leucæ longa, et tantundem lata. Valuit 4 libras; modo 100 solidos.

The Church itself holds *BOSCUMBE*. In the time of King Edward it paid geld for 4 hides. The land is 2 carucates. Of this land there are in demesne 2½ hides, and there is 1 carucate, with 1 serf. There are 2 villans, and 5 coscets, and 2 cottars, with 1 carucate. There are 4 acres of meadow. The pasture is one furlong long, and half a furlong broad. It was, and is, worth £3.

The Church itself holds *ALLENTONE*. In the time of King Edward it paid geld for 4 hides. The land is 2 carucates. Of this land there are in demesne 3 hides all but 1 virgate, and there is 1 carucate, and 3 serfs. There are 3 villans, and 5 coscets, and 1 cottar, with 1 carucate. There are 8 acres of meadow. The pasture is one mile long, and 1 furlong broad. It was worth £3; it is now worth £4.

The Church itself holds *CHELESTANESTONE*, and Alward holds it of the Abbess. In the time of King Edward it paid geld for 2½ hides. The land is 1 carucate and a half, and so much is there, with 2 serfs, and 3 coscets. There are 8 acres of meadow. The pasture is 5 furlongs long, and 1 furlong broad. It was worth 30 shillings; it is now worth 40 shillings.

The Church itself used to hold 2 hides in the time of King Edward, and held them afterwards in the time of King William, and they are for the support of the nuns. These hides Earl Morton now unjustly holds.

The Church itself holds 6 hides in *WINTREBURNE*. The land is 4 carucates. Of this land there are in demesne 3 hides, and there are 3 carucates and 2 serfs. There are 5 villans, and 10 bordars, with 1 carucate. There are 3 acres of meadow. The pasture is half a mile long, and as much broad. It was worth £4; it is now worth 100 shillings.

---

[1] These two hides appear to have belonged to the manor of *WINTRESLEU*. In the original, there is a marginal reference to the entry of *WINTRESLEU*, under the account of lands held by the Earl Morton. See below, *p.* 58.

IX a 68 c Ipsa Ecclesia tenet *WINTREBURNE.* Tempore Regis Edwardi geldabat pro 4 hidis et dimidio. Terra est 2 carucatæ. De hac terra sunt in dominio 2 hidæ et dimidium, et ibi 1 carucata. Ibi 4 villani, et 4 bordarii, et 2 cotarii, cum 1 carucata. Ibi 8 acræ prati, et 10 acræ pasturæ. Valuit, et valet, 4 libras.

The Church itself holds *WINTREBURNE.* In the time of King Edward it paid geld for 4½ hides. The land is 2 carucates. Of this land there are in demesne 2 hides and a half, and there is 1 carucate. There are 4 villans, and 4 bordars, and 2 cottars, with 1 carucate. There are 8 acres of meadow, and 10 acres of pasture. It was, and is worth, £4.

XVII. TERRA SANCTÆ MARIÆ DE BECH.

Ecclesia S. Mariæ de Bech[1] tenet de Rege *DEVREL.* Brictric tenuit tempore Regis Edwardi, et geldabat pro 10 hidis. Terra est 7 carucatæ. De hac terra sunt in dominio 6 hidæ et dimidium, et ibi 3 carucatæ, et 8 servi. Ibi 8 villani, et 7 coscez, et 2 bordarii, cum 4 carucatis. Ibi molinus de 30 denariis, et 4 acræ prati. Pastura 1 leuca longa, et 5 quarentenis lata. Silvæ 3 quarentenæ longitudine, et 2 quarentenæ latitudine.

Ecclesia ejusdem manerii habet 1 hidam de eadem terra. Totum manerium valet 12 libras. Valebat 15 libras, vivente Regina Mathilda,[2] quæ dedit eidem ecclesiæ.

XVII. LAND OF SAINT MARY OF BECH.

The Church of S. Mary of Bech holds *DEVREL* of the King. Brictric held it in the time of King Edward, and it paid geld for 10 hides. The land is 7 carucates. Of this land there are in demesne 6½ hides, and there are 3 carucates, and 8 serfs. There are 8 villans, and 7 coscets, and 2 bordars, with 4 carucates. There is a mill worth 30 pence, and 4 acres of meadow. The pasture is 1 mile long, and 5 furlongs broad. Of wood there are 3 furlongs in length, and 2 furlongs in breadth.

The church of the same manor has 1 hide of the same land. The whole manor is worth £12. It was worth £15, during the life-time of Queen Matilda, who gave it to the same church.

XVIII. TERRA GIRALDI DE WILTUNE.

Giraldus de Wiltune tenet de Rege *UPTONE* in elemosina. Idem tenebat tempore Regis Edwardi, et geldabat pro 10 hidis. Terra est 6 carucatæ. De hac terra sunt in dominio 6 hidæ et una virgata et

XVIII. THE LAND OF GIRALD OF WILTON.

Girald of Wilton holds *UPTONE* of the King in frank-almoigne. He also held it in the time of King Edward, and paid geld for 10 hides. The land is 6 carucates. Of this land there are in

---

[1] The Benedictine abbey of Bec, in Normandy, was originally founded by Hellouin, or Herluin, its first abbot, in 1034. It was re-founded by Lanfranc, its prior, afterwards Archbishop of Canterbury. Lanfranc has already been alluded to (p. 12, *note*) as having been the first abbot of St. Stephen, Caen. *Ellis*, i. 378.

[2] This entry shows that the survey of the county of Wilts was not taken by the Domesday Commissioners till *after the decease* of Matilda, the Queen of the Conqueror; that is, till after November, 1083. The same may be said of the survey of Dorsetshire. Thus, in *fol.* 83 b., Anschitil is stated to have held 'Tingeham' of Queen Matilda, but, it is added, that "*After her death* he did not petition the King for the land." *Ellis*, i. 7.

Fol. { IX a / 68 c } dimidium, et ibi 3 carucatæ, et 4 servi. Ibi 9 villani, et 6 bordarii, et 4 coscez, cum 3 carucatis. Ibi molinus, reddens 20 solidos, et 15 acræ prati. Pastura dimidio leucæ longa, et 2 quarentenis lata. Valet 10 libras.

demesne 6 hides and 1 virgate and a half, and there are 3 carucates, and 4 serfs. There are 9 villans, and 6 bordars, and 4 coscets, with 3 carucates. There is a mill, paying 20 shillings, and 15 acres of meadow. The pasture is half a mile long, and 2 furlongs broad. It is worth £10.

REINBALDI.[1]

Reinbaldus, presbyter, tenet *LATONE* et *AISI.* Duo Taini tenuerunt pro 2 maneriis tempore Regis Edwardi. Heraldus Comes junxit in unum, et geldabat pro 9 hidis. Terra est 8 carucatæ. De hac terra sunt in dominio 3 hidæ, et 8 servi. Ibi 15 villani, et 6 bordarii, et 4 cotarii, cum 5 carucatis; et in dominio 3 carucatæ. Ibi 2 molini, et 200 acræ prati. Pastura 1 leuca longa, et dimidio leucæ lata. Valuit, et valet, 10 libras.

REINBALD'S (LAND).

Reinbald, the priest, holds *LATONE* and *AISI.* Two Thanes held them for 2 manors in the time of King Edward. Earl Harold united them into one manor, and paid geld for 9 hides. The land is 8 carucates. Of this land there are in demesne 3 hides, and 8 serfs. There are 15 villans, and 6 bordars, and 4 cottars, with 5 carucates; and there are in demesne 3 carucates. There are 2 mills, and 200 acres of meadow. The pasture is 1 mile long, and half a mile broad. It was, and is, worth £10.

XIX. CANONICI LISIACENSES.

Canonici Lisiacenses tenent *DEVREL.* Eddeva tenuit tempore Regis Edwardi, et geldabat pro 4 hidis. Terra est 3 carucatæ. De ea sunt in dominio 3 hidæ et dimidium 3 acris minus, et ibi 1 carucata, et 2 servi; et 6 coscez, cum 1 villano, habentes 1 carucatam. Ibi 3 acræ prati. Pastura 4 quarentenis longa, et 3 quarentenis lata. Valuit 40 solidos; modo 70 solidos.

Alwardus, presbyter, habet 5 hidas, quæ pertinent ad ecclesiam *ALWARBERIE* de elemosina Regis.

XIX. THE CANONS OF LISIEUX.

The Canons of Lisieux hold *DEVREL.* Eddeva held it in the time of King Edward, and it paid geld for 4 hides. The land is 3 carucates. Of this there are in demesne $3\frac{1}{2}$ hides all but 3 acres, and there is 1 carucate, and 2 serfs; and there are 6 coscets, with 1 villan, having 1 carucate. There are 3 acres of meadow. The pasture is 4 furlongs long, and 3 furlongs broad. It was worth 40 shillings; it is now worth 70 shillings.

Alward, the priest, has 5 hides, which belong to the church of *ALWARBERIE* of the free gift of

[1] As these manors, which are on the borders of Gloucestershire, belonged to the Abbey of Cirencester (according to the Testa de Nevil, p. 154) "de veteri feoffamento," it is highly probable that this owner was the Reinbald who was Dean of the Collegiate Church at Cirencester, and Chancellor to King Edward the Confessor. Leland in his Itinerary ii. 49, speaking of Cirencester, says: "There was afore the Conquest a fair and rich College of Prebendaries in this Town, but of what Saxon's foundation no man can telle. Rumbaldus, chauncelar to King Edward the Confessor, was Dene of this house, and buried in the body of the Church, as it appeareth by the Epitaphy on his tumbe."—He gives the epitaph of Reinbald in Vol. v. 66. 'Reinbaldus *Canceler*' occurs in Domesday, (*Hereford*, 180*b*,) in the time of King Edward the Confessor. Ellis I. 398.

{IX a 68 c} Terra est 3 carucatæ. In dominio est 1 carucata; et 4 villani, et 8 bordarii, cum 2 carucatis. Ibi 10 acræ prati, et 4 quarentenæ silvæ in longitudine, et 4 in latitudine. Huic eidem ecclesiæ adjacet 1 hida, quæ nunquam geldavit. Totum valet 70 solidos.

the King. The land is 3 carucates. In demesne is 1 carucate; and there are 4 villans, and 8 bordars with 2 carucates. There are 10 acres of meadow, and 4 furlongs of wood in length, and 4 in breadth. There is 1 hide, adjacent to the same church, which never paid geld. The whole is worth 70 shillings.

Osbernus, presbyter, habet 2 hidas de Rege in ecclesia *ALWARESBERIE.* Valet 20 solidos.

Osbern, the priest, has 2 hides of the King in the Church of *ALWARESBERIE.* It is worth 20 shillings.

Agenulfus tenet *HORNINGESHAM.* Pater ejus tenuit de Rege Edwardo in elemosina. Ibi est dimidium hidæ. Terra est 1 carucata. Ibi est unus coscet, et 2 acræ prati, et 2 acræ silvæ. Valet 5 solidos.

Agenulf holds *HORNINGESHAM.* His father held it of King Edward in frank-almoigne. There is half a hide. The land is 1 carucate. There is 1 coscet, and 2 acres of meadow, and 2 acres of wood. It is worth 5 shillings.

XX. TERRA COMITIS MORITONIENSIS.

{IX b 68 d} Comes Moritoniensis[1] tenet *COWIC*, et S. Maria de Grestain de eo. Tempore Regis Edwardi, geldabat pro 10 hidis. Terra est 4 carucatæ. De hac terra sunt in diminio 6 hidæ et dimidium, et ibi 2 carucatæ, et 3 servi. Ibi 6 villani, et 9 bordarii, cum 2 carucatis. Ibi 20 acræ prati. Pastura dimidio leuca longa, et 3 quarentenis lata. Valuit 8 libras; modo 9 libras.

XX. LAND OF THE EARL MORTON.

The Earl Morton holds *COWIC*, and the Church of S. Mary of Grestain holds it of him. In the time of King Edward it paid geld for 10 hides. The land is 4 carucates. Of this land there are in demesne 6½ hides, and there are 2 carucates, and 3 serfs. There are 6 villans, and 9 bordars, with 2 carucates. There are 20 acres of meadow. The pasture is half a mile long, and 3 furlongs broad. It was worth £8; it is now worth £9.

Idem Comes tenet *NECHENDUNE*, et Gislebertus de eo. Godvinus tenuit tempore Regis Edwardi, et geldabat pro 3 hidis. Terra est 2

The same Earl holds *NECHENDUNE*, and Gilbert holds it of him. Godwin held it in the time of King Edward, and paid geld for 3 hides. The

[1] Robert, Earl of Moretaine, in Normandy was half-brother to William the Conqueror, being the son of Harleta and Herluin de Contaville. He was possessed, at the general survey, of almost the whole of Cornwall, except the lands of the King and the Church, and was advanced to the earldom of Cornwall. He married Matilda the youngest daughter of Roger de Montgomery, Earl of Shrewsbury. According to some accounts he was slain in Northumberland, in 1087; Kelham however says that he died 1091. *Illustr.* p. 31. His son William de Moretaine was dispossessed of his estates by King Henry I. in 1104, and died, without issue, as a monk at Bermondsey.

The first Earl was a great benefactor to the abbey of Grestein, situated near the mouth of the river Seine, in Normandy, which had been founded by his father. It was he that annexed the Priory of St. Michael's Mount in Cornwall, to the similarly situated Norman abbey of St. Michael in Periculo Maris. See p. 13, *note*. The charter of Robert, Earl of Moretain, by which he made this donation, is printed in the New Monast. vi. 289.

Fol. { IX b 68 d } carucatæ. De hac terra sunt in dominio 2 hidæ, et ibi 1 carucata, et 2 servi. Ibi 1 villanus, et 8 bordarii, cum 1 carucata. Ibi 20 acræ prati, et 15 acræ pasturæ. Valuit 30, valet modo 40, solidos.

Idem Comes tenet *CLIVE*, et Gislebertus de eo. Godvinus tenuit tempore Regis Edwardi, et geldabat pro 3 hidis. Terra est 1 carucata et dimidium. In dominio est 1 carucata, et 2 servi; et 10 acræ prati. Valuit 20 solidos; modo 40 solidos.

Idem Comes tenet *CLIVE*, et Gislebertus de eo. Godvinus tenuit tempore Regis Edwardi, et geldabat pro 4 hidis una virgata minus. Terra est 1 carucata et dimidium. Ibi est unus villanus, et 3 bordarii, et 16 acræ prati, et 14 acræ pasturæ. Valet 40 solidos.

Ipse Comes tenet *LANGEFORD*. Chetel tenuit tempore Regis Edwardi, et geldabat pro 5 hidis. Terra est 2 carucatæ et dimidium. De hac terra sunt in dominio 4 hidæ et una virgata terræ, et ibi 2 carucatæ. Ibi 2 villani, et 4 bordarii, cum dimidia carucata. Ibi dimidium molini reddens 30 denarios, et 20 acræ prati, et 30 acræ pasturæ. Valuit, et valet, 100 solidos.

Ipse Comes tenet *WINTRESLEU*. Harding tenuit tempore Regis Edwardi, et geldabat pro 6 hidis et dimidio. Terra est 7 carucatæ. De hac terra sunt in dominio 3 hidæ, et ibi 3 carucatæ, et 6 servi. Ibi 6 villani, et 12 coscez, cum 3 carucatis. Ibi molinus, de 5 solidis, et 3 acræ prati. Pastura una leuca longa, et tantundem lata. Silva 1 leuca longa, et dimidio leucæ lata. Valet 10 libras.

De hoc manerio tenebat Abbatissa Ambresberiensis 2 hidas tempore Regis Edwardi.[1]

land is 2 carucates. Of this land there are in demesne 2 hides, and there is 1 carucate, and 2 serfs. There is 1 villan, and 8 bordars, with 1 carucate. There are 20 acres of meadow, and 15 acres of pasture. It was worth 30, it is now worth 40, shillings.

The same Earl holds *CLIVE*, and Gilbert holds it of him. Godwin held it in the time of King Edward, and it paid geld for 3 hides. The land is 1 carucate and a half. In demesne is 1 carucate, and 2 serfs; and there are 10 acres of meadow. It was worth 20 shillings; it is now worth 40 shillings.

The same Earl holds *CLIVE*, and Gilbert holds it of him. Godwin held it in the time of King Edward, and it paid geld for 4 hides all but 1 virgate. The land is 1 carucate and a half. There is one villan, and 3 bordars, and 16 acres of meadow, and 14 acres of pasture. It is worth 40 shillings.

The Earl himself holds *LANGEFORD*. Chetel held it in the time of King Edward, and it paid geld for 5 hides. The land is 2½ carucates. Of this land there are in demesne 4 hides and 1 virgate of land, and there are 2 carucates. There are 2 villans, and 4 bordars, with half a carucate. There is half a mill paying 30 pence, and 20 acres of meadow, and 30 acres of pasture. It was, and is worth, 100 shillings.

The Earl himself holds *WINTRESLEU*. Harding held it in the time of King Edward, and paid geld for 6½ hides. The land is 7 carucates. Of this land there are in demesne 3 hides, and there are 3 carucates, and 6 serfs. There are 6 villans, and 12 coscets, with 3 carucates. There is a mill, worth 5 shillings, and 3 acres of meadow. The pasture is 1 mile long, and as much broad. The wood is 1 mile long, and half a mile broad. It is worth £10.

Of this manor the Abbess of Ambresbury held 2 hides in the time of King Edward.

[1] See, with reference to this holding, the note on p. 54.

IX b
68 d

XXI. TERRA ROGERII COMITIS.[1]

Comes Rogerius tenet *ETTONE.* Tempore Regis Edwardi geldabat pro 15 hidis. Terra est 12 carucatæ. De hac terra medietas est in dominio, et ibi 3 carucatæ et dimidium, et 6 servi. Ibi 8 villani, et 8 coscez, cum 5 carucatis. Ibi molinus, reddens 15 solidos et 6 denarios, et 100 acræ prati. Pastura 6 quarentenis longa, et 3 quarentenis lata. Valuit 15 libras tempore Regis Edwardi; modo 12 libras.

Ipse Comes tenet *MILDESTONE.* Tempore Regis Edwardi geldabat pro 3 hidis et dimidio. Terra est 2 carucatæ. De hac terra sunt in dominio 2 hidæ, et ibi 1 carucata; et 3 villani, et 5 coscez, cum 1 carucata et dimidio. Ibi 8 acræ prati. Pastura 1 leuca longa, et 3 quarentenis lata. Valuit, et valet, 70 solidos.

Hæc 2 maneria tenet Turoldus de Comite. Osmundus, Tainus, tenuit tempore Regis Edwardi.

Idem Comes tenet *POLTONE.* Siwardus tenuit tempore Regis Edwardi, et geldabat pro 5 hidis. Terra est 8 carucatæ. De hac terra sunt in dominio 3 hidæ et dimidium, et ibi 4 carucatæ, et 8 servi; et 8 villani, et 7 coscez, cum 4 carucatis. Ibi 15 acræ prati. Pastura 3 quarentenis longa, et una quarentena lata. Valuit 12 libras; modo 16 libras.

XXI. LAND OF EARL ROGER.

Earl Roger holds *ETTONE.* In the time of King Edward it paid geld for 15 hides. The land is 12 carucates. Of this land a moiety is in demesne, and there are 3½ carucates, and 6 serfs. There are 8 villans, and 8 coscets, with 5 carucates. There is a mill, paying 15 shillings and sixpence, and 100 acres of meadow. The pasture is 6 furlongs long, and 3 furlongs broad. It was worth £15 in the time of King Edward; it is now worth £12.

The same Earl holds *MILDESTONE.* In the time of King Edward it paid geld for 3½ hides. The land is 2 carucates. Of this land there are 2 hides in demesne, and there is 1 carucate; and there are 3 villans, and 5 coscets, with 1 carucate and a half. There are 8 acres of meadow. The pasture is 1 mile long, and 3 furlongs broad. It was, and is worth, 70 shillings.

Turold holds these 2 manors of the Earl. Osmund, a Thane, held them in the time of King Edward.

The same Earl holds *POLTONE.* Siward held it in the time of King Edward, and it paid geld for 5 hides. The land is 8 carucates. Of this land there are in demesne 3½ hides, and there are 4 carucates, and 8 serfs; and there are 8 villans, and 7 coscets, with 4 carucates. There are 15 acres of meadow. The pasture is 3 furlongs long, and 1 furlong broad. It was worth £12; it is now worth £16.

---

[1] This was Roger de Montgomery, son to Hugh de Montgomery and Josceline his wife, daughter of Turolf of Pont-Audomare, by Weva, sister to Gunnora Duchess of Normandy, great-grandmother to the Conqueror. He led the centre of the army at the battle of Hastings, and was afterwards governor of Normandy. William the Conqueror gave him the earldoms of Arundel and Shrewsbury. He was also one of the party who joined against William Rufus in favour of Robert Courthose, but was afterwards reconciled to the King. He founded the Abbey of St. Peter and St. Paul at Shrewsbury, and several religious houses in Normandy. See Dugd. Baron, i. 26. He died in 1094, having, according to some authorities, been slain by the Welsh, between Cardiff and Brecknock. *Ellis*, i. 480.

Fol. {IX b / 68 d}

XXII. TERRA HUGONIS COMITIS.

Comes Hugo[1] tenet *RETMORE*, et Willelmus de eo. Tempore Regis Edwardi geldabat pro dimidia hida. Terra est 3 carucatæ. In dominio sunt 2 carucatæ, cum 1 servo. Ibi 1 villanus, et 3 bordarii, et 11 coscez, cum 1 carucata. Ibi molinus reddens 14 solidos, et 5 acræ prati. Pastura 3 quarentenis longa, et una quarentena lata. Silva 3 quarentenis longa, et 2 quarentenis lata. Valuit 50 solidos; modo 60 solidos.

Idem Comes tenet *WIFLESFORDE*, et Haimo de eo. Tempore Regis Edwardi geldabat pro 1 hida. Terra est 1 carucata, et ipsa est in dominio, et 2 servi, et 3 coscez. Ibi 6 acræ prati. Pastura 8 quarentenis longa, et una quarentena lata. Valet 40 solidos.

Idem Comes tenet *HEORTHAM*, et Edwardus de eo. Tempore Regis Edwardi geldabat pro 2 hidis. Terra est 3 carucatæ. De hac terra una hida est in dominio, et ibi 2 carucatæ, et 2 servi. Ibi 1 miles, et 3 coscez, et 5 acræ prati, et 3 acræ silvæ, et 12 acræ pasturæ. Valet 40 solidos.

Idem Comes tenet *BREDECUMBE*, et Haimo de eo. Tempore Regis Edwardi geldabat pro 4 hidis. Terra est 2 carucatæ. De hac terra sunt in dominio 3 hidæ, et ibi 1 carucata, cum 1 servo. Ibi 1 villanus, et 4 bordarii, et molinus de 10 solidis, et 6 acræ prati, et 10 acræ silvæ, et 20 acræ pasturæ. Valuit 3 libras; modo 4 libras.

XXII. LAND OF EARL HUGO.

Earl Hugo holds *RETMORE*, and William of him. In the time of King Edward it paid geld for half a hide. The land is 3 carucates. In demesne are 2 carucates, with 1 serf. There is 1 villan, and 3 bordars, and 11 coscets, with 1 carucate. There is a mill paying 14 shillings, and 5 acres of meadow. The pasture is 3 furlongs long, and 1 furlong broad. The wood is 3 furlongs long, and 2 furlongs broad. It was worth 50 shillings; it is now worth 60 shillings.

The same Earl holds *WIFLESFORDE*, and Haimo holds it of him. In the time of King Edward it paid geld for 1 hide. The land is 1 carucate, and this is in demesne, and 2 serfs, and 3 coscets. There are 6 acres of meadow. The pasture is 8 furlongs long, and 1 furlong broad. It is worth 40 shillings.

The same Earl holds *HEORTHAM*, and Edward holds it of him. In the time of King Edward it paid geld for 2 hides. The land is 3 carucates. Of this land 1 hide is in demesne, and there are 2 carucates, and 2 serfs. There is 1 'miles,' and 3 coscets, and 5 acres of meadow, and 3 acres of wood, and 12 acres of pasture. It is worth 40 shillings.

The same Earl holds *BREDECUMBE*, and Haimo holds it of him. In the time of King Edward it paid geld for 4 hides. The land is 2 carucates. Of this land there are in demesne 3 hides, and there is 1 carucate, with 1 serf. There is 1 villan, and 4 bordars, and a mill worth 10 shillings, and 6 acres of meadow, and 10 acres of wood, and 20 acres of pasture. It was worth £3; it is now worth £4.

---

[1] Hugh de Abrincis (Avranches, in Normandy), surnamed Lupus, was nephew of William the Conqueror, being his half-sister's son. He received the Earldom of Chester, A.D. 1070. Together with Hugh Montgomery, Earl of Shrewsbury, in 1098 he took the Isle of Anglesea from the Welsh. He refounded the Abbey of St. Sever, in the diocese of Coutance, in 1085, and re-endowed the monastery of St. Werburgh, Chester, A.D. 1093. He died in 1101, having been a professed monk of Chester a few days. Some more particulars of Hugh Lupus may be found in Ordericus Vitalis, p. 787, and in Ormerod's Hist. Cheshire, i. 10. *Ellis*, i. 437.

X a 69 a Idem Comes tenet *CADEHAM*, et Willelmus de eo. Tempore Regis Edwardi geldabat pro 2 hidis. Terra est 2 carucatæ. De his 1 hida in dominio, et 1 carucata, et 2 servi; et 8 bordarii, cum 1 carucata. Ibi 5 acræ prati. Silva 2 quarentenis longa, et una quarentena lata. Valuit 30 solidos; modo 40 solidos.

The same Earl holds *CADEHAM*, and William holds it of him. In the time of King Edward it paid geld for 2 hides. The land is 2 carucates. Of these 1 hide is in demesne, and 1 carucate, and 2 serfs; and there are 8 bordars, with 1 carucate. There are 5 acres of meadow. The wood is 2 furlongs long, and 1 furlong broad. It was worth 30 shillings; it is now worth 40 shillings.

Hæc 5 maneria tenuit Ednod dapifer tempore Regis Edwardi.

Ednod, the steward, held these 5 manors in the time of King Edward.

Idem Comes tenet *FISCARTONE*, et Haimo de eo. Godricus tenuit tempore Regis Edwardi, et geldabat pro 3 hidis. Terra est 2 carucatæ. In dominio sunt 2 hidæ de hac terra, et ibi 1 carucata, et 1 servus. Ibi 3 villani, et 5 bordarii, et molinus de 10 solidis, et 40 acræ prati, et 40 acræ pasturæ. Valuit, et valet, 3 libras.

The same Earl holds *FISCARTONE*, and Haimo holds it of him. Godric held it in the time of King Edward, and it paid geld for 3 hides. The land is 2 carucates. In demesne are 2 hides of this land, and there is 1 carucate, and 1 serf. There are 3 villans, and 5 bordars, and a mill worth 10 shillings, and 40 acres of meadow, and 40 acres of pasture. It was, and is, worth £3.

XXIII. TERRA QUÆ FUIT ALBERICI COMITIS.

Comes Albericus[1] tenuit *CONTONE*. Tempore Regis Edwardi geldabat pro 7 hidis. Terra est 6 carucatæ; de qua sunt in dominio 3 hidæ et una virgata terræ, et ibi 1 carucata, et 6 servi. Ibi 5 villani, et 5 coscez, cum 3 carucatis. Ibi molinus, de 10 solidis, et 5 acræ prati. Pastura 3 quarentenis longa, et una quarentena lata. Valuit, et valet, 10 libras.

DERINTONE geldabat, tempore Regis Edwardi, pro una hida et dimidio. Terra est 1 carucata.

XXIII. LAND WHICH BELONGED TO EARL ALBERIC. [AUBREY.]

Earl Alberic held *CONTONE*. In the time of King Edward it paid geld for 7 hides. The land is 6 carucates; of which there are in demesne 3 hides and 1 virgate of land, and there is 1 carucate, and 6 serfs. There are 5 villans, and 5 coscets, with 3 carucates. There is a mill, worth 10 shillings, and 5 acres of meadow. The pasture is 3 furlongs long, and 1 furlong broad. It was, and is, worth £10.

DERINTONE used to pay geld in the time of King Edward for 1 hide and a half. The land is 1

[1] According to Kelham (p. 53.) this was Alberic de Vere, a son of Alphonsus, Count of Ghisnes, within the county of Flanders, who came over with the Conqueror, and received from him numerous lordships, principally in Essex and Suffolk. He is said to have been created Earl of Northumberland, and to have been the progenitor of the Veres, Earls of Oxford. Ellis (i. 367) expresses a doubt as to the accuracy of this statement, inasmuch as the Albericus, who was made Earl of Northumberland, returned to Normandy shortly after 1080, and thinks the Earl of present references must have been a different person, though of what county he was Earl does not appear. At the time of the survey all his lands were in the hands of the King. Of those in Warwickshire, Geoffrey de Wirce had the custody.

Fol. { X a, 69 a } In dominio est 1 hida, et aliam terram habent ibi 4 coscez. Ibi 5 acræ prati.

In ipsa villa est una hida. Terra 1 carucata. Hanc tenuit unus Tainus tempore Regis Edwardi. Ibi est unus bordarius, et 5 acræ prati.

Hæ 2 hidæ et dimidium valent 4 libras.

WINTRESLEI geldabat, tempore Regis Edwardi, pro 2 hidis. Terra est 2 carucatæ. Ibi est unus villanus, et 3 bordarii; et silva 2 quarentenis longa, et dimidio quarentenæ lata. Valet 20 solidos.

ALBOLDINTONE geldabat pro 3 hidis. Terra est 2 carucatæ. In dominio sunt 2 hidæ de hac terræ et dimidium, et ibi 1 carucata, et 4 coscez. Ibi 35 acræ prati, et pastura 3 quarentenis longa, et una quarentena lata. Valet 4 libras.

CHELTRE geldabat, tempore Regis Edwardi, pro 6 hidis. Terra est 5 carucatæ. De hac terra sunt in dominio 3 hidæ, et ibi 1 carucata, et 4 servi. Ibi 4 villani, et 2 bordarii, cum 2 carucatis. Pastura 4 quarentenis longa, et 2 quarentenis lata. Valuit 4 libras; modo 6 libras.

TEDRINTONE geldabat, tempore Regis Edwardi, pro 2 hidis. Terra est 2 carucatæ. Ibi est unus villanus, et dimidium molini reddens 30 denarios, et 5 acræ prati. Valet 20 solidos.

Has 6 terras tenuit Hardingus tempore Regis Edwardi.

ALENTONE geldabat, tempore Regis Edwardi, pro 4 hidis. Terra est 2 carucatæ. In dominio sunt 2 hidæ et dimidium de hac terra, et ibi est 1 carucata, et 3 servi. Ibi 1 villanus, et 4 coscez, cum 1 carucata. Ibi molinus, reddens 20 solidos, et 5 acræ prati. Pastura 3 quarentenis longa, et una quarentena lata. Hanc terram tenuit Comes Heraldus.

carucate. In demesne is 1 hide, and 4 coscets hold the rest of the land. There are 5 acres of meadow.

In this same vill is 1 hide. The land is 1 carucate. A Thane held this land in the time of King Edward. There is 1 bordar, and 5 acres of meadow.

These 2 hides and a half are worth £4.

WINTRESLEI used to pay geld, in the time of King Edward, for 2 hides. The land is 2 carucates. There is 1 villan, and 3 bordars; and the wood is 2 furlongs long, and half a furlong broad. It is worth 20 shillings.

ALBOLDINTONE used to pay geld for 3 hides. The land is 2 carucates. Of this land 2½ hides are in demesne, and there is 1 carucate, and 4 coscets. There are 35 acres of meadow, and the pasture is 3 furlongs long, and 1 furlong broad. It is worth £4.

CHELTRE used to pay geld, in the time of King Edward, for 6 hides. The land is 5 carucates. Of this land there are in demesne 3 hides, and there is 1 carucate, and 4 serfs. There are 4 villans, and 2 bordars, with 2 carucates. The pasture is 4 furlongs long, and 2 furlongs broad. It was worth £4; it is now worth £6.

TEDRINTONE paid geld, in the time of King Edward, for 2 hides. The land is 2 carucates. There is 1 villan, and half a mill paying 30 pence, and 5 acres of meadow. It is worth 20 shillings.

Harding held these 6 estates in the time of King Edward.

ALENTONE paid geld, in the time of King Edward, for 4 hides. The land is 2 carucates. Of this land there are in demesne 2½ hides, and there is 1 carucate, and 3 serfs. There is 1 villan, and 4 coscets, with 1 carucate. There is a mill, paying 20 shillings, and 5 acres of meadow. The pasture is 3 furlongs long, and 1 furlong broad. Earl Harold held this estate.

In eadem villa sunt 4 hidæ terræ quas injuste abstraxit Heraldus ab ecclesia Ambresberiensi testimonio Tainorum Sciræ. Modo tamen habet ecclesia.

ELECOME geldabat, tempore Regis Edwardi, pro 27 hidis. Terra est 8 carucatæ. De hac terra sunt in dominio 24 hidæ, et ibi 2 carucatæ, et 6 servi. Ibi 3 villani, et 14 bordarii, cum 3 carucatis. Ibi 60 acræ prati, et tantundem pasturæ, et 20 acræ silvæ. Valuit 27 libras; modo 20 libras.

STRADFORD geldabat, tempore Regis Edwardi, pro 13 hidis. Terra est 7 carucatæ. De hac terra sunt in dominio 9 hidæ et una virgata terræ, et ibi 2 carucatæ, et 7 servi. Ibi 6 villani, et 4 bordarii, et 10 coscez, cum 4 carucatis. Ibi 2 molini, reddentes 17 solidos et 6 denarios, et 15 acræ prati, et 2 acræ pasturæ juxta flumen, et alia pastura 1 leuca longa, et 6 quarentenis lata.

In Wiltune, 1 burgensis, reddens 20 denarios, pertinet huic manerio. Valet 20 libras.

GESSIC geldabat, tempore Regis Edwardi, pro 10 hidis. Terra est 12 carucatæ. De hac terra sunt in dominio 4 hidæ et dimidium, et ibi 2 carucatæ, et 8 servi. Ibi 5 villani, et 8 bordarii, cum 4 carucatis. Ibi 40 acræ prati. Pastura 1 leuca longa, et dimidio leucæ lata, et tantundem silvæ. Valuit 40 libras quando Albericus recepit; modo 10 libras.

Hæc 3 maneria tenuit Azor tempore Regis Edwardi.

Tota hæc terra fuit Alberici Comitis. Modo est in manu Regis.

In the same vill are 4 hides of land which Harold unjustly took away from the church of Ambresbury according to the testimony of the Thanes of the Shire. The church however now possesses it.

ELECOME paid geld, in the time of King Edward, for 27 hides. The land is 8 carucates. Of this land there are in demesne 24 hides, and there are 2 carucates, and 6 serfs. There are 3 villans, and 14 bordars, with 3 carucates. There are 60 acres of meadow, and as much pasture, and 20 acres of wood. It was worth £27; it is now worth £20.

STRADFORD paid geld, in the time of King Edward, for 13 hides. The land is 7 carucates. Of this land there are in demesne 9 hides and 1 virgate of land, and there are 2 carucates, and 7 serfs. There are 6 villans, and 4 bordars, and 10 coscets, with 4 carucates. There are 2 mills, paying 17 shillings and 6 pence, and 15 acres of meadow, and 2 acres of pasture near the river, and other pasture 1 mile long, and 6 furlongs broad.

In Wilton, one burgess, paying 20 pence, belongs to this manor. The whole estate is worth £20.

GESSIC paid geld, in the time of King Edward, for 10 hides. The land is 12 carucates. Of this land there are in demesne 4½ hides, and there are 2 carucates, and 8 serfs. There are 5 villans, and 8 bordars, with 4 carucates. There are 40 acres of meadow. The pasture is 1 mile long, and half a mile broad, and there is as much wood. It was worth £40 when Alberic received it; it is now worth £10.

Azor held these 3 manors in the time of King Edward.

The whole of this land belonged to the Earl Alberic. It is now in the hand of the King.

Fol. { X a
69 a

REDDITUS EDWARDI SARISBERIENSIS.

EDWARDUS[1] VICECOMES[2] habet per annum de denariis[3] quæ pertinent ad vicecomitatum, 130 porcos, et 32 bacons; frumenti 2 modios et 8 sextarios, et tantundem brasii; avenæ 5 modios et 4 sextarios; mellis 16 sextarios, vel pro melle 16 solidos; gallinas 480; ova 1600; caseos 100; agnos 52; vellera ovium 240; annonæ[4] 162 acras. Habet etiam 8 libras valentiis inter Reveland, et quod inde habet. Quando propositis firma deficit, necesse est Edwardo restaurare de suo.

RENTS OF EDWARD OF SALISBURY.

EDWARD, THE SHERIFF, has yearly from the profits which belong to the shrievalty, 130 porkers and 32 bacon-hogs; of wheat, 2 bushels and 8 sextaries, and as much barley; of oats, 5 bushels and 4 sextaries; of honey, 16 sextaries, or instead of honey 16 shillings; 480 hens; 1600 eggs; 100 cheeses; 52 lambs; 240 fleeces; of corn unreaped, 162 acres. He has also £80 in value between the Reeve-land, and what he receives thence. When the farm-rent fails with the bailiffs, then it is incumbent for Edward to supply the deficiency in the stores from his own lands.

---

[1] EDWARD OF SALISBURY was the son of a valiant Norman soldier, Walter le Ewrus, Count of Rosmar, to whom, in consideration of his services, William the Conqueror gave the whole of Salisbury and Ambresbury. See Bowles' History of Lacock, p. 39. He was standard-bearer to Henry the First in the twentieth year of his reign at the famous battle of Brenmule by which an end was put to the rebellion in Normandy. His large estates were divided between his son Walter of Salisbury, the founder of Bradenstoke Priory, and his daughter Matilda who married Humphrey de Bohun the founder of the Priory at Monkton Farleigh. The great granddaughter of Walter of Salisbury, was the celebrated ELA, Countess of Salisbury, who was married to William de Longespee, son of Henry II. by Rosamond Clifford. After her husband's death ELA founded the Abbeys of Lacock, and Hinton Charterhouse, and became the first Abbess of the former religious house. See *Journal of Arch. Inst.* (1849,) p. 213.—*Journal of Brit. Arch. Assoc.* (1859,) p. 38.

[2] The office of '*Vice-comes*' was one of high trust and responsibility. "If the designation were to be regarded" says Mr. J. G. Nichols, "as we now regard titles of dignity, we might fairly translate it as '*Viscount*,' though this term was not really introduced into England as a title of peerage until the reign of Henry VI. But in early feudal times titles independent of office did not exist: the 'Comites' or Earls, were actual officers; and the 'Vice-comes' who acted in the absence of an Earl, is usually considered as identical with the functionary known by the English term 'Shire-reeve,' or 'Sheriff.' The latin records of many centuries down to modern times confirm this interpretation. For many of the reigns of our Norman monarchs this office was commonly hereditary. Afterwards it was granted to the same person for several successive years, at the King's pleasure; and lastly the modern practice obtained of appointing a new Sheriff every year."—*Journal of Arch. Inst.* (1849,) p. 211. See also *Wilts. Arch. Mag.* III., 190, in an article, by Canon Jackson, on 'Sheriffs of Wiltshire.'

[3] By the term '*denariis*' is meant the profits arising from the 'Denarius tertius Comitatus' or the 'Third penny of the County,' which was granted to him. "In the fines and other emoluments," says Bishop Kennett, "arising from the County Courts, two parts were allotted to the king, and a third part or penny to the Earl of the County, who either received it in specie, at the assizes and trials, or had an equivalent composition paid from the exchequer." Madox (Baron. p. 137) says that the most ancient way of creating an Earl was by Charter; the King thereby granted the Earl 'tertium Denarium Comitatus,' and then girded him with the sword of the County or Earldom. The King at times derived a portion of his revenue from the '*third penny*' of Boroughs, or Towns. See above, p. 6. Other illustrations of this custom may be seen in Heywood's Dissertation on the "*Ranks of the people under the Anglo-Saxon Government*," pp. 100, 101. See also, *Ellis*, i. 168.

[4] In the original, the world *bled.* (intended for *bladi*) is written over the word *annonæ*. By 'bladum' is meant commonly, says Kennett, 'every sort of *standing* corn in the blade and ear.' Ducange also gives as one of its meanings,—'any kind of corn *growing* in the field' (quando est in herba ante messem). In the History of Lacock, *p.* 38, the expression is translated '*corn-rents*,' but the Latin in that case would rather have been, '*annonam* 162 *acrarum*.' Moreover the context implies that some specific produce is intended, which was to be received in gross, as grown on the 162 acres, and not as a corn-rent, that is, as a composition, or so many bushels one year with another, no matter what the acres might yield.

X b
69 b

XXIV. TERRA EJUSDEM EDWARDI SARISBERIENSIS.

Edwardus de Sarisberie tenet de Rege *WILCOTE*. Tempore Regis Edwardi geldabat pro 15 hidis et dimidio. Terra est 10 carucatæ. De hac terra sunt in dominio 7 hidæ, et ibi 3 carucatæ, et 6 servi. Ibi 19 villani, et 6 bordarii, et 12 coscez. Ibi 40 acræ prati, et 20 acræ pasturæ, et 50 acræ silvæ minutæ, et ecclesia nova, et domus optima, et vinea bona. Valuit 12 libras; modo 16 libras.

Idem Edwardus tenet *AULTONE*. Tempore Regis Edwardi geldabat pro 5 hidis. Terra est 4 carucatæ. In dominio sunt 2 carucatæ, et 4 servi. Ibi 3 villani, et 1 bordarius, et 6 coscez, cum 1 carucata. Ibi molinus, reddens 10 solidos, et 25 acræ prati. Pastura 3 quarentenis longa, et 2 quarentenis lata. Valuit 100 solidos; modo 6 libras.

Idem Edwardus tenet *ECESATINGETONE*. Tempore Regis Edwardi geldabat pro 7 hidis. Terra est 4 carucatæ. De hac terra sunt in dominio 4 hidæ, et ibi 3 carucatæ. Ibi 12 bordarii, et 6 cotarii, et 2 francigenæ[1] tenentes 2 hidas et unam virgatam terræ, et habent 2 carucatas. Ibi 6 acræ prati, et 50 acræ pasturæ. Valuit 6 libras; modo, dominium Edwardi 6 libras et dimidium; francigenarum, 40 solidos.

Idem Edwardus tenet *EDINTONE*. Tempore Regis Edwardi geldabat pro 10 hidis. Terra est 6 carucatæ. In dominio sunt 3 carucatæ, et 4 servi. Ibi 9 villani, et 2 cotarii, et 24 coscez, cum 3

XXIV. LAND OF THE SAME EDWARD OF SALISBURY.

Edward of Salisbury holds *WILCOTE* of the King. In the time of King Edward it paid geld for 15½ hides. The land is 10 carucates. Of this land there are in demesne 7 hides, and there are 3 carucates, and 6 serfs. There are 19 villans, and 6 bordars, and 12 coscez. There are 40 acres of meadow, and 20 acres of pasture, and 50 acres of coppice, and a new church, and excellent house, and a good vineyard. It was worth £12; it is now worth £16.

The same Edward holds *AULTONE*. In the time of King Edward it paid geld for 5 hides. The land is 4 carucates. In demesne are 2 carucates and 4 serfs. There are 3 villans, and 1 bordar, and 6 coscets, with 1 carucate. There is a mill, paying 10 shillings, and 25 acres of meadow. The pasture is 3 furlongs long, and 2 furlongs broad. It was worth 100 shillings; it is now worth £6.

The same Edward holds *ECESATINGETONE*. In the time of King Edward it paid geld for 7 hides. The land is 4 carucates. Of this land there are in demesne 4 hides, and there are 3 carucates. There are 12 bordars, and 6 cottars, and 2 foreigners holding 2 hides and 1 virgate of land, and they have 2 carucates. There are 6 acres of meadow, and 50 acres of pasture. It was worth £6; the demesne of Edward is now worth £6 10s.; that of the foreigners is worth 40 shillings.

The same Edward holds *EDINTONE*. In the time of King Edward it paid geld for 10 hides. The land is 6 carucates. In demesne are 3 carucates, and 4 serfs. There are 9 villans, and 2 cottars, and

---

[1] Kelham (p. 216) defines 'Francigena,' a "Frenchman born, a foreigner, an alien, in contradistinction to an Englishman." It seems to have been a general name for all persons who could not prove themselves to be English. Among the laws of William the Conqueror is one, 'De jure Normannorum qui ante adventum Gulielmi cives fuerunt Anglicani' which is as follows:—"Et omnis *Francigena* qui tempore Edwardi propinqui nostri fuit in Anglia particeps consuctudinum Anglorum, quod ipsi dicunt *an hlote* et *an scote*, persolvat secundum legem Anglorum."—*Thorpe's Ancient Laws and Institutes*, i. 491.

Fol. { X b 69 b } carucatis. Ibi 10 acræ prati, et 8 acræ pasturæ, et 8 acræ silvæ. Valuit 8 libras; modo 12 libras. Heraldus Comes tenuit.

Idem Edwardus tenet 6 hidas in Hundredo de *WRDERUSTESELLE*, et pro 6 hidis geldabat tempore Regis Edwardi. Terra est 3 carucatæ. In dominio sunt 2 carucatæ, et 4 villani, et 2 coscez, cum 1 carucata. Ibi molinus, reddens 18 denarios, et 24 acræ prati, et una quarentena pasturæ. Valuit 100 solidos; modo 6 libras. Brictric tenuit. Huardus tenet de Edwardo.

Idem tenet in *ROTEFELD* 1 hidam. Aluric tenuit tempore Regis Edwardi, et pro 1 hida geldabat. Herveus tenet de Edwardo. Terra est dimidium carucatæ. Ibi 3 bordarii, et 4 acræ prati. Pastura dimidio quarentenæ longa, et tantundem lata. Valet 15 solidos.

Idem Edwardus tenet *WINTREBURNE*. Ulveva tenuit tempore Regis Edwardi, et geldabat pro 3 hidis. Terra est 3 carucatæ. Godefridus tenet de Edwardo. De hac terra tenet 2 hidas in dominio; et ibi 2 carucatæ, et 4 servi. Ibi 4 villani, et 4 bordarii, cum 1 carucata. Ibi molinus, reddens 5 solidos, et 6 acræ prati, et 30 acræ silvæ. Pastura 6 quarentenis longa, et 4 quarentenis lata. Valuit, et valet, 3 libras.

Idem Edwardus tenet in *WINTREBURNE-STOCH* 1 hidam et dimidium, et Walterus tenet de eo. Terra est 1 carucata, quæ ibi est. Valet 30 solidos.

Idem Edwardus tenet in eadem villa 1 hidam. Terra 1 carucata. Walterus tenet de Edwardo. Ibi habet 1 carucatam cum 2 cotariis, et 1 acram prati, et 6 acras pasturæ. Valet 20 solidos. Alwius tenuit tempore Regis Edwardi, cujus uxor ibidem tenet hidam dimidiam de Rege.

24 coscets, with 3 carucates. There are 10 acres meadow, and 8 acres of pasture and 8 acres of woo It was worth £8; it is now worth £12. The E Harold held it.

The same Edward holds 6 hides in the Hundred *WRDERUSTESELLE*, and the estate was assess for 6 hides in the time of King Edward. The land 3 carucates. In demesne are 2 carucates, and 4 villa and 2 coscets, with 1 carucate. There is a m paying 18 pence, and 24 acres of meadow, and furlong of pasture. It was worth 100 shillings; is now worth £6. Brictric held it. Huard hol the estate of Edward.

The same Edward holds 1 hide in *ROTEFEL* Aluric held it in the time of King Edward, and paid geld for 1 hide. Hervey holds it of Edwar The land is half a carucate. There are 3 borda and 4 acres of meadow. The pasture is half furlong long, and as much broad. It is worth shillings.

The same Edward holds *WINTREBURN* Ulveva held it in the time of King Edward, and paid geld for 3 hides. The land is 3 carucate Godfrey holds it of Edward. Of this land he hol 2 hides in demesne; and there are 2 carucates, and serfs. There are 4 villans, and 4 bordars, with carucate. There is a mill, paying 5 shillings, and acres of meadow, and 30 acres of wood. The pastu is 6 furlongs long, and 4 furlongs broad. It wa and is, worth £3.

The same Edward holds in *WINTREBURN STOCH* 1 hide and a half, and Walter holds it him. The land is 1 carucate, which is there. It worth 30 shillings.

The same Edward holds in the same vill 1 hid The land is 1 carucate. Walter holds it of Edwar There he has 1 carucate with 2 cottars, and 1 acre meadow, and 6 acres of pasture. It is worth shillings. Alwi held it in the time of King Edwa and his wife holds there a half hide of the King.

X b
69 b Idem Edwardus tenet *WINTREBURNE.* Alric tenuit tempore Regis Edwardi, et geldabat pro 13 hidis, et 3 virgatis. Terra est 7 carucatæ. De hac terra sunt in dominio 7 hidæ, et ibi 4 carucatæ, et 7 servi. Ibi 12 villani, et 5 bordarii, cum 3 carucatis. Ibi 10 acræ prati. Pastura 1 leuca longa, et dimidio leucæ lata. Valuit 6 libras; modo 10 libras.

The same Edward holds *WINTREBURNE.* Alric held it in the time of King Edward, and it paid geld for 13 hides, and 3 virgates. The land is 7 carucates. Of this land there are in demesne 7 hides, and there are 4 carucates, and 7 serfs. There are 12 villans, and 5 bordars, with 3 carucates. There are 10 acres of meadow. The pasture is 1 mile long, and half a mile broad. It was worth £6; it is now worth £10.

Idem Edwardus tenet *ORCESTONE*; Hugo de eo. Godricus tenuit tempore Regis Edwardi, et geldabat pro 4 hidis et dimidio. Terra est 2 carucatæ. In dominio est 1 carucata, et 4 bordarii, cum 4 servis, habentes 1 carucatam. Ibi pastura 8 quarentenis longa, et 2 quarentenis lata. Valuit 3 libras; modo 4 libras.

The same Edward holds *ORCESTONE*; Hugh holds it of him. Godric held it in the time of King Edward, and it paid geld for 4½ hides. The land is 2 carucates. In demesne is 1 carucate, and there are 4 bordars, with 4 serfs, having 1 carucate. There is pasture 8 furlongs long, and 2 furlongs broad. It was worth £3; it is now worth £4.

Willelmus tenet de Edwardo in *ORCESTONE* 2 hidas. Alwinus tenuit tempore Regis Edwardi. Terra est 1 carucata, quæ ibi est, cum 1 bordario, et 3 servis; et 80 acræ pasturæ. Valuit 20 solidos; modo 30.

William holds of Edward in *ORCESTONE* 2 hides. Alwin held them in the time of King Edward. The land is 1 carucate, which is there, with 1 bordar, and 3 serfs; and there are 80 acres of pasture. It was worth 20 shillings; it is now worth 30.

Ipse Edwardus tenet *TODEWORDE.* Alward tenuit tempore Regis Edwardi, et geldabat pro 4 hidis. Terra est 2 carucatæ. In dominio sunt 3 hidæ de eadem, et ibi 2 carucatæ, et 3 servi. Ibi 1 villanus, et 2 coscez, cum dimidio carucatæ. Pastura 4 quarentenis longa, et 3 quarentenis lata. Valuit 50 solidos; modo 60 solidos.

Edward himself holds *TODEWORDE.* Alward held it in the time of King Edward, and it paid geld for 4 hides. The land is 2 carucates. In demesne are 3 hides of the same, and there are 2 carucates, and 3 serfs. There is 1 villan, and 2 coscets, with half a carucate. The pasture is 4 furlongs long, and 3 furlongs broad. It was worth 50 shillings; it is now worth 60 shillings.

In *TODEWORDE* est una virgata terræ quam Croc diratiocinavit sibi pertinere debere. Hanc tamen tenet Edwardus.

In *TODEWORDE* is one virgate of land which Croc claimed as belonging of right to him. This land, however, Edward holds.

Ipse Edwardus tenet *LITLEGARSELE.* Elwardus tenuit tempore Regis Edwardi, et geldabat pro 1 hida. Terra est 3 carucatæ. In dominio sunt 2 carucatæ, et 3 servi; et 8 coscez, cum 1 carucata. Ibi pastura 3 quarentenis longa, et una quarentena lata. Silva dimidio leucæ longa, et 2 quarentenis lata. Valuit 100 solidos; modo 6 libras et 10 solidos.

Edward himself holds *LITLEGARSELE.* Elward held it in the time of King Edward, and it paid geld for 1 hide. The land is 3 carucates. In demesne are 2 carucates, and 3 serfs; and there are 8 coscets, with 1 carucate. There is pasture 3 furlongs long, and 1 furlong broad. The wood is half a mile long, and 2 furlongs broad. It was worth 100 shillings; it is now worth £6 10*s.*

Fol. { XI a / 69 c } Osmundus tenet de Edwardo *AMBRESBERIE.* Ulmer tenuit tempore Regis Edwardi, et geldabat pro 1 hida. Terra est 1 carucata. Ibi sunt 3 coscez, et 6 acræ prati. Pastura 2 quarentenis longa, et dimidio quarentenæ lata. Valuit 10 solidos; modo 20 solidos.

Idem Osmundus tenet de Edwardo 3 virgatas terræ quæ adjacent ad *AMBRESBERIE.* Terra est 1 carucata, quæ ibi est cum 2 coscez, et 3 servis. Unus Anglicus tenet de eadem terra 1 virgatam et dimidium, et ibi habet dimidium carucatæ, et 1 coscet, et 3 servos. Totum valet 40 solidos. Alric et Cole tenuerunt tempore Regis Edwardi.

Ipse Edwardus tenet *DEVREL,* et Adelelmus de eo. Saulf tenuit tempore Regis Edwardi, et geldabat pro 4 hidis. Terra est 2 carucatæ. In dominio 2 hidæ et dimidium de eadem terra, et ibi 2 carucatæ, cum 1 servo. Ibi 1 villanus, et 9 coscez, cum 1 carucata. Ibi 2 acræ prati, et 3 acræ silvæ. Pastura 3 quarentenis longa, et 2 quarentenis lata. Valuit 40 solidos; modo 60 solidos.

Ipse Edwardus tenet *STOCHE* Stremius tenuit tempore Regis Edwardi, et geldabat pro 16 hidis et una virgata. Terra est 10 carucatæ. De hac sunt in dominio 7 hidæ et dimidium, et ibi 4 carucatæ, et 2 servi. Ibi 8 villani, et 16 bordarii, et 16 cotarii, cum 6 carucatis. Ibi molinus, reddens 30 denarios, et 4 acræ prati, et 12 acræ pasturæ. Silva dimidio leucæ longa, et 3 quarentenis lata. Valuit 6 libras; modo 10 libras.

Huic Manerio adjacet una hida et una virgata terræ, sicut diratiocinati sunt Angli. Hanc terram tenet Willelmus de Pinchengi.

Teodricus tenet de Edwardo in *SOMREFORDE* 3½ virgatas terræ, et pro tanto geldabat. Terra est 1 carucata, quæ ibi est cum 3 bordariis, et 3 coscez. Ibi pars molini reddens 15 denarios, et 5 acræ prati, et 7 acræ pasturæ.

Osmund holds *AMBRESBERIE* of Edwar[d]. Ulmer held it in the time of King Edward, and [it] paid geld for 1 hide. The land is 1 carucate. The[re] are 3 coscets, and 6 acres of meadow. The pasture [is] 2 furlongs long, and half a furlong broad. It wa[s] worth 10 shillings; it is now worth 20 shillings.

The same Osmund holds of Edward 3 virgate[s] of land which are adjacent to *AMBRESBERIE.* The land is 1 carucate, which is there with 2 coscet[s] and 3 serfs. One Englishman holds of the sam[e] land 1 virgate and a half, and has there half [a] carucate, and 1 coscet, and 3 serfs. The whol[e] estate is worth 40 shillings. Alric and Cole held i[t] in the time of King Edward.

Edward himself holds *DEVREL,* and Adelelm holds it of him. Saulf held it in the time of King Edward, and it paid geld for 4 hides. The land is 2 carucates. In demesne are 2½ hides of the same land, and there are 2 carucates, with 1 serf. There is 1 villan, and 9 coscets, with 1 carucate. There are 2 acres of meadow and 3 acres of wood. The pasture is 3 furlongs long, and 2 furlongs broad. It was worth 40 shillings; it is now worth 60 shillings.

Edward himself holds *STOCHE.* Strem[ius] held it in the time of King Edward, and it paid geld for 16 hides and 1 virgate. The land is 10 carucates. Of this there are in demesne 7 hides and a half, and there are 4 carucates, and 2 serfs. There are 8 villans, and 16 bordars, and 16 cottars, with 6 carucates. There is a mill, paying 30 pence, and 4 acres of meadow, and 12 acres of pasture. The wood is half a mile long, and 3 furlongs broad. It was worth £6; it is now worth £10.

Adjacent to this manor there is 1 hide and 1 virgate of land belonging to it, as the Englishmen have decided. This land William de Pinchengi holds.

Teodric holds of Edward 3½ virgates of land in *SOMREFORDE,* and it paid geld for so much. The land is 1 carucate, which is there with 3 bordars, and 3 coscets. There is part of a mill paying 15 pence, and 5 acres of meadow, and 7 acres of pasture.

XI a 69 c In Malmesberie una domus reddit 15 denarios.

Valuit 15 solidos; modo 20 solidos. Scirold tenuit tempore Regis Edwardi.

Robertus tenet de Edwardo *BLONTESDONE.* Achi tenuit tempore Regis Edwardi, et geldabat pro 5 hidis. Terra est 3 carucatæ. De ea sunt in dominio 4 hidæ et dimidium, et ibi 2 carucatæ; et 4 bordarii, cum 1 carucata. Ibi molinus, reddens 25 denarios, et 30 acræ prati, et totidem pasturæ. Valuit 40 solidos; modo 60 solidos.

Ipse Edwardus tenet *CHETRE.* Azor tenuit tempore Regis Edwardi, et geldabat pro 11 hidis et una virgata terræ. Terra est 14 carucatæ. De ea sunt in dominio 6 hidæ et una virgata terræ, et ibi 1 carucata, et 4 servi, et 11 coliberti; et 10 villani, et 3 coscez, cum 5 carucatis. Ibi 18 acræ prati, et pastura 1 leuca longa, et dimidio leucæ lata, et tantundem silvæ. Valuit 20 libras; modo 30 libras.

Ipse Edwardus tenet *CHETRE.* Chenvin tenuit tempore Regis Edwardi, et geldabat pro 5 hidis. Terra est 4 carucatæ. De ea sunt in dominio 3 hidæ, et ibi 2 carucatæ, et 4 servi; et 5 villani, et 3 coscez, cum 2 carucatis. Ibi 8 acræ prati, et pastura 5 quarentenis longa, et una quarentena lata. Valuit 8 libras; modo 10 libras.

Robertus tenet de Edwardo *CHETRE.* Ulwen tenuit tempore Regis Edwardi, et geldabat pro 5 hidis. Terra est 4 carucatæ. De ea sunt in dominio 4 hidæ et dimidium, et ibi 2 carucatæ, et 4 servi; et 4 villani, et 2 bordarii, cum 2 carucatis. Ibi pastura 6 quarentenis longa, et 2 quarentenis lata. Valuit 60 solidos; modo 100 solidos.

Ipse Edwardus tenet *BOIENTONE.* Alwinus tenuit tempore Regis Edwardi, et geldabat pro 11

In Malmesberie one house pays 15 pence.

It was worth 15 shillings; it is now worth 20 shillings. Scirold held it in the time of King Edward.

Robert holds *BLONTESDONE* of Edward. Achi held it in the time of King Edward, and it paid geld for 5 hides. The land is 3 carucates. Of this there are in demesne 4½ hides, and there are 2 carucates; and there are 4 bordars, with 1 carucate. There is a mill, paying 25 pence, and 30 acres of meadow, and as much pasture. It was worth 40 shillings; it is now worth 60 shillings.

Edward himself holds *CHETRE.* Azor held it in the time of King Edward, and it paid geld for 11 hides and 1 virgate of land. The land is 14 carucates. Of this there are in demesne 6 hides and 1 virgate of land, and there is 1 carucate, and 4 serfs, and 11 coliberts; and there are 10 villans, and 3 coscets, with 5 carucates. There are 18 acres of meadow, and the pasture is 1 mile long, and half a mile broad, and as much wood. It was worth £20; it is now worth £30.

Edward himself holds *CHETRE.* Chenvin held it in the time of King Edward, and it paid geld for 5 hides. The land is 4 carucates. Of this there are in demesne 3 hides, and there are 2 carucates, and 4 serfs; and 5 villans, and 3 coscets, with 2 carucates. There are 8 acres of meadow, and the pasture is 5 furlongs long, and 1 furlong broad. It was worth £8; it is now worth £10.

Robert holds *CHETRE* of Edward. Ulwen held it in the time of King Edward, and it paid geld for 5 hides. The land is 4 carucates. Of this there are in demesne 4½ hides, and there are 2 carucates, and 4 serfs; and there are 4 villans, and 2 bordars, with 2 carucates. The pasture there is 6 furlongs long, and 2 furlongs broad. It was worth 60 shillings; it is now worth 100 shillings.

Edward himself holds *BOIENTONE.* Alwin held it in the time of King Edward, and it paid geld

Fol. { XI a 69 c } hidis et dimidio. Terra est 6 carucatæ. De ea sunt in dominio 8 hidæ et dimidium, et ibi 3 carucatæ, et 5 servi; et 7 villani, et 5 coscez, cum 2 carucatis. Ibi molinus, reddens 15 solidos, et 10 acræ prati, et pastura 4 quarentenis longa, et 3 quarentenis lata. Silva 3 quarentenis longa, et totidem lata. Valuit 8 libras; modo 11 libras et 10 solidos.

for 11½ hides. The land is 6 carucates. Of thi there are in demesne 8½ hides, and there are 3 caru cates, and 5 serfs; and there are 7 villans, and coscets, with 2 carucates. There is a mill, paying 1 shillings, and 10 acres of meadow, and the pasture i 4 furlongs long, and 3 furlongs broad. The wood i 3 furlongs long, and as many broad. It was wort £8; it is now worth £11 10*s*.

Adelelmus tenet de Edwardo *BALLOCHELIE.* Winegod tenuit tempore Regis Edwardi, et geldabat pro una hida. Terra est 2 carucatæ, quæ ibi sunt in dominio cum 10 bordariis. Silva 3 quarentenis longa, et una quarentena lata. Valuit 20 solidos; modo 40 solidos.

Adelelm holds *BALLOCHELIE* of Edward Winegod held it in the time of King Edward, and i paid geld for one hide. The land is 2 carucates which are there in demesne with 10 bordars. Th wood is 3 furlongs long, and one furlong broad. I was worth 20 shillings; it is now worth 40 shillings

Azelinus tenet de Edwardo *POLE.* Wlwen tenuit tempore Regis Edwardi, et geldabat pro 5 hidis. Terra est 5 carucatæ. De ea sunt in dominio 3 hidæ, et ibi 3 carucatæ, et 6 servi; et 6 villani, et 2 bordarii, cum 2 carucatis. Ibi molinus, reddens 10 solidos, et 60 acræ prati. Pastura 3 quarentenis longa, et 2 quarentenis lata. Silva 1 leuca in longitudine et latitudine. Valuit 100 solidos; modo 6 libras.

Azelin holds *POLE* of Edward. Wlwen hel it in the time of King Edward, and it paid geld fo 5 hides. The land is 5 carucates. Of this ther are in demesne 3 hides, and there are 3 carucates and 6 serfs; and there are 6 villans, and 2 bordars with 2 carucates. There is a mill, paying 10 shillings and 60 acres of meadow. The pasture is 3 furlong long, and 2 furlongs broad. The wood is 1 mile in length and breadth. It was worth 100 shillings; i is now worth £6.

Ipse Edwardus tenet *BISCOPESTREU.* Edred tenuit tempore Regis Edwardi, et geldabat pro 7 hidis. Terra est 6 carucatæ. De ea sunt in dominio 4 hidæ, et ibi 3 carucatæ, et 4 servi; et 9 villani, et 6 bordarii, et 2 cotarii, cum 3 carucatis. Ibi molinus, reddens 15 solidos, et 8 acræ prati, et 8 acræ silvæ. Pastura 5 quarentenis longa, et 3 quarentenis lata. Valuit 7 libras; modo 11 libras.

Edward himself holds *BISCOPESTREU* Edred held it in the time of King Edward, and it paid geld for 7 hides. The land is 6 carucates Of this there are in demesne 4 hides, and there are carucates, and 4 serfs; and there are 9 villans, and 6 bordars, and 2 cottars, with 3 carucates. There is a mill, paying 15 shillings, and 8 acres of meadow and 8 acres of wood. The pasture is 5 furlongs long and 3 furlongs broad. It was worth £7; it is now worth £11.

Ipse Edwardus tenet in *MIDELTONE* 3 virgatas terræ. Lewinus et Alric tenuerunt tempore Regis Edwardi, et pro tanto geldabant. Terra est 1 carucata, quæ ibi est cum uno villano; et 4 acræ prati, et 6 acræ pasturæ, et una acra silvæ. Valuit, et valet, 27 solidos.

Edward himself holds in *MIDELTONE* virgates of land. Lewin and Alric held them i the time of King Edward, and they paid geld for s much. The land is 1 carucate, which is there wit 1 villan; and there are 4 acres of meadow, and acres of pasture, and 1 acre of wood. It was, and is worth 27 shillings.

XI b
69 d
Gislebertus tenet de Edwardo *TICOODE*. Svain tenuit tempore Regis Edwardi, et geldabat pro 2 hidis. Terra est 2 carucatæ et dimidium. Ibi sunt 2 carucatæ in dominio, cum 6 coscez; et 3 acræ prati, et totidem pasturæ. Valuit 30 solidos; modo 40 solidos.

Borel tenet de Edwardo *LANGEFEL*. Ulwi tenuit tempore Regis Edwardi, et geldabat pro 7 hidis. Terra est 6 carucatæ. De ea sunt in dominio 2 hidæ, et ibi 2 carucatæ, et 2 servi; et 4 villani, et 9 cotarii, et 7 coscez, cum 3 carucatis. Ibi 8 acræ prati, et 6 acræ silvæ. Valuit 40 solidos; modo 4 libras.

Idem Ulwi tenet de eadem terra 1 hidam. Valet 10 solidos.

Borel tenet de Edwardo *TERINTONE*. Elric tenuit tempore Regis Edwardi, et geldabat pro 2 hidis. Terra est 1 carucata, quæ ibi est, et 2 servi, et 3 coscez. Ibi quarta pars molini, reddens 20 denarios, et 6 acræ prati. Valuit 10 solidos; modo 20 solidos.

Ipse Edwardus tenet *LACOCH*. Edwinus tenuit tempore Regis Edwardi, et geldabat pro 7 hidis. Terra est 9 carucatæ. De ea sunt in dominio 3 hidæ et dimidium, et ibi 3 carucatæ, et 7 servi; et 12 villani, et 16 coscez, et 3 cotarii. Ibi 2 molini, reddentes 17 solidos et 6 denarios, et 20 acræ prati, et dimidia acra vineæ. Silva 1 leuca inter longitudinem et latitudinem. Valuit, et valet, 7 libras.

Ipse Edwardus tenet in *ROCHELIE* 1 hidam. Azor tenuit tempore Regis Edwardi, et [1]
Terra est 2 carucatæ. In dominio est una carucata; et unus villanus, et 3 bordarii, cum 1 carucata; et 20 acræ pasturæ. Valuit, et valet, 40 solidos.

Gilbert holds *TICOODE* of Edward. Svain held it in the time of King Edward, and it paid geld for 2 hides. The land is 2 carucates and a half. There are 2 carucates in demesne, with 6 coscets; and there are 3 acres of meadow, and as many of pasture. It was worth 30 shillings; it is now worth 40 shillings.

Borel holds *LANGEFEL* of Edward. Ulwi held it in the time of King Edward, and it paid geld for 7 hides. The land is 6 carucates. Of this there are 2 hides in demesne, and there are 2 carucates, and 2 serfs; and there are 4 villans, and 9 cottars, and 7 coscets, with 3 carucates. There are 8 acres of meadow, and 6 acres of wood. It was worth 40 shillings; it is now worth £4.

The same Ulwi holds 1 hide of the same land. It is worth 10 shillings.

Borel holds *TERINTONE* of Edward. Elric held it in the time of King Edward, and it paid geld for 2 hides. The land is 1 carucate, which is there, and there are 2 serfs, and 3 coscets. There is the fourth part of a mill paying 20 pence, and 6 acres of meadow. It was worth 10 shillings; it is now worth 20 shillings.

Edward himself holds *LACOCH*. Edwin held it in the time of King Edward, and it paid geld for 7 hides. The land is 9 carucates. Of this there are in demesne 3 hides and a half, and there are 3 carucates, and 7 serfs; and there are 12 villans, and 16 coscets, and 3 cottars. There are 2 mills, paying 17 shillings and 6 pence, and 20 acres of meadow, and half an acre of vineyard. The wood is 1 mile between length and breadth. It was, and is, worth £7.

Edward himself holds 1 hide in *ROCHELIE*. Azor held it in the time of King Edward, and
The land is 2 carucates. In demesne is 1 carucate; and there is 1 villan, and 3 bordars, with 1 carucate; and there are 20 acres of pasture. It was, and is, worth 40 shillings.

---

[1] The blank in the original manuscript should be probably supplied with—'pro tanto geldabat.'

Fol. { XI b 69 d

Tetbaldus tenet de Edwardo *WINTREBURNE.* Alwardus tenuit tempore Regis Edwardi, et geldabat pro 3 hidis, et una virgata terræ, et 4 acris. Terra est 2 carucatæ. In dominio est 1 carucata, cum 1 villano, et 6 bordariis; et 13 acræ pasturæ. Valuit 30 solidos; modo 4 libras.

Azelinus tenet de Edwardo in *DEPEFORD* 2 hidas terræ. Oswardus et Godvinus tenebant tempore Regis Edwardi, et pro tanto geldabant. Terra est 2 carucatæ. De ea in dominio est hida et dimidium, et ibi 2 carucatæ, cum 1 villano, et 3 bordariis, et 2 cotariis. Ibi molinus, reddens 10 solidos, et 8 acræ prati, et 16 acræ pasturæ. Valuit 20 solidos; modo 40 solidos. Qui tenebant poterant ire quo volebant.[1]

Turchitil tenet de Edwardo in *HERTHAM* 1 hidam terræ. Duo Taini tenuerunt tempore Regis Edwardi, et pro tanto geldabat. Terra est 6 bobus. Ibi est 1 carucata, cum 1 servo, et 4 coscez; et 4 acræ prati, et 12 acræ pasturæ, et 3 acræ silvæ parvæ. Valuit 10 solidos; modo 15 solidos.

Godefridus tenet de Edwardo *WEROCHESHALLE.* Baldvinus tenuit tempore Regis Edwardi, et geldabat pro 7 hidis. Terra est 9 carucatæ. De ea sunt in dominio 3 hidæ, et ibi 4 carucatæ, et 3 servi; et 16 villani, et 5 bordarii, et 6 coscez, cum 5 carucatis. Ibi 2 molini, reddentes 18 solidos, et dimidia acra prati. Silva 6 quarentenis longa, et 4 quarentenis lata; et 2 burgenses in Malmesberie reddunt 2 solidos. Valuit 100 solidos; modo 6 libras.

Tetbald holds *WINTREBURNE* of Edward. Alward held it in the time of King Edward, and it paid geld for 3 hides, and 1 virgate of land, and 4 acres. The land is 2 carucates. In demesne is 1 carucate, with 1 villan, and 6 bordars; and there are 13 acres of pasture. It was worth 30 shillings; it is now worth £4.

Azelin holds 2 hides of land of Edward in *DEPEFORD.* Osward and Godwin held them in the time of King Edward, and they paid geld for so much. The land is 2 carucates. Of this there is a hide and a half in demesne, and there are 2 carucates, with 1 villan, and 3 bordars, and 2 cottars. There is a mill paying 10 shillings, and 8 acres of meadow, and 16 acres of pasture. It was worth 20 shillings; it is now worth 40 shillings. They who held this land could go whither they wished.

Turchitil holds of Edward 1 hide of land in *HERTHAM.* Two Thanes held it in the time of King Edward, and it paid geld for so much. The land is sufficient for 6 oxen. There is 1 carucate, with 1 serf, and 4 coscets; and there are 4 acres of meadow, and 12 acres of pasture, and 3 acres of coppice-wood. It was worth 10 shillings; it is now worth 15 shillings.

Godfrey holds *WEROCHESHALLE* of Edward. Baldwin held it in the time of King Edward, and it paid geld for 7 hides. The land is 9 carucates. Of this there are in demesne 3 hides, and there are 4 carucates, and 3 serfs; and there are 16 villans, and 5 bordars, and 6 coscets, with 5 carucates. There are 2 mills, paying 18 shillings, and half an acre of meadow. The wood is 6 furlongs long, and 4 furlongs broad; and 2 burgesses in Malmesbury pay 2 shillings. It was worth 100 shillings; it is now worth £6.

---

[1] The phrase "potuit ire quo volebat," which is frequent in Domesday, is equivalent to "*liber* fuit." Thus in Dorsetshire under CNOLLE *(fol. 82)* it is said, "Unus Tainus tenuit tempore Regis Edwardi et *liber erat* cum hac terra." In the Exon Domesday *(fol. 48)* we have in the account of WAIA, in Dorset, the following,—"Quinque Taini tenuerunt ea die qua Rex Edwardus fuit vivus et mortuus qui *poterant ire ad quemlibet dominum* cum suis terris." Persons under this description were attached to no lord in a seignorial, but to the king only in a political, capacity. They might remove to any other part of the kingdom without alienating the possessions they quitted; or they were at liberty to part with their land, or to put themselves and their property under a different seignorial protection. This was termed "*commendare se,*" *i.e.* to recommend, or submit themselves to such a protection. *See Nichols' Leicester,* p. xli. *Ellis* i. 70.

XIb 69 d Aiulfus tenet de Edwardo *TOLLARD*. Rozo tenuit tempore Regis Edwardi, et geldabat pro 2 hidis et dimidio. Terra est totidem carucatæ. De ea sunt in dominio 2 hidæ et dimidia virgata terræ, et ibi 2 carucatæ; et 3 villani, et 7 coscez, cum dimidia carucata. Ibi pastura 2 quarentenis longa, et una quarentena lata, et tantundem silvæ. Valuit 40 solidos; modo 50 solidos.

Petrus tenet de Edwardo in *POERTONE* 1 hidam. Gode tenuit tempore Regis Edwardi. Terra est 1 carucata, quæ ibi est, cum 1 servo, et 1 bordario. Ibi molinus, reddens 32 denarios, et 2 acræ prati. Pastura 50 ovibus. Valet 20 solidos.

Ipse Edwardus tenet *WINTREBURNE*. Wlwen tenuit tempore Regis Edwardi, et geldabat pro 7 hidis. Terra est 6 carucatæ. De ea sunt in dominio 3 hidæ, et ibi 2 carucatæ, et 8 servi; et 8 villani, et 12 coscez, cum 3 carucatis. Ibi molinus, reddens 15 solidos, et 13 acræ prati. Pastura 5 quarentenis longa, et 3 quarentenis lata. Valuit 8 libras; modo 12 libras.

Letardus tenet de Edwardo in *LANGEFORDE* 1 hidam terræ. Azor tenuit tempore Regis Edwardi, et pro tanto geldabat. Terra est dimidium carucatæ. Ibi 9 acræ prati, et 10 acræ pasturæ. Valuit, et valet, 20 solidos.

Taini diratiocinantur hanc terram Ecclesiæ Glastingeberiensi.[1]

Aiulf holds *TOLLARD* of Edward. Rozo held it in the time of King Edward, and it paid geld for 2 hides and a half. The land is as many carucates. Of this there are in demesne 2 hides and half a virgate of land, and there are 2 carucates; and there are 3 villans, and 7 coscets, with a half carucate. There is pasture 2 furlongs long, and 1 furlong broad, and as much wood. It was worth 40 shillings; it is now worth 50 shillings.

Peter holds 1 hide of Edward in *POERTONE*. Gode held it in the time of King Edward. The land is 1 carucate, which is there, with 1 serf, and 1 bordar. There is a mill, paying 32 pence, and 2 acres of meadow. There is pasture for 50 sheep. It is worth 20 shillings.

Edward himself holds *WINTREBURNE*. Wlwen held it in the time of King Edward, and it paid geld for 7 hides. The land is 6 carucates. Of this there are in demesne 3 hides, and there are 2 carucates, and 8 serfs; and there are 8 villans, and 12 coscets, with 3 carucates. There is a mill, paying 15 shillings, and 13 acres of meadow. The pasture is 5 furlongs long, and 3 furlongs broad. It was worth £8; it is now worth £12.

Letard holds of Edward 1 hide in *LANGEFORDE*. Azor held it in the time of King Edward, and it paid geld for so much. The land is half a carucate. There are 9 acres of meadow, and 10 acres of pasture. It was, and is worth, 20 shillings.

The Thanes adjudge this land to the Church at Glastonbury.

---

[1] See above, *p.* 33, under "LANGEFORD."

XXV. TERRA ERNULFI DE HESDING.

Fol. {XI b, 69 d} Ernulfus de Hesding[1] tenet de Rege *CHIVELE.* Brixi tenuit tempore Regis Edwardi, et geldabat pro 16 hidis. Terra est 16 carucatæ. De hac terra sunt in dominio 7 hidæ, et ibi 6 carucatæ, et 10 servi; et 18 villani, et 14 bordarii, cum 12 carucatis. Ibi molini 2, reddentes 55 solidos, et 16 acræ prati. Pastura 4 quarentenis longa, et 4 lata. Silva 1 leuca longa, et 2 quarentenis lata. Valet 26 libras.

Quando recepit valebat 20 libras, excepta firma 2 Tainorum quæ in mansione[2] erat.

Ipse Ernulfus tenet in *POTERNE* 3 hidas et unam virgatam terræ, quæ geldabant cum Poterne, manerio Episcopi Sarisberiensis, tempore Regis Edwardi. Hanc terram clamat Osmundus Episcopus. Algarus, qui tenuit tempore Regis Edwardi, non poterat ab ecclesia separari. Robertus tenet de Ernulfo. Terra est 2 carucatæ, et sunt in dominio; et unus villanus ibi habet dimidiam carucatam; et 6 servi, et 3 bordarii. Ibi molinus, reddens 7 solidos et 6 denarios, et 14 acræ prati. [3] 3 quarentenis longa, et una quarentena lata. Valuit 4 libras; modo 100 solidos.

Fol. {XII a, 70 a} Lethelinus tenet de Ernulfo *CHEVREL.* Alwardus tenuit tempore Regis Edwardi, et geldabat pro 3 hidis et dimidio. Terra est 3 carucatæ. In dominio sunt 2 carucatæ; et 12 bordarii cum 1 carucata. Ibi dimidium molini reddens 30 denarios, et 3 acræ prati. Pastura 10 quarentenis longa, et una lata. Valuit 60 solidos; modo 100 solidos.

XXV. LAND OF ERNULF DE HESDING.

Ernulf de Hesding holds *CHIVELE* of th King. Brixi held it in the time of King Edwarc and it paid geld for 16 hides. The land is 1 carucates. Of this land 7 hides are in demesne, an there are 6 carucates, and 10 serfs; and there are 1 villans, and 14 bordars, with 12 carucates. Ther are 2 mills, paying 55 shillings, and 16 acres c meadow. The pasture is 4 furlongs long, and broad. The wood is 1 mile long, and 2 furlong broad. It is worth £26.

When he received it, it was worth £20, nc reckoning the holding of 2 Thanes which was in th manor.

Ernulf himself holds 3 hides and 1 virgate c land in *POTERNE,* which paid geld with Potern the manor of the Bishop of Sarum, in the time c King Edward. Bishop Osmund claims this lan Algar, who held this land in the time of Kin Edward, could not be separated from the churc Robert holds it of Ernulf. The land is 2 carucate and they are in demesne; and 1 villan has there half carucate; and there are 6 serfs, and 3 bordar There is a mill, paying 7 shillings and 6 pence, an 14 acres of meadow. The is 3 furlongs lon and 1 furlong broad. It was worth £4; it is no worth 100 shillings.

Lethelin holds *CHEVREL* of Ernulf. Alwa held it in the time of King Edward, and it paid ge for 3 hides and a half. The land is 3 carucate There are 2 carucates in demesne; and there are 1 bordars with 1 carucate. There is half a mi paying 30 pence, and 3 acres of meadow. Tl pasture is 10 furlongs long, and 1 broad. It w worth 60 shillings; it is now worth 100 shillings.

---

[1] Ernulf de Hesding was the first Earl of Perch, and father of Earl Rotrock, who married Matilda the natural daughter of King Henry I. See *Sandford's Genealog. Hist.* p. 32. *Ellis* i., 434.

[2] This use of the word 'mansio' to denote a 'manor' is not common, though, according to Kelham, occasionally to be m with. It is not easy, however, to suggest another translation this sentence that would be more satisfactory.

[3] The missing word is no doubt either 'Silva' or 'Pastur The scribe has omitted to insert it in the original manuscript.

XII a 70 a In *ECESATINGETONE* sunt 2 hidæ. Terra 1 carucata. Edricus tenuit tempore Regis Edwardi, et uxor ejus tenet modo de Ernulfo et ibi habet 1 carucatam; et 7 bordarii, cum 1 cotario. Ibi 12 acræ prati, et 12 acræ pasturæ. Valuit, et valet, 40 solidos.

Eadem uxor Edrici tenet de Ernulfo *CALESTONE.* Vir ejus tenuit tempore Regis Edwardi, et geldabat pro 2 hidis et dimidio. Terra est 3 carucatæ. De ea in dominio est 1 hida et una virgata, et ibi 1 carucata; et unus villanus, et 10 bordarii, et 18 coscez, cum 1 carucata. Ibi molinus, reddens 15 solidos, et 12 acræ prati, et 6 acræ silvæ. Pastura 3 quarentenis longa, et una quarentena lata. In *CALNE* unus burgensis reddit 11 denarios. Valuit, et valet, 4 libras.

[In *PEVESIE*[1] tenet idem Ernulfus de Rege 2 hidas. Tempore Regis Edwardi tenebat eas unus Tainus de Abbatia Wintoniensi, et non poterat ab ea separari. Valuit, et valet, 40 solidos.]

Benzelinus tenet de Ernulfo *STANDONE.* Brictric tenuit tempore Regis Edwardi, et geldabat pro 2 hidis. Terra est 2 carucatæ. In dominio est una; et molinus, reddens 6 solidos, et 4 acræ prati. Pastura 3 quarentenis longa, et 3 lata. Silva 3 quarentenis longa, et una quarentena lata. Valet 40 solidos.

Ipse Ernulfus tenet *CALDEFELLE.* Wallefus tenuit tempore Regis Edwardi, et geldabat pro 2 hidis et dimidio. Terra est 2 carucatæ. De ea est in dominio 1 hida et dimidium, et ibi 1 carucata, cum 1 servo, et 4 bordariis. Ibi dimidium molini reddens 18 denarios, et 6 acræ prati, et 6 acræ silvæ, et 8 acræ pasturæ. Valuit 4 libras; modo 50 solidos.

In *ECESATINGETONE* are 2 hides. The land is 1 carucate. Edric held it the time of King Edward, and his wife holds it now of Ernulf and has there 1 carucate; and there are 7 bordars, with 1 cottar. There are 12 acres of meadow, and 12 acres of pasture. It was, and is, worth 40 shillings.

The same wife of Edric holds *CALESTONE* of Ernulf. Her husband held it in the time of King Edward, and it paid geld for 2 hides and a half. The land is 3 carucates. Of this there is 1 hide and 1 virgate in demesne, and there is 1 carucate; and there is 1 villan, and 10 bordars, and 18 coscets, with 1 carucate. There is a mill, paying 15 shillings, and 12 acres of meadow, and 6 acres of wood. The pasture is 3 furlongs long, and 1 furlong broad. In *CALNE* 1 burgess pays 11 pence. It was, and is, worth £4.

[In *PEVESIE* the same Ernulf holds 2 hides of the King. In the time of King Edward a certain Thane held them of the Abbey of Winchester, and he could not be separated from it. It was, and is, worth 40 shillings.]

Benzelin holds *STANDONE* of Ernulf. Brictric held it in the time of King Edward, and it paid geld for 2 hides. The land is 2 carucates. In demesne is one; and there is a mill, paying 6 shillings, and 4 acres of meadow. The pasture is 3 furlongs long, and 3 broad. The wood is 3 furlongs long, and 1 furlong broad. It is worth 40 shillings.

Ernulf himself holds *CALDEFELLE.* Wallef held it in the time of King Edward, and it paid geld for 2 hides and a half. The land is 2 carucates. Of this there is one hide and a half in demesne, and there is 1 carucate, with 1 serf, and 4 bordars. There is half a mill paying 18 pence, and 6 acres of meadow, and 6 acres of wood, and 8 acres of pasture. It was worth £4; it is now worth 50 shillings.

---

[1] In the original manuscript this paragraph has been erased with the pen, and is therefore printed above within brackets. The same entry will be found, in substance, at *p.* 41, under "PEVESIE."

Fol. { XII a / 70 a }

Ipse Ernulfus tenet in eadem villa tantundem terræ pro uno Manerio. Godvinus tenuit tempore Regis Edwardi. Ibi tantundem habet quantum in superiori continetur, et tantundem appreciatur.

Ipse Ernulfus tenet 5 acras terræ in *BUTREMARE*.

Robertus tenet de Ernulfo *SCLIVE*. Chetel tenuit tempore Regis Edwardi, et geldabat pro 3 hidis. Terra est 2 carucatæ. De ea sunt in dominio 2 hidæ et dimidium, et ibi 2 carucatæ, cum 4 coscez. Ibi 20 acræ prati, et 15 acræ pasturæ, et 4 acræ silvæ. Valuit 30 solidos; modo 40 solidos.

Robertus tenet de Ernulfo *BICHENEHILDE*. Chetel tenuit tempore Regis Edwardi, et geldabat pro 1 hida. Terra est dimidia carucata, quæ ibi est, cum 1 coscet; et 6 acræ prati, et 4 acræ silvæ. Valuit 10 solidos; modo 15 solidos.

Robertus tenet de Ernulfo *WIDECOME*. Brictric tenuit tempore Regis Edwardi, et geldabat pro 2 hidis. Terra est 2 carucatæ. Ibi 7 coscez, cum 1 carucata; et 12 acræ prati, et 6 acræ pasturæ, et 12 acræ silvæ. Valuit 20 solidos; modo 30 solidos.

Robertus tenet de Ernulfo *HELMERINTONE*. Aschil tenuit tempore Regis Edwardi, et geldabat pro 1 hida. Terra est 1 carucata, quæ ibi est, cum 3 coscez. Ibi molinus, reddens 7 solidos et dimidium; et 6 acræ prati, et una acra pasturæ, et 8 acræ silvæ. Valuit 15 solidos; modo 30 solidos.

Ulward tenet de Ernulfo ad firmam *CELDRINTONE*. Ipse tenuit tempore Regis Edwardi, et geldabat pro 1 hida et 4 acris. Terra est 1 carucata, quæ ibi est in dominio; et pastura 2 quarentenis

Ernulf himself holds in the same vill the same quantity of land for one manor. Godwin held it in the time of King Edward. It has there as much as is contained in the above manor, and it is valued at a like sum.

Ernulf himself holds 5 acres of land in *BUTREMARE*.

Robert holds *SCLIVE* of Ernulf. Chetel held it in the time of King Edward, and it paid geld for 3 hides. The land is 2 carucates. Of this there are in demesne 2 hides and a half, and there are 2 carucates, with 4 coscets. There are 20 acres of meadow, and 15 acres of pasture, and 4 acres of wood. It was worth 30 shillings; it is now worth 40 shillings.

Robert holds *BICHENEHILDE* of Ernulf. Chetel held it in the time of King Edward, and it paid geld for 1 hide. The land is a half carucate, which is there, with 1 coscet; and there are 6 acres of meadow, and 4 acres of wood. It was worth 10 shillings; it is now worth 15 shillings.

Robert holds *WIDECOME* of Ernulf. Brictric held it in the time of King Edward, and it paid geld for 2 hides. The land is 2 carucates. There are 7 coscets, with 1 carucate; and there are 12 acres of meadow, and 6 acres of pasture, and 12 acres of wood. It was worth 20 shillings; it is now worth 30 shillings.

Robert holds *HELMERINTONE* of Ernulf. Aschil held it in the time of King Edward, and it paid geld for 1 hide. The land is 1 carucate, which is there, with 3 coscets. There is a mill, paying 7 shillings and sixpence; and there are 6 acres of meadow, and 1 acre of pasture, and 8 acres of wood. It was worth 15 shillings; it is now worth 30 shillings.

Ulward holds *CELDRINTONE* of Ernulf at a farm-rent. He himself held it in the time of King Edward, and it paid geld for 1 hide and 4 acres. The land is 1 carucate, which is there in demesne

XII a 70 a longa, et una quarentena lata. Valuit 25 solidos; modo 40 solidos.

and the pasture is 2 furlongs long and 1 furlong broad. It was worth 25 shillings; it is now worth 40 shillings.

Ipse Ernulfus tenet *CELDRINTONE.* Sewi tenuit tempore Regis Edwardi, et geldabat pro 1 hida. Terra est 1 carucata, quæ ibi est cum 1 coscet; et pastura 2 quarentenis longa, et una quarentena lata. Valuit 25 solidos; modo 40 solidos.

Ernulf himself holds *CELDRINTONE.* Sewi held it in the time of King Edward, and it paid geld for 1 hide. The land is 1 carucate, which is there with 1 coscet; and the pasture is 2 furlongs long, and 1 furlong broad. It was worth 25 shillings; it is now worth 40 shillings.

Godric tenet de Ernulfo in *CELDRINTONE* 1 hidam. Alwinus et Uluricus tenuerunt tempore Regis Edwardi pro 2 maneriis, et pro una hida geldabant. Terra est 1 carucata et dimidium, et tantum est ibi, cum 2 coscez. Ibi pastura 2 quarentenis longa, et una quarentena lata. Valuit 20 solidos; modo 40 solidos.

Godric holds 1 hide of Ernulf in *CELDRINTONE.* Alwin and Uluric held it in the time of King Edward for 2 manors, and paid geld for 1 hide. The land is 1 carucate and a half, and as much as this is there, with 2 coscets. There is pasture 2 furlongs long, and 1 furlong broad. It was worth 20 shillings; it is now worth 40 shillings.

Robertus tenet de Ernulfo *BECHENEHILDE.* Turgot tenuit tempore Regis Edwardi, et geldabat pro 1 hida. Terra est dimidium carucatæ. Ibi est unus coscet, et 6 acræ prati, et 6 acræ silvæ. Valuit 10 solidos; modo 15 solidos.

Robert holds *BECHENEHILDE* of Ernulf. Turgot held it in the time of King Edward, and it paid geld for 1 hide. The land is half a carucate. There is 1 coscet, and 6 acres of meadow, and 6 acres of wood. It was worth 10 shillings; it is now worth 15 shillings.

Urso tenet de Ernulfo *CHENEBUILD.* Ulwid tenuit tempore Regis Edwardi, et geldabat pro 2 hidis et dimidio. Terra est 2 carucatæ. In dominio est una, et 2 servi; et 6 acræ prati, et 2 acræ silvæ. Valuit 20 solidos; modo 25 solidos.

Urso holds *CHENEBUILD* of Ernulf. Ulwid held it in the time of King Edward, and it paid geld for $2\frac{1}{2}$ hides. The land is 2 carucates. In demesne is one, and 2 serfs; and there are 6 acres of meadow, and 2 acres of wood. It was worth 20 shillings; it is now worth 25 shillings.

XII b 70 b Ipse Ernulfus tenet *CHEIESLAVE.* Ulwi tenuit tempore Regis Edwardi, et geldabat pro una hida et una virgata et dimidio. Terra est 1 carucata; et una acra prati et dimidium; et una acra silvæ. Valet 20 solidos.

Ernulf himself holds *CHEIESLAVE.* Ulwi held it in the time of King Edward, and it paid geld for 1 hide and 1 virgate and a half. The land is 1 carucate; and there is 1 acre and a half of meadow; and 1 acre of wood. It is worth 20 shillings.

In eadem villa tenet unus Tainus de Ernulfo 2 virgatas terræ et dimidium. Hic, tempore Regis Edwardi, poterat ire ad quem vellet dominum,[1] et

In the same vill a Thane holds of Ernulf $2\frac{1}{2}$ virgates of land. He, in the time of King Edward, could go to what lord he thought proper, and in the

[1] On the meaning of this expression see the note on *p.* 72.

Fol. { XII b / 70 b } tempore Regis Willelmi sponte se vertit ad Ernulfum. Valebat hæc terra 15 solidos; modo 40 denarios, quos reddit Ernulfo de firma.

Urso tenet de Ernulfo *DEVREL.* Ulmarus tenuit tempore Regis Edwardi, et geldabat pro 2 hidis et dimidio, et dimidia virgatæ terræ. Terra est 3 carucatæ. De ea est in dominio 1 hida et dimidium, et ibi 2 carucatæ, et 3 servi; et 2 bordarii, et 6 coscez, cum 1 carucata. Ibi molinus, reddens 5 solidos, et 2 acræ prati. Pastura dimidio leucæ longa, et una quarentena lata; et tantundem silvæ. Valuit 30 solidos; modo 50 solidos.

Rainboldus tenet de Ernulfo *OPETONE.* Tous tenuit tempore Regis Edwardi, et geldabat pro 2 hidis et dimidio. Terra est 3 carucatæ. De ea est in dominio hida et dimidium, et ibi 2 carucatæ, cum 1 villano, et 5 bordariis. Ibi 4 acræ prati, et 3 acræ silvæ. Valet 40 solidos.

In hac terra est dimidia hida comprehensa quæ geldabat tempore Regis Edwardi, sed postquam Rex Willelmus in Angliam venit geldum non reddidit.

Infra eandem terram tenet Ernulfus, de terra Willelmi de Ow, dimidiam hidam; et etiam, de terra dominica Regis, tantum quod valet 1 hidam.

Nuboldus tenet de Ernulfo *WINTREBURNE.* Edricus tenuit tempore Regis Edwardi, et geldabat pro 1 hida, et 2½ virgatis terræ. Terra est 1 carucata, quæ ibi est cum 2 servis; et 8 acræ pasturæ. Valuit 20 solidos; modo 40 solidos.

Turchil tenet de Ernulfo *HARDENEHUS.* Alwardus tenuit tempore Regis Edwardi, et geldabat pro 3 hidis. Terra est 4 carucatæ. Ibi sunt 3 bordarii, et 12 acræ prati. Silva 1 quarentena longa, et 1 quarentena lata. Valuit 4 libras; modo 40 solidos.

time of King William of his own accord he return to Ernulf. This land was worth 15 shillings; wh the Thane now pays to Ernulf for the rent of t said land is worth 40 pence.

Urso holds *DEVREL* of Ernulf. Ulmar he it in the time of King Edward, and it paid geld f 2½ hides, and half a virgate of land. The land is carucates. Of this there is in demesne one hide a a half, and there are 2 carucates, and 3 serfs; a there are 2 bordars, and 6 coscets, with 1 caruca There is a mill, paying 5 shillings, and 2 acres meadow. The pasture is half a mile long, and furlong broad; and there is as much wood. It w worth 30 shillings; it is now worth 50 shillings.

Rainbold holds *OPETONE* of Ernulf. To held it in the time of King Edward, and it pa geld for 2½ hides. The land is 3 carucates. Of th there is in demesne 1 hide and a half, and there a 2 carucates with 1 villan, and 5 bordars. There a 4 acres of meadow, and 3 acres of wood. It worth 40 shillings.

In this land is included a half hide which pa geld in the time of King Edward, but since Kir William came into England it has paid no geld.

Within the same land Ernulf holds, of the la of William de Ow, a half hide; and also, of t demesne land of the King, as much as is worth hide.

Nubold holds *WINTREBURNE* of Ernu Edric held it in the time of King Edward, a it paid geld for 1 hide and 2½ virgates of land. T land is 1 carucate, which is there with 2 serfs; a there are 8 acres of pasture. It was worth shillings; it is now worth 40 shillings.

Turchil holds *HARDENEHUS* of Ernu Alward held it in the time of King Edward, a it paid geld for 3 hides. The land is 4 carucat There are 3 bordars, and 12 acres of meadow. T wood is 1 furlong long, and 1 furlong broad. It w worth £4; it is now worth 40 shillings.

{XII b / 70 b} Ipse Ernulfus tenet *ESTONE*. Godus tenuit tempore Regis Edwardi, et geldabat pro 5 hidis. Terra est 3 carucatæ. In dominio sunt 2 carucatæ, cum 1 servo, et 3 bordariis. Ibi 10 acræ prati, et 12 acræ pasturæ. Valuit 60 solidos; modo 100 solidos.

Ernulf himself holds *ESTONE*. Godus held it in the time of King Edward, and it paid geld for 5 hides. The land is 3 carucates. In demesne are 2 carucates, with 1 serf, and 3 bordars. There are 10 acres of meadow, and 12 acres of pasture. It was worth 60 shillings; it is now worth 100 shillings.

Judichel tenet de Ernulfo *ETONE*. Duo Taini tenebant tempore Regis Edwardi, et geldabat pro 5 hidis. Terra est 3 carucatæ. De ea sunt in dominio 3 hidæ et dimidium, et ibi 2 carucatæ; et 2 villani, et 6 bordarii; et 20 acræ prati, et totidem pasturæ, et 10 acræ silvæ. Valuit 30 solidos; modo 50 solidos.

Judichel holds *ETONE* of Ernulf. Two Thanes held it in the time of King Edward, and it paid geld for 5 hides. The land is 3 carucates. Of this there are in demesne 3½ hides, and there are 2 carucates; and there are 2 villans, and 6 bordars; and there are 20 acres of meadow, and as much pasture, and 10 acres of wood. It was worth 30 shillings; it is now worth 50 shillings.

Huboldus tenet unum manerium de Ernulfo. Aluric tenuit tempore Regis Edwardi, et geldabat pro 1 hida. Terra est 1 carucata; et 3 acræ prati. Valuit 5 solidos; modo 10 solidos.

Hubold holds one manor of Ernulf. Aluric held it in the time of King Edward, and it paid geld for 1 hide. The land is 1 carucate; and there are 3 acres of meadow. It was worth 5 shillings; it is now worth 10 shillings.

XXVI. TERRA ALUREDI DE MERLEBERG.

XXVI. LAND OF ALURED OF MARLBOROUGH.

Aluredus de Merleberg[1] tenet *ADELINGTONE*. Tempore Regis Edwardi geldabat pro 11 hidis et dimidio, et 5 acris terræ. Terra est 7 carucatæ. De ea sunt in dominio 7 hidæ et dimidium, et ibi 4 carucatæ, et 7 servi; et 6 villani, et 7

Alured of Marlborough holds *ADELINGTONE*. In the time of King Edward it paid geld for 11½ hides, and 5 acres of land. The land is 7 carucates. Of this there are in demesne 7½ hides, and there are 4 carucates, and 7 serfs; and there are

[1] Besides these possessions in Wilts, Alured of Marlborough had, at the general survey, estates in Surrey, Hants, Somerset, Devon, and Herefordshire. In the last named county he possessed, by gift it would seem of Earl William, the castle of Ewias *(Hereford* 186 *a)*; and under this, as the head of his Barony, many of the estates enumerated above were afterwards held. Hence the distinctive names given to some of them, as *e. g.* Somerford *Ewyas*, and Teffont *Ewyas*. The chief of this family in the time of Henry II. was Robert, Lord of Ewyas. He died without male issue, and his daughter Sybil was married first of all to Sir Robert Tregoz, and afterwards to Roger de Clifford. Many of the estates were held subsequently by members of the Tregoz family. See 'Testa de Nevil,' 136 *a*. For an account of this family,—from a branch of which descended the St. Johns, ancestors of Lord Bolingbroke the present owner of Lydiard *Tregoz*,—see Jackson's Aubrey, 170. Full accounts of them may be seen in the Topographer and Genealogist, ii. 124, and pedigrees of Ewyas and Tregoz are given in Hoare's 'Warminster,' p. 54, and 'Dunworth,' p. 110.

Fol. { XII b / 70 b } bordarii, cum 1 carucata. Ibi 20 acræ prati. Pastura 6 quarentenis longa, et 3 quarentenis lata.

De hac terra habet unus miles 2 hidas, et ibi 1 carucata. Totum valebat 12 libras; modo 15 libras.

Willelmus [18 hidas], et Gislebertus [1 hidam], et Ulvict [1 hidam], tenent de Aluredo, *RODE.* Tempore Regis Edwardi geldabat pro 20 hidis. Terra est 8 carucatæ. In dominio sunt 4 carucatæ, et 4 servi; et 4 villani, et 8 bordarii, et 11 coscez, et presbyter, cum 4 carucatis. Ibi 2 molini Willelmi, reddentes 9 solidos et 8 denarios, et 20 acræ prati. Silva 6 quarentenis longa, et una quarentena et dimidio lata. Valuit totum 6 libras; modo 8 libras.

Ipse Aluredus tenet *TEFONTE.* Tempore Regis Edwardi geldabat pro 6 hidis et dimidio. Terra est 5 carucatæ. De ea sunt in dominio 4 hidæ, et ibi 2 carucatæ, et 9 servi; et 4 villani, et 3 bordarii, et unus francus,[1] cum 2 carucatis. Ibi molinus, reddens 10 solidos, et 6 acræ prati, et 6 pasturæ, et 6 silvæ. Valuit, et valet, 6 libras.

Hugo tenet de Aluredo *CROSTONE.* Tempore Regis Edwardi geldabat pro 8 hidis. Terra est 5 carucatæ. De ea sunt in dominio 3 hidæ, et ibi 3 carucatæ, et 3 servi; et 2 villani, et 5 coscez, cum 2 carucatis. Ibi molinus, reddens 30 solidos, et 10 acræ prati, et pastura 6 acris longa, et totidem lata. Silva 3 quarentenis longa, et una quarentena lata. Valuit, et valet, 7 libras.

Ipse Aluredus tenet *NEWENTONE.* Tempore Regis Edwardi geldabat pro 11 hidis. Terra est 7 carucatæ. De ea sunt in dominio 6 hidæ, et ibi 2 carucatæ, et 6 servi; et 6 villani, et 4 bordarii, cum 3 carucatis. Ibi molinus, reddens 10 solidos, et 3

6 villans, and 7 bordars, with 1 carucate. There a 20 acres of meadow. The pasture is 6 furlongs lon and 3 furlongs broad.

Of this land a certain 'miles' has 2 hides, ar there is 1 carucate. The whole estate was wor £12; it is now worth £15.

William holds 18 hides, and Gilbert 1 hide, ar Ulviet 1 hide, of Alured in *RODE.* In the time King Edward it paid geld for 20 hides. The land 8 carucates. In demesne are 4 carucates, and 4 serf and there are 4 villans, and 8 bordars, and 11 cosce and a priest, with 4 carucates. There are 2 mills William's paying 9 shillings and 8 pence, and acres of meadow. The wood is 6 furlongs long, ar one furlong and a half broad. The whole was wor £6; it is now worth £8.

Alward himself holds *TEFONTE.* In the tin of King Edward it paid geld for 6½ hides. The lar is 5 carucates. Of this there are in demesne 4 hide and there are 2 carucates, and 9 serfs; and there a 4 villans, and 3 bordars, and 1 foreigner, with 2 car cates. There is a mill, paying 10 shillings, and acres of meadow, and 6 of pasture, and 6 of woo It was, and is, worth £6.

Hugo holds *CROSTONE* of Alured. In t time of King Edward it paid geld for 8 hides. T land is 5 carucates. Of this there are in demesne hides, and there are 3 carucates, and 3 serfs; ar there are 2 villans, and 5 coscets, with 2 carucat There is a mill, paying 30 shillings, and 10 acres meadow, and the pasture is 6 acres long, and much broad. The wood is 3 furlongs long, and furlong broad. It was, and is worth £7.

Alured himself holds *NEWENTONE.* In t time of King Edward it paid geld for 11 hides. T land is 7 carucates. Of this there are in demesne hides, and there are 2 carucates, and 6 serfs; a there are 6 villans, and 4 bordars, with 3 carucat

[1] On the meaning of this term see the note on *p.* 65.

XII b 70 b acræ prati: et pastura 3 quarentenis longa, et 3 quarentenis lata.

De eadem terræ habet Girardus 3 hidas; et ibi 4 villani, et 5 bordarii, cum 2 carucatis.

Valuit 10 libras: modo 18 libras. Ab Anglis appreciatur 12 libris.

Edwardus tenet de Aluredo in *WINTREBURNE* 1 hidam. Terra 1 carucata, quæ ibi est cum 1 servo, et 1 bordario. Valuit 10 solidos; modo 20 solidos.

Ipse Aluredus tenet *LEDIAR*. Tempore Regis Edwardi geldabat pro 7 hidis. Terra est 7 carucatæ. De ea sunt in dominio 3 hidæ, et ibi 1 carucata, et 3 servi; et 8 villani, et 10 coscez, cum 4 carucatis; et 40 acræ prati, et 30 acræ pasturæ. Silva 1 leuca longa, et dimidio lata. Valuit 10 libras; modo 6 libras.

In Crichelade 7 burgenses reddunt 5 solidos.

XIII a 70 c Ipse Aluredus tenet in *SVINDONE* 1 hidam et dimidium. Terra 6 bovatæ.[1] Valet 12 solidos.

Albertus tenet de Aluredo *MORDONE*. Tempore Regis Edwardi, geldabat pro 6 hidis. Terra est 4 carucatæ. De ea sunt in dominio 3 hidæ, et ibi 2 carucatæ, et 3 servi; et 3 villani, et 5 bordarii, cum 2 carucatis. Ibi 30 acræ prati. Pastura dimidio leucæ longa, et 2 quarentenis lata. Valuit 100 solidos; modo 4 libras.

Gunfridus tenet de Aluredo *WILDEHILLE*. Tempore Regis Edwardi geldabat pro 5 hidis. Terra

There is a mill, paying 10 shillings, and 3 acres of meadow: and the pasture is 3 furlongs long, and 3 furlongs broad.

Of this same land Girard has 3 hides; and there are 4 villans, and 5 bordars, with 2 carucates.

It was worth £10; it is now worth £18. By the English it is valued at £12.

Edward holds of Alured 1 hide in *WINTREBURNE*. The land is 1 carucate, which is there with 1 serf, and 1 bordar. It was worth 10 shillings; it is now worth 20 shillings.

Alured himself holds *LEDIAR*. In the time of King Edward it paid geld for 7 hides. The land is 7 carucates. Of this there are in demesne 3 hides, and there is 1 carucate, and 3 serfs; and there are 8 villans, and 10 coscets, with 4 carucates; and there are 40 acres of meadow, and 30 acres of pasture. The wood is 1 mile long, and half a mile broad. It was worth £10; it is now worth £6.

In Crichelade 7 burgesses pay 5 shillings.

Alured himself holds in *SVINDONE* 1 hide and a half. The land is 6 bovates. It is worth 12 shillings.

Albert holds *MORDONE* of Alured. In the time of King Edward, it paid geld for 6 hides. The land is 4 carucates. Of this there are in demesne 3 hides, and there are 2 carucates, and 3 serfs; and there are 3 villans, and 5 bordars, with 2 carucates. There are 30 acres of meadow. The pasture is half a mile long, and 2 furlongs broad. It was worth 100 shillings; it is now worth £4.

Gunfrid holds *WILDEHILLE* of Alured. In the time of King Edward it paid geld for 5 hides.

[1] The BOVATA, or Ox-gang, was originally as much as an ox-team could plough in a year. Eight bovates are usually said to have made a carucate; but the number of acres contained in a Bovate are variously stated in different records. Dr. Nash, in his 'Observations on Domesday for Worcester,' *p.* 9, gives quotations in which there are various Bovates mentioned containing respectively, *eight*, *sixteen*, and *seventeen* acres. No doubt, like carucates, and other portions of land, the exact measurement was uncertain, and depended on the soil, whether it were harder or easier to plough. *Ellis*, i. 156; *Kelham*, 164.

Fol. {XIII a / 70 c} est 3 carucatæ. De ea sunt in dominio 4 hidæ, et ibi 2 carucatæ; et 2 villani, et 4 bordarii, cum 1 carucata. Ibi molinus, reddens 25 denarios, et 30 acræ prati, et totidem pasturæ. Valuit 40 solidos; modo 60 solidos.

Radulfus tenet de Aluredo *OPETONE*. Tempore Regis Edwardi geldabat pro 9 hidis. Terra est 6 carucatæ. De ea sunt in dominio 5 hidæ, et ibi 2 carucatæ, et 5 servi; et 9 villani, et 22 bordarii, cum 4 carucatis. Ibi molinus, reddens 20 solidos, et 5 acræ prati, et 30 acræ pasturæ. Silva 3 quarentenis longa, et una quarentena lata. Valuit 8 libras; modo 9 libras.

Ipse Aluredus tenet *NORTONE*. Tempore Regis Edwardi geldabat pro 11 hidis. Terra est 8 carucatæ. De ea sunt in dominio 6 hidæ, et ibi 2 carucatæ, et 2 servi; et 12 villani, et 8 bordarii, cum 6 carucatis. Ibi 2 molini, reddentes 40 solidos, et 10 acræ prati. Pastura 4 quarentenis longa, et 2 quarentenis lata. Silva dimidio leucæ longa, et 4 quarentenis lata. Valuit 24 libras; modo 14 libras.

Ipse Aluredus tenet *ROCHELIE*. Tempore Regis Edwardi geldabat pro 10 hidis. Terra est 6 carucatæ. De ea sunt in dominio 6 hidæ et 3 virgatæ terræ, et ibi 1 carucata, cum 1 servo. Ibi 7 villani, et 12 bordarii, cum 3 carucatis. Ibi 3 acræ prati. Pastura dimidio leucæ longa, et 4 quarentenis lata. Valet 8 libras.

Ipse Aluredus tenet *FIFHIDE*. Radulfus de eo. Tempore Regis Edwardi geldabat pro 5 hidis. Terra est 4 carucatæ. De ea sunt in dominio 3 hidæ, et ibi 1 carucata, et 3 servi. Ibi 9 villani, et 6 bordarii, cum 2 carucatis. Ibi 2 acræ prati. Pastura dimidio leucæ longa, et 2 quarentenis lata. Silva dimidio leucæ longa, et dimidio quarentenæ lata. Valuit 4 libras; modo 100 solidos.

The land is 3 carucates. Of this there are in demesne 4 hides, and there are 2 carucates; and there are 2 villans, and 4 bordars, with 1 carucate. There is a mill, paying 25 pence, and 30 acres of meadow, and as much pasture. It was worth 40 shillings; it is now worth 60 shillings.

Radulf holds *OPETONE* of Alured. In the time of King Edward it paid geld for 9 hides. The land is 6 carucates. Of this there are in demesne 5 hides, and there are 2 carucates, and 5 serfs; and there are 9 villans, and 22 bordars, with 4 carucates. There is a mill, paying 20 shillings, and there are 5 acres of meadow, and 30 acres of pasture. The wood is 3 furlongs long, and 1 furlong broad. It was worth £8; it is now worth £9.

Alured himself holds *NORTONE*. In the time of King Edward it paid geld for 11 hides. The land is 8 carucates. Of this there are in demesne 6 hides, and there are 2 carucates, and 2 serfs; and there are 12 villans, and 8 bordars, with 6 carucates. There are 2 mills, paying 40 shillings, and 10 acres of meadow. The pasture is 4 furlongs long, and 2 furlongs broad. The wood is half a mile long, and 4 furlongs broad. It was worth £24; it is now worth £14.

Alured himself holds *ROCHELIE*. In the time of King Edward it paid geld for 10 hides. The land is 6 carucates. Of this there are in demesne 6 hides and 3 virgates of land, and there is 1 carucate with 1 serf. There are 7 villans, and 12 bordars with 3 carucates. There are 3 acres of meadow. The pasture is half a mile long, and 4 furlongs broad. It is worth £8.

Alured himself holds *FIFHIDE*. Radulf holds it of him. In the time of King Edward it paid geld for 5 hides. The land is 4 carucates. Of this there are in demesne 3 hides, and there is 1 carucate, and 3 serfs. There are 9 villans, and 6 bordars, with 2 carucates. There are 2 acres of meadow. The pasture is half a mile long, and 2 furlongs broad. The wood is half a mile long, and half a furlong broad. It was worth £4; it is now worth 100 shillings.

XIII a 70 c Ibi 1 ferraria reddit 12 denarios per annum. In Wiltune 2 burgenses reddunt 18 denarios.

One smith's forge pays 12 pence by the year. In Wilton 2 burgesses pay 18 pence.

Ipse Aluredus tenet unam virgatam terræ in *LACOC.* Terra est 1 carucata, quæ ibi est cum 1 bordario, et 2 acræ prati. Valuit 10 solidos; modo 5 solidos.

Alured himself holds 1 virgate of land in *LACOC.* The land is 1 carucate, which is there with 1 bordar, and there are 2 acres of meadow. It was worth 10 shillings; it is now worth 5 shillings.

Omnes has prescriptas terras tenuit Carlo tempore Regis Edwardi.

Carlo held all the before-mentioned lands in the time of King Edward.

Rogerius tenet de Aluredo *CLIVE.* Godric, et Tedgar, et Aluric, et Uluric tenuerunt pro 4 maneriis tempore Regis Edwardi, et geldabant pro 4 hidis. Terra est 2 carucatæ. In dominio est una carucata, et 3 servi, et 2 coscez. Ibi 24 acræ prati, et 20 acræ pasturæ, et 6 acræ silvæ. Valuit 40 solidos; modo 50 solidos.

Roger holds *CLIVE* of Alured. Godric, and Tedgar, and Aluric, and Uluric held it for 4 manors in the time of King Edward, and they paid geld for 4 hides. The land is 2 carucates. In demesne is 1 carucate, and 3 serfs, and 2 coscets. There are 24 acres of meadow, and 20 acres of pasture, and 6 acres of wood. It was worth 40 shillings; it is now worth 50 shillings.

Robertus tenet de Aluredo in *CLIVE* 2 hidas et dimidium, et pro tanto geldabat tempore Regis Edwardi. Sigar et Carman tenebant. Terra est 1 carucata et dimidium. Ibi sunt 3 servi, cum 1 bordario, et molinus reddens 5 solidos, et 12 acræ prati, et 20 acræ pasturæ, et 50 acræ silvæ. Valuit 20 solidos; modo 30 solidos.

Robert holds 2½ hides of Alured in *CLIVE,* and it paid geld for so much in the time of King Edward. Sigar and Carman held it. The land is 1 carucate and a half. There are 3 serfs, with 1 bordar, and a mill paying 5 shillings, and 12 acres of meadow, and 20 acres of pasture, and 50 acres of wood. It was worth 20 shillings; it is now worth 30 shillings.

Siwardus tenet de Aluredo *SUMREFORD.* Alnodus tenuit tempore Regis Edwardi, et geldabat pro 3 hidis, et 24 acris terræ. Terra est 3 carucatæ. De ea sunt in dominio 2 hidæ, et ibi 1 carucata, et 2 servi; et 3 villani, et 2 bordarii, et 8 coscez, cum 2 carucatis. Ibi molinus reddens 5 solidos, et 6 acræ prati. Silva 2 quarentenis longa, et una quarentena lata. Valuit, et valet, 40 solidos.

Siward holds *SUMREFORD* of Alured. Alnod held it in the time of King Edward, and it paid geld for 3 hides, and 24 acres of land. The land is 3 carucates. Of this there are in demesne 2 hides, and there is 1 carucate, and 2 serfs; and there are 3 villans, and 2 bordars, and 8 coscets, with 2 carucates. There is a mill paying 5 shillings, and 6 acres of meadow. The wood is 2 furlongs long, and 1 furlong broad. It was, and is, worth 40 shillings.

Edwardus tenet de Aluredo in *CHEGESLEI* 1 hidam et 1 virgatam terræ. Terra est 1 carucata. In dominio est dimidium carucatæ cum 1 servo, et 1 cotario; et 1 acra prati, et 1 acra silvæ, in longitudine et latitudine.

Edward holds of Alured in *CHEGESLEI* 1 hide and 1 virgate of land. The land is 1 carucate. In demesne is half a carucate with 1 serf, and 1 cottar; and there is 1 acre of meadow, and 1 acre of wood, in length and breadth.

In *MALMESBERIE* dimidia domus reddit 6 denarios. Valuit 40 solidos; modo 10 solidos.

In *MALMESBERIE* half a tenement pays 6 pence. It was worth 40 shillings; it is now worth 10 shillings.

Fol. { XIII a / 70 c } Præter hanc terram habet Durandus de Glowecestre dimidiam virgatam terræ, quam idem Edwardus tenebat tempore Regis Edwardi. Hanc ei abstulit injuste Amalricus de Drewes, ut testantur omnes Taini Sciræ.

Osmundus tenet de Aluredo in *HORNINGHAM* dimidiam hidam, et pro tanto geldabat tempore Regis Edwardi. Colsuen tenebat, et poterat ire quo volebat.[1] Terra est 1 carucata, quæ ibi est, cum 4 bordariis. Ibi 8 acræ silvæ, et una leuca pasturæ, et molinus reddens 7 solidos et 6 denarios. Valuit 5 solidos; modo 10 solidos.

In *CHENETE* tenet Aluredus 13 hidas et dimidium, et 2 acras terræ. De his habet Nicolaus 2 hidas; Turstinus, 3 hidas et dimidium; Ulviet, 2 hidas; Leuric, 3 hidas et dimidium; Ulmar 2 hidas et dimidium, et 2 acras terræ. Terra est 6 carucatæ. Ibi sunt 4 carucatæ, cum 1 villano, et 15 bordariis. Ibi molinus, reddens 12 solidos, et 11 acræ prati, et 106 acræ pasturæ, et 7 acræ silvæ. Totum valebat, quando receperunt, 4 libras et 10 solidos; modo, 8 libras et 10 solidos.

Has hidas in *CHENET*, tempore Regis Edwardi, tenuerunt Ulviet, Alnod, Edmar, Leuric, et Ulmar.

Willelmus Durus tenet de Aluredo *TEDELINTONE.* Ulveva et Alveve tenebant pro 2 maneriis, tempore Regis Edwardi, et geldabant pro 4 hidis. Terra est 4 carucatæ. De ea sunt in dominio 2 hidæ, et ibi 1 carucata, et 2 villani, et 4 bordarii, et 2 cotarii. Ibi 2 partes molini, reddentes 40 denarios, et 10 acræ prati. Valuit, et valet, 60 solidos.

Ulmarus tenet de Aluredo in *FIFHIDE* 1 hidam. Idem tenebat tempore Regis Edwardi. Valuit, et valet, 10 solidos.

Besides this land Durand of Gloucester has hal[f] a virgate of land, which the same Edward held i[n] the time of King Edward. This land Amalric d[e] Drewes took from him unjustly, as all the Thanes o[f] the Shire testify.

Osmund holds of Alured in *HORNINGHAM* [a] half hide, and it paid geld for so much in the tim[e] of King Edward. Colsuen held it, and he could g[o] whither he wished. The land is 1 carucate, which i[s] there, with 4 bordars. There are 8 acres of wood and 1 mile of pasture, and a mill paying 7 shilling[s] and 6 pence. It was worth 5 shillings; it is now worth 10 shillings.

Alured holds in *CHENETE* 13½ hides and [2] acres of land. Of these Nicholas has 2 hides; Turstin, 3½ hides; Ulviet, 2 hides; Leuric, 3½ hides; Ulmar 2½ hides, and 2 acres of land. The land is 6 carucates. There are there 4 carucates, with 1 villan, and 15 bordars. There is a mill, paying 12 shillings, and 11 acres of meadow, and 106 acres o[f] pasture, and 7 acres of wood. The whole was worth, when they received it, £4 10*s.*; it is now worth £8 10*s.*

Ulviet, Alnod, Edmar, Leuric, and Ulmar held these hides in *CHENET* in the time of King Edward.

William 'Durus' holds *TEDELINTONE* of Alured. Ulveva and Alveve held it for 2 manors, in the time of King Edward, and paid geld for 4 hides. The land is 4 carucates. Of this there are in demesne 2 hides, and there is 1 carucate, and 2 villans, and 4 bordars, and 2 cottars. There are 2 parts of a mill paying 40 pence, and 10 acres of meadow. It was, and is worth, 60 shillings.

Ulmar holds 1 hide in *FIFHIDE* of Alured. The same held it in the time of King Edward. It was, and is, worth 10 shillings.

[1] See, as to the meaning of this expression, the note at *p.* 72.

XXVII. TERRA HUNFRIDI DE INSULA.

{XIII b / 70 d} HUNFRIDUS DE INSULA[1] tenet de Rege *BROCTONE.* Tres Taini in paragio[2] tenuerunt tempore Regis Edwardi, et geldabant pro 12 hidis. Terra est 8 carucatæ. De ea sunt in dominio 4 hidæ et dimidium, et ibi 3 carucatæ, et 2 servi; et 17 villani, et 4 bordarii, cum 7 carucatis. Ibi 2 molini, reddentes 9 solidos, et 12 acræ prati, et 8 acræ pasturæ. Silva 1 leuca longa, et 2 quarentenis lata. Valuit 13 libras; modo 10 libras.

Pagen tenet de Hunfrido *CONTONE.* Levenot tenuit tempore Regis Edwardi, et geldabat pro 5 hidis et dimidio. Terra est 4 carucatæ. De ea sunt in dominio 2 hidæ, et una virgata terræ, et ibi 2 carucatæ, et 4 servi; et 4 villani, et 4 coscez, cum 2 carucatis. Ibi tercia pars 2 molinorum reddens 10 solidos, et 20 acræ prati, et 10 acræ pasturæ, et totidem silvæ. Valuit, et valet, 4 libras et 10 solidos.

Ipse Hunfridus tenet *STERTE.* Aluric tenuit tempore Regis Edwardi, et geldabat pro 5 hidis et

XXVII. THE LAND OF HUMFREY DE L'ISLE.

HUMFREY DE L'ISLE holds *BROCTONE* of the King. Three Thanes held it in parage in the time of King Edward, and they paid geld for 12 hides. The land is 8 carucates. Of this there are in demesne 4½ hides, and there are 3 carucates, and 2 serfs; and there are 17 villans, and 4 bordars, with 7 carucates. There are 2 mills, paying 9 shillings, and 12 acres of meadow, and 8 acres of pasture. The wood is 1 mile long and 2 furlongs broad. It was worth £13; it is now worth £10.

Pagen holds *CONTONE* of Humfrey. Levenot held it in the time of King Edward, and it paid geld for 5½ hides. The land is 4 carucates. Of this there are in demesne 2 hides and 1 virgate of land, and there are 2 carucates, and 4 serfs; and there are 4 villans, and 4 coscets, with 2 carucates. There is the third part of 2 mills paying 10 shillings, and 20 acres of meadow, and 10 acres of pasture, and as much wood. It was, and is worth £4 10s.

Humfrey himself holds *STERTE.* Aluric held it in the time of King Edward, and it paid geld with

---

[1] In the Wilts Arch. Mag. II., 261, a detailed account is given by Mr. Poulett Scrope of the various estates here enumerated as having belonged to HUMFREY DE L'ISLE. Their owner was no doubt one of William the Conqueror's Norman followers, and probably the LIELE of the Battle Abbey Roll. The entire seignory descended, by the marriage of Adeliza, heiress of the family, to the Dunstanvilles, powerful barons during the twelfth and thirteenth centuries, and by one of them a castle was built at Combe, in or about the reign of Henry I. This became, as was the custom of the time, the head seat of the barony, and the Dunstanvilles were thence styled Barons of Castle Combe.

The subsequent partition of these estates is thus explained by Mr. Scrope:—"In the year 1313, Bartholomew, Lord Badlesmere, became possessed of the barony by purchase from the last heir of the Dunstanvilles, William de Montfort; and on the partition of his great estates among his four daughters and co-heiresses, A.D. 1340, the several manors and knights' fees, composing the Barony of Combe, were distributed in separate portions among some of the greatest families of the time—those of De Vere,—Arundel,—Roos,—Mortimer,—Bohun,—and Titot. The disjointed fragments were still, however, held as 'parcels of the Barony of Combe' for some centuries after the partition of the estates."

[2] Sir H. Ellis (I. 241) has the following observations on the meaning of this term:—"Cowel says, from Spelman, that *Parage* signifies equality of name, blood, or dignity; but more especially of land, in the partition of all inheritance between co-heirs. Brady, from Dufresne, says,—'Or it is when the younger brothers hold their share of the fee of the elder brother, and he of the lord, and does the homage and service, they contributing their shares.' *Paragium*, however, in the language of Domesday, meant holding in equal portions, as well in rights and privileges as in actual property."

Fol. { XIII b, 70 d } una virgata et dimidio cum appendicibus. Terra est 3 carucatæ. De ea sunt in dominio 4 hidæ, et ibi 3 carucatæ, et 6 servi; et 15 bordarii, et unus francigena, habentes unam virgatam et dimidium. Ibi 2 molini, reddentes 8 solidos, et 30 acræ prati, et 10 acræ pasturæ, et 2 acræ silvæ. Valuit 100 solidos; modo 6 libras.

Blacheman tenet de Hunfrido *BURBETC*. Edric tenuit tempore Regis Edwardi, et geldabat pro 2 hidis et dimidio. Terra est 2 carucatæ et dimidium. De ea est in dominio hida et dimidium, et ibi 1 carucata; et 2 villani, et 3 coscez, cum 1 carucata. Silva ibi 3 quarentenis longa, et 2 quarentenis lata. Valuit 50 solidos; modo 40 solidos.

Pagen tenet de Hunfrido *CUMBREWELLE*. Levenot tenuit tempore Regis Edwardi, et geldabat pro 4 hidis. Terra est 5 carucatæ. In dominio sunt 2 carucatæ, cum 1 servo; et 2 villani, et 4 bordarii, cum 3 carucatis. Ibi 4 acræ prati, et 5 acræ silvæ. Valet 3 libras.

De eadem terra habet Rex 1 hidam in suo dominio, et nil ibi est, et unus Anglicus tenet dimidium de Rege. Valet 8 solidos.

Gunter tenet de Hunfrido *RUSTESELLE*. Uluric tenuit tempore Regis Edwardi, et geldabat pro 4 hidis. Terra est 2 carucatæ. In dominio est una, cum 2 bordariis. Et de molino 12 denarii. Et 8 acræ prati, et dimidia quarentena pasturæ. Valet 40 solidos.

Robertus tenet de Hunfrido *WERTUNE*. Alnod tenuit tempore Regis Edwardi, et geldabat pro 10 hidis. Terra est 4 carucatæ. De ea sunt in dominio 5 hidæ et dimidium, et ibi 2 carucatæ; et 6 villani, et 9 bordarii, cum 2 carucatis. Et ibi unus francigena tenet 2 hidas de eadem terra. Ibi molinus de

its appendages for 5 hides and 1 virgate and a half. The land is 3 carucates. Of this there are in demesne 4 hides, and there are 3 carucates, and 6 serfs; and there are 15 bordars, and one foreigner, having 1 virgate and a half. There are 2 mills, paying 8 shillings, and 30 acres of meadow, and 10 acres of pasture, and 2 acres of wood. It was worth 100 shillings; it is now worth £6.

Blacheman holds *BURBETC* of Humfrey. Edric held it in the time of King Edward, and it paid geld for 2½ hides. The land is 2½ carucates. Of this a hide and a half is in demesne, and there is 1 carucate; and there are 2 villans, and 3 coscets, with 1 carucate. The wood is 3 furlongs long, and 2 furlongs broad. It was worth 50 shillings; it is now worth 40 shillings.

Pagen holds *CUMBREWELLE* of Humfrey. Levenot held it in the time of King Edward, and it paid geld for 4 hides. The land is 5 carucates. In demesne are 2 carucates, with 1 serf; and there are 2 villans, and 4 bordars, with 3 carucates. There are 4 acres of meadow, and 5 acres of wood. It is worth £3.

Of the same land the King has 1 hide in his demesne, and there is no land in tillage,[1] and an Englishman holds half of it of the King. It is worth 8 shillings.

Gunter holds *RUSTESELLE* of Humfrey. Uluric held it in the time of King Edward, and it paid geld for 4 hides. The land is 2 carucates. In demesne is 1, with 2 bordars. And from a mill are received 12 pence. And there are 8 acres of meadow, and half a furlong of pasture. It is worth 40 shillings.

Robert holds *WERTUNE* of Humfrey. Alnod held it in the time of King Edward, and it paid geld for 10 hides. The land is 4 carucates. Of this there are in demesne 5½ hides, and there are 2 carucates; and there are 6 villans, and 9 bordars, with 2 carucates. And a foreigner holds 2 hides of the same

[1] This is the translation given by Wyndham of the expression, 'et nil ibi est,' and is perhaps the correct one. There is however, in § 68, under ULFELA, a somewhat similar entry,—'Terra est 3 carucatæ, et nil *pecuniæ*.' The conjecture is therefore hazarded, that possibly the scribe may have intended in the passage to have written,—'et nil *pecuniæ* ibi est,' *i.e.* 'there is no stock of cattle there.'

XIIIb 70 d 15 denariis, et 30 acræ pasturæ, et 2 acræ silvæ. Valuit, et valet, 100 solidos.

Robertus tenet de Hunfrido *SALTEHARPE.* Ulwinus tenuit tempore Regis Edwardi, et geldabat pro 10 hidis. Terra est 4 carucatæ. De ea sunt in dominio 8 hidæ, et ibi 2 carucatæ, et 3 servi; et 9 bordarii, cum 1 carucata. Ibi 20 acræ prati, et 30 acræ pasturæ. Valuit 100 solidos; modo 4 libras.

Robertus tenet de Hunfrido *CLIVE.* Edwinus tenuit tempore Regis Edwardi, et geldabat pro 8 hidis. Terra est 4 carucatæ. De ea sunt in dominio 6 hidæ, et ibi 2 carucatæ, et 4 servi; et 2 villani, et 7 bordarii, cum 2 carucatis. Ibi 20 acræ prati, et tantundem pasturæ. Et 3 burgenses in Crichelade reddunt 3 denarios. Valuit, et valet, 4 libras.

Robertus tenet de Hunfrido *SUMREFORD.* Edwinus tenuit tempore Regis Edwardi, et geldabat pro 3 hidis, et 24 acris. Terra est 3 carucatæ. De ea sunt in dominio 2 hidæ. Ibi 7 bordarii, et 16 coscez, habentes 2 carucatas; et tercia pars molini reddens 8 solidos; et 10 acræ prati. Pastura 3 quarentenis longa, et una quarentena lata. In Malmesberie 1 burgensis reddit 12 denarios. Valuit, et valet, 60 solidos.

Elbertus tenet de Hunfrido *SMITECOTE.* Sawinus tenuit tempore Regis Edwardi, et geldabat pro 5 hidis. Terra est 4 carucatæ. De ea sunt in dominio 2 hidæ et dimidium, et ibi 3 carucatæ, et 2 servi; et 3 villani, et 4 bordarii, cum 1 coscet, habent 2 carucatas. Ibi molinus de 5 solidis, et 20 acræ prati. Silva 4 quarentenis longa, et una quarentena lata. Et unus burgensis reddit 8 denarios. Valuit 40 solidos; modo, 60 solidos.

Ilbertus tenet de Hunfrido *BLUNTESDONE.* Edric tenuit tempore Regis Edwardi, et geldabat pro 5 hidis. Terra est 2 carucatæ et dimidium. De ea sunt in dominio 2 hidæ et dimidium, et ibi 1 carucata,

land. There is a mill worth 15 pence, and 30 acres of pasture, and 2 acres of wood. It was, and is worth 100 shillings.

Robert holds *SALTEHARPE* of Humfrey. Ulwin held it in the time of King Edward, and it paid geld for 10 hides. The land is 4 carucates. Of this there are in demesne 8 hides, and there are 2 carucates, and 3 serfs; and there are 9 bordars, with 1 carucate. There are 20 acres of meadow, and 30 acres of pasture. It was worth 100 shillings; it is now worth £4.

Robert holds *CLIVE* of Humfrey. Edwin held it in the time of King Edward, and it paid geld for 8 hides. The land is 4 carucates. Of this there are in demesne 6 hides, and there are 2 carucates, and 4 serfs; and there are 2 villans, and 7 bordars, with 2 carucates. There are 20 acres of meadow, and as much pasture. And 3 burgesses in Cricklade pay 3 pence. It was, and is, worth £4.

Robert holds *SUMREFORD* of Humfrey. Edwin held it in the time of King Edward, and it paid geld for 3 hides, and 24 acres. The land is 3 carucates. Of this there are in demesne 2 hides. There are 7 bordars, and 16 cosets, having 2 carucates; and the third part of a mill paying 8 shillings; and 10 acres of meadow. The pasture is 3 furlongs long, and 1 furlong broad. In Malmesbury 1 burgess pays 12 pence. It was, and is, worth 60 shillings.

Elbert holds *SMITECOTE* of Humfrey. Sawin held it in the time of King Edward, and it paid geld for 5 hides. The land is 4 carucates. Of this there are 2½ hides in demesne, and there are 3 carucates, and 2 serfs; and 3 villans, and 4 bordars, with 1 coset, have 2 carucates. There is a mill worth 5 shillings, and 20 acres of meadow. The wood is 4 furlongs long, and 1 furlong broad. And 1 burgess pays 8 pence. It was worth 40 shillings; it is now worth 60 shillings.

Ilbert holds *BLUNTESDONE* of Humfrey. Edric held it in the time of King Edward, and it paid geld for 5 hides. The land is 2½ carucates. Of this there are in demesne 2½ hides, and there is 1

Fol. { XIII b 70 d } cum 1 servo; et 2 bordarii, cum 1 carucata et dimidio. Valuit 30 solidos; modo 50 solidos.

Hugo et Giraldus tenent de Hunfrido *GRENDEWELLE.* Ordulfus tenuit tempore Regis Edwardi, et geldabat pro 5 hidis. Terra est 3 carucatæ. De ea sunt in dominio 4 hidæ, et ibi 2 carucatæ, cum 1 servo; et 1 villanus, et 2 bordarii, cum 1 carucata. Ibi 12 acræ prati. Valuit 40 solidos; modo 70 solidos.

Robertus tenet de Hunfrido *SCHETONE.* Chenvi tenuit tempore Regis Edwardi, et geldabat pro 6 hidis. Terra est 4 carucatæ. De ea sunt in dominio 3 hidæ, et ibi 2 carucatæ, et 3 servi; et 4 villani, et 3 coscez, cum 2 carucatis. Ibi dimidium molini, reddens 6 solidos et 3 denarios, et 12 acræ prati. Pastura 6 quarentenis longa, et tantundem lata. Valuit 4 libras; modo 6 libras.

Fol. { XIV a 71 a } Ipse Hunfridus tenet *WILI.* Aluric tenuit tempore Regis Edwardi, et geldabat pro 3 hidis et 3 virgatis. Terra est 4 carucatæ. De ea est in dominio 1 hida et 1 virgata terræ, et ibi 3 carucatæ, et 12 servi; et 2 villani, et 6 coscez, cum 1 carucata et dimidio. Ibi molinus de 15 solidis, et 10 acræ prati. Pastura dimidio leucæ longa, et tantundem lata. Valuit 3 libras; modo 4 libras.

Ipse Hunfridus tenet *WILRENONE.* Edvinus tenuit tempore Regis Edwardi, et geldabat pro 3 hidis. Terra est 2 carucatæ. De ea sunt in dominio 2 hidæ, et ibi una carucata; et 2 villani, et 1 coscet, cum 1 carucata. Ibi molinus, reddens 6 solidos, et 5 acræ prati, et 8 acræ pasturæ. Valuit 40 solidos; modo 60 solidos.

Ipse Hunfridus tenet *COLERNE.* Levenot tenuit tempore Regis Edwardi, et geldabat pro 10 hidis. Terra est 12 carucatæ. De ea sunt in dominio 4 hidæ et dimidium, et ibi 3 carucatæ, et 10 servi; et 13 villani, et 5 coscez, cum 8 carucatis.

carucate, with 1 serf; and there are 2 bordars, with 1 carucate and a half. It was worth 30 shillings; it is now worth 50 shillings.

Hugo and Girald hold *GRENDEWELLE* of Humfrey. Ordulf held it in the time of King Edward, and it paid geld for 5 hides. The land is 3 carucates. Of this there are in demesne 4 hides, and there are 2 carucates, with 1 serf; and there is 1 villan, and 2 bordars, with 1 carucate. There are 12 acres of meadow. It was worth 40 shillings; it is now worth 70 shillings.

Robert holds *SCHETONE* of Humfrey. Chenvi held it in the time of King Edward, and it paid geld for 6 hides. The land is 4 carucates. Of this there are in demesne 3 hides, and there are 2 carucates, and 3 serfs; and there are 4 villans, and 3 coscets, with 2 carucates. There is half a mill, paying 6 shillings and 3 pence, and 12 acres of meadow. The pasture is 6 furlongs long, and as much broad. It was worth £4; it is now worth £6.

Humfrey himself holds *WILI.* Aluric held it in the time of King Edward, and it paid geld for 3 hides and 3 virgates. The land is 4 carucates. Of this there is in demesne 1 hide and 1 virgate of land, and there are 3 carucates, and 12 serfs; and there are 2 villans, and 6 coscets, with 1 carucate and a half. There is a mill worth 15 shillings, and 10 acres of meadow. The pasture is half a mile long, and as much broad. It was worth £3; it is now worth £4.

Humfrey himself holds *WILRENONE.* Edwin held it in the time of King Edward, and it paid geld for 3 hides. The land is 2 carucates. Of this there are in demesne 2 hides, and there is 1 carucate; and there are 2 villans, and 1 coscet, with 1 carucate. There is a mill, paying 6 shillings, and 5 acres of meadow, and 8 acres of pasture. It was worth 40 shillings; it is now worth 60 shillings.

Humfrey himself holds *COLERNE.* Levenot held it in the time of King Edward, and it paid geld for 10 hides. The land is 12 carucates. Of this there are in demesne 4½ hides, and there are 3 carucates, and 10 serfs; and there are 13 villans

XIVa 71 a Ibi molinus, reddens 13 solidos et 6 denarios, et 8 acræ prati. Silva parva 1 leuca longa, et alia lata. Valuit, et valet, 10 libras.

Ipse Hunfridus tenet *WINTREBURNE.* Duo Taini tenebant tempore Regis Edwardi, et geldabant pro 10 hidis. Terra est 6 carucatæ. De ea sunt in dominio 4 hidæ et 10 acræ terræ, et ibi 3 carucatæ, et 8 servi; et 4 villani, et 8 bordarii, cum 3 carucatis. Ibi 14 acræ prati, et 20 acræ pasturæ. Valuit, et valet, 10 libras.

Ipse Hunfridus tenet *POLTONE.* Tovi tenuit tempore Regis Edwardi, et geldabat pro 10 hidis. Terra est 4 carucatæ. De ea sunt in dominio 8 hidæ, et ibi 2 carucatæ, et 2 servi; et 2 villani, et 7 bordarii, cum 1 carucata. Ibi molinus, reddens 15 solidos, et 4 acræ prati, et 10 acræ pasturæ, et 8 acræ silvæ. Valuit, et valet, 8 libras.

Ranulfus tenet de Hunfrido *HANTONE.* Ulgar tenuit tempore Regis Edwardi, et geldabat pro 10 hidis. Terra est 4 carucatæ. De ea sunt in dominio 6 hidæ, et ibi 1 carucata, cum 1 servo; et 4 villani, et 6 bordarii, cum 2 carucatis. Ibi 12 acræ prati, et 14 acræ pasturæ. Valuit, et valet, 100 solidos.

Turchitil tenet de Hunfrido *BEDESTONE.* Aluric tenuit tempore Regis Edwardi, et geldabat pro 1 hida et una virgata. Terra est . Ibi sunt 4 coscez, et 3 acræ prati, et 2 acræ silvæ. Valuit 10 solidos; modo 20 solidos.

Hugo tenet de Hunfrido *HEORTHAM.* Godric tenuit tempore Regis Edwardi, et geldabat pro 1 hida. Terra est dimidium carucatæ. Ibi sunt 2 coscez, et 2 acræ prati, et 7 acræ pasturæ, et 2 acræ silvæ. Valuit 8 solidos; modo 12 solidos.

Ipse Hunfridus tenet *COME.* Svain tenuit tempore Regis Edwardi, et geldabat pro 10 hidis.

and 5 coscets, with 8 carucates. There is a mill, paying 13 shillings and 6 pence, and 8 acres of meadow. The coppice wood is 1 mile long, and another broad. It was, and is, worth £10.

Humfrey himself holds *WINTREBURNE.* Two Thanes held it in the time of King Edward, and paid geld for 10 hides. The land is 6 carucates. Of this there are in demesne 4 hides and 10 acres of land, and there are 3 carucates, and 8 serfs; and there are 4 villans, and 8 bordars, with 3 carucates. There are 14 acres of meadow, and 20 acres of pasture. It was, and is, worth £10.

Humfrey himself holds *POLTONE.* Tovi held it in the time of King Edward, and it paid geld for 10 hides. The land is 4 carucates. Of this there are in demesne 8 hides, and there are 2 carucates, and 2 serfs; and there are 2 villans, and 7 bordars, with 1 carucate. There is a mill, paying 15 shillings, and 4 acres of meadow, and 10 acres of pasture, and 8 acres of wood. It was, and is, worth £8.

Ranulf holds *HANTONE* of Humfrey. Ulgar held it in the time of King Edward, and it paid geld for 10 hides. The land is 4 carucates. Of this there are in demesne 6 hides, and there is 1 carucate, with 1 serf; and there are 4 villans, and 6 bordars, with 2 carucates. There are 12 acres of meadow, and 14 acres of pasture. It was, and is, worth 100 shillings.

Turchitil holds *BEDESTONE* of Humfrey. Aluric held it in the time of King Edward, and it paid geld for 1 hide and 1 virgate. The land is . There are 4 coscets, and 3 acres of meadow, and 2 acres of wood. It was worth 10 shillings; it is now worth 20 shillings.

Hugo holds *HEORTHAM* of Humfrey. Godric held it in the time of King Edward, and it paid geld for 1 hide. The land is half a carucate. There are 2 coscets, and 2 acres of meadow, and 7 acres of pasture, and 2 acres of wood. It was worth 8 shillings; it is now worth 12 shillings.

Humfrey himself holds *COME.* Svain held it in the time of King Edward, and it paid geld for 10

Fol. { XIV a / 71 a } Terra est 10 carucatæ. De ea sunt in dominio 5 hidæ una virgata minus, et ibi 4 carucatæ, et 13 servi; et 5 villani, et 7 bordarii, et 5 cotarii, cum 6 carucatis. Ibi 3 molini, reddentes 31 solidos et 6 denarios, et 12 acræ prati. Silva 1 leuca longa, et dimidio leucæ lata. In Wiltune 1 burgensis reddit 5 solidos, et 2 burgenses in Malmesberie reddunt 18 denarios. Valuit, et valet, 10 libras.

hides. The land is 10 carucates. Of this there are in demesne 5 hides, all but 1 virgate, and there are 4 carucates, and 13 serfs; and there are 5 villans, and 7 bordars, and 5 cottars, with 6 carucates. There are 3 mills, paying 31 shillings and 6 pence, and 12 acres of meadow. The wood is 1 mile long, and half a mile broad. In Wilton 1 burgess pays 5 shillings, and 2 burgesses in Malmesbury pay 18 pence. It was, and is, worth £10.

Robertus tenet de Hunfrido *SORESTONE*. Godus tenuit tempore Regis Edwardi, et geldabat pro 6 hidis et dimidio. Terra est 5 carucatæ. De ea sunt in dominio 3 hidæ et dimidium, et ibi 3 carucatæ, et 2 servi; et 3 villani, et 9 bordarii, cum 2 carucatis. Ibi 2 molini, reddentes 10 solidos, et 6 acræ prati, et 10 acræ silvæ minutæ. Valuit 3 libras; modo 4 libras.

Robert holds *SORESTONE* of Humfrey. Godus held it in the time of King Edward, and it paid geld for 6½ hides. The land is 5 carucates. Of this there are in demesne 3½ hides, and there are 3 carucates, and 2 serfs; and there are 3 villans, and 9 bordars, with 2 carucates. There are 2 mills, paying 10 shillings, and 6 acres of meadow, and 10 acres of coppice-wood. It was worth £3; it is now worth £4.

Ipse Hunfridus tenet *HARDICOTE*. Aluric tenuit tempore Regis Edwardi, et geldabat pro 3 hidis. Terra est 4 carucatæ. De ea sunt in dominio 2 hidæ, et ibi 2 carucatæ, cum 1 servo; et 2 villani, et 12 bordarii, cum 2 carucatis. Ibi molinus, reddens 6 solidos, et 6 acræ prati, et 8 acræ pasturæ. Valuit 40 solidos; modo 60 solidos.

Humfrey himself holds *HARDICOTE*. Alurie held it in the time of King Edward, and it paid geld for 3 hides. The land is 4 carucates. Of this there are in demesne 2 hides, and there are 2 carucates, with 1 serf; and there are 2 villans, and 12 bordars, with 2 carucates. There is a mill, paying 6 shillings, and 6 acres of meadow, and 8 acres of pasture. It was worth 40 shillings; it is now worth 60 shillings.

Ipse Hunfridus tenet *FISTESFERIE*. Edricus tenuit tempore Regis Edwardi, et geldabat pro 3 hidis. Terra est 4 carucatæ. De ea sunt in dominio 2 hidæ, et ibi 1 carucata, et 3 servi; et 4 villani, et 2 bordarii, et 2 coliberti, cum 3 carucatis. Ibi 12 acræ prati. Silva 2 quarentenis longa, et una quarentena lata. Valuit 40 solidos; modo, 50 solidos.

Humfrey himself holds *FISTESFERIE*. Edrie held it in the time of King Edward, and it paid geld for 3 hides. The land is 4 carucates. Of this there are in demesne 2 hides, and there is 1 carucate, and 3 serfs; and there are 4 villans, and 2 bordars, and 2 coliberts, with 3 carucates. There are 12 acres of meadow. The wood is 2 furlongs long, and 1 furlong broad. It was worth 40 shillings; it is now worth 50 shillings.

Gozelinus tenet de Hunfrido in *MELEFORD* dimidiam hidam terræ, et pro tanto geldabat tempore Regis Edwardi. Sawold ot Sawardus tenebant. Terra est 1 carucata. Ibi sunt 6 cotarii, et 3 acræ prati. Valuit 15 denarios; modo 7 solidos.

Gozelin holds half a hide of land of Humfrey in *MELEFORD*, and it paid geld for so much in the time of King Edward. Sawold and Saward held it. The land is 1 earueate. There are 6 cottars, and 3 acres of meadow. It was worth 15 pence; it is now worth 7 shillings.

Medietas hujus terræ est in foresta Regis.

Half this land is in the King's forest.

XXVIII. TERRA MILONIS CRISPIN.

XIV b
71 b
MILO CRISPIN[1] tenet de Rege *WODETONE.* Levenod tenuit tempore Regis Edwardi, et geldabat pro 12 hidis. Terra est 12 carucatæ. De ea sunt in dominio 6 hidæ, et ibi 3 carucatæ, et 5 servi; et 11 villani, et 14 bordarii, cum 6 carucatis. Ibi molinus reddens 30 denarios, et 24 acræ prati, et 33 acræ pasturæ. Silva 2 leucis longa, et una leuca lata. In Malmesberie una domus reddit 13 denarios. Valuit 10 libras; modo 9 libras.

Rainaldus tenet de Milone *CILLETONE.* Heraldus Comes tenuit tempore Regis Edwardi, et geldabat pro 10 hidis. Terra est 12 carucatæ. De ea sunt in dominio 6 hidæ et dimidium, et ibi 2 carucatæ, et 2 servi; et 7 villani, et 10 coscez, cum 5 carucatis. Ibi 2 molini reddentes 40 solidos, et pratum 2 quarentenis longum et una quarentena latum, et tantundem pasturæ. Silva 1 leuca longa, et 2 quarentenis lata. Valuit 12 libras; modo 10 libras.

Hunfridus tenet de Milone *CLIVE.* Heraldus tenuit tempore Regis Edwardi, et geldabat pro 5 hidis. Terra est 2 carucatæ. De ea sunt in dominio 3 hidæ et dimidium, et ibi 1 carucata, cum 1 servo. Ibi 3 villani, et 4 bordarii, et 1 cotarius, cum dimidia carucata. Ibi 20 acræ prati, et 12 acræ pasturæ. Valuit 30 solidos; modo 50 solidos.

XXVIII. LAND OF MILO CRISPIN.

MILO CRISPIN holds *WODETONE* of the King. Levenod held it, in the time of King Edward, and it paid geld for 12 hides. The land is 12 carucates. Of this there are in demesne 6 hides, and there are 3 carucates, and 5 serfs; and there are 11 villans, and 14 bordars, with 6 carucates. There is a mill paying 30 pence, and 24 acres of meadow, and 33 acres of pasture. The wood is 2 miles long, and 1 mile broad. In Malmesbury 1 house pays 13 pence. It was worth £10; it is now worth £9.

Rainald holds *CILLETONE* of Milo. Earl Harold held it, in the time of King Edward, and it paid geld for 10 hides. The land is 12 carucates. Of this there are in demesne 6½ hides, and there are 2 carucates, and 2 serfs; and there are 7 villans, and 10 coseets, with 5 carucates. There are 2 mills paying 40 shillings, and the meadow is 2 furlongs long and 1 furlong broad, and as much pasture. The wood is 1 mile long, and 2 furlongs broad. It was worth £12; it is now worth £10.

Humfrey holds *CLIVE* of Milo. Harold held it in the time of King Edward, and it paid geld or 5 hides. The land is 2 carucates. Of this there are in demesne 3½ hides, and there is 1 carucate, with 1 serf. There are 3 villans, and 4 bordars, and 1 cottar, with a half carucate. There are 20 acres of meadow, and 12 acres of pasture. It was worth 30 shillings; it is now worth 50 shillings.

---

[1] Amongst the principal supporters of William the Conqueror was ROBERT DE OILGI, who was well rewarded for his fidelity with estates in no less than *eight* counties. His daughter and heiress Maud married MILO CRISPIN, who through her became possessed of the honor and castle of Wallingford. Many of the estates above enumerated are recorded in the 'Testa de Nevil' as having been held of the 'honor of Wallingford.'

Bishop Kennett (Paroch. Antiq. I. 76) says, on the authority of William of Poictou,—"After the decisive battle of Hastings, the Conqueror carried his forces into Kent, and marching back from thence passed by London, possessed by the party of Edgar Atheling, and came to Wallingford, when the lord of that town, WIGOD DE WALINGFORD, went out to meet him, delivered the town to him, and entertained him there, till Archbishop Stigand and many of the grandees of Edgar's faction came and offered their submission. For which service and merit of the lord of that place, the victorious prince in policy to ingratiate himself with the Saxons, and to reward his Normans, gave Aldith, only daughter of the said Wigod, in marriage to Robert de Oily, who, after her father's death, in right of her, became possessed of that great estate."

Fol. { XIV b / 71 b } In eadem *CLIVE* tenet Milo 1 hidam. Terra dimidium carucatæ. Valet 6 solidos. Qui tenebat tempore Regis Edwardi poterat ire ad quem dominum volebat.[1]

Turchetil tenet de Milone *LITLECOTE*. Godric tenuit tempore Regis Edwardi, et pro una hida et una virgata geldabat. Terra est dimidia carucata, quæ ibi est cum 1 bordario. Ibi 4 acræ prati, et totidem pasturæ, et totidem spineti. Valet 10 solidos.

Rainaldus tenet de Milone in *WALECOTE* 2 hidas et dimidium. Alnod tenuit tempore Regis Edwardi; et ibidem 3 virgatæ terræ quas tenuit Levenot tempore Regis Edwardi. Totum valet 23 solidos.

Rainaldus tenet de Milone *DRACOTE*. Levenot tenuit tempore Regis Edwardi, et geldabat pro 10 hidis. Terra est 6 carucatæ. De ea sunt in dominio 5 hidæ, et ibi 2 carucatæ, cum 1 servo; et 4 villani, et 7 bordarii, cum 3 carucatis. Ibi 18 acræ prati, et 40 acræ pasturæ. Valuit, et valet, 100 solidos.

Hunfridus tenet de Milone *BRENCHEWRDE*. Tochi tenuit tempore Regis Edwardi, et geldabat pro 5 hidis. Terra est 3 carucatæ. De ea sunt in dominio 4 hidæ, et ibi 1 carucata. Ibi 8 bordarii, et 8 coscez, cum 1 carucata. Ibi 24 acræ prati, et 3 acræ pasturæ. Silva 4 quarentenis longa, et tantundem lata. Valuit, et valet, 50 solidos.

Iste Tochi poterat ire quo volebat.[1]

Rainoldus tenet de Milone *REDBORNE*. Wigot tenuit tempore Regis Edwardi, et geldabat pro 5 hidis. Terra est 4 carucatæ. De ea sunt in dominio 2 hidæ [et ibi 1 carucata].[2] Ibi 3 villani, et 5

In the same *CLIVE* Milo holds 1 hide. The land is half a carucate. It is worth 6 shillings. He who held it in the time of King Edward could go to what lord he pleased.

Turchetil holds *LITLECOTE* of Milo. Godric held it in the time of King Edward, and it paid geld for 1 hide and 1 virgate. The land is a half carucate, which is there with 1 bordar. There are 4 acres of meadow, and as much pasture, and as much bramble-wood. It is worth 10 shillings.

Rainald holds of Milo in *WALECOTE* 2½ hides. Alnod held them in the time of King Edward; and there are also 3 virgates of land which Levenot held in the time of King Edward. The whole is worth 23 shillings.

Rainald holds *DRACOTE* of Milo. Levenot held it in the time of King Edward, and it paid geld for 10 hides. The land is 6 carucates. Of this there are in demesne 5 hides, and there are 2 carucates, with 1 serf; and there are 4 villans, and 7 bordars, with 3 carucates. There are 18 acres of meadow, and 40 acres of pasture. It was, and is, worth 100 shillings.

Humfrey holds *BRENCHEWRDE* of Milo. Tochi held it in the time of King Edward, and it paid geld for 5 hides. The land is 3 carucates. Of this there are in demesne 4 hides, and there is 1 carucate. There are 8 bordars, and 8 coscets, with 1 carucate. There are 24 acres of meadow, and 3 acres of pasture. The wood is 4 furlongs long, and as much broad. It was, and is, worth 50 shillings.

This same Tochi could go whither he wished.

Rainald holds *REDBORNE* of Milo. Wigot held it in the time of King Edward, and it paid geld for 5 hides. The land is 4 carucates. Of this there are in demesne 2 hides [and there is 1 carucate].

---

[1] As to the meaning of this expression see the note at *p.* 72.

[2] The words within brackets are given from conjecture. In the original there is a blank space left, which was never filled up. It will be observed that out of the *four* carucates, *three* are immediately afterwards accounted for, thus rendering it probable that the missing words should be supplied as is above suggested.

XIVb
71 b
bordarii, et 1 servus, cum 3 carucatis. Pratum 6 quarentenis longum, et 2 quarentenis latum. Pastura 2 quarentenis longa, et tantundem lata. Valuit 100 solidos; modo 4 libras.

There are 3 villans, and 5 borders, and 1 serf, with 3 carucates. The meadow is 6 furlongs long, and 2 furlongs broad. The pasture is 2 furlongs long, and as many broad. It was worth 100 shillings; it is now worth £4.

Unus Tainus, Siwardus, tenet de Milone *CHEGESLAUE.* Duo Taini tenuerunt tempore Regis Edwardi, et geldabant pro 1 hida et una virgata et dimidio. Terra est 6 boum qui ibi sunt arantes, et 1 cotarius cum uno servo.[1] Ibi 1 acra prati, et 1 virgata et dimidium [pasturæ],[2] et 1 acra silvæ. Valuit, et valet, 10 solidos.

Siward, a Thane, holds *CHEGESLAUE* of Milo. Two Thanes held it in the time of King Edward, and paid geld for 1 hide and 1 virgate and a half. There is land sufficient for 6 oxen which are at plough there, and there is 1 cottar with 1 serf. There is 1 acre of meadow, and 1 virgate and a half [of pasture], and 1 acre of wood. It was, and is, worth 10 shillings.

Qui tenebant tempore Regis Edwardi poterant ire quo volebant.

They who held this land in the time of King Edward could go whither they wished.

Præter hanc terram habet Durandus dimidiam virgatam terræ quam tenebat Siwardus tempore Regis Edwardi. Hanc abstulit ei injuste Amalricus de Drewes, ut dicunt Taini Scira.

Besides this land Durand has a half virgate of land which Siward held in the time of King Edward. Amalric de Drewes took away this land from him unjustly, as the Thanes of the Shire allege.

Ipse Milo tenet *OCHEBURNE.* Heraldus Comes tenuit tempore Regis Edwardi, et geldabat pro 10 hidis. Terra est 8 carucatæ. De ea sunt in dominio 6 hidæ, et ibi 3 carucatæ, et 4 servi; et 11 villani, et 4 bordarii, cum 3 carucatis. Ibi molinus reddens 30 solidos, et 8 acræ prati. Pastura dimidio leucæ longa, et tantundem lata. Valuit, et valet, 15 libras.

Milo himself holds *OCHEBURNE.* Earl Harold held it in the time of King Edward, and it paid geld for 10 hides. The land is 8 carucates. Of this there are 6 hides in demesne, and there are 3 carucates and 4 serfs; and there are 11 villans, and 4 bordars, with 3 carucates. There is a mill paying 30 shillings, and 8 acres of meadow. The pasture is half a mile long, and as much broad. It was, and is, worth £15.

Rainaldus tenet de Milone *MANETUNE.* Wigot tenuit tempore Regis Edwardi, et geldabat pro 3 hidis. Terra est 3 carucatæ. De ea est in dominio 1 hida, et ibi 1 carucata, et 2 servi; et 5 villani, et 5 bordarii, cum 2 carucatis. Ibi 4 acræ prati, et 40 acræ pasturæ, et totidem silvæ. Valuit, et valet, 3 libras.

Rainald holds *MANETUNE* of Milo. Wigot held it in the time of King Edward, and it paid geld for 3 hides. The land is three carucates. Of this there is in demesne 1 hide, and there is 1 carucate, and 2 serfs; and there are 5 villans, and 5 bordars, with 2 carucates. There are 4 acres of meadow, and 40 acres of pasture, and as many of wood. It was, and is, worth £3.

[1] In the original it is, '1 cotarius *et* uno servo.' This is so evidently a mistake of the scribe that the rendering in the text has been substituted for it.

[2] The word '*pasturæ*' seems to be necessary to complete the account, and is therefore inserted, though not in the original.

Fol. { XIV b / 71 b } Rainaldus tenet de Milone *HASEBERIE.* Levenot tenuit tempore Regis Edwardi, et geldabat pro 5 hidis. Terra est 5 carucatæ. De ea est in dominio 1 hida, et ibi 2 carucatæ, et 2 servi; et 5 villani, et 13 coscez, et 2 cotarii, cum 3 carucatis. Ibi 2 molini reddentes 35 solidos, et 22 acræ prati; et silva 2 quarentenis longa, et una quarentena lata. Valuit, et valet, 6 libras.

Rainald holds *HASEBERIE* of Milo. Levenot held it in the time of King Edward, and it paid geld for 5 hides. The land is 5 carucates. Of this there is in demesne 1 hide and there are 2 carucates, and 2 serfs; and there are 5 villans, and 13 coscets, and 2 cottars, with 3 carucates. There are 2 mills paying 35 shillings, and 22 acres of meadow; and the wood is 2 furlongs long, and 1 furlong broad. It was, and is, worth £6.

XXIX. TERRA GISLEBERTI DE BRETEVILE.

Gislebertus de Bretevile[1] tenet de Rege *CHESEBERIE.* Edricus tenuit tempore Regis Edwardi, et geldabat pro 5 hidis. Terra est 9 carucatæ. In dominio sunt 4 carucatæ, et 7 servi; et 12 villani, et 3 bordarii, et 14 coscez, cum 5 carucatis. Ibi 2 molini reddentes 20 solidos, et 15 acræ prati, et 40 acræ silvæ. Pastura 15 quarentenis longa, et 3 quarentenis lata. Valuit 8 libras; modo 12 libras.

Idem Gislebertus tenet in *BECHENHALLE* 5 hidas. Hacun tenuit tempore Regis Edwardi. Terra est 2 carucatæ. De ea sunt in dominio 4 hidæ, et ibi 1 carucata, et 4 servi; et 1 villanus, et 3 bordarii, cum 1 carucata. Ibi 10 acræ prati, et 12 acræ pasturæ, et 4 acræ silvæ. Valuit 40 solidos; modo 50 solidos.

In eadem villa 2 hidas una virgata minus tenuit Toli tempore Regis Edwardi. Terra 6 bovatæ. Ibi habet Gislebertus 1 villanum. Valet 18 solidos.

XXIX. LAND OF GILBERT DE BRETEVILE.

Gilbert de Bretevile holds *CHESEBERIE* of the King. Edric held it in the time of King Edward, and it paid geld for 5 hides. The land is 9 carucates. In demesne are 4 carucates, and 7 serfs; and there are 12 villans, and 3 bordars, and 14 coscets, with 5 carucates. There are 2 mills paying 20 shillings, and 15 acres of meadow, and 40 acres of wood. The pasture is 15 furlongs long, and 3 furlongs broad. It was worth £8; it is now worth £12.

The same Gilbert holds 5 hides in *BECHENHALLE.* Hacun held it in the time of King Edward. The land is 2 carucates. Of this there are 4 hides in demesne, and there is 1 carucate, and 4 serfs; and there is 1 villan, and 3 bordars, with 1 carucate. There are 10 acres of meadow, and 12 acres of pasture, and 4 acres of wood. It was worth 40 shillings; it is now worth 50 shillings.

In the same vill Toli held 2 hides all but 1 virgate in the time of King Edward. The land is 6 bovates. Gilbert has there 1 villan. It is worth 18 shillings.

---

[1] The name of Breteville, which is still that of a town in Normandy, occurs on the Battle Abbey Roll. William de Breteville, who was with William Rufus, in the New Forest, when that king was accidentally shot by Sir Walter Tyrrel, was most probably one of this family. He at the first opposed Henry I. in his endeavours to secure the crown, and espoused the cause of Duke Robert his elder brother. The estates enumerated above as having belonged at the great survey to Gilbert de Breteville afterwards formed part of the Fee of Bigod, Earl Marshal. Under him they were held by the family of Columbars, and under them by the Pipards. One of these estates,—Cliff-*Pipard*,—still preserves in its name the memorial of some of its early possessors. See '*Jackson's Aubrey*,' p. 164.

XV a 71 c In eadem villa 3 hidas et unam virgatam terræ tenebant Saul et Alwinus tempore Regis Edwardi. Terra est 10 bovatæ. Ibi habet Gislebertus 2 villanos, et 4 acras prati, et 6 acras pasturæ. Valebat 20 solidos; modo 27 solidos.

In the same vill Saul and Alwin held 3 hides and 1 virgate of land in the time of King Edward. The land is 10 bovates. Gilbert has there 2 villans, and 4 acres of meadow, and 6 acres of pasture. It was worth 20 shillings; it is now worth 27 shillings.

Ipse Gislebertus tenet *CLIVE.* Aluric et Burgel et Godeve tenuerunt tempore Regis Edwardi, et geldabant pro 16 hidis una virgata minus. Terra est 7 carucatæ. De eadem terra habet Ansfridus 11 hidas de Gisleberto, et ibi 3 carucatas in dominio, et 7 servos; et 3 villanos, et 2 bordarios, et 10 coscez, cum 2 carucatis et dimidio. Ibi molinus reddens 5 solidos, et 50 acræ prati, et 70 acræ pasturæ, et 18 acræ silvæ.

Gilbert himself holds *CLIVE.* Aluric and Burgel and Godeve held it in the time of King Edward, and paid geld for 16 hides all but 1 virgate. The land is 7 carucates. Of this same land Ansfrid has 11 hides under Gilbert, and has there in demesne 3 carucates, and 7 serfs; and 3 villans, and 2 bordars, and 10 coscets, with 2½ curucates. There is a mill paying 5 shillings, and 50 acres of meadow, and 70 acres of pasture, and 18 acres of wood.

De his 11 hidis est una in *TORNELLE,* quæ jacebat in *CLIVE* tempore Regis Edwardi.

One of these 11 hides, which used to lie in *CLIVE* in the time of King Edward, is in *TORNELLE.*

Ibi in *CLIVE* sunt 2 bordarii, et 2 servi, et 16 acræ prati, et 17 acræ pasturæ, sub Gisleberto. Hoc valet 35 solidos. Quod Ansfridus tenet valet 6 libras.

There are in *CLIVE* 2 bordars, and 2 serfs, and 16 acres of meadow, and 17 acres of pasture, under Gilbert. This holding is worth 35 shillings. What Ansfrid holds is worth £8.

Turstinus tenet de Gisleberto *MORTUNE.* Ulgar tenuit tempore Regis Edwardi, et geldabat pro 3 hidis una virgata minus. Terra est 2 carucatæ. De ea sunt in dominio 1 hida et 1 virgata terræ, et ibi 1 carucata; et 2 villani, et 4 bordarii, cum 2 carucatis. Ibi 20 acræ prati, et 80 acræ pasturæ. Valuit, et valet, 40 solidos.

Turstin holds *MORTUNE* of Gilbert. Ulgar held it in the time of King Edward, and it paid geld for 3 hides all but 1 virgate. The land is 2 carucates. Of this there are in demesne 1 hide and 1 virgate of land, and there is 1 carucate; and there are 2 villans, and 4 bordars, with 2 carucates. There are 20 acres of meadow, and 80 acres of pasture. It was, and is, worth 40 shillings.

Ipse Gislebertus tenet *HENTONE.* Ulgar tenuit tempore Regis Edwardi, et geldabat pro 11 hidis et 1 virgata. Terra est 5 carucatæ. De ea sunt in dominio 9 hidæ et 1 virgata terræ, et ibi 2 carucatæ; et 4 villani, et 5 bordarii, cum 2 carucatis. Ibi 16 acræ prati, et 30 acræ pasturæ. Valuit 100 solidos; modo 7 libras.

Gilbert himself holds *HENTONE.* Ulgar held it in the time of King Edward, and it paid geld for 11 hides and 1 virgate. The land is 5 carucates. Of this there are in demesne 9 hides and 1 virgate of land, and there are 2 carucates; and there are 4 villans, and 5 bordars, with 2 carucates. There are 16 acres of meadow, and 30 acres of pasture. It was worth 100 shillings; it is now worth £7.

Ansfridus tenet de Gisleberto *BACHENTUNE.* Edric tenuit tempore Regis Edwardi, et geldabat pro 2 hidis. Terra est 3 carucatæ. De ea est in

Ansfrid holds *BACHENTUNE* of Gilbert. Edric held it in the time of King Edward, and it paid geld for 2 hides. The land is 3 carucates. Of this there

Fol. { XV a / 71 c } dominio 1 hida, et ibi 2 carucatæ; et 4 villani, et 7 bordarii, et 3 cotarii, cum 2 carucatis. Ibi 8 acræ prati, et 40 acræ pasturæ. Valuit, et valet, 6 libras.

is 1 hide in demesne, and there are 2 carucates; and there are 4 villans, and 7 bordars, and 3 cottars, with 2 carucates. There are 8 acres of meadow, and 40 acres of pasture. It was, and is, worth £6.

Ansfridus tenet de Gisleberto *STAMERE.* Bruning tenuit tempore Regis Edwardi, et geldabat pro 2 hidis et dimidio. Terra est 2 carucatæ. De ea sunt in dominio 2 hidæ, et ibi 1 carucata, et 2 servi; et unus villanus, et 3 bordarii, cum dimidia carucata. Valuit 20 solidos; modo 40 solidos.

Ansfrid holds *STAMERE* of Gilbert. Bruning held it in the time of King Edward, and it paid geld for 2½ hides. The land is 2 carucates. Of this there are in demesne 2 hides, and there is 1 carucate, and 2 serfs; and there is 1 villan, and 3 bordars, with a half carucate. It was worth 20 shillings; it is now worth 40 shillings.

XXX. TERRA DURANDI DE GLOWECESTRE.

XXX. LAND OF DURAND OF GLOUCESTER.

Durandus de Glowecestre[1] tenet de Rege *CERITONE.* Almarus tenuit tempore Regis Edwardi, et geldabat pro 10 hidis. Terra est 5 carucatæ. De ea sunt in dominio 7 hidæ, cum 1 carucata et dimidio; et 7 villani, et 10 bordarii, cum 2 carucatis. Ibi molinus reddens 10 solidos, et 30 acræ prati. Pastura dimidio leucæ longa, et 3 quarentenis lata. Valuit 11 libras; modo 10 libras.

Durand of Gloucester holds *CERITONE* of the King. Almar held it in the time of King Edward, and it paid geld for 10 hides. The land is 5 carucates. Of this there are in demesne 7 hides, with 1 carucate and a half; and there are 7 villans, and 10 bordars, with 2 carucates. There is a mill paying 10 shillings, and 30 acres of meadow. The pasture is half a mile long, and 3 furlongs broad. It was worth £11; it is now worth £10.

Rogerius tenet de Durando *TOCHEHAM.* Dodo tenuit tempore Regis Edwardi de Ecclesia Malmesberiensi, et non poterat ab ea separari, et geldabat pro 5 hidis. Terra est [4 carucatæ]. In dominio est dimidium [hidæ], et ibi 2 carucatæ, cum 1 servo; et 7 villani, et 3 bordarii, cum 2 carucatis. Ibi molinus reddens 50 denarios, et 12 acræ prati, et 4 acræ pasturæ, et 2 acræ silvæ. Valuit 40 solidos; modo 4 libras.

Roger holds *TOCHEHAM* of Durand. Dodo held it in the time of King Edward of the Church at Malmesbury, and it could not be separated from it, and it paid geld for 5 hides. The land is [4 carucates]. In demesne is half [a hide] and there are 2 carucates with 1 serf; and there are 7 villans, and 3 bordars, with 2 carucates. There is a mill paying 50 pence, and 12 acres of meadow, and 4 acres of pasture, and 2 acres of wood. It was worth 40 shillings; it is now worth £4.

Idem tenet in *UFECOTE* 1 hidam et dimidium. Terra est 1 carucata. Hæc est in dominio. Valuit,

The same Roger holds 1 hide and a half in *UFECOTE.* The land is 1 carucate. This is in

[1] Durand of Gloucester was Sheriff of Gloucester at the time of the survey. Besides these estates in Wilts, he had others in Hants, Gloucestershire, and Herefordshire. In the Domesday account of the last-named county he is called 'Durandus *Vicecomes*.' (*Domesday, Hereford*, 180.)

[2] The words within brackets are supplied from conjecture. In the original manuscript the scribe has omitted to complete the sentences.

XVa 71 c et valet, 15 solidos. Almarus tenuit tempore Regis Edwardi.

Ipse Durandus tenet *SEGRETE.* Duo Taini tenuerunt tempore Regis Edwardi, et geldabant pro 5 hidis. Terra est 4 carucatæ. De ea sunt in dominio 2 hidæ, et ibi 1 carucata; et 3 villani, et 2 bordarii, cum 3 carucatis. Ibi 40 acræ prati. Valuit 40 solidos; modo 50 solidos.

Duo milites tenent de Durando. Qui tenebant tempore Regis Edwardi poterant ire quo volebant.

Ipse Durandus tenet *ESSELIE.* Eldred tenuit tempore Regis Edwardi, et geldabat pro 5 hidis una virgata minus. Terra est 4 carucatæ. De his sunt in dominio 3 hidæ, et ibi 2 carucatæ et 3 servi; et 5 villani, et 3 bordarii, cum 2 carucatis, et 2 cotarii. Ibi 5 acræ prati, et 5 acræ silvæ. Valuit, et valet, 4 libras.

Unam virgatam terræ in ipsa villa calumniatur unus miles Milonis Crispin.

Ipse Durandus tenet *LOCHERIGE.* Elmar tenuit tempore Regis Edwardi, et reddidit geldum pro 2 hidis. Terra est 1 carucata. De hac est in dominio 1 hida. Ibi 1 villanus, et 2 bordarii, cum 1 servo; et una acra prati, et 12 acræ pasturæ, et 6 acræ silvæ. Valuit 40 solidos; modo 30 solidos.

Herman tenet de Durando *LOCHINTONE.* Heraldus Comes tenuit tempore Regis Edwardi, et geldabat pro 4 hidis. Terra est 5 carucatæ. De ea sunt in dominio 2 hidæ, et ibi 2 carucatæ, cum 1 servo; et 6 villani, et 8 bordarii, cum 2 carucatis. Ibi molinus reddens 5 solidos, et 10 acræ prati, et 8 acræ pasturæ, et 4 acræ silvæ. Valuit 100 solidos; modo 4 libras.

demesne. It was, and is, worth 15 shillings. Almar held it in the time of King Edward.

Durand himself holds *SEGRETE.* Two Thanes held it in the time of King Edward, and they paid geld for 5 hides. The land is 4 carucates. Of this there are in demesne 2 hides, and there is 1 carucate; and there are 3 villans, and 2 bordars, with 3 carucates. There are 40 acres of meadow. It was worth 40 shillings, it is now worth 50 shillings.

Two 'milites' hold the manor of Durand. They who held it in the time of King Edward could go whither they wished.

Durand himself holds *ESSELIE.* Eldred held it in the time of King Edward, and it paid geld for 5 hides all but 1 virgate. The land is 4 carucates. Of this there are in demesne 3 hides, and there are 2 carucates, and 3 serfs; and there are 5 villans, and 3 bordars, with 2 carucates, and 2 cottars. There are 5 acres of meadow, and 5 acres of wood. It was, and is, worth £4.

One of Milo Crispin's retainers claims 1 virgate of land in this same vill.

Durand himself holds *LOCHERIGE.* Elmar held it in time of King Edward, and paid geld for 2 hides. The land is 1 carucate. Of this 1 hide is in demesne. There is 1 villan, and 2 bordars, with 1 serf; and there is 1 acre of meadow, and 12 acres of of pasture, and 6 acres of wood. It was worth 40 shillings; it is now worth 30 shillings.

Herman holds *LOCHINTONE* of Durand. Earl Harold held it in the time of King Edward, and it paid geld for 4 hides. The land is 5 carucates. Of this there are in demesne 2 hides, and there are 2 carucates, with 1 serf; and there are 6 villans, and 8 bordars, with 2 carucates. There is a mill paying 5 shillings, and 10 acres of meadow, and 8 acres of pasture, and 4 acres of wood. It was worth 100 shillings; it is now worth £4.

Fol. { XV a / 71 c }

XXXI. TERRA WALTERII GIFARD.

WALTERIUS GIFARD[1] tenet de Rege *BRADELIE.* Tosti Comes tenuit tempore Regis Edwardi, et pro 10 hidis se defendebat.[2] Terra est 10 carucatæ. De ea sunt in dominio 4 hidæ, et ibi 2 carucatæ, et 4 servi; et 6 villani, et 13 bordarii, cum 6 carucatis. Ibi duo molini, reddentes 12 solidos et 6 denarios, et 10 acræ prati. Pastura dimidio leucæ longa, et 2 quarentenis lata. Silva 1 leuca longa, et una lata. Valuit 12 libras; modo 10 libras.

XXXI. LAND OF WALTER GIFARD.

WALTER GIFARD holds *BRADELIE* of the King. Earl Tosti held it in the time of King Edward, and it was assessed at 10 hides. The land is 10 carucates. Of this there are in demesne 4 hides, and there are 2 carucates, and 4 serfs; and there are 6 villans, and 13 bordars, with 6 carucates. There are 2 mills paying 12 shillings and 6 pence, and 10 acres of meadow. The pasture is half a mile long, and 2 furlongs broad. The wood is 1 mile long, and 1 mile broad. It was worth £12; it is now worth £10.

XXXII. TERRA WILLELMI DE OW.

WILLELMUS DE OW[3] tenet de Rege *DIARNEFORD.* Tempore Regis Edwardi geldabat pro 16 hidis. Terra est 14 carucatæ. De ea sunt in dominio 4 hidæ, et ibi 2 carucatæ, et 2 servi; et 26 villani, et 37 bordarii, cum 12 carucatis. Ibi 3 molini reddentes 24 solidos et 6 denarios, et 30 acræ prati. Pastura 10 quarentenis longa, et 2 quarentenis lata. Silva 4 quarentenis longa, et 2 quarentenis

XXXII. LAND OF WILLIAM DE OW.

WILLIAM DE OW holds *DIARNEFORD* of the King. In the time of King Edward it paid geld for 16 hides. The land is 14 carucates. Of this there are in demesne 4 hides, and there are 2 carucates, and 2 serfs; and there are 26 villans, and 37 bordars, with 12 carucates. There are 3 mills paying 24 shillings and 6 pence, and 30 acres of meadow. The pasture is 10 furlongs long, and 2

---

[1] WALTER GIFARD was the son of Osbern de Bolebec and Aveline his wife, sister to Gunnora, Duchess of Normandy, great grandmother to the Conqueror. With Odo, the Bishop, and Robert Montaigne, he was of William's council held at Lillebonne, to consider the descent upon England. He distinguished himself at the battle of Hastings, though then advanced in years, and for his bravery and services was created Earl of Buckingham. He died in England in 1102, and, as he had directed, his corpse was carried into Normandy, and buried in the porch of the Abbey Church at Longueville. His wife was Agnes, daughter of Gerard Flaitel, and sister to the Bishop of Evreux. See *Hoare's 'Hundred of Mere,'* p. 93.

[2] *Se defendebat,* i.e., literally, *defended* itself; because the rates or taxes imposed on lands were raised for the defence of the realm against foreign invasions. Each manor was said to defend itself (an equivalent to being rated) at so many hides, because the taxes raised for its defence were in proportion to the value of it, which was estimated in hides.

[3] WILLIAM DE OW or EU, was the son of Robert Earl of Eu, in Normandy, one of the chief counsellors of William's invasion, and who received from the Conqueror the castelry of Hastings. William de Ow married the daughter of Hugh, Earl of Chester. At one time he favoured the succession of Robert Courthose to the English throne, but afterwards forsook his cause. In the year 1096, he was accused at Salisbury by Geoffrey Bainard of having been in treason against William Rufus, whereupon that king, though the Saxon Chronicle speaks of him as his kinsman, ordered him to be put to death with unusual cruelty. *Ellis,* i. 463.

XV b
71 d
lata. In Wiltone 4 domus reddunt 4 solidos. Valuit et valet, 24 libras.

furlongs broad. The wood is 4 furlongs long, and 2 furlongs broad. In Wilton 4 houses pay 4 shillings. The estate was, and is, worth £24.

Willelmus de Aldrie tenet de Willelmo *LITELTONE.* Tempore Regis Edwardi geldabat pro 6 hidis et una virgata terræ. Terra est 6 carucatæ. In dominio sunt 2 carucatæ, cum 1 servo; et 3 villani, et 21 bordarii, cum 3 carucatis. Ibi 2 molini reddentes 30 solidos, et 12 acræ prati. Pastura 10 quarentenis longa, et 2 quarentenis lata. Valuit 10 libras; modo 8 libras.

William de Aldrie holds *LITELTONE* of William. In the time of King Edward it paid geld for 6 hides and 1 virgate of land. The land is 6 carucates. In demesne are 2 carucates, with 1 serf; and there are 3 villans, and 21 bordars, with 3 carucates. There are 2 mills paying 30 shillings, and 12 acres of meadow. The pasture is 10 furlongs long, and 2 furlongs broad. It was worth £10; it is now worth £8.

Hæc terra fuit, tempore Regis Edwardi, Tainlande[1] Ecclesiæ Sarisberiensis. Alestan [de] Boscumbe tenuit.

In the time of King Edward this was Tainland belonging to the Church of Salisbury. Alestan [de] Boscumbe held it.

Idem Willelmus tenet de Willelmo *CONTONE.* Tempore Regis Edwardi geldabat pro 6 hidis. Terra est 4 carucatæ. In dominio sunt 2 carucatæ, et 5 servi; et 3 villani, et 11 bordarii, cum 2 carucatis. Ibi tercia pars 2 molinorum reddens 10 solidos, et 24 acræ prati, et 10 acræ pasturæ, et totidem silvæ. Valuit, et valet, 100 solidos.

The same William holds *CONTONE* of William. In the time of King Edward it paid geld for 6 hides. The land is 4 carucates. In demesne are 2 carucates, and 5 serfs; and there are 3 villans, and 11 bordars, with 2 carucates. There is the third part of 2 mills paying 10 shillings, and 24 acres of meadow, and 10 acres of pasture, and as many of wood. It was, and is, worth 100 shillings.

Willelmus de Mara tenet de Willelmo *BREVRESBROC.* Tempore Regis Edwardi geldabat pro 2 hidis et dimidio. Terra est 2 carucatæ. De ea est in dominio 1 hida et dimidium, et ibi 2 carucatæ, et 2 servi; et 1 villanus, et 8 bordarii. Valuit, et valet, 30 solidos.

William de Mara holds *BREVRESBROC* of William. In the time of King Edward it paid geld for $2\frac{1}{2}$ hides. The land is 2 carucates. Of this there is in demesne 1 hide and a half, and there are 2 carucates, and 2 serfs; and there is 1 villan, and 8 bordars. It was, and is, worth 30 shillings.

Hugo tenet de Willelmo *CERLETONE.* Tempore Regis Edwardi geldabat pro 5 hidis. Terra est 7 carucatæ. De ea sunt in dominio 4 hidæ et dimidium, et ibi 1 carucata; et 2 villani, et 7 bordarii, cum dimidio carucatæ. Ibi 2 molini reddentes 8 solidos et 4 denarios, et 15 acræ prati. Pastura 4

Hugo holds *CERLETONE* of William. In the time of King Edward it paid geld for 5 hides. The land is 7 carucates. Of this there are $4\frac{1}{2}$ hides in demesne, and there is 1 carucate; and there 2 villans, and 7 bordars, with half a carucate. There are 2 mills paying 8 shillings and 4 pence, and 15

[1] TAINLAND, (or THANE-LAND), is thus defined by Spelman, "Terra hæreditaria, et colonorum servituti non obnoxia." Jacob, in his Law Dictionary, explains the expression as denoting "such lands as were granted by charter of the Saxon kings to their Thanes, and which were held with all immunities, except the three-fold necessity of expeditions, repairs of castles, and mending of bridges." See also, *Ellis* i. 231.

Fol. { XV b / 71 d } quarentenis longa, et una quarentena lata. Silva 6 quarentenis longa, et 3 quarentenis lata. Valuit, et valet, 100 solidos.

Idem Hugo tenet de Willelmo *GRAFTONE.* Tempore Regis Edwardi, geldabat pro una hida. Terra est 1 carucata et dimidium. Ibi sunt 3 bordarii. Pastura 2 quarentenis longa, et una quarentena lata. Valuit 60 solidos ; modo 40 solidos.

Edwardus tenet de Willelmo *BOSCUMBE.* Tempore Regis Edwardi geldabat pro 7 hidis. Terra est 4 carucatæ. De ea sunt in dominio 4 hidæ et dimidium, et ibi 2 carucatæ, et ibi 2 servi; et 3 villani, et 4 coscez, cum 1 carucata et dimidio. Ibi 6 acræ prati. Pastura 12 quarentenis longa, et totidem lata. Valet 10 libras.

Bernardus tenet *CELDRETONE.* Tempore Regis Edwardi geldabat pro 3 hidis et dimidio, 4 acris minus. Terra est 2 carucatæ. De ea sunt in dominio 3 hidæ, et ibi 2 carucatæ, et 2 servi ; et 5 bordarii, et 2 coscez. Ibi pastura 6 quarentenis longa, et 5 quarentenis lata. Valuit 100 solidos; modo 9 libras.

Radulfus tenet de Willelmo *ADHELMERTONE.* Tempore Regis Edwardi geldabat pro 9 hidis. Terra est 8 carucatæ. De ea sunt in dominio 3 hidæ, et ibi 2 carucatæ; et 7 villani, et 10 bordarii, cum 6 carucatis. Ibi molinus reddens 7 solidos, et 50 acræ prati, et 40 acræ pasturæ. Valuit, et valet, 7 libras.

Bernardus tenet de Willelmo *COTEFORD.* Tempore Regis Edwardi geldabat pro 1 hida et dimidio. Terra est 2 carucatæ. De ea in dominio 1 hida, et ibi 1 carucata, cum 1 servo; et 2 coscez, cum 1 carucata. Ibi 10 acræ prati, et quarta pars molini reddens 3 solidos. Pastura 4 quarentenis

acres of meadow. The pasture is 4 furlongs long, and 1 furlong broad. The wood is 6 furlongs long, and 3 furlongs broad. It was, and is, worth 100 shillings.

The same Hugo holds *GRAFTONE* of William. In the time of King Edward it paid geld for 1 hide. The land is 1 carucate and a half. There are 3 bordars. The pasture is 2 furlongs long, and 1 furlong broad. It was worth 60 shillings; it is now worth 40 shillings.

Edward holds *BOSCUMBE* of William. In the time of King Edward it paid geld for 7 hides. The land is 4 carucates. Of this there are in demesne 4½ hides, and there are 2 carucates, and 2 serfs ; and there are 3 villans, and 4 coscets, with 1 carucate and a half. There are 6 acres of meadow. The pasture is 12 furlongs long, and as many broad. It is worth £10.

Bernard holds *CELDRETONE.* In the time of King Edward it paid geld for 3½ hides, wanting 4 acres. The land is 2 carucates. Of this there are in demesne 3 hides, and there are 2 carucates, and 2 serfs ; and there are 5 bordars, and 2 coscets. The pasture there is 6 furlongs long, and 5 furlongs broad. It was worth 100 shillings ; it is now worth £9.

Radulf holds *ADHELMERTONE* of William. In the time of King Edward it paid geld for 9 hides. The land is 8 carucates. Of this there are in demesne 3 hides, and there are 2 carucates ; and there are 7 villans, and 10 bordars, with 6 carucates. There is a mill paying 7 shillings, and 50 acres of meadow, and 40 acres of pasture. It was, and is, worth £7.

Bernard holds *COTEFORD* of William. In the time of King Edward it paid geld for 1 hide and a half. The land is 2 carucates. Of this 1 hide is in demesne, and there is 1 carucate, with 1 serf; and there are 2 coscets, with 1 carucate. There are 10 acres of meadow, and the fourth part of a mill

XV b 71 d longa, et 2 quarentenis lata. Valuit 4 libras; modo 3 libras.

Warnerus tenet de Willelmo *DIGERIC.* Tempore Regis Edwardi geldabat pro 1 hida et 3 virgatis terræ. Terra est 1 carucata, quæ ibi est in dominio; et 2 villani, et 4 coscez. Ibi dimidium molini reddens 5 solidos, et 7 acræ prati, et 15 acræ pasturæ, et 17 acræ silvæ minutæ. Valet 30 solidos.

De hac terra 1 hidam præstitit Alestano quidam Abbas Malmesberiensis.

Radulfus tenet de Willelmo *LACHAM.* Tempore Regis Edwardi geldabat pro 7 hidis et dimidio. Terra est 10 carucatæ. De ea in dominio est 1 hida et dimidium, et ibi 2 carucatæ, et 2 servi; et 10 villani, et 4 bordarii, et 24 coscez, cum 8 carucatis. Ibi 2 molini reddentes 30 solidos, et 15 acræ prati. Silva 1 leuca longa, et tantundem lata. Valuit 6 libras; modo similiter.

Willelmus tenet de Willelmo *SEVAMENTONE.* Tempore Regis Edwardi geldabat pro 10 hidis. Terra est 7 carucatæ. De ea sunt in dominio 4 hidæ, et ibi 2 carucatæ; et 10 villani, et 5 bordarii, cum 5 carucatis. Ibi 20 acræ prati. Silva 2 quarentenis longa, et una quarentena lata. Valuit 6 libras; modo 7 libras.

Unus Anglicus tenet de Willelmo *GETONE.* Tempore Regis Edwardi geldabat pro una virgata terræ. Terra est dimidia carucata, quæ ibi est. Reddit 5 solidos.

Has omnes præscriptas terras Willelmi de Ow tenuit Alestan de Boscumbe.

Hugo tenet de Willelmo *SOPEWORDE.* Aluric tenuit tempore Regis Edwardi, et geldabat pro 5 hidis. Terra est 6 carucatæ. De ea sunt in dominio 3 hidæ et dimidium, et ibi 2 carucatæ, et 6

paying 3 shillings. The pasture is 4 furlongs long, and 2 furlongs broad. It was worth £4; it is now £3.

Warner holds *DIGERIC* of William. In the time of King Edward it paid geld for 1 hide and 3 virgates of land. The land is 1 carucate, which is there in demesne; and there are 2 villans, and 4 coscets. There is half a mill paying 5 shillings, and 7 acres of meadow, and 15 acres of pasture, and 17 acres of coppice-wood. It is worth 30 shillings.

A certain Abbot of Malmesbury granted 1 hide of this land to Alestan.

Radulf holds *LACHAM* of William. In the time of King Edward it paid geld for 7½ hides. The land is 10 carucates. Of this there is in demesne 1 hide and a half, and there are 2 carucates, and 2 serfs; and there are 10 villans, and 4 bordars, and 24 coscets, with 8 carucates. There are 2 mills paying 30 shillings, and 15 acres of meadow. The wood is a mile long, and as much broad. It was worth £6; it is now of like value.

William holds *SEVAMENTONE* of William. In the time of King Edward it paid geld for 10 hides. The land is 7 carucates. Of this there are in demesne 4 hides, and there are 2 carucates; and there are 10 villans, and 5 bordars, with 5 carucates. There are 20 acres of meadow. The wood is 2 furlongs long, and 1 furlong broad. It was worth £6; it is now worth £7.

An Englishman holds *GETONE* of William. In the time of King Edward it paid geld for 1 virgate of land. The land which is there is a half carucate. It pays 5 shillings.

Alestan of Boscumbe held all these above mentioned lands now belonging to William de Ow.

Hugo holds *SOPEWORDE* of William. Aluric held it in the time of King Edward, and it paid geld for 5 hides. The land is 6 carucates. Of this there are 3½ hides in demesne, and there are 2 caru-

Fol. { XV b, 71 d } servi; et 3 villani, et 5 bordarii, cum 3 carucatis. Valuit 6 libras; modo 4 libras.

Idem Willelmus tenet *TOLLARD.* Toli tenuit tempore Regis Edwardi pro uno manerio, et geldabat pro 1 hida. Terra est 1 carucata. Ibi sunt coscez, et 5 acræ prati, et una quarentena silvæ. Valuit, et valet, 20 solidos.

Ansfridus tenet de Willelmo *OPETONE.* Toli tenuit tempore Regis Edwardi, et geldabat pro 3 hidis. Terra est 2 carucatæ et dimidium. De ea sunt in dominio 2 hidæ, et ibi 1 carucata; et 2 villani, et 5 bordarii, cum 1 carucata. Ibi molinus reddens 5 solidos, et 4 acræ prati. Silva 2 quarentenis longa, et una quarentena lata, et 20 acræ pasturæ. Valuit 15 solidos; modo 60 solidos.

Pro dimidia hida non reddidit geldum postquam Willelmus Rex venit in Angliam; et Hernulfus de Hesding tenet injuste dimidiam hidam in ipsa villa.

cates, and 6 serfs; and there are 3 villans, and 5 bordars, with 3 carucates. It was worth £6; it is now worth £4.

The same William holds *TOLLARD.* Toli held it in the time of King Edward for 1 manor, and it paid geld for 1 hide. The land is 1 carucate. There are coseets, and 5 acres of meadow, and 1 furlong of wood. It was, and is, worth 20 shillings.

Ansfrid holds *OPETONE* of William. Toli held it in the time of King Edward, and it paid geld for 3 hides. The land is 2½ carucates. Of this there are in demesne 2 hides, and there is 1 carucate; and there are 2 villans, and 5 bordars, with 1 carucate. There is a mill paying 5 shillings, and 4 acres of meadow. The wood is 2 furlongs long, and 1 furlong broad, and there are 20 acres of pasture. It was worth 15 shillings; it is now worth 60 shillings.

For a half hide he has not paid geld since King William came into England; and Ernulf de Hesding holds unjustly a half hide in the same vill.

XXXIII. TERRA WILLELMI DE BRAIOSE.

Willelmus de Braiose[1] tenet de Rege *ESSAGE.* Alwinus tenuit tempore Regis Edwardi, et geldabat pro 2 hidis et una virgata terræ et dimidio. Terra est 1 carucata et dimidium. De ea sunt in dominio 2 hidæ. Ibi 1 villanus, et 2 bordarii, cum dimidia carucata. Ibi 40 acræ pasturæ, et silva 1 leuca longa, et 3 quarentenis lata. Valuit 10 solidos; modo 20 solidos. Robertus tenet de Willelmo.

XXXIII. LAND OF WILLIAM DE BRAIOSE.

William de Braiose holds *ESSAGE* of the King. Alwin held it in the time of King Edward, and it paid geld for 2 hides and 1 virgate and a half of land. The land is 1 carucate and a half. Of this there are 2 hides in demesne. There is 1 villan, and 2 bordars, with a half carucate. There are 40 acres of pasture, and the wood is 1 mile long, and 3 furlongs broad. It was worth 10 shillings; it is now worth 20 shillings. Robert holds it of William.

[1] William de Braiose was a benefactor to the Abbey of St. Florent at Saumur, and the founder of Sele Priory in Sussex. He possessed, besides this small holding in Wilts, estates in Sussex, Surrey, Hants, Berks, and Dorset. His family continued in the male line, till the latter end of the reign of Edward III. See *Dugd. Baron.*, i. 414.

XXXIV. TERRA WILLELMI DE MOIUN.

XVI a WILLELMUS DE MOIUN[1] tenet de Rege *SUTONE*,[2]
72 a et Walterus de eo. Colo tenuit tempore Regis Edwardi, et geldabat pro 5 hidis. Terra est 4 carucatæ. De ea sunt in dominio 3 hidæ et una virgata terræ, et ibi 2 carucatæ, et 3 servi; et 3 villani, et 6 bordarii, cum 2 carucatis. Ibi molinus reddens 4 solidos, et 4 acræ prati, et 2 acræ silvæ. Pastura dimidio leucæ longa, et una lata. Valuit 4 libras; modo 100 solidos.

XXXIV. LAND OF WILLIAM DE MOIUN.

WILLIAM DE MOIUN holds *SUTONE* of the King, and Walter of him. Colo held it in the time of King Edward, and it paid geld for 5 hides. The land is 4 carucates. Of this there are in demesne 3 hides and 1 virgate of land, and there are 2 carucates, and 3 serfs; and there are 3 villans, and 6 bordars, with 2 carucates. There is a mill paying 4 shillings, and 4 acres of meadow, and 2 acres of wood. The pasture is half a mile long, and one mile broad. It was worth £4; it is now worth 100 shillings.

XXXV. TERRA WILLELMI DE FALEISE.

WILLELMUS DE FALEISE[3] tenet de Rege dimidiam hidam in *STANINGES*, et Alwardus de eo. Terra est dimidia carucata, quæ ibi est; et 4 acræ prati. Valuit 20 solidos; modo reddit 10 solidos. Leuing tenuit tempore Regis Edwardi.

XXXV. LAND OF WILLIAM DE FALEISE.

WILLIAM DE FALEISE holds of the King a half hide in *STANINGES*, and Alward holds it of him. The land which is there is a half carucate; and there are 4 acres of meadow. It was worth 20 shillings; it now pays 10 shillings. Leuing held it in the time of King Edward.

---

[1] Leland (Collect. I. 203) quoting an old roll in Norman-French, in which were contained the names of those who came over to England with King William, mentions "William de Moion" as "the most noble of all the host." He had possessions also in Dorset, Devon, and Somerset; in the last named county he held no less than fifty-six manors *(Somerset, 95 b)*. The first William de Moiun, who was also, according to Leland, called Capel, built the priory of Dunster, where he was buried, as was also his son who bare the same name as his father. The grandson, also a William de Moiun, surnamed Meschin, was created Earl of Somerset, but he does not appear to have left any children to inherit his title.

[2] This manor of SUTONE is the only one in Wiltshire of which a detailed account is given in the Exon Domesday (p. 41). In the introduction to the Wiltshire portion of that record, contained in this volume, some remarks will be found upon the entry in question. We learn from it the surname of the tenant, viz., Walter *Hosatus* (the same which appears in later times as HUSEE, and HUSSEY) and are able from this additional information to identify the manor alluded to with tolerable certainty.

[3] WILLIAM DE FALEISE held manors also in Dorset, Devon, and Somerset. From an entry under the last named county *(fol. 96 b)*, we learn that he was married to the daughter of Serlo de Burci, who is recorded as holding a small estate at Dobreham (Domerham), under the Abbot of Glastonbury. See above, *p.* 29.

XXXVI. TERRA WALSCINI DE DOWAI.

Fol. { XVI a / 72 a } WALSCINUS DE DOWAI tenet de Rege *CELDEWELLE*, et Godescal de eo. Alsi tenuit tempore Regis Edwardi, et geldabat pro 5 hidis. Terra est 3 carucatæ. De ea sunt in dominio 3 hidæ, et 3 virgatæ terræ, et ibi 1 carucata, cum 1 servo, et 1 villano, et 6 bordariis, cum dimidia carucata. Ibi 10 acræ prati, et 7 acræ pasturæ, et 8 acræ silvæ. Valuit, et valet, 3 libras.

Radulfus tenet de Walscino *STORTONE*. Alwacre tenuit tempore Regis Edwardi, et geldabat pro 8 hidis. Terra est 6 carucatæ. De ea sunt in dominio 5 hidæ, et ibi 2 carucatæ, cum 1 servo; et 6 villani, et 13 coscez, et 8 cotarii, cum 4 carucatis. Ibi 2 molini, reddentes 20 denarios, et 60 acræ pasturæ. Silva 1 leuca longa, et una lata. Valuit 4 libras; modo 7 libras.

XXXVI. LAND OF WALSCIN DE DOWAI [DOUAY].

WALSCIN DE DOWAI holds *CELDEWELLE* of the King, and Godescal holds it of him. Alsi held it in the time of King Edward, and it paid geld for 5 hides. The land is 3 carucates. Of this there are 3 hides and 3 virgates of land in demesne, and there is 1 carucate, with one serf, and one villan, and 6 bordars, with a half carucate. There are 10 acres of meadow, and 7 acres of pasture, and 8 acres of wood. It was, and is, worth £3.

Radulf holds *STORTONE* of Walscin. Alwacre held it in the time of King Edward, and it paid geld for 8 hides. The land is 6 carucates. Of this there are in demesne 5 hides, and there are 2 carucates, with 1 serf; and there are 6 villans, and 13 coscets, and 8 cottars, with 4 carucates. There are 2 mills paying 20 pence, and 60 acres of pasture. The wood is 1 mile long, and one broad. It was worth £4; it is now worth £7.

XXXVII. TERRA WALERANNI VENATORIS.

WALERANNUS[1] tenet de Rege *COTEFORD*. Erlebald tenuit tempore Regis Edwardi, et geldabat pro 6 hidis. Terra est 6 carucatæ. De ea sunt in diminio 3 hidæ, et ibi 2 carucatæ, et 3 servi; et 7 villani, et 6 bordarii, cum 3 carucatis. Ibi molinus

XXXVII. LAND OF WALERAN THE HUNTSMAN.

WALERAN holds *COTEFORD* of the King. Erlebald held it in the time of King Edward, and it paid geld for 6 hides. The land is 6 carucates. Of this there are in demesne 3 hides, and there are 2 carucates, and 3 serfs; and there are 7 villans, and

[1] WALERAN was one of the Conqueror's principal huntsmen. He is entered in Hampshire as holding several manors in that county *in capite*, and had still larger possessions in Dorsetshire, and Wilts. He also held lands in Hampshire under the Abbey of St. Peter, Winchester. His descendants for many generations remained in possession of the manors enumerated above. They were held by Walter Waleran, Lord of Grimstead, who was married to Isabel, grand-daughter of William Longespée, Earl of Salisbury, and who died, A.D. 1200. Through his daughters and co-heiresses, the several estates were taken by marriage into the families of Ingham, and St. Martin and held by them during great part of the fourteenth century. See Hoare's '*Branch and Dole*,' p. 10.

VI a reddens 10 solidos, et 10 acræ prati. Pastura dimidio
2 a leucæ longa, et 5 quarentenis lata. Valuit 10 libras;
modo 12 libras.

6 bordars, with 3 carucates. There is a mill paying 10 shillings, and 10 acres of meadow. The pasture is half a mile long, and 5 furlongs broad. It was worth £10; it is now worth £12.

Walterus tenet de Waleranno *ANESTIGE.* Aluric et Ulwardus tenebant tempore Regis Edwardi, et geldabant pro 7 hidis. Terra est 4 carucatæ. De ea sunt in dimidio 5 hidæ et una virgata terræ, et ibi 2 carucatæ, et 2 servi; et 6 villani, et 4 bordarii, cum 2 carucatis. Ibi molinus reddens 5 solidos, et 16 acræ prati, et 15 acræ silvæ. Pastura dimidio leucæ longa, et 3 quarentenis lata. Valuit, et valet, 100 solidos.

Walter holds *ANESTIGE* of Waleran. Aluric and Ulward held it in the time of King Edward, and paid geld for 7 hides. The land is 4 carucates. Of this there are in demesne 5 hides and 1 virgate of land, and there are 2 carucates, and 2 serfs; and there are 6 villans, and 4 bordars, with 2 carucates. There is a mill paying 5 shillings, and 16 acres of meadow, and 15 acres of wood. The pasture is half a mile long, and 3 furlongs broad. It was, and is, worth 100 shillings.

Azelinus tenet de Waleranno *BUTREMARE.* Octo Taini tenuerunt tempore Regis Edwardi, et geldabant pro 1 hida et una virgata terræ. Terra est 2 carucatæ. Valet 20 solidos.

Azelin holds *BUTREMARE* of Waleran. Eight Thanes held it in the time of King Edward, and paid geld for 1 hide and 1 virgate of land. The land is 2 carucates. It is worth 20 shillings.

Ipse Walerannus tenet 1 hidam in *STANINGES.* Colo tenuit tempore Regis Edwardi. Terra est dimidium carucatæ. Ibi sunt 6 acræ prati. Valuit 5 solidos; modo 10 solidos.

Waleran himself holds 1 hide in *STANINGES.* Colo held in the time of King Edward. The land is half a carucate. There are 6 acres of meadow. It was worth 5 shillings; it is now worth 10 shillings.

Ricardus tenet de Waleranno *CHENETE.* Leveclai tenuit tempore Regis Edwardi, et geldabat pro una hida et dimidio et una virgata terræ. Terra est 1 carucata, quæ ibi est, cum 1 servo, et 2 bordariis, et una acra prati, et 4 acris pasturæ. Valuit, et valet, 20 solidos.

Richard holds *CHENETE* of Waleran. Leveclai held it in the time of King Edward, and it paid geld for 1 hide and a half and 1 virgate of land. The land is 1 carucate, which is there, with one 1 serf, and 2 bordars, and 1 acre of meadow, and 4 acres of pasture. It was, and is, worth 20 shillings.

Azelinus tenet de Waleranno *STANLEGE.* Selewinus tenuit tempore Regis Edwardi, et geldabat pro una hida et 3 virgatis terræ. Terra est 1 carucata. Ibi sunt 3 villani, et 3 bordarii, et 10 acræ prati. Valuit 15 solidos; modo 30 solidos.

Azelin holds *STANLEGE* of Waleran. Selewin held it in the time of King Edward, and it paid geld for 1 hide and 3 virgates of land. The land is 1 carucate. There are 3 villans, and 3 bordars, and 10 acres of meadow. It was worth 15 shillings; it is now worth 30 shillings.

Ipse Walerannus tenet *LANGEFORD.* Osulf tenuit tempore Regis Edwardi, et geldabat pro 10 hidis. Terra est 5 carucatæ. De ea sunt in dominio 5 hidæ, et ibi 2 carucatæ, et 5 servi; et 8 villani, et 4 bordarii, cum 3 carucatis. Ibi molinus reddens

Waleran himself holds *LANGEFORD.* Osulf held it in the time of King Edward, and it paid geld for 10 hides. The land is 5 carucates. Of this there are 5 hides in demesne, and there are 2 carucates, and 5 serfs; and there are 8 villans, and 4 bordars with

Fol. {XVI a / 72 a} 15 solidos, et 30 acræ prati. Pastura dimidio leucæ longa, et 2 quarentenis lata. Valuit, et valet, 10 libras.

Erenburgis tenet de Waleranno *LANGEFORD.* Norman tenuit tempore Regis Edwardi, et geldabat pro 5 hidis. Terra est 2 carucatæ. De ea sunt in dominio 4 hidæ, et ibi 1 carucata, cum 1 servo, et 1 villano, et 5 bordariis, cum dimidio carucatæ. Ibi dimidium molini reddens 30 denarios, et 20 acræ prati. Pastura 4 quarentenis longa, et una quarentena lata. Valuit, et valet, 100 solidos.

Engenoldus tenet de Waleranno dimidium hidæ in *BEREFORD*, et pro tanto geldabat tempore Regis Edwardi. Bolle tenuit. Terra est dimidium carucatæ. Ibi sunt 2 bordarii, et 3 acræ prati. Valuit, et valet, 7 solidos.

Robertus tenet de Waleranno in *WITFORD*, 3 virgatas terræ, et pro tanto geldabat tempore Regis Edwardi. Bolle tenuit. Terra est dimidium carucatæ. Ibi sunt 2 bordarii, et 4 acræ prati. Valuit, et valet, 10 solidos.

Herbertus tenet de Waleranno *GREMESTEDE.*
Fol. {XVI b / 72 b} Agemundus tenuit tempore Regis Edwardi, et geldabat pro 3 hidis. Terra est 3 carucatæ. De ea est in dominio 1 hida et dimidium, et ibi 1 carucata, et 2 servi; et 5 villani, et 7 coscez, cum 3 carucatis. Ibi 10 acræ prati. Silva 5 quarentenis longa, et 2 quarentenis lata. Valuit, et valet, 60 solidos.

Engenulfus tenet de Waleranno *WATEDENE.* Bolle tenuit tempore Regis Edwardi, et geldabat pro 2 hidis. Terra est 1 carucata et dimidium. De ea in dominio est hida et dimidium, et ibi 1 carucata; et 4 coscez cum dimidia carucata. Ibi 7 acræ prati. Silvæ 2 quarentenæ longitudine, et dimidium quarentenæ latitudine. Valuit 15 solidos; modo 25 solidos.

3 carucates. There is a mill paying 15 shillings, and 30 acres of meadow. The pasture is half a mile long, and 2 furlongs broad. It was, and is, worth £10.

Erenburgis holds *LANGEFORD* of Waleran. Norman held it in the time of King Edward, and it paid geld for 5 hides. The land is 2 carucates. Of this there are in demesne 4 hides, and there is 1 carucate, with 1 serf, and 1 villan and 5 bordars, with half a carucate. There is half a mill paying 30 pence, and 20 acres of meadow. The pasture is 4 furlongs long, and 1 furlong broad. It was, and is, worth 100 shillings.

Engenold holds half a hide of Waleran in *BEREFORD*, and it paid geld for so much in the time of King Edward. Bolle held it. The land is half a carucate. There are two bordars and 3 acres of meadow. It was, and is, worth 7 shillings.

Robert holds of Waleran 3 virgates of land in *WITFORD*, and it paid geld for so much in the time of King Edward. Bolle held it. The land is half a carucate. There are 2 bordars, and 4 acres of meadow. It was, and is worth, 10 shillings.

Herbert holds *GREMESTEDE* of Waleran. Agemund held it in the time of King Edward, and it paid geld for 3 hides. The land is 3 carucates. Of this there is one hide and a half in demesne, and there is 1 carucate, and 2 serfs; and there are 5 villans, and 7 coscets, with 3 carucates. There are 10 acres of meadow. The wood is 5 furlongs long, and 2 furlongs broad. It was, and is, worth 60 shillings.

Engenulf holds *WATEDENE* of Waleran. Bolle held it in the time of King Edward, and it paid geld for 2 hides. The land is 1 carucate and a half. Of this there is in desmesne one hide and a half and there is 1 carucate; and there are 4 coscets with a half carucate. There are 7 acres of meadow. Of wood there are 2 furlongs in length, and half a furlong in breadth. It was worth 15 shillings; it is now worth 25 shillings.

XVI b
72 b In *WATEDENE* tenent 2 milites 3 virgatas terræ et dimidium, 2 acris minus. Tempore Regis Edwardi tenebant 4 Taini, qui poterant ire quo volebant.[1] Terra est dimidia carucata, quæ ibi est, cum 2 coscez, et una acra prati et dimidio. Valet 12 solidos.

In *WATEDENE* 2 'milites' hold 3½ virgates of land, all but 2 acres. In the time of King Edward 4 Thanes held them and they were able to go whither they wished. The land is half a carucate which is there, with 2 coscets, and 1 acre and a half of meadow. It is worth 12 shillings.

Engenulfus tenet de Waleranno unam virgatam terræ in *ALWARBERIE*, et ibi habet 1 coscet. Valet 2 solidos. Bode tenuit tempore Regis Edwardi.

Engenulf holds 1 virgate of land of Waleran in *ALWARBERIE*, and has there 1 coscet. It is worth 2 shillings. Bode held it in the time of King Edward.

Ipse Walerannus tenet *DUENE*. Godric tenuit tempore Regis Edwardi, et geldabat pro 2 hidis et una virgata terræ. Terra est 3 carucatæ. De ea est in dominio 1 hida, et ibi carucata et dimidium, et 2 servi; et unus villanus, et 10 coscez, cum carucata et dimidio. Ibi molinus et dimidium reddens 16 solidos, et 5 acræ prati. Silva 1 quarentena inter longitudinem et latitudinem. Valuit, et valet, 60 solidos.

Waleran himself holds *DUENE*. Godric held it in the time of King Edward, and it paid geld for 2 hides and 1 virgate of land. The land is 3 carucates. Of this there is in demesne 1 hide, and there is a carucate and a half, and 2 serfs; and there is 1 villan, and 10 coscets, with a carucate and a half. There is a mill and a half paying 16 shillings, and 5 acres of meadow. The wood is 1 furlong between length and breadth. It was, and is, worth 60 shillings.

In *HERDICOTE* tenet [Walerannus] dimidium hidæ. Terra est dimidium carucatæ. Ibi habet dimidium molinum reddentem 6 solidos. Totum valet 20 solidos. Ednod tenuit tempore Regis Edwardi.

In *HERDICOTE* [Waleran] holds half a hide. The land is half a carucate. He has there a half mill paying 6 shillings. The whole is worth 20 shillings. Ednod held it in the time of King Edward.

XXXVIII. TERRA WILLELMI FILII WIDONIS.

XXXVIII. LAND OF WILLIAM, SON OF WIDON. [FITZ-WIDON.]

WILLELMUS FILIUS WIDONIS tenet de Rege *SUTONE*. Alwold et soror ejus tenuerunt tempore Regis Edwardi, et geldabat pro 8 hidis. Terra est 6 carucatæ. De ea sunt in dominio 4 hidæ, et ibi 2 carucatæ, et 4 servi; et 6 villani, et 8 bordarii, cum 4 carucatis. Ibi 2 partes molini reddentes 13 solidos et 4 denarios, et 6 acræ prati. Pastura 1 leuca longa, et 2 quarentenis lata, et tantundem silvæ. Valuit 8 libras; modo 10 libras.

WILLIAM FITZ-WIDON holds *SUTONE* of the King. Alwold and his sister held it in the time of King Edward, and it paid geld for 8 hides. The land is 6 carucates. Of this there are in demesne 4 hides, and there are 2 carucates, and 4 serfs; and there are 6 villans, and 8 bordars, with 4 carucates. There are 2 parts of a mill paying 13 shillings and 4 pence, and 6 acres of meadow. The pasture is 1 mile long, and 2 furlongs broad, and there is as much wood. It was worth £8; it is now worth £10.

[1] See the note on p. 72.

XXXIX. TERRA HENRICI DE FERIERES.

Fol. { XVI b 72 b } HENRICUS DE FERIERES[1] tenet de Rege *STANDENE.* Godric tenuit tempore Regis Edwardi, et geldabat pro 1 hida. Terra est 5 carucatæ. In dominio sunt 4, et 4 servi; et 8 acræ prati, et 10 acræ pasturæ, et 6 acræ silvæ. Valet 100 solidos.

Ibi est silva pertinens ad *BEDVINE* tempore Regis Edwardi.

Idem tenet *CLIVE.* Godric tenuit tempore Regis Edwardi, et geldabat pro 5 hidis una virgata minus. Terra est 3 carucatæ. De ea sunt in dominio 4 hidæ et una virgata, et ibi 3 carucatæ, et 6 servi, et 5 bordarii, et 30 acræ prati, et 12 acræ pasturæ. Valuit, et valet, 4 libras.

XXXIX. LAND OF HENRY DE FERIERES.

HENRY DE FERIERES holds *STANDENE* of the King. Godric held it in the time of King Edward, and it paid geld for 1 hide. The land is 5 carucates. There are in demesne 4, and 4 serfs; and there are 8 acres of meadow, and 10 acres of pasture, and 6 acres of wood. It is worth 100 shillings.

There is a wood there which belonged to *BEDVINE* in the time of King Edward.

The same holds *CLIVE.* Godric held it in the time of King Edward, and it paid geld for 5 hides all but 1 virgate. The land is 3 carucates. Of this there are in demesne 4 hides and 1 virgate, and there are 3 carucates, and 6 serfs, and 5 bordars, and 30 acres of meadow, and 12 acres of pasture. It was, and is, worth £4.

XL. TERRA RICARDI FILII GISLEBERTI.

RICARDUS FILIUS GISLEBERTI[2] COMITIS tenet de Rege *SUDTONE,* et Berengerus de eo. Ulwardus tenuit tempore Regis Edwardi, et geldabat pro 10 hidis. Terra est 6 carucatæ. De ea sunt in dominio

XL. LAND OF RICHARD, SON OF EARL GILBERT [FITZ-GILBERT].

RICHARD SON OF EARL GILBERT holds *SUDTONE* of the King, and Berenger of him. Ulward held it in the time of King Edward, and it paid geld for 10 hides. The land is 6 carucates. Of

---

[1] HENRY DE FERIERES was the ancestor of the family of Ferrers, Earls of Derby, and one of the Conqueror's commissioners for the formation of the Domesday survey. He had possessions in no less than fourteen counties. One of them was Tutbury, in Staffordshire. Towards the end of the eleventh century, he founded the Priory at Tutbury, which afterwards became a cell to the Abbey of St. Peter super Divam, in Normandy. *Ellis* i., 418.

[2] RICHARD FITZ-GILBERT is also known by the name of RICHARD DE TONEBRIGE *(Kent, p. 14).* He was the ancestor of the noble family of CLARE. His father was Gislebert, (surnamed Crispin,) Earl of Brion, in Normandy, and son of Geoffrey, the natural son of Richard, Duke of Normandy. He was himself Justice of England, and was joined in that office with William de Warren. He assumed the name of De Tonebrige, from his seat at Tunbridge, in Kent, the town and castle of which he had obtained from the Archbishop of Canterbury, in exchange for the castle of Brion in Normandy. In Suffolk he seems to have had the name of CLARE, from one of his lordships in that county, and his descendants are known as Earls Clare, or De Clare, till they obtained the English Earldoms of Gloucester and Hertford. His wife Rothais, daughter of Walter Giffard, Earl of Buckingham, is entered in the record as a holder of lands in Hertfordshire *(fol 142 b.)* and Huntingdonshire *(fol 207).* After the decease of her first husband she married Eudo Dapifer. *Ellis* I., 477, 481.

XVI b 2 b 7 hidæ, et ibi 3 carucatæ, et 5 servi; et 6 villani, et 9 bordarii, cum 3 carucatis. Ibi molinus reddens 10 solidos, et 12 acræ prati, et 3 acræ silvæ. Pastura 6 quarentenis longa, et 3 quarentenis lata; et 5 burgenses reddentes 50 denarios. Valuit, et valet, 6 libras.

this there are in demesne 7 hides, and there are 3 carucates, and 5 serfs; and there are 6 villans, and 9 bordars, with 3 carucates. There is a mill paying 10 shillings, and 12 acres of meadow, and 3 acres of wood. The pasture is 6 furlongs long, and 3 furlongs broad; and there are 5 burgesses paying 50 pence. It was, and is, worth £6.

XLI. TERRA RADULFI DE MORTEMER.

Radulfus de Mortemer[1] tenet *HUNLAVINTONE.* Heraldus Comes tenuit, et geldabat pro 20 hidis. Terra est 14 carucatæ. De ea sunt in dominio 14 hidæ, et ibi 4 carucatæ, et 8 servi; et 19 villani, et 8 coscez, cum 6 carucatis. Ibi 12 acræ prati, et 10 acræ pasturæ, et 8 acræ silvæ. Valuit, et valet, 12 libras.

In Malmesberie una domus reddit 12 denarios.

Oidelardus tenet de Radulfo *TOCHEHAM.* Alwinus tenuit tempore Regis Edwardi, et geldabat pro 2 hidis et dimidio. Terra est 3 carucatæ. De ea sunt in dominio 2 hidæ, et ibi 2 carucatæ, cum 1 servo, et 1 villano, et 3 coscez cum dimidia carucata. Ibi 12 acræ prati, et totidem pasturæ, et 2 acræ silvæ. Valuit 30 solidos; modo 50 solidos.

Edwardus tenet de Radulfo *BRADEFELDE.* Bristwi et Elwi tenuerunt tempore Regis Edwardi, et geldabant pro 2 hidis et dimidio. Terra est 2 carucatæ. De ea est in dominio 1 hida et dimidium,

XLI. LAND OF RADULF DE MORTEMER.

Radulf de Mortemer holds *HUNLAVINTONE* of the King. Earl Harold held it, and it paid geld for 20 hides. The land is 14 carucates. Of this there are in demesne 14 hides, and there are 4 carucates, and 8 serfs; and there are 19 villans, and 8 coscets, with 6 carucates. There are 12 acres of meadow, and 10 acres of pasture, and 8 acres of wood. It was, and is, worth £12.

In Malmesbury 1 house pays 12 pence.

Oidelard holds *TOCHEHAM* of Radulf. Alwin held it in the time of King Edward, and it paid geld for $2\frac{1}{2}$ hides. The land is 3 carucates. Of this there are in demesne 2 hides, and there are 2 carucates, with 1 serf, and 1 villan, and 3 coscets with a half carucate. There are 12 acres of meadow, and as many of pasture, and 2 acres of wood. It was worth 30 shillings; it is now worth 50 shillings.

Edward holds *BRADEFELDE* of Radulf. Bristwi and Elwi held it in the time of King Edward, and they paid geld for $2\frac{1}{2}$ hides. The land is 2 carucates. Of this there is in demesne 1 hide and a

---

[1] Ralph de Mortemer, was the son of Roger de Mortemer, founder of the Abbey of St. Victor in Normandy. He was allied to the Conqueror, and received from him many grants in different counties. Wigmore Castle, in Shropshire, was given to him for his services in subduing and taking prisoner, Edric, Earl of Shrewsbury. He founded Wigmore Abbey; and died some time towards the close of the reign of Henry I. His son, Hugh de Mortemer, married Matilda Longespée, and from their son Roger, who died in 1215, were descended the Earls of March. *Dugd. Baron.* i., 138.

Fol. { XVI b, 72 b } et ibi 2 carucatæ, et 3 villani, et 2 coscez, et 12 acræ prati. Valuit, et valet, 30 solidos.

In *HIWI* tenet Radulfus 1 hidam, et ibi habet 1 bordarium, et 4 acras prati. Valet 15 solidos. Toti emit eam tempore Regis Edwardi, de Ecclesia Malmesberiensi, ad ætatem trium hominum, et infra hunc terminum poterat ire cum ea ad quem vellet dominum.[1]

Ipse Radulfus tenet *CLATFORD*. Alwinus tenuit tempore Regis Edwardi, et geldabat pro 5 hidis. Terra est 3 carucatæ. De ea sunt in dominio 3 hidæ, et ibi 2 carucatæ, cum 1 servo, et 1 villano, et 7 bordariis, cum 1 carucata. Ibi molinus, reddens 20 solidos, et 5 acræ prati. Pastura dimidio leucæ longa, et 3 quarentenis lata. Silva dimidio leucæ longa, et tantundem lata. Valuit, et valet, 100 solidos.

Ipse Radulfus tenet *IMEMERIE*. Alwinus tenuit tempore Regis Edwardi, et geldabat pro 2 hidis. Terra est 2 carucatæ. In dominio est 1 1 carucata, et 2 servi; et 1 villanus, et 4 bordarii. Ibi pastura 3 quarentenis longa, et 2 quarentenis lata. Valuit 3 libras; modo 4 libras.

Fol. { XVII a, 72 c } Ricardus tenet de Radulfo *SIRENDONE*. Alwi tenuit, tempore Regis Edwardi, et geldabat pro 5 hidis. Terra est 6 carucatæ. De ea sunt in dominio 2 hidæ et dimidium, et ibi 2 carucatæ, et 4 servi; et 12 villani, et 3 bordarii, cum 4 carucatis. Ibi 7 acræ prati. Valuit, et valet, 7 libras.

Rogerius tenet de Radulfo *CHINTONE*. Alwinus tenuit tempore Regis Edwardi, et geldabat pro 1 hida et dimidio. Terra est 1 carucata, quæ ibi est in dominio, cum 1 servo, et 2 bordariis. Ibi molinus, reddens 2 solidos, et 4 acræ prati, et 6 acræ silvæ. Valuit 20 solidos; modo 30 solidos.

half, and there are 2 carucates, and 3 villans, and 2 coscets, and 12 acres of meadow. It was, and is, worth 30 shillings.

In *HIWI* Radulf holds 1 hide, and has there 1 bordar, and 4 acres of meadow. It is worth 15 shillings. Toti purchased it, in the time of King Edward, of the Church of Malmesbury, for the lives of three men, and within that term could go with the land to what lord he pleased.

Radulf himself holds *CLATFORD*. Alwin held in the time of King Edward, and it paid geld for 5 hides. The land is 3 carucates. Of this there are in demesne 3 hides, and there are 2 carucates, with 1 serf, and 1 villan, and 7 bordars, with 1 carucate. There is a mill, paying 20 shillings, and 5 acres of meadow. The pasture is half a mile long, and 3 furlongs broad. The wood is half a mile long, and as much broad. It was, and is, worth 100 shillings.

Radulf himself holds *IMEMERIE*. Alwin held it in the time of King Edward, and it paid geld for 2 hides. The land is 2 carucates. In demesne is 1 carucate, and 2 serfs; and there is 1 villan, and 4 bordars. The pasture there is 3 furlongs long, and 2 furlongs broad. It was worth £3; it is now worth £4.

Richard holds *SIRENDONE* of Radulf. Alwi held it in the time of King Edward, and it paid geld for 5 hides. The land is 6 carucates. Of this there are in demesne 2½ hides, and there are 2 carucates and 4 serfs; and there are 12 villans, and 3 bordars with 4 carucates. There are 7 acres of meadow. It was, and is, worth £7.

Roger holds *CHINTONE* of Radulf. Alwin held it in the time of King Edward, and it paid geld for 1 hide and a half. The land is 1 carucate, which is there in demesne, with 1 serf, and 2 bordars. There is a mill, paying 2 shillings, and 4 acres of meadow and 6 acres of wood. It was worth 20 shillings; it is now worth 30 shillings.

---

[1] As to the meaning of this expression, see the note on p. 72.

XVII a
72 c
Hic Alwinus tenebat hanc terram de Ecclesia Glastingeberiensi, et non poterat ab ea separari, et inde serviebat Abbati.

This Alwin used to hold this land of the Church of Glastonbury, and could not be separated from it, and rendered the customary services therefrom to the Abbot.

Ricardus tenet de Radulfo 3 hidas in *ALDRITONE*, et Walterus 1 hidam tenet ibidem. Alric, Godwin, Algar, et Godric, in paragio[1] tenuerunt, tempore Regis Edwardi, et geldabant pro 4 hidis. Terra est 4 carucatæ. Ibi sunt 4 villani, et 5 bordarii, et 2 servi, et molendinum de 37 denariis, et 25 acræ prati. In Malmesberie 1 burgensis reddit 7 denarios. Valuit, et valet, 60 solidos.

Richard holds 3 hides of Radulf in *ALDRITONE*, and Walter holds 1 hide there. Alric, Godwin, Algar, and Godric, held them in parage in the time of King Edward, and paid geld for 4 hides. The land is 4 carucates. There are 4 villans and 5 bordars, and 2 serfs, and a mill worth 37 pence, and 25 acres of meadow. A burgess in Malmesbury pays 7 pence. It was, and is, worth 60 shillings.

Edwardus tenet de Radulfo *LOCHINTONE*. Alwardus tenuit tempore Regis Edwardi, et geldabat pro 3 hidis. Terra est 4 carucatæ. De ea sunt in dominio 2 hidæ una virgata minus, et ibi 2 carucatæ; et 2 villani, et 4 bordarii, cum 2 carucatis. Ibi 8 acræ prati, et 4 acræ silvæ. Valuit, et valet, 3 libras.

Edward holds *LOCHINTONE* of Radulf. Alward held it in the time of King Edward, and it paid geld for 3 hides. The land is 4 carucates. Of this there are in demesne 2 hides all but 1 virgate, and there are 2 carucates; and there are 2 villans, and 4 bordars, with 2 carucates. There are 8 acres of meadow, and 4 acres of wood. It was, and is, worth £3.

XLII. TERRA ROBERTI FILII GIROLDI.

Robertus filius Giroldi tenet de Rege *WITEBERGE*. Saulf tenuit tempore Regis Edwardi, et geldabat pro 10 hidis. Terra est 5 carucatæ. De ea sunt in dominio 7 hidæ, et ibi 4 carucatæ, et 5 servi; et 5 villani, et 11 coscez, cum 1 bordario, habentes 1 carucatam. Ibi molinus, reddens 12 solidos et 6 denarios, et 50 acræ prati, et 50 acræ pasturæ, et 10 acræ silvæ minutæ. Valuit 7 libras; modo 10 libras. Gozelinus tenet de Roberto.

XLII. LAND OF ROBERT, SON OF GIROLD. [FITZ-GIROLD.]

Robert Fitz-Girold holds *WITEBERGE* of the King. Saulf held it in the time of King Edward, and it paid geld for 10 hides. The land is 5 carucates. Of this there are in demesne 7 hides, and there are 4 carucates, and 5 serfs; and there are 5 villans, and 11 coscets, with one bordar, having 1 carucate. There is a mill paying 12 shillings and 6 pence, and 50 acres of meadow, and 50 acres of pasture, and 10 acres of brush-wood. It was worth £7; it is now worth £10. Gozelin holds it of Robert.

Rainerius tenet de Roberto *FISTESBERIE*. Vitel tenuit tempore Regis Edwardi, et geldabat pro 10 hidis. Terra est 5 carucatæ. De ea sunt in dominio 6 hidæ, et ibi 2 carucatæ, et 2 servi; et 7 villani, et 2 bordarii, cum 1 carucata et dimidio. Ibi pastura

Rainer holds *FISTESBERIE* of Robert. Vitel held it in the time of King Edward, and it paid geld for 10 hides. The land is 5 carucates. Of this there are in demesne 6 hides, and there are 2 carucates, and 2 serfs; and there are 7 villans, and 2

[1] See note 2, on p. 85.

Fol. { XVII a 72 c } 5 quarentenis longa, et 3 quarentenis lata. Silva dimidio leucæ longa, et 3 quarentenis lata. Valuit, et valet, 100 solidos.

Rainerus tenet de Roberto *FOSTESBERGE.* Alwinus tenuit tempore Regis Edwardi, et geldabat pro 2 hidis. Terra est 2 carucatæ. Ibi sunt 3 bordarii, cum 1 carucata. Pastura 2 quarentenis longa, et una quarentena et dimidio lata. Silva 2 quarentenis longa, et 2 quarentenis lata. Valuit 15 solidos; modo 30 solidos.

Robertus tenet *BEDESDENE.* Coolle tenuit tempore Regis Edwardi, et geldabat pro una virgata terræ. Terra est 1 carucata, quæ ibi est, cum 1 villano, et 2 bordariis, et 4 servis; et pastura 2 quarentenis longa, et una lata. Reddit 30 solidos.

Robertus tenet de Roberto *BRISMARTONE.* Brismar tenuit tempore Regis Edwardi, et geldabat pro 4 hidis. Terra est 2 carucatæ, quæ ibi sunt in dominio, cum 11 bordariis. Ibi molinus, reddens 12 solidos, et 10 acræ prati. Pastura 12 quarentenis longa, et 4 quarentenis lata. Valuit 10 solidos; modo 4 libras.

Idem Robertus tenet Roberto *MILDESTONE.* Brismar tenuit tempore Regis Edwardi, et geldabat pro hida et dimidio. Terra est 1 carucata quæ ibi [est] cum 2 servis, et 4 coscez. Ibi molinus, reddens 18 solidos, et 4 acræ prati. Pastura 12 quarentenis longa, et una quarentena lata. Valuit 20 solidos; modo 30 solidos.

Hugo tenet de Roberto *WIFLESFORD.* Tovi tenuit tempore Regis Edwardi, et geldabat pro 1 hida. Terra est 1 carucata, quæ ibi est, cum 1 villano, et 3 coscez. Ibi molinus, reddens 10 solidos, et 6 acræ prati. Pastura 9 quarentenis longa, et 2 quarentenis lata. Valuit 30 solidos; valet 60 solidos.

bordars, with 1 carucate and a half. The pasture there is 5 furlongs long, and 3 furlongs broad. The wood is half-a-mile long, and 3 furlongs broad. It was, and is, worth 100 shillings.

Rainer holds *FOSTESBERGE* of Robert. Alwin held it in the time King Edward, and it paid geld for 2 hides. The land is 2 carucates. There are 3 bordars, with one carucate. The pasture is 2 furlongs long, and 1 furlong and a half broad. The wood is 2 furlongs long, and 2 furlongs broad. It was worth 15 shillings; it is now worth 30 shillings.

Robert holds *BEDESDENE.* Coolle held it in the time of King Edward, and it paid geld for 1 virgate of land. The land is 1 carucate, which is there, with 1 villan, and 2 bordars, and 4 serfs; and the pasture is 2 furlongs long, and 1 broad. It pays 30 shillings.

Robert holds *BRISMARTONE* of Robert. Brismar held it in the time of King Edward, and it paid geld for 4 hides. The land is 2 carucates, which are there in demesne, with 11 bordars. There is a mill, paying 12 shillings, and 10 acres of meadow. The pasture is 12 furlongs long, and 4 furlongs broad. It was worth 10 shillings; it is now worth £4.

The same Robert holds *MILDESTONE* of Robert. Brismar held it in the time King Edward, and it paid geld for a hide and a half. The land is 1 carucate which is there, with 2 serfs, and 4 coscets. There is a mill paying 18 shillings, and 4 acres of meadow. The pasture is 12 furlongs long, and 1 furlong broad. It was worth 20 shillings; it is now worth 30 shillings.

Hugo holds *WIFLESFORD* of Robert. Tovi held it in the time of King Edward, and it paid geld for 1 hide. The land is 1 carucate, which is there, with 1 villan, and 3 coscets. There is a mill, paying 10 shillings, and 6 acres of meadow. The pasture is 9 furlongs long, and 2 furlongs broad. It was worth 30 shillings; it is now worth 60 shillings.

XVII a 72 c Rainerus tenet de Roberto *VITELETONE.* Vitel tenuit tempore Regis Edwardi, et geldabat pro 10 hidis. Terra est 12 carucatæ. De ea sunt in dominio 5 hidæ et una virgata terræ, et ibi 3 carucatæ, et 6 servi; et 6 villani, et 12 bordarii, cum 3 carucatis. Ibi molinus, reddens 22 solidos et 6 denarios, et 3 acræ prati. Pastura 1 leuca longa, et dimidio leucæ lata. Valuit, et valet, 12 libras.

Hugo tenet de Roberto *SCAGE.* Cudulf tenuit tempore Regis Edwardi, et geldabat pro 2 hidis et una virgata et dimidio. Terra est 1 carucata. Ibi est unus villanus, et 2 servi, et 30 acræ pasturæ. Silva 1 leuca longa, et una quarentena lata. Valuit 20 solidos; modo 40 solidos.

Robertus tenet de Roberto *EBLESBORNE.* Alwardus et Fitheus tenuerunt, tempore Regis Edwardi, pro 2 maneriis, et geldabant pro 14 hidis. Terra est 10 carucatæ. De ea sunt in dominio 10 hidæ, et ibi 6 carucatæ, et 4 servi; et 18 villani, et 7 bordarii, cum 4 carucatis. Ibi 14 acræ prati. Pastura 14 quarentenis longa, et 4 quarentenis lata. Silva 2 leucæ inter longitudinem et latitudinem. Valuit 12 libras; modo 14 libras.

Rainer holds *VITELETONE* of Robert. Vitel held it in the time of King Edward, and it paid geld for 10 hides. The land is 12 carucates. Of this there are in demesne 5 hides and 1 virgate of land, and there are 3 carucates, and 6 serfs; and there are 6 villans, and 12 bordars, with 3 carucates. There is a mill, paying 22 shillings and 6 pence, and 3 acres of meadow. The pasture is 1 mile long, and half a mile broad. It was, and is, worth £12.

Hugo holds *SCAGE* of Robert. Cudulf held it in the time of King Edward, and it paid geld for 2 hides and 1 virgate and a half. The land is 1 carucate. There is 1 villan, and 2 serfs, and 30 acres of pasture. The wood is 1 mile long, and 1 furlong broad. It was worth 20 shillings; it is now worth 40 shillings.

Robert holds *EBLESBORNE* of Robert. Alward and Fitheus held it, in the time of King Edward, for 2 manors, and paid geld for 14 hides. The land is 10 carucates. Of this there are 10 hides in demesne, and there are 6 carucates, and 4 serfs; and there are 18 villans, and 7 bordars, with 4 carucates. There are 14 acres of meadow. The pasture is 14 furlongs long, and 4 furlongs broad. The wood is 2 miles between length and breadth. It was worth £12; it is now worth £14.

XLIII. TERRA ROBERTI FILII ROLF.

Robertus Filius Rolf tenet in *MORDONE* 1 hidam et unam virgatam terræ. Ulgar tenuit tempore Regis Edwardi, et geldabat pro 5 virgatis terræ. Terra est 1 carucata, quæ ibi est in dominio cum 1 servo, et 1 villano; et 10 acræ prati, et 40 acræ pasturæ. Valuit, et valet, 20 solidos.

Robertus Filius Rolf tenet *HANTONE.* Ulgar tenuit tempore Regis Edwardi, et geldabat pro 9 hidis una virgata minus. Terra est 5 carucatæ. De

XLIII. LAND OF ROBERT SON OF ROLF. [FITZ-ROLF.]

Robert Fitz-rolf holds in *MORDONE* 1 hide and 1 virgate of land. Ulgar held it in the time of King Edward, and it paid geld for 5 virgates of land. The land is 1 carucate, which is there in demesne with 1 serf and 1 villan; and there are 10 acres of meadow, and 40 acres of pasture. It was, and is, worth 20 shillings.

Robert Fitz-Rolf holds *HANTONE.* Ulgar held it in the time of King Edward, and it paid geld for 9 hides all but 1 virgate. The land is 5

Fol. {XVIIa 72 c} ea sunt in dominio 6 hidæ, et ibi 2 carucatæ, cum 1 servo; et 6 villani, et 6 bordarii. Ibi 12 acræ prati. Pastura 1 quarentena longa, et tantundem lata. Valuit, et valet, 6 libras.

carucates. Of this there are in demesne 6 hides and there are 2 carucates, with 1 serf; and there are 6 villans, and 6 bordars. There are 12 acres of meadow. The pasture is 1 furlong long, and as much broad. It was, and is, worth £6.

XLIV. [TERRA] ROGERII DE CORCELLE.

Fol. {XVIIa 72 c} ROGERIUS DE CORCELLE[1] tenet de Rege *FISERTONE.* Bondi tenuit tempore Regis Edwardi, et geldabat pro 10 hidis. Terra est 10 carucatæ. De ea sunt in dominio 5 hidæ et dimidium, et ibi 3 carucatæ; et 16 villani, et 12 bordarii, et 14 cotarii, cum 7 carucatis. Ibi molinus, 20 solidos reddens, et 12 acræ prati, et 10 acræ silvæ. Pastura dimidio leucæ longa, et tantundem lata. Valuit, et valet, 25 libras.

XLIV. LAND OF ROGER DE CORCELLE.

ROGER DE CORCELLE holds *FISERTONE* of the King. Bondi held it in the time of King Edward, and it paid geld for 10 hides. The land is 10 carucates. Of this there are in demesne 5½ hides and there are 3 carucates; and there are 16 villans and 12 bordars, and 14 cottars, with 7 carucates. There is a mill, paying 20 shillings, and 12 acres of meadow and 10 acres of wood. The pasture is half a mile long and as much broad. It was, and is, worth £25.

XLV. [TERRA] ROGERII DE BERCHELAI.

ROGERIUS DE BERCHELAI[2] tenet de Rege *FOXELEGE.* Aldret tenuit tempore Regis Edwardi, et geldabat pro 2 hidis. Terra est 4 carucatæ. De ea est in dominio 1 hida, et ibi 2 carucatæ, et 3 servi; et 4 villani, et 3 coscez, cum 3 carucatis. Ibi molinus, [de] 7 solidis et 6 denariis, et 4 acræ prati, et 8 acræ pasturæ, et una domus[3] in Malmesberie. Valuit, et valet, 40 solidos.

XLV. LAND OF ROGER DE BERCHELAI.

ROGER DE BERCHELAI holds *FOXELEGE* of the King. Aldret held it in the time of King Edward and it paid geld for 2 hides. The land is 4 carucates. Of this there is 1 hide in demesne, and there are 2 carucates, and 3 serfs; and there are 4 villans, and 3 coscets, with 3 carucates. There is a mill, worth 7 shillings and 6 pence, and 4 acres of meadow, and 8 acres of pasture, and 1 house in Malmesbury. It was, and is, worth 40 shillings.

---

[1] Kelham, quoting Collins (Peerage, i. p. 191), says that this ROGER DE CORCELLE accompanied William the Conqueror into England, and, for his services, had several lands in Wilts, Dorset, and Somerset. He adds that he was the ancestor of the Churchills, Dukes of Marlborough. *Kelham,* p. 54.

[2] ROGER DE BERCHELAI was owner of the lordship of Berkeley, in Gloucester, but divested of it afterwards for taking part with King Stephen. He became, in 1091, a monk of Gloucester. The estate at Berkeley was given subsequently by Henry II. to Robert Fitz-Harding, whose second son Maurice was ancestor to the Earls of Berkeley. *Ellis,* i. 381.

[3] This is described at p. 4, as "una masura in Malmesberie de firma Regis."

XVII a
72 c
Idem Rogerius tenet 1 hidam dimidio virgatæ minus de dominica firma de *CEPEHAM*. Celeinus tenuit tempore Regis Edwardi, purpresturam[1] Edrici Vice-Comitis.

Ipse Rogerius tenet *ESTONE*. Alwi tenuit tempore Regis Edwardi, et geldabat pro 3 hidis dimidio virgatæ minus. Terra est 3 carucatæ. De ea sunt 2 hidæ in dominio, et ibi 2 carucatæ, et 4 servi; et 2 villani, et 3 bordarii, cum 1 carucata. Ibi molinus reddens 6 solidos. Valuit 30 solidos; modo 40 solidos.

The same Roger holds 1 hide all but half a virgate of the demesne farm of *CEPEHAM*. Celein held in the time of King Edward, as a purpresture of Edric the Sheriff.

Roger himself holds *ESTONE*. Alwi held it in the time of King Edward, and it paid geld for 3 hides, all but half a virgate. The land is 3 carucates. Of this there are 2 hides in demesne, and there are 2 carucates, and 4 serfs; and there are 2 villans, and 3 bordars, with 1 carucate. There is a mill paying 6 shillings. It was worth 30 shillings; it is now worth 40 shillings.

XLVI. [TERRA BERNARDI PANCEVOLT.]

XVII b
72 d
Bernardus Pancevolt tenet *FERSTESFELD*. Godvinus tenuit tempore Regis Edwardi, et geldabat pro una virgata terræ et dimidio. Terra est dimidium carucatæ. Valet 5 solidos.

XLVI. [LAND OF BERNARD PANCEVOLT.]

Bernard Pancevolt holds *FERSTESFELD*. Godwin held it in the time of King Edward, and it paid geld for 1 virgate and a half of land. The land is half a carucate. It was worth 5 shillings.

XLVII. TERRA BERENGERI GIFARD.

Berenger Gifard tenet de Rege *FONTEL*. Euing tenuit tempore Regis Edwardi, et geldabat pro 5 hidis. Terra est 7 carucatæ. De ea est in dominio 1 hida, et ibi 3 carucatæ, et 4 servi; et 6 villani, et 16 bordarii, cum 4 carucatis. Ibi molinus, reddens 5 solidos, et 7 acræ prati. Pastura dimidio leucæ longa, et 3 quarentenis lata. Silva 4 quarentenis longa, et 2 quarentenis lata. Valuit 100 solidos; modo 6 libras.

XLVII. LAND OF BERENGER GIFARD.

Berenger Gifard holds *FONTEL* of the King. Euing held it in the time of King Edward, and it paid geld for 5 hides. The land is 7 carucates. Of this there is in demesne 1 hide, and there are 3 carucates, and 4 serfs; and there are 6 villans, and 16 bordars, with 4 carucates. There is a mill, paying 5 shillings, and 7 acres of meadow. The pasture is half a mile long, and 3 furlongs broad. The wood is 4 furlongs long, and 2 furlongs broad. It was worth 100 shillings; it is now worth £6.

---

[1] "Pourpresture," says Jacob (Law Dict. *sub voce.*) "from the French *pour-pris, (conseptum*, an enclosure,) denotes anything done to the hurt of the King's demesnes, or the highways, &c., by inclosure or buildings, endeavouring to make that private which ought to be public." He adds, from Crompton, the following extended meaning,—"Pourpresture is properly when a man taketh unto himself, or encroacheth anything he ought not, whether it be in jurisdiction, land, or franchise, and generally when anything is done to the nuisance of the King's tenants." Skene, after defining three sorts of this offence, explains "Pourpresture against the King as happening by the negligence of the Sheriff or his deputy, or by the long continuance of wars, inasmuch as those who have lands near the crown lands take or inclose a part of them, and add it to their own."

Fol. { XVIIb 72 d } Idem tenet 1 hidam in *BEREFORD*. Heraldus Comes tenuit tempore Regis Edwardi, et pro tanto geldabat. Terra est 1 carucata. Ibi sunt 6 bordarii, et 6 acræ prati. Valuit 60 (9 ?) solidos; modo 20 solidos.

The same holds 1 hide in *BEREFORD*. Ear Harold held it in the time of King Edward, and i paid geld for so much. The land is 1 carucate There are 6 bordars, and 6 acres of meadow. It wa worth 60 (9?) shillings; it is now worth 20 shillings

---

XLVIII. TERRA OSBERNI GIFARD.

Osbernus Gifard[1] tenet de Rege *WINTREBURNE*. Domne tenuit tempore Regis Edwardi, et geldabat pro 11 hidis. Terra est 6 carucatæ. De ea sunt in dominio 9 hidæ, et ibi 4 carucatæ, et 5 servi; et 4 villani, et 5 bordarii, cum 2 carucatis. Ibi 6 acræ prati, et pastura 9 quarentenis longa, et 6 quarentenis lata. Valuit 7 libras; modo 9 libras.

Idem Osbernus tenet 2 hidas in *WINTREBURNE*. Terra est 1 carucata. Ibi 2 acræ prati, et 3 acræ pasturæ. Valuit 30 solidos; modo 40 solidos.

Idem Osbernus tenet 3 hidas et dimidium in *ORCESTONE*. Ulmarus et Alwinus tenuerunt tempore Regis Edwardi. Terra est 2 carucatæ, quæ ibi sunt in dominio, et 3 servi. Pastura dimidio leucæ et 40 acris longa, et lata. Valuit 40 solidos; modo 50 solidos.

Ipse Osbernus tenet *STANTONE*. Brictric tenuit tempore Regis Edwardi, et geldabat pro 18 hidis. Ibi habet 2 carucatas in dominio in 9 hidis, et ibi 7 servi; et 9 villani, et 3 coscez, cum 6 carucatis. Ibi 6 acræ prati. Pastura 1 leuca longa, et 1 lata. Silva 1 leuca longa, et 3 quarentenis lata. Valuit 9 libras; modo 8 libras.

XLVIII. LAND OF OSBERN GIFARD.

Osbern Gifard holds *WINTREBURNE* of the King. Domne held it in the time of King Edward and it paid geld for 11 hides. The land is 6 carucates. Of this there are 9 hides in demesne, and there are 4 carucates, and 5 serfs; and there are 4 villans, and 5 bordars, with 2 carucates. There are 6 acres of meadow, and the pasture is 9 furlongs long, and 6 furlongs broad. It was worth £7; it is now worth £9.

The same Osbern holds 2 hides in *WINTREBURNE*. The land is 1 carucate. There are 2 acres of meadow, and 3 acres of pasture. It was worth 30 shillings; it is now worth 40 shillings.

The same Osbern holds 3½ hides in *ORCESTONE*. Ulmar and Alwin held them in the time of King Edward. The land is 2 carucates which are there in demesne, and 3 serfs. The pasture is in length and breadth half a mile and 40 acres. It was worth 40 shillings; it is now worth 50 shillings.

Osbern himself holds *STANTONE*. Brictric held it in the time of King Edward, and it paid geld for 18 hides. He has there 2 carucates in demesne in 9 hides, and there are 7 serfs; and there are 9 villans, and 3 coscets, with 6 carucates. There are 6 acres of meadow. The pasture is 1 mile long, and 1 broad. The wood is 1 mile long, and 3 furlongs broad. It was worth £9; it is now worth £8.

---

[1] Osbern Gifard was the first of the family of the Giffards, of Brimsfield, the chief seat of their barony, in Gloucestershire. Their chief seat in Wiltshire was at Sherrington.

VIIb Ecclesia S. STEFANI DE FONTENED[1] tenet de
d Osberno 2 hidas et unam virgatam terræ in *MIDELTONE.* Domno tenuit tempore Regis Edwardi, et pro tanto geldabat. Terra est 2 carucatæ, quæ ibi sunt in dominio cum 1 servo, et 2 bordariis. Ibi 5 acræ prati, et 20 acræ pasturæ, et una acra silvæ. Valuit 20 solidos; modo 50 solidos.

The Church of S. STEPHEN of FONTENED holds of Osbern 2 hides and 1 virgate of land in *MIDELTONE.* Domno held it in the time of King Edward, and it paid geld for so much. The land is 2 carucates, which are there in demesne with one serf, and 2 bordars. There are 5 acres of meadow, and 20 acres of pasture, and 1 acre of wood. It was worth 20 shillings; it is now worth 50 shillings.

Ipse Osbernus tenet *COTEFORD.* Aluric tenuit tempore Regis Edwardi, et geldabat pro una hida et dimidio. Terra est 2 carucatæ. De ea est in dominio 1 hida, et ibi 1 carucata et dimidium, et 2 servi; et 6 çoscez, et 1 cotarius, cum dimidia carucata. Ibi quarta pars molini, reddens 3 solidos et 3 obolos, et 10 acræ prati. Pastura 4 quarentenis longa, et una quarentena lata. Valebat 50 solidos; modo 60 solidos.

Osbern himself holds *COTEFORD.* Aluric held it in the time of King Edward, and it paid geld for 1 hide and a half. The land is 2 carucates. Of this there is in demesne 1 hide, and there is there 1 carucate and a half, and 2 serfs; and there are 6 coscets, and 1 cottar, with a half carucate. There is the fourth part of a mill, paying 3 shillings and 3 half-pence, and 10 acres of meadow. The pasture is 4 furlongs long, and 1 furlong broad. It was worth 50 shillings; it is now worth 60 shillings.

Ipse Osbernus tenet *ORCHESTONE.* Trasemundus tenuit tempore Regis Edwardi, et geldabat pro 5 hidis. Terra est 3 carucatæ. De ea sunt in dominio 4 hidæ, et ibi 2 carucatæ, et 3 servi; et 4 villani, et 3 coscez, et 5 cotarii, cum 1 carucata et dimidio. Ibi pastura 3 quarentenis longa, et una quarentena lata. Valuit 4 libras; modo 100 solidos.

Osbern himself holds *ORCHESTONE.* Trasemund held it in the time of King Edward, and it paid geld for 5 hides. The land is 3 carucates. Of this there are 4 hides in demesne, and there are 2 carucates, and 3 serfs; and there are 4 villans, and 3 coscets, and 5 cottars, with 1 carucate and a half. The pasture there is 3 furlongs long, and 1 furlong broad. It was worth £4; it is now worth 100 shillings.

Ipse Osbernus tenet *DEVREL.* Smail tenuit tempore Regis Edwardi, et geldabat pro 3 hidis et dimidia virgata terræ. Terra est 3 carucatæ. De ea sunt in dominio 2 hidæ, et ibi 2 carucatæ, cum 1 servo, et 9 coscez, et 3 bordariis. Ibi molinus, reddens 30 denarios, et 2 acræ prati, et pastura 2 quarentenis longa, et una quarentena lata. Silva dimidio leucæ longa, et tantundem lata. Valuit 40 solidos; modo 60 solidos.

Osbern himself holds *DEVREL.* Smail held it in the time of King Edward, and it paid geld for 3 hides and half a virgate of land. The land is 3 carucates. Of this there are 2 hides in demesne, and there are 2 carucates, with 1 serf, and 9 coscets, and 3 bordars. There is a mill, paying 30 pence, and 2 acres of meadow, and the pasture is 2 furlongs long, and 1 furlong broad. The wood is half a mile long, and as much broad. It was worth 40 shillings; it is now worth 60 shillings.

---

[1] It is so spelt in the original. In other records we have it written 'Funtenay.' Test. de Nev. 156. This was an Abbey of the Benedictine Order at Fontenay in Normandy, founded by St. Evremond, about A.D. 568 or 570. Having been destroyed by the Normans, it was re-founded by Ralph Taisson, whose Charter of Foundation, in the time of the Conqueror, is given in the New Monast. vi. 1084. Dugdale also gives a charter of Robert Marmion. Brimsfield, in Gloucestershire, was an alien cell to this Abbey. See note on p. 116.

Fol. { XVIIb / 72 d } Ipse Osbernus tenet *TERINTONE.* Domno tenuit tempore Regis Edwardi, et geldabat pro 10 hidis. Terra est 6 carucatæ. De ea sunt in dominio 9 hidæ, et ibi 3 carucatæ, et 4 servi; et 2 villani, et 4 coscez, et 3 bordarii, cum 3 carucatis. Ibi 10 acræ prati. Valuit 4 libras; modo 100 solidos.

Osbern himself holds *TERINTONE.* Domno held it in the time of King Edward, and it paid geld for 10 hides. The land is 6 carucates. Of this there are in demesne 9 hides, and there are 3 carucates, and 4 serfs; and there are 2 villans, and 4 coscets, and 3 bordars, with 3 carucates. There are 10 acres of meadow. It was worth £4; it is now worth 100 shillings.

Ipse Osbernus tenet *SCARENTONE.* Algar tenuit tempore Regis Edwardi, et geldabat pro 5 hidis. Terra est 2 carucatæ et dimidium. De ea sunt in dominio 4 hidæ et dimidium, et ibi 2 carucatæ, et 5 servi; et 2 villani, cum dimidia carucata. Ibi dimidium molini reddens 7 solidos et 6 denarios, et 6 acræ prati, et 60 acræ pasturæ, et 40 acræ silvæ. Valuit 4 libras; modo 100 solidos.

Osbern himself holds *SCARENTONE.* Algar held it in the time of King Edward, and it paid geld for 5 hides. The land is 2½ carucates. Of this there are in demesne 4½ hides, and there are 2 carucates, and 5 serfs; and there are 2 villans, with a half carucate. There is half a mill paying 7 shillings and 6 pence, and 6 acres of meadow, and 60 acres of pasture, and 40 acres of wood. It was worth £4; it is now worth 100 shillings.

Ipse Osbernus tenet *SCARENTONE.* Smalo tenuit tempore Regis Edwardi, et geldabat pro 5 hidis. Terra est 2 carucatæ et dimidium. De ea sunt in dominio 4 hidæ et dimidium, et ibi 2 carucatæ, et 5 servi; et 2 villani, cum dimidia carucata. Ibi dimidium molini reddens 7 solidos et 6 denarios, et 6 acræ prati, et 60 acræ pasturæ, et 40 acræ silvæ, et in Wiltune 1 burgensis reddens 3 solidos. Valuit 4 libras; modo 100 solidos.

Osbern himself holds *SCARENTONE.* Smalo held it in the time of King Edward, and it paid geld for 5 hides. The land is 2½ carucates. Of this there are 4½ hides in demesne, and there are 2 carucates, and 5 serfs; and there are 2 villans, with a half carucate. There is half a mill paying 7 shillings and 6 pence, and 6 acres of meadow, and 60 acres of pasture, and 40 acres of wood, and 1 burgess in Wilton paying 3 shillings. It was worth £4; it is now worth 100 shillings.

Gunduinus tenet de Osberno *OGEFORD.* Ednodus tenuit tempore Regis Edwardi, et geldabat pro 2 hidis et dimidio. Terra est 1 carucata, quæ ibi est cum 1 servo, et 1 bordario. Ibi molinus, reddens 4 solidos, et 4 acræ prati, et 10 acræ pasturæ. Valuit 30 solidos; modo 40 solidos.

Gunduin holds *OGEFORD* of Osbern. Ednod held it in the time of King Edward, and it paid geld for 2½ hides. The land is 1 carucate, which is there with 1 serf, and 1 bordar. There is a mill, paying 4 shillings, and 4 acres of meadow, and 10 acres of pasture. It was worth 30 shillings; it is now worth 40 shillings.

Hanc terram abstulit Godvinus Comes [ecclesia] S. Mariæ Wiltunensis, et tunc eam recuperavit Ednodus.

Earl Godwin took away this estate from the church of S. Mary at Wilton, and then Ednod recovered it.

XLIX. TERRA DROGONIS FILII PONZ.

XVIII a DROGO FILIUS PONZ[1] tenet de Rege *SEGRIE.*
73 a Wiflet tenuit tempore Regis Edwardi, et geldabat pro 5 hidis. Terra est 4 carucatæ. De ea sunt in dominio 2 hidæ, et ibi 1 carucata; et 5 villani, et 6 bordarii, et 5 coscez, cum 1 carucata. Ibi 2 molini reddentes 22 solidos et 4 denarios, et 30 acræ prati. In Malmesberie una domus reddit 9 denarios. Valuit 60 solidos; modo 70 solidos.

Rogerius de Laci, et Turstinus filius Rolf, et Willelmus Leuric tenent 1 hidam in *COLESELLE.* Tres Taini tenebant tempore Regis Edwardi. Pars omnium valet 4 libras.

Gislebertus tenet de Drogone *ESTONE.* Oswardus tenuit tempore Regis Edwardi, et geldabat pro 5 hidis. Terra est 3 carucatæ. De ea sunt in dominio 4 hidæ, et ibi 2 carucatæ, et 2 servi; et 1 villanus, et 4 bordarii, et 2 coscez. Ibi 10 acræ prati. Silva 2 quarentenis longa, et 2 quarentenis lata. Valuit 40 solidos; modo 50 solidos.

Hugo tenet de Drogone *ALDRINTONE.* Edricus tenuit tempore Regis Edwardi, et geldabat pro 3 hidis. Terra est 3 carucatæ. De ea sunt in dominio 2 hidæ et 3 virgatæ terræ, et ibi 1 carucata, cum 1 servo, et 2 bordariis. De parte molini 22 denarii; et 15 acræ prati. Valuit, et valet, 60 solidos.

XLIX. LAND OF DROGO, SON OF PONZ. [FITZ-PONZ.]

DROGO FITZ-PONZ holds *SEGRIE* of the King. Wiflet held it in the time of King Edward, and it paid geld for 5 hides. The land is four carucates. Of this there are in demesne 2 hides, and there is 1 carucate; and there are 5 villans, and 6 bordars, and 5 coscets, with 1 carucate. There are 2 mills paying 22 shillings and 4 pence, and 30 acres of meadow. A house in Malmesbury pays 9 pence. It was worth 60 shillings; it is now worth 70 shillings.

Roger de Laci, and Turstin Fitz-Rolf, and William Leuric hold 1 hide in *COLESELLE.* Three Thanes held it in the time of King Edward. The shares of all are worth £4.

Gislebert holds *ESTONE* of Drogo. Osward held it in the time of King Edward, and it paid geld for 5 hides. The land is 3 carucates. Of this there are 4 hides in demesne, and there are 2 carucates, and 2 serfs; and there is 1 villan, and 4 bordars, and 2 coscets. There are 10 acres of meadow. The wood is 2 furlongs long, and 2 furlongs broad. It was worth 40 shillings; it is now worth 50 shillings.

Hugo holds *ALDRINTONE* of Drogo. Edric held it in the time of King Edward, and it paid geld for 3 hides. The land is 3 carucates. Of this there are in demesne 2 hides and 3 virgates of land, and there is 1 carucate, with one serf, and 2 bordars. From part of a mill there are 22 pence; and there are 15 acres of meadow; it was, and is, worth 60 shillings.

---

[1] DROGO, or DRU, was a noble Norman, son of Walter de Ponz, and brother of Richard de Ponz, ancestor of the noble family of Clifford. He held no less than 73 estates, many of them, however, of but small extent, in Devonshire, as under-tenant to the Bishop of Coutance. *Ellis, I.* 406.

L. TERRA HUGONIS LASNE.

Fol. { XVIII a / 73 a } HUGO LASNE[1] tenet 1 hidam terræ et 3 virgatas de Rege in *SCALDEBURNE*, et Willelmus tenet de eo. Unus Tainus tenuit de Rege Edwardo, et pro tanto geldabat. Terra est 2 carucatæ. Ibi est unus villanus, et 4 coscez, cum 1 carucata. Ibi 1 arpenna[2] prati, et 2 acræ silvæ. Valet 30 solidos.

Heraldus tenet de Hugone *WICHELESTOTE*. Leuric tenuit tempore Regis Edwardi, et geldabat pro 5 hidis. Terra est 2 carucatæ. De ea sunt in dominio 4 hidæ, et ibi 1 carucata et dimidium, cum 1 servo; et 3 villani, et 6 bordarii, cum dimidia carucata. Ibi molinus, reddens 5 solidos, et 25 acræ prati, et 30 acræ pasturæ. Valuit, et valet, 40 solidos.

Ipse Hugo tenet in *CLIVE* 2 hidas. Godeva tenuit pro uno manerio. Terra est 1 carucata. Ibi est unus coscet, et 12 acræ prati. Valet 12 solidos.

Willelmus tenet de Hugone *CORTITONE*. Dene tenuit tempore Regis Edwardi, et geldabat pro 6 hidis. Terra est 4 carucatæ. De ea sunt in dominio 4 hidæ, et ibi 1 carucata et dimidium, et 2 servi; et 4 bordarii, cum dimidia carucata. Ibi molinus, reddens 20 solidos, et 6 acræ prati. Pastura 3 quarentenis longa, et 2 quarentenis lata, et tantundem silvæ. Valuit 100 solidos; modo 6 libras.

L. LAND OF HUGO LASNE.

HUGO LASNE holds 1 hide and 3 virgates of land of the King in *SCALDEBURNE*, and William holds them of him. A Thane held the estate of King Edward, and it paid geld for so much. The land is 2 carucates. There is 1 villan, and 4 coscets, with 1 carucate. There is 1 arpen of meadow, and 2 acres of wood. It is worth 30 shillings.

Harold holds *WICHELESTOTE*. Leuric held it in the time of King Edward, and it paid geld for 5 hides. The land is 2 carucates. Of this there are 4 hides in demesne, and there is 1 carucate and a half, with 1 serf; and there are 3 villans, and 6 bordars with a half carucate. There is a mill, paying 5 shillings, and 25 acres of meadow, and 30 acres of pasture. It was, and is, worth 40 shillings.

Hugo himself holds 2 hides in *CLIVE*. Godeve held them for 1 manor. The land is 1 carucate. There is 1 coscet, and 12 acres of meadow. It is worth 12 shillings.

William holds *CORTITONE* of Hugo. Dene held it in the time of King Edward, and it paid geld for 6 hides. The land is 4 carucates. Of this there are in demesne 4 hides, and there is 1 carucate and a half, and 2 serfs; and there are 4 bordars with a half carucate. There is a mill, paying 20 shillings, and 6 acres of meadow. The pasture is 3 furlongs long, and 2 furlongs broad, and there is as much wood. It was worth 100 shillings; it is now worth £6.

---

[1] In the body of the entry of the lands belonging to HUGO LASNE in Worcestershire, he is called "Hugo *Asinus*" (as though the name were originally 'L'asne,' the older form of what is now contracted into 'L'âne'), whether in reference to his personal or mental peculiarities we are not informed. This sort of name was not uncommon in the Norman times. The first of the Bohun family was called "*Barbatus*," or "Hunfridus *cum barba*." The Earl Hugo was surnamed "*Lupus*"; see above, p. 60. Ellis (I. 436) gives an amusing instance out of the Consuetudinarium of the Abbey of St. Edmondsbury (MS. Harl., 3977, *fol.* 19,) of the practice of bestowing these appellations:—"Erat quidam vir strenuus Reynaldus Stanceberd DENASEZ, sic vocatus quia *nasum in bello cum rege Willelmo seniore amiserat*," &c. The names given to somo of our early Norman kings, such as *Rufus*, *Beauclerc*, and *Cœur de Lion*, are illustrations of this custom.

[2] See, on the "Arpenna" as a measure of land, the note on *p.* 44.

XVIII a 73 a Ecclesia S. MARIÆ WINTONIENSIS tenet de Hugone *CHENETE* pro filia[1] ejus. Honewinus tenuit tempore Regis Edwardi, et geldabat pro 2 hidis una virgata minus. Terra est 1 carucata, quæ ibi est in dominio cum 2 bordariis, et una acra prati, et 6 acris pasturæ. Valuit 10 solidos; modo 20 solidos.

The Church of S. MARY AT WINTON holds *CHENETE* of Hugo for his daughter. Honewin held it in the time of King Edward, and it paid geld for 2 hides all but 1 virgate. The land is 1 carucate, which is there in demesne with 2 bordars, and 1 acre of meadow, and 6 acres of pasture. It was worth 10 shillings; it is now worth 20 shillings.

LI. TERRA HUGONIS FILII BALDRICI.

HUGO FILIUS BALDRICI[2] tenet *MERESDENE*, et Walterus, gener ejus, de eo. Wenesi tenuit tempore Regis Edwardi, et geldabat pro 10 hidis. Terra est 8 carucatæ. In dominio sunt 2 carucatæ, et 3 servi; et 9 villani, et 14 coscez, et 2 bordarii, cum 5 carucatis. Ibi molinus, reddens 7 solidos et dimidium, et 24 acræ prati. Pastura 3 quarentenis longa, et 2 quarentenis lata. In Wiltune 1 domus reddit 10 denarios. Valuit 7 libras; modo 10 libras.

LI. LAND OF HUGO, SON OF BALDRIC. [FITZ-BALDRIC.]

HUGO FITZ-BALDRIC holds *MERESDENE*, and Walter, his son-in-law, holds it of him. Wenesi held it in the time of King Edward, and it paid geld for 10 hides. The land is 8 carucates. In demesne are 2 carucates, and 3 serfs; and there are 9 villans, and 14 coscets, and 2 bordars, with 5 carucates. There is a mill, paying 7 shillings and 6 pence, and 24 acres of meadow. The pasture is 3 furlongs long, and 2 furlongs broad. A house in Wilton pays 10 pence. It was worth £7; it is now worth £10.

LII. [TERRA] HUNFRIDI CAMERARII.

HUNFRIDUS, CAMERARIUS,[3] tenet de Rege *SCHERNECOTE*. Alwardus tenuit tempore Regis Edwardi, et geldabat pro 5 hidis. Terra est 4 carucatæ. De ea sunt in dominio 2 hidæ et dimidium, et ibi 2 carucatæ, et 3 servi; et 8 villani, cum 2 carucatis. Ibi 50 acræ prati, et pastura 2 quarentenis longa, et una quarentena lata. Valuit 40 solidos; modo 60 solidos.

LII. LAND OF HUMFREY THE CHAMBERLAIN.

HUMFREY, THE CHAMBERLAIN, holds *SCHERNECOTE* of the King. Alward held it in the time of King Edward, and it paid geld for 5 hides. The land is 4 carucates. Of this $2\frac{1}{2}$ hides are in demesne and there are 2 carucates, and 3 serfs; and there are 8 villans, with 2 carucates. There are 50 acres of meadow, and the pasture is 2 furlongs long, and 1 furlong broad. It was worth 40 shillings; it is now worth 60 shillings.

[1] His daughter, it is implied, was a Nun at Winchester, and this estate was her "portion." See note on p. 50.

[2] HUGO FITZ-BALDRIC occurs in the Domesday for Nottingham *(fol. 280)* with the word "Vice-Comes" written above. Kelham *(p. 43)* says that he was Sheriff of Northumberland. From the Exon Domesday, in the account of the Hundred of Swanborough, we may infer, that the tenant's name was 'Walter de Rivera,' and that this estate was the dowry of the daughter of Hugo Fitz-Baldric, to whom he was married.

[3] The office of the "Camerarius," says Kelham, p. 171, was to take charge of the King's "camera," or treasury. He considers that it answered to the present Treasurer of the Household.

LIII. TERRA GUNFRIDI MALDOITH.

Fol. {XVIIIa 73 a} GUNFRIDUS MALDUIT[1] tenet de Rege *CALESTONE.* Algarus tenuit tempore Regis Edwardi, et geldabat pro 2 hidis et una virgata terræ. Terra est 2 carucatæ. De ea sunt in dominio 5 virgatæ terræ, et ibi 2 carucatæ, et 3 servi; et 6 bordarii cum dimidia carucata. Ibi molinus, reddens 15 solidos, et 8 acræ prati. Pastura 2 quarentenis longa, et una quarentena lata. Valuit 40 solidos; modo 50 solidos.

Idem Gunfridus tenet *WITELIE.* Appe tenuit tempore Regis Edwardi, et geldabat pro una hida. Terra est 2 carucatæ, quæ ibi sunt in dominio cum 1 servo, et 6 bordariis. Ibi 8 acræ prati. Silva 3 quarentenis longa, et una quarentena lata. Valuit 40 solidos; modo 50 solidos.

LIII. LAND OF GUNFRID MALDOITH.

GUNFRID MALDUIT holds *CALESTONE* of the King. Algar held it in the time of King Edward, and it paid geld for 2 hides and 1 virgate of land. The land is 2 carucates. Of this there are in demesne 5 virgates of land, and there are 2 carucates, and 3 serfs; and there are 6 bordars with half a carucate. There is a mill, paying 15 shillings, and 8 acres of meadow. The pasture is 2 furlongs long, and 1 furlong broad. It was worth 40 shillings; it is now worth 50 shillings.

The same Gunfrid holds *WITELIE.* Appe held it in the time of King Edward, and it paid geld for 1 hide. The land is 2 carucates, which are there in demesne with 1 serf, and 6 bordars. There are 8 acres of meadow. The wood is 3 furlongs long, and 1 furlong broad. It was worth 40 shillings; it is now worth 50 shillings.

LIV. TERRA ALUREDI ISPANIENSIS.

ALUREDUS DE ISPANIA[2] tenet de Rege *ETESBERIE.* Alwi tenuit tempore Regis Edwardi, et geldabat pro 5 hidis. Terra est 4 carucatæ. De ea sunt in dominio 3 hidæ et dimidium, et ibi 2 carucatæ, et 2 servi; et 7 bordarii, et unus miles, cum 1 carucata. Ibi 20 acræ pasturæ. Valuit 3 libras; modo 4 libras.

LIV. LAND OF ALURED OF SPAIN.

ALURED OF SPAIN holds *ETESBERIE* of the King. Alwi held it in the time of King Edward, and it paid geld for 5 hides. The land is 4 carucates. Of this there are $3\frac{1}{2}$ hides in demesne, and there are 2 carucates, and 2 serfs; and there 7 bordars, and one 'miles,' with 1 carucate. There are 20 acres of pasture. It was worth £3; it is now worth £4.

---

[1] In the Exon Domesday this name is written "Gunfridus *Maledoctus*," another instance of the Norman custom of giving names from some personal or mental peculiarities, to which allusion has been made. (p. 120 note.) In after times this surname assumed the form of "Mauduit." See *Hoare's Warminster Hundr.* p. 2.

[2] KELHAM (p. 55) says that this ALURED was originally of Spain, and that hence came his distinctive designation. ELLIS (I. 370) says that the family of 'Hispaine,' in Essex, were descended from him, and refers to Morant's Essex, II., pp. 301, 363, 380.

LV. [TERRA] AIULFI, VICECOMITIS.

{XVIIIa 73 a} AIULFUS, VICECOMES,[1] tenet de Rege 5 hidas in *TOLLARD*, et dimidiam hidam. Quinque Taini tenuerunt tempore Regis Edwardi, et pro 5 hidis et dimidio geldabant. Terra est 4 carucatæ. De ea sunt in dominio 4 hidæ, et ibi 2 carucatæ, et 2 servi, et 3 villani, et 14 bordarii. Ibi 2 arpennæ vineæ, et 20 acræ pasturæ, et 4 acræ silvæ. Valuit 4 libras; modo 6 libras.

Idem Aiulfus tenet dimidiam hidam in *BERMENTONE.* Terra est dimidium carucatæ. Reddit 12 solidos. Radulfus tenuit tempore Regis Edwardi.

LV. LAND OF AIULF, THE SHERIFF.

AIULF, THE SHERIFF, holds 5 hides, and a half hide, of the King, in *TOLLARD.* Five Thanes held it in the time of King Edward, and they paid geld for 5½ hides. The land is 4 carucates. Of this there are in demesne 4 hides, and there are 2 carucates, and 2 serfs, and 3 villans, and 14 bordars. There are 2 arpens of vineyard, and 20 acres of pasture, and 4 acres of wood. It was worth £4; it is now worth £6.

The same Aiulf holds a half hide in *BERMENTONE.* The land is half a carucate. It pays 12 shillings. Radulf held it in the time of King Edward.

LVI. TERRA NIGELLI MEDICI.

NIGELLUS, MEDICUS,[2] tenet de Rege *STRATONE.* Tempore Regis Edwardi geldabat pro 30 hidis. Terra est 14 carucatæ. De ea sunt in dominio 5 hidæ, et ibi 3 carucatæ, et 2 servi; et 24 villani, et 18 bordarii, cum 12 carucatis. Ibi molinus, reddens 2 solidos, et pratum 8 quarentenis longum, et 5 quarentenis latum. Pastura 1 leuca longa, et 5 quarentenis lata. Valuit 18 libras; modo 16 libras.

Idem Nigellus tenet *CHESIGEBERIE.* Tempore Regis Edwardi geldabat pro 8 hidis. Terra est

LVI. LAND OF NIGEL THE PHYSICIAN.

NIGEL, THE PHYSICIAN, holds *STRATONE* of the King. In the time of King Edward it paid geld for 30 hides. The land is 14 carucates. Of this there are in demesne 5 hides, and there are 3 carucates, and 2 serfs; and there are 24 villans, and 18 bordars, with 12 carucates. There is a mill, paying 2 shillings, and the meadow is 8 furlongs long, and 5 furlongs broad. The pasture is 1 mile long, and 5 furlongs broad. It was worth £18; it is now worth £16.

The same Nigel holds *CHESIGEBERIE.* In the time of King Edward it paid geld for 8 hides. The

[1] AIULF was Sheriff of Dorset in the time of King Edward the Confessor. In the list of Tenants in capite prefixed to the Domesday for Dorset he is called 'VICE-COMES', whilst in the accounts of the various manors that belonged to him, he is entered as "CAMERARIUS."—One of his possessions in Dorset is called 'Hampreston *Chamberlain*' to the present day.

[2] NIGEL was the Conqueror's physician. Lands were granted to him not only in Wilts, but in Hants, Herefordshire, and Shropshire. See Domesday, *fol.* 49, 183, 260 *b.* Many of the lands so granted, like most of these belonging to NIGEL in Wilts, had been previously held by SPIRTES, a priest, and, in several instances, under some religious house. This was the case with some of the manors in Herefordshire, which had belonged in the Confessor's time, to the Church of St. Guthlac, at Hereford.

Fol. { XVIII b 73 b } 5 carucatæ. De ea sunt in dominio 4 hidæ et dimidium, et ibi 2 carucatæ et dimidium, et 2 servi; et 8 villani, et 12 bordarii, cum 2 carucatis. Ibi molinus, reddens 7 solidos et dimidium, et 20 acræ prati, et pastura 1 leuca longa, et 5 quarentenis lata. Valuit, et valet, 13 libras.

Idem Nigellus tenet 1 hidam in *NIGRAVRE*, et Durandus de eo. Terra est 1 carucata. Ibi sunt 3 bordarii cum dimidia carucata, et 6 acræ prati. Pastura 4 quarentenis longa, et 2 quarentenis lata. Valuit, et valet, 3 libras.

Hæc 3 maneria pertinent ad Ecclesiam de *NIGRAVRE*.

Idem Nigellus tenet 4 hidas in *SUDTONE*, et pro tanto geldabat tempore Regis Edwardi. Terra est 3 carucatæ. S. Maria de Monteburg[1] tenet de Nigello. De hac terra sunt in dominio 2 hidæ, et ibi 1 carucata, et 3 servi; et 5 villani, et 5 bordarii, cum 2 carucatis. Ibi tercia pars molini, reddens 6 solidos et 8 denarios, et 3 acræ prati. Pastura dimidio leucæ longa, et 1 quarentena lata. Silva 1 leuca longa, et 1 quarentena lata. Valuit 4 libras; modo 100 solidos.

Hæc 4 maneria tenuit Spirtes presbyter tempore Regis Edwardi.

Nigellus tenet dimidiam hidam in *BEVRESBROC*, et pro tanto geldabat tempore Regis Edwardi. Ibi habet 1 villanum, et 1 bordarium; et silva 1 quarentena longa, et dimidio quarentenæ lata. Valet 7 solidos.

Idem Nigellus tenet *HASEBERIE*. Tempore Regis Edwardi geldabat pro una virgata terræ.

land is 5 carucates. Of this there are 4½ hides in demesne, and there are 2½ carucates, and 2 serfs; and there are 8 villans, and 12 bordars, with 2 carucates. There is a mill, paying 7 shillings and sixpence, and 20 acres of meadow, and the pasture is 1 mile long and 5 furlongs broad. It was, and is, worth £13.

The same Nigel holds 1 hide in *NIGRAVRE*, and Durand holds it of him. The land is 1 carucate. There are 3 bordars with a half carucate, and 6 acres of meadow. The pasture is 4 furlongs long, and 2 furlongs broad. It was, and is, worth £3.

These 3 manors belong to the Church of *NIGRAVRE*.

The same Nigel holds 4 hides in *SUDTONE*, and it paid geld for so much in the time of King Edward. The land is 3 carucates. The abbey of S. Mary de Monteburg holds it of Nigel. Of this there are in demesne 2 hides, and there is 1 carucate, and 3 serfs; and there are 5 villans, and 5 bordars, with 2 carucates. There is the third part of a mill, paying 6 shillings and 8 pence, and 3 acres of meadow. The pasture is half a mile long, and 1 furlong broad. The wood is 1 mile long, and 1 furlong broad. It was worth £4; it is now worth 100 shillings.

Spirtes, a priest, held these 4 manors in the time of King Edward.

Nigel holds half a hide in *BEVRESBROC*, and it paid geld for so much in the time of King Edward. He has there 1 villan, and 1 bordar; and the wood is one furlong long, and half a furlong broad. It is worth 7 shillings.

The same Nigel holds *HASEBERIE*. In the time of King Edward it paid geld for 1 virgate of

[1] The Abbey of S. MARY DE MONTEBURG was in the diocese of Coutance in Normandy. It was founded, according to Dugdale, in 1090, by Baldwin de Redvers. This entry in Domesday, however, shews, that it must have been founded at least as early as 1086. The Abbey held a manor in Somersetshire, the name of which is not expressly mentioned, also by the gift of Nigel, the Conqueror's physician. That manor had been held by SPIRTES, a priest, in the time of King Edward. *Somerset, fol.* 91.

I. {XVIIIb 73 b} Terra est 6 bovatæ. Ibi sunt 3 bordarii, et 3 acræ prati. Pastura 4 quarentenis longa, et una quarentena lata. Valet 10 solidos.

Has 2 terras tenuit Alsi presbyter tempore Regis Edwardi.

land. The land is 6 bovates. There are three bordars, and 3 acres of meadow. The pasture is 4 furlongs long, and 1 furlong broad. It is worth 10 shillings.

Alsi, a priest, held these 2 estates in the time of King Edward.

LVII. TERRA OSBERNI PRESBYTERI.

OSBERNUS PRESBYTER[1] tenet *HUMITONE.* Alsi tenuit tempore Regis Edwardi, et geldabat pro 2 hidis. Terra est 1 carucata. Ibi sunt 2 coscez, et 3 acræ prati, et 6 acræ pasturæ. Valet 30 solidos.

LVII. LAND OF OSBERN THE PRIEST.

OSBERN THE PRIEST holds *HUMITONE.* Alsi held it in the time of King Edward, and it paid geld for 2 hides. The land is 1 carucate. There are 2 coscets, and 3 acres of meadow, and 6 acres of pasture. It is worth 30 shillings.

LVIII. TERRA RICARDI PUINGIANT.

RICARDUS PUINGIANT tenet de Rege *CALESTONE.* Gunnar tenuit tempore Regis Edwardi, et geldabat pro 4 hidis una virgata minus. Terra est 4 carucatæ. De ea sunt in dominio 2 hidæ et una virgata, et ibi 3 carucatæ, et 2 servi; et 16 coscez, et 3 bordarii, cum 1 carucata. Ibi 2 molini, reddentes 33 solidos et 6 denarios, et 15 acræ prati, et totidem pasturæ. Silva 3 quarentenis longa, et 2 quarentenis lata. Et in Calne 2 burgenses reddunt 20 denarios. Valuit 4 libras; modo 100 solidos.

Idem Ricardus tenet *TROI.* Tempore Regis Edwardi geldabat pro 7 hidis et dimidio. Terra est 4 carucatæ. De ea sunt in dominio 5 hidæ, et ibi 3

LVIII. LAND OF RICHARD PUINGIANT.

RICHARD PUINGIANT holds *CALESTONE* of the King. Gunnar held it in the time of King Edward, and it paid geld for 4 hides all but one virgate. The land is 4 carucates. Of this there are in demesne 2 carucates and 1 virgate, and there are 3 carucates, and 2 serfs; and there are 16 coscets, and 3 bordars, with 1 carucate. There are 2 mills paying 33 shillings and 6 pence, and 15 acres of meadow, and as much pasture. The wood is 3 furlongs long, and 2 furlongs broad. And in Calne 2 burgesses pay 20 pence. It was worth £4; it is now worth 100 shillings.

The same Richard holds *TROI.* In the time of King Edward it paid geld for 7 hides and a half. The land is 4 carucates. Of this there are in demesne

---

[1] This is probably the same OSBERN, the priest, who held the Church at BRETFORD, *p.* 10, and possessed a small estate under the Church of ALWARESBERIE, *p.* 57, both these places being in the neighbourhood of HUMITONE (Humington), the manor described above.

Fol. { XVIIIb 73b } 5 carucatæ. Ibi sunt 3 villani, cum 1 carucata, et 2 acræ prati. Pastura 4 quarentenis longa, et 3 quarentenis lata. Silva 6 quarentenis longa, et 3 quarentenis lata. Valuit 100 solidos; modo 7 libras.

Hanc terram tenebat S. Maria de Wiltune tempore Regis Edwardi, et non poterat ab ecclesia separari.

hides, and there are 3 carucates. There are 3 villans with 1 carucate, and 2 acres of meadow. The pasture is 4 furlongs long, and 3 furlongs broad. The wood is 6 furlongs long, and 3 furlongs broad. It was worth 100 shillings; it is now worth £7.

The Church of S. Mary at Wilton held this estate in the time of King Edward, and it could not be alienated from the church.

LIX. TERRA ROBERTI MARESCAL.

Robertus Marescal tenet de Rege *LAVENTONE.* Eddid Regina tenuit, et geldabat pro 15 hidis. Terra est 10 carucatæ. De ea sunt in dominio 7 hidæ, et ibi 4 carucatæ, et 7 servi; et 14 villani, et 17 bordarii, cum 5 carucatis. Ibi 2 molini, reddentes 16 solidos et 4 denarios, et 20 acræ prati, et 12 acræ silvæ. Pastura 1 leuca longa, et tantundem lata. Valuit, et valet, 20 libras.

Idem Robertus tenet *GARE.* Oswardus tenuit tempore Regis Edwardi, et geldabat pro 3 hidis. Terra est 3 carucatæ. De ea sunt in dominio 2 hidæ, et ibi 2 carucatæ, et 6 servi; et 3 villani, et 1 bordarius, cum 1 carucata; et 40 acræ pasturæ. Valuit 30 solidos; modo 50 solidos.

LIX. LAND OF ROBERT MARESCAL.

Robert Marescal holds *LAVENTONE* of the King. Queen Eddid held it, and it paid geld for 15 hides. The land is 10 carucates. Of this there are 7 hides in demesne, and there are 4 carucates, and 7 serfs; and there are 14 villans, and 17 bordars, with 5 carucates. There are 2 mills, paying 16 shillings and 4 pence, and 20 acres of meadow, and 12 acres of wood. The pasture is 1 mile long, and as much broad. It was, and is, worth £20.

The same Robert holds *GARE.* Osward held it in the time of King Edward, and it paid geld for 3 hides. The land is 3 carucates. Of this there are in demesne 2 hides, and there are 2 carucates, and 6 serfs; and there are 3 villans, and 1 bordar, with 1 carucate; and there are 40 acres of pasture. It was worth 30 shillings; it is now worth 50 shillings.

LX. [TERRA ROBERTI FLAVI.]

Robertus Flavus[1] tenet de Rege *LAVENTONE.* Achi tenuit tempore Regis Edwardi, et

LAND OF ROBERT BLOND.

Robert Blond holds *LAVENTONE* of the King. Achi held it in the time of King Edward

[1] That is literally, Robert "the fair," or "le *blond.*" Hence the family name of "Blount." In the Testa de Nevil we have, at pp. 141, 153, the name of one knight's fee, held by Roger Gernon "apud Laventon de Willelmo *Blundo.*" The fee was still, as at the time of Domesday, held by William Blount of the king, as chief lord. Moreover, in the Inquis. Nonar. (1340) we have 'Galfridus le *Blount*' among the jurors in the account of the prebends of Poterne and Lavington Episcopi.

{XVIIIb 73 b} geldabat pro 10 hidis. Terra est 7 carucatæ. De ea sunt in dominio 1 hida, et 1 virgata; et 1 carucata. Duo generi ejus[1] tenent de eo 7 hidas et unam virgatam, et ibi habent 5 carucatas, cum hominibus suis. Ibi molinus reddens 5 solidos, et pastura 1 leuca et dimidio longa, et 4 quarentenis lata. Valuit 15 libras; modo 12 libras.

and it paid geld for 10 hides. The land is 7 carucates. Of this there are in demesne 1 hide and 1 virgate; and there is 1 carucate. His two sons-in-law hold of him 7 hides and 1 virgate, and they have there 5 carucates, with their dependents. There is a mill paying 5 shillings, and pasture is 1 mile and a half long, and 4 furlongs broad. It was worth £15; it is now worth £12.

LXI. TERRA RICARDI STURMID.

Ricardus Sturmid tenet de Rege *CUVLESTONE.* Aluric tenuit tempore Regis Edwardi, et geldabat pro 2 hidis. Terra est 2 carucatæ. De ea est in dominio 1 hida, et ibi 1 carucata; et 2 villani, et 8 coscez, cum 2 carucatis. Ibi pastura 2 quarentenis longa, et una quarentena lata; et tantundem silvæ. Valuit 15 solidos; modo 30 solidos.

LXI. LAND OF RICHARD STURMID.

Richard Sturmid holds *CUVLESTONE* of the King. Aluric held it in the time of King Edward, and it paid geld for 2 hides. The land is 2 carucates. Of this there is in demesne 1 hide, and there is 1 carucate; and there are 2 villans, and 8 coscets, with 2 carucates. The pasture there is 2 furlongs long, and 1 furlong broad; and there is as much wood. It was worth 15 shillings; it is now worth 30 shillings.

LXII. TERRA RAINALDI CANUT.

Rainaldus Canut tenet de Rege 1 hidam in *CHIPEHAM.* Tochi tenuit tempore Regis Edwardi. Terra est 1 carucata. Ibi 2 bordarii habent dimidiam carucatam; et 20 acræ prati, et dimidium molini reddens 15 solidos. Totum valuit, et valet, 20 solidos.

LXII. LAND OF RAINALD CANUT.

Rainald Canut holds 1 hide in *CHIPEHAM* of the King. Tochi held it in the time of King Edward. The land is 1 carucate. Two bordars there have a half carucate; and there are 20 acres of meadow, and half a mill paying 15 shillings. The whole was, and is, worth 20 shillings.

[1] The names of these two sons-in-law are given in the Exon Domesday in the account of the Hundred of Rugeberg. They were "Willelmus de Aldeleia" and "Robertus de Albemarle."

LXIII. TERRA MACI DE MORETANIA.

Fol. {XVIII b, 73 b} MACI DE MORETANIA tenet de Rege *WINTREBURNE.* Ulwardus tenuit tempore Regis Edwardi, et geldabat pro 4 hidis. Terra est 2 earucatæ. De ea sunt in dominio 2 hidæ, et ibi 1 carucata, cum 1 servo; et 2 villani, et 4 bordarii, cum 1 earucata. Ibi pastura 4 quarentenis longa, et tantundem lata. Valuit 40 solidos; modo 60 solidos.

LXIII. LAND OF MACI OF MORETANIA.

MACI OF MORETANIA holds *WINTREBURNE* of the King. Ulward held it in the time of King Edward, and it paid geld for 4 hides. The land is 2 earucates. Of this there are in demesne 2 hides, and there is 1 earucate, with 1 serf; and there are 2 villans, and 4 bordars, with 1 earucate. The pasture there is 4 furlongs long, and as much broad. It was worth 40 shillings; it is now worth 60 shillings.

LXIV. TERRA GOZELINI RIVEIRE.

GOZELINUS RIVEIRE tenet de Rege *SELE.* Almarus tenuit tempore Regis Edwardi, et geldabat pro 2 hidis et dimidio. Terra est 3 carucatæ. In dominio est 1 carucata, et 2 servi; et 5 villani, et 3 coscez, cum 2 carucatis. Ibi molinus 40 denarios reddens, et 3 acræ prati. Pastura 3 quarentenis longa, et 3 lata. Silva dimidio leucæ longa, et tantundem lata. Valuit, et valet, 30 solidos.

LXIV. LAND OF GOZELIN RIVEIRE.

GOZELIN RIVEIRE holds *SELE* of the King. Almar held it in the time of King Edward, and it paid geld for 2½ hides. The land is 3 carucates. In demesne is 1 carucate, and 2 serfs; and there are 5 villans, and 3 eoscets, with 2 carucates. There is a mill paying 40 pence, and 3 acres of meadow. The pasture is 3 furlongs long, and 3 broad. The wood is half a mile long, and as much broad. It was, and is, worth £30 shillings.

LXV. [TERRA] GODESCALLI.

GODESCAL tenet de Rege *WINTREBURNE.* Alwi tenuit tempore Regis Edwardi, et geldabat pro 2 hidis. Terra est 2 carucatæ. In dominio est 1 carucata, et 3 servi; et 4 bordarii, et 5 coscez. Ibi dimidium molini, reddens 3 solidos et 9 denarios, et dimidium acræ prati. Silva 2 quarentenis longa, et tantundem lata. Valuit 30 solidos; modo 40 solidos.

LXV. LAND OF GODESCAL.

GODESCAL holds *WINTREBURNE* of the King. Alwi held it in the time of King Edward, and it paid geld for 2 hides. The land is 2 earucates. In demesne is 1 carucate, and 3 serfs; and there are 4 bordars, and 5 coscets. There is half a mill paying 3 shillings and 9 pence, and half an acre of meadow. The wood is 2 furlongs long, and as much broad. It was worth 30 shillings; it is now worth 40 shillings

XVIII b 73 b IDEM GODESCAL tenet dimidiam hidam quam Gudmund tenuit tempore Regis Edwardi, et pro tanto geldabat. Ibi est 1 coscet. Valet 12 solidos.

THE SAME GODESCAL holds a half hide which Gudmund held in the time of King Edward, and it paid geld for so much. There is 1 coscet. It is worth 12 shillings.

LXVI. [TERRA] SERVIENTIUM REGIS.[1]

HERMAN DE DREWES tenet de Rege *ETONE.* Edric tenuit tempore Regis Edwardi, et geldabat pro 2 hidis. Terra est 2 carucatæ. In dominio est 1 carucata; et 2 bordarii, et 2 coscez, et 1 villanus, cum 1 carucata. Ibi 2 acræ prati. Silva 2 quarentenis longa, et una quarentena lata. Valuit, et valet, 30 solidos.

XIX a 73 c AMELRICUS DE DREWES tenet de Rege *MANIFORD.* Godric tenuit tempore Regis Edwardi, et geldabat pro 3 hidis et dimidio. Terra est 1 carucata et dimidium. Ibi sunt 4 bordarii, et tercia pars molini reddens 50 denarios, et 12 acræ prati. Pastura 4 quarentenis longa, et una quarentena et dimidio lata. Valuit 30 solidos; modo 60 solidos.

ANSGERUS, COQUUS, tenet *HELPRINTONE.* Tres Taini tenuerunt pariter[2] tempore Regis Edwardi, et geldabat pro 4 hidis, et una virgata, et 6 acris. Terra est 3 carucatæ, quæ ibi sunt in dominio, cum 1 servo, et 9 coscez. Ibi 12 acræ prati, et 20 acræ pasturæ. Valuit 4 libras; modo 10 solidos minus.

WILLELMUS CORNIOLE tenet de Rege *HELPRINTONE.* Quatuor Taini tenuerunt pariter[2] tempore Regis Edwardi, et geldabat pro 5 hidis et una virgata terræ. Terra est 5 carucatæ. In do-

LXVI. LAND OF THE KING'S SERVANTS.

HERMAN DE DREWES holds *ETONE* of the King. Edric held it in the time of King Edward, and it paid geld for 2 hides. The land is 2 carucates. There is 1 carucate in demesne; and there are 2 bordars, and 2 coscets, and 1 villan, with 1 carucate. There are 2 acres of meadow. The wood is 2 furlongs long, and 1 furlong broad. It was, and is, worth 30 shillings.

AMELRIC DE DREWES holds *MANIFORD* of the King. Godric held it in the time of King Edward, and it paid geld for 3½ hides. The land is 1 carucate and a half. There are 4 bordars, and the third part of a mill paying 50 pence, and 12 acres of meadow. The pasture is 4 furlongs long, and one furlong and a half broad. It was worth 30 shillings; it is now worth 60 shillings.

ANSGER, THE COOK, holds *HELPRINTONE.* Three Thanes held it in parage in the time of King Edward, and it paid geld for 4 hides and 1 virgate, and 6 acres. The land is 3 carucates, which are there in demesne, with 1 serf, and 9 coscets. There are 12 acres of meadow, and 20 acres of pasture. It was worth £4; it is now worth 10 shillings less.

WILLIAM CORNIOLE holds *HELPRINTONE* of the King. Four Thanes held it in parage in the time of King Edward, and it paid geld for 5 hides and 1 virgate of land. The land is 5 carucates. In

---

[1] In the Introduction to this Volume will be found accounts of the various classes of persons mentioned in Domesday, and amongst them of the SERVIENTES,—TAINI,—and MINISTRI REGIS. In the General Index, references are given to the pages in which these several terms are explained.

[2] See note on p. 85.

Fol. XIX a 73 c minio sunt 2 carucatæ; et unus villanus cum 1 carucata, et 12 acræ prati, et 20 acræ pasturæ. Reddit 40 solidos.

demesne are 2 carucates; and there is 1 villan wit 1 carucate, and 12 acres of meadow, and 20 acres c pasture. It pays 40 shillings.

FULCHEREDUS tenet 3 virgatas terræ in *GELINGEHAM.* Algar tenuit tempore Regis Edwardi. Terra est 2 carucatæ, quæ ibi sunt cum 1 bordario. Valuit, et valet, 15 solidos.

FULCHERED holds 3 virgates of land in *GE LINGEHAM.* Algar held them in the time c King Edward. The land is 2 carucates, which ar there with 1 bordar. It was, and is, worth 1 shillings.

STEFANUS, CARPENTARIUS, tenet 1 hidam et unam virgatam terræ in *ARDESCOTE.* Odo tenuit tempore Regis Edwardi. Terra est 2 carucatæ, quæ ibi sunt cum 1 servo, et 3 villanis, et 2 bordariis. Ibi 30 acræ prati, et 8 acræ pasturæ. Et in Crichelade unus ortus reddit 2 denarios. Valuit 30 solidos; modo 60 solidos.

STEPHEN, THE CARPENTER, holds 1 hide and virgate of land in *ARDESCOTE.* Odo held it i the time of King Edward. The land is 2 carucates which are there with 1 serf, and 3 villans, and bordars. There are 30 acres of meadow, and 8 acre of pasture. And in Crichelade a garden pays pence. It was worth 30 shillings; it is now wort 60 shillings.

IDEM STEFANUS tenet 3 hidas. Achil tenuit tempore Regis Edwardi. Terra est 1 carucata, quæ ibi est cum 1 villano, et 4 bordariis. Ibi pastura dimidio leucæ longa, et 3 quarentenis lata. Valuit 20 solidos; modo 40 solidos.

THE SAME STEPHEN holds 3 hides. Achil hel them in the time of King Edward. The land is carucate which is there with 1 villan, and 4 bordars The pasture there is half a mile long, and 3 furlong broad. It was worth 20 shillings; it is now wort 40 shillings.

OSMUNDUS tenet 1 hidam in *PONBERIE.* Alnod tenuit tempore Regis Edwardi. Terra est 1 carucata, quæ ibi est in dominio. Valuit 5 solidos; modo 10 solidos.

OSMUND holds 1 hide in *PONBERIE.* Alno held it in the time of King Edward. The land is carucate, which is there in demesne. It was wort 5 shillings; it is now worth 10 shillings.

LXVII. TERRA ODONIS ET ALIORUM TAINORUM[1] REGIS.

ODO DE WINCESTRE tenet de Rege *COLECOTE.* Ibi sunt 5 hidæ. Tempore Regis Edwardi geldabat pro dimidia hida. Terra est 3 carucatæ. De ea sunt in dominio 4 hidæ et dimidium. Ibi 1 villanus, et 4 bordarii, cum 1 servo, habentes 1 carucatam; et 60 acræ prati. In Crichelade 3 burgenses reddunt 21 denarios. Valet 4 libras.

LXVII. LAND OF ODO AND OTHER OF THE KING'S THANES.

ODO OF WINCHESTER holds *COLECOTE* of th King. There are 5 hides. In the time of Kin Edward it paid geld for half a hide. The land is carucates. Of this there are in demesne 4½ hide There is 1 villan, and 4 bordars, with 1 serf, havin 1 carucate; and there are 60 acres of meadow. I Crichelade 3 burgesses pay 21 pence. It is wort £4.

[1] See note on p. 129.

{XIX a / 73 c} BRICTRIC[1] tenet de Rege *COVELESTONE.* Tempore Regis Edwardi geldabat pro 5 hidis. Terra est 4 carucatæ. In dominio sunt 2 carucatæ, et 6 servi; et 5 villani, et 3 bordarii, cum 2 carucatis. Ibi molinus reddens 10 solidos, et 30 acræ prati, et 5 quarentenæ pasturæ. Valet 100 solidos.

BRICTRIC holds *COVELESTONE* of the King. In the time of King Edward it paid geld for 5 hides. The land is 4 carucates. In demesne are 2 carucates, and 6 serfs; and there are 5 villans, and 3 bordars, with 2 carucates. There is a mill paying 10 shillings, and 30 acres of meadow, and 5 furlongs of pasture. It is worth 100 shillings.

BRICTRIC tenet 1 hidam in *SVALOCLIVE* et 1 virgatam terræ et dimidium. Terra est 1 carucata, quæ ibi est cum 2 villanis. Valet 15 solidos.

BRICTRIC holds in *SVALOCLIVE* 1 hide and 1 virgate and half of land. The land is 1 carucate, which is there with 2 villans. It is worth 15 shillings.

BRICTRIC tenet 1 hidam in *TROLE.* Terra est 1 carucata, quæ ibi est cum 1 villano. Valet 10 solidos.

BRICTRIC holds 1 hide in *TROLE.* The land is 1 carucate, which is there with 1 villan. It is worth 10 shillings.

BRICTRIC tenet *FARLEGE*, et frater ejus de eo. Tempore Regis Edwardi geldabat pro 5 hidis. Terra est 4 carucatæ. In dominio est 1 carucata, et 4 servi; et 5 villani, et 3 bordarii, cum 3 carucatis. Ibi 20 acræ pasturæ, et 3 acræ silvæ. Valet 70 solidos.

BRICTRIC holds *FARLEGE*, and his brother holds it of him. In the time of King Edward it paid geld for 5 hides. The land is 4 carucates. In demesne is 1 carucate, and 4 serfs; and there are 5 villans, and 3 bordars, with 3 carucates. There are 20 acres of pasture, and 3 acres of wood. It is worth 70 shillings.

BRICTRIC tenet *WOCHESIE.* Pater ejus tenuit tempore Regis Edwardi, et geldabat pro 10 hidis, Terra est 6 carucatæ. In dominio sunt 2 carucatæ, et 10 servi; et 6 villani, et 12 coscez, cum 4 carucatis. Ibi molinus 5 solidos reddens, et 40 acræ prati, et 30 acræ pasturæ. Silva 1 leuca longa, et dimidio leucæ lata. Valuit 8 libras; modo 6 libras.

BRICTRIC holds *WOCHESIE.* His father held it in the time of King Edward, and it paid geld for 10 hides. The land is 6 carucates. In demesne are 2 carucates, and 10 serfs; and there are 6 villans, and 12 coscets, with 4 carucates. There is a mill paying 5 shillings, and 40 acres of meadow, and 30 acres of pasture. The wood is 1 mile long, and half a mile broad. It was worth £8; it is now worth £6.

BRICTRIC tenet *STRABURG.* Pater ejus tenuit tempore Regis Edwardi, et geldabat pro 10 hidis.

BRICTRIC holds *STRABURG.* His father held in the time of King Edward, and it paid geld for 10

[1] BRICTRIC, who held the nine Manors above enumerated, was, it is conceived, the distinguished man who, in the days of Edward the Confessor, had been his ambassador at the Court of Flanders. Matilda, daughter of Earl Baldwin, who afterwards became the wife of William the Conqueror, in revenge, it is said, from some real or supposed slight from Brictric, induced her husband to confiscate his estates, and to bestow them on herself. With some of them she endowed foreign monasteries. See above, p. 55, under 'DEVREL.' If our conjecture be correct as to the same person being intended in both entries, it would appear that BRICTRIC, if deprived of all his estates during Queen Matilda's life, was allowed, after her death, which occurred before the Wiltshire Domesday was completed, to enjoy some of them again. Those alluded to above were for the most part bestowed on the BOHUN family, by some of whom was founded the Priory at Monkton Farleigh. *Wilts. Arch. Mag.* iv. 267.

Fol. { XIX a / 73 c } Terra est 9 carucatæ. In dominio sunt 2 carucatæ, et 7 servi; et 11 villani, et 6 coscez, cum 7 carucatis. Ibi molinus 10 solidos reddens, et 10 acræ prati, et 12 acræ pasturæ. Silva 5 quarentenis longa, et 3 quarentenis lata. Valuit 4 libras; modo 8 libras.

Brictric tenet *STAVRETONE.* Pater ejus tenuit tempore Regis Edwardi, et geldabat pro 5 hidis. Terra est 3 carucatæ. In dominio sunt 2 carucatæ, et 7 servi; et 3 villani, et 2 coscez, cum 1 carucata. Ibi molinus reddens 20 solidos, et 20 acræ prati, et 20 acræ pasturæ. Valet 70 solidos.

Brictric tenet *ODESTOCHE.* Pater ejus tenuit tempore Regis Edwardi, et geldabat pro 12 hidis. Terra est 6 carucatæ. In dominio est 1 carucata, et 3 servi; et 9 villani, et 16 coscez, cum 2 carucatis et dimidio. Ibi molinus reddens 7 solidos et 6 denarios, et 40 acræ prati. Pastura 1 leuca longa, et 3 quarentenis lata, et in alia parte 5 acræ pasturæ. Silva 3 quarentenis longa, et 3 quarentenis lata. In Wiltune 1 burgensis reddit 12 denarios. Valet 10 libras.

Brictric et Alwi frater ejus tenent *COLESFELD.* Tempore Regis Edwardi geldabat pro 1 hida et dimidio. Terra est 1 carucata, quæ ibi est cum 3 coscez. Ibi 2 quarentenæ silvæ minutæ. Valet 10 solidos.

Alwardus tenet 3 hidas in *POTERNE.*[1] Tempore Regis Edwardi geldabat cum manerio Episcopi. Terra est 3 carucatæ. In dominio est una; et 3 villani, et 4 bordarii, cum 2 carucatis. Ibi 4 quarentenis longa, et 3 quarentenis lata. Valet 70 solidos. Episcopus Osmundus calumniatur.

hides. The land is 9 carucates. In demesne are 2 carucates, and 7 serfs; and there are 11 villans, and 6 coscets, with 7 carucates. There is a mill paying 10 shillings, and 10 acres of meadow, and 12 acres of pasture. The wood is 5 furlongs long, and 3 furlongs broad. It was worth £4; it is now worth £8.

Brictric holds *STAVRETONE.* His father held it in the time of King Edward, and it paid geld for 5 hides. The land is 3 carucates. In demesne are 2 carucates, and 7 serfs; and there are 3 villans, and 2 coscets, with 1 carucate. There is a mill paying 20 shillings, and 20 acres of meadow, and 20 acres of pasture. It is worth 70 shillings.

Brictric holds *ODESTOCHE.* His father held it in the time of King Edward, and it paid geld for 12 hides. The land is 6 carucates. One carucate is in demesne, and 3 serfs; and there are 9 villans, and 16 coscets, with $2\frac{1}{2}$ carucates. There is a mill paying 7 shillings and 6 pence, and 40 acres of meadow. The pasture is 1 mile long, and 3 furlongs broad, and in another part are 5 acres of pasture. The wood is 3 furlongs long, and 3 furlongs broad. One burgess in Wilton pays 12 pence. The estate is worth £10.

Brictric and his brother Alwi hold *COLESFELD.* In the time of King Edward it paid geld for 1 hide and a half. The land is 1 carucate, which is there with 3 coscets. There are 2 furlongs of coppice wood. It is worth 10 shillings.

Alward holds 3 hides in *POTERNE.* In the time of King Edward it paid geld with the manor of the Bishop. The land is 3 carucates. One is in demesne; and there are 3 villans, and 4 bordars, with 2 carucates. The there is 4 furlongs long, and 3 furlongs broad. It is worth 70 shillings. Bishop Osmund claims it.

[1] This holding is referred to at p. 22.

XIX a
73 c
ALWARDUS tenet 1 hidam in *TIDULFHIDE.* Terra est 1 carucata quæ ibi est, et 1 quarentena pasturæ. Valet 20 solidos.

ALWARD holds 1 hide in *TIDULFHIDE.* The land which is there is 1 carucate, and there is 1 furlong of pasture. It is worth 20 shillings.

ALWARDUS tenet *SVALOCLIVE.* Tempore Regis Edwardi geldabat pro 3 hidis, dimidio virgatæ minus. Terra est 1 carucata et dimidium. Villani tenent. Valet 30 solidos.

ALWARD holds *SVALOCLIVE.* In the time of King Edward it paid geld for 3 hides all but half a virgate. The land is 1 carucate and a half. Villans held it. It is worth 30 shillings.

ALWARDUS COLLINC tenet *CUNUCHE.* Tempore Regis Edwardi geldabat pro 4 hidis. Terra est 3 carucatæ. In dominio est una carucata, et 3 servi; et 4 villani, et 3 bordarii, cum 2 carucatis. Ibi molinus reddens 15 solidos, et 5 acræ prati. Pastura dimidio leucæ longa, et una quarentena lata. Valet 4 libras.

ALWARD COLLINC holds *CUNUCHE.* In the time of King Edward it paid geld for 4 hides. The land is 3 carucates. In demesne is 1 carucate, and 3 serfs; and there are 4 villans, and 3 bordars, with 2 carucates. There is a mill, paying 15 shillings, and 5 acres of meadow. The pasture is half a mile long, and 1 furlong broad. It is worth £4.

XIX b
73 d
ALURIC DE MELCHESAM tenet de Rege *WIVLESFORD.* Brismar tenuit tempore Regis Edwardi, et geldabat pro 5 hidis. Terra est 2 carucatæ et dimidium, quæ ibi sunt cum 10 bordariis. Ibi 8 acræ prati. Pastura 5 quarentenis longa, et una quarentena lata. Valuit 100 solidos; modo 8 solidos.[1] Edwardus tenet in vadimonio.

ALURIC OF MELKSHAM holds *WIVLESFORD* of the King. Brismar held it in the time of King Edward, and it paid geld for 5 hides. The land is 2½ carucates which are there with 10 bordars. There are 8 acres of meadow. The pasture is 5 furlongs long, and 1 furlong broad. It was worth 100 shillings; it is now worth 8 shillings [pounds?]. Edward holds it in mortgage.

ALURIC tenet *FARLEGE.* Brismar tenuit tempore Regis Edwardi, et geldabat pro 5 hidis. Terra est 4 carucatæ. In dominio est 1 carucata, et 4 servi; et 5 villani, et 3 bordarii, cum 3 carucatis. Ibi 20 acræ pasturæ, et 3 acræ silvæ. Valet 70 solidos.

ALURIC holds *FARLEGE.* Brismar held it in the time of King Edward, and it paid geld for 5 hides. The land is 4 carucates. In demesne is 1 carucate, and 4 serfs; and there are 5 villans, and 3 bordars, with 3 carucates. There are 20 acres of pasture, and 3 acres of wood. It is worth 70 shillings.

ALURIC tenet *WADONE.* Ipse tenuit tempore Regis Edwardi, et geldabat pro 3 hidis. Terra est 2 carucatæ. In dominio est una, et 3 servi, et 3 coscez. Ibi molinus reddens 5 solidos, et 8 acræ prati. Una quarentena pasturæ in longitudine et latitudine. Valet 20 solidos.

ALURIC holds *WADONE.* He held it in the time of King Edward, and it paid geld for 3 hides. The land is 2 carucates. One of them is in demesne, and 3 serfs, and 3 coscets. There is a mill paying 5 shillings, and 8 acres of meadow. There is 1 furlong of pasture in length and breadth. It is worth 20 shillings.

ALURIC [2] 'Parvus' tenet 2 virgatas terræ et dimidium in *TIDULFHIDE.* Terra est dimidia carucata. Valet 7 solidos et 6 denarios.

ALURIC 'Parvus' holds 2½ virgates of land in *TIDULFHIDE.* The land is a half carucate. It is worth 7 shillings and 6 pence.

---

[1] It is so written in the original, but it would seem most probably to be a mistake for '*libras.*'

[2] In the Hants Domesday (*fol.* 50 b.) we have "Aluric *Petit*" described as holding a small estate near the New Forest.

Fol. { XIX b, 73 d } IDEM tenet 1 hidam in *HELMERTUNE*. Terra est 1 carucata, et ibi habet unum servum. Valet 15 solidos.

THE SAME holds 1 hide in *HELMERTUNE*. The land is 1 carucate, and he has there 1 serf. It is worth 13 shillings.

IDEM tenet 1 hidam in *TOCHEHAM*, et pro tanto geldabat. Terra est 1 carucata. Ibi 6 acræ prati, et 6 acræ pasturæ. Valet 13 solidos.

THE SAME holds 1 hide in *TOCHEHAM*, and it paid geld for so much. The land is 1 carucate. There are 6 acres of meadow, and 6 acres of pasture. It is worth 13 shillings.

IDEM tenet 2 hidas una virgata minus quas 2 Taini tenuerunt tempore Regis Edwardi. Terra est 6 bovatæ. Valet 15 solidos.

THE SAME holds 2 hides all but 1 virgate which 2 Thanes held in the time of King Edward. The land is 6 bovates. It is worth 15 shillings.

ALWINUS, presbyter, tenet *SUMREFORD*. Tempore Regis Edwardi geldabat pro 2 virgatis terræ et dimidio. Terra est dimidia carucata. Ibi sunt 2 coscez, et 1 cotarius, et pars molini reddens 15 denarios, et 4 acræ prati, et 4 acræ pasturæ. Valet 11 solidos.

ALWIN, a priest, holds *SUMREFORD*. In the time of King Edward it paid geld for 2½ virgates of land. The land is a half carucate. There are 2 coscets, and 1 cottar, and part of a mill paying 15 pence, and 4 acres of meadow, and 4 acres of pasture. It is worth 11 shillings.

In eadem villa tenet ALWIUS 2 virgatas terræ et dimidium, et pro tanto geldabat tempore Regis Edwardi. Terra est dimidia carucata. Ibi sunt 2 coscez, et pars molini [reddens] 15 denarios, et 4 acræ prati, et 4 acræ pasturæ. Valuit, et valet, 8 solidos.

In the same vill ALWI holds 2½ virgates of land, and it paid geld for so much in the time of King Edward. The land is a half carucate. There are 2 coscets, and part of a mill [paying] 15 pence, and 4 acres of meadow, and 4 acres of pasture. It was, and is, worth 8 shillings.

In eadem villa tenet EDWARDUS dimidiam hidam. Terra est dimidia carucata. Valet 40 denarios.

In the same vill EDWARD holds a half hide. The land is a half carucate. It is worth 40 pence.

In eadem villa tenet SAIEVA 2 virgatas terræ et dimidium. Terra est dimidia carucata. Ibi est unus coscet, et 1 cotarius; pars molini reddens 15 denarios, et 4 acræ prati, et 4 acræ pasturæ. Valet 11 solidos.

In the same vill SAIEVA holds 2½ virgates of land. The land is a half carucate. There is 1 coscet, and 1 cottar; there is part of a mill paying 15 pence, and 4 acres of meadow, and 4 acres of pasture. It is worth 11 shillings.

ALWI, FILIUS TURBER, tenet dimidiam hidam in *STANINGES*. Terra est dimidia carucata. Ibi 4 acræ prati. Valet 5 solidos.

ALWI, the son of Turber, holds half a hide in *STANINGES*. The land is a half carucate. There are 4 acres of meadow. It is worth 5 shillings.

ALRIC tenet dimidiam hidam [geldantem] in *TOCHEHAM*. Terra est dimidia carucata. Ibi 3 acræ prati, et 3 acræ pasturæ. Valet 7 solidos.

ALRIC holds a half hide [that pays geld] in *TOCHEHAM*. The land is a half carucate. There are 3 acres of meadow, and 3 acres of pasture. It is worth 7 shillings.

AZOR tenet 2 hidas in *BERRELEGE*. Done tenuit tempore Regis Edwardi. Terra est 4 carucatæ.

AZOR holds 2 hides in *BERRELEGE*. Done held them in the time of King Edward. The land

XIX b 78 d In dominio sunt 2 carucatæ, cum 1 bordario, et 2 villanis. Valuit, et valet, 40 solidos.

ALESTAN tenet dimidiam hidam terræ in *TIDULFHIDE.* Valet 5 solidos.

ALMAR tenet 2 virgatas terræ et dimidium in *TIDULFHIDE.* Valet 5 solidos.

ALGAR tenet 1 hidam [geldantem] in *TOCHEHAM.* Terra est 1 carucata. Ibi habet dimidiam carucatam, cum 1 bordario, et 6 acras prati, et totidem pasturæ. Valet 13 solidos.

ALVIED tenet *SELA.* Tempore Regis Edwardi geldabat pro 2 hidis et dimidio. Terra est 3 carucatæ. In dominio est 1 carucata, et 4 servi, et 8 villani, et 9 bordarii, cum 2 carucatis. Ibi molinus reddens 3 solidos, et 4 acræ prati, et 40 acræ pasturæ. Silva dimidio leucæ longa, et dimidio leucæ lata. Valet 30 solidos.

AZOR tenet 1 hidam in *CORSELIE.* Terra est 1 carucata, quæ ibi est in dominio cum 4 bordariis. Ibi molinus reddens 40 denarios, et silva 1 quarentena longa, et dimidio quarentenæ lata. Valet 20 solidos.

ALDRED tenet *BIMERTONE.* Ipse tenuit tempore Regis Edwardi, et geldabat pro 2 hidis. Terra est 2 carucatæ. Ibi est 1 villanus, et 3 bordarii, et 4 acræ prati, et molinus reddens 12 solidos et 6 denarios. Valet 40 solidos.

ALDRED tenet *FERSTESFELD.* Ipse tenuit tempore Regis Edwardi, et geldabat pro 1 hida. Terra est 2 carucatæ. Ibi est 1 carucata, cum 1 villano, et 3 coscez. Ibi pastura 1 quarentena longa, et una lata. Silva 2 quarentenis longa, et 1 quarentena lata. Valet 10 solidos.

ALDRED tenet *WINTREBURNE.* Godvinus tenuit tempore Regis Edwardi, et geldabat pro 1 hida et dimidio. Terra est 1 carucata. Ibi est dimi-

is 4 carucates. In demesne are 2 carucates, with 1 bordar, and 2 villans. The estate was, and is, worth 40 shillings.

ALESTAN holds a half hide of land in *TIDULFHIDE.* It is worth 5 shillings.

ALMAR holds 2 virgates and a half of land in *TIDULFHIDE.* It is worth 5 shillings.

ALGAR holds 1 hide [that pays geld] in *TOCHEHAM.* The land is 1 carucate. He has there 1 carucate, with 1 bordar, and 6 acres of meadow, and as much pasture. It is worth 13 shillings.

ALVIED holds *SELA.* In the time of King Edward it paid geld for 2½ hides. The land is 3 carucates. In demesne is 1 carucate, and there are 4 serfs, and 8 villans, and 9 bordars, with 2 carucates. There is a mill paying 3 shillings, and 4 acres of meadow, and 40 acres of pasture. The wood is half a mile long, and half a mile broad. It is worth 30 shillings.

AZOR holds 1 hide in *CORSELIE.* The land is 1 carucate, which is there in demesne with 4 bordars. There is a mill, paying 40 pence, and the wood is 1 furlong long, and half a furlong broad. It is worth 20 shillings.

ALDRED holds *BIMERTONE.* He held it in the time of King Edward, and it paid geld for 2 hides. The land is 2 carucates. There is 1 villan, and 3 bordars, and 4 acres of meadow, and a mill paying 12 shillings and 6 pence. It is worth 40 shillings.

ALDRED holds *FERSTESFELD.* He held it in the time of King Edward, and it paid geld for 1 hide. The land is 2 carucates. There is 1 carucate, with 1 villan, and 3 coscets. The pasture is 1 furlong long, and 1 broad. The wood is 2 furlongs long, and 1 furlong broad. It is worth 10 shillings.

ALDRED holds *WINTREBURNE.* Godwin held it in the time of King Edward, and it paid geld for 1 hide and a half. The land is 1 carucate. There

Fol. { XIX b / 73 d } dia carucata cum 1 villano, et 1 bordario; et pars molini reddens 22 denarios et obolum. Pastura 2 quarentenis longa, et tantundem lata. Valet 30 solidos.

Aldred tenet in *ANESTIGE* 3 hidas. Terra est 2 carucatæ, quæ ibi sunt cum 1 servo, et 1 villano, et 3 bordariis. Ibi molinus reddens 25 denarios, et 5 acræ silvæ, et 5 acræ prati, et 2 quarentenæ pasturæ. Valet 30 solidos.

Aldred tenet in *WERVETONE* 10 hidas. Terra est 4 carucatæ, quæ ibi sunt cum 5 servis, et 3 villanis, et 3 bordariis. Valuit, et valet, 100 solidos.

Has 2 terras tenuerunt Bricnod et Alwin tempore Regis Edwardi.

Cudulfus tenet *WINTREBURNE.* Ipse tenuit tempore Regis Edwardi. Ibi habet 6 hidas. Terra est 3 carucatæ. In dominio sunt 2 carucatæ, et 5 servi; cum 1 villano, et 2 bordariis, habentibus 1 carucatam. Ibi 4 acræ prati, et dimidia leuca pasturæ. Valet 3 libras.

Chetel tenet 1 hidam in *MALMESBERIE.* Godvinus tenuit tempore Regis Edwardi. Terra est 1 carucata, quæ ibi est cum 2 bordariis. Ibi 6 acræ prati. Pastura 3 quarentenis longa, et dimidio quarentenæ lata. Valet 20 solidos.

Cheping tenet *HASEBERIE.* Ipse tenuit tempore Regis Edwardi, et geldabat pro una virgata terræ. Terra est 1 carucata quæ ibi est; et silva 2 quarentenis longa, et una quarentena lata. Valet 7 solidos.

Cola tenet *GRAMESTEDE.* Pater ejus tenuit tempore Regis Edwardi, et geldabat pro 1 hida et dimidio. Terra est 1 carucata. Ibi sunt 4 villani. Valet 15 solidos.

Grimbaldus, aurifaber, tenet *MANIFORD.* Edwardus tenuit tempore Regis Edwardi, et geldabat pro 6 hidis et dimidio. Terra est 4 carucatæ. In

is a half carucate, with 1 villan, and 1 bordar; and part of a mill paying 22 pence and 1 half-penny. The pasture is 2 furlongs long, and as much broad. It is worth 30 shillings.

Aldred holds 3 hides in *ANESTIGE.* The land is 2 carucates, which are there with 1 serf, and 1 villan, and 3 bordars. There is a mill paying 25 pence, and 5 acres of wood, and 5 acres of meadow, and 2 furlongs of pasture. It is worth 30 shillings.

Aldred holds 10 hides in *WERVETONE.* The land is 4 carucates, which are there with 5 serfs, and 3 villans, and 3 bordars. It was, and is, worth 100 shillings.

Bricnod and Alwin held these two manors in the time of King Edward.

Cudulf holds *WINTREBURNE.* He held it in the time of King Edward. He has there 6 hides. The land is 3 carucates. There are 2 carucates in demesne, and 5 serfs; with 1 villan, and 2 bordars, having 1 carucate. There are 4 acres of meadow, and half a mile of pasture. It is worth £3.

Chetel holds 1 hide in *MALMESBERIE.* Godwin held it in the time of King Edward. The land is 1 carucate, which is there with 2 bordars. There are 6 acres of meadow. The pasture is 3 furlongs long, and half a furlong broad. It is worth 20 shillings.

Cheping holds *HASEBERIE.* He held it in the time of King Edward, and it paid geld for 1 virgate of land. The land which is there is 1 carucate; and the wood is 2 furlongs long, and 1 furlong broad. It is worth 7 shillings.

Cola holds *GRAMESTEDE.* His father held it in the time of King Edward, and it paid geld for 1 hide and a half. The land is 1 carucate. There are 4 villans. It is worth 15 shillings.

Grimbald, the goldsmith, holds *MANIFORD.* Edward held it in the time of King Edward, and it paid geld for 6½ hides. The land is 4 carucates. In

XX a 74 a dominio sunt 2 carucatæ; et unus villanus, et 10 coscez, et 2 bordarii, cum 1 carucata. Ibi 2 partes molini reddentes 12 solidos et 6 denarios, et 20 acræ prati. Pastura 12 quarentenæ in longitudine et latitudine. Valuit 100 solidos; modo 6 libras.

demesne are 2 carucates; and there is 1 villan, and 10 coscets, and 2 bordars, with 1 carucate. There are 2 parts of a mill paying 12 shillings and 6 pence, and 20 acres of meadow. The pasture is 12 furlongs in length and breadth. It was worth 100 shillings; it is now worth £6.

IDEM GRIMBALDUS tenet *STANTONE.* Lange tenuit tempore Regis Edwardi, et geldabat pro 10 hidis. Terra est 6 carucatæ. In dominio sunt 2 carucatæ, et 2 servi; et 4 villani, et 10 coscez, cum 3 carucatis. Ibi 3 acræ prati. Pastura 6 quarentenis longa, et 4 lata. Valet 12 libras.

THE SAME GRIMBALD holds *STANTONE.* Lange held it in the time of King Edward, and it paid geld for 10 hides. The land is 6 carucates. In demesne are 2 carucates, and 2 serfs; and there are 4 villans, and 10 coscets, with 3 carucates. There are 3 acres of meadow. The pasture is 6 furlongs long, and 4 broad. It is worth £12.

GODRIC, venator, tenet unam virgatam terræ [geldantem] in *MERA.* Terra est dimidia carucata. Ibi habet 1 coscet, et dimidiam acram prati. Valet 5 solidos.

GODRIC, the huntsman, holds 1 virgate of land [which pays geld] in *MERA.* The land is a half carucate. He has there 1 coscet, and a half acre of meadow. It is worth 5 shillings.

GODRIC tenet *HERTHAM.* Pater ejus tenuit tempore Regis Edwardi, et geldabat pro 3 virgatis et dimidio. Terra est dimidia carucata. Ibi 2 acræ prati, et 3 acræ pasturæ. Valet 10 solidos.

GODRIC holds *HERTHAM.* His father held it in the time of King Edward, and it paid geld for 3½ virgates. The land is a half carucate. There are 2 acres of meadow, and 3 acres of pasture. It is worth 10 shillings.

GODVINUS CLEC tenet unam virgatam terræ in *HELPERITUNE.* Valet 2 solidos.

GODWIN CLEC holds 1 virgate of land in *HELPERITUNE.* It is worth 2 shillings.

GODE tenet 1 hidam in *STOTECOME.* Ipsa tenuit tempore Regis Edwardi. Terra est 3 carucatæ. In dominio est 1 carucata; et 2 villani, et 5 bordarii, cum 2 carucatis. Ibi molinus de 15 solidis, et 50 acræ silvæ. Valet 50 solidos.

GODE holds 1 hide in *STOTECOME.* She held it in the time of King Edward. The land is 3 carucates. In demesne is 1 carucate; and there are 2 villans, and 5 bordars, with 2 carucates. There is a mill worth 15 shillings, and 50 acres of wood. It is worth 50 shillings.

ERLECHING tenet unam virgatam terræ et dimidium in *ECHESATINGETONE.* Terra est 2 bovatæ. Valet 7 solidos et 6 denarios.

ERLECHING holds 1 virgate and a half of land in *ECHESATINGETONE.* The land is 2 bovates. It is worth 7 shillings and 6 pence.

EDRIC tenet 1 hidam in *PEVESIE.* Terra est 1 carucata et dimidium. Valet 20 solidos.

EDRIC holds 1 hide in *PEVESIE.* The land is 1 carucate and a half. It is worth 20 shillings.

EDVINUS tenet *CHIGELEI.* Ipse tenuit tempore Regis Edwardi, et geldabat pro una virgata

EDWIN holds *CHIGELEI.* He held it in the time of King Edward, and it paid geld for 1 virgate

Fol. {XX a / 74 a} terræ et dimidio. Terra est dimidia carucata quæ ibi est. Valet 3 solidos.

EDGAR, presbyter, tenet dimidiam hidam in *DEVREL.* Algar tenuit tempore Regis Edwardi, et pro tanto geldabat. Terra est dimidia carucata. Ibi habet 2 coscez. Pastura 3 quarentenis longa, et una lata. Valet 12 solidos.

EDRIC, cecus, tenet *HERTHAM.* Ipse tenuit tempore Regis Edwardi, et geldabat pro una virgata terræ. Terra est 2 boum qui ibi sunt. Valet 30 denarios.

EDWARDUS tenet *WIDETONE.* Pater ejus tenuit tempore Regis Edwardi, et geldabat pro 3 hidis. Terra est 3 carucatæ. In dominio est 1 carucata; et 4 villani, et 5 coscez, et 3 bordarii, cum 1 carucata. Ibi molinus reddens 10 solidos, et 20 acræ prati, et 3 quarentenæ silvæ. Valuit 3 libras; modo 4 libras.

EDMUNDUS tenet dimidiam virgatam terræ in *BRAMESSAGE.* Valet 30 denarios.

EDMUNDUS tenet *PLEITEFORD.* Algar tenuit tempore Regis Edwardi, et geldabat pro una virgata terræ. Terra est dimidia carucata, quæ ibi est cum 2 bordariis, et 2 coscez. Ibi molinus reddens 10 denarios. Silva 3 quarentenis longa, et una quarentena lata.

IDEM EDMUNDUS tenet unam virgatam terræ, in qua habet dimidiam carucatam, et 4 bordarios, et 2 cotarios.

Hæ duæ terræ simul valent 40 solidos.

EDMUNDUS, FILIUS AIULF, tenet 1 hidam in *BREDFORD.* Reddit 12 solidos et 6 denarios.

FILIUS AIULF tenet *GRAMESTEDE.* Pater ejus tenuit tempore Regis Edwardi, et geldabat pro una hida et dimidio. Terra est 2 carucatæ. In dominio est 1 carucata, cum 1 villano, et 2 coscez, et 2

and a half of land. The land which is there is a half carucate. It is worth 3 shillings.

EDGAR, the priest, holds a half hide in *DEVREL.* Algar held it in the time of King Edward, and it paid geld for so much. The land is a half carucate. He has there 2 coscets. The pasture is 3 furlongs long, and 1 broad. It is worth 12 shillings.

EDRIC, the blind, holds *HERTHAM.* He held it in the time of King Edward, and it paid geld for 1 virgate of land. There is land sufficient for 2 oxen which are there. It is worth 30 pence.

EDWARD holds *WIDETONE.* His father held it in the time of King Edward, and it paid geld for 3 hides. The land is 3 carucates. In demesne is 1 carucate; and there are 4 villans, and 5 coscets, and 3 bordars, with 1 carucate. There is a mill, paying 10 shillings, and 20 acres of meadow, and 3 furlongs of wood. It was worth £3; it is now worth £4.

EDMUND holds a half virgate of land in *BRAMESSAGE.* It is worth 30 pence.

EDMUND holds *PLEITEFORD.* Algar held it in the time of King Edward, and it paid geld for 1 virgate of land. The land is a half carucate, which is there with 2 bordars, and 2 coscets. There is a mill paying 10 pence. The wood is 3 furlongs long, and 1 furlong broad.

THE SAME EDMUND holds 1 virgate of land, in which he has a half carucate, and 4 bordars, and 2 cottars.

These two estates together are worth 40 shillings.

EDMUND, SON OF AIULF, holds 1 hide in *BREDFORD.* It pays 12 shillings and 6 pence.

THE SON OF AIULF holds *GRAMESTEDE.* His father held it in the time of King Edward, and it paid geld for one hide and a half. The land is 2 carucates. In demesne is 1 carucate, with 1

XXa 74a cotariis. Ibi molinus reddens 10 solidos, et 14 acræ prati, et 4 quarentenæ pasturæ. Silva 4 quarentenis longa, et 4 quarentenis lata. Valet 40 solidos.

HARDING tenet de Rege *WENISTETONE.* Ipse tenuit tempore Regis Edwardi, et geldabat pro 11 hidis. Terra est 6 carucatæ. In dominio sunt 2 carucatæ, et 6 servi; et 7 villani, et 6 coscez, cum 3 carucatis. Ibi molinus reddens 10 solidos, et 20 acræ prati. Pastura 12 quarentenis longa, et 4 quarentenis lata. Valet 11 libras.

HARDING tenet *FISGLEDENE.* Ipse tenuit tempore Regis Edwardi, et geldabat pro 11 hidis et dimidio. Terra est 5 carucatæ. In dominio est 1 carucata, et 6 servi; et 7 villani, et 8 bordarii, cum 4 carucatis. Ibi molinus reddens 15 solidos, et 24 acræ prati. Pastura 12 quarentenis longa, et 3 quarentenis lata. Valet 9 libras.

De hac terra habuit Albericus Comes 4 hidas et dimidium. Modo tenet Rex.

HARDING tenet *OCHEBURNE.* Ipse tenuit tempore Regis Edwardi, et geldabat pro 5 hidis. Terra est 3 carucatæ. In dominio est 1 carucata, cum 1 servo; et 3 villani, et 4 bordarii, cum 1 carucata. Ibi 2 acræ prati. Pastura 2 quarentenis longa, et una quarentena lata. Valet 4 libras.

TURCHIL tenet in *CONTONE.* Ipse tenuit tempore Regis Edwardi, et geldabat pro 6 hidis. Terra est 4 carucatæ. In dominio est 1 carucata, et 4 servi; et 5 villani, et 10 coscez, et 3 bordarii, cum 2 carucatis. Ibi tercia pars 2 molinorum reddens 10 solidos, et 24 acræ prati, et 10 acræ pasturæ, et 10 acræ silvæ. Valet 100 solidos.

ULF tenet 1 hidam in *BODEBERIE.* Terra est 1 carucata. Ibi sunt 4 bordarii, et 3 servi, et 3 acræ silvæ. Valet 10 solidos.

villan, and 2 coscets, and 2 cottars. There is a mill paying 10 shillings, and 14 acres of meadow, and 4 furlongs of pasture. The wood is 4 furlongs long, and 4 furlongs broad. It is worth 40 shillings.

HARDING holds *WENISTETONE* of the King. He held it in the time of King Edward, and it paid geld for 11 hides. The land is 6 carucates. In demesne are 2 carucates, and 6 serfs; and there are 7 villans, and 6 coscets, with 3 carucates. There is a mill paying 10 shillings, and 20 acres of meadow. The pasture is 12 furlongs long, and 4 furlongs broad. It is worth £11.

HARDING holds *FISGLEDENE.* He held it in the time of King Edward, and it paid geld for 11½ hides. The land is 5 carucates. In demesne is 1 carucate, and 6 serfs; and there are 7 villans, and 8 bordars, with 4 carucates. There is a mill paying 15 shillings, and 24 acres of meadow. The pasture is 12 furlongs long, and 3 furlongs broad. It is worth £9.

Of this land the Earl Alberic had 4½ hides. The King now holds them.

HARDING holds *OCHEBURNE.* He held it in the time of King Edward, and it paid geld for 5 hides. The land is 3 carucates. In demesne is 1 carucate, with 1 serf; and there are 3 villans, and 4 bordars, with 1 carucate. There are 2 acres of meadow. The pasture is 2 furlongs long, and 1 furlong broad. It is worth £4.

TURCHIL holds an estate in *CONTONE.* He held it in the time of King Edward, and it paid geld for 6 hides. The land is 4 carucates. In demesne is 1 carucate, and 4 serfs; and there are 5 villans, and 10 coscets, and 3 bordars, with 2 carucates. There is the third part of 2 mills, paying 10 shillings, and 24 acres of meadow, and 10 acres of pasture, and 10 acres of wood. It is worth 100 shillings.

ULF holds 1 hide in *BODEBERIE.* The land is 1 carucate. There are 4 bordars, and 3 serfs, and 3 acres of wood. It is worth 10 shillings.

Fol. XX a, 74 a. Ulric tenet 1 hidam et 1 virgatam terræ in *SCALDEBURNE.* Ordwoldus tenuit tempore Regis Edwardi, et pro tanto geldabat. Terra est 1 carucata et dimidium, et ibi sunt 3 bordarii. Valet 20 solidos.

Uluric holds 1 hide and 1 virgate of land in *SCALDEBURNE.* Ordwold held it in the time of King Edward, and it paid geld for so much. The land is 1 carucate and a half, and there are 3 bordars. It is worth 20 shillings.

Uluric tenet 3 virgatas terræ in *WINTRESLEI*, et 1 virgatam terræ in *TUDERLEGE.* Pater ejus tenuit tempore Regis Edwardi, et pro una hida geldabat. Terra est 1 carucata. Hanc habent ibi 4 rustici. Silva 4 quarentenis longa, et una quarentena lata. Valet 20 solidos.

Uluric holds 3 virgates of land in *WINTRESLEI*, and 1 virgate of land in *TUDERLEGE.* His father held it in the time of King Edward, and it paid geld for 1 hide. The land is 1 carucate. This land 4 countrymen hold. The wood is 4 furlongs long, and 1 furlong broad. It is worth 20 shillings.

Uluric tenet 3 hidas et dimidium in *ULFECOTE.* Pater ejus tenuit tempore Regis Edwardi. Terra est 1 carucata et dimidium. Valet 30 solidos.

Uluric holds 3½ hides in *ULFECOTE.* His father held it in the time of King Edward. The land is 1 carucate and a half. It is worth 30 shillings.

Uluric tenet *MERA.* Allic tenuit tempore Regis Edwardi, et geldabat pro 1 virgata terræ et dimidio. Terra est dimidia carucata, quæ ibi est cum 4 bordariis, et dimidia acra prati, et una acra pasturæ. Valet 7 solidos et 6 denarios.

Uluric holds *MERA.* Allic held it in the time of King Edward, and it paid geld for 1 virgate and a half of land. The land is a half carucate, which is there with 4 bordars, and half an acre of meadow, and 1 acre of pasture. It is worth 7 shillings and 6 pence.

Fol. XX b, 74 b. Uluric tenet 1 hidam et 1 virgatam terræ in *SVINDONE.* Terra est dimidia carucata. Valet 7 solidos.

Uluric holds 1 hide and 1 virgate of land in *SVINDONE.* The land is a half carucate. It is worth 7 shillings.

Uluric tenet 1 hidam in *BREDFORD.* Terra est dimidia carucata. Valet 12 solidos et 6 denarios.

Uluric holds 1 hide in *BREDFORD.* The land is a half carucate. It is worth 12 shillings and 6 pence.

Uluric tenet 1 hidam in *FRISTESFELD*, et ibi habet 6 bordarios. Valet 20 solidos.

Uluric holds 1 hide in *FRISTESFELD*, and has there 6 bordars. It is worth 20 shillings.

Uluric tenet *PORTONE.* Pater ejus tenuit tempore Regis Edwardi, et geldabat pro 2 hidis. Terra est 2 carucatæ. In dominio est 1 carucata, cum 1 servo; et 2 villani, et 3 coscez, cum 1 carucata. Ibi 6 acræ prati, et 3 quarentenæ pasturæ. Valet 40 solidos.

Uluric holds *PORTONE.* His father held it in the time of King Edward, and it paid geld for 2 hides. The land is 2 carucates. In demesne is 1 carucate, with 1 serf; and there are 2 villans, and 3 coscets, with 1 carucate. There are 6 acres of meadow, and 3 furlongs of pasture. It is worth 40 shillings.

Ulward tenet 4 hidas in *WINTRESLEI.* Terra est 3 carucatæ. In dominio est 1 carucata, et

Ulward holds 4 hides in *WINTRESLEI.* The land is 3 carucates. In demesne is 1 carucate, and

XX b 74 b 2 servi; et 1 villanus, et 3 bordarii. Silva 3 quarentenis longa, et 1 quarentena lata. Valet 40 solidos.

ULWARD, prebendarius Regis, tenet 2 hidas in *SVINDONE.* Terra est 6 bovatæ. Valet 15 solidos.

ULURIC WAULA tenet dimidiam hidam in *CLIVE.* Terra est dimidia carucata. Valet 4 solidos.

ULNOD tenet 1 hidam in *MERE*, et pro tanto geldabat tempore Regis Edwardi. Terra est 1 carucata, quæ ibi est cum 6 cotariis, et 4 acris prati, et 1 acra pasturæ. Valet 20 solidos.

ULVIET, venator, tenet *LANGEFORD.* Tempore Regis Edwardi geldabat pro 4 hidis. Terra est 2 carucatæ. In dominio est 1 carucata, cum 1 servo; et 2 villani, et 6 bordarii, et 3 cotarii. Ibi molinus reddens 5 solidos, et 20 acræ prati. Pastura 5 quarentenis longa, et 2 quarentenis lata. Valet 60 solidos.

ULNOD tenet dimidiam hidam [geldantem] in *BRAMESSAGE.* Pater ejus tenuit. Terra est dimidia carucata. Valet 10 solidos.

ULVIET tenet dimidiam hidam in *MELEFORD.* Terra est 2 bovatæ. Valet 2 solidos. Dimidia hæc terra est in foresta.

WENESII UXOR tenet *TITICOME.* Vir ejus tenuit tempore Regis Edwardi, et geldabat pro 2 hidis. Terra est 3 carucatæ. In dominio est 1 carucata, cum 1 servo; et 2 villani, et 6 bordarii, cum 2 carucatis. Ibi molinus reddens 15 solidos, et 4 acræ silvæ. Pastura 5 quarentenis longa, et 2 quarentenis lata. Valet 70 solidos.

WADO tenet 1 hidam in *BEREFORD.* Ipse tenuit tempore Regis Edwardi. Terra est 1 carucata, quæ ibi est cum 1 bordario; et 6 acræ prati. Valet 15 solidos.

2 serfs; and there is 1 villan, and 3 bordars. The wood is 3 furlongs long, and 1 furlong broad. It is worth 40 shillings.

ULWARD, the King's purveyor, holds 2 hides in *SVINDONE.* The land is 6 bovates. It is worth 15 shillings.

ULURIC WAULA holds a half hide in *CLIVE.* The land is a half carucate. It is worth 4 shillings.

ULNOD holds 1 hide in *MERE*, and it paid geld for so much in the time of King Edward. The land is 1 carucate, which is there with 6 cottars, and 4 acres of meadow, and 1 acre of pasture. It is worth 20 shillings.

ULVIET, the huntsman, holds *LANGEFORD.* In the time of King Edward it paid geld for 4 hides. The land is 2 carucates. In demesne is 1 carucate, with 1 serf; and there are 2 villans, and 6 bordars, and 3 cottars. There is a mill paying 5 shillings, and 20 acres of meadow. The pasture is 5 furlongs long, and 2 furlongs broad. It is worth 60 shillings.

ULNOD holds half a hide [that pays geld] in *BRAMESSAGE.* His father held it. The land is a half carucate. It is worth 10 shillings.

ULVIET holds a half hide in *MELEFORD.* The land is 2 bovates. It is worth 2 shillings. Half this land is in the forest.

The WIFE OF WENESIUS holds *TITICOME.* Her husband held it in the time of King Edward, and it paid geld for 2 hides. The land is 3 carucates. In demesne is 1 carucate, with 1 serf; and there are 2 villans, and 6 bordars, with 2 carucates. There is a mill paying 15 shillings, and 4 acres of wood. The pasture is 5 furlongs long, and 2 furlongs broad. It is worth 70 shillings.

WADO holds 1 hide in *BEREFORD.* He held it in the time of King Edward. The land is 1 carucate, which is there with 1 bordar; and there are 6 acres of meadow. It is worth 15 shillings.

Fol. { XX b / 74 b } Osgot tenet dimidiam hidam in *SCALDEBURNE.* Terra est dimidia carucata. Valet 5 solidos.

Osgot holds a half hide in *SCALDEBURNE.* The land is a half carucate. It is worth 5 shillings.

Odolina tenet dimidiam hidam in *MARTONE.* Terra est 1 carucata et dimidium. Ibi 30 acræ inter pratum et pasturam. Valet 40 solidos.

Odolina holds a half hide in *MARTONE.* The land is one carucate and a half. There are 30 acres between meadow and pasture. It is worth 40 shillings.

Saulf tenet 1 hidam [geldantem] in *GATEGRAM.* Pater ejus tenuit. Terra est dimidia carucata. Valet 10 solidos.

Saulf holds 1 hide [that pays geld] in *GATEGRAM.* His father held it. The land is a half carucate. It is worth 10 shillings.

Turchil tenet 2 hidas in *OCHEBURNE.* Pater ejus tenuit. Terra est 1 carucata. Ibi 30 acræ pasturæ. Valet 10 solidos.

Turchil holds 2 hides in *OCHEBURNE.* His father held it. The land is 1 carucate. There are 30 acres of pasture. It is worth 10 shillings.

Leviet tenet *CUNUCHE.* Vir ejus tenuit tempore Regis Edwardi, et geldabat pro 3 hidis et dimidio. Terra est 2 carucatæ et dimidium, quæ ibi sunt cum 1 servo; et 4 villani, et 4 bordarii. Ibi molinus reddens 15 solidos, et 5 acræ prati. Pastura dimidio leucæ longa, et una quarentena lata. Valet 3 libras.

Leviet holds *CUNUCHE.* Her husband held it in the time of King Edward, and it paid geld for 3½ hides. The land is 2½ carucates which are there with 1 serf; and there are 4 villans, and 3 bordars. There is a mill paying 15 shillings, and 5 acres of meadow. The pasture is half a mile long, and 1 furlong broad. It is worth £3.

Hæc Leviede fecit, et facit, aurifrisium Regis et Reginæ.

This Leviede used to make, and still makes, the embroidery of the King and the Queen.

Alfildis tenet *HEORTHAM.* Vir ejus tenuit tempore Regis Edwardi, et geldabat pro 1 virgata. Terra est dimidia carucata quæ ibi est; et 1 acra prati. Valet 3 solidos.

Alfildis holds *HEORTHAM.* Her husband held it in the time of King Edward, and it paid geld for 1 virgate. The land is a half carucate which is there; and there is 1 acre of meadow. It is worth 3 shillings.

Saieva tenet unam virgatam terræ [geldantem]. Alwi tenuit tempore Regis Edwardi. Terra est 2 bobus. Ibi 1 acra prati. Valet 3 solidos.

Saieva holds 1 virgate of land [that pays geld]. Alwi held it in the time of King Edward. The land is sufficient for two oxen. There is 1 acre of meadow. It is worth 3 shillings.

Liseman tenet 3 hidas in *MELCHESHAM.* Ipse tenuit tempore Regis Edwardi, et pro tanto geldabat. Terra est 2 carucatæ et dimidium. In dominio est 1 carucata; et 4 villani, et 3 bordarii, et 3 cotarii, cum 1 carucata. Ibi 10 acræ prati, et 5 acræ pasturæ, et 5 acræ silvæ. Valet 30 solidos.

Liseman holds 3 hides in *MELCHESHAM.* He held it in the time of King Edward, and it paid geld for so much. The land is 2½ carucates. There is 1 carucate in demesne; and there are 4 villans and 3 bordars, and 3 cottars, with 1 carucate. There are 10 acres of meadow, and 5 acres of pasture, and 5 acres of wood. It is worth 30 shillings.

XX b
74 b
Eldild tenet 1 hidam et 6 acras terræ in *HELPERINTONE.* Vir ejus tenuit tempore Regis Edwardi. Terra est 1 carucata. Ibi est 1 bordarius, et 4 acræ prati. Valet 8 solidos.

Osward tenet 1 hidam [geldantem] in *BRETFORD.* Terra est dimidia carucata. Pater ejus tenuit. Valet 12 solidos et 6 denarios.

Otho tenet *LANGEFORD.* Pater ejus tenuit tempore Regis Edwardi, et geldabat pro 2 hidis. Terra est 2 carucatæ. Ibi sunt 6 bordarii, et molinus reddens 20 denarios. Ibi pastura 1 leuca longa, et dimidio leucæ lata. Silva 4 quarentenis longa, et 4 quarentenis lata. Valet 15 solidos.

Sbernus tenet 1 virgatam terræ in *CRISTESFELD.* Valet 15 denarios.

Svain tenet *STAPLEFORD.* Pater ejus tenuit tempore Regis Edwardi, et geldabat pro 10 hidis et dimidio. Terra est 10 carucatæ. In dominio sunt 2 carucatæ, cum 1 servo ; et 17 villani, et 10 bordarii, cum 8 carucatis. Ibi 2 molini reddentes 30 solidos, et 40 acræ prati. Pastura dimidio leucæ longa, et tantundem lata. Silva 1 leuca longa, et dimidio leucæ lata. Valet 12 libras.

Saric tenet *WINTREBURNE.* Alwinus tenuit tempore Regis Edwardi, et geldabat pro 1 hida et dimidio. Terra est 1 carucata quæ ibi est in dominio, cum 1 villano, et 4 cosecez. Ibi pars molini reddens 22 denarios et obolum. Silva 2 quarentenis longa, et una quarentena lata. Valet 30 solidos.

Saric tenet *LAVERTESTOCHE.* Gest, frater ejus, tenuit tempore Regis Edwardi, et geldabat pro dimidia hida. Terra est dimidia carucata quæ ibi est. Valet 10 solidos.

Saward tenet 3 hidas in *BROCTUNE.* Alwold tenuit tempore Regis Edwardi. Terra est 2 carucatæ quæ ibi sunt. Valet 40 solidos.

Eldild holds 1 hide and 6 acres of land in *HELPERINTONE.* Her husband held it in the time of King Edward. The land is 1 carucate. There is 1 bordar, and 4 acres of meadow. It is worth 8 shillings.

Osward holds 1 hide [paying geld] in *BRETFORD.* The land is a half carucate. His father held it. It is worth 12 shillings and 6 pence.

Otho holds *LANGEFORD.* His father held it in the time of King Edward, and it paid geld for 2 hides. The land is 2 carucates. There are 6 bordars, and a mill paying 20 pence. There is pasture 1 mile long, and half a mile broad. The wood is 4 furlongs long, and 4 furlongs broad. It is worth 15 shillings.

Sbernus holds 1 virgate of land in *CRISTESFELD.* It is worth 15 pence.

Svain holds *STAPLEFORD.* His father held in the time of King Edward, and it paid geld for 10½ hides. The land is 10 carucates. In demesne are 2 carucates, with 1 serf; and there are 17 villans, and 10 bordars, with 8 carucates. There are 2 mills paying 30 shillings, and 40 acres of meadow. The pasture is half a mile long, and as much broad. The wood is one mile long, and half a mile broad. It is worth £12.

Saric holds *WINTREBURNE.* Alwin held it in the time of King Edward, and it paid geld for 1 hide and a half. The land is one carucate which is there in demesne, with 1 villan, and 4 coscets. There is part of a mill paying 22 pence and a half-penny. The wood is 2 furlongs long, and 1 furlong broad. It is worth 30 shillings.

Saric holds *LAVERTESTOCHE.* Gest, his brother, held it in the time of King Edward, and it paid geld for a half hide. The land is a half carucate which is there. It is worth 10 shillings.

Saward holds 3 hides in *BROCTUNE.* Alwold held it in the time of King Edward. The land is 2 carucates which are there. It is worth 40 shillings.

Fol. {XX b, 74 b} RAINBURGIS tenet unum manerium quod Godric tenuit tempore Regis Edwardi, et geldabat pro 5 hidis. Terra est 3 carucatæ quæ ibi sunt; et 5 servi, et 6 villani, et 1 bordarius, et 4 acræ prati. Pastura 5 quarentenis longa, et 2 quarentenis lata. Valuit 4 libras; modo 100 solidos.

RAINBURGIS holds a manor which Godric held in the time of King Edward, and it paid geld for 5 hides. The land is 3 carucates which are there; and there are 5 serfs, and 6 villans, and 1 bordar, and 4 acres of meadow. The pasture is 5 furlongs long, and 2 furlongs broad. It was worth £4; it is now worth 100 shillings.

FORESTARII REGIS tenent 1 hidam et dimidium in foresta de *GRAVELINGES*. Valet 30 solidos.

THE KING'S FORESTERS hold 1 hide and a half in the forest of *GRAVELINGES*. It is worth 30 shillings.

LANCH tenuit de Rege Edwardo *BLONTESDONE*, et defendebat se pro 2 hidis. Modo tenet Edwardus, Vicecomes, in manu Regis, et ibi sunt 3 bordarii. Valuit 20 solidos; modo 7 solidos.

LANCH held *BLONTESDONE* of King Edward, and it was assessed at 2 hides. Edward the sheriff now holds it, as in the hands of the King, and there are 3 bordars. It was worth 20 shillings; it is now worth 7 shillings.

LXVIII. TERRA MINISTRORUM[1] REGIS.

LXVIII. LAND OF THE KING'S OFFICERS.

HERVEUS DE WILTUNE tenet de Rege 1 hidam in *EDENDONE*. Fol. {XXI a, 74 c} Oswardus tenuit tempore Regis Edwardi. Terra est 1 carucata. Ibi sunt 3 bordarii, et tantum prati et pasturæ quantum convenit 1 hidæ. Valet 30 solidos.

HERVEY OF WILTON, holds 1 hide in *EDENDONE* of the King. Osward held it in the time of King Edward. The land is 1 carucate. There are 3 bordars, and as much meadow and pasture as is sufficient for 1 hide. It is worth 30 shillings.

HERVEUS tenet 1 hidam et dimidium. Hanc tenuit Edvinus tempore Regis Edwardi. Terra est 1 carucata. Ibi sunt 4 acræ pasturæ. Valuit, et valet, 30 solidos.

HERVEY holds 1 hide and a half. Edwin held this in the time of King Edward. The land is 1 carucate. There are 4 acres of pasture. It was, and is, worth 30 shillings.

Hæc est in *NIGRAVRA*.

This land is in *NIGRAVRA*.

RICARDUS STURMID tenet 1 hidam et unam virgatam terræ et dimidium in *IWIS*. Terra est 3 carucatæ. In dominio est 1 carucata, et 4 servi; et 3 villani, et 4 coscez, cum 2 carucatis. Ibi 4 acræ prati, et silva 1 leuca longa, et 4 quarentenis lata. Valuit 30 solidos; modo 60 solidos.

RICHARD STURMID holds 1 hide and a virgate and a half of land in *IWIS*. The land is 3 carucates. In demesne is 1 carucate, and 4 serfs; and there are 3 villans, and 4 coscets, with 2 carucates. There are 4 acres of meadow, and the wood is 1 mile long, and 4 furlongs broad. It was worth 30 shillings; it is now worth 60 shillings.

IDEM RICARDUS tenet *BUBERGE*, et Willelmus

THE SAME RICHARD holds *BUBERGE*, and Wil-

[1] See the note on p. 129.

XXI b 74 c de eo. Aluric tenuit tempore Regis Edwardi, et geldabat pro 2 hidis et dimidio. Terra est 2 carucatæ, quæ ibi sunt cum 1 servo, et 1 villano, et 4 coscez. Ibi 2 arpenz prati; et silva 4 quarentenis longa, et 2 quarentenis lata. Valet 30 solidos.

IDEM tenet in *GRASTONE* 1 hidam. Valet 20 solidos.

IDEM tenet in *HAREDONE* 1 hidam et dimidium, et Robertus de eo. Aluric tenuit tempore Regis Edwardi. Terra est 1 carucata, quæ ibi est in dominio. Valet 10 solidos.

IDEM tenet in *SALDEBORNE* 1 hidam et 3 virgatas terræ. Ordwoldus tenuit tempore Regis Edwardi, et pro tanto geldabat. Terra est 3 carucatæ. In dominio sunt 2 carucatæ, et 4 servi; et 3 villani, et 3 coscez, cum 1 carucata. Ibi 3 arpenz prati, et silva 4 quarentenis longa, et 2 quarentenis lata. Valet 40 solidos.

ROBERTUS FILIUS RADULFI tenet in *GRASTONE* 1 hidam et 2 virgatas terræ et dimidium. Ulmar tenuit tempore Regis Edwardi. Terra est 2 carucatæ, quæ ibi sunt in dominio, cum 1 servo, et 5 coscez; et 2 arpenz silvæ. Valet 30 solidos.

RADULFUS DE HALVILE tenet in *GRASTONE* 3 hidas et unam virgatam terræ et dimidium. Alwinus et Alwold, et Lewinus, et Celestan, tenuerunt tempore Regis Edwardi de eo. Terra est 4 carucatæ et dimidium. In dominio sunt 3 carucatæ, et 3 servi; et 4 coscez cum 1 carucata et dimidio. Ibi pastura 2 quarentenis longa, et dimidio quarentenæ lata. Valet 7 libras.

IDEM RADULFUS tenet in *MERTONE* 1 hidam. Duo Taini tenebant tempore Regis Edwardi. Terra est 1 carucata, quæ ibi est in dominio cum 2 servis, et 2 coscez. Ibi 2 arpenz prati, et 2 acræ pasturæ. Valet 40 solidos.

liam holds it of him. Aluric held it in time of King Edward, and it paid geld for 2½ hides. The land is 2 carucates, which are there with 1 serf, and 1 villan, and 4 coscets. There are 2 arpens of meadow; and the wood is 4 furlongs long, and 2 furlongs broad. It is worth 30 shillings.

THE SAME holds 1 hide in *GRASTONE*. It is worth 20 shillings.

THE SAME holds 1 hide and a half in *HAREDONE*, and Robert holds it of him. Aluric held it in the time of King Edward. The land is 1 carucate which is there in demesne. It is worth 10 shillings.

THE SAME holds 1 hide and 3 virgates of land in *SALDEBORNE*. Ordwold held it in the time of King Edward, and it paid geld for so much. The land is 3 carucates. In demesne are 2 carucates, and 4 serfs; and there are 3 villans, and 3 coscets, with 1 carucate. There are 3 arpens of meadow, and the wood is 4 furlongs long, and 2 furlongs broad. It is worth 40 shillings.

ROBERT, SON OF RADULF, [FITZ-ROLF] holds 1 hide and 2½ virgates of land in *GRASTONE*. Ulmar held it in the time of King Edward. The land is 2 carucates, which are there in demesne, with 1 serf, and 5 coscets; and there are 2 arpens of wood. It is worth 30 shillings.

RADULF DE HALVILE holds 3 hides and 1 virgate and a half of land in *GRASTONE*. Alwin, and Alwold, and Lewin, and Celestan, held the lands of him in the time of King Edward. The land is 4½ carucates. In demesne are 3 carucates, and 3 serfs; and there are 4 coscets, with 1 carucate and a half. The pasture there is 2 furlongs long, and half a furlong broad. It is worth £7.

THE SAME RADULF holds 1 hide in *MERTONE*. Two Thanes held it in the time of King Edward. The land is 1 carucate, which is there in demesne, with 2 serfs, and 2 coscets. There are 2 arpens of meadow, and 2 acres of pasture. It is worth 40 shillings.

Fol. { XXI a / 74 c } IDEM RADULFUS tenet in *BURBED* 2 hidas et unam virgatam terræ. Alric tenuit tempore Regis Edwardi. Terra est 2 carucatæ, quæ ibi sunt cum 1 servo; et 2 villani, et 1 bordarius. Silva 3 quarentenis longa, et 2 quarentenis lata. Valet 30 solidos.

THE SAME RADULF holds in *BURBED* 2 hides and 1 virgate of land. Alric held it in the time of King Edward. The land is 2 carucates, which are there with 1 serf; and there are 2 villans, and 1 bordar. The wood is 3 furlongs long, and 2 furlongs broad. It is worth 30 shillings.

In *ULFELA* habet [Radulfus] 4 hidas. Turoldus et Alwinus tenebant tempore Regis Edwardi, et pro tanto geldabant. Terra est 3 carucatæ, et nil pecuniæ. Ibi molinus reddens 16 solidos, et 4 villani, et 4 coscez. Silva 2 quarentenis longa, et tantundem lata. Valet 30 solidos.

In *ULFELA* [Radulf] has 4 hides. Turold and Alwin held them in the time of King Edward, and paid geld for so much. The land is 3 carucates, and there is no stock of cattle. There is a mill paying 16 shillings, and 4 villans, and 4 coscets. The wood is 2 furlongs long, and as much broad. It is worth 30 shillings.

TURBERTUS tenet in *MERTONE* 1 hidam. Lewinus tenuit tempore Regis Edwardi, et pro tanto geldabat. Terra est 1 carucata. Ibi sunt 2 coscez, et 6 acræ prati, et 10 acræ pasturæ. Valuit, et valet, 40 solidos.

TURBERT holds 1 hide in *MERTONE*. Lewin held it in the time of King Edward, and it paid geld for so much. The land is 1 carucate. There are 2 coscets, and 6 acres of meadow, and 10 acres of pasture. It was, and is, worth 40 shillings.

CROC tenet *TODEWRDE*. Tres Taini tenuerunt tempore Regis Edwardi, et geldabat pro 3 hidis. Terra est 1 carucata et dimidium. De ea tenet Croc 3 virgatas terræ, et unus miles ejus 2 hidas. Ibi est 1 carucata, et 2 bordarii, et 1 villanus; et pastura 2 quarentenis longa, et una quarentena lata. Valuit 20 solidos; modo 50 solidos.

CROC holds *TODEWRDE*. Three Thanes held it in the time of King Edward, and it paid geld for 3 hides. The land is 1 carucate and a half. Of this Croc holds 3 virgates of land, and a military retainer of his hold 2 hides. There is 1 carucate, and 2 bordars, and 1 villan; and the pasture is 2 furlongs long, and 1 furlong broad. It was worth 20 shillings; it is now worth 50 shillings.

Edwardus, Vicecomes, tenet unam virgatam terræ quæ pertinet his 3 hidis.

Edward, the sheriff, holds 1 virgate of land which belongs to these 3 hides.

HERVEUS tenet *ROTEFELDE*. Heraldus Comes tenuit tempore Regis Edwardi, et geldabat pro 2 hidis. Terra est 1 carucata, quæ ibi est in dominio; et 5 bordarii. Ibi 8 acræ prati, et pastura 2 quarentenis longa, et una quarentena lata. Valuit 30 solidos; modo 40 solidos.

HERVEY holds *ROTEFELDE*. Earl Harold held it in the time of King Edward, and it paid geld for 2 hides. The land is 1 carucate, which is there in demesne; and there are 5 bordars. There are 8 acres of meadow, and the pasture is 2 furlongs long, and 1 furlong broad. It was worth 30 shillings; it is now worth 40 shillings.

TETBALDUS et HUNFRIDUS tenent *WIDEHILLE*. Robertus filius Wimarc tenuit, et geldabat pro 5 hidis. Terra est 5 carucatæ. In dominio sunt 2 carucatæ, et 2 servi, et 6 bordarii. Ibi 50 acræ prati, et 60 acræ pasturæ. Valuit 20 solidos; modo 40 solidos.

TETBALD and HUMFREY hold *WIDEHILLE*. Robert the son of Wimarc [Fitz-Wimarc] held it, and it used to pay geld for 5 hides. The land is 5 carucates. In demesne are 2 carucates, and 2 serfs, and 6 bordars. There are 50 acres of meadow, and 60 acres of pasture. It was worth 20 shillings; it is now worth 40 shillings.

XI a ANSCHITIL tenet *BUTREMERE.* Godvinus
c tenuit tempore Regis Edwardi, et geldabat pro dimidia virgata terræ. Terra est 2 bovatæ. Valet 40 denarios.

ANSCHITIL holds *BUTREMERE.* Godwin held it in the time of King Edward, and it paid geld for a half virgate of land. The land is 2 bovates. It is worth 40 pence.

JOHANNES, hostiarius, tenet *ELTONE.* Godric et Bollo tenuerunt tempore Regis Edwardi, et geldabat pro 5 hidis. Terra est 4 carucatæ. In dominio sunt 2 carucatæ, et 3 servi; et 4 villani, et 2 cotarii, cum dimidia carucata. Ibi 8 acræ prati, et pastura 3 quarentenis longa, et 2 quarentenis lata.

JOHN, the door-keeper, holds *ELTONE.* Godric and Bollo held it in the time of King Edward, and it paid geld for 5 hides. The land is 4 carucates. In demesne are 2 carucates, and 3 serfs; and there are 4 villans, and 2 cottars, with a half carucate. There are 8 acres of meadow, and the pasture is 3 furlongs long, and 2 furlongs broad.

De hac terra tenet TURSTINUS 1 hidam, et FRAWINUS 1 hidam. Ibi est 1 bordarius, et 1 cotarius, cum dimidia carucata; et 2 acræ prati. Pastura 4 quarentenis longa, et 2 quarentenis lata. Totum valet 100 solidos.

Of this land TURSTIN holds 1 hide, and FRAWIN 1 hide. There is 1 bordar, and 1 cottar, with a half carucate; and there are 2 acres of meadow. The pasture is 4 furlongs long, and 2 furlongs broad. The whole estate is worth 100 shillings.

IDEM [JOHANNES] tenet dimidiam hidam in *BEREFORD.* Aluric tenuit tempore Regis Edwardi. Terra est 1 carucata. Ibi est 1 bordarius, cum 1 servo, et 8 acræ prati. Valuit, et valet, 10 solidos.

THE SAME [JOHN] holds a half hide in *BEREFORD.* Aluric held it in the time of King Edward. The land is 1 carucate. There is 1 bordar, with 1 serf, and 8 acres of meadow. It was, and is, worth 10 shillings.

WILLELMUS SCUDET tenet *WESBERIE.* Ulward tenuit tempore Regis Edwardi, et geldabat pro 4 hidis et dimidio. Terra est 7 carucatæ. In dominio sunt 4 carucatæ, et 4 servi; et 20 bordarii, cum 3 carucatis. Ibi 20 acræ prati, et 4 acræ silvæ, et 2 molini reddentes 25 solidos. Valuit, et valet, 8 libras.

WILLIAM SCUDET holds *WESBERIE.* Ulward held it in the time of King Edward, and it paid geld for 4 and a half hides. The land is 7 carucates. There are 4 carucates in demesne, and 4 serfs; and 20 bordars, with 3 carucates. There are 20 acres of meadow, and 4 acres of wood, and 2 mills paying 25 shillings. It was, and is, worth £8.

GOISFRIDUS tenet *DRAICOTE.* Edric tenuit tempore Regis Edwardi, et geldabat pro 5 hidis. Terra est 5 carucatæ. In dominio sunt 2 carucatæ, et 4 servi; et 7 villani, et 10 coscez, cum 3 carucatis. Ibi molinus reddens 5 solidos, et 40 acræ prati. Pastura 2 quarentenis longa, et una quarentena lata. Silva 4 quarentenis longa, et 2 quarentenis lata; et 1 burgensis reddit 12 denarios. Valet 100 solidos.

GOISFRID [GEOFFREY] holds *DRAICOTE.* Edric held it in the time of King Edward, and it paid geld for 5 hides. The land is 5 carucates. In demesne are 2 carucates, and 4 serfs; and there are 7 villans, and 10 coscets, with 3 carucates. There is a mill paying 5 shillings, and 40 acres of meadow. The pasture is 2 furlongs long, and 1 furlong broad. The wood is 4 furlongs long, and 2 furlongs broad; and 1 burgess pays 12 pence. It is worth 100 shillings.

WILLELMUS FILIUS ANSCULF tenet *TORNVELE.* Strami tenuit tempore Regis Edwardi, et

WILLIAM, THE SON OF ANSCULF, holds *TORNVELE.* Strami held it in the time of King Ed-

Fol. { XXI b / 74 d } geldabat pro 7 hidis et dimidio. Terra est 5 carucatæ. In dominio sunt 2 carucatæ; et 5 villani, et 5 bordarii, et 5 coscez, cum 3 carucatis. Ibi molinus reddens 5 solidos, et 11 acræ prati, et 10 acræ silvæ, et pastura 2 quarentenis longa, et 2 lata. Valuit, et valet, 100 solidos.

Willelmus tenet 2 hidas prope istas 7 hidas supradictas. Una pertinet ad Bradenestoch, manerium Edwardi Vicecomitis, et altera ad Clive, manerium Gisleberti de Bretevile, secundum testimonium Tainorum. Valent 20 solidos.

Wibertus tenet *CLIVE.* Hæc fuit de terra Ulvevæ Beteslau, et geldabat tempore Regis Edwardi pro 5 hidis et una virgata terræ. Terra est 3 carucatæ. In dominio sunt 2 carucatæ; et 3 villani, et 1 bordarius, et 1 coscez, cum 1 carucata. In Crichelade una domus reddit 3 denarios. Ibi 42 acræ prati et dimidium, et 84 acræ pasturæ, et 24 acræ silvæ. Valuit 20 solidos; modo 3 libras et 10 solidos.

Odinus, camerarius,[1] tenet *SVINDONE.* Torbertus tenuit tempore Regis Edwardi, et geldabat pro 12 hidis. Terra est 6 carucatæ. In dominio sunt 2 carucatæ, et 2 servi; et 6 villani, et 8 bordarii, cum 3 carucatis. Ibi molinus reddens 4 solidos, et 30 acræ prati, et 20 acræ pasturæ. Valuit 60 solidos; modo 100 solidos.

De hac terra tenet Milo Crispin 2 hidas, et ibi habet 1 carucatam. Odinus eas calumniatur.

Turstinus, camerarius, tenet *CLIVE.* Alwinus tenuit tempore Regis Edwardi, et geldabat pro 4 hidis. Terra est 1 carucata et dimidium. In dominio est 1 carucata, cum 1 servo, et 4 coscez. Ibi molinus, reddens 5 solidos, et 12 acræ prati, et 8 acræ pasturæ. Valet 50 solidos.

ward, and it paid geld for 7½ hides. The land is carucates. In demesne are 2 carucates; and ther are 5 villans, and 5 bordars, and 5 coscets, with carucates. There is a mill paying 5 shillings, and 1 acres of meadow, and 10 acres of wood, and the pasture is 2 furlongs long, and 2 broad. It was, and is worth 100 shillings.

William holds 2 hides near the above mentione 7 hides. One of them belongs to Bradenestoch, th manor of Edward the sheriff, and the other to Clive the manor of Gilbert de Bretevile, according to th testimony of the Thanes. They are worth 20 shillings.

Wibert holds *CLIVE.* This was of the land c Ulveve Beteslau, and paid geld in the time of King Edward for 5 hides and 1 virgate of land. The land is 3 carucates. In demesne are 2 carucates; and there are 3 villans, and 1 bordar, and 1 coscet, with 1 carucate. A house in Cricklade pays 3 pence There are 42½ acres of meadow, and 84 acres o pasture, and 24 acres of wood. It was worth 2 shillings; it is now worth £3 10*s.*

Odin, the chamberlain, holds *SVINDONE* Torbert held it in the time of King Edward, and it paid geld for 12 hides. The land is 6 carucates. In demesne are 2 carucates, and 2 serfs; and there are 6 villans, and 8 bordars, with 3 carucates. There is a mill paying 4 shillings, and 30 acres of meadow, and 20 acres of pasture. It was worth 60 shillings, it is now worth 100 shillings.

Of this land Milo Crispin holds 2 hides, and has there 1 carucate. Odin claims them.

Turstin, the chamberlain, holds *CLIVE.* Alwin held it in the time of King Edward, and it paid geld for 4 hides. The land is 1 carucate and a half In demesne is 1 carucate, with 1 serf, and 4 coscets There is a mill paying 5 shillings, and 12 acres of meadow, and 8 acres of pasture. It is worth 5 shillings.

[1] The office of the 'Camerarius' was to take charge of the kings 'camera', or treasury, and answered to the Treasurer of the household at present. Kelham, p. 171.

XXI b ALBERICUS, camerarius, tenet *SMALEBROC*
74 d Mainard tenuit tempore Regis Edwardi, et geldabat pro 2 hidis. Terra est 3 carucatæ. In dominio est 1 carucata; et 1 villanus, et 12 bordarii, cum 2 carucatis. Ibi 6 acræ prati, et 9 acræ silvæ. Valuit 30 solidos; modo 40 solidos.

ALBERICUS, camerarius, tenet *DEVREL*. Duo Taini tenuerunt tempore Regis Edwardi, et geldabant pro 1 hida. Terra est 1 carucata. Ibi sunt 8 coscez cum 1 carucata, et molinus reddens 4 solidos, et 1 acra prati. Pastura 4 quarentenis longa, et 2 quarentenis lata. Silva 5 quarentenis longa, et 1 quarentena lata. Valuit 40 solidos; modo 29 solidos.

GUNDVINUS, granetarius, tenet *WITECLIVE*. Alwi tenuit tempore Regis Edwardi, et geldabat pro 2 hidis. Terra est 1 carucata quæ ibi est in dominio, cum 1 servo, et 1 coscet. Ibi 2 acræ prati, et pastura 4 quarentenis longa, et una quarentena lata. Silva 1 quarentena longa, et altera lata. Valuit 20 solidos; modo 35 solidos.

WARINUS, arbalistarius,[1] tenet *CELEWRDE*. Edric tenuit tempore Regis Edwardi, et geldabat pro 2 hidis. Terra est 2 carucatæ. In dominio est 1 carucata, cum 4 bordariis. Ibi 8 acræ prati, et 10 acræ silvæ. Valuit, et valet, 40 solidos.

CROC tenet dimidiam hidam in *STOCHE*. Terra est dimidia carucata. Valet 10 solidos.

WILLELMUS CORNIOLE tenet *WICHEFORD*. Avitius tenuit tempore Regis Edwardi, et geldabat pro 2 hidis. Terra est 2 carucatæ. Ibi sunt 3 villani, et 3 bordarii, cum 1 carucata, et molinus reddens 15 solidos. Ibi 8 acræ prati. Valuit, et valet, 40 solidos.

EDWARDUS tenet unam virgatam terræ in *ALWARBERIE*. Bode tenuit tempore Regis Edwardi. Valet 40 denarios.

ALBERIC, the chamberlain, holds *SMALEBROC*. Mainard held it in the time of King Edward, and it paid geld for 2 hides. The land is 3 carucates. In demesne is 1 carucate; and there is 1 villan, and 12 bordars, with 2 carucates. There are 6 acres of meadow, and 9 acres of wood. It was worth 30 shillings; it is now worth 40 shillings.

ALBERIC, the chamberlain, holds *DEVREL*. Two Thanes held it in the time of King Edward, and paid geld for 1 hide. The land is 1 carucate. There are 8 coscets with 1 carucate, and a mill paying 4 shillings, and 1 acre of meadow. The pasture is 4 furlongs long, and 2 furlongs broad. The wood is 5 furlongs long, and 1 furlong broad. It was worth 40 shillings; it is now worth 29 shillings.

GUNDVIN, the keeper of the granaries, holds *WITECLIVE*. Alwi held it in the time of King Edward, and it paid geld for 2 hides. The land is 1 carucate which is there in demesne, with 1 serf, and 1 coscet. There are 2 acres of meadow, and the pasture is 4 furlongs long, and 1 furlong broad. The wood is 1 furlong long, and another broad. It was worth 20 shillings; it is now worth 35 shillings.

WARIN, the bow-man, holds *CELEWRDE*. Edric held it in the time of King Edward, and it paid geld for 2 hides. The land is 2 carucates. In demesne is 1 carucate, with 4 bordars. There are 8 acres of meadow, and 10 acres of wood. It was, and is, worth 40 shillings.

CROC holds a half hide in *STOCHE*. The land is a half carucate. It is worth 10 shillings.

WILLIAM CORNIOLE holds *WICHEFORD*. Avitius held it in the time of King Edward, and it paid geld for 2 hides. The land is 2 carucates. There are 3 villans, and 3 bordars, with 1 carucate, and a mill paying 15 shillings. There are 8 acres of meadow. It was, and is, worth 40 shillings.

EDWARD holds 1 virgate of land in *ALWARBERIE*. Bode held it in the time of King Edward. It is worth 40 pence.

[1] "Our Kings," says KELHAM, p. 157, "had an officer styled Arbalistarius' or 'Balistarius Regis', and lands were held in capite of the King, by the service of presenting annually a cross-bow, and of finding thread to make a cross-bow string, as often as he passed through a certain district."

THE

EXON DOMESDAY

FOR

WILTSHIRE.

INTRODUCTION.

THE EXON DOMESDAY is so designated because the original manuscript is preserved among the muniments and charters belonging to the Cathedral at Exeter. This record contains a description of the western parts of the kingdom, comprising the counties of Wilts, Dorset, Somerset, Devon, and Cornwall. The same returns, made by the Conqueror's Commissioners at the time of the general survey, which furnished the materials for the Great Domesday, would seem to have been made use of for the compilation of the Exon Domesday.

In one respect the portion of this record relating to Wilts, differs materially from those which refer to Dorset, Somerset, Devon, and Cornwall. In the accounts of each of the last named counties we have uniformly supplied to us the enumeration of live stock on every estate, a statement of the number not only of the hides, carucates, and various classes of owners or occupiers, but also of the number of oxen, sheep, goats, horses, pigs, &c.; just as it is given, in fact, in the second volume of the Great Survey. But all that this Record supplies us with in its Wiltshire portion is a list of the various hundreds and of those who were owners of some of the principal estates contained in them. The only land accounted for by name is the manor of SUTONA (Sutton) belonging to William de Moione, *fol.* 47. [See above, p. 103.] There is also contained in a summary at *folios* 527 *b*, 528, and 530, the number of manors in Wiltshire, belonging to Glastonbury Abbey, Ralph de Mortemer, Milo Crispin, Robert Fitz-Girold, and the Earl Morton. These fragments would seem to imply either that some portion of the Record was lost, or that the Exon Domesday was never complete in its contents.

But fragmentary and meagre as is the Wiltshire portion of this Record, it is invaluable to us as a means of interpreting the contents of the Exchequer Domesday. Indeed without its help it would be impossible, save by the merest conjecture, to suggest in the case of many manors what particular estate is alluded to. The omission of the Hundreds in the Great Domesday for Wiltshire, makes its interpretation more than usually difficult, and a glance at the numerous entries in the subjoined lists under the generic names of CLIVE,—CONTONE,—DEVEREL,—LANGEFORD,—SUDTONE,—WINTREBURNE,—will show how impossible it is, without some clue to the Hundred in which they are situated, to attempt to identify the several estates. In the Exchequer Domesday only *three* Hundreds are mentioned at all, and these but incidentally, namely, CICEMERTONE (*p.* 6), SUTELESBERG (*p.* 6), and WRDERUSTESELLE (*p.* 66), and singularly enough the two last are not found under those designations in the Exon Domesday.

An illustration of the utility of the information supplied by this Record occurs in connexion with the estate held at SUTONE by William de Moione to which reference has just been made. The tenant, who in the Exchequer Domesday is designated simply WALTER, is called in the Exon Domesday WALTER *Hosatus*. This is the same name which in later times occurs as HUSEY and HUSSEY. In the Hundred Rolls [ii. 277] under the Hundred of Warminster, we have the "Heirs of Hubert *Husee*" holding one Knight's fee at "Sutton Parva" in the time of Edward I. Moreover in the Test. de Nev. 150, we have the following entry:—"Walter de Limesye holds in Parva Sutton one Knight's fee of Henry *Husee*, and he of Reginald de *Mohun* and he of the King as of the honor of Dunster."—A comparison of these entries makes it certain that the manor alluded to is "Little Sutton" now a tithing in the parish of Sutton Veney in the Hundred of Warminster. The almost incidental entry in the Exon Domesday of the tenant's surname supplies the link without which our conclusions must have been, after all, but conjectural.

It must be borne in mind that the manors referred to, under the different Hundreds, in the Exon Domesday, though in many instances by far the greater number, are not the whole of them. The object of the Record was to a great extent fiscal, to determine, that is, the "geld" or tax due to the Crown from the various estates. Certain claims of exemption from this payment were allowed. The demesne lands of religious houses, and also of the great Lords and Barons who held by military service, were all exempted; much also of what was Thane-land was free; and some exemptions were claimed under especial grants from the Crown. In the Exon Domesday, we have a summary of the whole number of Hides in each Hundred, and then follows a *special* notice of such portions of the several estates as were exempt from payment of "geld." Hence we have but few notices of such manors as were held subordinately by some tenant under a Chief-Lord. Those referred to, however, together with a few incidental notices of others scattered here and there throughout the Record, are sufficiently numerous to enable us, with their help, to identify, with tolerable certainty, by far the greater number of those described in the Exchequer Domesday.

There are no less than *three* copies of the Exon Domesday for Wiltshire. It is alluded to as the "INQUISITIO GELDI" or the "Taxation of the Hundreds" for this county. These copies vary slightly from one another in substance, as well as in mode of expression, and also in the names and order of the Hundreds. Internal evidence seems to show them to have been made at different times, and by different persons. The *first* of the three copies appears to be the least complete of the three; the *second* contains nearly all the matter of the first with some corrections and additions in the margin; the *third* incorporates these additions with the text, and seems a corrected edition of the other two. The text of this third copy has been adopted for the present work;—the portions included within brackets are from one or other of the first named copies, and consist of such additions or modifications as seemed calculated to throw light on the entries in the Exchequer Domesday.

The Inquisition for each Hundred states; I.—The total number of Hides; II.—The number held by the King and his Barons in demesne, or which for other reasons were exempt from 'geld'; III.—The number of Hides for which the tax was paid, and the amount received; IV.—The tax in arrear, or withheld, with the reason for it so remaining; V.—The money retained by the Collectors (in one instance they are called 'Congregatores geldi' for their own use, where such was the case, though the principle on which their remuneration was apportioned, does no[t] clearly appear.

It may be observed that the tax in the Exon Domesday is computed at the rate of *Six shillings* for every hid[e] In the hundred of Mere, for example, *fifty-one* hides paid £15 6s. ($51 \times 6 = 306$ shillings). In the hundred of Ramsbur[y] *sixty* hides paid £18 ($60 \times 6 = 360$ shillings). In the hundred of Dunelawe *twenty-four* hides paid £7 4s. ($24 \times 6 = 14$

shillings). In the hundred of Scipe *sixty-three* hides paid £18 18*s*. (63 × 6 = 378 shillings). Under Chippenham hundred (*p*. 161) the 'geld' of *one* hide is expressly stated to have been *six shillings*, and that of *three* virgates,—four of them making up the hide,—*four shillings and sixpence*. So uniformly is this the case, that when the total differs from this reckoning it is probably owing either to some not having been paid, or to a mistake of the copyist. This is, no doubt, the case in the hundred of Alwarberie, in which *thirty-five hides and a half* are said to have paid £10 14*s*., whereas the proper sum would seem to have been £10 13*s*. (35½ × 6 = 213 shillings). These entries abundantly confirm the statements made by early historians on the subject.*

Amongst other matters on which the Exon Domesday throws light must be mentioned the Ancient Hundreds of Wiltshire. Some remarks will be found in the general Introduction to this work on the institution of Hundreds and Tithings, but as the list given to us in the Exon Domesday is the earliest which we have, this would seem the best place in which to offer some observations on those for Wiltshire, at all events as regards their relation to the present Hundreds of the County.

At the time of Domesday there would seem to have been *forty* distinct Hundreds in Wilts. Of these, *twenty-two* were in what we now call North Wilts, and *eighteen* in South Wilts. The following tables will show how they corresponded with the present hundreds. †

NORTH WILTS.

	Ancient Hundreds.	*Modern Hundreds.*
1.	CICEMETHORN	MALMESBURY.
2.	STERCHELEE (Sterkley)	
3.	THORNGRAVE	CHIPPENHAM, with the exception of a few manors, formerly belonging to the Abbot of Glastonbury, placed in the Hundred of NORTH DAMERHAM.
4.	DUNELAWE (Dunley)	
5.	CEPEHAM	
6.	CRECHELADE	These form the united Hundred of HIGHWORTH, CRICKLADE, and STAPLE.
7.	SCIPE	
8.	WURDE (High-*worth*)	
9.	STAPLE	
10.	CHINGBRIGE	KINGSBRIDGE.
11.	BLACHEGRAVE	
12.	THORNHYLLE	
13.	SELCHELAI	SELKLEY.
14.	RAMESBERIE	RAMSBURY.
15.	BRADEFORD	BRADFORD.
16.	MELCHESAM	MELKSHAM.
17.	CALNE	CALNE (including also Bromham, now reckoned in the Hundred of Pottern and Cannings.)

---

* Thus Matthew of Westminster says,—"De unoquoque aratro, id est hyda terræ totius regni, *sex solidos* extorsit truculenter."—See Ellis, II, 350.

† It may be observed, that in several of the Modern Hundreds are to be found manors, or parishes, now reckoned as belonging to a "Ragged Hundred," called that of ELSTUB, which consists of estates from various parts of the County, as *e.g.*, WESTWOOD from the Hundred of Bradford,—HAM from that of Kinwardstone,—STOCKTON from that of Branche,—ALTON (Priors) from that of Swanborough,—PATNEY from that of Stodfald. It seemed hardly necessary to particularise them under each Hundred, the more so, as they do not seem to have been so transferred to the Hundred of ELSTUB till after the reign of Edward I.

Ancient Hundreds.	Modern Hundreds.
18. WERVESDONE	WHERWELSDOWN.
19. CANENGE	The present parish of BISHOP'S CANNINGS, including South Broom, &c.
20. RUGEBERGE ... ... 21. STODFALD ... ... 22. SWANEBERG	These Hundreds,—with the exception of West Lavington, Pottern, and Rowde, which, together with Bishop's Cannings and Bromham, are now in a separate Hundred, called that of POTTERN and CANNINGS,—are all now included in that of SWANBOROUGH.

SOUTH WILTS.

Ancient Hundreds.	Modern Hundreds.
23. WESTBERIE	WESTBURY.
24. WARMINISTRE	WARMINSTER.
25. HESTREDEBERIE	HEYTESBURY.
26. EILESTEBBE	Such portions of the present Hundred of ELSTUB AND EVERLEIGH, as are comprised in Netheravon Enford, Fittleton, and that immediate neighbourhood.
27. CHENEWARESTAN	KINWARDSTONE.
28. MERE	MERE, including East Knoyle, now transferred to the Hundred of DOWNTON.
29. DONWORTH	DUNWORTH, including Fonthill Episcopi, now transferred to the Hundred of DOWNTON.
30. DOLESFELD ... ... 31. BRENCHESBEROE	The united Hundred of BRANCH AND DOLE.
32. AMBRESBERIE	AMBRESBURY.
33. STANFORD	CHALK.
34. CAUDUNE ... ... 35. CADEWORDE	The united Hundred of CAWDON AND CADWORTH.
36. DOMERHAM	SOUTH DAMERHAM. (See above under 'Chippenham for *North* Damerham).
37. WINDREDIC	UNDERDITCH.
38. FERSTESFELD	FRUSTFIELD.
39. ALWARBERIE	ALDERBURY.
40. DUNTONE	DOWNTON, but not including, as now, Fonthill Episcopi and East Knoyle.

A close comparison of the Exchequer with the Exon Domesday, as far as the abbreviated form of the Wiltshire portion of the latter permits it to be carried out, shews that, though for the most part they agree as to their general contents, a few variations nevertheless may be observed. Some changes in occupation or ownership would appear to have taken place during the interval that elapsed between the completion of the two records, and the Exon Domesday is probably corrected to a slightly later date than the Exchequer Domesday. These trifling variations are noticed in the succeeding pages under the Hundreds in which they occur.

It will be observed that in the spelling of the names both of places and persons there is a considerable difference between the two records. Indeed the caprice with which the Norman Scribes wrote the various names seems unaccountable. Instances are so numerous, that it is needless to particularise. One example may be seen at *p.* 142, where in the same entry we have the name of the tenant written first as Leviet, and in the next clause as Leviede.

In the Exon Domesday we have frequently supplied to us the 'surnames' of persons, which are commonly omitted in the other record. Thus we have Rainald *Canut* in the Hundred of Scipe,—Walter *Hosatus* in that of Warminster,—Alward *Culling* in that of Heytesbury,—Osmund *Latimarus* in that of Bradford. In some instances the two records help to interpret the names found in each other; thus the 'Gunfrid *Maldoith*' (*p.* 122) in the one, is the 'Gunfridus *Maledoctus*' of the other; and 'Robertus *Flavus*' of the Exchequer Domesday (*p.* 126), is the 'Robert *Blond*' of the other record.

A difference also may be marked in one or two cases as to diction. Examples are given by Ellis, in his Introduction to the Exon Domesday, taken from various parts of that record. This difference, however, is not so marked in the Wiltshire portion which is given in an abbreviated form, as in other cases where the record goes more into detail, and appears to be not so much a summary, as an abstract, of the original Rolls.

EXON DOMESDAY.

1. CICEMETHORN HUNDRED.

IN hundreto de CICEMETHORN sunt 169 hid. et dimid. De his habent Barones in dominio 76 hid. et dimid. et dimid. virg. Inde habet Abbas Malmesberiensis 66 hid. et dimid.; Brictricus 7 hid.; Durandus* de Glowecestra 3 hid. dimid. virg. minus; et pro 93 hid. dimid. virg. minus redditæ sunt Regi [in constitutis terminis] 27 libr. et 3 sol. et 3 denar. Quatuor collectores geldi retinuerunt 14 sol.

* Robertus nepos Durandi. A.†

In the hundred of CICEMETHORN are 169½ hides. Of these the Barons have in demesne 76½ hides and half a virgate. Of them, the Abbot of Malmesbury has 66½ hides ; Brictric 7 hides ; Durand of Gloucester 3 hides all but half a virgate ; and for 93 hides all but half a virgate are paid to the King at the appointed terms, £27 3s. 3d. The four collectors of the geld retained 14 shillings.

The Hundred of CICEMETHORN, or, as it is written in the Exchequer Domesday, *p.* 6, CICEMERTONE, is situated in the North-West portion of the County. It was, no long time afterwards, called CHEGGELAWE, for it is so designated in the list of Wiltshire Hundreds given in the Abbrev. Placit (*p.* 15) of the date of Rich. I. This last name is still retained in CHEDGELOW, a small hamlet in the parish of Crudwell. This ancient Hundred is now merged in that of Malmesbury. It is named as a distinct Hundred as late as A.D. 1340. Non. Inq., *p.* 66. See on this and the adjoining Hundreds some remarks in Jackson's Aubrey, *p.* 207.

---

† The letters A. and B., added to the various readings given in notes to the original of the Exon Domesday, denote respectively those derived rom the *first* or *second* copy of that record; the *third* copy, as has been already intimated, being apparently the most complete, has been chosen as the text for this work. In the subjoined list of manors under the various Hundreds, the number following each name denotes the page at which an account of it may be found. Where no modern name is given, the reader, by referring to the alphabetical analysis in a subsequent part of this volume, will find the best conjecture that can be formed as to the estate alluded to.

The estates alluded to in the above summary, together with their modern names, and their several owners at the time of Domesday, would seem to be the following:—

BROCHENEBERGE	p. 35	...	*Brokenborough*		ABBOT OF MALMESBURY.
CHEMELE	„ 36	...	*Kemble*		
NEWENTONE	„ 36	...	*Long Newnton*		
CERLETONE	„ 37	...	*Charlton*		
GARDONE	„ 37	...	*Garsdon.*		
CREDVELLE	„ 37	...	*Crudwell.*		
WOCHESIE	„ 131	...	*Oaksey*	...	BRICTRIC.
ESSELIE	„ 97	...	*Ashley*	...	DURAND OF GLOUCESTER.

2. STERKLEY HUNDRED.

In hundreto de STERCHELEE sunt 152 hid. et 1 virg. De his habent Barones 43 hid. et 1 virg. in dominio. Inde habet Radulfus de Mortuo Mari 14 hid. in dominio; Osbernus Gifard 8 hid. et 1 virg.; Abbas Malmesberiensis 3 hid. et dimid.; Rogerius de Bercheleia 1 hid.; Abbas de Glastingeberia 14 hid.; Gosfridus Marescal 2 hid. et dimid.; et pro 108 hid. et dimid. redditæ sunt Regi 32 libr. et 10 sol. et 10 denar.

De terra Ernulfi de Hesding [pro dimid. hid. et dimid. virg.] retenti sunt 3 sol. et 9 denar. usque modo, [et modo redditi sunt. A.].

In the hundred of STERKLEY are 152 hides and 1 virgate. Of these the Barons have 43 hides and 1 virgate in demesne. Of these Radulf de Mortemer has 14 hides in demesne; Osbern Gifard 8 hides and 1 virgate; the Abbot of Malmesbury 3½ hides; Roger de Berkeley 1 hide; the Abbot of Glastonbury 14 hides; Geoffrey Marescal 2½ hides; and for 108½ hides have been paid to the King £32 10*s.* 10*d.*

Of the land of Ernulf de Hesding, for half a hide and half a virgate, 3 shillings and 9 pence have been retained till now, and now they have been paid.

The Hundred of STERKLEY comprised a considerable portion of the county immediately adjoining the hundred just described, and is like it now included in that of Malmesbury, with the exception of the parish of Christian Malford, which was afterwards, together with other estates in the neighbourhood, belonging to the Abbot of Glastonbury, placed in a hundred called NORTH DAMERHAM. See p. 28. The name Storkley (or Starkley) is still preserved in a hamlet belonging to the parish of Broad Somerford. Jackson's Aubrey, 207.

The following would appear to be the estates and their owners alluded to in the above summary.

HUNLAVINTONE *	p. 109	...	*Hullavington*	...	RADULPH DE MORTEMER.
STANTONE	„ 116	...	*Stanton St. Quintin*	...	OSBERN GIFARD.
BRECHEORDE	„ 35	...	*Brinkworth*	...	ABBOT OF MALMESBURY.
NORTONE †	„ 35	...	*Norton*		

* Abbrev. Plac. 13.

† NORTON appears at different times to have been considered in different hundreds. In the Abbrev. Plac. it is given as in CHEGGELEWE (CICEMETHORN); in the Hundred Rolls. II. 272, and the Inq. Non. 165, it is spoken of as in STERKELEE.

FOXELEGE	p.	114	...	*Foxley*	...	ROGER DE BERCHELAI.
CRISTEMELEFORDE*	,,	30	...	*Christian Malford*	...	ABBOT OF GLASTONBURY.
DRAICOTE	,,	147	...	*Draycote Cerne*	...	GEOFFREY MARESCAL.
CHEIESLAVE	,,	77	...	*Chedglow*	...	ERNULF DE HESDING.

* Abbrev. Plac. 13.

3. THORNGRAVE HUNDRED.

In hundreto de THORNGRAVA sunt 113 hid. Inde habent Barones in dominio 47 hid. dimid. virg. minus. Abbas de Glastingeberia habet inde 32 hid.; Willelmus de Ow 5 hid.; Ernulfus de Hesding 5 hid. dimid. virg. minus; Hunfridus de Insula 5 hid.; et pro 66 hid. et dimid. virg. redditæ sunt Regi 9 libr. et 16 sol. et 9 denar.

In the hundred of THORNGRAVE are 113 hides. Of these the Barons have in demesne 47 hides, all but half a virgate. The Abbot of Glastonbury has of them 32 hides; William de Ow 5 hides; Ernulf de Hesding 5 hides all but half a virgate; Humphrey de L'Isle 5 hides; and for 66 hides and half a virgate are paid to the King £9 16*s*. 9*d*.

It is by no means easy to state the exact limits of this ancient Hundred. There is a passing allusion to it in the Abbrev. Plac., *p.* 13 (*temp.* Rich. I.), in its account of the Hundred of 'Dunilewe,' but no particulars are furnished concerning it. It is not mentioned under the name of *Thorngrave*, either in the Hundred Rolls, or in the Nomina Villarum.

By a close comparison of the entries in the Exchequer and Exon Domesday, with lists given in subsequent documents, we may infer that the whole of this once extensive Hundred, containing no less than 113 hides (probably some 18,000 acres), was merged, in the first instance in the Hundred of CHIPPENHAM. At the commencement of the 14th century, those estates comprised within it belonging to the Abbot of Glastonbury were transferred to NORTH DAMERHAM. See Jackson's Aubrey, *p.* 124.

The following would seem in all probability to be the manors, and their respective owners, alluded to above :—

NITELETONE	p.	31	...	*Nettleton*	}	ABBOT OF GLASTONBURY.
GRETELINTONE	,,	32	...	*Grittleton*	}	
LANGHELEI	,,	32	...	*Kington Langley*	}	
SEVAMENTONE	,,	101	...	*Sevington*	...	WILLIAM DE OW.
ESTONE	,,	79	...	*Easton Piers*	...	ERNULF DE HESDING.
COME	,,	89	...	*Castle Combe*	...	HUMFREY DE L'ISLE.

4. DUNELAWE HUNDRED.

In hundreto de DUNELAWE sunt 28 hid. Inde habent Barones in dominio 4 hid. Inde habet Hermannus 2 hid.; Rogerus 2 hid. ; et pro 24 hid. redditæ sunt Regi 7 libr. et 4 sol.

In the hundred of DUNLEY are 28 hides. Of these the Barons have in demesne 4 hides. Herman has of them 2 hides; Roger 2 hides; and for 24 hides are paid to the King £7 4*s*.

This small Hundred was in the north-west portion of the county. The Foss Road, running from Bath to Cirencester, would seem, for a little distance, to have been its boundary on the East. Besides the places mentioned below, the following are conjectured to have been included in it:—ALDRITONE, *pp.* 111, 119 (Alderton); LITELTONE, *p.* 27 (Littleton Drew); and SIRENDONE, *p.* 110 (Surrendall). See Abbrev. Plac. 13, and Jackson's Aubrey, 104. DUNLEY is still the name of a farm, the lands belonging to which are on either side of the Foss and situated partly in Littleton Drew, partly in Hullavington. This Hundred was afterwards merged in that of CHIPPENHAM.

The MANORS above alluded to are most probably the following:—

LOCHINTONE	*p.* 97	...	*Luckington*	...	HERMAN [UNDER DURAND OF GLOUCESTER.]
ESTONE	„ 115	...	*Easton Grey*	...	ROGER [DE BERCHELAI.]

5. CHIPPENHAM HUNDRED.

In hundreto de CEPEHAM sunt 142 hid. De his habent Barones in dominio 44 hid. et 1 virg. et dimid. Inde habet Rex de terra Tostig 10 hid. in dominio; Edwardus Vice-comes 3 hid. et dimid.; Ecclesia de Cossam 2 hid. et dimid.; Hunfridus de Insula 4 hid. et. dimid.; Abbas Malmesberiensis 14 hid. et dimid. et dimid. virg.; Ulwi 1 hid. quam Edwardus Vice-comes dedit sibi precepto Regis; Saieva vidua 1 virg.; Osbernus Gifard 9 hid.; et pro 80 hid. redditæ sunt Regi 24 libr. 21 denar. minus. Hos 21 denar. et 9 sol. retinuerunt 4 collectores geldi.

Warnerus retinuit geldum 1 hid. scilicet 6 sol. [qui modo redditi sunt]; Ulwi retinuit geldum 1 hid.; Turstin, homo Gisleberti Maminot, retinuit geldum 3 virg. scilicet 4 sol. et 6

In the hundred of CHIPPENHAM are 142 hides. Of these the Barons have in demesne 44 hides and 1 virgate and a half. Of these the King has of the land of Tostig 10 hides in demesne; Edward the Sheriff has 3½ hides; the Church of Corsham 2½ hides; Humfrey de L'Isle 4½ hides; the Abbot of Malmesbury 14½ hides and ½ virgate; Ulwi 1 hide, which Edward the Sheriff gave at the command of the King; Saieva, a widow, 1 virgate; Osbern Gifard 9 hides; and for 80 hides have been paid to the King £24 all but 21 pence. These 21 pence and 9 shillings the 4 collectors of the geld retained.

Warner retained the geld of 1 hide, to wit, 6 shillings (which are now paid); Ulwi retained the geld of 1 hide; Turstin, the tenant of Gislebert Maminot, retained the geld of 3 virgates,

denar., [qui modo* redditi sunt]; et de 14 hid. et dimid. de terra Tostig quas tenent villani Regis non habet Rex geldum.

* Qui modo *non* redditi sunt (A); shewing that the various manuscripts were not of precisely the same date.

to wit, 4 shillings and 6 pence (which are now paid); and from 14½ hides from the land of Tostig which the King's villans hold, the King has no geld.

The Hundred of CHIPPENHAM was formerly of much less extent than now. The two ancient hundreds which have been just described, *viz.*, THORNGRAVE and DUNELAWE, were subsequently merged in it. The estates belonging to the Abbot of Glastonbury, which were originally comprised within it, were afterwards transferred to a separate and scattered hundred, called that of NORTH DAMERHAM. See above, *p.* 160, under "Thorngrave Hundred."

The manors alluded to in the above summary, and their respective owners, appear to be the following:—

COSSEHAM	*p.* 11	...	*Corsham*	...	THE KING, OF THE LAND OF EARL TOSTIG.
LACOCH	„ 71	...	*Lacock*	...	EDWARD OF SALISBURY.
COSSEHAM*	„ 11	...	*Corsham*	...	CHURCH OF CORSHAM.
COLERNE	„ 88	...	*Colerne*	...	HUMFREY DE L'ISLE.
A small holding not named	„ 142	...		...	SAIEVA, a Widow.
BREME	„ 38	...	*Bremhill*	...	ABBOT OF MALMESBURY.
LANGEFEL	„ 71	...	*Langley Burrel*	...	WLWI.
TERINTONE	„ 118	...	*Tytherton*	...	OSBERN GIFARD.
DIGERIC	„ 101	...	*Ditteridge*	...	WARNER, under WILLIAM DE OW.
ETONE	„ 28	...	*Yatton Keynes*	...	TURSTIN, under GISLEBERT MAMINOT, Bishop of Lisieux.

* This refers to the manor which belonged to the Church at CORSHAM. According to the Exchequer Domesday, this manor was in the hands of the Abbey of St. STEPHEN, at CAEN.

6. CRICKLADE HUNDRED.

In hundreto de CRECHELADE* sunt 49 hid. Ex his habent Barones 20 hid. in dominio. Inde habet Abbas de Craneburna 10 hid. in dominio; Rainbold 5 hid.; Hunfridus [de Insula] 2 hid. et dimid.; Comes Rogerius 2 hid. et dimid.; et pro 29 hid. redditæ sunt Regi 8 libr. et 14 sol. et 6† denar.

* Crichalade A. Crichelada B. † Et 1 denar A.

In the hundred of CRICKLADE are 49 hides. Of these the Barons have 20 hides in demesne. Of them the Abbot of Cranbourn has 10 hides in demesne; Rainbold 5 hides; Humfrey de L'Isle 2½ hides; the Earl Roger 2½ hides; and for 29 hides have been paid to the King £8 14*s.* 6*d.*

The Hundred of CRICKLADE, together with those of STAPLE and HIGHWORTH, form now a united Hundred. At the time of Domesday they were distinct. The Hundred of Cricklade was the smallest of the *three,*—or rather *four,* for in the present Highworth is included the Hundred of SCIPE,—and consisted of a few manors lying near the north-western boundary of the county. Those referred to in the above summary would appear to be the following :—

ESSITONE	p. 41	...	*Ashton Keynes*	...	ABBOT OF CRANBOURN.
LATONE AISI	„ 56	...	*Latton* *Eisey*	...	RAINBOLD.
SCHERNECOTE	„ 121	...	*Sharncote*	...	HUMFREY DE L'ISLE.*
POLTONE	„ 59	...	*Poulton*	...	EARL ROGER.

* In the Exchequer Domesday he is described as "HUMFREY, the *Chamberlain.*"

7. SCIPE HUNDRED.

In hundreto de SCIPE sunt 80 hid. De his habent Barones Regis in dominio 15 hid. Inde habet Nigellus medicus 5 hid. Raginaldus Canut 2 hid. [quas ipse tenet de Milone Crispino]; Gislebertus de Breteville [de terra Rogeri Comitis] 5 hid. et 3 virg.; Hunfridus coquus, et Teodbald medicus, 4 hid. et 1 virg.; et pro 63 hid. redditæ sunt Regi 18 libr. et 18 sol.

In the hundred of SCIPE are 80 hides. Of these the King's Barons have 15 hides in demesne. Of these, Nigel the Physician has 5 hides; Reginald Canut 5 hides, which he holds of Milo Crispin; Gilbert de Breteville, of the land of the Earl Roger, 5 hides and 3 virgates; Humfrey the cook, and Teodbald the physician, 4 hides and 1 virgate; and for 63 hides are paid to the King £18 18*s*.

We have no records relating to this ancient Hundred;—hence it is by no means easy to define its exact limits. It would seem, from the number of hides at which it was assessed, to have comprised the larger portion of the present hundred of HIGHWORTH, with which it was afterwards united. Most probably all the manors on the *western* side of that hundred, such as BLUNSDON,—RODBOURN CHENEY,—STRATTON ST. MARGARET,—and others, constituted the Hundred of SCIPE.

There is some little difficulty in identifying *all* the estates referred to in the summary given above. Some change of ownership, it may be, took place between the date of the completion of the two records which may account for the apparent discrepancy. There is no manor, for instance, named in the Exchequer Domesday as having belonged to the Earl Roger, and held under him by Gilbert de Breteville.

The following is a list of those which can be identified with tolerable certainty :—

STRATONE	p. 123	...	*Stratton St. Margaret's*	...	NIGEL, THE PHYSICIAN.
REDBORNE	„ 92	...	*Rodbourn Cheney*	...	REGINALD CANUT, of the land of MILO CRISPIN.
WIDEHILLE	„ 146	...	*Widhill*	...	HUMFREY, THE COOK. TEODBALD, THE PHYSICIAN.

8. WORTH [HIGHWORTH] HUNDRED.

In hundreto de WORDE* sunt 60 hid. De his habent Barones 22 hid. et dimid. in dominio. Inde habet Rex 4 hid. in dominio. Turoldus 6 hid. et dimid.; Robertus filius Roulfi 7 hid.; Grimbaldus 5 hid.; et pro 30 hid. et dimid. et tercia parte dimid. hid. redditæ sunt Regi 9 libr. et 4 sol.

De 5 hid. quas tenent villani de terra Haroldi non habet Rex geldum. De 2 hidis [quas Turoldus dedit nepti suæ] Gunterus retinuit geldum præter 12 denar.

* Worda. C.

In the hundred of WORTH are 60 hides. Of these the Barons have 22½ hides in demesne. Of them the King has 4 hides in demesne. Turold 6½ hides; Robert Fitz-Rolf 7 hides; Grimbald 5 hides; and for 30½ hides and the third part of half a hide are paid to the King £9 4*s*.

From 5 hides which the King's villans hold of the land of Harold, the King has no geld. From 2 hides, which Turold gave to his granddaughter, Gunter retained the geld except 12 pence.

This Hundred contained originally a few estates lying in the north-east portion of the county, and was of much smaller extent than now. In the Hundred Rolls it is called "ALTEL-BURGH," and sometimes "WORTH." Some information will be found in Jackson's Aubrey, *p*. 150, relating to this Hundred.

As far as they can be identified, the manors above alluded to, and their respective owners, are conjectured to be the following :—

ETTONE	*p.* 59	...	*Eaton*	...	TUROLD.
RUSTESELLE	,, 86	...	*Lushill*	...	GUNTER, under HUMFREY DE L'ISLE.
HANTONE	,, 113	...	*Hinton*	...	ROBERT FITZ-ROLF.
STANTONE	,, 137	...	*Stanton Fitz-Waryn*	...	GRIMBALD.

---

9. STAPLE HUNDRED.

In hundreto de STAPLA sunt 52 hid. De his habent Barones in dominio 32 hid. et 3 virg. et dimid. Inde habet Rex 5 hid. in dominio de terra Haroldi;* Abbas de Malmesberia 21 hid. et dimid; Odo de Wincestra 4 hid. et dimid.; Warinus 2 hid. dimid. virg. minus; et pro 14 hid. et dimid. virg. redditæ sunt Regi 4 libr. et 4 sol. et 9 denar. De 5 hid. de terra Haroldi quas tenent villani Regis non habet Rex geldum.

* Terra Comitis Haroldi. B.

In the hundred of STAPLE are 52 hides. Of these the Barons have 32 hides and 3½ virgates in demesne. Of these the King has 5 hides in demesne of the land of Harold; the Abbot of Malmesbury 21½ hides; Odo of Winchester 4½ hides; Warin 2 hides all but half a virgate; and for 14 hides and half a virgate, are paid to the King £4 4*s*. 9*d*. From the five hides of the land of Harold which the King's villans hold the King has no geld.

The Hundred of STAPLE is now united with those of HIGHWORTH and CRICKLADE. Some particulars respecting it will be found in Jackson's Aubrey, *p.* 150.

The manors above alluded to are, it is conceived, the following:—

LIDIARDE	*p.* 15	...	*Lydiard Millicent*	...	THE KING.
PIRITONE	,, 39	...	*Pirton*	...	ABBOT OF MALMESBURY.
COLECOT	,, 130	...	*Colecot*	...	ODO OF WINCHESTER.
CELEWRDE	,, 149	...	*Chelworth*	...	WARIN, THE BOWMAN.

10. KINGSBRIDGE HUNDRED.

In hundreto de CHINGBRIGGE sunt 110 hid. et dimid. De his habent Barones 40 hid. et dimid. in dominio. Inde habet Edwardus Vicecomes 8 hid.; Walchelinus Episcopus 5 hid.; Henricus de Ferieres 4 hid. et dimid.; Wilbertus 3 hid. et dimid.; Rogerius 1 virg.; Abbas Malmesberiensis 8 hid.; Gislebertus de Bretevilla* 4 hid. et 1 virg.; Turstin, camerarius, 2 hid. et dimid.; Hunfridus 4 hid. et dimid.; et pro 64 hid. et dimid. redditæ sunt Regi 19 lib. et 6 sol. et 10 denar. Turchitillus et Hugolinus retinuerunt geldum dimid. hid. [de qua debet reddi geldum]. Odo, homo Baiocensis Episcopi, retinuit geldum 5 hid.

* Gislebertus de Cliva. A.

In the hundred of KINGSBRIDGE are 110½ hides. Of these the Barons have 40½ hides in demesne. Of them, Edward the Sheriff has 8 hides; Bishop Walchelin 5 hides; Henry de Ferieres 4½ hides; Wilbert 3½ hides; Roger 1 virgate; the Abbot of Malmesbury 8 hides; Gilbert de Breteville 4 hides and 1 virgate; Turstin, the chamberlain, 2½ hides; Humfrey 4½ hides; and for 64½ hides are paid to the King £19 6*s.* 10*d.* Turchitil and Hugolin retained the geld of half a hide from which geld ought to have been paid. Odo, tenant of the Bishop of Baieux, retained the geld of 5 hides.

The Hundred of KINGSBRIDGE was formerly of much smaller extent than at the present time. It now includes the old Hundreds of BLACHEGRAVE and THORNHILL. See Jackson's Aubrey, *p.* 162.

Many of the manors alluded to above are described in the Exchequer Domesday under the generic term—CLIVE. For such as are left without the modern names being added, the reader is referred to the alphabetical analysis in a subsequent part of this volume, where, in most cases, some conjecture is given as to what manor is intended.

STOCHE	*p.* 68	...	*Braden-Stoke*	...	EDWARD [OF SALISBURY], THE SHERIFF.
CLIVE	,, 19	...	*Bush-ton* [=*Bishops-ton*]	...	BISHOP WALCHELIN [OF WINCHESTER].
WADHULLE	,, 25	...	*Woodhill (in Cliff Pipard)*	...	BISHOP OF BAIEUX.
CLIVE	,, 108	...		...	HENRY DE FERIERES.
CLIVE	,, 148	...		...	WILBERT.
CLIVE	,, 83	...	*Clevancy*	...	ROGER.
HIWEI	,, 34	...	*Highway*	...	ABBOT OF MALMESBURY.
CLIVE	,, 95	...	*Cliff Pipard*	...	GILBERT DE BRETEVILLE.

CLIVE	p. 148	...		... TURSTIN, THE CHAMBERLAIN.
CLIVE?	" 87	...	*Cliff Pipard*	... HUMFREY [DE L'ISLE].
LITTLECOTE	" 92	...	*Littlecote*	... TURCHITIL and HUGOLIN.

11. BLACHEGRAVE HUNDRED.

In hundreto de BLACHEGRAVE sunt 165 hid. et dimid. virg. De his habent Rex et Barones in dominio 71 hid. et dimid. virg. Inde Rex habet de terra Alberici Comitis 24 hid.; Episcopus Walchelinus 15 hid.; Aldredus frater Odonis 8 hid.; Gislebertus de Bretevilla 8 hid.; Milo Crispinus 6 hid.; Aluredus de Merleberge 3 hid.; Odinus camerarius 6 hid.; Aluric parvus dimid. hid.; Uluricus 1 virg.; Alnotus dimid. virg.

Raginaldus Canutus de terra Milonis retinuit geldum dimid. hid.; Alduinus et frater ejus retinuerunt geldum dimid. hid. et dimid. virg. quas tenent de Aluredo; Uluricus 1 virg. quam tenet de Rege; Wadardus retinuit geldum 1 hid.; et pro 91 hid. et 3 virg. et dimid. sunt redditæ Regi 27 lib. et 10 sol. et 6 denar.

In the hundred of BLACHEGRAVE are 165 hides and half a virgate. Of these the King and Barons have in demesne 71 hides and half a virgate. Of these the King has of the land of Earl Alberic 24 hides; Bishop Walchelin 15 hides; Aldred, the brother of Odo, 8 hides; Gilbert de Breteville, 8 hides; Milo Crispin 6 hides; Alured of Marlborough 3 hides; Odin, the chamberlain, 6 hides; Aluric 'parvus' a half hide; Uluric 1 virgate; Alnot half a virgate.

Reginald Canut retained the geld of half a hide of the land of Milo; Alduin and his brother retained the geld of half a hide and half a virgate which they hold of Alured; Uluric, of one virgate which he holds of the King; Wadard retained the geld of 1 hide; and for 91 hides and $3\frac{1}{2}$ virgates are paid to the King £27 10*s.* 6*d.*

This is now part of the Hundred of KINGSBRIDGE. It is mentioned as a distinct hundred in the Nomina Villarum (A.D. 1316), where it occurs as 'BLAKINGROVE,' though several manors originally belonging to it seem by that time to have been transferred to that of KINGSBRIDGE. The name 'BLAGROVE' still remains as the designation of two farms in the neighbourhood of LYDIARD TREGOZ.

The manors and owners referred to are conjectured to be the following:—

ELECOMF	p. 63	...	*Elcomb*	... THE KING [of the land of EARL ALBERIC].
ELENDUNE	" 19	...	*Elingdon*	... BISHOP WALCHELIN [WINCHESTER].
WERVETONE	" 136	...	*Wroughton*	... ALDRED.
BECHENHALLE	" 94	...	*Binknoll*	... GILBERT DE BRETEVILLE.
WODETONE	" 91	...	*Wootton Basset*	... MILO CRISPIN.

LEDIAR	p. 81	...	*Lydiard Tregoz*	...	ALURED OF MARLBOROUGH.
SVINDONE	„ 81	...	*Swindon*	...	
TOCHEHAM	„ 134	...	*Tockenham*	...	ALURIC 'PARVUS.'
SVINDONE	„ 140	...	*Swindon*	...	ULURIC.
WALECOTE	„ 92	...	*Walcot*	...	ALNOT.

SVINDUNE	„ 25	...	*Swindon*	...	WADARD [UNDER THE BISHOP OF BAIEUX].

12. THORNHILL HUNDRED.

In hundreto de THORNEHELLE* sunt 170 hid. De his habent Barones in dominio 66 hid. et dimid. Inde habet Rex in dominio 15 hid. de terra Haroldi; Walchelinus Episcopus 9 hid.; Abbas Glastingeberiensis 9 hid. et dimid.; Abbas Wincestriensis 14 hid.; Stephanus 1 hid.; Abbatissa Sancti Edwardi 18 hid.; et pro 63 hid. et 3 virg. redditæ sunt Regi 19 lib. et 2 sol. et 4 denar. Collectores geldi retinuerunt 15 sol. et 2 denar.

De 27 hid. quas tenent villani de terra Haroldi non habet Rex suum geldum. Prepositus Abbatis Glastingeberiensis retinuit geldum de 3 hid. et dimid.;† prefectus Abbatissæ Sancti Edwardi retinuit geldum de 6 hid.;† prefectus Abbatis Rualon‡ retinuit geldum 3 hid.†

* Tornhylle. B. Torenhella. C.

† In *MS.* A. there is added to each of these entries—"quæ erant terræ villanorum ea die qua Rex Edwardus fuit vivus et mortuus"—*i.e.*, on the day when King Edward died.

In the hundred of THORNHILL are 170 hides. Of these the Barons have 66½ hides in demesne. Of these the King has 15 hides in demesne of the land of Harold; Bishop Walchelin 9 hides; the Abbot of Glastonbury 9½ hides; the Abbot of Winchester 14 hides; Stephen 1 hide; the Abbess of St. Edward 18 hides; and for 63 hides and 3 virgates are paid to the King £19 2*s.* 4*d.* The collectors of the geld retained 15 shillings and 2 pence.

From 27 hides which the King's villans hold of the land of Harold, the King has not his proper geld. The bailiff of the Abbot of Glastonbury retained the geld from 3½ hides; the bailiff of the Abbess of St. Edward retained the geld from 6 hides; the bailiff of the Abbot of Rualon‡ retained the geld of 3 hides.

‡ This is a designation of the Abbot of St. PETER'S, WINCHESTER, or, as it was afterwards called, HYDE ABBEY. See *p.* 39, *note.*

This ancient Hundred, like that of BLACHEGRAVE, is now part of the Hundred of KINGSBRIDGE. It remained as a separate hundred at least till A.D. 1316, for it occurs as such, not only in the Hundred Rolls, but in the Nomina Villarum.

The manors alluded to above appear to be the following:—

WEMBERGE	p. 20	...	*Wanborough*	...	BISHOP WALCHELIN [WINCHESTER].
BADEBERIE	„ 31	...	*Badbury*	...	ABBOT OF GLASTONBURY.
CHISELDENE	„ 41	...	*Chiselden*	...	ABBOT OF ST. PETER'S, WINCHESTER.

ARDESCOTE	p. 130	...	*Erdescote (now Earlscourt)* ...	STEPHEN [THE CARPENTER].
LEDENTONE	,, 44	...	*Liddington* ...	ABBESS OF SHAFTESBURY.

13. SELKLEY HUNDRED.

In hundreto de SELCHELAI sunt 197 hid. dimid. virg. minus. De his habent Barones in dominio 94 hid. et 3 virg. et dimid. Rex habet de terra Wigodi 18 hid.; Milo Crispin 6 hid.; Harding 3 hid.; Stephanus carpentarius 3 hid. et dimid.; Hunfridus 8 hid.; Alueredus 6 hid. et 3 virg.; Radulfus 3 hid.; Durandus vicecomes 1 hid. et dimid.; Robertus [de Braiosa] 2 hid.* [quas tenet de Willelmo de Braiosa]; Walchelinus Episcopus 8 hid. et dimid. virg.; Abbatissa de Wiltonia 7 hid.; Abbatissa de Wincestra 1 hid. et dimid.; Abbas de Glastingeberia 9 hid.; Gislebertus Gifard 2 hid. et dimid. et dimid. virg.* [quas tenet de Abbate Glastingeberiensi]; Abbatissa Ambresberiensis 3 hid.; Hunfridus de Insula 4 hid. et 1 virg.; Robertus filius Roulfi 5 hid.; Gislebertus de Bretevilla 7 hid. et 1 virg.; Edwardus† vicecomes dimid. hid. [quam tenet predecessor ejus ad gablam]; et pro 97 hid. dimid. virg. minus redditæ sunt Regi 29 lib. et.16 denar.

* To each of these entries *MS.* C. adds 'retinuit geldum.'

† In *MS.* C. we have it, 'Tainus quidam Edwardi vicecomitis retinuit geldum dimid. hid.'

In the hundred of SELKLEY are 197 hides, all but half a virgate. Of these the Barons have in demesne 94 hides and 3½ virgates. The King has of the land of Wigod 18 hides; Milo Crispin 6 hides; Harding 3 hides; Stephen the carpenter 3½ hides; Humfrey 8 hides; Alured 6 hides and 3 virgates; Radulf 3 hides; Durand the Sheriff 1 hide and a half; Robert de Braiose 2 hides, which he holds of William de Braiose; Bishop Walchelin 8 hides and half a virgate; the Abbess of Wilton 7 hides; the Abbess of Winchester 1 hide and a half; the Abbot of Glastonbury 9 hides; Gilbert Gifard 2½ hides and half a virgate, which he holds of the Abbot of Glastonbury; the Abbess of Ambresbury 3 hides; Humfrey de L'Isle 4 hides and 1 virgate; Robert Fitz-Rolf 5 hides; Gilbert de Breteville 7 hides and 1 virgate; Edward the Sheriff half a hide, which his predecessor holds at a rent; and for 97 hides all but half a virgate there are paid to the King £29 1*s.* 4*d.*

The Hundred of SELKLEY would seem to be of the same extent now as in ancient times. In the Hundred Rolls II., 256, 263, a number of details are given concerning the estates and their owners, in the time both of Henry III., and of Edward I.

It is not quite easy to identify all the manors above alluded to. In the case of two or three they have been supplied from conjecture.

ALDEBORNE	p. 11	...	*Aldbourn* ...	THE KING.
OCHEBORNE	,, 15	...	*Ogbourn* ...	
OCHEBURNE	,, 93	...	*Ogbourn* ...	MILO CRISPIN.
OCHEBURNE	,, 139	...	*Ogbourn* ...	HARDING.
[Manor not named]	,, 130	...	...	STEPHEN, THE CARPENTER.

POLTONE	*p* 89	...	*Polton*	...	HUMFREY [DE L'ISLE].
ROCHELIE	„ 82	...	*Rockley*	...	ALURED [OF MARLBOROUGH].
CLATFORD	„ 110	...	*Clatford*	...	RADULPH [DE MORTEMER].
LOCHERIGE	„ 97	...	*Lockeridge*	...	DURAND, THE SHERIFF [OF GLOUCESTER].
ESSAGE	„ 102	...	*Shaw*	...	ROBERT DE BRAIOSE [OF WILLIAM DE BRAIOSE].
OVRETONE	„ 20	...	*Overton*	...	BISHOP WALCHELIN [WINCHESTER].
OVRETONE	„ 47	...	*Overton*	...	ABBESS OF WILTON.
CHENETE	„ 121	...	*Kennet*	...	ABBESS OF WINCHESTER.
WINTREBORNE	„ 31	...	*Winterbourn Monkton*	...	ABBOT OF GLASTONBURY.
WINTREBORNE	„ 31	...	*Winterbourn Monkton*	...	GILBERT GIFARD, under the ABBOT OF GLASTONBURY.
WINTREBURNE	„ 54	...	*Robson (in Winterbourn Basset)*		ABBESS OF AMBRESBURY.
WINTREBURNE	„ 89	...	*Winterbourn Basset*	...	HUMFREY DE L'ISLE.
MORDONE?	„ 113	...	*Moredon*	...	ROBERT FITZ-ROLF.
HENTONE	„ 95	...	*Broad Hinton*	...	GILBERT DE BRETEVILLE.
ROCHELIE?	„ 71	...	*Rockley*	...	EDWARD THE SHERIFF [OF SALISBURY].

14. RAMSBURY HUNDRED.

In hundreto de RAMESBERIA sunt 90 hid. De his habet Osmundus Episcopus 30 hid. in dominio, et pro 60 hid. redditæ sunt Regi 18 libr.

In the hundred of RAMSBURY are 90 hides. Of these, Bishop Osmund has 30 hides in demesne, and for 60 hides are paid to the King £18.

This is described in the Hundred Rolls II., 231, as a "free Hundred belonging to the church at Sarum, in virtue of an ancient grant by King Offa." The seat of the first Bishopric established for Wiltshire was at RAMSBURY. The name was originally "*hræfenes-byrig*," *i.e.* Ravens-bury,—hence its Bishops styled themselves "Episcopi *Corvinensis* Ecclesiæ."

The manor of RAMSBURY, which was co-extensive with the Hundred, included BISHOPSTON,—BAYDON,—and AXFORD.

RAMESBERIE	*p.* 23	...	*Ramsbury*	...	BISHOP OSMUND [OF SARUM].

15. BRADFORD HUNDRED.

In hundreto de BRADEFORD sunt 99 hid. Ex his habent Barones 24 hid. et dimid. virg. in dominio. Inde habet Abbatissa Sancti Edwardi 14 hid.; Hunfridus 4 hid. et dimid. ; Sawardus 2 hid. et dimid. et dimid. virg.; Ulf dimid. hid.; Osmundus Latimarus 3 virg. et dimid.; Ascerus 1 hid. et dimid. virg. Rex habet dimid. hid. vastatæ terræ, et pro 73 hid. et 3 virg. et dimid. redditæ sunt Regi 22 libr. et 9 sol. et 1 denar.

In the hundred of BRADFORD are 99 hides. Of these the Barons have 24 hides and half a virgate in demesne. Of these the Abbess of St. Edward has 14 hides; Humphrey 14½ hides; Saward 2½ hides and half a virgate; Ulf half a hide; Osmund Latimar 3½ virgates; Ascer 1 hide and half a virgate. The King has half a hide of waste land, and for 73 hides and 3½ virgates are paid to the King £22 9*s.* 1*d.*

It would appear probable that CHALDFIELD, now in this Hundred, was originally in that of MELKSHAM, see below, *p.* 171. Moreover, WESTWOOD,—now, as part of the possessions of the monastery of St. Swithin, Winchester, transferred to the ragged Hundred of ELSTUB—was originally part of that of BRADFORD. With these exceptions, the Hundred of BRADFORD would seem anciently to have been of the same extent as now. The Manor and Hundred were granted to the Abbess of Shaftesbury by King Ethelred, A.D. 1001, and they continued to be held by that religious house till the dissolution of monasteries in the time of Henry VIII.

The manors and owners alluded to in the above summary are the following :—

BRADEFORD	*p.* 43	...	*Bradford*	...	ABBESS OF ST. EDWARD [SHAFTESBURY].
BROCTONE	„ 85	...	*Broughton Gifford*	...	HUMFREY [DE L'ISLE].
BROCTUNE	„ 143	...	*Broughton Parva (Monkton)*...		SAWARD.
BODEBERIE	„ 139	...	*Budbury*	...	ULF.
PONBERIE	„ 130	...	*Pomeroy*	...	OSMUND [LATIMAR].
BERRELEGE	„ 134	...	*Berlegh*	...	ASCER [AZOR].

---

16. MELKSHAM HUNDRED.

In hundreto de MELCHESAM sunt 86 hid. et 13 carucatæ nunquam geldantes de terra Haroldi. Has habet Rex in dominio. De predictis hidis habent Barones in dominio 32 hid. et dimid. virg. Inde habet Rex de terra Haroldi 9 hid. in dominio ; Brictricus 8 hid. et dimid.; Aluricus 2 hid. ; Liesman 2 hid.; Ernulfus de Hesding 1 hid. et 3 virg.; Willelmus Corniola

In the hundred of MELKSHAM are 86 hides and 13 carucates paying no geld of the land of Harold. These the King has in demesne. Of the aforesaid hides the Barons have in demesne 32 hides and half a virgate. Of these the King has of the land of Harold 9 hides in demesne; Brictric 8 hides and a half; Aluric 2 hides; Liesman 2 hides; Ernulf de Hesding 1 hide and

3 hid. et 3 virg.; Ansgerus 4 hid. et 1 virg.; Eldild vidua 1 hid. et 1 virg. et dimid.; et pro 15 hid. et dimid. virg. sunt redditæ Regi in constitutis terminis 4 libr. et 11 sol.

3 virgates; William Corniole 3 hides and 3 virgates; Ansger 4 hides and 1 virgate; Eldild, a widow, 1 hide and 1 virgate and a half; and for 15 hides and a half virgate are paid to the King in the appointed terms £4 11*s*.

Odo Culus-lupi* et Godvinus retinuerunt geldum dimid. hid.;† villani Regis retinuerunt geldum de 38 hid. de terra Haroldi.

Odo Cul-de-lou and Godwin retained the geld of half a hide; the King's villans retained the geld of 38 hides of the land of Harold.

* Cul-de-lou. A. B. No such name as that of Odo Cul-de-lou is recorded among the holders of land in the Great Domesday. The reference would seem, in all probability, to be, to the land at HILPERTON held by Eldild. *p.* 143.

† In MS. A. is added,—"modo recuperaverunt Walterus et socii ejus 3 sol. de terra Odonis Cul-de-lou, scilicet 1 virg., et de terra Godvini alia virg."

This Hundred, in addition to what is now contained in it, comprised also, it is conjectured, the manor of CHALDFIELD. See above, *p.* 170. In other respects it is of the same extent now as in olden times.

The manors and owners referred to in the above summary would seem to be the following:—

MELCHESHAM	*p.* 12	*Melksham*	THE KING, of the land of EARL HAROLD.
TROLE	" 131	*Trowle*	BRICTRIC.
STRABURG	" 131	*Trowbridge (?)*	BRICTRIC.
STAVRETONE	" 132	*Staverton*	BRICTRIC.
WADONE	" 133	*Whaddon*	ALURIC [OF MELKSHAM].
MELCHESHAM	" 142	*Melksham*	LISEMAN.
CALDEFELLE (?)	" 75	*Chaldfield*	ERNULF DE HESDING.
HELPRINTONE	" 129	*Hilperton*	ANSGER.
HELPRINTONE	" 129	*Hilperton*	WILLIAM CORNIOLE.
HELPERINTONE	" 143	*Hilperton*	ELDILD.
HELPERITUNE	" 137	*Hilperton*	GODWIN [CLEC].

---

17. CALNE HUNDRED.

In hundreto de CALNA sunt 91 hid. De his habent Barones in dominio 26 hid. et dimid. et 2 partes 1 virg. Inde habet Rex de terra Reginæ Edithæ in Brumham 10 hid. in dominio; Edwardus vice-comes 5 hid.; Abbatissa de Wiltona 1 hid.; Ricardus Puignant 2 hid. et dimid.; Aluredus de Ispania 3 hid. et 3 virg.; uxor Edrici 1 hid. et 1 virg.; Gunfridus maledoctus

In the hundred of CALNE are 91 hides. Of these the Barons have in demesne 26½ hides and two parts of 1 virgate. Of these the King has, of the land of Queen Editha in Bromham, 10 hides in demesne; Edward the Sheriff 5 hides; the Abbess of Wilton 1 hide; Richard Puignant 2½ hides; Alured of Spain 3 hides and 3 virgates; the wife of Edric 1 hide and 1 virgate; Gunfrid

2 hid. et* 2 partes 1 virg.; Nigellus presbyter 1 hid.; et pro 50 hid. et 3 virg. et† tertia parte 1 virg. redditæ sunt Regi 15 libr. et 5 sol. De 10 hid. quas tenent villani Regi de terra Haroldi non habet Rex geldum. Collectores geldi de Cepeham receperunt [21 sol.] in hoc hundreto geldum de 3 hid. et dimid. [quæ adjacent hundreto de Calna] et hoc retinuerunt.

* 7 acras. A.B. † 3 acris. A.B.

Maldoith 2 hides and 2 parts of 1 virgate; Nigel a priest 1 hide; and for 50 hides and 3 virgates and the third part of 1 virgate are paid to the King £15 5*s.* From 10 hides, which the King's villans hold of the land of Harold, the King has no geld. The collectors of the geld for Chippenham received 21 shillings in this hundred as geld for $3\frac{1}{2}$ hides which are adjacent to the hundred of Calne, and this they retained.

The Hundred of CALNE would seem to be of the same extent as formerly with the exception of BROMHAM, which is now in the hundred of POTTERNE and CANNINGS.

What is the manor alluded to in the above entry, as possessed by the Abbess of Wilton, has not been ascertained. None of those so held, according to the Great Domesday (see *pp.* 45, 51), appear to have been in this Hundred. The rest, together with their respective owners, would appear to be the following:—

BROMHAM	*p.* 13	*Bromham*	THE KING, of the land of QUEEN EDITHA.*
EDINTONE	„ 65	*Heddington*	EDWARD, THE SHERIFF [OF SALISBURY].
CALESTONE	„ 125	*Calston*	RICHARD PUIGNANT.
ETESBERIE	„ 122	*Yatesbury*	ALURED OF SPAIN.
CALESTONE	„ 75	*Calston*	THE WIFE OF EDRIC [under ERNULF DE HESDING].
CALESTONE	„ 121	*Calston*	GUNFRID MALDOITH.
CAUNA, CHURCH OF	„ 7	*Lands belonging to the Church of Calne*	NIGEL, A PRIEST.

---

* In the Exchequer Domesday it is spoken of as the land of 'Earl Harold,' *p.* 13.

18. WHERWELSDOWN HUNDRED.

In hundreto de WERVESDONE sunt 78 hid. De his habent Barones in dominio 21 hid. et dimid. et dimid. virg. Inde habet Abbatissa de Rumeseio 11 hid.; Ernulfus de Hesding 6 hid. et 1 virg.; Brictricus 3 hid. et dimid. et dimid. virg.; Herveius de Wiltona 3 virg. et 1 acram; et pro 56 hid. et 1 virg. et dimid. redditæ sunt Regi 16 libr. et 18 sol. et 3 denar.

In the hundred of WHERWELSDOWN are 78 hides. Of these the Barons have $21\frac{1}{2}$ hides and half a virgate in demesne. Of these, the Abbess of Romsey has 11 hides; Ernulf de Hesding 6 hides and 1 virgate; Brictric $3\frac{1}{2}$ hides and half a virgate; Hervey of Wilton 3 virgates and 1 acre; and for 56 hides and 1 virgate and a half are paid to the King £16 18*s.* 3*d.*

This corresponds with the present hundred of WHERWELSDOWN. As far as we can judge, its limits have remained unaltered from very early times. The Lordship of the Hundred was bestowed on the Abbess of Romsey by King Edgar. The manors and owners alluded to are the following:—

EDENDONE	p. 52	...	*Edington*	...	ABBESS OF ROMSEY.
AISTONE	,, 53	...	*Steeple Ashton*		
CHIVELE	,, 74	...	*Keevil*	...	ERNULF DE HESDING.
COVELESTONE	,, 131	...	*East Coulston*	...	BRICTRIC.
EDENDONE	,, 144	...	*Edington*	...	HERVEY OF WILTON.

19. CANNINGS HUNDRED.

In hundreto de CANINGA* sunt 70 hid. Inde habet Osmundus Episcopus 10 hid. in dominio, et pro 60 hid. redditæ sunt Regi 18 libr.

* Canenge. A.

In the hundred of CANNINGS are 70 hides. Of these, Bishop Osmund has 10 hides in demesne, and for 60 hides there are paid to the King £18.

The Hundred of CANNINGS belonged to the Bishops of Sarum. In the Hundred Rolls (II. 231) it is described as a "free hundred of the Bishop of Sarum, appertaining to the Church of Sarum from an ancient grant." It comprised the present parish of Bishop's CANNINGS, including SOUTH BROOM,—RYNDWEY (Roundway),—and COTES. HYWEY (Highway) was afterwards included in this hundred (Nom. Vill.), that manor having been ceded to the Bishops of Sarum by the Abbots of Malmesbury. See Jackson's Aubrey, *p.* 60.

CAININGHAM	p. 22	...	*Bishop's Cannings*	...	BISHOP OSMUND [OF SARUM].

20. RUGEBERG HUNDRED.

In hundreto de RUGEBERGA sunt 96 hid. et 3 virg. et dimid. De his habent Barones 22 hid. in dominio. Inde habet Rex 5 hid. in dominio; Osmundus Episcopus 10 hid. in dominio; Robertus Blondus 1 hid.; Robertus Marescal 7 hid.; et pro 60 hid. et 3 virg. et dimid. redditæ sunt Regi 18 libr. et 5 sol. et 4 denar.

Willelmus de Aldeleia retinuit geldum 1 hid. et dimid. quas Robertus Blondus dedit sibi de dominio suo cum filia. Robertus de Albamarla retinuit geldum 2 hid. et dimid. quas Robertus Blondus dedit sibi de dominio suo cum filia. Et villani Regis retinuerunt geldum 5 hid. de terra Tostig.*

* De terra Haroldi. B.

In the hundred of RUGEBERG are 96 hides and 3½ virgates. Of these the Barons have 22 hides in demesne. Of these the King has 5 hides in demesne; Bishop Osmund 10 hides in demesne; Robert Blond 1 hide; Robert Marescal 7 hides; and for 60 hides and 3½ virgates are paid to the King £18 5*s.* 4*d.*

William de Aldeleia retained the geld of 1 hide and a half which Robert Blond gave him from his demesne with his daughter. Robert de Albemarle retained the geld of 2 hides and a half which Robert Blond gave him from his demesne with his daughter. And the King's villans retained the geld of 5 hides from the land of Tostig.

This ancient Hundred, the name of which, RUGE-BERG, means the "*rough*," or hoar, "*barrow*," is now divided between those of POTTERNE, CANNINGS, and SWANBOROUGH. At the commencement of the 14th century there were two hundreds of this name, one called "RUGEBERG REGIS," and the other "RUGEBERG EPISCOPI." See Hund. R. II., 231, and Jackson's Aubrey, *p.* 308.

The manors alluded to, with their respective owners, appear to be the following :—

THEODULVESIDE	*p.* 10	...	*Tilshead*	...	THE KING.
POTERNE	" 21	...	*Pottern*	...	BISHOP OSMUND [OF SARUM.]
LAVENTONE	" 126	...	*West Lavington*	...	ROBERT BLOND.
LAVENTONE	" 126	...	*East Lavington*	...	ROBERT MARESCAL.

21. STODFALD HUNDRED.

In hundreto de STODFALDA sunt 93 hid. et 1 virg. De his habent Barones in dominio 41 hid. et 3 virg. et dimid. Inde habet Abbatissa Wintoniæ* 10 hid. et dimid.; Hunfridus 4 hid.; Edwardus vicecomes 2 hid. et 3 virg. et dimid.; Estrit 1 hid. et dimid.; Aluredus de Merlberg 8 hid. et dimid.; Durandus de Glowecestra 7 hid. et dimid.; Comes Moritonii 7 hid.; et pro 51 hid. et 1 virg. redditæ sunt Regi 15 libr. et 7 sol. et 7 denar.

Tres Taini Edwardi vice-comitis [qui tenent ad gablam 1 hid. et dimid. et qui prius tenuerunt] retinuerunt geldum.

* Wiltoniæ, C., but this must evidently be a mistake of the scribe.
† Estrild. C.

In the hundred of STODFALD are 93 hides and 1 virgate. Of these the Barons have in demesne 41 hides and 3½ virgates. Of these, the Abbess of Winchester has 10½ hides; Humfrey 4 hides; Edward, the Sheriff, 2 hides and 3½ virgates; Estrit 1 hide and a half; Alured of Marlborough 8½ hides; Durand of Gloucester 7½ hides; the Earl Morton 7 hides; and for 51 hides and 1 virgate are paid to the King £15 7*s.* 7*d.*

Three Thanes of Edward the Sheriff, who hold at a rent 1 hide and a half, and who formerly held the land, retained the geld of the same.

The Hundred of STODFALD is now included in that of SWANBOROUGH. The name is from the Anglo-Saxon *Stód-fald*, and means simply the "*fold*," or place, for horses. The estates alluded to, and their respective owners, would seem to be the following :—

JERCHESFONTE	*p.* 51	...	*Erchfont* }	...	ABBESS OF ST. MARY, WINCHESTER.
CANINGE	" 52	...	*All-Cannings* }	...	
STERTE	" 85	...	*Stert*	...	HUMFREY [DE L'ISLE].
ECESATINGETONE	" 65	...	*Etchilhampton (spelt sometimes Ashlington, or Ashelton)*	...	EDWARD THE SHERIFF [OF SALISBURY].
ECESATINGETONE	" 75	...	*Etchilhampton*	...	ESTRIT [? THE WIFE OF EDRIC].
ADELINGTONE	" 79	...	*Allington*	...	ALURED OF MARLBOROUGH.
CERITONE	" 96	...	*Chirton*	...	DURAND OF GLOUCESTER.
COWIC	" 57	...	*Conock*	...	EARL MORTON.

22. SWANBOROUGH HUNDRED.

In hundreto de SWANEBERGA sunt 183 hid. et 1 virg. et dimid. De his habent Barones 70 hid. et 1 virg. et dimid. Inde habet Rex [de terra Comitis Haroldi] 25 hid. et 3 virg. in dominio; Edwardus vice-comes 7 hid.; Gosfridus Episcopus 4 hid.; Episcopus Wintoniensis 6 hid.; Abbas de Wincestra* 5 hid. et dimid. virg.; Abbatissa Wiltoniæ 13 hid.; Walterus de Rivera 5 hid. [quas Hugo dedit filiæ suæ]; Grimboldus 4 hid. et dimid.; et pro 83 hid. et 3 virg. redditæ sunt Regi 25 libr. et 2 sol. et 9 denar. De 29 hid. et 1 virg. de terra Haroldi quas tenent villani Regis non habet Rex geldum.

* Wintoniensis. A.

In the hundred of SWANBOROUGH are 183 hides and 1 virgate and a half. Of these the Barons have 70 hides and 1 virgate and a half. The King has of them of the land of Earl Harold 25 hides and 3 virgates in demesne; Edward the Sheriff has 7 hides; Bishop Geoffrey 4 hides; the Bishop of Winchester 6 hides; the Abbot of Winchester 5 hides and half a virgate; the Abbess of Wilton 13 hides; Walter de Rivera 5 hides which Hugo gave to his daughter; Grimbold 4½ hides; and for 83 hides and 3 virgates are paid to the King £25 2*s.* 9*d.* From 29 hides and 1 virgate of the land of Harold, which the King's villans hold, the King has no geld.

The original Hundred of SWANBOROUGH comprised only the eastern portion of what is now included in it. Dr. Ingram conjectured that the name was a corruption of '*Sand-beorg*,' that is literally '*Sand-hill*,' from a large tumulus bearing that name, and which is alluded to in an Anglo-Saxon charter relating to North Newnton. Cod. Dipl., 1109.

The manors referred to above, and their respective owners, would appear to be the following:—

RUSTESELVE	p. 10	...	*Rushall*	... THE KING, of the land of HAROLD.
AULTONE	„ 65	...	*Alton Berners*	... EDWARD THE SHERIFF [OF SALISBURY].
WILCOTE	„ 65	...	*Wilcot*	
DRAICOTE	„ 26	...	*Draycot*	... GEOFFREY, BISHOP OF COUTANCE.
AWLTONE	„ 18	...	*Alton Priors*	... BISHOP OF WINCHESTER.
MANEFORDE	„ 39	...	*Manningford Abbas*	... ABBOT OF ST. PETER'S, WINCHESTER.
STANTONE	„ 45	...	*Stanton Bernard*	... ABBESS OF WILTON.
NEWETONE	„ 45	...	*North Newnton*	
MERESDENE	„ 121	...	*Marden*	... WALTER DE RIVERA, Son-in-law of HUGO [FITZ-BALDRIC].
MANIFORD	„ 136	...	*Manningford (Bohun?)*	... GRIMBOLD.

23. WESTBURY HUNDRED.

In hundreto de WESTBERIA sunt 40 hid. et 7 carucatæ nunquam geldantes; has habet Rex in doninio ; et Willelmus Scuet * [de his habet] 2 hid. et dimid. in dominio; et pro 2 hid. redditi sunt Regi 12 sol.; et pro 35 hid. et dimid. quas tenent villani Regis de terra Reginæ Edithæ non habet Rex geldum.

* Escuet. A.

In the hundred of WESTBURY are 40 hides and 7 carucates paying no geld; these the King has in demesne ; and William Scuet has of these 2½ hides in demesne and for 2 hides are paid to the King 12 shillings; and for 35½ hides which the King's villans hold of the land of Queen Editha the King has no geld.

The Hundred of WESTBURY would seem to be the same extent now as formerly, and to be co-extensive with the Manor which included BRATTON, DILTON, and LEIGH. The manors alluded to, and their owners, are the following :—

WESTBERIE	p. 13	...	*Westbury*	...	THE KING, OF THE LAND OF QUEEN EDITHA.
WESTBERIE	„ 147	...	*Westbury*	...	WILLIAM SCUET [SCUDET].

---

24. WARMINSTER HUNDRED.

In hundreto de WARMINSTER sunt 89 hid. et dimid. De his habent Barones in dominio 30 hid. et 1 virg. Inde habet Abbatissa de Sancto Edwardo 7 hid. et 3 virg.; Rogerus de Curcello 5 hid. et dimid.; Aluredus de Merleberg 6 hid.; Edwardus vice-comes 4 hid.; Nigellus medicus 2 hid.; Willelmus filius Widonis 4 hid.; Albericus 1 hid.; Sanctus Stephanus de Fonteneio 2 hid. quas tenet adhuc Alricus* predecessor ejus; et pro 56 hid. redditæ sunt Regi 16 libr. et 16 sol.

[Hic est inventa 1 hida quæ non reddidit geldum postquam Willelmus Rex habuit regnum; eam tenent Ansfridus et Rainboldus. A.]

* In *MS.* C. this entry is thus given,—"Alricus prepositus S. Stephani de Fonteneio retinuit geldum de 2 hidis."

In the hundred of WARMINSTER are 89½ hides. Of these the Barons have in demesne 30 hides and 1 virgate. Of these the Abbess of St. Edward has 7 hides and 3 virgates; Roger de Curcelle 5½ hides; Alured of Marlborough 6 hides; Edward the sheriff 4 hides; Nigel the physician 2 hides; William Fitz-Widon 4 hides; Alberic 1 hide; The Abbey of St. Stephen of Fontenay 2 hides which Alric the previous tenant still holds; and for 56 hides are paid to the King £16 16*s*.

Here was found 1 hide which has not paid geld since King William had the kingdom; Ansfrid and Rainbold hold it.

The Hundred of WARMINSTER would appear to be of the same extent now as in olden times, even to the including of certain manors, such as DINTON, and FISHERTON DELAMERE, which are locally situated in other hundreds.

The manors alluded to, and their respective owners, are the following :—

DOMNITONE	p. 44	...	*Dinton*	...	ABBESS OF ST. EDWARD [SHAFTESBURY.]
FISERTONE	„ 114	...	*Fisherton Delamere*	...	ROGER DE CORCELLE.
NORTONE	„ 82	...	*Norton Bavent*	...	ALURED OF MARLBOROUGH.
BISCOPESTREU	„ 70	...	*Bishopstrow*	...	EDWARD THE SHERIFF [OF SALISBURY].
SUDTONE	„ 124	...	*Sutton*	...	NIGEL, THE PHYSICIAN.
SUTONE	„ 107	...	*Sutton*	...	WILLIAM FITZ-WIDON.
SMALEBROC	„ 149	...	*Smallbrook*	...	ALBERIC [THE CHAMBERLAIN.]
MIDELTONE	„ 117	...	*Middleton*	...	ABBEY OF ST. STEPHEN OF FONTENAY.
OPETONE	„ 78	...	*Upton Scudamore*	...	RAINBOLD AND ANSFRID.
OPETONE	„ 102	...			

25. HEYTESBURY HUNDRED.

In hundreto de HESTREDEBERIA* sunt 137 hid. et dimid. De his habent Barones Regis 52 hid. in dominio. Edwardus vice-comes habet 17 hid. et dimid. et dimid. virg.; Osbernus Gifard 5 hid. [et de dimid. hid. Ailsi prefectus ejus retenuit geldum, et pro hac dimid. hid. vadiavit Regi 3 sol.]; Rainburgis 3 hid. et dimid.; Hunfridus 3 hid. et dimid.; Walerannus 3 hid. et dimid.; Giraldus 6 hid. et 1 virg. et dimid.; Alwardus Culling 2 hid.; Levit 2 hid.; Abbas de Glastingeberia 5 hid.; Ecclesia Beccensis [per monachum qui custodit villam] retinuit geldum de 10 hid. quæ datæ fuerunt pro anima Reginæ; Abbatissa de Romeseia 1 hid. et dimid.; Gunduinus 2 hid. 4 acris minus, et de his 4 acris debet geldum [et vadiavit Waltero 5 denar.]; et pro 74 hid. redditæ sunt Regi 21 libr. et 13 sol. et 8 denar. Quatuor collectores geldi retinuerunt 10 sol. et 4 denar. quos recuperaverunt Walterus et socii ejus; et super 1

* Extredeberie. A.

In the hundred of HEYTESBURY are 137½ hides. Of these the King's Barons have 52 hides in demesne. Edward the sheriff has 17½ hides and half a virgate; Osbern Gifard 5 hides, and of half a hide Ailsi his bailiff retained the geld, and for this half hide gave security to the King for 3 shillings; Rainburgis 3½ hides; Humfrey 3½ hides; Waleran 3½ hides; Girald 6 hides and 1 virgate and a half; Alward Culling 2 hides; Levit 2 hides; the Abbot of Glastonbury 5 hides; the church of Bec by the monk who has custody of the manor, retained the geld of 10 hides which were given for the soul of the Queen; the Abbess of Romsey 1 hide and a half; Gunduin 2 hides all but 4 acres, and for these 4 acres he owes geld, and gave security to Walter for 5 pence: and for 74 hides are paid to the King £21 13s. 8d. The four collectors of the geld retained 10 shillings and 4 pence which Walter and his colleagues recovered; and for one

hid. quam invenerunt homines hundreti, de qua tenent Vrso dimid. virg., Ricardus, homo Osmundi, dimid. virg., Durandus dimid. virg., Albericus dimid. virg., Edgarus dimid. hid., debent habere predicti 6 sol.†

† In *MS. C.* the names of the five holders are given with the simple addition, "retinuerunt geldum 1 hid." The details of the last clause are given from *MS. A.*

hide which the men of the hundred discovere[d], of which Urso holds half a virgate, Richar[d] the tenant of Osmund, half a virgate, Duran[d] half a virgate, Alberic half a virgate, Edga[r] half a hide, the aforesaid collectors ought to hav[e] 6 shillings.

With the exception of the transfer of the manor of LONGBRIDGE DEVEREL to the Hundred of SOUTH DAMERHAM, as part of th[e] possessions of the Abbot of Glastonbury (*p.* 28, note), the Hundred of HEYTESBURY would appear to be of the same extent now a[s] formerly. Of the manors alluded to above, two, of small extent, cannot be satisfactorily accounted for by any entry in the Excheque[r] Domesday. The others are probably as follows :—

CHETRE	*p.* 69	...	*Chittern*	EDWARD THE SHERIFF [OF SALISBURY.]
CHETRE	,, 69	...	*Chittern*	
BOIENTONE	,, 69	...	*Boyton*	
ORCESTONE	,, 116	...	*Orcheston St. George*	OSBERN GIFARD.
COTEFORD	,, 117	...	*Ashton Giffard, in Codford St. Peter*	
DEVREL	,, 117	...	*Hill Deverel*	
[ESTATE NOT NAMED]	,, 144	...		RAINBURGIS.
WILI	,, 88	...	*Great & Little Bathampton on Wyly.*	HUMFREY DE L'ISLE.
WILRENONE	,, 89			
COTEFORD	,, 104	...	*Codford St. Mary*	WALERAN, THE HUNTSMAN.
UPTONE	,, 55	...	*Upton Lovel*	GIRALD [OF WILTON].
CUNUCHE	,, 133	...	*Knook*	ALWARD CULLING.
CUNUCHE	,, 142	...	*Knook*	LEVIT [LEVIET].
DEVREL	,, 30	...	*Longbridge Deverel*	ABBOT OF GLASTONBURY.
DEVREL	,, 55	...	*Brixton Deverel*	CHURCH OF S. MARY AT BEC.
WITECLIVE	,, 149	...	*White-Cleeve*	GUNDUIN.
DEVREL	,, 78	...	*Hill Deverel*	URSO.
HORNINGHAM	,, 84	...	*Horningsham*	RICHARD [HOMO OSMUNDI].
DEVREL	,, 149	...	*Hill Deverel*	ALBERIC [THE CHAMBERLAIN].
DEVREL	,, 138	...	*Hill Deverel*	EDGAR.

26. ELSTUB HUNDRED.

In hundreto de AILESTEBBA* sunt 73 hid., et 8 carucatæ nunquam geldantes; has habet Rex in dominio. De predictis hidis habent Barones in dominio 16 hid. Inde habet Episcopus Wintoniensis 10 hid. in dominio; Nigellus medicus 4 hid. et dimid.; Herveius de Wiltona 1 hid. et dimid.; et pro 37 hid. redditæ sunt Regi 11 libr. et 2 sol.; et pro 20 hid. de terra Haroldi quas tenent villani non habet Rex geldum.

* Alestabe. A. Eilestebba. B.

In the hundred of ELSTUB are 73 hides, and 8 carucates paying no geld; these the King has in demesne. Of the aforesaid hides the Barons have 16 hides in demesne. Of them the Bishop of Winchester has 10 hides in demesne; Nigel the physician 4½ hides; Hervey, of Wilton, 1 hide and a half; and for 37 hides are paid to the King £11 2s., and for 20 hides of the land of Harold which the villans hold the King has no geld.

There is a separate entry in the Exon Domesday for the manor of COLLINGBOURN DUCIS, which now belongs to this Hundred (though in the Hundred Rolls ii. 259, 'COLINGEBURN' and 'EVERLEY' are named under that of KINWARDSTONE), and which is as follows:—

In COLINGEBURNA de terra Haroldi sunt 14 hid., et 10 carucatæ nunquam geldantes; has habet Rex in dominio, et pro his 14 hid. quas tenent villani non habet Rex geldum.

In COLLINGBOURN of the land of Harold are 14 hides, and 10 carucates never paying geld; these the King has in demesne, and for these 14 hides which the villans hold the King has not any geld.

The corresponding Hundred to the one above described is now called that of ELSTUB and EVERLEY. It is of larger extent now than formerly, inasmuch as within that of ELSTUB are included a number of manors from various parts of Wilts belonging formerly to the Priory of St. Swithin, at Winchester; such, for example, as ALTON PRIORS,—STOCKTON,—WESTWOOD,—HAM,—OVERTON. The word 'Elstub' is still retained as the name of a field in the parish of Enford. It means literally the "stump or stowl of the elder" (A.S. *Ellen-stub*), which is of most frequent occurrence in the recital of ancient boundaries. The following are the manors and owners alluded to in the entry above:—

NIGRAVRE	p. 14	...	*Nether-Avon*	...	THE KING, of the land of HAROLD.
ENEDFORDE	„ 20	...	*Enford*	...	BISHOP OF WINCHESTER.
CHESIGEBERIE	„ 123	...	*Chisenbury de La Folye*	...	NIGEL, the PHYSICIAN.
NIGRAVRA	„ 144	...	*Nether-Avon*	...	HERVEY OF WILTON.
COLINGEBURNE	„ 14	...	*Collingbourn Ducis*	...	THE KING, of the land of HAROLD.

27. KINWARDSTONE HUNDRED.

In hundreto de CHENEWARESTAN* sunt 196 hid. et 1 virg. De his habent Rex et Barones 48 hid. et 3 virg. in dominio. Inde habet Rex in dominio de terra Reginæ Edithæ 13 hid. et 1 virg.; Walchelinus Episcopus 5 hid. et dimid.; Abbas Wintoniensis 16 hid. et 1 virg.; Goda 1 hid. et dimid.; Edricus dimid. hid.; Turoldus 2 hid. et 1 virg.; Turbertus 1 hid.; Radulfus de Halvilla 3 hid. et dimid.; Henricus de Ferrariis 1 hid.; Robertus filius Radulfi 1 hid. et 1 virg.; Uluricus venator 1 hid.; Ricardus Estormit 1 hid. et 3 virg.

Radulfus de Halvilla retinuit geldum de 1 hid. quam tenet quidam Anglus de eo; Hugo grandis retinuit geldum de 1 hid. et dimid. virg.; Willelmus filius Hugonis retinuit geldum dimid. hid. vastatæ terræ; et de 16 hid. et dimid. de terræ Regina Edithæ, quas tenet villani, Rex non habet geldum; et pro 128 hid. et dimid. redditæ sunt Regi 37 libr. et 12 sol. et 6 denar.

* *MS.* A. has no account of this Hundred.

In the hundred of KINWARDSTONE are 196 hides and 1 virgate. Of these the King and the Barons have 48 hides and 3 virgates in demesne. Of these the King has in demesne of the land of Queen Editha 13 hides and 1 virgate; Bishop Walchelin 5½ hides; the Abbot of Winchester 16 hides and 1 virgate; Goda 1 hide and a half; Edric half a hide; Turold 2 hides and 1 virgate; Turbert 1 hide; Radulf de Halville 3½ hides; Henry de Ferieres 1 hide; Robert Fitz-Rolf 1 hide and 1 virgate; Uluric the huntsman 1 hide; Richard Sturmid 1 hide and 3 virgates.

Radulf de Halville retained the geld of 1 hide which a certain Englishman holds of him; Hugo 'grandis' retained the geld of 1 hide and half a virgate; William, son of Hugo, retained the geld of half a hide of waste land; and from 16½ hides of the land of Queen Editha, which the villans hold, the King has no geld; and for 128½ hides are paid to the King £37 12*s.* 6*d.*

The Hundred of KINWARDSTONE, with the exception of one or two manors transferred to that of ELSTUB and EVERLEY, would appear to be of the same extent now as formerly. It was the largest of all the Wiltshire Hundreds. Many of the manors were of small extent. It is not easy to say precisely what manors are alluded to in every case in the above summary. The subjoined list is conjectured to be correct, as far as it goes, of the various holders, and the manors possessed by them, in this Hundred:—

OTONE	p. 13	...	*Wootton*	...	THE KING, of the Land of QUEEN EDITHA.
HAME	,, 18	...	*Ham*	...	BISHOP WALCHELIN [OF WINCHESTER].
COLEBURNE	,, 40	...	*Collingbourn Kingston*	...	ABBOT OF ST. PETER'S WINCHESTER.
PEVESIE	,, 40	...	*Pewsey*		
STOTECOME	,, 137	...	*Stitchcomb*	...	GODA.
PEVESIE	,, 137	...	*Pewsey*	...	EDRIC.
ULFELA	,, 146	...	*Wolfhall*	...	TUROLD.*
MERTONE	,, 146	...	*Marten*	...	TURBERT.

---

* In the Exchequer Domesday, TUROLD is entered only as one of the tenants in the time of the Confessor. This manor nevertheless seems clearly to be the one referred to in the Exon Domesday.

GRASTONE	*p.* 145	...	*Grafton*	...	RADULF DE HALVILLE.
MERTONE	,, 145	...	*Marten*		
BURBED	,, 146	...	*Burbage*		
ULFELA	,, 146	...	*Wolfhall*		
STANDENE	,, 108	...	*Standen Chaworth*	...	HENRY DE FERIERES.
GRASTONE	,, 145	...	*Grafton*	...	ROBERT FITZ-ROLF.
SCALDEBURNE	,, 140	...	*Shalbourn*	...	ULURIC, THE HUNTSMAN.
BUBERGE	,, 144	...	*Burbage*	...	RICHARD ESTURMY [STURMID].
GRASTONE	,, 145	...	*Grafton*		
HAREDONE	,, 145	...	*Harding*		
SALDEBORNE	,, 145	...	*Shalbourn*		
GRAFTONE	,, 100	...	*Grafton*	...	HUGO [GRANDIS ?] under WILLIAM DE OW.
SCALDEBURNE	,, 120	...	*Shalbourn*	...	WILLIAM [FITZ-HUGH.]

28. MERE HUNDRED.

In hundredo de MERA sunt 86 hid. et dimid. et 1 virg. Inde habent Barones in dominio 34 hid. et dimid. et dimid. virg. De his habet Rex in Chenuuel 17 hid. et dimid. in dominio. Abbas de Glastingeberia 5 hid. Abbatissa de Wiltona 4 hid. et 1 virg. Walterus Gifard 4 hid. Gislebertus Maminot* 3 hid. et dimid. et dimid. virg. Godricus venator 1 virg. Et pro 51 hid. redditæ sunt Regi 15 libr. et 6 solid. Sed de his denariis non fuerunt redditi 74 solid. de Chenuuel Regis [de terra Comitis Willelmi] in nullo terminorum sed pro eo 4 collectores geldi retinuerunt 12 denar. Saulfus autem retinuit geldum de 1 hid. et 1 virg. quas tenet de Godselino de Riveria, scilicet 9 solid. et 6 denar.

* Episcopus Luxoniensis. A. [Bishop of Lisieux.]

In the hundred of MERE are 86 hides and a half and 1 virgate. Of these the Barons have in demesne 34 hides and a half, and half a virgate. Of them, the king has, in Knoyle, 17 hides and a half in demesne. The Abbot of Glastonbury 5 hides. The Abbess of Wilton 4 hides and 1 virgate. Walter Gifard 4 hides. Gilbert Maminot 3 hides and a half and half a virgate. Godric, the huntsman, one virgate. And for 51 hides are paid to the king 15 pounds and 6 shillings. But of this money there were not paid 74 shillings from Knoyle Regis, the land of Earl William, at any of the usual terms, but for it the 4 collectors of the tax retained 12 pence. Saulf, however, retained the tax of 1 hide and 1 virgate which he holds of Gozelin de Riveire, to wit, seven shillings and six pence.

The Hundred of MERE is situated in the south-west portion of Wiltshire. For some distance it forms the *boundary* of the county :—hence its name, which seems to be derived from the word *ge-mære* (a boundary), so constantly employed in Anglo-Saxon charters in describing the land-limits of estates. Several places were formerly included in this Hundred which were subsequently transferred to others. The estates alluded to in the summary given above would seem to be the following :—

CHENVEL	p. 15	...	*East Knoyle*	...	THE KING.
DEVREL	„ 34	...	*Monkton Deverel*	...	ABBOT OF GLASTONBURY.
CHENVEL	„ 47	...	*West Knoyle*	...	ABBESS OF WILTON.
BRADELIE	„ 98	...	*Maiden Bradley*	...	WALTER GIFARD.
DEVREL	„ 56	...	*Kingston Deverel*	...	BISHOP OF LISIEUX.
MERA	„ 137	...	*Mere*	...	GODRIC, THE HUNTSMAN.
SELE	„ 128	...	*Zeals*	...	GOZELIN RIVEIRE.

29. DUNWORTH HUNDRED.

In hundreto de DONWORTH* sunt 121 hid. De his habent Barones in dominio 38 hid. Abbatissa Sancti Edwardi habet inde 17 hid.; Walchelinus episcopus 5 hid.; Aluereduus 4 hid. et dimid.; Aldredus 2 hid. et dimid.; Abbatissa Wiltoniæ 8 hid.; Berengerus Cotel 1 hid.; et pro 83 hid. redditæ sunt Regi 24 libr. et 18 sol.

De his collectores retinuerunt 27 solidos; istorum, 6 solidos recuperaverunt Walterus et socii ejus.

* Donoworde. A. Doneworda. C.

In the hundred of DUNWORTH are 121 hides. Of these the Barons have 38 hides in demesne. The Abbess of St. Edward has of them 17 hides; Bishop Walchelin 5 hides; Alured 4½ hides; Aldred 2½ hides; the Abbess of Wilton 8 hides; Berenger Cotel 1 hide; and for 83 hides are paid to the King £24 18*s*.

Of these the collectors retained 27 shillings; of these Walter and his assistants recovered 6 shillings.

With the exception of the transfer of Fonthill Episcopi to the Hundred of DOWNTON, this Hundred of DUNWORTH would appear to be of the same extent now as formerly. The estates alluded to, and their respective owners, are as follows:—

TISSEBERIE	p. 42	...	*Tisbury*	...	ABBESS OF ST. EDWARD [SHAFTESBURY].
DUNEHEVE	„ 43	...	*Donhead*		
FONTEL	„ 17	...	*Fonthill Episcopi*	...	BISHOP WALCHELIN [OF WINCHESTER].
TEFONTE	„ 80	...	*Teffont Evias*	...	ALURED OF MARLBOROUGH.
ANESTIGE	„ 136	...	*Anstey*	...	ALDRED.
CHILMERC	„ 46	...	*Chilmark*	...	ABBESS OF WILTON.
FONTEL	„ 115	...	*Fonthill Giffard*	...	BERENGER COTEL.*

* In the Exchequer Domesday this name is given as BERENGER *GIFARD* for there can be no doubt of 'FONTEL' being the manor alluded to in the above summary.

30. DOLE HUNDRED.

In hundreto de DOLESFELD sunt 70 hid. dimid. virg. minus, et 3 carucatæ nunquam geldantes de terra Reginæ Edithæ. Has habet Rex in dominio. De predictis hid. habent Barones in dominio 35 hid. et 1 virg. et dimid. Inde habet Edwardus vice-comes 7 hid. in dominio; Osbernus Gifard 14 hid. et 1 virg.; Abbatissa Wiltoniensis 3 hid.; Mattheus de Moretania 2 hid. et dimid.; Cudulfus 5 hid. et dimid. et dimid. virg.; Abbas Wintoniensis 1 hid.; Robertus Marescal 1 hid. et 3 virg. et dimid.; et pro 32 hid. et 1 virg. et 1 acra redditæ sunt Regi 9 libr. et 13 sol. et 7 denar. Sed de his denariis non fuerunt redditi 10 solidi, qui primo termino debuerunt reddi, usque ad ultimum terminum. Prefectus Regis de Winterburnestoca retinuit geldum de 2 hid. et 1 virg.

In the hundred of DOLE are 70 hides all but half a virgate, and 3 carucates which pay no geld of the land of Queen Editha. These the King has in demesne. Of the aforesaid hides the Barons have in demesne 35 hides and 1 virgate and a half. Edward the Sheriff has 7 hides in demesne; Osbern Gifard 14 hides and 1 virgate; the Abbess of Wilton 3 hides; Matthew of Moretania 2 hides and a half; Cudulf 5 hides and a half, and half a virgate; the Abbot of Winchester 1 hide; Robert Marescal 1 hide and 3 virgates and a half; and for 32 hides and 1 virgate and 1 acre, are paid to the King £9 13*s.* 7*d.* But of this money, 10 shillings, which ought to have been paid at the first term of payment, were not accounted for till the last. The King's bailiff of Winterbourn Stoke retained the geld from 2 hides and one virgate.

It is by no means easy to identify several of the manors referred to in the above summary, in consequence of their being described under the generic word 'WINTERBOURN,' a name properly attributable to several districts in Wilts (this being the most extensive of them), in which the "*Winter-bourns,*" *i.e., streams,* rise. Where no modern name is given, the reader will find the best interpretation that can be suggested in the alphabetical list of names in a subsequent part of this volume. With regard to the manor said to be held by the "Abbess of Wilton," no conjecture can be offered. None of those entered in the Exchequer Domesday (*pp.* 45—51) answer to the description. It may be either an illustration of what we have noticed in a previous page, of the change of ownership that would seem to have taken place between the dates of the completion of the two records respectively, or may be a mistake of the scribe for the 'Abbess of *Ambresbury.*' Certainly some land in what is now called MADDINGTON, in this Hundred, belonged from early times to that religious house.

WINTREBURNE	*p.* 14	*Winterbourn Stoke*	THE KING, of the land of QUEEN EDITHA.
WINTREBURNE	„ 67	*Shrewton*	EDWARD OF SALISBURY.
WINTREBURNE	„ 116	} *Elston, in Orcheston St. George*	} OSBERN GIFARD.
WINTREBURNE	„ 116		
ORCHESTON	„ 117		
WINTREBURNE	„ 128		MATTHEW* OF MORETANIA.

---

* *Maci* de Moretainia, *p.* 128.

WINTREBURNE	„ 136	...		... CUDULF.
WINTREBURNE	„ 41	...	*Rolleston*	... ABBOT OF ST. PETER'S, WINCHESTER.
GARE	„ 126	...	*Gore*	... ROBERT MARESCAL.

31. BRANCHE HUNDRED.

In hundreto de BRENCESBERGE sunt 108 hid. et dimid. De his habent Barones in dominio 35 hid. et 3 acras. Inde habet Osbernus Gifard 9 hid.; Walchelinus episcopus 3 hid. et dimid; Abbatissa Wiltoniensis 10 hid. et 3 virg.; Waleranus 5 hid.; Comes Moritonii 4 hid. et 1 virg. et 3 acras; Sueinus 2 hid. et dimid.; et pro 71 hid. et 1 virg. et 2 partibus 1 virg. redditæ sunt Regi 21 libr. et 8 sol. et 6 denar. De his retinuerunt collectores 12 denar. Robertus Dispensator retinuit geldum de 2 hid. dimid. virg. minus.

In the hundred of BRANCHE are 108½ hides. Of these the Barons have in demesne 35 hides and 3 acres. Of these Osbern Gifard has 9 hides; Bishop Walchelin 3½ hides; the Abbess of Wilton 10 hides and 3 virgates; Waleran 5 hides; the Earl Morton 4 hides, and 1 virgate, and 3 acres; Svain 2½ hides; and for 71 hides and 1 virgate and 2 parts of 1 virgate, are paid to the King £21 8*s.* 6*d.* Of those the collectors retained 12 pence. Robert 'Dispensator' retained the geld of 2 hides all but half a virgate.

This Hundred, together with the one just described, constitutes now the united Hundred of BRANCHE and DOLE. In Sir R. C. Hoare's Heytesb. Hundr., *p.* 234, it is stated, though on what authority we are not told, that the original name of Sherrington was "Brenchesborow." No doubt the Hundred, the present appellation of which is a contracted form, was called from some '*beorg*,' *i.e.*, "*barrow*" or "tumulus" of sufficient size or traditional importance to assign its name to it.

The manors alluded to, and their respective owners, are the following:—

SCARENTONE	*p.* 118	...	*Sherrington*	... OSBERN GIFARD.
SCARENTONE	„ 118	...	*Sherrington*	
STOTTUNE	„ 21	...	*Stockton*	... BISHOP WALCHELIN [OF WINCHESTER].
NEWENTONE	„ 48	...	*South Newton*	... ABBESS OF WILTON.
WILGI	„ 48	...	*Wyly*	
WICHEFORD	„ 48	...	*Wishford*	
OCHEFORDE	„ 49	...	*Ugford*	
LANGEFORD	„ 105	...	*Steeple Langford*	... WALERAN, THE HUNTSMAN.
LANGEFORD	„ 58	...	*Hanging Langford*	... EARL MORTON.
STAPLEFORD	„ 143	...	*Stapleford*	... SVAIN.
DECHEMENTONE	„ 25	...	*Ditchhampton*	... ROBERT, DISPENSATOR.

32. AMBRESBURY HUNDRED.

In hundrcto de AMBRESBERIA sunt 127 hid. et dimid. De his habent Barones in dominio 42 hid. et dimid. virg. Inde habet Aluredus 6 hid.; Turoldus 2 hid.; Johannes hostiarius 2 hid. et dimid.; Abbatissa de Ambresberia 12 hid. et 3 virg.; Ricardus, de terra quæ fuit Alberici, 6 hid.; Harding 7 hid. et dimid.; Croc 3 virg.; Robertus filius Geroldi dimid. hid.; Herveius 1 hid. et dimid.; Comes Moritonensis 2 hid.; Edwardus vice-comes 2 virg. et dimid.; et pro 78 hid. et dimid. redditæ sunt Regi 23 libr. et 11 sol.

Taini Ernulfi de Hesding [qui prius eas tenuerunt] retinuerunt geldum 3 hid. et 4 acrarum. Cudulfus [de terra Roberti filii Giroldi quam ipse Cudulfus prius tenuit] retinuit geldum dimid. virg. Odo [homo Baiocensis Episcopi] retinuit geldum de 3 hid. et 3 virg.

In the hundred of AMBRESBURY are 127½ hides. Of these the Barons have in demesne 42 hides and half a virgate. Of these Alured has 6 hides; Turold 2 hides; John, the door-keeper, 2½ hides; the Abbess of Ambresbury 12 hides and 3 virgates; Richard, of the land which belonged to Earl Alberic, 6 hides; Harding 7½ hides; Croc 3 virgates; Robert Fitz-Girold half a hide; Hervey 1 hide and a half; the Earl Morton 2 hides; Edward the sheriff 2½ virgates; and for 78½ hides are paid to the King £23 11s.

The Thanes of Ernulf de Hesding, who formerly held the lands, retained the geld of 3 hides and 4 acres. Cudulf of the land of Robert Fitz-Girold which Cudulf himself formerly held, retained the geld of half a virgate. Odo, the tenant of the Bishop of Baieux, retained the geld of 3 hides and 3 virgates.

The Hundred of AMBRESBURY would appear to be of the same extent now as formerly. The manors and their respective owners alluded to in the above summary are probably the following:—

NEWENTONE	p. 80	...	*Newton Tony*	... ALURED OF MARLBOROUGH.
MILDESTONE	„ 59	...	*Milston*	... TUROLD, under the EARL ROGER.
ELTONE	„ 147	...	*Alton*	... JOHN, the Door-Keeper.
ALLENTONE	„ 54	...	*Allington*	... ABBESS OF AMBRESBURY.
BOSCUMB	„ 54	...	*Boscombe*	
BOLTINTONE	„ 53	...	*Bullford*	
CHELSTANESTONE	„ 54	...	*Cholston*	
WINTRESLIE	„ 62	...	*Winterslow*	... RICHARD, of the land which belonged to EARL ALBERIC.
CONTONE	„ 61	...	*Compton*	
DERINTONE	„ 61	...	*Durrington*	
FISGLEDENE	„ 139	...	*Figheldean*	... HARDING.
ALBOLDINTONE	„ 62	...	*Ablington*	
TODEWRDE	„ 146	...	*Tidworth*	... CROC.
MILDESTONE	„ 112	...	*Milston*	... ROBERT FITZ-GIROLD.
BEDESDENE	„ 112	...	*Biddesden*	

ROTEFELDE	p. 146	...	*Ratfyn*	...	HERVEY.
NECHENDONE	„ 57	...		...	EARL MORTON.
TODEWORDE	„ 67	...	*Tidworth*	...	EDWARD, THE SHERIFF [OF SALISBURY].
LITLEGARSELE	„ 67	...	*Ludgarshall*		
CELDRINTONE	„ 76–77	...	*Cholderton*	...	THANES OF ERNULF DE HESDING.
SCAGE	„ 113	...	*Shaw*	...	CUDULF, of land belonging to Robert Fitz-Girold.
TODEWORDE	„ 24	...	*Tidworth*	...	ODO, under the Bishop Baieux.

33. STANFORD HUNDRED.

In hundreto de STANFORD* sunt 105 hid. De his habent Barones in dominio 19 hid. et dimid. Inde habet Abbatissa Wiltoniensis 10 hid.; Ricardus Puignant 5 hid. et 3 virg; Aiulfus 3 hid. et 3 virg.; et pro 85 hid. et dimid. redditæ sunt Ręgi 25 libr. et 13 sol. Collectores retinuerunt 10 solidos.†

* Stafort. B. Staford. C.

† *MS.* A. adds, "et modo redditi sunt."

In the hundred of STANFORD are 105 hides. Of these the Barons have in demesne 19½ hides. Of them the Abbess of Wilton has 10 hides; Richard Puignant 5 hides and 3 virgates; Aiulf 3 hides and 3 virgates; and for 85½ hides are paid to the King £25 13*s*. The collectors retained 10 shillings.

This Hundred is now called by the name of CHALK. Its original designation was derived from the A.S. *Stán-ford, i.e.*, the 'paved' or '*stone-ford*' over the stream called the 'Ebele,' whence we have the name 'Eblesbourn,' now contracted into 'Ebbesbourn.' There is still the name 'STOW-FORD' given to a little place close by Fifield Bavent. In the Abbrev. Placit, *p.* 19, this Hundred is named as that of 'STAFFORD.' In the Inq. p. m. of 36 Edw. III., under the manors of Roger Bavent, is mentioned, "Chalke apud *Stonforth* Hundred."

The manors alluded to above, are the following:—

CHELCHE	p. 47	...	*Chalk*	...	ABBESS OF WILTON.
TROI	„ 125	...	*Trow*	...	RICHARD PUIGNANT.
TOLLARD	„ 123	...	*Tollard*	...	AIULF, the Sheriff.

34. CAWDON HUNDRED.

In hundreto de CAWADONE* sunt 59 hid. et 3 carucatæ; has habet Rex in dominio. De predictis hidis habent Barones in dominio 34 hid.

* Cauduna. C.

In the hundred of CAWDON are 59 hides, and 3 carucates, these the King has in demesne. Of the aforesaid hides the Barons have in

et dimid. Rex inde habet de terra Haroldi 12 hid. et de terra Alberici 9 hid. et dimid.; Brictricus 6 hid.; Osbernus presbyter 2 hid. et dimid.; Ulviet 3 hid.; Uluricus venator et cognatus ejus 1 hid. et dimid.; et pro 13 hid. redditæ sunt Regi 3 libr. et 18 sol.; et pro 11 hid. et dimid. de terra Haroldi quas villani Regis tenent non habet Rex geldum.

demesne 34½ hides. Of these, of the land of Harold, the King has 12 hides, and of the land of Alberic 9½ hides; Brictric 6 hides; Osbern the priest 2½ hides; Ulviet 3 hides; Uluric the huntsman and his kinsman 1 hide and a half; and for 13 hides are paid to the King £3 18*s.*; and for 11½ hides of the land of Harold, which the King's villans hold, the King has no geld.

This Hundred, together with the one next described, constitutes now the united Hundred of CAWDON and CADWORTH. The manors alluded to above, and their respective owners, would appear to be the following:—

BRETFORD	*p.* 9	...	*Britford*	...	THE KING.
CUMBE	„ 12	...	*Combe Bisset*	...	THE KING, of the land of HAROLD.
STRADFORD	„ 63	...	*Stratford Tony*	...	THE KING, of the land of EARL ALBERIC.
ODESTOCHE	„ 132	...	*Odstock*	...	BRICTRIC.
HUMITONE	„ 125	...	*Homington*	...	OSBERN, the Priest.
LANGEFORD	„ 141	...	*Longford*	...	ULVIET.
BREDFORD	„ 140	...	*Britford*	...	ULURIC, the Huntsman.

---

35. CADWORTH HUNDRED.

In hundreto de CADEWORDA* sunt 45 hid. et dimid. Inde habent Barones in dominio 13 hid. et dimid. Inde habet Abbatissa de Wiltona 11 hid.; Hunfridus de Insula 2 hid.; Johannes hostiarius dimid. hid.; et pro 32 hid. redditæ sunt Regi 9 libr. et 12 sol., 2 denar. minus. Collectores geldi retinuerunt 4 denarios.

* Cadeworde. A. Cadworde. B.

In the hundred of CADWORTH are 45½ hides. Of these the Barons have in demesne 13½ hides. Of them, the Abbess of Wilton has 11 hides; Humfrey de L'Isle 2 hides; John the door-keeper half a hide; and for 32 hides are paid to the King £9 12*s.*, all but 2 pence. The collectors of the geld retained 4 pence.

This Hundred is now united with the one just described. The manors, with their respective owners, referred to in the above summary, appear to be as follows:—

BREDECUMBE	*p.* 49	...	*Burcombe*	...	ABBESS OF WILTON.
BABESTOCHE	„ 49	...	*Baverstock*		
WAISEL	„ 49	...			
FEBEFONTE	„ 50	...	*Fovant*		
HARDICOTE	„ 90	...	*Hurcot*	...	HUMFREY DE L'ISLE.
BEREFORD	„ 147	...	*Barford*	...	JOHN, the door-keeper.

36. DAMERHAM HUNDRED.

In hundreto de DOMERHAM* sunt 63 hid. De his habent Barones in dominio 18 hid. Rex habet inde de terra Haroldi 2 hid.; Abbas de Glastingeberia 16 hid.; et pro 14 hid. 4 acris minus redditæ sunt Regi 4 libr. et 3 sol. et 8 denar. De terra Abbatis de 18 hid. non habet Rex geldum. De terra Serlonis de Burci [de terra Abbatis] de 5 hid. non habet Rex geldum. De 8 hid.† quas tenent villani Regis non habet Rex geldum.

In the hundred of DAMERHAM are 63 hides. Of these the Barons have in demesne 10 hides. The King has of them of the land of Harold 2 hides; the Abbot of Glastonbury 16 hides; and for 14 hides, all but 4 acres, are paid to the King £4 3*s.* 8*d.* From the land of the Abbot, from 18 hides, the King has no geld. From the land of Serlo de Burci, of the land of the Abbot, from 5 hides, the King has no geld. From 8 hides which the King's villans hold the King has no geld.

* Damreham. A. Domraham. B.

† These *eight* hides are no doubt part of CONTONE, the whole of which estate was assessed at *ten* hides, *two* of them being held by the king, as above stated, in demesne. See above, *p.* 10.

This Hundred corresponds with that of SOUTH DAMERHAM. A distinct Hundred, called that of NORTH DAMERHAM was formed of the estates in North Wilts belonging to the Abbey of Glastonbury. See above, *p.* 28, note. It would appear that from very early times COMPTON, though not locally situated within its proper limits, was nevertheless included in this Hundred.

The estates and owners alluded to are the following:—

CONTONE	*p.*	10	...	*Compton Chamberlain*	...	THE KING, of the land of HAROLD.
DOBREHAM	,,	28	...	*Damerham*	...	ABBOT OF GLASTONBURY.
DOBREHAM	,,	29	...	*Part of Damerham*	...	SERLO DE BURCI, under the ABBOT OF GLASTONBURY.

---

37. UNDERDITCH HUNDRED.

In hundreto de WINDREDIC sunt 70 hid. De his habet Osmundus Sarisberiensis episcopus 10 hid. in dominio; et pro 60 hid. redditæ sunt Regi 18 libr. et 6 denar.

In the hundred of UNDERDITCH are 70 hides. Of these Osmund, Bishop of Sarum, has 10 hides in demesne; and for 60 hides are paid to the King £18 0*s.* 6*d.*

The name of this Hundred is derived from one of those ancient '*dykes*,' of which there are several near the southern borders of the county. In old documents we meet with it as WONDRE-DIC and WONDER-DIC. In the Nom. Vill. it is WONDER-DYCH. It embraces OLD SARUM,—WILSFORD,—LAKE,—WOODFORD,—and STRATFORD. The manor alluded to is the following, which must have included some of the others just named:—

SARISBERIE	*p.*	23	...	*Sarum*	...	OSMUND, Bishop of Sarum

38. FRUSTFIELD HUNDRED.

In hundreto de FERSTESFELD sunt 11 hid. et dimid. virg. De his habent Barones in dominio 4 hid. et 1 virg. Inde habet Hunfridus de Insula 2 hid.; Ricardus Estormid 1 hid.; Otre 1 hid.; Aldret 1 virg.; et pro 7 hid. dimid. virg. minus habet Rex 41 sol. et 2 denar. Collectores hujus geldi retinuerunt 1 denar.*

* *MS.* A. adds,—"Illi qui collegerunt geldum reddiderunt modo denar. 1 qui remanserat."

In the hundred of FRUSTFIELD are 11 hides and half a virgate. Of these the Barons have in demesne 4 hides and 1 virgate. Of these Humfrey de L'Isle has 2 hides; Richard Estormid 1 hide; Otre 1 hide; Aldret 1 virgate; and for 7 hides all but half a virgate the King has 41 shillings and 2 pence. The collectors of this geld retained 1 penny.

This was the smallest in extent of all the Wiltshire Hundreds, and would seem now to be confined within the same limits as in olden time. The manors, and their respective owners referred to above, are the following:—

FISTESFERIE	*p.* 90	...	*Welpley*	...	HUMFREY DE L'ISLE.
CUVLESTONE	„ 127	...	*Coulesfield Esturmy*	...	HENRY ESTORMID [STURMID].
LANGEFORD	„ 143	...	*Landford*	...	OTRE [OTHO].
FERSTESFELD	„ 135	...	*Aldreston*	...	ALDRET [ALDRED].

---

39. ALDERBURY HUNDRED.

In hundreto de ALWAREBERIA* sunt 65 hid. et 1 virg. et dimid. Inde habent Barones in dominio 29 hid. et 3 virg. et dimid. Abbas de Glastingeberia 5 hid. et 1 virg. et dimid.; Edwardus vice-comes 3 hid. [de his sunt 2 hid. in foresta Regis]; Gosfridus Episcopus 1 hid. et dimid.; Uluric 1 hid.; Godescal 2 hid. et dimid. virg.; Aldret 1 hid. et dimid. virg.; Saricus 1 hid. et dimid. virg.; Suainus 1 virg.; Ulviet dimid. hid.; Comes Moritonii 3 hid.; Edwardus† presbyter 3 hid.; Edgiva 2 hid.; Walerannus 2 hid. et 1 virg. et dimid.; Cola 1 hid.; Goscelinus 1 virg.; Godemannus 1 virg.; Nigellus dimid.

In the hundred of ALDERBURY are 65 hides and 1 virgate and a half. Of these the Barons have in demesne 29 hides and 3½ virgates. The Abbot of Glastonbury has 5 hides and 1 virgate and a half; Edward the Sheriff 3 hides, of these, 2 hides are in the King's forest; Bishop Geoffrey 1 hide and a half; Uluric 1 hide; Godescal 2 hides and half a virgate; Aldret 1 hide and half a virgate; Saric 1 hide and half a virgate; Svain 1 virgate; Ulviet half a hide; Earl Morton 3 hides; Edward the priest 3 hides; Edgiva 2 hides; Waleran 2 hides and 1 virgate and a half; Cola 1 hide; Goscelin 1 virgate; Godeman

* Alwartberie. A.

† This is possibly an error of the scribe's for "*Al*-wardus presbyter," and the manor alluded to the one held in ALWARBERIE, *p.* 56. Among the Ministri Regis' one by name 'EDWARD' possessed land in "ALWARBERIE," *p.* 149, but it was in extent only *one virgate*, and he is not described as '*presbyter*.'

virg.; Edit 3 virg. et dimid.; Osbernus* 1 hid.; et pro 35 hid. et dimid. redditæ sunt Regi 10 libr. et 14 sol.

* Osbertus. C.

1 virgate; Nigel half a virgate; Edith 3½ virgates; Osbern 1 hide; and for 35½ hides are paid to the King £10 14*s*.

The Hundred of ALDERBURY—the more usual form of the name is ALWARD-BURY—is probably of the same extent now as formerly. There is some difficulty in identifying a few of the manors alluded to in the above summary, partly from some being described under the generic term 'WINTREBURNE' (as in DOLE Hundred), and partly from the circumstance that several of the owners of the smaller holdings are not named in the Exchequer Domesday as possessing property in this Hundred. Of the rest, the following would appear to be a correct list of manors and their respective owners:—

EUNESTETONE	p. 33	...	*Idmeston*	...	ABBOT OF GLASTONBURY.
WINTREBURNE	„ 33	...	*Gomeldon (?)*		
WINTREBURNE	„ 73	...	*Winterbourn Earls*	...	EDWARD, THE SHERIFF [OF SALISBURY].
WINTREBURNE	„ 27	...		...	BISHOP GEOFFREY [OF COUTANCE].
PORTONE	„ 140	...	*Porton*	...	ULURIC.
WINTREBURNE	„ 128	...		...	GODESCAL.
WINTREBURNE	„ 135	...		...	ALDRET [ALDRED].
WINTREBURNE	„ 143	...		...	SARIC.
LAVERTESTOCHE	„ 143	...	*Laverstock*		
MELEFORD	„ 141	...	*Milford*	...	ULVIET.
WINTRESLEU	„ 58	...	*Winterslow*	...	EARL MORTON.
DUENE	„ 107	...	*West Dean*	...	WALERAN.
HERDICOTE	„ 107	...	*Hurcot*		
WINTREBURNE	„ 33	...			
GRAMESTEDE	„ 136	...	*East Grimstead*	...	COLA.
MELEFORD	„ 90	...	*Milford*	...	GOSCELIN [under HUMFREY DE L'ISLE.
ALWARESBERIE	„ 57	...	*Alderbury*	...	OSBERN [the Priest?].

40. DOWNTON HUNDRED.

In hundreto de DUNTONE sunt 97 hid. Inde habent Barones in dominio 31 hid. et dimid. Walchelinus Episcopus inde habet 30 hid.;* Walerannus dimid. hid.; Willelmus de Faleise dimid. hid.; Ragenild dimid. hid.; et pro 63 hid. et dimid. redditæ sunt Regi 19 libr. et 15 denar.;

In the hundred of DOWNTON are 97 hides. Of these the Barons have in demesne 31½ hides. Bishop Walchelin has of them 30 hides; Waleran half a hide; William de Faleise half a hide; Ragenild half a hide; and for 63½ hides are paid to the King, £19 1*s*. 3*d*.; but of these, 9 pence

* *MS.* A. adds, "Et 2 hid. de quibus homines ibi manentes ibi fugati sunt propter forestam Regis."

sed de his denariis 9 non fuerunt redditi usque nunc de 1 virg. terræ Waleranni.* Duo hidæ de terra Walchelini Episcopi sunt ibi wastæ propter forestam Regis.

have not been paid to the present time from 1 virgate of Waleran's land. Two hides of the land of Bishop Walchelin are waste on account of the King's forest.

* *MS.* A. has it thus, "Sed de his denariis redditi sunt modo 9 qui erant retenti de 1 virg. terræ Waleranni."

The Hundred of DOWNTON comprised at the first the large estate of 100 hides granted originally by Cœnwealha, King of Wessex, A.D. 688, to the Church of St. Peter and Paul, Winchester. It included EBLESBOURN, now called BISHOPSTON. In the course of the 14th century, EAST KNOYLE, and FONTHILL EPISCOPI, estates also belonging to the Bishop of Winchester, were added to this Hundred. The manors alluded to in the above summary would seem to be the following. With reference to the one last-named it is conjectured that possibly the 'ENGENOLD' of the Exchequer Domesday may be intended for the 'RAGENILD' mentioned above.

DUNTONE	*p.* 17	...	*Downton*	...	BISHOP OF WINCHESTER.
STANINGES	,, 105	...	*Stanlinch*	...	WALERAN.
STANINGES	,, 103	...	*Stanlinch*	...	WILLIAM DE FALEISE.
BEREFORD	,, 106	...	*Barford*	...	RAGENILD [ENGENOLD ?] under WALERAN.

ANALYSIS

OF THE

DOMESDAY FOR WILTSHIRE.

ABBREVIATIONS.

Arch. Journ. ...	Journal of the Archæological Institute.
Arch. Assoc. Journ...	Journal of the British Archæological Association.
Abbr. Plac. ...	Abbreviatio Placitorum (Rich. I.—Edw. II).
Aubrey ...	Aubrey's Collections, edited and enlarged by Canon Jackson.
Cod. Dipl. ...	Kemble's 'Codex Diplomaticus,' or collection of Anglo-Saxon charters.
Hund. R. ...	Rotuli Hundredorum (or Hundred Rolls), *temp.* Hen. III. and Edw. I.
Inq. Non. ...	Nonarum Inquisitiones, A.D. 1340.
Inq. p. m. ...	Calendar of 'Inquisitiones post mortem.'
Mon. Hist. Brit. ...	Monumenta Historica Britannica.
N. Mon. ...	The new edition of the 'Monasticon Anglicanum.'
Not. Mon. ...	Tanner's 'Notitia Monastica.'
Nom. Vill. ...	'Nomina Villarum,' or Names of the Lords of Manors in Wilts, A.D. 1316 (Harl. MS. 6281, *p.* 231).
Tax. Eccl. ...	'Taxatio Ecclesiastica' of Pope Nicholas, c. 1292.
Test. de Nev. ...	Testa de Nevill, or 'Liber Feodorum,' *temp.* Hen. III. and Edw. I.
T.R.E. ...	Tempore Regis Edwardi, *i.e.*, in the time of King Edward the Confessor.
T.R.W. ...	Tempore Regis Willelmi, *i.e.*, in the time of King William.
Wilts. Mag. ...	Magazine of Wiltshire Archæological Society.
Wilts. Inst. ...	Wiltshire Institutions, or List of Incumbents instituted to benefices from A.D. 1297 downwards, printed privately by Sir Thomas Phillipps.

Where the name of a HUNDRED with a number following it is given, as *e.g.*, HEYTESBURY 32, it refers to the page in the account of that Hundred in Sir R. C. Hoare's "History of Modern Wiltshire."

ANALYSIS.

NAME.	T. R. E. Owner, or Tenant.	T. R. W. Tenant in Capite.	T. R. W. Under-Tenant.	MODERN NAME, &c.
ADELINGTONE p. 79	Carlo	ALURED of Marlborough.	Miles,—2 hides	*ALLINGTON*, now in the hundred of Swanborough, but originally in that of Stodfald. It is reckoned as a tithing of All-Cannings. Robert Tregoz (p. 79, *note*) held land at "Kainges (=Cannings) and Alington," c. 1270, Test. de Nev. 137. John Tregoz held the manor, as of the barony of Ewyas, in 1278 (Hundr. R. II. 273), and died siesed of it in 1304. Inq. p. m. 28 Edw. I.
ADHELMERTONE p. 100	Alestan of Boscumbe.	WILLIAM DE OW	Radulf	Most probably a portion of *HELMARTON*. A reference to the Test. de Nev. 137, will shew that many of the manors possessed by William de Ow were afterwards held by the Earl Marescal. Amongst the latter was a knight's fee at "Helmarton," which was held subordinately by Radulf de Wancy, from whose family Clevancy (originally Clive-*Wancy*) which is in the parish, derives its distinctive name.
AISI and LATONE p. 56	Held by 2 Thanes as 2 manors. United into *one* manor by the Earl Harold.	REINBALD, the Priest.		*EISEY* and *LATTON* in the hundred of Cricklade. Aubrey, 153.
AISTONE p. 53	Abbess of Romsey	ABBESS OF ROMSEY.	Edward,—3 hides William,—1 hide Some Englishmen,—4 hides	*STEEPLE ASHTON*, in the hundred of Wherwelsdown, the gift of King Edgar (c. 967) to the Abbey at Romsey. This parish includes SEMINGTON, LITTLETON, HENTON, WEST ASHTON, and ROOD ASHTON. In the Edington Chartulary is an extent of the manor of "Aistone," taken, most probably, from the Chartulary of Romsey which is now lost. In Aubrey (p. 392), is an account of the principal and subordinate manors, and of their successive owners.
ALBOLDINTONE p. 62	Harding	EARL ALBERIC		From the Exon Domesday, p. 185, we may infer that this estate was in the hundred of Ambresbury. It is no doubt *ABLINGTON*, a name now applied to a farm in the parish of Figheldean. See below, under "FISGLEDENE."

NAME.	T. R. E. Owner, or Tenant.	T. R. W. Tenant in Capite.	T. R. W. Under-Tenant.	MODERN NAME, &c.
ALDEBORNE p. 11	Ghida	THE KING		*ALDBOURN*, in the hundred of Selkley. This manor afterwards parcel of the estates of the Duchy of Lancas A survey of the manor, in 1591, is given in W Mag. vi. 188. The patronage of the church has fr earliest times been vested in the Bishops of Sarum.
ALDEBORNE, Church of p. 11		THE PRIEST OF THE CHURCH		
ALDRITONE p. 111	Alric, Godwin, Algar, Godric "in paragio"	RADULF DE MORTEMER	Richard,—3 hides Walter,— 1 hide	These are different portions of *ALDERTON*, in the hund of Chippenham, but, originally, it would seem, in that Dunelawe (Dunley). Aubrey, 104. In the time Edw. I., lands, to the extent of one-third of a Knig fee, were held under Ralph de *Mortimer*, at "Audrinto and Henry de Hertham held *three hides* in the same pla under Walter de Clifford, a descendant of Drogo Fitz-P (p. 119, *note*). Test. de Nev. 150, 154. Aubrey, 47.
ALDRINTONE p. 119	Edric	DROGO FITZ-PONZ	Hugo	
ALLENTONE p. 54	Abbess of Ambresbury	ABBESS OF AMBRESBURY		A remark, under the second of these entries, to the ef that there were *four* hides in the *same vill*, which E Harold, at one time, unjustly took away from the Abb of Ambresbury (p. 63), shows that they both refer to p tions of the same estate, viz., *ALLINGTON*, in the hu dred of Ambresbury. The whole parish contains 9 acres. Ambresb. Hundr., 107.
ALENTONE p. 62	Earl Harold	EARL ALBERIC		
ALVESTONE p. 44	Abbess of Shaftesbury	ABBESS OF SHAFTESBURY		This estate is described as appurtenant to the manor Bradford. The name is now lost. It may possibly be memorial of *Alwi*, brother of Brictric, who is recorded being the tenant of the neighbouring estate of Farle (Monkton). See below, under "FARLEGE."
ALWARBERIE, Church of p. 56, 57.		CANONS OF LISIEUX (?)	Alward, a Priest, —5 hides Osbern, a Priest, —2 hides	*ALDERBURY*, which may have derived its name, most common form of which is "Alwardberie," fr *Alward*, the Priest, who held so large a portion the estate. From the way in which it is ente in the Record, it would seem to have belonged to Canons of Lisieux. The Church of "Alwardberie" v afterwards granted to the cathedral at Sarum. Alde Hundr., 3.
ALWARBERIE p. 107	Bolle	WALERAN, the huntsman	Engenulf	A small holding in *ALDERBURY*. Waleran posses lands at Watedene (Waddon), and Gramestede (Gri stead), in the immediate neighbourhood.
ALWARBERIE p. 149	Bode	EDWARD [the Priest]: as one of the King's Officers.		This would seem to be the small holding in the hundred *ALDERBURY*, which, according to the Exon Dom day, p. 190, was possessed by Edward "the Priest."
AMBLESBERIE p. 8	King Edward. [Three Thanes held lands in this manor. The Abbess of Wilton also held 2 hides which were the gift of King Edward.]	THE KING		*AMBRESBURY*, the name of a large parish, and of hundred in which it is situated. A full account of parish, which contains some 5,296 acres, will be found Ambresb. Hundr., 81.
AMBRESBERIE p. 68	Ulmer	EDWARD of Salisbury	Osmund	These two holdings, the latter of which is described as joining Ambresberie, would seem to be portions of same estate. A manor in the parish is called "Ambr bury *Earls*," and a farm to this day is designated "*Ea* Farm," memorials possibly of its ancient chief Lords, Earls of Salisbury.
AMBRESBERIE p. 68	Alric, Cole	EDWARD of Salisbury	Osmund	

NAME.	T. R. E. Owner, or Tenant.	T. R. W. Tenant in Capite.	T. R. W. Under-Tenant.	MODERN NAME, &c.
ANESTIGE p. 105	Aluric / Ulward	WALERAN, the huntsman	Walter	These two holdings are different portions of *ANSTEY*, in the hundred of Dunworth. Originally, a part of what is now called WARDOUR may have been included in the former, as Laurence St. Martin, a descendant of Waleran, held "Verdure" in 1316. Nom. Vill. Dunw. Hundr., 59, 212.
ANESTIGE p. 136	Bricnod	ALDRED, as one of the King's Thanes.		
ARDESCOTE p. 130	Odo	STEPHEN, the carpenter, as one of the King' Servants.		According to the Exon Domesday (p. 168), this was in the hundred of Thornhill. It is the *Erdescote* which belonged (35 Edw. III.) to Blount (holding under Bohun, Earl of Hereford), and afterwards to the Lovels. The name seems now to be corrupted to *EARLSCOURT*. Aubrey, 196.
.... p. 130	Achil	STEPHEN, the carpenter		The name of this holding is not given, but from the Exon Domesday (p. 168), it may be inferred that it was in the hundred of Selkley.
AULTONE p. 65		EDWARD of Salisbury		*ALTON BERNERS* [or *BARNES*], in the hundred of Swanborough. In 3 Edw. I. it was held by the Earl of Lincoln, in right, as it would seem, of his wife, Margaret Longespée, a direct descendant of Edward of Salisbury. Hund. R. II., 277. It was afterwards held by the Earls of Lancaster, one of whom married the only daughter and heiress of Henry de Lacy, Earl of Lincoln. It derives its distinctive name from John Bourchier, Lord Berners. Aubrey, 302.
AWLTONE p. 18	Bishop of Winchester	BISHOP OF WINCHESTER, "pro victu monachorum."	William Scudet, —3 hides, under the Bishop	*ALTON PRIORS*, originally in the hundred of Swanborough, afterwards, like other manors belonging to St. Swithin, Winchester, transferred to that of Elstub. The estate was given to the monastery by King Egbert, in 825. Charters, containing land-limits, are given in Cod. Dipl. 1035, 1070. The parish comprises some 2,530 acres, and is now reckoned as a chapelry of OVERTON.
AVREBERIE, Church of p. 16		RAINBOLD, a Priest		This is entered under the "King's Land." It is a *portion* of *AVEBURY*, in the hundred of Selkley, for the name, we may perhaps infer from this entry, was applied at first only to a small part of the *present* parish. The rest, amounting in all to some 15½ hides, is accounted for in the record under the entries of "CHENETE" and "BACHENTUNE." Aubrey, 325.
BABESTOCHE p. 49	Abbess of Wilton	ABBESS OF WILTON		*BAVERSTOCK*, in the hundred of Cadworth. It was given to the Abbey at Wilton, by King Edgar, in 968. Cadw. Hundr., 96.
BACHENTUNE p. 95	Edric	GILBERT DE BRETEVILE	Ansfrid	*BECKHAMPTON*, now a tithing of the parish of Avebury. There was a free chapel here, dedicated to St. Vincent, and the names of the Incumbents are given in the Wilts Institutions. It was endowed partly with lands at Stanmore. See below, under "STAMERE." Aubrey, 163.
BADEBERIE p. 31	Abbot of Glastonbury	ABBOT OF GLASTONBURY		*BADBURY*, in the parish of Chiselden. It was originally in the hundred of Thornhill (p. 167); it is now in that of Kingsbridge. The manor was given by King Edred, in 995, to Dunstan, Abbot of Glastonbury. A copy of the Charter is given in N. Mon. I. 51. Aubrey, 163.
BALLOCHELIE p. 70	Winegod	EDWARD of Salisbury	Adelelm	This is no doubt the "Baileclive" of the Test. de Nev. 138, where, as elsewhere in the same record, it is mentioned among the fees of the Earl of Sarum, and immediately after "Hulle Deverel." Its present name is *BAYCLIFFE*, the designation of a farm in the parish of Hill Deverel, and hundred of Heytesbury. The same tenant held "Devrel," under Edward of Salisbury. Heytesb. Hund., 32.

NAME.	T. R. E. Owner, or Tenant.	T. R. W. Tenant in Capite.	T. R. W. Under-Tenant.	MODERN NAME, &c.
BECHENHALLE p. 94	Hacun Toli Saul Alwin	GILBERT DE BRETEVILE		*BINKNOLL*, a tithing of the parish of Broad Hinton. was originally in the hundred of Blachsgrave (p. 166); is now in that of Kingsbridge. Matthew de Columb (p. 94, *note*) held "Bsnknoll" in 3 Edw. I. Hund R. 244. Aubrey, 167.
BECHENEHILDE p. 77	Turgot	ERNULF DE HESDING	Robert	Thess ars evidently differsnt portions of the same esta which may be what in Andrews and Dury's map of Wi is called *BIGNALL* (corrupted now into *BACON-HIL* close by Widcomb, in the parish of Helmarton. Seve of the adjoining manors belonged to Ernulf de Hesding.
BICHENEHILDE p. 76	Chetel	ERNULF DE HESDING	Robert	
BEDESDENE p. 112	Coolle	ROBERT FITZ-GIROLD		*BIDDESDEN*, in the parish of Ludgershall, and hundr of Ambresbury. It would seem from the Wilts Inst. have been the mother church of Ludgershall. Robert Fi Girold held also the neighbouring estate of "Tedords (S. Tidworth). Hants Domesd. fol. 46 b. Aubrey, 35
BEDESTONE p. 89	Aluric	HUMFREY DE L'ISLE	Turchitil	*BIDDESTON*, in the hundred of Chippenham. This esta would seem to be part of the present parish called Bi deston St. Peter's, the Rectory of which, by gift of t Dunstanvilles, descendants of Humfrey de L'Isle, belong to the Priory of Monkton Farleigh. See below, und "HEORTHAM." Wilts Mag. II., 285. Aubrey, 54.
BEDVINDE p. 7	King Edward	THE KING	Henry de Ferreres, — a grove within the manor	*BEDWIN*, in the hundred of Kinwardstone. With the e ception of sundry holdings separately accounted for—s below under ULFELA, HAREDONE, CHESEBERIE, GRA TONE, and MERTONE—this estate would seem to incl both Little and Great Bedwin. A full account of t parish, by a former vicar, will be found in the Wilts Ma VI. 260. The wood alluded to in the entry is clearly t one described (at p. 108) as at "STANDENE" (Stand Hussey).
BEDVINDE Church of p. 16	The father of Bristoard	BRISTOARD, a Priest		
BEREFORD p. 147	Aluric	JOHN "Hostiarius," as one of the King's Officers		This small holding, according to the Exon Domesday, p. 18 was in the hundred of Cadworth. It is no doubt a pa of *BARFORD ST. MARTIN*. Cadw., Hundr., 88.
BEREFORD p. 115	Earl Harold	BERENGER GIFARD		A comparison of entries in Hund. R. II. 244. and Test. d Nev. 156, leads to the conjecture that these were also po tions of *BARFORD ST. MARTIN*. There seem to ha been *three* subordinate holdings (two of them of *one car cate* each, as are these) in this estate. The whols paris comprises more than 2,000 acres.
BEREFORD p. 141	Wado	WADO, as one of the King's Thanes.		
BEREFORD p. 106	Bolle	WALERAN, the huntsman	Engenold	This is most probably *BARFORD*, in the hundred of Dow ton. Several small estates in that immediate neighbou hood belonged to Waleran. See below, undor "DUENE and "STANINGES."
BERMENTONE p. 123	Radulf	AIULF, the sheriff		The conjecture is hazarded that these *may be* portions *BEMERTON* in the hundred of Branche. There were tw holdings (c. 1270) at BIMERTON (Test. de Nev. 152, 155 and one of them was possessed by the Abbess of Wilto under "Galfridus *Camerarius*," the last being also a usu appellatiou of AIULF (p. 123, *note*).
BIMERTONE p. 135	Aldred	ALDRED, as one of the King's Thanes		
BERRELEGE p. 134	Done	AZOR, as one of the King's Thanes.		This manor, according to the Exon Domesday, p. 170, was the hundred of Bradford. In the Wilts Institutions we ha a list of presentations to the chapel of *BERLEGH*, the Prior of Monkton Farleigh, but the name is now los and the manor itself cannot bo identified. It was pr bably near Monkton Farleigh and Cumberwell. See A brey, 26. Azor is recordod, in the Somerset Domesda as having held "Herlei" (Warleigh), an adjoining estat in the time of tho Confessor, and a district in ths imm diate neighbourhood is still called "Berrifield," thoug oftsn contracted into "Berfield" and "Bearfisld."

NAME.	T. R. E. Owner, or Tenant.	T. R. W. Tenant in Capite.	T. R. W. Under-Tenant.	MODERN NAME, &c.
BICHENESTOCH p. 42	Harding, under the Abbess of Shaftesbury	ABBESS OF SHAFTESBURY	Turstin	*BEECHINGSTOKE*, in the hundred of Swanborough. A Charter by King Edmund (A.D. 941), relating to this manor, which is there called simply "STOKE," extracted from the Shaftesbury Chartulary, is given in Cod. Dipl., III. 416.
BISCOPESTREU p. 70	Edred	EDWARD of Salisbury		*BISHOPSTROW*, in the hundred of Warminster. Its name, *Biscopes treow*, i.e., "Bishop's-tree," or "Cross," may be a memorial of Bishop Aldhelm, to whom the church is dedicated. He was, no doubt, often in that neighbourhood, his monasteries of Bradford and Frome being at no great distance. Wilts Mag. viii., 78. Warminst. Hund., 69, 113.
BLONTESDONE p. 69	Achi	EDWARD of Salisbury	Robert	These would seem to be *BROAD BLUNSDON* and *BURY BLUNSDON* respectively. These are both regarded now as part of the parish of Highworth. Aubrey, 151.
BLONTESDUNE p. 144	Lanch, as one of the King's Thanes.	EDWARD, the sheriff, —held "in manu Regis"		
BLUNTESDONE p. 87	Edric	HUMFREY DE L'ISLE	Ilbert	*BLUNSDON ST. ANDREW*, in the hundred of Highworth. Wilts Mag. II., 282. Aubrey, 150.
BODEBERIE p. 139		ULF, as a King's Thane		This holding is in the hundred of Bradford. The name *BUDBURY* is now given to a small portion of the upper part of the town of Bradford-on-Avon, but formerly was applied to a larger extent of land. A tithing adjoining it is called Wool-ley, which, from its ancient spelling, WILF-LEGE, or ULF-LEGE (Test. de Nev., 153), may be conjectured to be a memorial of Ulf, the King's Thane.
BOIENTONE p. 69	Alwin	EDWARD of Salisbury		*BOYTON*, in the hundred of Heytesbury. Various members of the Giffard family (Test. de Nev., 138), held lands here under the Earls of Sarum, as chief lords. Heytesb. Hund., 197. Wilts Mag. I. 233.
BOLTINTONE p. 53	Abbess of Ambresbury	ABBESS OF AMBRESBURY	Alward,—3 hides	*BULLFORD*, in the hundred of Ambresbury. In the Nom. Vill. it is spelt *Bolt-ford*. Alward, the tenant of a portion of this manor, held also the neighbouring estate of CHELSTANESTON (Cholston). Ambresb. Hundr., 44.
BOSCUMBE p. 100	Alestan	WILLIAM DE OW	Edward	East and West Boscumbe, containing respectively 950 and 740 acres, and making up the present parish of *BOSCUMBE* in the hundred of Ambresbury. A detailed account of the two estates is given in Ambresb. Hund., 110.
BOSCUMBE p. 54	Abbess of Ambresbury	ABBESS OF AMBRESBURY		
BRADELIE p. 98	Earl Tosti	WALTER GIFARD		*MAIDEN BRADLEY*, in the hundred of Mere. It derives its distinctive name from a hospital for "leprous *maidens*," founded there by Manasser Bisset, about the year 1154. Test. de Nev., 156. The Church of Bradley was alienated by Henry Bisset, his son, and bestowed on the Priory of Notley (Buckinghamshire), which was founded by Walter Giffard. In 1401, the church was appropriated to the convent at Maiden Bradley. Dugd. Baron. I. 632. Mere Hundr., 94. Aubrey, 383.
BRADEFELDE p. 109	Bristwi Elwi	RADULF DE MORTEMER	Edward	*BRADFIELD*, in the parish of Hullavington. See below, under "Hunlavintone." In the Test. de Nev., 150, there are recorded *two* holdings, each of one fourth of a knight's fee, under Ralph de Mortimer (c. 1240), in Bradefeld. Aubrey, 248.

NAME.	T. R. E. Owner, or Tenant.	T. R. W. Tenant in Capite.	T. R. W. Under-Tenant.	MODERN NAME, &c.
BRADEFORD p. 43	Abbess of Shaftesbury	ABBESS OF SHAFTESBURY		*BRADFORD-ON-AVON*, the gift of King Ethelred, A 1001, to the Abbess of Shaftesbury. A full account this parish will be found in vol. v. of the Wilts Mag.
BRADENESTOCH p. 148		EDWARD of Salisbury [the sheriff.]	William, son of Ansculf [de Pinchengi]	This is described as near Tornvele (Thorn hill), and belo ing to *BRADENESTOCH*. In the entry of that ma which is given under "STOCHE" (p. 68), the tena name is given as William de Pinchengi. He was the of Ansculf de Pinchengi. Ellis, I. 511.
BRAMESSAGE p. 138		EDMUND, as a King's Thane		These would appear to be portions, one of them of small extent, of *BRAMSHAW*, which, though situ locally in the southern part of Alderbury hundred reckoned, in the Nom. Vill., in that of Cawden. Par this parish is in Hampshire. The manor of Britford from an early period connected with Bramshaw, hence, perhaps, they were placed in the same hund "Edmund," the owner of the smaller of these two man may possibly be the same as "Edmund" who held a tion of "BREDFORD." Frustf. Hundr., 100.
BRAMESSAGE p. 141	Ulnod's father	ULNOD, as a King's Thane		
BRECHEORDE p. 35	Abbot of Malmesbury	ABBOT OF MALMESBURY	"Miles,"—1 hide	A portion of *BRINKWORTH*, originally in the hundred Sterkeley (p. 159), now in that of Malmesbury. This ma was given by a Saxon nobleman, by name Leofsi, to Abbey of Malmesbury. See Cod. Dipl. 817, from an exp sion in which it appears that *GRITTENHAM*, now pa this parish, was included in the gift of Brokenborough adjoining manors to Malmesbury. The land-limits of estate at Brinkworth (from the Add. MSS., No. 15,667 the British Museum), are given by Akerman, in his pa on the "Possessions of Malmesbury Abbey" (p. 14), printed from the 27th vol. of the Archæologia. Aub 208.
BRENCHWRDE p. 92	Tochi	MILO CRISPIN	Humfrey	This is also an estate at or near Brinkworth. An entr Test. de Nev., 137, from which it appears that "Roger *Dantesey*" held a knight's fee, under the manor of W lingford (page 91, *note*) at *TYDOVRE* [= *IDOVI* leads to the conjecture that that estate, though now Dantsey parish, may be the one intended. See Aub 216.
BREDECUMBE p. 49	Abbess of Wilton	ABBESS OF WILTON	Edward,—1 hide	*SOUTH BURCOMB*, in the hundred of Cadworth. charter by which King Æthelstan gives "Brydan-cum to the Abbey at Wilton (A.D. 937) is to be found in C Dipl. 1115. See also Hoare's "Registrum Wiltunen Cadw. Hundr., 95.
BREDECUMBE p. 60	Ednod, "the steward"	EARL HUGO	Kaimo	*NORTH BURCOMB*, in the hundred of Branche. T estate would seem to have been held (c. 1270) under Earl of Sarum, as chief Lord of the fee. Test. de Nev. Branche Hund., 151.
BREME p. 38	Abbot of Malmesbury	ABBOT OF MALMESBURY	Edward,—4 hides Edward,—2 hides, of the King, which were held under him by Gislebert Teodric,—4 hides, and also 1 hide, of the land of the villans, given to him by the Abbot William de Ow,—1 hide, given by the Abbot to Alestan, in the time of King Edward	*BREMHILL*, in the hundred of Chippenham, given King Æthelstan (c. 935) to the Abbey at Malmesbury. "Bremele," according to a charter by King Edw (A.D. 1065) reciting the various lands belonging to Malm bury, were included YWERIG, (Ewridge), see below un "Digeric,"—SPEERFUL (Spirit Hill),—CHEDECOTE (Ch cott)—FOXHAM,—and AVENE. An account of this pa was published, some years ago, by the Rev. W. L Bowles. Aubrey, 60.

NAME.	T. R. E. Owner, or Tenant.	T. R. W. Tenant in Capite.	T. R. W. Under-Tenant.	MODERN NAME, &c.
BRETFORD p. 9	King Edward	THE KING		*BRITFORD*, in the hundred of Cawden. Osbern, the priest, held also the neighbouring estate of Hnmitone (Homington). There are still vestiges, in the north and south doorways, of the church which existed at Britford in Anglo-Saxon times. See Parker's "Glossary of Architecture," plate xviii. Bloxam's "Gothic Architecture," p. 90.
.... Church of p. 10		OSBERN, the Priest		
BREDFORD p. 140		ULURIC, as a King's Thane		An entry in the Exon Domesday (p. 187) shews that the *first* of these three holdings, all of them of small extent, was in the hundred of Cawden. There can be little doubt, therefore, that it was at *BRITFORD*. It is most probable that the other two were there also; the possessor of the *third* holding is recorded as the owner of a small estate at Gramestede (Grimstead), which is but a short distance from Britford. Cawd. Hund., 53—59.
BREDFORD p. 138		EDMUND, son of AIULF, as a King's Thane		
BRETFORD p. 143	Osward's father	OSWARD, as a King's Thane		
BREVRESBROC p. 99	Alestan, of Boscumbe	WILLIAM DE OW	William de Mara	These two holdings are portions of *BEVERSBROOK*, close by Calne. Under the fees of the Earl Marshal (c. 1250)—together with many others of the manors held by William de Ow—is one of half a knight's fee at Bevresbrok, held by Robert *de la Mare* under Andrew Blund, and by the latter of Peter *de la Mare*. Test. de Nev. 136. In the Nom. Vill. (c. 1316), the manor of "BLAKELONDE" (Blacklands), in the hundred of Calne, is said to be held by Alexander le *Blount*, and three others.
BEVRESBROC p. 124	Alsi, a Priest	NIGEL, the physician		
BRISMARTONE p. 112	Brismar	ROBERT FITZ-GIROLD	Robert	*BRIGMERSTON* (or, as it is now sometimes written, *BRIGMILSTON*), in the hundred of Ambresbury. The original name is no doubt derived from "Brismar," its Anglo-Saxon owner, who also held the adjoining estate of Mildestone (Milston). Ambresb. Hundr., 37.
BROCHENEBERGE p. 35	Abbot of Malmesbury	ABBOT OF MALMESBURY	Ranulf Flambard,—6 hides in Corston Robert,—3½ hides William,—2 hides An Englishwoman —1 hide 2 "milites,"—3½ hides	*BROKENBOROUGH*, in the old hundred of Cicemethorn (p. 158), now in that of Malmesbury. This extensive estate, consisting in all of 100 mansæ, was bestowed on the Abbey of Malmesbury by King Edwy, in 956. Cod. Dipl. 460. The original grant included estates at CORSTON,—RONBOURN,—CUSFALDE (*Cole*-Park),—BREMELHAM,—GRITTENHAM, and SUTTON (Benger). Cod. Dipl., 817. None of these are separately mentioned in the record, because they are all comprised under the larger estate of Brokenborough. See Aubrey, 211, 266, 280, 291.
BROCTONE p. 85	Three Thanes, holding "in paragio"	HUMFREY DE L'ISLE		*BROUGHTON GIFFORD*, in the hundred of Bradford. A full account of this parish by the present Rector is printed in the Wilts Mag., v. 265. From 1269 to 1322 the Lords of the manor were members of the family of GIFFARD, and from them is derived the distinctive name of the parish. The church at Broughton was given to Shaftesbury Abbey by one Gundreda, on the dedication of a kinswoman as a nun. Harl. MS. 61, fol. 54.
BROCTUNE p. 143	Alwold	SAWARD, as a King's Thane		*MONKTON*, a tithing in the parish of Broughton Gifford, and hundred of Bradford (p. 170). It was formerly called "Broctune Parva," or "Little Broughton." It was given in the twelfth century by Ilbert de Chat, its then owner, to the priory of Farleigh *Monkton*, and hence its present name. Wilts Mag., V. 330.
.... p. 144	Godric	RAINBURGIS, as a King's Thane		The *name* of this manor is not given; it is simply described as "the manor which Godric held T. R. E." The only hundred in which, according to the Exon Domesday, Rainburgis held lands, was that of Heytesbury. See below, p. 178.

NAME.	T. R. E. Owner, or Tenant.	T. R. W. Tenant in Capite.	T. R. W. Under-Tenant.	MODERN NAME, &c.
BROMHAM p. 13	Earl Harold	THE KING	A Priest,—1¼ hide	*BROMHAM*, at the time of Domesday (p. 171), and for some centuries afterwards, in the hundred of Calne (Nom. Vill.), subsequently placed in that of Pottern and Cannings. The parish of Bromham (exclusive of Chittoe, which, though locally situated in it, belongs to Bishops Cannings) contains 3,597 acres. The manor and church were bestowed on the "Abbey of Bataile" (Battle) by one of the early Kings, and the patronage was in the hands of that religious house till the sixteenth century, after which time it was held by the Baynton family. Test. de Nev., 155.
BURBED p. 146	Alric	RADULF DE HALVILE as one of the King's Officers	William	These three holdings are all portions of *BURBAGE*, in the hundred of Kinwardstone, the entire parish containing 3,332 acres, but much of it originally no doubt forest land. The *first* entry, which seems referred to in the Exon Domesday p. 181, would probably embrace the part of the parish where now the church and village are, as ULFELA (Wolfhall), which immediately adjoins that portion of Burbage, also belonged to Radulf de Halville. The *second* holding, we may perhaps infer from an entry in the Test. de Nev. 143, in which "Galfridus *Sturmi*" is recorded as possessed of "Burbach *Durle*," comprises *DURLEY*, now a hamlet in the north-east portion of the parish. The *third* entry is the half knight's fee that was held in "Burbache" (c. 1270) by "Walter de Dunstanville of the manor of Wallingford," though it is not easy to say what part of the parish it comprised. Test. de Nev. 141, 157. Wilts Mag. II., 276.
BUBERGE p. 144	Aluric	RICHARD STURMID, as one of the King's Officers	Blacheman	
BURBETC p. 86	Edric	HUMFREY DE L'ISLE		
BURBETCE Church of p. 16		VITALIS, the Priest		The Church at *BURBAGE* was given by Henry I. to Old Sarum Cathedral, and with Husseborne (Hurstborne, Hants), became a prebend. In the Taxat. Eccl. 194 *b*, it is spoken of as the "Chapel of Burbache annexed to the prebend of Husebyrn." The Vicarage was in the gift and under the jurisdiction of the Prebendary. The Bishop of Sarum now presents to it. Aubrey, 381.
BUTREMARE p. 105	Eight Thanes	WALERAN, the huntsman	Azelin	These are different portions of *BUTTERMERE*, in the hundred of Kinwardstone, a parish containing 1,502 acres. "Willelmus de Sancto Martino," a descendant of Waleran, held "one fourth of a knight's fee at Butremere," in the time of Edw. I. Hundr. R. II., 260. The manor of Buttermere was given by Wotwyn, a monk of Winton, to the church of St. Swithin, and the Bishops of Winchester have presented to the living from an early period. Leland. Collect., I. 613.
BUTREMARE p. 76		ERNULF DE HESDING		
BUTREMERE p. 147		ANSCHITIL, as one of the King's officers		
CADEHAM p. 61	Ednod,—'dapifer'	EARL HUGO	William	Most probably *CADENHAM*, in the parish of Bremhill and hundred of Chippenham. Aubrey, 61.
CALDEFELLE p. 75	Wallef	ERNULF DE HESDING		These two estates would seem to be *GREAT* and *LITTLE CHALDFIELD*, now in the hundred of Bradford, but, probably, at the time of Domesday, in that of Melksham (p. 171). An account of the Manor House and Church of Great Chaldfield, with a description of the architectural peculiarities, was published a few years ago by Mr. T. L. Walker.
CALDEFELLE p. 76	Godwin	ERNULF DE HESDING		
CAININGHAM p. 22	Bishop of Sarum	BISHOP OF SARUM	The Priest, — 2 hides Ebrard,--10 hides Herman,--4 hides Quintin,--3 hides Walter,—2 hides Brictward, — 5 hides Alward,—1 hide Wife of Bailiff, 1 hide	*BISHOP'S CANNINGS*, comprising HORTON,—COATES,—SOUTH BROOM,—ROUNDWAY,—CHITTOE (locally situated in Bromham), and BUPTON (locally situated in Cliff Pipard). In the Hundred Rolls (II. 236) we have "William *Quintin*" (the name of one of the under-tenants at the time of Domesday) and "William *Bubbe*," recorded as holding one knight's fee (39 H. 3) at CLYVE. This clearly alludes to Bup-ton (formerly *Bubbe*-ton). Aubrey, 165. A full account of this parish, by its late Vicar, Archdeacon Macdonald, will be found in the Wilts Mag. VI., 129.

NAME.	T. R. E. Owner, or Tenant.	T. R. W. Tenant in Capite.	Under-Tenant.	MODERN NAME, &c.
NINGE p. 52	Abbess of St. Mary, Winchester	ABBESS OF ST. MARY, WINCHESTER		*ALL-CANNINGS*, in the hundred of Stodfald (p. 174); now in that of Swanborough. The parish—exclusive of chapelries now considered part of it but separately accounted for in the record—(see under "ADELINGTONE" and "ECESATINGETONE")—contains 3,221 acres.
LESTONE p. 125	Gunnar	RICHARD PUINGIANT		All these, according to the Exon Domesday (p. 172), were in the hundred of Calne. They refer to holdings at *CALSTON* and its neighbourhood, for the land represented by the three entries must have been at least 1,400 acres. *CALSTON WILLINGTON*—so called from John de Wilinton, a Baron of the time of Edw. III.—is no doubt one of the manors intended, but that parish contains only 308 acres. Of estates in the immediate vicinity, apparently not otherwise accounted for in Domesday, *QUEMERFORD* (anciently *CUMBREFORD*) was, in 1257, together with several other manors possessed by Ernulf de Hesding, held by Patrick de Chaworth (Aubrey, 37);—and *BLACKLAND* was held, in 1316, in part at least, by one of the *Mauduit* family, a descendant of Gunfrid Maldoith. Nom. Vill. Aubrey 39.
LESTONE p. 75	Edric	ERNULF DE HESDING	Edric's wife	
LESTONE p. 122	Algar	GUNFRID MALDOITH		
UNA p. 7	King Edward	THE KING		*CALNE*;—a full account of this manor, which embraced several neighbouring estates, *e.g.*, BERWICK [Basset], and CHERHILL, now formed into independent parishes, is given in Aubrey 31–37.
UNA Church of p. 7		NIGEL	Alured of Spain, —5 hides— these claimed by Nigel, as having belonged to the Church, T.R.E.	The Churches of CALNE, with the tithes thereto belonging, formed part of the endowment by St. Osmund of his Cathedral at Sarum. Hatcher's Salisbury, 717.
LDEWELLE p. 104	Alsi	WALSCIN DE DOWAI	Godescal	Though the name cannot as yet be identified, yet from being mentioned in connexion with STORTONE (Stourton), and belonging to the same owner, this manor may be conjectured to have been near the south-western border of the county. ALSI occurs also as the tenant, in the time of the Confessor, of CANDELLE (Caundel), in Dorset, an estate which at the time of Domesday was possessed by WALSEIN DE DOWAI. Domesd. I. *fol.* 82.
LDRINTONE p. 76	Ulward	ERNULF DE HESDING	Ulward	The entry in the Exon Domesday (p. 186), identifies these three holdings, all of which are but of small extent, as different parts of *CHOLDERTON*, in the hundred of Ambresbury. Ambresh. Hund., 100.
LDRINTONE p. 77	Sewi	ERNULF DE HESDING		
LDRINTONE p. 77	Alwin } as two Uluric } manors	ERNULF DE HESDING	Godric	
LDRETONE p. 100	Alestan, of Boscumbe	WILLIAM DE OW	Bernard	This holding is also a portion of *CHOLDERTON*. In the Test. de Nev., 144, under the fees of the Earl Marescal, is one held, by subordinate tenants, of Eudo de *Bernard* in "Cheldrintone." Moreover, in the year 1175, the church at Cholderton was given by "Roger *Bernard*" to the Priory of St. Neot's, in Huntingdonshire.
ERLETONE p. 99	Alestan, of Boscumbe	WILLIAM DE OW	Hugo	*CHARLTON*, "juxta Hungerford" (Inq. p. m. 53, Hen. III.), in the hundred of Kinwardstone. The heirs of the Earl Marescal were possessed of it in 2 Edw. I. (Hund. Rolls II., 260.) See also Test. de Nev., 156. In the Inq. Non. 174, "Charlton," though in Wilts, is said to be part of the parish of Hungerford.
RLETONE p. 37	Abbot of Malmesbury	ABBOT OF MALMESBURY	Radulf Flambard —3 hides	*CHARLTON* (close to Malmesbury), in the old hundred of Cicemethorn, now in that of Malmesbury. This was granted to the monastery, as early as A.D. 681, by Æthelred, King of Mercia. A charter containing the land-limits of "Cherletone" is given in Cod. Dipl. III., 374. Aubrey, 212.

NAME.	T. R. E. Owner, or Tenant.	T. R. W.		MODERN NAME, &c.
		Tenant in Capite.	Under-Tenant.	
CERITONE p. 96	Almar	DURAND of Gloucester		*CHIRTON*, originally in the hundred of Stodfald (p. 17 now in that of Swanborough.
CELEORDE p. 36	Abbot of Malmesbury	ABBOT OF MALMESBURY	Tovi,—2¼ hides William,— 4 hides	This is spoken of as part of the manor of CHEMELE. It *CHELWORTH*, now a portion of the parish of Crudwe The land-limits of this estate are given in a charter Cod. Dipl. III., 402.
CELEWRDE p. 149	Edric	WARIN, the bowman, as one of the King's Officers		This is *CHELWORTH*, close by Cricklade. It is referr to in the Exon Domesday (p. 165) as in the hundred Staple.
CHEDELWICH p. 24	Algar	BISHOP OF SALISBURY	Hugo	*CHADENWYCH*, a tithing in the parish and hundred Mere, containing about 725 acres. Test. de Nev., 15 Mere Hund., 31.
CHEGESLAUE p. 93	Two Thanes Siward	MILO CRISPIN	Siward Durand of Gloucester	These entries, which are but of small extent, refer *CHEDGLOW*, now a hamlet in the parish of Crudwe but formerly the name of a hundred and denoting probab a larger extent of land. The *first* was held (c. 1,270) Henry de Puriton and Hugo de Peverel of the "honor Wallingford" (Test. de Nev., 155);—the *second* by Willia Foliot and Radulf de Sterklee, as one of the fees of Robe Tregoz. See the notes on pp. 91, 79.
CHEGESLIE p. 83	Edward	ALURED of Marlborough	Edward Durand of Gloucester	
CHEIESLAUE p. 77	Ulwi A Thane,—2½ virgates	ERNULF DE HESDING	The same Thane	This holding appears to be alluded to in the Exon Domesd (p. 160), under the hundred of Sterkeley. It is no doubt portion of *CHEDGLOW*, which was on the borders the two hundreds of Cicemethorne and Sterkeley. In th Test. de Nev., 150, it is recorded as having been held Hugo de Standen as among the fees of Patrick de Ch worth, like many others held at Domesday by Ernulf Hesding. See Inq. p. m. xlii. Henr. III.
CHELCHE p. 47	Abbess of Wilton Aileva,—2 hides	ABBESS OF WILTON	Girard,—3 hides Richard Poingiant, — 7½ hides	This large estate at *CHALK*, which includes BROAD CHAL —BOWER CHALK,—ALVEDISTON,—BERWICK ST. JOHN,- and SEMLEIGH,—was granted to the Abbey at Wilton King Edwy, A.D. 955. The charter, with the land-limit is given in Cod. Dipl., 436 The name of the tenant in the time of the Confessor seer preserved in *Alvedes*-ton, *i. e.*, the *town* (or village) AILEVA;—that of "GIRARD," in Guston (a contracted for of *Girardes*-ton), Test. de Nev., 141, 157;—the holding Richard Poingiant was at TROI (now TROW), in the pari of Alvedeston. See below, p. 125.
CHELESTANESTONE p. 54	Abbess of Ambresbury	ABBESS OF AMBRESBURY	Alward	Most probably *CHOLSTON*, the name now of a farm in t parish of Figheldean, and hundred of Ambresbury.
CHEMELE p. 36	Abbot of Malmesbury	ABBOT OF MALMESBURY	Tovi, 2¼ hides William 4 hides } in Celeorde. Anschitil,—1 hide	*KEMBLE*, in the hundred of Cicemethorn, (p. 159) now that of Malmesbury. This was given as early as A.D. 682, Cædwealha, King of Wessex, to the monastery at Malme bury. Cod. Dipl. 24, 29. In this manor was includ some land at CHELWORTH. Cod. Dipl., 817. Aubrey, 24
CHENEBUILD p. 77	Ulwid	ERNULF DE HESDING	Urso	From the name of the tenant, URSO, who also held DEVR (p. 78), it is probable that this small estate was near t south-west borders of the county. It is not easy to tra the name in any existing manors. URSO is recorded the tenant of an estate at MELESBERIE (Melbury), Dorset, close by the border of the county, also und ERNULF DE HESDING. Domesd. I., *fol.* 80*b*.

NAME.	T. R. E. Owner, or Tenant.	T. R. W. Tenant in Capite.	T. R. W. Under-Tenant.	MODERN NAME, &c.
CHENETE p. 84	Alnod Edmar Ulviet Leuric Ulmar	ALURED of Marlborough	Nicholas, — 2 hides Turstin, — 3½ hides Ulviet,—2 hides Leuric,—3 hides Ulmar,—2½	An entry in the Test. de Nev., 153, in which the Abbess of Winchester, Walter Walerand, and Robert Tregoz (see above, p. 79) are said to hold fees in the same place, identifies these several estates as parts of *KENNET*, in the hundred of Selkley, a name attributed formerly to a much larger tract of country than now, in the neighbourhood of the river of the same name. The *larger portion*, comprising the greater part, if not all, held by Alured of Marlborough, may be *WEST KENNET*, now a tithing of Avebury. The *other two* are probably portions of *EAST KENNET*, a separate parish, containing 776 acres. Aubrey, 337.
CHENETE p. 121	Honewin	HUGO LASNE	Church of St. Mary, Winton, in trust for the daughter of Hugo Lasne	
CHENETE p. 105	Leveclai	WALERAN, the huntsman	Richard	
CHENVEL p. 15	Eileva, under Earl William	THE KING	Gilbert,—1 hide	*EAST KNOYLE*, or, as it is also called, *BISHOP'S KNOYLE*. At the time of Domesday it was in the hundred of Mere (p. 182). From having belonged to the King, it was formerly called "KNOYLE REGIS." It was purchased by Richard Tocliffe, Bishop of Winchester (A.D. 1173–1189), and by him given to the Church at Winton. Abbr. Plac., 29. Leland Coll. I., 613. In the time of Edw. I. a small hundred, called that of "KNOWEL EPISCOPI," was formed, which comprised this place and Bishop's Fonthill. It is now, with other estates belonging to the see of Winchester, in the hundred of Downton. Mere Hundr., 182.
CHENVEL p. 47	Abbess of Wilton	ABBESS OF WILTON		*WEST KNOYLE* (or, *KNOYLE ODIERNE*), in the hundred of Mere. Lands in the parish belonged at one time to a person described as "Hodierna Nutrix" (*i. e.*, Hodierne, the nurse), who was thus pensioned by Richard I. Wilts Mag. III., 30. The estate was given to the Abbey at Wilton by King Eadred, A.D. 948. Charters relating to it will be found in Hoare's Reg. Wiltun. p. 1, and in Cod. Dipl., 422, 462. Mere Hundr., 38, 176.
CHEPEHAM p. 9	King Edward [Ulviet, 1 hide Edric,—½ virgate]	THE KING		All these entries relate to *CHIPPENHAM*, the name of a large parish, and of the hundred in which it is situated. In this manor are included the several tithings of ALLINGTON,—STANLEY,—NETHERMORE,—and originally, it would seem, SLAUGHTERFORD. Abbr. Plac., 243. A full account of the parish will be found in the Wilts. Mag. III., 19, and in Aubrey, 66.
CEPEHAM p. 115	Celein (as a purpresture of Edric the sheriff.)	ROGER DE BERCHELA		
CHEPEHAM Church of p. 9	Bishop Osbern	BISHOP OSBERN		
CHIPEHAM p. 127	Tochi	RAINALD CANUD		
CHELTRE p. 62	Harding	EARL ALBERIC		The *last three* of these entries, and most probably also the *first* of them, relate to different portions of *CHITTERNE* [or, *CHILTERNE*], in the hundred of Heytesbury (p. 178). In CHITTERNE ST. MARY are 1,203 acres,—in CHITTERNE ALL SAINTS (which included the chapelry of CHITTERNE ST. ANDREW), 4,411 acres. In the Nom. Vill. (A.D. 1316), there seem to be four lordships implied, held respectively by John Syfrewast, under the Earl of Salisbury,—Alicia de Pickford,—the Prior of Bradenstock,—the Abbess of Lacock. The gifts of lands to the two religious houses were made by descendants of Edward of Salisbury. Heytesbury Hund., 165, 171.
CHETRE p. 69	Azor	EDWARD of Salisbury		
CHETRE p. 69	Chenvin	EDWARD of Salisbury		
CHETRE p. 69	Ulwen	EDWARD of Salisbury	Robert	

NAME.	T. R. E. Owner, or Tenant.	T. R. W. Tenant in Capite.	T. R. W. Under-Tenant.	MODERN NAME, &c.
CHEVREL p. 74	Alward	ERNULF DE HESDING	Lethelin	*CHEVEREL*, in the old hundred of Rugeberg, afterwa in that of Swanborough. There are now two villages, t one CHEVEREL MAGNA, containing 1,870 acres, the oth CHEVEREL PARVA, containing 690 acres. Much of what now included in these parishes was probably, at the ti of Domesday, forest-land. See below, under "POTERNE
CHESEBERIE p. 94	Edric	GILBERT DE BRETEVILLE		*CHISBURY*, in the parish of Little Bedwin, and hund of Kinwardstone. It was held, 3 Edw. I., by Matthew Columbars (p. 94 *note*), of the heirs of Bigod, Earl M shall. Hundr. R. II., 260. Wilts Mag. VI., 272. Aubr 164, 380.
CHESIGEBERIE p. 123	Spirtes, a Priest	NIGEL, the physician		*CHISENBURY DE LA FOLYE*, in the hundred Elstub (p. 179). The manor was held, 2 Edw. I., Richard de la Folye, of the Earl of Hereford, as chief lo of the fee. Though at some distance from NETHER-AVO it is still, as at the time of Domesday, connected with being now reckoned as part of that parish. See belo under "NIGRAVRE." Elstub Hundr., 17, 189.
CHIGELIE p. 137	Edwin	EDWIN, as a King's Thane		As DEVREL is named next after this small manor, we m conjecture that it is possibly *CHICKLADE* that is he intended; but as we have no clue to the hundred in whi it was situated, we can form no trustworthy opinion.
CHILMERC p. 46	Abbess of Wilton	ABBESS OF WILTON		*CHILMARK*, in the hundred of Dunworth (p. 182), the gi as it would appear, of King Æthelstan to the Abbess Wilton. Hoare's Reg. Wiltun., 46. The whole paris including the tithing of RUDGE, contains 3,116 acre A mill, locally situated at CHICKSGROVE, in Tisbury, reckoned as belonging to this parish. Dunw. Hundr., 12
CHINTONE p. 110	Alwin	RADULF DE MORTEMER	Roger	This is probably *WEST KINGTON*, or, as it is sometim spelt, *KEINTON*, originally, it would seem, in the hu dred of Thorngrave,—now in that of Chippenham. Radu de Mortimer held the neighbouring manors of ALDRITON —BRADEFELDE,—and SIRENDONE. It is stated that Alwi held this manor in the time of Edward the Confessor the Church of Glastonbury, to whom the immediate adjoining estate of NETTLETON still belonged.
CHISELDENE p. 41	Abbey of St. Peter, Winchester	ABBEY OF ST. PETER, WINCHESTER.		*CHISELDEN*, in the old hundred of Thornhill (p. 167), no in that of Kingsbridge. This estate, together with i Church, was given by King Edward the elder to the Abbe of St. Peter, at Winchester, of which he was the actu founder, though it had been projected by his father, Alfre the Great. Cod. Dipl., 336. Aubrey, 162.
CHIVELE p. 74	Brixi	ERNULF DE HESDING		*KEEVIL*, in the hundred of Whorwelsdown (p. 173). Th *manor* together with that of BULKINGTON, which, though i the hundred of Melksham, is reckoned as a tithing of Kee vil, belonged afterwards to the Fitz-Alans, Earls Arunde The *church* was given by Ernulf de Hesding to Shaftes bury, on his dedicating a certain kinswoman as a nun i that convent. In 1393 it was purchased for Edingto Priory. All the deeds are contained in the Edingto Chartulary. Wilts Mag. VII., 298.
CILLETONE p. 91	Earl Harold	MILO CRISPIN	Rainald	*CHILTON FOLIOT*, in the hundred of Kinwardston Sampson Foliot held CHILTON, and DREYCOT (Foliot) to wards the end of the 13th century, both of them havin been at the time of Domesday entered among the lands o Milo Crispin. Test. de Nev., 145.

NAME.	T. R. E. Owner, or Tenant.	T. R. W. Tenant in Capite.	T. R. W. Under-Tenant.	MODERN NAME, &c.
CLATFORD p. 110	Alwin	RADULF DE MORTEMER		*CLATFORD*, in the hundred of Selkley. There was an alien Priory here, which was a cell to the Abbey of St. Victor "in Caleto," (*i.e.* at Caux,) a few miles to the north of Rouen in Normandy, founded by Sir Roger Mortemer, father, it is supposed, of Radulf de Mortemer. Dugd. Baron I., 138. The manor of CLATFORD was given to that Abbey by one of the Mortimer family, about the time of Henry III. It was granted by Henry VI. to Eton College. It was afterwards resigned to the Crown, in exchange for other lands, and bestowed (1 Edw. VI.) on Edward, Duke of Somerset. New Mon. VI., 1055. Aubrey, 246.
CLIVE p. 19	Bishop of Winchester	BISHOP OF WINCHESTER "pro victu monachorum."		This is the *BISHOPPESTON* (now corrupted into *BUSHTON*) of the Nom. Vill., in the hundred of Kingsbridge (p. 165), which, together with Thornhill in the same hundred, belonged to the Bishop of Winchester, as "custos" of the Priory of St. Swithin. Charters concerning CLIFE, containing land-limits, are given in the Cod. Dipl. 636, 638. BUSHTON is in the parish of Cliff-Pypard. Aubrey, 166.
CLIVE p. 83	Godric, Tedgar, Aluric, Uluric } held it for 4 manors	ALURED of Marlborough	Roger	Most probably a portion of *CLEVANCY* (originally *CLIVE-WANCY*, so called from Radulf de Wancy, who held lands here, c. 1275, Test. de Nev., 137), in the parish of Helmarton, and hundred of Kingsbridge. Among the fees of Robert Tregoz was one at CLYVE-WANCY. Inq. p. m., 28 Edw. I. (See note on p. 79.)
CLIVE p. 83	Sigar and Carman	ALURED of Marlborough	Robert	This manor is described as "*in* CLIVE." It was probably in the same neighbourhood as the one just described. The present parishes of Helmarton and Cliff-Pipard both consist of a number of what were formerly separate and independent manors. One of these is probably alluded to, but which of them, from want of more information, it is impossible to say.
CLIVE p. 141		ULURIC WAULA, as one of the King's Thanes		If ULURIC WAULA be the same as the ULURIC named in the last entry but one, as holding a portion of that estate, T. R. E., this small manor was also probably in the same vicinity. This, however, is mere conjecture.
CLIVE p. 87	Edwin	HUMFREY DE L'ISLE	Robert	A portion of the present parish of *CLIFF-PIPARD*, in the hundred of Kingsbridge. Richard *Pipard* held several fees here (c. 1275), and hence the distinctive name. Test. de Nev., 140, 149, 156. In the Castle Combe Court Rolls for 1454, Agnes de Cobham is entered as holding a knight's fee in PIPPARDESCLYVE of the lordship of Combe. Wilts Mag. ii., 279.
CLIVE p. 95	Aluric, Burgel, Godeve	GILBERT DE BRETEVILE	Ansfrid,—11 hides	The mention of one of these hides having formerly been in TORNELLE (Thornhill), which is in CLIFF-PIPARD, identifies this holding as being the eastern part of that parish. The neighbouring estate of STAMERE (Stanmore) also was held by the same tenant under Gilbert de Bretevile.
CLIVE p. 120	Godeve	HUGO LASNE		The name of the tenant T. R. E. being the same as one of those in the preceding entry, suggests the probability that this holding, which was but of small extent, was in the same neighbourhood.
CLIVE p. 91	Harold	MILO CRISPIN	Humfrey }	These two holdings are said to be in the same CLIVE. An entry in the Test. de Nev., 137, makes it tolerably clear that they were at *BRODETON* (*BROAD-TOWN*), a part of the parish of Cliff-Pipard, where (c. 1275) one knight's fee was held by Fulco Basset, as of the "honor of Wallingford." (See p. 91, note.)
CLIVE p. 92		MILO CRISPIN		

NAME.	T. R. E. Owner, or Tenant.	T. R. W. Tenant in Capite.	T. R. W. Under-Tenant.	MODERN NAME, &c.
CLIVE p. 108	Godric	HENRY DE FERIERES		All these holdings are referred to in the Exon Domesday 165), as in the hundred of Kingsbridge. GODRIC, the te ant T. R. E. of the first, also possessed, it will be observ a small estate in this neighbourhood, which, at the time Domesday was held in chief by Alured of Marlboroug See under CLIVE (p. 83).
CLIVE p. 148	Ulveva	WIBERT, as one of the King's Officers.		
CLIVE p. 148		TURSTIN, the Chamberlain, as one of the King's Officers.		
CLIVE p. 58	Godwin	EARL MORTON	Gilbert	These would seem to be different portions of the same esta An entry in the Hund. R. ii., 243, in which the Earl Cornwall is said to be possessed of "Wasturne," in the hu dred of Blachegrave, leads to the conjecture that possi *FASTERN*, now in the parish of Wootton-Bassett, may intended; but this is mere supposition, as we have no re clue even to the hundred in which the manor alluded was situated.
CLIVE p. 58	Godwin	EARL MORTON	Gilbert	
COLEBURNE p. 40	Abbey of St. Peter, Winchester	ABBEY OF ST. PETER, WINCHESTER.	Croc, — 10½ hides Fulcred,—2 hides	*COLLINGBOURN ABBAS*, in the hundred of Kinwar stone. This extensive manor, containing 7,190 acres, w bestowed on the Abbey of St. Peter, Winchester, by Ki Edward the Elder. Hund. R. ii., 260. See also Cod. Dip 336. Since the end of the 16th century it has been call COLLINGBOURN REGIS, or, as now, COLLINGBOURN KINGSTO
COLINGEBURNE p. 14	Earl Harold	THE KING		*COLLINGBOURN DUCIS.* At the time of Domesday, being mentioned separately in the Exon Domesday (p. 17 it would seem not to have been then included in any hu dred. It would appear afterwards to have been reckon as part of the hundred of Kinwardstone. Hund. R. i 260. The manor was given by Henry III. to his half-br ther, William de Valence, and hence for some time it w called COLLINGBOURN VALENCE. Edmund, Earl of La caster, died siezed of it in 1279, and from him it probab derived its name of COLLINGBOURN COMITIS, or EARL' When it was possessed by his grandson Henry, who w created Duke of Lancaster, it obtained the name which still retains, COLLINGBOURN DUCIS. It is now in t hundred of Elstub and Everley. Elstub Hund., 14.
COLINGEBURNE Church of p. 15		GIRALD, priest of Wilton		The Church at *COLLINGBOURN* was bestowed on Whe well Monastery, and the Abbess of that religious hou presented to the Rectory from 1306–1545.
COLECOTE p. 130		ODO of Winchester, as one of the King's Thanes.		*COLCOTE* (or *COLCUT*), in the hundred of Staple (165). It is situated close by Cricklade, and on the line the Roman road that runs from Cirencester to Speen. I the Inq. p. m., 48 Edw. III., it occurs as "Colcote jux Chelesworth."
COLESELLE p. 119	Three Thanes	DROGO FITZ-PONZ	Roger de Laci Turstin Fitz-Rolf William Leuric	This is, without doubt, a small manor at or adjoinin *COLESHILL*, a parish now in Berks, but close by th north-east boundary of Wiltshire. Turstin Fitz-Rolf, on of the subordinate holders, is recorded in Domesday as th tenant in capite of COLESELLE in Berks. (Vol. i., *fol.* 63 Moreover the Church of St. Mary, Winchester, held a estate at COLESELLE, according to the same record (Berk i., *fol.* 59b), by gift of Walter de *Laci* (no doubt, of th same family as *another* of the subordinate holders) wh his daughter became a nun in the convent. The manor COLESHILL was afterwards given to Edington Priory, by i founder, William of Edington, Bishop of Winchester. Se Lyson's Magn. Brit. (Berks.), p.p. 166, 265.
COLESFELDE p. 132		BRICTRIC & ALWI, as King's Thanes		Most probably a portion of *COWLESFIELD* (now *COW FIELD*) in the hundred of Frustfield. There are sever small manors here. See below, under CUVLESTON Frustfield Hund., 69.

NAME.	T. R. E. Owner, or Tenant.	T. R. W. Tenant in Capite.	T. R. W. Under-Tenant.	MODERN NAME, &c.
COLERNE p. 88	Levenot	HUMFREY DE L'ISLE		*COLERNE*, in the hundred of Chippenham. Its manorial history is given in Wilts Mag. ii., 269, and its church described in Wilts Mag. iii., 358. See also an account of Roman remains then in Arch. Journ., 1856. (p. 328.) Aubrey, 75.
COME p. 89	Svain	HUMFREY DE L'ISLE		*CASTLE COMBE*, originally in the hundred of Thorngrave (p. 160), now in that of Chippenham. A full account of this parish was printed by G. P. Scrope, Esq., M.P., and an abridgment of the same will be found in the Wilts Mag. ii., 133. Aubrey, 63.
CONTONE p. 10	Earl Harold	THE KING		*COMPTON CHAMBERLAIN*, in the hundred of Damerham (p. 188). It was held in the time of Rich. I. by the serjeantcy of being one of the king's *chamberlains* and hence its distinctive name. Hund. R. ii., 253.
CONTONE p. 85	Levenot	HUMFREY DE L'ISLE	Pagen	A portion of *COMPTON BASSET*, in the hundred of Calne. The whole parish, including the tithing of COMPTON CUMBERWELL, contains 2,631 acres. This manor was held in 1233 by Gilbert Bassett, and shortly afterward by Fulke Bassett, Bishop of London. Test. de Nev., 141. Aubrey, 41. See below, under CUMBREWELLE.
CONTONE p. 139	Turchil	TURCHIL, as one of the King's Thanes		As TURCHIL is mentioned (p. 142) as the possessor of a small estate in OCHEBURNE (Ogbourn), and this holding, which is described as "*in* Contone," follows the mention also of OCHEBURNE, it probably was at no great distance from it. It *may* be a part of *COMPTON BASSET*, which is hardly sufficiently accounted for, as to its actual extent, by other entries.
CONTONE p. 61	Harding	EARL ALBERIC		*COMPTON*, an outlying portion of the hundred of Ambresbury (p. 185). Though not in the same hundred, it is a tithing now of the parish of ENFORD. It contains about 1,100 acres. Elstub. Hund., 18.
CONTONE p. 99	Alestan of Boscumbe	WILLIAM DE OW	William de Aldrie	From the name of the tenant, who is probably the same as the "William de Aldeleia" mentioned in the Exon Domesday (p. 173); it seems likely that this estate is in the neighbourhood of the one just described. Compare the entry under LITELTONE. It is *possibly COMBE*, which is now reckoned as a tithing of ENFORD. Though a separate tithing, or manor, it does not seem otherwise accounted for in the Record.
CORSELIE p. 135		AZOR, as one of the King's Thanes		*CORSLEY*, in the hundred of Warminster. The Prioress of 'Stodlegh' had the manor in 1316. Nom. Vill. Warm. Hund., 63.
CORSTONE p. 35	Abbot of Malmesbury	ABBOT OF MALMESBURY	Ranulf Flambard	*CORSTON*, near Malmesbury. See above, under BROCHENEBERGE.
CORTITONE p. 120	Dene	HUGO LASNE	William	This is probably *CORTON* (or *CORTYNTONE*), now a tithing within the parish of BOYTON. It was formerly a separate lordship. In the Wilts Inst. are given the names of the incumbents of its chapel from 1304–1395, after which time it appears to have been annexed to Boyton.
COSSEHAM p. 11	Earl Tosti	THE KING		*CORSHAM*, in the hundred of Chippenham (p. 162). The history both of the manor and church is given by Canon Jackson, in Aubrey, 79.
COSSEHAM Church of p. 12		ABBEY OF ST. STEPHEN, at CAEN		*CORSHAM*, in the hundred of Chippenham (p. 162). The history both of the manor and church is given by Canon Jackson, in Aubrey, 79.
COTEFORD p. 100	Alestan of Boscumb	WILLIAM DE OW	Bernard	A portion of *CODFORD ST. PETER*, in the Hundred of Heytesbury. Roger *Bernard* was an owner of lands here in the time of Henry III. Test. de Nev., 136. Heytesbury Hundr., 220.

NAME.	T. R. E. Owner, or Tenant.	T. R. W. Tenant in Capite.	T. R. W. Under-Tenant.	MODERN NAME, &c.
COTEFORD p. 117	Aluric	OSBERN GIFARD		This is no doubt *ASHTON GIFFARD*, a tithing in t parish of Codford St. Peter. This will be tolerably e dent by comparing the entry under ASTON, in Test. Nev., 137, with the one just given relating to COTEFO Heytesb. Hundr., 225.
COTEFORD p. 104	Erlebald	WALERAN, the huntsman		*CODFORD ST. MARY*, in the hundred of Heytesbu (p. 178). The manor of EAST CODFORD was held, c. 128 by Oliver de Ingham (Inq. p. m., 10 Edw. I.), a lineal de scendant of Waleran. Dr. Ingram published an account this parish, under the title of "Memorials of Codford S Mary." Heytesb. Hundr., 228.
COVELESTONE p. 131		BRICTRIC, as one of the King's Thanes		*COULSTON*, in the hundred of Whorwelsdown (p. 17 Like several other of the estates belonging to Brictr CUVELESTON became afterwards part of the possessio of the Bohuns, Earls of Hereford, and was held as app taining to the office of "Constable of England." Hund R. ii., 278.
COWIC p. 57		EARL MORTON	Church of St. Mary of Grestain.	*CONOCK*, in the hundred of Stodfald (p. 174), now in th of Swanborough. In the Hund. R. ii., 235, the Abbey Grestain is recorded as holding the manor of Couc 3 Edw. I. In the Nom. Vill. it is spelt CONEK, an said to be still held (1316) by the same Abbey. See Tes de Nev., 153. This is now reckoned as a tithing of t parish of CHIRTON.
CREDVELLE p. 37	Abbot of Malmesbury Guerlin,—3 hides	ABBOT OF MALMESBURY	Ebrard,—3 hides	*CRUDWELL*, in the hundred of Cicemethorn (p. 159), no in that of Malmesbury. This manor, which included HAN KYNTON (Hankerton), MORCOTE, and EASTCOTE, was giv to Malmesbury by King Æthelwulf. Cod. Dipl. 82 Land-limits will be found in charters in Add. MSS. (Br Mus.), 15,667, fol. 34–36; extracts from which are giv in the Archæologia, vol. 37. See Aubrey, 213.
CRICHELADE Church of p. 39		CHURCH OF ST. PETER, WESTMINSTER		*CRICKLADE*, in a hundred of the same name. A fe notices of this place, which includes some tithings sep rately accounted for in Domesday, will be found in Wilt Mag. vii., 137.
CRISTEMELEFORDE p. 30	Abbot of Glastonbury	ABBOT OF GLASTONBURY	Robert,—1 hide Edward, —1 virgate	*CHRISTIAN-MALFORD*, originally (p. 160) in the hundr of Sterkeley (Abb. Plac. 13), afterwards, like other estat belonging to the Abbot of Glastonbury, transferred to hundred called that of North Damerham. This estate w given by King Edmund, in 940, to Dunstan, Abbot Glastonbury. Cod. Dipl., 384. See Aubrey, 124, 422.
CRISTESFELDE p. 143		SBERNUS, as one of the King's Thanes		It looks as though the scribe had made a mistake in bo names, and that one was intended for *Osbernus*, and t other for *Fristesfelde* (Frustfield). This is mere suppo tion, but a reference to ALWARBERIE and HUMITONE w show that "OSBERN, a priest," had possessions at great distance from FRUSTFIELD.
CROSTONE p. 80	Carlo	ALURED OF MARLBOROUGH	Hugo	Conjectured to be *CORTON* (formerly *CORSTON*), in t parish of Helmarton. Lands in that parish were he under Alured of Marlborough. See above, under CLIV There was a free chapel at CORTON, and a list of t Incumbents from 1344–1524 is given in the Wiltshi Institutions. Aubrey, 168.
CUMBE p. 12	Ghida	THE KING		*COMBE BISSET*, in the hundred of Cawdon (p. 18 Included in this large manor is WEST HARNHAM. T manor belonged, in the time of Henry III., to John *Biss* Chief Forester of England, and descended to two of h sons-in-law, John de Wolyton (or Wotton), and Hugo Plessetis. Hund. R. ii., 247, See also Test de Nev., 1 Cawdon Hund., 10.
Church of p. 12			Leuric, the priest	

NAME.	T. R. E. Owner, or Tenant.	T. R. W. Tenant in Capite.	T. R. W. Under-Tenant.	MODERN NAME, &c.
CUMBREWELLE p. 86	Levenot	HUMFREY DE L'ISLE	Pagen	The names of the tenants, both before and after the Conquests, lead to the probable conclusion that this is *COMPTON-CUMBERWELL*, a tithing of Compton Bassett. See above, under CONTONE. Mr. Scrope suggests CUMBERWELL, near Bradford-on-Avon, but that tithing contains only 297 acres (probably only *half the extent* of the manor here referred to), and there is no actual *proof* that it belonged to the Dunstanvilles, the descendants of Humfrey de L'Isle, before the fourteenth century. Wilts Mag. II., 277. Test. de Nev., 141. Aubrey, 42.
CUNUCHE p. 133		ALWARD COLLINC, as one of the King's Thanes		These two holdings are, according to the Exon Domesday (p. 178), in the hundred of Heytesbury. They are no doubt different portions of *KNOOK*, a chapelry of Heytesbury, which contains, in all, some 1250 acres. Heytesb. Hundr., 187.
CUNUCHE p. 142	Leviet's husband	LEVIET, embroideress to the King and Queen, as one of the King's Thanes		
CUVLESTONE p. 127	Aluric	RICHARD STURMID		*COWESFIELD* [formerly *COWLESFIELD*] in the hundred of Frustfield (p. 189). One of the manors here belonged in 1316 to Henry *Sturmy*. Nom. Vill. See also Test. de Nev., 143, and Frustfield Hundr., 75.
DANTESIE p. 34	Alward, under the Abbot of Malmesbury	ABBOT OF MALMESBURY	Robert	*DAUNTSEY*, in the hundred of Sterkley, now in that of Malmesbury. This estate was given by King Æthelwulf, in 850, to Malmesbury. A charter with land-limits is to be found in Cod. Dipl., 263. Aubrey, 216.
DIARNEFORD p. 98		WILLIAM DE OW	Edward	These would seem to be respectively *GREAT* and *LITTLE DURNFORD*, now one parish, in the hundred of Ambresbury. The whole parish comprising the tithings of NORMANTON, NETTON, and SALTERTON, contains about 3,500 acres. The church of "DERNEFORD" is mentioned in a charter of Henry II., [New Mon. vi., 1296] as having been given to the cathedral at Sarum for the purpose of constituting a prebend, by "Walter, Son of Richard and Isabel de Thorny, and others, patrons of the same." Ambresb. Hundr., 120.
DARNEFORD p. 46	Three Englishmen, under the Abbess of Wilton.	ABBESS OF WILTON	Edward	
DECHEMENTONE p. 25	Azor	BISHOP OF BAIEUX	Robert, [Dispensator.] p. 184	These two estates would seem to make up *DITCHAMPTON*, near Wilton, the one being the portion of Ditchampton belonging to BURCOMBE, the other that annexed to WILTON. See note on p. 50. There was a church at Ditchampton, dedicated to St. Andrew, which in 1564 was annexed, by Bishop Jewell, to the Rectory of St. Mary, Wilton. Branche Hundr., 75, 152.
DICEHANTONE p. 49	Abbess of Wilton	ABBESS OF WILTON		
DEPEFORD p. 72	Osward Godwin	EDWARD OF SALISBURY	Azelin	*DEPTFORD*, now a tithing in the parish of WYLY, though in a distinct hundred, namely that of Heytesbury. This may be explained perhaps by the fact that the possessions of Edward of Salisbury lay chiefly in that hundred. Branche Hundr., 8.
DERINTONE p. 61	Harding, a Thane,—1 hide	EARL ALBERIC		*DURRINGTON*, in the hundred of Ambresbury. An account of successive owners of this manor is given in Aubrey, p. 356. The church is now in the gift of the Dean and Chapter of Winchester. Ambresb. Hundr., 41.
DEVREL p. 30	Abbot of Glastonbury	ABBOT OF GLASTONBURY	A Thane,—$1\frac{1}{2}$ hide	*LONGBRIDGE DEVEREL*, in the hundred of Heytesbury (p. 178), now, like other estates belonging to Glastonbury, in that of Damerham. In early times it would seem to have formed a separate hundred of itself. Abbrev. Plac., 16. Heytesb. Hundr., 35.
DEVREL p. 34	Abbot of Glastonbury Eisi,—$1\frac{1}{4}$ hide	ABBOT OF GLASTONBURY	"Miles,"—$1\frac{1}{4}$ hide	*MONKTON DEVEREL*, in the hundred of Mere (p. 182), now, for the same reason as the preceding manor, with which it is united in one parish, in that of Damerham. Mere Hundr., 176.

2 F

NAME.	T. R. E. Owner, or Tenant.	T. R. W. Tenant in Capite.	Under-Tenant.	MODERN NAME, &c.
Devrel p. 55	Brictric	Church of St. Mary at Bec.		*BRIXTON DEVEREL*, in the hundred of Heytesb[ury] (p. 178). Its distinctive name is clearly derived from Anglo-Saxon possessor. In the Test. de Nev., 154, is spelt "Brichtriches-ton." See note on p. 1[…] Heytesb. Hundr., 3.
Devrel p. 68	Saulf	Edward of Salisbury	Adelelm	This is no doubt the estate of 'one knight's fee' held, 1276, by John de Vernun, of the Earl of Hereford. Te[st.] de Nev., 139. It is a portion of *KINGSTON DEV[E]REL*, which parish is now in two hundreds, Mere [and] Ambresbury. The tenants, both before and after the Co[n]quest, held lands in this neighbourhood. See under B[a]lochelie and Sele.
Devrel p. 56	Eddeva	Canons of Lisieux		This is most probably the other portion of *KINGST[ON] DEVEREL*, and that which is now considered to be in *A[m]bresbury* Hundred. Originally it was in Mere Hund[r.] (p. 182). See Mere Hundr., 138.
Devrel p. 117	Smail	Osbern Gifard		All these four holdings, some of them of small extent, a[re] according to the Exon Domesday (p. 178), in the hundr[ed] of Heytesbury, and are no doubt portions of *HIL[L] DEVEREL*. In the Test de Nev., pp. 139, 142, 1[…] there are clearly *four* sub-infeudations, of varying exte[nt] in Hulle, or Hulle-Devrel. The *first* of these entr[ies] is the estate given, in 1180, by Elias Giffard, for t[he] purpose of constituting a prebend in the church [of] Heytesbury. See Heytesb. Hundr., 8.
Devrel p. 78	Ulmar	Ernulf de Hesding	Urso	
Devrel p. 138	Algar	Edgar, a priest, as one of the King's Thanes		
Devrel p. 149	Two Thanes	Alberic, the chamberlain, as one of the King's Officers		
Digeric p. 101	Alcstan of Boscumbe. [Alcstan,—1 hide, granted by an Abbot of Malmesbury]	William de Ow	Warner	*DITTERIDGE*, in the hundred of Chippenham (p. 16[…]). A comparison of the entries under "Breme" and "Di[g]eric" would lead to the probable conclusion that the *hi[de]* held by Alcstan, in the days of the Confessor, was Ywerig (Ew-ridge), now in the parish of Colerne, a pa[rt] of the original grant included in Bremhill to the Abb[ot] at Malmesbury. Aubrey, 78, 84.
Dobreham p. 28	Abbot of Glastonbury	Abbot of Glastonbury	Serlo [de Burei],—3 hides; Hugo's wife,—3 hides; Roger,—1 hide and 8 acres	*DAMERHAM*, in a hundred of the same name. Th[is] estate includes Tidpit, at which place there was [an] ancient church, (the names of the Incumbents bei[ng] still preserved,) and Marton, which is recorded also as [a] chapelry of Damerham. See Hoare's "South Damerham," 11, 22.
Dobreham p. 42		Church of Cranbourn		An entry in the Hund. R. II., 253, seems to imply that th[e] small holding of *one hide*, which is described as "[…] Damerham," was what was called "*LA HYDE*,"—n[ow] "*HIDE FARM*."
Domnitone p. 44	Abbess of Shaftesbury	Abbess of Shaftesbury	Gunfrid, 2 hides	*DINTON*, in the hundred of Warminster, though loca[lly] situated in that of Dunworth. This manor includes Te[f]font Magna. Wilts Arch. Mag. VII., 296 Dunwo[rth] Hundr., 102.
Dracote p. 92	Levenot	Milo Crispin	Rainald	*DRAYCOT FOLIOT*, in the hundred of Thornhill, (Hun[d.] R. II., 275,) now in that of Kingsbridge. See und[er] Cilletone. Wilts Mag. I., 93; III., 280.
Draicote p. 26	Alward } as *two* Elnod } manors	Bishop of Coutance	Roger	*DRAYCOT*, in the parish of Wilcot, and hundred of Swa[n]borough. See Exon. Domesd. (p. 175).

NAME.	T. R. E. Owner, or Tenant.	T. R. W. Tenant in Capite.	T. R. W. Under-Tenant.	MODERN NAME, &c.
DRAICOTE p. 147	Edric	GEOFFREY [MARESCAL],—as one of the King's Officers		*DRAYCOT CERNE*, in the hundred of Sterkley (p. 160), now in that of Malmesbury. In the Exon Domesday the owner is called "Gosfridus *Marescal*." This estate was held by the "CERNES" and their predecessors, the family of "VENOIR" by the service of supplying the "Third rod of the *Marshalsea*." See Aubrey, 229, and also Hund. R. II., 235. This tenure, we may perhaps infer from the above notice in the Exon Domesday, is probably of an earlier date than has hitherto been supposed.
DUNTONE p. 17	Bishop of Winchester	BISHOP OF WINCHESTER	William de Braiose,—14 hides. Waleran,—5 hides. Ralph,—5 hides. Ansgot,—$3\frac{1}{2}$ hides.	*DOWNTON*, in a hundred of the same name. This extensive manor, which includes BISHOPSTON (formerly Ebbesbourn Episcopi),—CHARLTON,—HAMPTWORTH,—WITHERINGTON,—NUNTON,—and BODENHAM,—was given at the first by Cenwalch, King of Wessex, about the middle of the seventh century, to the church of St. Peter and Paul, Winchester. A series of charters, recording successive grants of this large manor, will be found in Cod. Dipl., 985, 1108, 1036. Of the subordinate holdings the *first* would seem to include the "Knight's fee" held, in 1278, by William de *Brewes* in FALLERSTONE (Fallston, in Bishopston parish),—and the *second*, that held by Oliver de Ingham, a direct descendant of Waleran, at HAMPTWORTH, on the south-east boundary of Downton. Hund. R. II., 256.
DUNEHEVE p. 43	Abbess of Shaftesbury	ABBESS OF SHAFTESBURY	Turstin—6 hides A Thane, — 1 hide	From the large extent of this estate it would seem to have included *DONHEAD ST. ANDREW* and *DONHEAD ST. MARY*, the latter comprising also the Chapelry of CHARLTON. This was a gift, according to the Test. de Nev., 155, of King Edgar. See Wilts Mag. VII., 281. Dunworth Hundr., 29, 49.
DUENE p. 107	Godric	WALERAN, the huntsman		*WEST DEAN*, in the hundred of Alderbury. The adjoining estate of EAST DEAN, which is in Hants, belonged also to Waleran.—Hants Domesd., *fol.* 48. The Wiltshire portion, together with the neighbouring estate of GRYMSTEAD, [see below, under GREMESTEDE] belonged (3 Edw. I.) to Oliver Ingham, and William de St. Martin, both of them being direct descendants of Waleran. Alderb. Hundr., 9, 17.
EBLESBORNE p. 113	Alward, Fitheus } for two manors	ROBERT FITZ-GIROLD	Robert	This is no doubt *EBBESBOURN WAKE*, in the hundred of Stanford (Chalk). This manor was held by several in succession of the family of WAKE during the 13th and 14th centuries. Hund. R. II., 248. Test. de Nev., 142. Chalk Hundr., 161.
ECESATINGETONE p. 65		EDWARD OF SALISBURY		This is clearly *ETCHILHAMPTON* (near Devizes), originally in the hundred of Stodfald (p. 174), now in that of Swanborough. It is spelt in various ways,—HOCHELHAMPTON,—ETHEL-HAMPTON, &c., and is now pronounced ASHLINGTON, or, ASHELTON. See Hundr. R. II., 235. Test. de Nev., 152, 153. It is a chapelry of ALL-CANNINGS.
ECESATINGETONE p. 75	Edric	ERNULF DE HESDING	The wife of Edric	The wife of Edric would seem most probably to be the ESTRIT, named in the Exon Domesday (p. 174) as holding land in the hundred of Stodfald. These two possessions, the latter being of very small extent, would seem to be portions also of *ETCHILHAMPTON*.
ECHESATINGETONE p. 137		ERLECHING, as one of the King's Thanes		
EDINTONE p. 65	Earl Harold	EDWARD OF SALISBURY		*HEDDINGTON*, in the hundred of Calne (p. 172). A moiety of this estate was held in the time of Edw. I., by the Abbess of Lacock, the same having been given to that religious house by Ela, Countess of Sarum. Test. de Nev., 155

NAME.	T. R. E. Owner, or Tenant.	T. R. W. Tenant in Capite.	T. R. W. Under-Tenant.	MODERN NAME, &c.
EDENDONE p. 52	Abbess of Romsey	ABBESS OF ROMSEY	William, —4½ hides Osmund,—4 hides Englishmen—5 hides Hervey,—2 hides	*EDINGDON*, in the hundred of Whorwelsdown (p.173). T manor included the tithings of WEST COULSTON,—BA TON,—TINHEAD,—and also NORTH BRADLEY and SOU WICK. The "Osmund," mentioned among the tenants, most probahly the same person as held the neighbour estate of PONBERIE (Pomeroy). Aubrey, 346. Wilts M III., 47.—V. 193, 243.
EDENDONE p. 144	Osward	HERVEY OF WILTON as one of the King's Officers		The owner of this small estate of *one hide*, would seem be the same as one of the tenants in the preceding ent This holding is no doubt a part of the above estate.
ELENDUNE p. 19	Bishop of Winchester [Godric,—1½ hide, under the Bishop]	BISHOP OF WINCHESTER, "pro victu monachorum."	"Miles,"—1½ hide	This is the portion of what is now called *WROUGHT* which is in Elstub Hundred. The estate is sometin called 'ELINGDON-WROUGHTON,'—Hund. R. II., 244. is the "ELLENDUNE" of the Anglo-Saxon charters. S its land-limits, from the Codex Winton, printed in Co Dipl., 1184. It was at the time of Domesday, in Black grave Hundred (p. 166). Aubrey, 367.
ELECOME p. 63	Azor	EARL ALBERIC		*ELCOMB* in the parish of ELINGDON (=WROUGHTON), a like it originally in the hundred of Blachegrave (p. 16 There was a chapel here to which the Lords Lovel p sented from 1308—1448, a list of the Incumbents bei still preserved in the Wilts Institutions. Aubrey, 369.
ELTONE p. 147	Godric Bollo	JOHN, the doorkeeper,—as one of the King's Officers	Turstin,—1 hide Frawin,—1 hide	This estate, according to the Exon Domesday (p. 185) was the hundred of Ambresbury. It is no doubt the ALETON the Nom. Vill., and most probably *ALTON*, in the pari of FIGHELDEAN. Ambresb. Hund., 36.
ENEDFORDE p. 20	Bishop of Winchester	BISHOP OF WINCHESTER, "pro victu monachorum."	William,—5 hides Harold,—2 hides An Englishman,—3 hides The Priest,—1 hide	*ENFORD*, in the hundred of Elstub (p. 179). The wh parish, comprising now the tithings of CHISENBU PRIORS,—FIFIELD,—LONG STREET,—COMBE,—and COM TON,—contains 6,975 acres. This estate was given to t church at Winchester by King Æthelstan, in 934. See t charter in Cod. Dipl., 1110. Elstub Hundr., 19.
ESSITONE p. 41	Church of Cranbourn	CHURCH OF CRANBOURN		*ASHTON KEYNES*, in the hundred of Cricklade (p. 16 Robert de Keynes died seized of part of this estate 1280. Aubrey, 160. The Abbot of Tewkesbury was p tron of the living from the 14th to the middle of the 16 century. See p. 41, *note*.
ESTONE p. 79	Godus	ERNULF DE HESDING		This is a portion of *EASTON PIERS* [or *PERCY*], in t hundred of Thorngrave (p. 160), now in that of Malme bury. Though in a different hundred, it is consider part of the parish of KINGTON ST. MICHAEL. It was fo merly a separate chapelry, with its own Incumbent a Patron. It is named among the fees of "Patricius Cadureis" (=Chaworth), and was held subordinately "Henry *Kaignel.*" Inq. p. m. 42, Henry III. Test. Nev., 150. A deed, given in Aubrey 444, seems to ide tify this holding with "OLD EASTON"; and the mention of BROMDUNE (now evidently Broomfield) in the same dee points out the locality as the *western* portion of the prese tithing. Aubrey, 235. Wilts Mag., IV., 72.

NAME.	T. R. E. Owner, or Tenant.	T. R. W. Tenant in Capite.	T. R. W. Under-Tenant.	MODERN NAME, &c.
ESTONE p. 119	Osward	DROGO FITZ-PONZ	Gislebert	This is most probably another portion of *EASTON PIERS*. The neighbouring estates of ALDRINTONE (Alderton) and SEGRIE were also held by, or under, Drogo Fitz-Ponz. In the Test. de Nev., 140, both SEGRE and ESTON are named among the fees of Walter de Clifford, a descendant of Drogo Fitz-Ponz. See p. 119, *note*. This holding may be conjectured to be at LOWER EASTON.
ESTONE p. 115	Alwi	ROGER DE BERCHELAI		*EASTON GREY*, in the old hundred of Dunelawe (p. 161), now in that of Chippenham. The patronage of the church belonged from an early period to the Abbey of St. Peter's, Gloucester, in which society Roger de Berchelai became a monk. Aubrey, 85.
ESSELIE p. 97	Eldred	DURAND OF GLOUCESTER		*ASHLEY*, near Tetbury, in the old hundred of Cicemethorn (p. 159), now in that of Malmesbury. Aubrey, 207. A survey of the manor (1591) is given in Wilts Mag. vi., 199.
ESSAGE p. 102	Alwin	WILLIAM DE BRAIOSE	Robert	This would seem from the Exon Domesday (p. 169) to be in the hundred of Selkley. In the Nom. Vill. under that hundred, is given the manor of SHAWE, held (c. 1316) by John de Hardyngton. It would seem to be *SHAW*, an outlying portion of the parish of ALTON BERNERS.
ETESBERIE p. 122	Alwi	ALURED OF SPAIN		*YATESBURY*, in the hundred of Calne (p. 172). The parish contains about 1600 acres. Aubrey, 46.
ETONE p. 79	Two Thanes	ERNULF DE HESDING	Judichel	This is most probably the "*one knight's fee* held by Henry Kaynel, at Yatton, of Patrick de Chaworth," in the time of Henry III. Test. de Nev., 142. It is a portion of *YATTON KAYNEL*, in the old hundred of Thorngrave, afterwards in that of Chippenham. Aubrey, 120.
.... p. 79	Aluric	ERNULF DE HESDING	Hubold	The *name* of this holding is not given; it was probably in the same neighbourhood as the one just described.
ETONE p. 28	Levenot	BISHOP OF LISIEUX	Turstin	According to the Exon Domesday (p. 162), this manor appears to be in the hundred of Chippenham. It is possibly *YATTON KEYNES*, or, as it is also called, *WEST YATTON*. Aubrey, 122.
ETONE p. 129	Edric	HERMAN DE DREWES, as one of the King's Servants		
ETTONE p. 59	Osmund, a Thane	EARL ROGER	Turold	This estate is alluded to in the Exon Domesday (p. 164) as having been in the hundred of Highworth. It is most probably *EATON MEYSY* (or *CASTLE EATON*), which, like POULTON, another of the Earl Roger's estates, belonged, in the time of Edw. III., to Sir Thomas de Sancto Mauro (Seymour). See below, under POLTONE.
EUNESTETONE p. 33	Abbot of Glastonbury	ABBOT OF GLASTONBURY		A portion of *IDMESTON*, in the hundred of Alderbury (p. 190). In the Hundr. Rolls, ii., 242, IDMESTON is spoken of as having belonged "ex antiquo" to the Abbot of Glastonbury. Charters containing land-limits will be found in the Cod. Dipl., 417, 419, 565, and in New Monast. i., 58. See below, under WENISTETONE. Alderb. Hund., 54, 208.
FARLEGE p. 131		BRICTRIC, as one of the King's Thanes	The brother of Brictric [Alwi (?)]	*MONKTON FARLEIGH*, in the hundred of Bradford. A history of the Priory at this place is given in Wilts Mag. iv., 267.

2 G

NAME.	T. R. E. Owner, or Tenant.	T. R. W. Tenant in Capite.	Under-Tenant.	MODERN NAME, &c.
FARLEGE p. 133	Brismar	ALURIC of Melksham as one of the King's Thanes		*FARLEIGH*, in the hundred of Alderbury. This is chapelry of the parish of ALDERBURY, and would seem have been included in the gift recited in the charter Henry I. to the cathedral at Sarum. Alderh. Hund., 37.
FERSTESFELD p. 135	Aldred	ALDRED, as one of the King's Thanes		This, according to the Exon Domesday (p. 189), is in th hundred of Fruetfield. It is conjectured to be *ALDERS TON* (formerly *Aldredes-ton*), which still retains the nam of its Anglo-Saxon owner. Frustf. Hundr., 4.
FERSTESFELD p. 115	Godwin	BERNARD PANCE-VOLT		These are also, no doubt, small holdings in FRUSTFIELD The owner of the former, Bernard Pancevolt, held estate on the Hampshire side of the border. See Moody Hants Domesd., p. 37.
FRISTESFELD p. 140		ULURIC, as one of the King's Thanes		
FEBEFONTE p. 50	Abbess of Wilton	ABBESS OF WILTON		*FOVANT*, in the hundred of Cadworth, given by Kin Æthelred, in 994, to the monastery at Wilton. A charte with land-limits, is given in Cod. Dipl., 687. Cadw Hundr., 76.
FIFHIDE p. 18	Alsi, under the Bishop of Winchester	BISHOP OF WIN-CHESTER	Edward	Most probably *FIFIELD*, in the hundred of Elstub. I the Hundr. R. ii., 258, it is called "Fifhide *Episcopi*. It is now regarded as a tithing of ENFORD. A charter containing land-limits, will be found in Cod. Dipl., 592.
FIFHIDE p. 82	Carlo	ALURED of Marl-borough	Radulf	These two entries refer to *FIFIELD BAVENT*, in th hundred of Stanford. Like other estates belonging t Alured of Marlborough, this was held under the family c Tregoz. Hundr. R. ii., 249; Chalk Hund., 115.
FIFHIDE p. 84	Ulmar	ALURED of Marl-borough	Ulmar	
FISCARTONE p. 61	Godric	EARL HUGO	Haimo	Most probably *FISHERTON ANGER*, next Salisbury, i the hundred of Branche. The second name is a corrup tion of AUCHER. Several persons bearing that family nam possessed the manor towards the close of the 13th century Test. de Nev., 140, 156. Branche Hundr., 162.
FISERTONE p. 114	Bondi	ROGER DE CORCELLE		*FISHERTON DELAMERE*, in the hundred of War minster (p 177), though locally situated in that of Heytes bury. In early times it was held under the manor o CURI (Curry Mallet), in Somerset (Test. de Nev., 151) which also belonged at the time of Domesday to ROGER D CORCELLE. The DELAMERE family, of Nunney, owne it A.D. 1390—hence its distinctive name. Heytesb. Hund. 252.
FISGLEDENE p. 139	Harding	HARDING, as one of the King's Thanes	Earl Alberic had $4\frac{1}{2}$ hides, now in the King's hand	A portion of the present parish of *FIGHELDEAN*, in th hundred of Ambresbury. See above, under ALBOLDIN TONE,—CHELESTANSTONE,—and ELTONE. The church of FICHELDENE was given to the cathedral at Sarum early in the 12th century. A charter of Henry I., con taining the grant, is among the Bishop's records, and is printed in New Mon. vi., 1296. The rectory was an nexed to the Treasurership of the Cathedral. Aubrey, 357 Ambresb. Hundr., 34.
FISTESFERIE p. 90	Edric	HUMFREY DE L'ISLE		This, according to the Exon Domesday (p. 189), was in th hundred of FRUSTFIELD, of the original form of which i is probably a corruption. It is most likely to b *WHELPLEY*, an estate which belonged to the Dunstan villes, descendants of Humfrey de L'Isle, from the 13th century downwards. Test. de Nev., 144. Wilts Mag ii., 272, 286. Frustf. Hundr., 30.

NAME.	T. R. E. Owner, or Tenant.	T. R. W.		MODERN NAME, &c.
		Tenant in Capite.	Under-Tenant.	
FISTESBERIE p. 111	Vitel	ROBERT FITZ-GIROLD	Rainer	From the principal and subordinate owners being the same, it is possible that these two are different portions of the same estate. The latter is most probably *FOSBURY*, a manor now absorbed into Tottenham park. Aubrey, 380. Robert Fitz-Girold was possessed of the neighbouring manor of BEDESDENE.
FOSTESBERGE p. 112	Alwin	ROBERT FITZ-GIROLD	Rainer	
FONTEL p. 17	Bishop of Winchester	BISHOP OF WINCHESTER		*FONTHILL EPISCOPI*, originally in the hundred of Dunworth (p. 182), then included in a small hundred called that of Knowel Episcopi, afterwards transferred to that of Downton. Dunw. Hundr., 10, 194, 210.
FONTEL p. 115	Euing	BERENGER GIFARD		*FONTHILL GIFFARD*, in the hundred of Dunworth. The Exon Domesday (p. 182) appears to give the name of the owner as 'Berenger *Cotel*.' Dunw. Hundr., 12.
FOXELEGE p. 114	Aldret	ROGER DE BERCHELSI		*FOXLEY*, in the old hundred of Sterkley (p. 160), now in that of Malmesbury. Aubrey, 275.
GARDONE p. 37	Ulveva, under the Abbot of Malmesbury	ABBOT OF MALMESBURY		*GARSDON*, in the hundred of Cicemethorn (p. 159), now in that of Malmesbury. This was one of the earliest possessions of Malmesbury. A charter reciting its gift to Aldhelm, by Ina, King of Wessex (A.D. 701), is given in Cod. Dipl., 48. It seems at one time to have been lost to the Abbey, for by a charter, dated 1081, Matilda, Queen of the Conqueror, makes a grant of it to Abbot Warin. Aubrey, 242.
GARE p. 126	Osward	ROBERT MARESCAL		*GORE*, a tithing now of MARKET LAVINGTON, which, like it, belonged to Robert Marescal. See under LAVENTONE. In the Nom. Vill. it is reckoned in the hundred of DOLESFELT, as it was at the time of Domesday (p. 184). Dole. Hundr., 208.
GATEGRAM p. 142	Saulf's father	SAULF, as one of the King's Thanes		Possibly *GOATACRE*, in the parish of Helmarton, but this is mere conjecture. See Aubrey, 168.
GELINGEHAM p. 130	Algar	FULCHERED, as one of the King's Servants		This small holding must be on the south-west border of the county, by *GILLINGHAM*, in Dorset. No part of that parish is in Wilts, but in old papers "MERE GILLINGHAM" occurs, as if at one time there was some commixture of parishes in that locality. In the Exon Domesday for Dorset (*fol.* 24), under the hundred of GELINGEHAM, we have FULCRED named as possessed of 2½ *virgates* in demesne.
GESSIC p. 63	Azor	EARL ALBERIC		This must be, most probably, a portion of *GUSSAGE*, which is also on the borders of the county, and close by Cranbourne chase. No part of GUSSAGE is now in Wilts, all the parishes bearing that name, and there are several, being wholly in Dorset.
GETONE p. 101	Alestan of Boscumbe	WILLIAM DE OW	An Englishman	A small holding possibly at or near *YATTON KEYNEL*, in the old hundred of Thorngrave. The neighbouring estates of SEVAMENTONE and SOPEWORDE belonged to William de Ow.
GRAFTONE p. 100	Alestan of Boscumbe	WILLIAM DE OW	Hugo	All these holdings are alluded to in the Exon Domesday (p. 181) under the hundred of Kinwardstone. They are different portions of *EAST* and *WEST GRAFTON*, in the parish of Great Bedwin. Wilts Mag. vi., 270, 274.
GRASTONE p. 145		RICHARD STURMID, as one of the King's Officers		
GRASTONE p. 145	Ulmar	ROBERT FITZ-ROLF, as one of the King's Officers		

NAME.	T. R. E. Owner, or Tenant.	T. R. W. Tenant in Capite.	T. R. W. Under-Tenant.	MODERN NAME, &c.
GRASTONE p. 145	Alwin, Alwold, Lewin, Celestan under Radulf de Halville	RADULF DE HALVILLE, as one of the King's Officers		This holding is also alluded to in the Exon Domesday (p. 181,) under the hundred of Kinwardstone. It is a portion of either *EAST* or *WEST GRAFTON*, in the parish of GREAT BEDWIN. Wilts Mag., vi., 270, 274.
GRAMESTEDE p. 136	Cola's father	COLA, as one of the King's Thanes		These two entries probably refer to different portions of *WEST GRIMSTEAD*, in the hundred of Alderbury. One of the large dykes called *Grimes-dic* (or Grims-ditch) is near the parish, and hence no douht its name is derived. Alderb. Hundr., 9.
GRAMESTEDE p. 138	Aiulf	EDMUND, son of Aiulf, as one of the King's Thanes		
GREMESTEDE p. 106	Agemund	WALERAN, the huntsman	Herbert	*EAST GRIMSTEAD*, a chapelry of WEST DEAN, in the hundred of Alderhury. This estate was held hy Waleran's descendants, the families of INGHAM, and ST. MARTIN, for some centuries afterwards. Hundr. R. ii., 243. Inq. p. m. 18, Ed. III. Alderh. Hund., 116.
GRAVELINGES FOREST p. 144		THE KING'S FORESTERS		The forest of *GROVELEY*, in South Wilts. Dunw. Hundr., 184–190, 226; Branche Hundr., 172.
GRENDEWELLE p. 88	Ordulf	HUMFREY DE L'ISLE	Hugo, Girald	*GROUNDWELL*, now a farm in the parish of LITTLE BLUNSDON, and hundred of Highworth. Wilts Mag., ii., 283.
GRETELINTONE p. 32	Abbot of Glastonbury	ABBOT OF GLASTONBURY	Bishop of Coutance, 5 hides; Urso,—4 hides	*GRITTLETON*, in the hundred of Thorngrave (p. 160), then included in that of Chippenham, and afterwards, like other estates belonging to Malmeshury, transferred to that of Damerham. A history of Grittleton, written hy Canon Jackson, was published some years ago hy the Wilts Topographical Society. Aubrey, 129.
GUERMINSTRE p. 8	King Edward	THE KING		*WARMINSTER*, the name of a principal town in South Wilts, and of the hundred in which it is situated. Warm. Hundr., 1–40.
HAME p. 18	Bishop of Winchester	BISHOP OF WINCHESTER "pro victu monachorum"	William,—2 hides	*HAM*, originally in the hundred of Kinwardstone (page 180), now, like other estates helonging to the Bishop of Winchester, in that of Elstuh. There is a charter, relating to HAMME, in Cod. Dipl., 1220. The estate at one time was lost to the monastery; for, in a document preserved by Leland, Collect. i., 613, relating to the founders of the cathedral church of St. Swithin, Winchester, it is said of Bishop Tochin (Toclive?) (c. 1180), "*Redemit* Hamme et suæ ecclesiæ Winton. dedit." N. Mon. i., 210.
HANINDONE p. 29	Abbot of Glastonbury	ABBOT OF GLASTONBURY	Robert	*HANNINGTON*, in the hundred of Highworth, the gift of Elfreda, Queen of Edward the Elder, to the Abhot of Glastonhury. N. Mon. i., 50. The manor, in 1316, belonged to Henry of Lancaster. Nom. Vill. A survey of it, as part of the possessions of the Duchy of Lancaster, in 1591, is given in Wilts Mag. vi., 189.
HANTONE p. 113	Ulgar	ROBERT FITZ-ROLF		This is possibly *LITTLE HINTON*, originally in the hundred of Highworth (p. 164). It is given under that of Thornhill, in the Nom. Vill. (1316). It is now in Elstub, as part of the possessions of the church of Winchester, to which it was given by Alwin, Bishop of Winchester (c. 1040). N. Mon. i., 195. If our conjecture be true, this estate must have been lost for a time to Winchester.

NAME.	T. R. E. Owner, or Tenant.	T. R. W. Tenant in Capite.	T. R. W. Under-Tenant.	MODERN NAME, &c.
HANTONE p. 89	Ulgar	HUMFREY DE L'ISLE	Ranulf	These are portions of *BROAD HINTON*, a parish which is situated in *two* hundreds. Aubrey, 331. The *former* of the entries is in the hundred of Kingsbridge. Among the fees of Egidius de Badlesmere, a descendant of Humfrey de L'Isle, is BRODHINTON. Inq. p. m. 12 Edw. III. See also Wilts Mag. ii., 284. The *latter* of the entries seems accounted for in the Exon Domesday (p. 169) under the hundred of Selkley, and the estate was held, like others belonging to Gilbert de Bretevile, as part of the fee of the Earl Marshal, in 3 Edw. I. Hund. R. ii., 269.
HANTONE p. 95	Ulgar	GILBERT DE BRETEVILE		
HARDENEHUS p. 78	Alward	ERNULF DE HESDING	Turchil	*HARDENHUISH*, in the old hundred of Thorngrave, now in that of Chippenham. Patricius de Cadurcis (Chaworth) died siesed of HARDENHEWISHE, 42 Henry III. (Inq. p. m.), and, under his family, many of the estates, possessed at the time of Domesday by Ernulf de Hesding, were afterwards held. Test. de Nev., 142. Inq. p. m. 4 Edw. II.
HASEBERIE p. 94	Levenot	MILO CRISPIN	Rainald	These entries, three of them of very small extent, refer to *HASELBURY*, in the hundred of Chippenham. This was formerly a distinct parish, though now deemed part of Box, the names of the Incumbents, who were appointed by the Priors of Bradenstoke, being still preserved. "ASELBIRI," like other manors belonging to Milo Crispin, was held (c. 1280) by Henry Crok, of the "honor of *Wallingford*." Test. de Nev., 156. Walter Croc gave property here to Bradenstoke Abbey. Aubrey, 58.
HASEBERIE p. 136	Cheping	CHEPING, as one of the King's Thanes		
HASEBERIE p. 124	Alsi, a priest	NIGEL, the Physician		
HASEBERIE Church of p. 16		BISHOP OSBERN		
HAREDONE p. 145	Aluric	RICHARD STURMID	Robert	*HARDING*, in the parish of Bedwin and hundred of Kinwardstone (p. 181). Its present form is a corruption of HAREDON, or, as it is also written, HARDEN. Test. de Nev., 143. Wilts Mag. vi., 272.
HARDICOTE p. 90	Aluric	HUMFREY DE L'ISLE		*HURDCOT* (or *HURCOT*), in the hundred of Cadworth (p. 187). It is situated between Barford St. Martin and Compton Chamberlain. It was held of the Barony of Combe, 3 Edw. I., by Petronilla de Montfort, a daughter of Walter de Dunstanville, and lineal descendant of Humfrey de L'Isle. Hundr. R. ii., 253. Wilts Mag. ii., 272.
HERDICOTE p. 107	Ednod	WALERAN, the huntsman.		According to the Exon Domesday (p. 190), this small estate was in the hundred of Alderbury. It is probably *HURCOT*, in the parish of WINTERBOURN EARLS.
HELMERINTONE p. 76	Aschil	ERNULF DE HESDING	Robert	These are two holdings, each of moderate extent, in the present parish of HELMARTON, in the hundred of Kingsbridge. The parish consists of *six* hamlets. See under ADHELMERTONE, CROSTONE, and WIDECOMBE. Aubrey, 167.
HELMERTUNE p. 134		ALURIC "parvus"		
HELPRINTONE p. 129	Three Thanes	ANSGER, the cook, as one of the King's Servants.		All these holdings, some of them of but small extent, are different portions of *HILPERTON*. The several owners are alluded to in the Exon Domesday (p. 171), under the hundred of Melksham.
HELPRINTONE p. 129	Four Thanes	WILLIAM CORNIOLE, as one of the King's Servants.		
HELPERITUNE p. 137		GODWIN CLEC, as one of the King's Thanes		
HELPERINTONE p. 143	Eldild's husband	ELDILD, as one of the King's Thanes		

NAME.	T. R. E. Owner, or Tenant.	T. R. W. Tenant in Capite.	T. R. W. Under-Tenant.	MODERN NAME, &c.
Heortham p. 60	Ednod	Earl Hugo	Edward	All these holdings,—several of them of very small extent, and amounting in the whole to rather less than *six hides*,—were no doubt at *HARTHAM*, near Chippenham. It is conjectured that they refer to lands, partly in the parish of Corsham, and partly in that of Biddeston St. Nicholas. Turchitil, the under-tenant of the *second* manor, was also tenant of the adjoining estate of Bedestone. (Biddeston St. Peter's). See Aubrey, 54, 83. Wilts Mag. ii., 285; iv., 143.
Hertham p. 72	Two Thanes	Edward of Salisbury	Turchitil	
Heortham p. 89	Godric	Humfrey de L'Isle	Hugo	
Hertham p. 137	Godric's father	Godric, the huntsman, as one of the King's Thanes		
Hertham p. 138	Edric, the blind	Edric, as one of the King's Thanes		
Heortham p. 142	Alfildis' husband	Alfildis, as one of the King's Thanes		
.... p. 142	Alwi	Saieva, as one of the King's Thanes		This small holding of *one virgate* is alluded to in the Exon Domesday (p. 161), under the hundred of Chippenham. The name of the estate is not given, but, following immediately after an entry relating to Hartham, it may be conjectured to have been in the same neighbourhood.
Hestrebe Church of p. 16		Alward, the Priest		This was at *HEYTESBURY*:—The glebe land is here reckoned at 2 *carucates*; so, in the Inq. Non. 155, under Heghtredebury we have this entry, "Rector habet *duas carucatas terræ*." A full history of the church at Heytesbury, which was collegiate, and had its Dean and Prebendaries, will be found in Heytesb. Hundr., 82.
Hiwei p. 34	Abbot of Malmesbury	Abbot of Malmesbury		*HIGHWAY*, originally in the hundred of Kingsbridge, (p. 165). This manor was surrendered, c. 1228, to the see of Salisbury, and was afterwards placed in the hundred of Cannings, in which it still remains. The full particulars of the transfer of the estate from the Abbot to the Bishop are given in Aubrey, 60.
Hiwi p. 110	Toti, for 3 lives, under the Abbot of Malmesbury	Radulf de Mortemer		
Horningesham p. 57	Agenulf's father	Canons of Lisieux	Agenulf	This would seem to be the estate at *HORNINGSHAM*, in the hundred of Heytesbury, which was afterwards given for the purpose of founding a prebend in the church of Heytesbury. Heytesb. Hundr., 45.
Horningham p. 84	Colsuen	Alured of Marlborough	Osmund	*LITTLE HORNINGSHAM*, in the parish of Maiden Bradley and Tithing of Baycliffe. It is alluded to in the Exon Domesday (p. 178), under the hundred of Heytesbury. There was a chapel here which was dependent on the church at Maiden Bradley. In the Test. de Nev., 154, Parva Horningesham is recorded as having been held subordinately by several persons under Robert Tregoz in chief. See p. 79, *note*.
Humitone p. 125	Alsi	Osbern, the Priest		*HOMINGTON*, close by Britford, in the hundred of Cawden. It is alluded to in the Exon Domesday (p. 187).
Hunlavintone p. 109	Earl Harold	Radulf de Mortemer		*HULLAVINGTON*, in the old hundred of Sterkley (p. 159); now in that of Malmesbury. This estate was given by Radulf de Mortemer for the endowment of the monastery of St. Victor in Normandy, which had been founded by his father. Test. de Nev., 155. See above, under Clatford. Hundr. R. ii., 272. Aubrey, 246.

NAME.	T. R. E. Owner, or Tenant.	T. R. W. Tenant in Capite.	T. R. W. Under-Tenant.	MODERN NAME, &c.
IMEMERIE p. 110	Alwin	RADULF DE MORTEMER		*IMBER*, now partly in the hundred of Heytesbury, and partly in that of Swanborough. In the Test. de Nev. 154, several infeudations are recorded of YMEMER; amongst others, one was held in chief of the honour of Wigmore, the principal seat of the MORTIMER family. Heytesb. Hundr., 158.
IWIS p. 144		RICHARD STURMID, as one of the King's Officers		*HUISH DOIGNEL*, in the hundred of Swanborough. ROBERT DOYNEL held the manor in the time of Henry III. (Hund. R. ii., 234), and hence comes its distinctive name. In 1414, SIR WILLIAM STURMY presented to the living. Wilts Inst.
JERCHESFONTE p. 51	Abbey of St. Mary, Winchester	ABBEY OF ST. MARY, Winchester	Edward,—$1\frac{1}{2}$ hide Walter, — 1 hide Englishmen, —$2\frac{1}{3}$ hides	*ERCHFONT*, in the hundred of Stodfald (p. 174), now in that of Swanborough. Hundr. R. ii., 273. Test. de Nev., 153.
LACOCH p. 71	Edwin	EDWARD OF SALISBURY		These two entries, the latter being of very small extent, refer to *LACOCK*, in the hundred of Chippenham (p. 162). A history of Lacock Abbey, by Bowles and Nichols, was published in 1835. Aubrey, 89.
LACOC p. 83	Carlo	ALURED OF MARLBOROUGH		
LANGEFEL p. 71	Ulwi	EDWARD OF SALISBURY	Borel Ulwi,—1 hide	*LANGLEY BURREL*, in the hundred of Chippenham; the name of the principal tenant at Domesday giving the parish its distinctive name. The family of BUREL continued to hold the manor till the commencement of the 14th century. The small holding of ULWI is referred to in the Exon Domesday (p. 162). Aubrey, 95.
LANGHELIE p. 32	Abbot of Glastonbury	ABBOT OF GLASTONBURY	Urso,—$2\frac{1}{2}$ hides Radulf,—$1\frac{1}{2}$hide Roger,—$1\frac{3}{4}$ hide	*KINGTON LANGLEY*, now a tithing in the parish of KINGTON ST. MICHAEL. From its extent,—it was assessed at *twenty-nine* hides,—it would seem to include the greater part of that parish, EASTON PIERS being separately accounted for under ESTONE. The name of one of the tenants, URSO, is perpetuated in LANGLEY FITZ-URSE, one of the subordinate manors. Aubrey, 146. This estate was first of all in the hundred of Thorngrave (p. 160), then in that of Chippenham, now in that of North Damerham. The history of the parish will be found in Aubrey. 130, and Wilts Mag. iv., 36–128.
LANGEFORD p. 105	Osulf	WALERAN, the huntsman.		*STEEPLE LANGFORD*, in the hundred of Branche. Sir Lawrence St. Martin, a lineal descendant of Waleran, died siesed of STUPEL LANGEFORD. Inq. p. m. 12 Edw. II. Branche Hundr., 171.
LANGEFORD p. 106	Norman	WALERAN, the huntsman	Erenburgis	By a comparison of notices in various records, this holding would seem probably to be at *LANDFORD*, in the hundred of Frustfield. Jacobus de Lye held (c. 1270) half a knight's fee at LANEFORD, under Albreda de Botreaux, a lineal descendant of Waleran. Test. de Nev., 141. In 1310, Willelmus de Lye presented to the church at LANEFORD (= Landford). Wilts Inst. Among the fees of Oliver de Ingham (also a descendant of Waleran) are reckoned LANEFORD, as well as STEPEL-LANGFORD. Inq. p. m., 17 Edw. III.
LANGEFORD p. 143	Otho's father	OTHO, as one of the King's Thanes		This is clearly the holding assigned to OTRE in the Exon Domesday (p. 189), under the hundred of Frustfield. It is no doubt, like the estate just described, a portion of *LANDFORD*. Frustf. Hundr., 81.

NAME.	T. R. E. Owner, or Tenant.	T. R. W. Tenant in Capite.	Under-Tenant.	MODERN NAME, &c.
LANGEFORD p. 58	Chetel	EARL MORTON		*HANGING LANGFORD*, in the parish of STEEPLE LANGFORD, and hundred of Branche (p. 184). In the Test. de Nev. 155, the following entry appears to relate to it, "Decanus de *Morton* tenet in HANGINDELANGEFORD 100 solidos terræ," &c. See also, Inq. Non. 177, under STUPELLANGEFORD. Branche Hundr., 16.
LANGEFORD p. 49	The father of the Englishmen who held it T. R. W., under the Abbess	ABBESS OF WILTON	Two Englishmen	*LITTLE LANGFORD*, in the hundred of Branche. This estate was granted by King Edmund, in 943, to the church at Wilton. The charter, with land-limits, is given in Cod. Dipl. iii., 419.
LANGEFORD p. 141		ULVIET, the huntsman, as one of the King's Thanes		According to the Exon Domesday (p. 187), this was in Cawden hundred. It is most probably *LONGFORD*, close by BRITFORD. Cawd. Hundr., 24.
LANGEFORD p. 33	Two Thanes, under the Abbot of Glastonbury	ABBOT OF GLASTONBURY	Edward [of Salisbury]	These were two small and contiguous estates. We have no certain clue to their locality. There is some slight reason for thinking that they were in Alderbury hundred, and probably some portion of what is now included in IDMESTON. This however is but conjecture.
LANGEFORDE p. 73	Azor	EDWARD OF SALISBURY	Letard	
LATONE See "AISI"				
LAVVRECESTOHES p. 50	Abbess of Wilton	ABBESS OF WILTON		These two entries relate to *LAVERSTOCK*, in the hundred of Alderbury (p. 190). Alderb. Hundr., 103.
LAVERTESTOCHE p. 143	Gest	SARIC, as one the King's Thanes		
LACHAM p. 101	Alestan of Boscumb	WILLIAM DE OW	Radulf	*LACKHAM*, in the parish of LACOCK, and hundred of Chippenham. It was held in the time of Henry III. under WILLIAM DE EWE, of the same family as its principal owner in Domesday. In 35 Edw. I. it occurs among the fees of Bigod, Earl Marshall, like some other estates, held under William de Ow as chief lord. Inq. p. m. Aubrey, 95.
LAVENTONE p. 126	Queen Editha	ROBERT MARESCAL		*MARKET* or *EAST LAVINGTON*, originally in the old hundred of Rugeberg (p. 174), now in that of Swanborough. A survey (1591) of EASTERTON GERNON in this parish, as part of the possessions of the Duchy of Lancaster, will be found in Wilts Mag. vi., 191. See above, under GARE.
LAVENTONE p. 126	Achi	ROBERT BLOND		*BISHOP'S* or *WEST LAVINGTON*, originally in the hundred of Rugeberg (p. 174), afterwards transferred to that of Potterne and Cannings. See note on p. 126, and also under LITELTONE.
LEDENTONE p. 44	Abbess of Shaftesbury	ABBESS OF SHAFTESBURY		*LIDDINGTON*, in the hundred of Thornhill (p. 168), now in that of Kingsbridge. A charter relating to LIDENTUNE is given in Cod. Dipl. iii., 415.
LITLEGARSELLE p. 67	Elward	EDWARD OF SALISBURY		*LUDGARSHALL*, in the hundred of Ambresbury (p. 186). See above, under BEDESDENE. Aubrey, 359. Ambresb. Hundr., 83.
LEDIAR p. 81	Carlo	ALURED OF MARLBOROUGH		*LIDIARD TREGOZ*, in the hundred of Blachegrave (p. 167), now in that of Kingsbridge. Its distinctive name is derived from the TREGOZ family, who, as successors of Alured of Marlborough, possessed it in the time of Edw. I. Hundr. R. ii., 244. Aubrey, 170.

NAME.	T. R. E. Owner, or Tenant.	T. R. W. Tenant in Capite.	T. R. W. Under-Tenant.	MODERN NAME, &c.
LIDIARDE p. 15	Godric, under the Earl William	THE KING		*LYDIARD MILICENT*, in the hundred of Staple (p. 165), now in that of Highworth. It derives its distinctive appellation from the Christian name of a lady who owned it in the time of King John. Aubrey, 153. Wilts Mag. vii. 142.
LITTLECOTE p. 92	Godric	MILO CRISPIN	Turchetil	According to the Exon Domesday (p. 166), this is in the hundred of Kingsbridge. It is most probably *LITTLECOTE*, in the parish of HELMARTON, a manor held in 1316, according to the Nom. Vill., by Ralph Bluet. Aubrey, 168.
LITELTONE p. 27	Alward, of the Church of Glastonbury	BISHOP OF COUTANCE	Robert	*LITTLETON DREW*, in the hundred of Dunelawe, now in that of Chippenham. DROGO (or DRU) FITZ-PONZ held no less than 73 estates in Devonshire, as tenant to the Bishop of Coutance, and also ALDRINTONE (Alderton), an adjoining estate; and hence it is possible that from him may have first come the distinctive name of this estate. WALTER DRU was Lord of Littelton about 1290. Test. de Nev., 142, 158. Aubrey, 103.
LITELTONE p. 99	Alestan de Boscumb, as Tainland belonging to the Church at Salisbury	WILLIAM DE OW	William de Aldrie	*LITTLETON*, a tithing of the parish of West Lavington, formerly in the hundred of Rugeberg, now in that of Potterne and Cannings. WILLIAM DE ALDRIE would seem to be the same as the WILLIAM DE ALDELEIA of the Exon Domesday (p. 173), there described as the son-in-law of Robert Blond, the owner of LAVENTONE (West Lavington). See p. 127.
LOCHERIGE p. 97	Elmar	DURAND OF GLOUCESTER		According to the Exon Domesday (p. 169), this is in the hundred of Selkley. It is *LOCKERIDGE*, which is situated between OVERTON and FIFIELD.
LOCHINTONE p. 97	Earl Harold	DURAND OF GLOUCESTER	Herman	These would seem to be different portions of *LUCKINGTON*, originally in the hundred of Dunelawe, afterwards in that of Chippenham. The *former* is alluded to in the Exon Domesday under the hundred of Dunelawe (p. 161). The fact of SIRENDONE, ALDRITONE, and CHINTONE,—all of them adjoining estates,—being held by Radulf de Mortemer, renders it most probable that the *latter* is also a portion of the same parish. In the Nom. Vill., A.D. 1316, under Chippenham hundred, there are *two* manors implied in the entry relating to LOKYNTONE. The whole parish contains 1627 acres. Aubrey, 105.
LOCHINTONE p. 111	Alward	RADULF DE MORTEMER	Edward	
MALMESBERIE Borough of pp. 3, 6		THE KING, and others		*MALMESBURY*;—the line separating the two hundreds of Sterkley and Cicemethorn (= Cheggelawe) ran originally through the centre of what is now the borough of Malmesbury. Moffat wrote a history of this town at the close of the last century. Wilts Mag. viii. 14. Aubrey, 251.
MAMESBERIE p. 26	Gilbert	BISHOP OF COUTANCE		These were two holdings, each of moderate extent, in the immediate neighbourhood of MALMESBURY, which it is not easy, or perhaps possible, accurately to identify.
MALMESBERIE p. 136	Godwin	CHETEL, as one of the King's Thanes		
MANEFORDE p. 39	Abbey of St. Peter, Winchester	ABBEY OF ST. PETER, WINCHESTER		*MANNINGFORD ABBAS*, in the hundred of Swanborough (p. 175). This is called MANINGFORD PARVA, in the Hund. R. ii. 234.
MANETUNE p. 93	Wigot	MILO CRISPIN	Rainald	*MANTON*, in the hundred of Selkley. This is now a tithing of PRESHUTE. It was held in the 13th century, like other estates belonging at Domesday to Milo Crispin, of the "honor of Wallingford." Hund. R. ii. 263.

NAME.	T. R. E. Owner, or Tenant.	T. R. W. Tenant in Capite.	T. R. W. Under-Tenant.	MODERN NAME, &c.
MANIFORD p. 129	Godric	AMELRIC DE DREWES, as one of the King's Servants		The *former* of these entries is most probably *MANNINGFORD BOHUN*, which contains about 1080 acres. It belonged to the BOHUN family, c. 1316, and is regarded as a tithing of WILSFORD, which was also a part of their possessions.—The *latter* is most probably *MANNINGFORD BRUCE*, which contains about 1300 acres. It derives its distinctive name from MARIA DE BREWOSE, who held the manor in 1316 (Nom. Vill.), and whose family were patrons of the living during the whole of the 14th century. Wilts Inst.
MANIFORD p. 136	Edward	GRIMBALD, the goldsmith, as one of the King's Thanes		
MARTONE p. 142		ODOLINA, as one of the King's Thanes		We have no clue to the hundred in which this small estate was situated. There is a MARTON by South Damerham, and a MARTEN close by Bedwin;—probably, from being named next to SCALDEBURNE (Shalbourn), a portion of the latter is referred to. See below, under MERTONE. In William the Conqueror's first charter to Westminster Abbey, there is mention of a "hide of land at MERTUNE, in Wiltshire," which had been given to the abbey by a "religious woman of the name of ODELINA." Reg. Westm. MS. Cotton. Faust. A. iii. fol. 42. See Ellis, i. 509.
MELCHESHAM p. 12	Earl Harold	THE KING		*MELKSHAM*, the name of a town, and of the hundred in which it is situated. The parish includes SHAW,—SEEND,—and ERLE-STOKE. Aubrey, 295.
MELCHESHAM, Church of p. 12		RUMOLD, the priest		The church at MELKSHAM was granted by King John to the cathedral at Salisbury. Hund. R. ii., 232. The deed is given in Hatcher and Benson's "Salisbury." Aubrey, 296.
MELCHESHAM p. 142	Liseman	LISEMAN, as one of the King's Thanes		This manor is alluded to in the Exon Domesday, under the hundred of Melksham (p. 171). It is most probably some estate in the immediate neighbourhood of the larger manor,—possibly POULSHOT, which does not appear to be otherwise accounted for; but this is simple conjecture.
MELEFORD p. 90	Sawold / Saward	HUMFREY DE L'ISLE	Gozelin	These two small holdings are both referred to in the Exon Domesday, under the hundred of Alderbury (p. 190). They are portions of *MILFORD*, close by Salisbury. The forest referred to, under the *second* entry, is that of CLARENDON. Wilts Mag. ii., 286. Alderb. Hund., 110.
MELEFORD p. 141		ULVICT, the huntsman, as one of the King's Thanes		
MERA p. 137		GODRIC, the huntsman, as one of the King's Thanes		These are three holdings, the first two of very small extent, in *MERE*. The first is alluded to in the Exon Domesday (p. 182), under the hundred of Mere. A moiety of the tithes of the church at MERE formed part of the endowment of the cathedral at Salisbury. Aubrey, 385. Mere Hund., 6.
MERE p. 140	Allic	ULURIC, as one of the King's Thanes		
MERE p. 141		ULNOD, as one of the King's Thanes		
MERESDENE p. 121	Wenesi	HUGO FITZ-BALDRIC	Walter [de Rivera], son-in-law of Hugo Fitz-Baldric	*MARDEN*, in the hundred of Swanborough (p. 175). This estate was forfeited to the Crown in the time of Henry III., "de terra Normannorum" (Hund. R. ii., 275), and was afterwards the possession of Ela, daughter of William Longespée (by her first marriage, Countess of Warwick), who had married Philip Bassett as her second husband. Her son-in-law, Hugh le Despencer, held the manor in 1316. Nom. Vill. The patronage of the church belonged from an early period to Bradenstoke Priory. Wilts Inst.

NAME.	T. R. E. Owner, or Tenant.	T. R. W. Tenant in Capite.	T. R. W. Under-Tenant.	MODERN NAME, &c.
MERLEBERGE Church of p. 16		WILLIAM DE BELFOU		The church of *MARLBOROUGH* was given by William I. to Osmund, Bishop of Sarum. As early as the reign of Henry III. there were *two* churches at MARLBOROUGH. Hund. R. ii., 256. The history of this town was written a few years ago by Mr. Waylen. See also Wilts Mag. vii., 1-29. Aubrey, 337.
MERTONE p. 145	Two Thanes	RADULF DE HALVILE, as one of the King's Officers		These are different portions of *MARTEN*, in the parish of GREAT BEDWIN. They are both alluded to in the Exon Domesday (pp. 180, 181), under the hundred of Kinwardstone. Wilts Mag. vi., 258, 273.
MERTONE p. 146	Lewin	TURBERT, as one of the King's Officers		
MIDELTONE p. 70	Lewin Alric	EDWARD, of Salisbury		These are portions of *MIDDLETON*, close by Warminster. They are referred to in the Exon Domesday (p. 177), under the hundred of Warminster. One of the Giffard family gave the latter estate to the Abbey of St. Stephen, Funtenay. Hund. R. ii., 276. Test. de Nev., 156.
MIDELTONE p. 117	Domno	OSBERN GIFARD	Church of St. Stephen, Funtenay	
MILDENHALLE p. 31	Hugolin, of the Abbot of Glastonbury	ABBOT OF GLASTONBURY	Edward	*MILDENHALL*, in the hundred of Selkley. The lordship of the manor belonged to Glastonbury till 3 Edw. I. (Hund. R. ii., 269), when it passed away from that religious house. For its subsequent history, see Aubrey, 338.
MILDESTONE p. 59	Osmund	EARL ROGER	Turold	These are portions of *MILSTON*, in the hundred of Ambresbury. The *former* is clearly alluded to in the Exon Domesday (p. 185), and also, as seems probable, the *latter*. A comparison of the entry with that respecting BRISMARTONE (p. 112), confirms the probability. Ambresb. Hund., 37.
MILDESTONE p. 112	Brismar	ROBERT FITZ-GIROLD	Robert	
MORDONE p. 81	Carlo	ALURED of Marlborough	Albert	*MORDON*, a hamlet now of the parish of RODBOURN CHENEY. It was seemingly at first in the old hundred of Scipe,—it is now in that of Highworth. John de Tregoz died siesed of it at the commencement of the 14th century. Inq. p. m. 28 Edw. I.
MORDONE p. 113	Ulgar	ROBERT FITZ-ROLF,		From the name of the possessor, T. R. E., who is also entered as holding HENTONE (Broad Hinton), we may conjecture that these two small estates were possibly in the same neighbourhood as the one just described, if not portions of it. In the Inq. p. m. 22 Edw. IV. the manor of LYDEYERD TREGOSE, together with lands at MORTON, WALCOTE, SWINDON, and elsewhere, are recorded as having been possessed by Agnes Dohyns. We have, however, no certain clue, as yet, to the exact locality of these two manors.
MORTUNE p. 95	Ulgar	GILBERT DE BRETEVILE	Turstin	
NEWENTONE p. 36	Abbot of Malmesbury. [The Abbot gave 1 hide 'cuidam militi suo']	ABBOT OF MALMESBURY	Osbern,—3 hides William,—2 hides	*LONG NEWNTON*, in the hundred of Cicemethorn (p. 158), now in that of Malmesbury. The manor was given to Malmesbury Abbey by Æthelred, king of Mercia, in 681. Cod. Dipl., 817. At the dissolution it was granted to the Estcourt family. Aubrey, 271.
NEWETONE p. 45	Abbess of Wilton	ABBESS OF WILTON	Richard Sturmid,—1 hide Aluric, the huntsman,—1 hide	*NORTH NEWNTON*, in the hundred of Swanborough (p. 175). This manor, which includes RAINSCOMB, was given to the monastery at Wilton, by King Æthelstan, in 933. Cod. Dipl. 320, 1109. The holding of Richard Sturmid was probably at RAINSCOMB. He was possessed of IWIS (Huish), an immediately adjoining estate (p. 144).

NAME.	T. R. E. Owner, or Tenant.	T. R. W. Tenant in Capite.	T. R. W. Under-Tenant.	MODERN NAME, &c.
NEWENTONE p. 48	Abbess of Wilton	ABBESS OF WILTON		*SOUTH NEWTON*, in the hundred of Branche (p. 184). A charter relating to this manor, which included "3 mansæ in FYRSTES-FELD" (Frustfield), now called the "EARLDOMS," is given in Cod. Dipl. iii., 418. Branche Hund., 51.
NEWENTONE p. 80	Carlo	ALURED of Marlborough	Girard,—3 hides	*NEWTON TONY*, in the hundred of Ambresbury (p. 185). The manor belonged in 1816 (Nom. Vill.) to ALICE DE TONI, Countess of Warwick. Ambresb. Hund., 103.
NECHENDUNE p. 57	Godwin	EARL MORTON	Gilbert	This would appear, from the Exon Domesday (p. 186), to have been in the hundred of Ambresbury. The name is now not easily recognized, unless *KNIGHTON DOWN* be intended. It would probably be in that neighbourhood, as most of the other manors in the hundred of Ambresbury are fully accounted for.
NIGRAVRE p. 14	Earl Harold	THE KING	A Thane,—2½ hides Hervey,—1½ hides	This is clearly what is now called *NETHER-AVON*, in the hundred of Elstub (p. 179). See above, under CHESIGEBERIE. The word NIGRAVRE is probably *nigrum arvum*, a translation of BLACK-HEATH, a name still given to the down-land not far from NETHER-AVON. The land in this parish is held under the Duchy of Lancaster. A survey of the manor, in 1591, is given in Wilts Mag. vi., 194. Elstub. Hund., 28.
NIGRAVRE p. 144	Edwin	HERVEY of Wilton, as one of the King's Officers		This is evidently the small estate alluded to, in the preceding entry, as having been held by HERVEY, as under-tenant.
NIGRAVRE Church of pp. 14, 124	Spirtes, a priest	NIGEL, the physician	Durand	The church of *NETHERAVON* was given, at the commencement of the 12th century, to the cathedral at Sarum, and constituted a prebend. The charter of Henry I., bestowing the church of "NEDHERAVEN" and other gifts on Sarum, is printed in New Mon. vi., 1296. STRATONE and CHESIGBERIE are said both to have belonged to the church of Nigravre (p. 124). They both belonged, in the time of Edw. I., to the family of DE LA FOLYE. Aubrey, 160.
NITELETONE p. 31	Abbot of Glastonbury	ABBOT OF GLASTONBURY		*NETTLETON*, in the old hundred of Thorngrave (p. 160), then comprehended in that of Chippenham, afterwards, like other Glastonbury estates, transferred to that of North Damerham. Charters relating to it are given in Cod. Dipl., 398, 439. Aubrey, 148, 435.
NORTONE p. 35	Abbot of Malmesbury	ABBOT OF MALMESBURY		*NORTON*, in the old hundred of Sterkley, p. 159 (see *note*), now in that of Malmesbury. It was given by King Æthelstan, in 931, to the monastery at Malmesbury. Cod. Dipl., 355. Aubrey, 274.
NORTONE p. 82	Carlo	ALURED of Marlborough		*NORTON BAVENT*, in the hundred of Warminster (p. 177). JOHN TREGOZ was chief lord in the 13th century (Hund. R. ii., 277), and under him PETRUS DE SKYDEMORE, whence it is sometimes called NORTON SKYDMORE (=Scudamore). In 1316, JOHN BAVENT held the manor. Nom. Vill. Warm. Hund., 77.
OCHEBORNE p. 15		THE KING		*NORTH OGBOURN*, or *OGBOURN MAGNA*, in the hundred of Selkley (p. 168). It is now commonly called OGBOURN ST. GEORGE.
OCHEBORNE p. 93	Earl Harold	MILO CRISPIN		*OGBOURN PARVA*, or *OGBOURN ST. ANDREW*, in the hundred of Selkley (p. 168). In *present* actual extent this is the larger of the two parishes, because it embraces ROCHELIE, and, possibly, other manors, which are separately accounted for in Domesday. Some particulars respecting these parishes will be found in N. Mon. vi., 1068. Abbrev. Plac., 313.

NAME.	T. R. E. Owner, or Tenant.	T. R. W. Tenant in Capite.	Under-Tenant.	MODERN NAME, &c.
OCHEBURNE p. 139	Harding	HARDING, as one of the King's Thanes		The *former* of these holdings is alluded to in the Exon Domesday (p. 168). There is no doubt they are both portions of one of the OGBOURNS. One of them is possibly *OGBOURN MEYSY*, now in the parish of OGBOURN ST. ANDREW. The Earl of Gloucester is named as holding *half a knight's fee* at OKEBURNE PARVA. Hund. R. ii., 269. EATON MEYSY, and MARSTON MEYSY, are both among the fees held under the honor of Gloucester, in Test. de Nev., 136.
OCHEBURNE p. 142	Turchil's father	TURCHIL, as one of the King's Thanes		
OCHEFORD p. 49	Abbess of Wilton	ABBESS OF WILTON		*UGFORD*, in the hundred of Branche (p. 184), now annexed to BURCOMBE, but till recently a tithing, or chapelry, in the parish of SOUTH NEWTON. Branche Hundr., 55.
OGEFORD p. 118	Ednod, under the Abbess of Wilton	OSBERN GIFARD	Gunduin	This was also a portion of *UGFORD*, which at one time belonged to Wilton, but was forcibly taken away from it by Earl Godwin, till Ednod temporarily recovered it.
ODESTOCHE p. 132	Brictric's father	BRICTRIC, as one of the King's Thanes		*ODSTOCK*, in the hundred of Cawdon (p. 187). The parish contains about 1100 acres. Cawd. Hundr., 19.
OPETONE p. 82	Carlo	ALURED OF MARLBOROUGH	Radulf	The largest portion of *UPTON SCUDAMORE*, in the hundred of Warminster. Peter de Skydemore held it, 3 Edw. I., under John Tregoz, as of the Barony of Ewyas. Hund. R. ii., 277. Warminster Hundr., 48.
OPETONE p. 78	Tous	ERNULF DE HESDING	Rainbold	A comparison of these two entries shows that they relate to immediately adjoining estates, and the mention in the Exon Domesday, under Warminster Hundred (p. 177), of the names of the two tenants, proves that they are in that hundred. They are no doubt holdings at or near *UPTON SCUDAMORE*. In the Nom. Vill. mention is made of THOLNESTON (Thoulston) and NORTHBRYGGE (Norridge) as separate manors. Possibly one, or both of these, may be the manors referred to in this entry.
OPETONE p. 102	Toli	WILLIAM DE OW	Ansfrid	
OPPAVRENE Church of p. 16		ABBEY OF ST. WANDREGISIL		There was an alien priory at *UPAVON*, which was a cell to the abbey of St. Wandregisil, at Fontanelle, in Normandy. On the dissolution of alien monasteries, the *Church* was given, 1 Henry VI., to the monastery of Ederose (Ivy Church). An extent of UPAVON PRIORY is among the Donat. MSS. in the British Museum. New Mon. vi., 1055. A survey of the *Manor* of UPAVON (1591), as part of the possessions of the Duchy of Lancaster, is given in Wilts Mag. vi., 190. See also Hundr. R. ii., 234.
ORCESTONE p. 67	Godric	EDWARD OF SALISBURY	Hugo	These are two different portions of *ORCHESTON ST. MARY*, sometimes called *ORCHESTON BOYVILLE*, in the hundred of Dole. They are both alluded to among the fees of the Earl of Sarum, in Test. de Nev., 138, one being held by HENRY DE BOYVILL, and the other by ADAM DE LITTLECOTE. Dole Hundr., 40.
ORCESTONE p. 67	Alwin	EDWARD OF SALISBURY	William	
ORCESTONE p. 116	Ulmar, Alwin	OSBERN GIFARD		*ORCHESTON ST. GEORGE*, in the hundred of Heytesbury (p. 178). Heytesb. Hundr., 178.
ORCHESTONE p. 117	Trasemund	OSBERN GIFARD		*ELSTON*, in the hundred of Dole (p. 183), but, though seemingly in a different hundred, now reckoned as a tithing of ORCHESTON ST. GEORGE. This is clearly included in the *two knights' fees*, held, according to Test. de Nev., 142, at Orcheston, by *Elias* Giffard, and from him perhaps comes the name, which is sometimes spelt *Elys*-ton. See Heytesb. Hundr., 182.

NAME.	T. R. E. Owner, or Tenant.	T. R. W. Tenant in Capite.	T. R. W. Under-Tenant.	MODERN NAME, &c.
OTNOE p. 13	Queen Editha	THE KING		An entry in the Abbrev. Plac. (p. 78), of a suit between WALTER DE RIPERIA (= Rivers) and the abbot of ST. MICHAEL DE MONTE, proves these entries to have reference to *WOOTTON RIVERS*, in the hundred of Kinwardstone (p. 180). The manor intended, from its large extent (which must have been some 5000 to 6000 acres at the least), must have embraced considerably more than the *present* parish, which contains but 1150 acres, and probably included the district of *CADLEY*, which immediately adjoins Savernake forest, if not some portions of neighbouring parishes, such as MIDDLETON, and EASTON (Royal), which do not seem otherwise accounted for in Domesday.
OTONE 2 Churches of p. 13		ABBEY OF ST. MICHAEL DE MONTE		
OVRETONE p. 20	Bishop of Winchester	BISHOP OF WINCHESTER, "pro victu monachorum"	Durand,—2 hides	*EAST OVERTON*, in the hundred of Selkley (p. 169). It is called, in the Nom. Vill., OVERTON FIFHIDE. Two copies, derived from different sources, of a charter of King Æthelstan's, A.D. 939, relating to this manor, are given in Cod. Dipl., 378, 1120. See also Arch. Journ. xiv., 133.
OVRETONE p. 47	Abbess of Wilton	ABBESS OF WILTON		*WEST OVERTON*, in the hundred of Selkley (p. 169). A charter of King Edgar's, A.D. 972, relating to this estate, which is described as "*æt Cynetan*," *i. e.* "at Kennet," is given in Cod. Dipl., 571, taken from the Wilton Chartulary. This manor is called, in the Nom. Vill., OVERTON ABBATISSÆ. See Hundr. R. ii., 269.
PEVESIE p. 40	Abbey of St. Peter's, Winchester	ABBEY OF ST. PETER'S, Winchester	A Thane,—2 hides Ernulf de Hesding, 2 hides, of the King	*PEWSEY*, in the hundred of Kinwardstone (p. 180), the gift of King Edmund, in 940, to Hyde Abbey. In the chartulary of that abbey (Harl. MS., 1761), are several documents relating to PEWSEY. King Edmund's charter is given in Cod. Dipl., 380. See also New Mon. ii., 438.
PEVESIE Church of p. 16		RAINBOLD, the Priest		
PEVESIE p. 75	A Thane, of the Abbot of Winchester	ERNULF DE HESDING		The *former* of these is the holding alluded to in the previous entry as held by Ernulf de Hesding, under the larger manor; the *latter* is alluded to in the Exon Domesday under the hundred of Kinwardstone (p. 180), and is no doubt some smaller portion of the same.
PEVESIE p. 137		EDRIC, as one of the King's Thanes		
PAVESHOU Church of p. 12	Father of Edgar	EDGAR		*PEWSHAM*, close by CORSHAM, in the hundred of Chippenham. See above, p. 12, *note*.
PERTEWORDE p. 27	Ulward	BISHOP OF COUTANCE	Osbert	*PERTWOOD*, near HINDON, in the hundred of Warminster, but locally situated in that of Mere. See Mere Hundr., 179.
PIRITONE p. 39	Abbot of Malmesbury	ABBOT OF MALMESBURY		*PURTON*, anciently spelt *PIRITONE* (A.S. *pirig-tun*), in the hundred of Staple (p. 165). This was one of the earliest endowments of Malmesbury, having been given to Aldhelm, whilst he was abbot of that monastery, by Cædwealha, King of Wessex, A.D. 688. Cod. Dipl., 29, 1065. Aubrey, 154.
POTERNE p. 21	Bishop of Sarum	BISHOP OF SARUM	Two Englishmen —6¼ hides Alward,—3 hides Ernulf de Hesding,—3¼ hides under the king, though claimed by the Bishop	*POTTERNE*, in the old hundred of Rugeberg (p. 174), now in that of Potterne and Cannings. In this manor are included WORTON and MARSTON. In Waylen's History of Devizes will be found some information concerning this parish and hundred.

NAME.	T. R. E. Owner, or Tenant.	T. R. W. Tenant in Capite.	T. R. W. Under-Tenant.	MODERN NAME, &c.
POTERNE p. 74	Algar, under the Bishop of Sarum	ERNULF DE HESDING	Robert	These are the two holdings alluded to in the preceding entry, and are portions of the manor of *POTTERNE.*
POTERNE p. 132	Bishop of Sarum	ALWARD, as one of the King's Thanes		
POLTONE p. 59	Siward	EARL ROGER		*POULTON*, an outlying part of Wilts, locally situated in Gloucestershire, reckoned in the hundred of Cricklade (p. 163). Hund. R. ii., 230. Nom. Vill. In 1316, the manor belonged to NICHOLAS DE SANCTO MAURO (= Seymour). Sir Thomas Seymour founded here, in the 14th century, a Gilbertine Priory, which he endowed with the Manor and Rectory of POULTON. New Mon. vi., 979.
POLTONE p. 89	Tovi	HUMFREY DE L'ISLE		*POLTON*, the name now of some farms in the Parish of MILDENHALL and hundred of Selkley (p. 169). Wilts Mag. ii., 271. Walter de Dunstanville confirmed to Tewkesbury Abbey, c. 1190, PULTON and WERFTON. See below, under WERTUNE. New Mon. ii., 54.
POLE p. 70	Ulwen	EDWARD OF SALISBURY	Azelin	*POOL KEYNES*, in the old hundred of Cicemethorn, now in that of Malmesbury. This estate came afterwards by inheritance to the Dukes of Lancaster, and the patronage is still in the hands of the Duchy of Lancaster. A survey of the estate, in 1591, is given in Wilts Mag. vi., 197. Aubrey, 278.
POERTONE p. 73	Gode	EDWARD OF SALISBURY	Peter	This is most probably *PORTON*, in the hundred of Alderbury. One fourth part of a knight's fee was held at PORTON, under the Earl of Sarum, c. 1270. Test. de Nev., 144. A list of the Incumbents of the Chapel of St. Nicholas, at PORTON, is given in the Wilts Inst. It is now united to IDMESTON. Alderb. Hundr., 73.
PORTONE p. 140	Uluric's father	ULURIC, the huntsman, as one of the King's Thanes		This, according to the Exon Domesday (p. 190), was in the hundred of Alderbury, and *may be* a portion of the manor just described. It is more likely to be *PITTON*, a chapelry now annexed to Alderbury parish. Uluric is called, in the Exon Domesday, "the huntsman" (p. 187), and the *half hide* in PUTTON (a common way of spelling that name) held on the service of being a warder of the forest of Clarendon, according to Test. de Nev., 143, would seem to be the same holding. Alderb. Hundr., 40.
PONBERIE p. 130	Alnod	OSMUND [Latimar]		According to the Exon Domesday (p. 170), this holding was in the hundred of Bradford. It is *POMEROY*, the name of a farm in the parish of WINFIELD.
-RAMESBERIE p. 23	Bishop of Sarum	BISHOP OF SARUM	The Priests, — 4 hides Otbold,—12 hides Herbert,—5 hides Quintin,—5 hides The Bailiff's Wife, —1 hide	*RAMSBURY*:—comprising BAYDON,—AXFORD,—EASTRIDGE,—and possibly BISHOPSTON. This was an early seat of the Bishops of Wiltshire, and the hundred was bestowed on the see by King Offa, at the close of the 8th century. Hund. R. ii., 231, 265. The name itself is a corruption of *hræfenes-byrig*, i. e. *raven's-bury*, and the early Bishops called themselves EPISCOPI CORVINENSIS ECCLESIÆ. Aubrey, 310.
RETMORE p. 60	Ednod	EARL HUGO	William	
-REDBORNE p. 92	Wigot	MILO CRISPIN	Rainald	*RODBOURN CHENEY*, in the old hundred of Scipe (p. 163), afterwards in that of Highworth. RADULF DE CHANU held this estate at the end of the 13th century, under the Earl of Cornwall, as of the honor of Wallingford. Test. de Nev., 138. Aubrey, 157.

NAME.	T. R. E. Owner, or Tenant.	T. R. W. Tenant in Capite.	T. R. W. Under-Tenant.	MODERN NAME, &c.
ROTEFELD p. 66	Aluric	EDWARD OF SALISBURY	Hervey	These are no doubt portions of one and the same estate. The *latter* is alluded to in the Exon Domesday (p. 186), under the hundred of Ambresbury. In Inq. Non., 171, mention is made of a prebend belonging to the church at Sarum within the parish of Ambresbury, and the latter is described in the charter of Henry I. as "*one hide*, which HERVEY the son of Walter, the son of Edward, held at ROTEFEN." Dodsworth's Salisb. Cath., 102. The name is preserved in *RATFYN*, the designation of a farm in Ambresbury parish.
ROTEFELDE p. 146	Earl Harold	HERVEY, as one of the King's Officers		
ROCHELIE p. 82	Carlo	ALURED OF MARLBOROUGH		*ROCKLEY*, in the parish of Ogburn St. Andrew, and hundred of Selkley. John Tregoz, a descendant of Alured of Marlborough, held it, 3 Edw. I., as of the barony of Ewyas. Hundr. R. ii., 269.
ROCHELIE p. 71	Azor	EDWARD OF SALISBURY		This comparatively small holding is described as "*i*... ROCHELIE." It is most probably a portion of the same *ROCKLEY*, in the hundred of Selkley.
RODE p. 80	Carlo	ALURED OF MARLBOROUGH	William, — 18 hides Ulviet,—1 hide Gilbert,—1 hide	This is probably *ROWDE*. It is named in the record next to ADELINGTONE (Allington); and CHENETE (Kennet), at no great distance, was also held in chief of Alured of Marlborough. Ulviet, one of the tenants, was also an occupier at CHENETE.—This manor of ROWDE was in the old hundred of Rugeberg; now in that of Potterne and Cannings. Aubrey, 309.
RUSTESELVE p. 10	Ghida	THE KING		*RUSHALL*, in the hundred of Swanborough (p. 175). This large manor must, with its appendages, have comprised at least 6000 acres, and therefore probably comprehended CHARLTON, which is not otherwise accounted for, and, it may be, a portion of what is now the parish of UPAVON, the church of which also belonged to the Abbey of St. Wandregisil.
RUSTESELVE Church of p. 11		ABBEY OF ST. WANDREGISIL		
RUSTESELLE p. 86	Aluric	HUMFREY DE L'ISLE	Gunter	There can be little doubt but that in this name there has been an error, and that it was meant for LUSTESELLE. The place alluded to is most probably *LUSHILL*, near Hannington, in the hundred of Highworth. It is referred to in the Exon Domesday under that hundred (p. 164). Wilts Mag. ii., 277.
SALTEHARPE p. 87	Ulwin	HUMFREY DE L'ISLE	Robert	*SALTHORP*, in the parish of WROUGHTON. It was in the old hundred of Blachegrave (Hund. R. ii., 244), now in that of Kingsbridge. Wilts Mag. ii., 279. Aubrey, 368.
SARISBERIE p. 23	Bishop of Sarum	BISHOP OF SARUM	Edward,—5 hides Odo,—5 hides Hugo,—2¾ hides	This manor, from its large extent, which was certainly not less than 11,000 acres, must have included, besides *OLD SARUM*, other neighbouring parishes, such as STRATFORD and WOODFORD. In the hundred of Underditch, according to the Exon Domesday (p. 188), were 70 *hides*, so that this estate, which was assessed at 50 *hides*, would probably include *five sevenths* of the land in that hundred.
SCALDEBURNE p. 120	A Thane	HUGO LASNE	William	These are all different portions, each of but small extent, of *SHALBOURN*, in the hundred of Kinwardstone. It lies on the eastern border of the county, close by TIDCOMB and the forest of CHUTE. The *last three* entries appear to be referred to in the Exon Domesday under the hundred of Kinwardstone (p. 188).
SCALDEBURNE p. 140	Ordwold	ULURIC, as one of the King's Thanes		
SCALDEBURNE p. 142		OSGOT, as one of the King's Thanes		
SALDEBORNE p. 145	Ordwold	RICHARD STURMID, as one of the King's Officers		

NAME.	T. R. E. Owner, or Tenant.	T. R. W. Tenant in Capite.	T. R. W. Under-Tenant.	MODERN NAME, &c.
SCHETONE p. 88	Chenvi	HUMFREY DE L'ISLE	Robert	Mr. Scrope conjectures this to be *CHADDINGTON*, in the parish of LYDIARD TREGOZ, and hundred of Blagrave,—now in that of Kingsbridge. Wilts Mag. ii., 283. That was certainly held by the descendants of Humfrey de L'Isle, and amongst others by Petronilla do Montfort. Hund. R. ii., 244. See also Test. de Nev., 137, where CHETINDON is named among the *fees* of Walter de Dunstanville. Aubrey, 171.
SCAGE p. 113	Cudulf	ROBERT FITZ-GIROLD	Hugo	This must be the manor alluded to in the Exon Domesday (p. 186) as land held, T. R. E., by Cudulf, and afterwards belonging to Robert Fitz-Girold, and would in that case be in the hundred of Ambresbury. *SHAW*, close by BEDESDENE (Biddesden) and FOSTESBERGE (Fosbury) (both of which also belonged to Robert Fitz-Girold), may probably be intended.
SCARENTONE p. 118	Algar	OSBERN GIFARD		These two entries refer to *SHERRINGTON*, in the hundred of Branche. They were assessed at *ten hides*, of which *nine* were held in demesne, the exact number stated, in the Exon Domesday (p. 184), so to be held by Osbern Gifard. The whole parish contains 1040 acres. See Heytesb. Hund., 238.
SCARENTONE p. 118	Smalo	OSBERN GIFARD		
SCHERNECOTE p. 121	Alward	HUMFREY, the Chamberlain		*SHARNCOTE*, in the hundred of Cricklade. From the Exon Domesday (p. 163), we infer that Humfrey, the Chamberlain, is the same as Humfrey de L'Isle. The parish contains about 600 acres.
SCLIVE p. 76	Chetel	ERNULF DE HESDING	Robert	
SEGRIE p. 119	Wiflet	DROGO FITZ-PONZ		This, without doubt, is a portion of *SEAGRY*, in the old hundred of Sterkley,—now in that of Malmeshury. It was held by WALTER CLIFFORD, who was nephew of DROGO (or DREW), and took the name on marrying the heiress of Clifford Castle. Test. de Nev., 140. Aubrey, 281.
SEGRETE p. 97	Two Thanes	DURAND OF GLOUCESTER	Two "milites"	This is most probably another portion of *SEAGRY*. The whole parish contains 1060 acres.
SEVAMENTONE p. 101	Alestan of Boscumbe	WILLIAM DE OW	William	*SEVINGTON*, the original name of the parish now called LEIGH DELAMERE. It was originally in the hundred of Thorngrave,—now in that of Chippenham. Aubrey, 101.
SELA p. 135		ALVIED, as one of the King's Thanes		These two holdings constitute the present tithing of *ZEALS*, in the parish and hundred of Mere. The latter is alluded to in the Exon Domesday (p. 182). There are *two manors* here, the one ZEALS CLEVEDON and the other ZEALS AILESBURY, or LOWER and HIGHER ZEALS. Mere Hund., 31.
SELE p. 128	Almar	GOZELIN RIVEIRE		
SIRENDONE p. 110	Alwi	RADULF DE MORTEMER	Richard	*SURRENDEN* (or *SURRENDELL*), in the old hundred of Dunelawe,—now in that of Chippenham. It is considered part of the parish of HULLAVINGTON, though they are in different hundreds. It was held under the fee of the MORTIMERS in the 13th century. Aubrey, 114.
SMITECOTE p. 87	Sawin	HUMFREY DE L'ISLE	Elbert	*SMITHCOTE*, in the parish of DAUNTSEY, and hundred of Sterkley,—now in the hundred of Malmesbury. Wilts Mag. ii., 281. Aubrey, 217.
SMALEBROC p. 149	Mainard	ALBERIC, the Chamberlain, as one of the King's Officers		*SMALLBROOK*, half-way between WARMINSTER and BISHOPSTROW, in the parish and hundred of Warminster. It is referred to in the Exon Domesday (p. 177). Hund. R. ii., 276.

NAME.	T. R. E. Owner, or Tenant.	T. R. W. Tenant in Capite.	T. R. W. Under-Tenant.	MODERN NAME, &c.
SOPEWORDE p. 101	Aluric	WILLIAM DE OW	Hugo	*SOPWORTH*, in the hundred of Chippenham. It is name c. 1272, among the fees of the EARL MARESCAL, lik several other estates belonging, at Domesday, to Willia de Ow. Test. de Nev., 137. Aubrey, 112.
SORSTAIN Church of p. 16		ABBEY OF ST. WANDRAGISIL		This is the church of *SHERSTON MAGNA*, or *MUC SHERSTON*, in the hundred of Chippenham. The char ter of William I. confirming, among other grants, th church of SCORESTAN to the abbey of St. Vandrille (*alia* Fontenelle), is given in New Mon. vi., 1107. Aubrey, 10
SORESTONE p. 90	Godus	HUMFREY DE L'ISLE	Robert	*SHERSTON PARVA*, in the hundred of Chippenham. I was held, c. 1270, under Walter de Dunstanvillo, as of th barony of Castle Combe, by Ralph de Pinkeny,—hence it usual designation SHERSTON PINKNEY. Wilts Mag. ii. 286. Aubrey, 109.
STAMERE p. 96	Bruning	GILBERT DE BRETEVILE	Ansfrid	*STANMORE*, in the hundred of Selkley. It lies on th borders of the two parishes of CLIFF PIPARD and WINTERBOURN BASSET. It was held, together with BECKHAMPTO (see under BACHENTUNE), in 2 Edw. I., by one of th Columbars family. Hund. R. ii., 269. To this day som lands in STANMORE are free of tithe, because formerly pa of the endowment of the "*free chapel* in BECKHAMPTON." Aubrey, 331.
STANINGES p. 103	Leuing	WILLIAM DE FALUISE	Alward	These three small holdings, amounting in all but to *two hides*, are no doubt different portions of *STANLINCH* (now called TRAFALGAR), in the hundred of Downton The *first two* are distinctly alluded to in the Exon Domesday (p. 190). WILLIAM DE ST. MARTIN, a descendant o WALERAN, held, 2 Edw. I., lands in CHERLTON and STANLING. Downton Hund., 46.
STANINGES p. 105	Colo	WALERAN, the huntsman		
STANINGES p. 134		ALWI, as one of the King's Thanes		
STANTONE p. 45	Abbess of Wilton	ABBESS OF WILTON		*STANTON BERNERS* (or *BERNARD*), in the hundre of Swanborough (p. 175). This estate was given to Wilton by King Edwy, A.D. 957. See charters relating to it and containing land-limits, in Cod. Dipl., 335, 467, 482.
STANTONE p. 116	Brictric	OSBERN GIFARD		*STANTON ST. QUINTIN*, in the hundred of Sterkley (p. 159),—now in that of Malmesbury. Sir Herbert de St. Quintin held the manor under the honor of Gloucester 3 Edw. I. Hund. R. ii., 272. An entry under CRISTEMALEFORD (p. 30) seems to imply that some land in STANTON once belonged to Glastonbury Abbey. Aubrey, 286.
STANTONE p. 137	Lange	GRIMBALD, the goldsmith, as one of the King's Thanes		*STANTON FITZ-WARYN*, in the hundred of Highwort (p. 164). FULCO FITZ-WARYN held lands here, and presented to the living in 1299. Wilts Inst. See also Test de Nev., 150. Tho parish is also called, from successiv owners, STANTON FITZ-HERBERT, and STANTON FITZ BRYNDE.
STANDONE p. 75	Brictric	ERNULF DE HESDING	Benzelin	*STANDEN CHAWORTH*, or *NORTH STANDEN*, i the hundred of Kinwardstone. In the Non. Inq., 174, i is described as situated in Wilts, with a chapel annexed t the parish church of HUNGERFORD. It was held unde PATRICK DE CHAWORTH, 3 Edw. I. Hundr. R. ii., 260 Test. de Nev., 144. A survey of the manor, in 1591, a parcel of tho possessions of the Duchy of Lancaster, i given in Wilts Mag. vi., 187.
STANDENE p. 108	Godric	HENRY DE FERIERES		*STANDEN HUSSEY* in the hundred of Kinwardstone (p 181). This manor is also described in Non. Inq., 174, a situated in Wilts, with a chapel annexed to HUNGERFORD RICHARD HUSEE died, siesed of a portion of the mano here in 1361, which he had held of tho honor of TUTBURY a principal possession of the FERIERES (Ferrers) family Inq. p. m., 35 Edw. III.

NAME.	T. R. E. Owner, or Tenant.	T. R. W.		MODERN NAME, &c.
		Tenant in Capite.	Under-Tenant.	
STANLEGE p. 105	Selewin	WALERAN, the huntsman	Azelin	This holding was probably at *STANLEY*, in the hundred of Chippenham, in the neighbourhood of the forests of Chippenham and Pewsham. An account of the Abbey, founded here in the middle of the 12th century, is given in Bowles' History of Bremhill. Aubrey, 113.
STAVRETONE p. 132	Brictric's father	BRICTRIC		*STAVERTON*, in the hundred of Melksham (p. 171). It is now considered as a tithing of the parish of TROWBRIDGE.
STRABURG p. 131	Brictric's father	BRICTRIC		Coming immediately before STAVERTON, it would seem probable that this manor is intended for *TROWBRIDGE*, though the scribe has strangely corrupted the name. See Exon Domesday (p. 171). Brictric also held TROLE (Trowle) and FARLEGE (Monkton Farleigh), both of which are in the immediate neighbourhood. Moreover HUMFREY BOHUN, by whom several other estates belonging at Domesday to BRICTRIC, were afterwards held, was possessed, in the 13th year of King John's reign, of STAVERTON and TROBRIGGE. Abbrev. Plac., 85.
STAPLEFORD p. 143	Svain's father	SVAIN, as one of the King's Thanes		*STAPLEFORD*, in the hundred of Branchs (p. 184). The parish contains 2004 acres. This estate afterwards came into the possession of the descendants of Waleran, the huntsman, as John Ingham and Reginald St. Martin owned the lordship of the manor in 1316. Nom. Vill. Branche Hundr., 20.
STERTE p. 85	Aluric	HUMFREY DE L'ISLE		*STERT*, in the old hundred of Stodfald (p. 174), now in that of Swanborough. It was held, 2 Edw. I., by Petronilla de Montfort, a descendant of Humfrey de L'Isle, of the barony of Castle Combe. Hundr. R. ii., 273. It is now connected with ERCHFONT, as a united parish. Wilts Mag. ii., 264.
STOCHE p. 68	Stremi	EDWARD, of Salisbury	William de Pinchengi,—$1\frac{1}{4}$ hide	*BRADENSTOKE*, in the hundred of Kingsbridge (p. 165). This entry includes, without doubt, LYNEHAM, in which parish Bradenstoke is now reckoned. The name of the tenant is still preserved in TOCKENHAM PINKNEY (Abbrev. Plac., 14), which is probably the holding alluded to, as WEST TOCKENHAM is in Lyneham parish. Aubrey, 187.
STOCHE p. 149		CROC, the huntsman, as one of the King's Officers		CROC "venator" occurs in a charter from William the Conqueror to the Abbey of Malmesbury respecting the Abbot's woods in the forest of BRADENE. New Mon. i., 261. It is probable therefore that this small holding was in the immediate vicinity of the estate just described.
STORTONE p. 104	Alwacre	WALSCIN DE DOWAI	Radulf	This is no doubt *STOURTON*, in the hundred of Mere. The parish contains 2210 acres. Mere Hundr., 42. Aubrey, 389.
STOTECOME p. 137	Gode	GODE		This holding, according to the Exon Domesday (p. 180), was in the hundred of Kinwardstone. It has been conjectured to be *STICHCOMB*, close by Mildenhall.
STOTTUNE p. 21	Bishop of Winchester	BISHOP OF WINCHESTER, "pro victu monachorum"	Richer,—5 hides Anschitil,—$2\frac{1}{2}$ hides	*STOCKTON*, now, like other estates held by the Bishop of Winchester, in the hundred of Elstub, but originally in that of Branche (p. 184). Hundr. R. ii., 233. A charter of King Edward the Elder, A.D. 991, respecting this estate, in which it is described as "10 cassates (=hides) *bi Wilig*," i.e., "*by the river Wyly*," extracted from the Cod. Winton, is given in Cod. Dipl., 1078. See Heytesb. Hundr., 241.

NAME.	T. R. E. Owner, or Tenant.	T. R. W. Tenant in Capite.	T. R. W. Under-Tenant.	MODERN NAME, &c.
STRADFORD p. 63	Azor	EARL ALBERIC		*STRATFORD TONY*, in the hundred of Cawdon (p. 187). RALPH DE THONEY was a landowner here in 1278 (Hundr. R. ii., 247), and ALICE DE TONY, Countess of Warwick, held the manor in 1316. Nom. Vill. From that family the parish derives its distinctive name. Cawdon Hundr., 4.
STRATONE p. 123	Spirtes, a priest	NIGEL, the physician		*STRATTON ST. MARGARET*, originally in the hundred of Seipe (p. 163), afterwards in that of Highworth. There are *two* manors, STRATTON SUPERIOR and INFERIOR, recorded in the Nom. Vill., both of which, from the large extent of this estate, which was assessed at ***thirty hides*** are no doubt included in it. Aubrey, 161.
SUTONE p. 107	Alwold and his sister	WILLIAM FITZ-WIDON		These two holdings are alluded to in the Exon Domesday (p. 177), under the hundred of Warminster. They are portions of *SUTTON MAGNA*, or *SUTTON FENNY* (now commonly written *VENEY*). In the Nom. Vill., c. 1316, there would seem to have been at least *two* lordships here. Warm. Hundr., 83.
SUDTONE p. 124	Spirtes, a priest	NIGEL, the physician	Abbey of St. Mary de Monteburg	
SUTONE p. 103	Colo	WILLIAM DE MOIUN	Walter [Hosatus]	*SUTTON PARVA*, now a tithing in SUTTON VENEY. See remarks on this entry at pp. 103, 154. There was a free chapel here, dedicated to St. Nicholas (Nom. Inq., 170), and the names of the Incumbents from 1312 to 1333 are still preserved. Warm. Hundr., 85.
SUDTONE p. 108	Ulward	RICHARD FITZ-GILBERT	Berenger	This seems clearly to be the estate held, c. 1270, by GALFRIDUS DE MANDEVILE, of the Earl of Clare, the lineal descendant of Richard Fitz-Gilbert (see p. 108, *note*), at SUTTON. Test. de Nev., 141. It is *SUTTON MANDEVILLE*, in the hundred of Cadworth. In 1316, Hugo le Despencer, who married Eleanor, daughter of Gilbert de Clare, is named as possessing part of this same manor. Nom. Vill. Cawd. Hundr., 71. [From the tenant's name a conjecture might have been hazarded that "SUTTON BERENGER" (now contracted into BENGER) was the estate intended, but that manor always belonged to Malmesbury, and is accounted for under BROCHENEBERGE, as parcel of the large grant made to that Abbey in 956, by King Edwy. For this same reason SUTTON BENGER was reckoned, in 1316, with Brokenborough, in the hundred of Cheggelewe (Nom. Vill.), though not locally situated within its proper limits, and is now in that of Malmesbury.]
SVALOCLIVE p. 46	Abbess of Wilton	ABBESS OF WILTON		These are different portions of *SWALLOWCLIFF*, in the hundred of Dunworth. The first entry was the half knight's fee held, 3 Edw. I., in SWALEWECLIVE, by John de Maundevyle, of the Abbess of Wilton. Hundr. R. ii., 258. A charter relating to SWEALEWANCLIF is given in Cod. Dipl., 387. See Heytesb. Hundr., 121. Dunw. Hundr., 67.
SVALOCLIVE p. 131		BRICTRIC, as one of the King's Thanes		
SVALOCLIVE p. 133		ALWARD, as one of the King's Thanes		
SUMREFORD p. 28	Alward	BISHOP OF LISIEUX		This is most probably *SOMERFORD KEYNES*, in the hundred of Cricklade. Hutchins (History of Dorset, i., 110) says that RALPH DE KAYNES had this manor given to him on his marriage with the daughter of Hugh Maminot, a baron in Kent, of the same family as Gilbert de Maminot, Bishop of Lisieux, who held it at the Conquest. Aubrey, 160.

NAME.	T. R. E. Owner, or Tenant.	T. R. W. Tenant in Capite.	T. R. W. Under-Tenant.	MODERN NAME, &c.
Sumreford p. 87	Edwin	Humfrey de L'Isle	Robert	All these appear to be portions of *SOMERFORD MAGNA*, or *BROAD SOMERFORD*, in the old hundred of Sterkley, now in that of Malmesbury. The *first* is the half knight's fee which was held, 3 Edw. I., under the barony of Castle Comb, by John Mautravers, and hence the name Somerford Maltravers;—the *second* is the half knight's fee owned by John Tregoz, under the barony of Ewyas, and hence this portion was anciently called Somerford Ewyas;—the *third* is the land possessed at the same date by the Earl of Hereford, a descendant of Edward of Salisbury, and is most likely the property held afterwards by the nuns of St. Mary's Priory, Kington St. Michael, under Bohun, Earl of Hereford. The prioress of that religious house presented to the living of Broad Somerford in 1324. See Hundr. R. ii., 272, where, under separate entries, these *three holdings* seem accurately accounted for. Aubrey, 283.
Sumreford p. 83	Alnod	Alured of Marlborough	Siward	
Somreforde p. 68	Scirold	Edward of Salisbury	Teodric	
Sumreford p. 35	Alward	Abbot of Malmesbury	Gunfrid	A comparison of entries in various records leads to the probable conclusion that this estate was at *LITTLE SOMERFORD*, or *SOMERFORD MAUDUIT*. The Hundr. Rolls ii., 272, speak of a manor held by John Mauduit, at Somerford, under the Abbot of Malmesbury. In the Nom. Vill., c. 1316, under the hundred of Sterkley, (the lordship of which was vested in the Abbot of Malmesbury,) John Mauduyt is named as lord of the manor of Somerford. If, as seems probable, the tenant be the same as Gunfrid Maldoith, who held Witelie (p. 122),—and the occurrence of Somerford Mauduit and Witlee among the manors held by successive generations of the Mauduit family seems to prove it—(see Inq. p. m., 31 Edw. I., and Inq. p. m., 20 Edw. III),—there would appear little room to doubt the correctness of the interpretation suggested. See Aubrey, 285.
Sumreford p. 134		Alwin, a priest; Alwi; Edward; Saieva } as King's Thanes		These were sundry small holdings, amounting in the whole to little more than *two hides*, under the King, in one of the Somerfords, but in which it is impossible now to say with accuracy. In the Inq. p. m., 36 Edw. III., Theobald Mounteney is recorded as having died siesed of land at Somerford Keynes; and in Test. de Nev., 151, one of the same family is named as holding *one-third* of a knight's fee there. This *may* comprise these four small holdings; but this is, of course, mere conjecture.
Svindune p. 25	Leviet	Bishop of Baieux	Wadard	These are all holdings, three of them but of moderate extent, in *SWINDON*, in the old hundred of Blagrave (p. 167), now in that of Kingsbridge. The *first* seems to correspond with the *one knight's fee* held in Alta (High) Swindon by William de Valence, 3 Edw. I., Hundr. R. ii., 244;—the *second* was probably a small estate at or near Even Swyndon, since both Lydiard (Tregoz) and Moredon, in that immediate neighbourhood, belonged to Alured of Marlborough;—the *third* seems, from its extent, to be the principal portion of the present parish, the *two hides* held by Milo Crispin being no doubt close by Walecote (Walcot), which also belonged to him, near its north-western boundary;—of the *other two*, which were but small holdings under the King, it is impossible now to identify the locality. In 1316, according to Nom. Vill., there seems to have been but one manor here, which was held by Adomar de Valence (Earl of Pembroke), and hence the name, which is sometimes met with, Swindon Valence. Inq. p.m. 17, Edw. II. Wilts Mag. vii., 123. Aubrey, 191.
Svindone p. 81	Carlo	Alured of Marlborough		
Svindone p. 148	Torbert	Odin, the chamberlain, as one of the King's Officers	Milo Crispin, —2 hides	
Svindone p. 140		Ulric, as one of the King's Thanes		
Svindone p. 141		Ulward, as one of the King's Thanes		
Tedelintone p. 84	{ Ulveva, Alveve, —for 2 manors	Alured of Marlborough	William 'Durus'	*TITHERINGTON LUCAS*, in the hundred of Chippenham. In Test. de Nev., 137, Adam Lucas is recorded as the holder of one knight's fee at Tuderinton, under Robert Tregoz, a descendant of Alured of Marlborough. Moreover, among the fees of John de Tregoz, who died in 1304, that of Tuderington Lucas is named. Inq. p. m., 28 Edw. I. Aubrey, 116.

NAME.	T. R. E. Owner, or Tenant.	T. R. W. Tenant in Capite.	T. R. W. Under-Tenant.	MODERN NAME, &c.
TERINTONE p. 118	Domno	OSBERN GIFARD		This estate seems clearly to be alluded to in the Exon Domesday (p. 162), under the hundred of Chippenham. It represents, without doubt, the *two knight's fees* held by GODFREY ESCUDEMOR and ELYAS DE KAYLEWEY at TUDERINTON, of ELYAS GIFFARD, c. 1270, recorded in Test. de Nev., 142, an estate which is also called (Test. de Nev., 144) KAYLEWENT. The name of one of its early owners is still preserved in *TITHERTON KELWAYS;* though more than the *present* parish, which comprises but 130 acres, must be included in the manor alluded to in this entry.
TERINTONE p. 71	Elric	EDWARD of Salisbury	Borel	From its being mentioned immediately after LANGEFEL (Langley Burrell), and being occupied by the same tenant, BOREL, the inference may fairly be drawn, that this holding, which was but of small extent, was in the same immediate neighbourhood as the *TITHERTON* just described.
TEDRINTONE p. 62	Harding	EARL ALBERIC		From this comparatively small holding being named next to CHELTRE (Chittern), and being occupied by the same tenant, T. R. E., it is conjectured that this may possibly be *TITHERINGTON*, in the hundred of Heytesbury. See Heytesb. Hundr., 155, 277.
THEODULVESIDE p. 10	King Edward	THE KING		*TILSHEAD*, at the time of Domesday in the hundred of Rugeberg (p. 174). It is so reckoned also in the Nom. Vill. In the Hundr. R., it is included in the hundred of Dolesfelt (Dole). At the present time, NORTH TILSHEAD, containing 2097 acres, is in Dole, and SOUTH TILSHEAD, containing 848 acres, in Wherwelsdown hundred. The principal *manor* at Tilshead was given by the Conqueror to the Abbey of Caen, and the gift was confirmed by Henry I. Hundr. R., ii., 254. N. Mon., vi., 1065. The Abbess of Romsey also, according to Non. Inq. 178, possessed a *manor* here, most probably the portion in Wherwelsdown hundred, the greater part of the property belonging to that religious house being situated in that hundred. See p. 172. The *church*, which is dedicated to St. Thomas à Becket, was given by Henry II. to the Priory of Ivychurch, which he had founded for canons of the order of St. Austin, near his palace at Clarendon. The first mention of the appropriation of the church to the said monastery is in the Patent Rolls, 10 Edw. II. (1317). A Vicarage however was established at Tilshead before 1291. Tax. Eccles., 181. Dole Hundr., 42.
TIDULFHIDE p. 133		ALURIC "Parvus" (as King's Thanes)		These are all small portions of the large manor of *TILSHEAD* just referred to. They were all held under the King.
TIDULFHIDE p. 133		ALWARD (as King's Thanes)		
TIDULFHIDE p. 135		ALESTAN (as King's Thanes)		
TIDULFHIDE p. 135		ALMAR (as King's Thanes)		
TICOODE p. 71	Svain	EDWARD of Salisbury	Gilbert	This it is conjectured may possibly be *THICK-WOOD*, near COLERNE. The same tenant, SVAIN, who occupied it T.R.E., is recorded also as the occupant of COME (Castle Combe), in the immediate neighbourhood. It may correspond with BOXE (Box), which would be in the same vicinity, and which is reckoned in Test. de Nev., 135, 138, among the fees of the Earl of Salisbury, and singularly, in both cases, in immediate connection, as in Domesday, with LANGLEY BURRELL. See Aubrey, 77.

NAME.	T. R. E. Owner, or Tenant.	T. R. W. Tenant in Capite.	T. R. W. Under-Tenant.	MODERN NAME, &c.
TISSEBERIE p. 42	Abbess of Shaftesbury	ABBESS OF SHAFTESBURY	Turstin,—3 hides Gunfrid,—3 hides Alheric,—2 hides Edward, the sheriff,—2 caruc.	*TISBURY*, in the hundred of Dunworth. This estate was given to the Abbess of Shaftesbury, in 984, by King Æthelred. The charter, with land-limits, may be seen in Cod. Dipl., 641. Of the subordinate holdings that belonged to GUNFRID (who was probably GUNFRID MALDOITH), is no doubt land at ABSHULL, NIPRED, and FERNHULL, since various tenants held there in all some *two-thirds* of a knight's fee of ROBERT MAUDUIT, c. 1270. Test. de Nev., 152. See Wilts Mag., vii., 286. Dunworth Hundr., 128.
TITICOME p. 141	Wenesius	THE WIFE OF WENESIUS, as one of the King's Thanes,		This is most probably *TIDCOMB*, in the hundred of Kinwardstone. The manor was held, 3 Edw. I., by Hubert Hussey, under the Earl of Warwick as chief lord. Hundr. R., ii., 260. The church afterwards formed part of the endowment of Easton Priory. Aubrey, 358, 382.
TORNVELE p. 147	Strami	WILLIAM FITZ-ANSULF, as one of the King's Officers		*THORNHILL*, in the parish of CLIFF PIPARD and hundred of Kingsbridge. The tenant, T. R. E., also held STOCHE (Bradenstoke). A comparison moreover of the entries at pp. 68, 95, and 148, would seem to make it probable that WILLIAM FITZ-ANSCULF and WILLIAM DE PINCHENGI may be the same person. Aubrey, 166.
.... p. 148		WILLIAM FITZ-ANSCULF, as one of the King's Officers		This estate, which is said to be near the preceding one, consists of *two hides*, which are described, *the one* as belonging to BRADENSTOKE, *the other* to CLIFF PIPARD. See above, under CLIVE, the manor of GILBERT DE BRETEVILLE, p. 95.
TODEWORDE p. 24	Eddulf	BISHOP OF BAIEUX	Odo	These holdings, all of which are alluded to in the Exon Domesday (p. 185), under the hundred Ambreshury, are different portions of the parish of *NORTH TIDWORTH*. There were at least *two* manors here in the 13th century, TIDWORTH MELEWIS, granted by William, Earl of Salisbury, to William de Melewis, and TIDWORTH ZOUCH, held in the time of Edward II. by Alan la Zouch. The patronage of the Church remained for some centuries in the hands of the Earls of Salisbury or their descendants. The adjoining estate of SOUTH TIDWORTH (Hants) was also held at Domesday by CROC, the huntsman, and ROBERT FITZ-GIROLD, the owner of BEDESDENE, which is in the immediate neighbourhood. Hants Domesd., 46*b*, 49. Amhresb. Hundr., 90.
TODEWORDE p. 67	Alward	EDWARD of Salisbury	[Croc,—1 virgate]	
TODEWORDE p. 146	Three Thanes	CROC, the huntsman, as one of the King's Officers	"Miles,"—2 hides [Edward of Salisbury,—1 virgate]	
TOLLARD p. 123	Five Thanes	AIULF, the Sheriff		These are all different portions of *TOLLARD ROYAL*, in the hundred of Stanford (= Chalk), at the south-western corner of the county. The *first* holding is alluded to in the Exon Domesday (p. 186). The *second* may possibly be RUSH-MERE, deriving its original name it may be from Rozo, the occupier T. R. E. From the tenant, or owner, of the *third*, TOLI, may perchance be derived the name TOL-LARD. King John had a hunting-seat at this place, and hence the designation TOLLARD ROYAL. Chalk Hundr., 170.
TOLLARD p. 73	Rozo	EDWARD of Salisbury	Aiulf	
TOLLARD p. 102	Toli	WILLIAM DE OW		
TROI p. 125	Abbess of Wilton	RICHARD PUINGIANT		*TROW*, in the parish of Berwick St. John, and hundred of Stanford (= Chalk). Exon Domesd., p. 186. This is clearly the same estate that is included as a subordinate holding under CHELCHE, p. 47.
TROLE p. 131		BRICTRIC, as one of the King's Thanes		*TROWLE*, in the hundred of Melksham (p. 171). It is a tithing of the parish of TROWBRIDGE. A tithing, immediately adjoining it, belonging to BRADFORD-ON-AVON, is also called by the same name.
TOCHEHAM p. 109	Alwin	RADULF DE MORTEMER	Oidelard	This is the *half knight's fee* held, c. 1270, under RADULF DE MORTEMER, by Thomas de Tockenham. Test. de Nev., 150. It is no doubt the land held afterwards by BRADENSTOKE PRIORY under the MORTIMERS, and is most probably a part of *WEST TOCKENHAM*. Aubrey, 189.

NAME.	T. R. E. Owner, or Tenant.	T. R. W. Tenant in Capite.	T. R. W. Under-Tenant.	MODERN NAME, &c.
TOCHEHAM p. 96	Dodo, under the Church of Malmesbury	DURAND of Gloucester	Roger	This is without doubt the *one knight's fee* held at TOCHEHAM by Herbert Fitz-Piers, as an inheritance from WALTER PINKNAY. Test. de Nev., 150. A comparison of entries in various records leads to the conclusion that it is a portion of *WEST TOCKENHAM*, which is in the parish of LINEHAM and hundred of Kingsbridge. In Abbrev. Plac. 14, it is called TOKENHAM PINKINNI. See above, under STOCHE, and also Aubrey, 194.
TOCHEHAM p. 134		ALRIC (as King's Thanes)		All these holdings making up in the whole about *four hides*, are most probably portions of *EAST TOCKENHAM*, formerly in the hundred of Blagrave, now in that of Kingsbridge. The name of the *fourth* holding is not given, but it seems to be implied that it was at TOCHEHAM. The *third* is alluded to in the Exon Domesday, under the hundred of Blagrave (p. 167). Aubrey, 194.
TOCHEHAM p. 135		ALGAR (as King's Thanes)		
TOCHEHAM p. 134		ALURIC 'Parvus' (as King's Thanes)		
.... p. 134	Two Thanes	ALURIC 'Parvus' (as King's Thanes)		
TUDERLEGE p. 140	Uluric's father	ULURIC, as one of the King's Thanes		This is a very small holding on the south-east borders of the county close by *TITHERLEY*. See below, under WINTRESLIE. The parish of TITHERLEY is in Hants.
ULFECOTE p. 140	Uluric's father	ULURIC, as one of the King's Thanes		From the circumstance of ULURIC being possessed of a small estate at SVINDONE (Swindon), it is conjectured that this may be *UFCOTT*, which is a few miles distant from that place.
UFECOTE p. 96	Almar	DURAND of Gloucester	Roger	This small holding is described as *in* UFECOTE. It *may* be a portion of the manor just described. A reference to TOCHEHAM (p. 96) will show that both the chief lord, and tenant, T. R. W., held lands in the neighbourhood. See Aubrey, 335.
ULFELA p. 146	Turold Alwin	RADULF DE HALVILLE, as one of the King's Officers		This is referred to in the Exon Domesday (p. 181), under the hundred of Kinwardstone. It is *WOLFHALL*, in the parish of GREAT BEDWIN. Wilts Mag., vi., 264. Aubrey, 379.
UPTONE p. 55	Girald of Wilton	GIRALD OF WILTON, 'in frank-almoigne'		*UPTON LOVEL*, in the hundred of Heytesbury (p. 178). A charter concerning this estate, which is there called UBBANTUNE, is contained in the Wilton Chartulary. Cod. Dipl., 468. It would seem at one time to have belonged to the Abbey at Wilton, and the tenure in *frank-almoigne* implies as much. It appears to be included in Test. de Nev., 151, 154, among the fees of the Abbess. Heytesb. Hundr., 190.
VITELETONE p. 113	Vitel	ROBERT FITZ-GIROLD	Rainer	*FITTLETON*, in the hundred of Elstub. It would seem most probably to derive its name from that of its possessor T. R. E. Robert Fitz-Girold held also several estates in the immediate neighbourhood as *e.g.* BEDESDENE (Biddesden), MILDESTONE (Milston), and BRISMARTONE (Brigmerston). Elstub Hundr., 26.
WADHULLE p. 25	Eddulf	BISHOP OF BAIEUX	Odo	*WODHULL* (now *WOOD-HILL*), in the parish of Cliff Pipard and hundred of Kingsbridge (p. 165). There was a chapel here in ancient times. Inq. Non., 162.
WADONE p. 133	Aluric	ALURIC of Melksham, as one of the King's Thanes		*WHADDON*, in the hundred of Melksham (p. 171). The parish contains 580 acres. Aubrey, 305.

NAME.	T. R. E. Owner, or Tenant.	T. R. W. Tenant in Capite.	T. R. W. Under-Tenant.	MODERN NAME, &c.
WAISEL p. 10	Abbess of Wilton	ABBESS OF WILTON		This is the manor of *WASSERN* (or *WASSHERNE*), which comprised a considerable portion of what is now included within the park at WILTON. (See below, p. 187.) It is mentioned in the Hundr. R., ii., 244, as being in the hundred of Cadworth, and belonging to Wilton; and (p. 281) under the heading BURGUS DE WYLTON, a house is spoken of as being "*in regio vico de* WASSERN." The name is now lost, but the manor was granted under this title to Sir W. Herbert, 33 Henry VIII. See Branche Hundr., 150.
WALECOTE p. 92	Alnod Levenot	MILO CRISPIN	Rainald	*WALCOT*, near Swindon, in the old hundred of Blagrave (p. 167), now in that of Kingsbridge. Like other estates belonging to Milo Crispin, it was held, c. 1270, under the honor of Wallingford. Test. de Nev., 137.
WATEDENE p. 106	Bolle	WALERAN, the huntsman	Engenulf	By a comparison of these entries with those under ALWARBERIE, it will be evident that these holdings were at *WHADDON*, in the hundred of Alderbury. The descendants of Waleran for many years continued to hold this estate. Test. de Nev., 142. Alderb. Hundr., 6.
WATEDENE p. 107	Four Thanes	WALERAN, the huntsman	Two "milites"	
WEMBERGE p. 20	Bishop of Winchester	BISHOP OF WINCHESTER, "pro victu monachorum"	Richer,—1 hide	*WANBOROUGH*, in the old hundred of Thornhill (p. 167), now in that of Kingsbridge. This estate was granted to the Church of St. Peter and St. Paul at Winton, by King Æthelwulf, in 854. The charter, with land-limits, is given in Cod. Dipl., 1053. Details concerning this parish will be found in Wilts Mag., vii., 132, and Aubrey, 195.
WENISTETONE p. 139	Harding	HARDING, as one of the King's Thanes		From the similarity of this name to EUNESTETONE (see p. 33), it would seem most probable that this manor is also some portion of *IDMESTON*, in the hundred of Alderbury. The whole parish, including PORTON and GOMELDON, contains more than 5000 acres. Alderb. Hundr., 61.
WERDORE p. 46	Abbess of Wilton	ABBESS OF WILTON	Britmar	A portion of the present estate of WARDOUR. William de St. Martin held it, c. 1270, under the Abbess of Wilton. Test. de Nev., 151. See above, under ANESTIGE.
WEROCHESHALLE p. 72	Baldwin	EDWARD of Salisbury	Godfrey	*NORTH WRAXALL*, in the hundred of Chippenham. This manor is named among the fees of the Earl of Sarum. Test. de Nev., 135. The parish contains 2104 acres. An interesting account of a Roman Villa discovered there by G. P. Scrope, Esq., in 1859, is given in Wilts Mag., vii., 59. See also Aubrey, 118.
WERTUNE p. 86	Alnod	HUMFREY DE L'ISLE	Robert	This is a portion of the parish of WROUGHTON, in the hundred of Blachegrave, now in that of Kingsbridge. It is commonly called in the records *OVER WROUGHTON* (=Upper Wroughton). Hundr. R., ii., 244. Wilts Mag., ii., 278. Aubrey, 367.
WERVETONE p. 136	Bricnod Alwin	ALDRED, as one of the King's Thanes		This is described as "*in* WERVETONE," and is no doubt another portion of *WROUGHTON*. It is alluded to in the Exon Domesday (p. 166), under the hundred of Blachegrave. The present parish of WROUGHTON (including ELINGDON, now reckoned as part of it) contains 6390 acres. See above, under ELENDUNE.
WESTBERIE p. 13	Queen Editha	THE KING	William Scudet,—4½ hides	*WESTBURY*, in a hundred of the same name. A full account of this parish—which comprises BRATTON, DILTON, and LEIGH—will be found in Hoare's MODERN WILTSHIRE. Some additional particulars are given in Aubrey, 402.
WESTBERIE, Church of p. 14		A certain CLERICOLUS		

NAME.	T. R. E. Owner, or Tenant.	T. R. W. Tenant in Capite.	T. R. W. Under-Tenant.	MODERN NAME, &c.
WESBERIE p. 147	Ulward	WILLIAM SCUDET, as one of the King's Officers.		This is evidently the subordinate holding under the larger manor alluded to in the preceding entry.
WESTWODE p. 19	Bishop of Winchester	BISHOP OF WINCHESTER, "pro victu monachorum."		*WESTWOOD*, originally in the hundred of Bradford (Wilts Mag., v., 22), now, like other estates belonging to St. Swithin, Winchester, in that of Elstub. The parish from time immemorial has been united with that of BRADFORD-ON-AVON. The lordship of the manor belongs to the Dean and Chapter of Winchester. Two charters relating to it, one of them with land-limits, are given in Cod. Dipl., 639, 658.
WICHEFORD p. 48	Abbess of Wilton	ABBESS OF WILTON		*LITTLE WISHFORD*, in the hundred of Branche (p. 184). It is reckoned as a tithing of the parish of SOUTH NEWTON. The charter of King Æthelstan (A.D. 937) respecting "*five mansæ in* NIWANTUNE," given in Cod. Dipl., 1114, appears to relate to this estate. Branche Hundr., 54.
WICHEFORD p. 149	Avitius	WILLIAM CORNIOLE, as one of the King's Officers		*GREAT WISHFORD*, in the hundred of Branche. The parish consists of 1610 acres. Most of what is now included in it was, without doubt, at the time of Domesday, part of GROVELY FOREST. Branche Hundr., 45.
WICHELESTOTE p. 120	Leuric	HUGO LASNE	Harold	Most probably *WICKLESCOT* (now corrupted into *WESTLECOT*), close by Swindon. Aubrey, 191, 368.
WIDECOME p. 76	Brictric	ERNULF DE HESDING	Robert	*WIDCOMB*, in the parish of HELMARTON and hundred of Kingsbridge. See above, under HELMERINTONE. Aubrey, 167.
WIDETON p. 138	Father of Edward	EDWARD, as one of the King's Thanes		
WIDEHILLE p. 146	Robert Fitz-Wimarc	TETBALD & HUMFREY, as King's Officers		These two entries refer to different portions of *WIDHILL*, the name now of some farms in the parishes of BROAD and LITTLE BLUNSDON. The *former* is alluded to in the Exon Domesday (p. 163), under the hundred of Scipe, and is probably NORTH WIDHILL. The *latter* is named among the fees of John Tregoz (Inq. p. m. 28, Edw. I.), and is there called WEST WIDEHULL. In Test. de Nev., 136, THOMAS MAUDUIT, a descendant possibly of the tenant GUNFRID [MALDOITH ?], is recorded as holding lands at WIDIHULL WASTEVILL, under Robert Tregoz as of the honor of Ewyas. (See p. 79, *note*). Both of these estates are now in the hundred of Highworth.
WILDEHILLE p. 81	Carlo	ALURED of Marlbrough	Gunfrid	
WIFLESFORDE p. 60	Ednod, the steward	EARL HUGO	Haimo	These are both, it is conjectured, portions of *WILSFORD*, in the hundred of Underditch. The *former* is clearly the *one-fourth* of a knight's fee held at PARVA WYVELESFORD, c. 1270 (Test. de Nev., 144), by RICARDUS FILIUS AUCHER. The same owner is recorded as possessed of FISSERTONE, also one of the possessions of Earl Hugo (p. 61). Test. de Nev., 140.—As regards the *latter* holding, a reference to the manors of Robert Fitz-Girold (see above, under BRISMARTONE and MILDESTONE), will show that he was possessed of lands in the neighbourhood.
WIFLESFORD p. 112	Tovi	ROBERT FITZ-GIROLD	Hugo	
WILCOTE p. 65		EDWARD of Salisbury		*WILCOT*, in the hundred of Swanborough (p. 175). From the large extent of this manor, which was assessed at $15\frac{1}{4}$ *hides*, and from the fact that a portion of the *present* parish (see above, under DRAICOTE) is separately accounted for, it is conjectured that it probably included WOODBOROUGH. The two are recorded in the Nom. Vill. as having been both held by the Earl of Lancaster, a lineal descendant of Edward of Salisbury. WILCOT was held, in the time of Edw. I. by the Prior of Bradenstock, by gift of the Earl of Sarum. Test. de Nev., 155.

NAME.	T. R. E. Owner, or Tenant.	T. R. W. Tenant in Capite.	Under-Tenant.	MODERN NAME, &c.
WILGI p. 48	Abbess of Wilton	ABBESS OF WILTON		*WYLY*, in the hundred of Branche (p. 184). A charter relating to this manor, containing land-limits, is given in Cod. Dipl., 379. Branche Hundr., 5. See above, under DEPEFORD.
WILI p. 88	Aluric	HUMFREY DE L'ISLE		These two manors make up the number of hides held by Humphrey de L'Isle in the hundred of Heytesbury (p. 178). They are respectively *GREAT* and *LITTLE BATHAMPTON ON WYLY*. Though in a different hundred, they are now considered tithings in the parish of STEEPLE LANGFORD. The two manors under the names of WYLI and BACHAMWYLI are recorded among the fees of Walter de Dunstanville, c. 1270, in Test. de Nev., 140. The word WILRENONE looks like a corruption for WYLYBOURN, a name applied to that part of the country. Wilts Mag., ii., 266. Branche Hundr., 15.
WILRENONE p. 88	Edwin	HUMFREY DE L'ISLE		
WINEFEL p. 26	Azor	BISHOP OF COUTANCE	Roger	*WINFIELD*, in the hundred of Bradford. This estate was afterwards bestowed on the Abbey of Keynsham (Test. de Nev. 136), and the patronage was exercised by the head of that religious house till the Reformation. Wilts Inst. See below, under WITHENHAM.
WINTREBURNE p. 14	Queen Editha	THE KING		These entries refer to *WINTERBOURN-STOKE*, in the hundred of Dole (p. 183), a manor which, it is conjectured, originally included also some portion of BERWICK ST. JAMES. The Abbey of Jumieges was possessed of the church. Wilts Inst. The *third* holding would seem to be probably *WINTERBOURN PARVA*, (or as it is now called, *ASSERTON*), since in Test. de Nev., 135, that is recorded as having been held by "Willelmus filius *Walteri*" of the Earl of Sarum, and to have amounted to *half a knight's fee*, which would correspond with the 2½ *hides* at which it was assessed. It is now part of *BERWICK ST. JAMES*. A survey of this last parish, 1591, as parcel of the possessions of the Duchy of Lancaster, is given in Wilts Mag., vi., 195.
WINTREBURNE, Church of p. 14		ABBEY OF JUMIEGES		
WINTREBURNE-STOCH p. 66	Alwi,—1 hide	EDWARD of Salisbury	Walter—2 hides Alwi's wife,—½ hide	
WINTREBURNE p. 128	Ulward	MACI OF MORETAINA		These two manors, according to the Exon Domesday (pp. 183, 184), were in the hundred of Dole. They are most probably some portions of the large manor just alluded to, which it is impossible now to identify.
WINTREBURNE p. 136	Cudulf	CUDULF, as one of the King's Thanes		
WINTREBURNE p. 78	Nubold	ERNULF DE HESDING	Nubold	This would seem to correspond with land in the hundred of Dole, held in chief, c. 1276, by Paganus de Cadurcis (=Chaworth), in whose family many of the estates held at Domesday by Ernulf de Hesding became afterwards vested. Both in the Hund. R., ii., 254, and Test. de Nev., 142, it is said to have been at BERWYKE, and hence it is conjectured to be a portion of *BERWICK ST. JAMES*.
WINTREBURNE p. 41	Abbey of St. Peter's, Winchester	ABBEY OF ST. PETER'S WINCHESTER		This is clearly the ABBODESTON of the Nom. Vill. It was granted under the name of WINTREBURN to the Abbess of St. Peter's, Winchester, by King Edgar, in 966. Cod. Dipl., 523. It is now called *ROLLESTON*. It was in the hundred of Dole originally (page 184); it was afterwards transferred to that of Elstub.
WINTREBURNE p. 55	Abbess of Ambresbury	ABBESS OF AMBRESBURY		These are without doubt the *two carucates* held in WINTREBURN MADINTON, 3 Edw. I., by the Abbess of Ambresbury. Hundr. R., ii., 254. It is a portion of *MADDINGTON*, a moiety of which manor belonged to the Abbess. Nom. Vill. Test. de Nev., 155.

NAME.	T. R. E. Owner, or Tenant.	T. R. W. Tenant in Capite.	T. R. W. Under-Tenant.	MODERN NAME, &c.
WINTREBURNE p. 116	Domne	OSBERN GIFARD		These two are conjectured to be also portions of *MADDIN-TON*, the *former* being referred to in the Exon Domesd (page 183) under the hundred of Dole, and entries Hundr. R., ii. 254, compared with those in Test. de Ne 138, leading to such a conclusion as being probab correct. The *latter* may be the *CLIFTON GIFFAR* referred to in the Hundred Rolls.
WINTREBURNE p. 116		OSBERN GIFARD		
WINTREBURNE p. 67	Alric	EDWARD of Salisbury		A comparison of entries in Hundr. R., ii., 254, and Test. Nev., 135, leads to the conclusion that the *first* of these the *two knight's fee* held at WINTREBURN SCIREVETON, a the *others* the two sub-infeudations, each of half a knigh fee, at the same place. They probably make up the pr sent parish of *SHREWTON*, in the hundred of Do The former part of the name would seem to be a co ruption of *Scir-gerefa*, i.e. *Shire-reeve* (=Sheriff), and to be still a memorial of the office borne by its Domesd owner.
WINTREBURNE p. 66	Ulveva	EDWARD of Salisbury	Godfrey	
WINTREBURNE p. 72	Alward	EDWARD of Salisbury	Tetbald	
WINTREBURNE p. 81		ALURED of Marlborough	Edward	
WINTREBORNE p. 31	Abbot of Glastonbury Orgar,—$3\frac{1}{2}$ hides	ABBOT OF GLASTONBURY	Gilbert,—$3\frac{1}{2}$ hides	*WINTERBOURN MONKTON* in the hundred of Selkl (page 169), a parish containing 1813 acres. The man was given to Glastonbury by Elfrida, Queen of Edward t Elder. N. Mon., i., 24. Aubrey, 341.
WINTREBURNE p. 54	Abbess of Ambresbury	ABBESS OF AMBRESBURY		This is clearly the RUBBEDESTON of the Nom. Vill., und the hundred of Selkley, which, in 1316, belonged to t Abbess of Ambresbury. It is now *ROBSON*, the name a farm in the parish of Winterbourn Bassett. See belo p. 169. In the N. Mon., under 'ministers' accounts, ap pended to the history of Ambresbury, it is called the man of NORTH WINTERBOURN. See Aubrey, 344.
WINTREBURNE p. 89	Two Thanes	HUMFREY DE L'ISLE		This is the principal portion of the present parish *WINTERBOURN BASSETT*, in the hundred of Sel ley (p. 169), which contains in the whole some 2210 acre Wilts Mag., ii., 270. Aubrey, 342.
WINTREBURNE p. 33	Abbot of Glastonbury	ABBOT OF GLASTONBURY	Waleran,—1 virgate	From GOMELDON being mentioned in the Hundr. R., ii., 24 under the hundred of Alderbury, in connection wi IDEMESTON, as belonging to Glastonbury, coupled wi the fact that in the Exon Domesday (p. 190), this esta is alluded to as having been in the same hundred, it wou seem probable that what is now called *GUMBLETO* which is in Idmiston parish, is intended by this entr The neighbouring estate of HURCOT (see under HERDICOT belonged to Waleran. Alderb. Hundr., 57.
WINTREBURNE p. 73	Ulwen	EDWARD of Salisbury		*WINTERBOURN EARLS*, in the hundred of Alderbu (p. 190). The parish contains 1619 acres. Alder Hundr., 85.
WINTREBURNE p. 128	Alwi	GODESCAL		This, according to the Exon Domesday (p. 190), was in t hundred of Alderbury. It seems to correspond with t *two carucates* held by Henry de la Mare, c. 1270 (Test. Nev., 143), and which had previously formed part at lea of the manor of GUNNORA DE LA MARE (Inq. p. m. 5 Henry III.), whence the name *WINTERBOURN GU NER*.
. . . . p. 129	Gudmund	GODESCAL		The *name* of this small holding is not given. It was, if n a portion of the same manor, probably in its immedi vicinity.

NAME.	T. R. E. Owner, or Tenant.	T. R. W. Tenant in Capite.	T. R. W. Under-Tenant.	MODERN NAME, &c.
Wintreburne p. 27	Lessid	Bishop of Coutance		These two estates, neither of them of any great extent, were, according to the Exon Domesday (p. 190), in the hundred of Alderbury. It is not easy to say precisely what manors are intended. The *former* may possibly be *WINTERBOURN DAUNTSEY.*
Wintreburne p. 135	Godwin	Aldred, as one of the King's Thanes		
Wintreburne p. 143	Alwin	Saric, as one of the King's Thanes		The Exon Domesday (p. 190) accounts for this estate under the hundred of Alderbury. As Saric held Laverstock, which is next named in the record, it seems very probable that *WINTERBOURN FORD*, which is in that parish, is the estate intended by this entry. Alderb. Hundr., 106.
Wintreslew p. 58	Harding Abbess of Ambresbury,—2 hides	Earl Morton		This, according to the Exon Domesday (p. 190), was in the hundred of Alderbury. It is *WEST WINTERSLOW.* On the attainder of William, Earl of Morton, in the reign of Henry I., it would seem to have escheated to the Crown, for, in 1215, it belonged to Isabella, Queen of England. Alderb. Hundr., 44.
Wintreslei p. 62	Harding	Earl Alberic		This is most probably *EAST WINTERSLOW*, an outlying portion of the hundred of Ambresbury, under which it is accounted for in the Exon Domesday (p. 185). An account of the descent of this manor is given in Alderb. Hundr., 47.
Wintreslei p. 140		Ulward, as one of the King's Thanes		These are probably portions, the second of but small extent, of *MIDDLE WINTERSLOW*, or, as it is sometimes called, *MIDDLETON.* Uluric possessed also *one virgate* of land in Tuderlege (Titherley), the adjoining manor. Alderb. Hundr., 49.
Wintreslei p. 140	Father of Uluric	Uluric, as one of the King's Thanes		
Witeberge p. 111	Saulf	Robert Fitz-Girold	Gozelin	This is *possibly WYCHBURY*, in the hundred of Cawdon. Robert Fitz-Girold was chief lord of Ebbesbourn Wake, which is situated at no great distance from it. See above, under Eblesborne. Cawd. Hundr., 67.
Witeclive p. 149	Alwi	Gundvin, as one of the King's Officers		The tithing of *WHITE-CLEEVE* (or *WHITE-CLIFT*), in the hundred of Heytesbury (p. 178). It comprises some 300 acres, and lies principally in Brixton Deverel, a few acres only being in Monkton Deverel. Heytesb. Hundr., 7.
Witelie p. 122	Appe	Gunfrid Maldoith		*WITLEY*, in the hundred and parish of Melksham. The Mauduit family, descendants of the Domesday owner, held property here. John Mauduyt died siesed of the manor, 31 Edw. I. Inq., p. m. Aubrey, 295.
Witford p. 106	Bolle	Waleran, the huntsman	Robert	
Withenham p. 26	Alvet	Bishop of Coutance		*WITHENHAM*, in the hundred of Bradford. Formerly this was a separate parish, the names of its incumbents from 1299—1421 being still preserved. In 1428, Walter, Lord Hungerford, obtained permission to unite Withenham *alias* Rowley church and parish with Farleigh Hungerford. See Wilts Mag., v., 20. The larger portion of this last-named parish is in Somerset; Withenham, which is the smaller part of it, is in Wilts.
Wivelesford p. 133	Brismar	Aluric of Melksham, as one of the King's Thanes		*WILSFORD*, near Pewsey, in the hundred of Swanborough. The Edward, who is said to have held it "*in mortgage*," was most probably Edward of Salisbury, as both Wyvelesford and Manyngford Bohun (which is a tithing in that parish) belonged, 3 Edw. I., to his descendant, the Earl of Hereford. Hundr. R., ii., 274.

2 O

NAME.	T. R. E. Owner, or Tenant.	T. R. W. Tenant in Capite.	T. R. W. Under-Tenant.	MODERN NAME, &c.
WOCHESIE p. 131	Brictric's father	BRICTRIC, as one of the King's Thanes		*OAKSEY*, in tho hundred of Cicemethorn (p. 159), now that of Malmesbury. This manor became afterwards p cel of the estates of the Duchy of Lancaster, and a s vey, 1591, is given in Wilts Mag., vi., 108. Aubrey, 2
WODETONE p. 91	Levenod	MILO CRISPIN		*WOOTTON BASSET*, in tho hundred of Blachegr (p. 166), now in that of Kingsbridge. It is inclu among tho fees held by Edmund, Earl of Cornw appertaining to the "honor of Wallingford." See p. *note*. Inq., p. m. 28 Edw. I. Aubrey, 202. [In Test. Nev., 137, BRODETON, said to be held by FULCO BASS among the fees of the "honor of Wallingford," is clea a misprint for WODETON.]
WURDE, Church of p. 15		RADULF, the priest		*HIGH-WORTH*, in a hundred of the same name. S above, under BLONTESDONE. Aubrey, 151.
An estate in the Hundred of WRDERUSTESELLE p. 66	Brictric	EDWARD of Salisbury	Huard	The *name* of this estate is not given, but it is simply scribed as *six hides* in the *Hundred* of WRDERUSTESEL What hundred is alluded to it is not easy to say, as no of those named in the Exon Domesday can as yet be ide tified with it. It has been conjectured that the hund of WHERWELSDOWN was intended, but all the manors that hundred (see p. 172) seem fully accounted f BRICTRIC, the Anglo-Saxon proprietor, certainly h several estates in that neighbourhood, all of which ca afterwards into the possession of the descendants of E WARD OF SALISBURY. See above, under COVELESTONE, STRABURG,—STAVRETONE,—and TROLE.

CORRIGENDA.

Page 17, line 6, *for* 'hæc,' *read* 'hac.'

" 19, " 8, *for* '*WESTWOODE*,' *read* '*WESTWODE*.'

" 30, " 27, *for* 'hæc,' *read* 'hæ.'

" 62, " 13, *for* 'terræ,' *read* 'terra.'

" 80, " 17, *for* 'Alward,' *read* 'Alured.'

" 112, " 23, *for* 'tenet Roberto' *read* 'tenet de Roberto.'

" 181, " 5, *for* 'Standen Chaworth,' *read* 'Standen Hussey.'

" 219, (second entry,) *for* 'HANTONE,' *read* 'HENTONE.'

" 225, (under the last entry,) *transfer* 'Aluric, the huntsman,' *to the column headed* T. R. E.

" 228, (first entry,) *for* 'OTNOE,' *read* 'OTONE.'

" 244, (under WODETONE,) *erase the words within brackets*,—[In Test. de Nev. 137, &c. . . . . WODETON.]

GENERAL INDEX.

LIST OF SUBSCRIBERS.

CHANCELLOR, The LORD (2 *Copies*)

AILESBURY, the Marquis of, Tottenham Park
ANTIQUARIES, SOCIETY OF, Somerset House, per C. WATSON, Esq., *Secretary*
ARCHÆOLOGICAL SOCIETY, THE WILTSHIRE, per Rev. Canon JACKSON, *Secretary*
ADLAM, W., Esq., Chew Magna
ATTWOOD, Francis, Esq., The Close, Sarum
AUSTEN, Rev. John, Tollard Royal

BATH, the Marquis of, Longleat
BROUGHTON, Lord, Tedworth
BRUCE, Lord Charles, M.P., Tottenham Park
BADEN, Miss, Longstreet, Pewsey
BAILWARD, J., Esq., Horsington
BAILWARD, Miss, Frankleigh House, Bradford-on-Avon
BARNES, Rev. H. M., Alton Barnes
BARON, Rev. J., Upton Scudamore, Warminster
BEACH, Sir M. Hicks, Bart., Williamstrip Park
BEACH, W. W., Esq., M.P., Oakley Hall, Basingstoke
BENNETT, Rev. Frederick, Shrewton
BICKNELL, Rev. Charles Brook, Stourton Rectory
BLANDFORD, Henry, Esq., Seend
BOSWORTH, Mr., 215, Regent Street, London
BOUVERIE, E. P., Esq., M.P., 44, Wilton Crescent, London
BRACKSTONE, R. H., Esq., Beechen Cliff, Bath
BRADFORD, R., Esq., Midge Hall, Wootton Bassett
BRADFORD, James, Esq., Swindon
BRIDGER, W. M., Esq., the late, Bradford-on-Avon
BROOKE, S. B., Esq., Cowbridge House, Malmesbury
BROWN and Co., Messrs., Salisbury (3 *Copies*)
BUCKLEY, General, M.P., New Hall, Salisbury
BUTCHER, W. H., Esq., Devizes

CLEVELAND, her Grace the Dowager Duchess of
CARNARVON, Countess Dowager, Pixton Park
CAILLARD, C. F. D., Esq., Judge of County Courts of Wiltshire and Somersetshire
CLARKE, Major, Trowbridge
CLARKE, W. P., Esq., Trowbridge
CLARKE, Thomas, Esq., Trowbridge
CONOLLY, C. J., Esq., Cottles House
COTTERELL, J. H., Esq., Bewdley Villa, Bath
CRAWLEY, Rev. R., Steeple Ashton, Trowbridge
CROWDY, F., Esq., Rowden, Berks
CROWDY, Dr., Beaufort Buildings, Bath
CROOK, Rev. H. S., Uphaven

DEVONSHIRE, his Grace the Duke of, Devonshire House, London
DYNEVOR, Lord, 19, Prince's Gardens, London
DORMAN, Mark, Esq., late Mayor of Northampton
De SALES, W. T., Esq., Dawley Court, Uxbridge

ESTCOURT, Right Hon. T. H. S., M.P., Estcourt, Tetbury (2 *Copies*)
EDGELL, Rev. E. B., Bromham
EDMONDS, E., Esq., Berryfield, Bradford-on-Avon
EMPSON, Rev. W., Royal Crescent, Bath
ESTCOURT, E. B., Esq., the late
EVERETT, Joseph, Esq., Greenhill, Warminster (2 *Copies*)
EWART, W., Esq., M.P., Broadleaze, Devizes
EARLE, Rev. A., Monkton Farleigh
EARLE, Rev. John, Swainswick

FALCONER, Dr. R. W., 22, Bennett Street, Bath
FALCONER, Thomas, Esq., Judge of the County Courts of Glamorganshire and Brecknockshire, Usk
FLOWER, Thomas Bruges, Esq., 7, Beaufort Buildings, Bath
FORESTER, William, Esq., Malmesbury
FULLER, J. B., Esq., Neston Park, Corsham

GLADSTONE, the late Captain, M.P., Bowden Park
GODDARD, Rev. F., Helmarton
GODDARD, H. N., Esq., Clyffe Manor, Wootton Bassett
GODDARD, A. L., Esq., M.P., The Lawn, Swindon
GODWIN, C., Esq., Norfolk Crescent, Bath
GOODWIN, Josiah, Esq., Edward Street, Bath
GORE, Arthur, Esq., Melksham
GRAVES, R., Esq., Charlton Ludwell, Salisbury

HERBERT OF LEA, Lady, Wilton House
HALE, R. B., Esq., Alderly, Wotton-under-Edge
HALE, Colonel, Ditto
HALL, Marshall, Esq., Blacklands Park, Calne
HASTINGS, Rev. Prebendary, Trowbridge
HEATHCOTE, Rt. Hon. Sir W., Bart., Hursley Park, Winchester
HEATHCOTE, Rev. G., Colerne
HENEAGE, G. H. W., Esq., Compton Bassett, Calne
HOLFORD, R. S., Esq., M.P., Weston Burt, Tetbury
HULBERT, H. P., Esq., Darlington Place, Bath

LIST OF SUBSCRIBERS.

INSKIPP, E. T., Esq., Bankruptcy Court, Bristol

JACKSON, Rev. Canon, Leigh De-la-mere
JAMES, Col. Sir Henry, Ordnance Office, Southampton
JOHNSON, Rev. J. H., Tilshead, Devizes
JONES, Colonel Inigo, Kelston
JONES, H. P., Esq., Portway House, Warminster

KEMM, W. C., Esq., Amesbury, Wilts
KITE, Mr. Edward, Devizes

LANSDOWNE, the late Marquis of, Bowood
LANSDOWNE, the Marquis of, Bowood
LITERARY INSTITUTION, Bradford-on-Avon, per Mr. MARKS, *Secretary*
LADD, J. N., Esq., Calne
LANCASTER, Rev. T. B., Rector of Grittleton
LANGTON, W. H. P. Gore, Esq., M.P., Newton Park
LEIGHTON, Rev. Baldwin, Bradford-on-Avon
LOPES, Sir M., Bart., M.P., Westbury
LOPES, the Dowager Lady, East Hill, Frome
LONG, W., Esq., M.P., Rood Ashton (2 *Copies*)
LONG, R. P., Esq., M.P., Dolforgan
LONG, Rev. Henry, Rood Ashton
LONG, W., Esq., Lansdown Crescent, Bath
LUKIS, Rev. W. C., Wath Rectory, Ripon

MANVERS, the Earl, Thoresby Park
METHUEN, Lord, Corsham Court
MAJOR, Rev. S. C., Devizes
MARKLAND, J. H., Esq., the late, Bath
MEEK, Alexander, Esq., Hillworth, Devizes
MERRIMAN, W. C., Esq., Marlborough
MERRIMAN, T. B., Esq., Marlborough
MEREWETHER, H. A., Esq., Q.C., Bowden Hill, Chippenham
MILES, Rev. T., Stockton
MORGELL, Rev. Crosbie, East Knoyle, Hindon
MOORE, Stuart A., Esq., General Record Office, London
MULLINGS, R., Esq., Stratton, Gloucestershire

NELSON, the Earl, Trafalgar
NELSON, the Countess Dowager, Landford House
NEELD, Sir John, Bart., Grittleton
NICHOLS, J. Gough, Esq., F.S.A., London
NOYES, Messrs., Chippenham (2 *Copies*)

ORDNANCE SURVEY OFFICE, Library of, per Sir H. JAMES

PARFITT, Rev. Canon, Cottle's House
PEACOCK, Rev. E., Road Hill, Bath
PEARSE, Rev. Thomas, Fittleton Rectory, Marlborough
PENRUDDOCK, Charles, Esq., Compton House
PHIPPS, C. P., Esq., Chalcot House, Westbury
PHIPPS, J. L., Esq., Leighton, Westbury
PHILLIPS, Jacob, Esq., Chippenham
PICKWICK, Captain, Frankleigh, Bradford-on-Avon
PRICE, Richard E., Esq., Marlborough

RADNOR, the Earl of, Coleshill House, Highworth
RANDALL, Thomas, Esq., Wilton, Salisbury
ROBINSON, Mrs. Henry, Effingham, Leatherhead

SALMON, Eyre, Esq., Holcombe House
SANDFORD, W. A., Esq., Nynehead Court
SAUNDERS, T. Bush, Esq., Bradford-on-Avon (2 *Copies*)
SCARTH, Rev. Prebendary, Bath
SCROPE, G. Poulett, Esq., M.P., Castle Combe
SKILLICORNE, W. N., Esq., 9, Queen's Parade, Cheltenham
SKRINE, H. D., Esq., Warleigh Manor, Bath
SLADEN, Rev. E. H. M., Alton Barnes
SMITH, Rev. A. C., Yatesbury
St. BARBE, Mrs., Green Park, Bath
STANCOMB, J. P., Esq., Trowbridge
STANCOMB, W., Esq., Trowbridge
STOCKWELL, Rev. J. S., Wylye
STRONG, Rev. A., Chippenham
SWAYNE, John, Esq., Wilton
SWAYNE, H. T. F., Esq., Netherhampton House, Salisbury

TAYLOR, S. Watson, Esq., Erlestoke Park
THURNAM, Dr., Devizes
TITE, W., Esq., M.P., Lowndes Square, London (2 *Copies*)
TOWER, Rev. C., Chilmark

VACHER & SONS, Messrs., Parliament Street, London (3 *Copies*)
VIVIAN, Mrs., Claverton Manor

WESTMINSTER, the Marquis of, Eaton Hall, Cheshire
WALSH, Rev. Digby, Trowbridge
WARD, Charles E., Esq., Bathford
WARDALE, Rev. C. Bradford, Grammar School, Trowbridge
WILLIAMS, Rev. F. D., the late, Wishford Magna
WILKINSON, Rev. Dr., West Lavington
WILKINSON, Rev. Prebendary, Broughton Gifford
WRANGHAM, the late Mr. Sergeant, The Rocks (2 *Copies*)

CPSIA information can be obtained
at www.ICGtesting.com
Printed in the USA
LVHW101621090422
715402LV00011B/65

9 783752 588217